FIVE VICTORIAN GHOST NOVELS

FIVE VICTORIAN GHOST NOVELS

Edited

WITH AN INTRODUCTION

by E. F. Bleiler

Dover Publications, Inc.
New York

Published in Canada by General Publishing Company, Ltd., 30 Lesmill Road, Don Mills, Toronto, Ontario.
Published in the United Kingdom by Constable and Company, Ltd., 10 Orange Street, London WC 2.

This Dover edition, first published in 1971, is a new selection of five novels, taken from the sources indicated on page 421. This material has been reprinted without abridgment or significant alteration. The selection was made by E. F. Bleiler, who also wrote the Introduction.

International Standard Book Number: 0-486-22558-5
Library of Congress Catalog Card Number: 77-102771

Manufactured in the United States of America
Dover Publications, Inc.
180 Varick Street
New York, N.Y. 10014

Contents

Introduction to the Dover Edition

One of the finer traditions of the Victorian period was the Christmas Annual or Special Christmas Number. Each year most of the major periodicals—Dickens's *Household Words* and *All the Year Round*, Mrs. Braddon's *Belgravia*, *London Society*, and others—devoted a single issue, out of series, to lighter amusements for Christmas. Charades, special adventure stories, pantomime humor, cartoons were all customary, but favorites with all were the ghost stories, long and short, that were usually concentrated around Christmas. Similarly certain book publishers, such as Routledge's, issued special Christmas Annuals, with somewhat more sophisticated supernatural material. Perhaps the publishers felt they were continuing the old tradition of ghost stories by a yule fire; perhaps they were simply increasing circulation. In any event, such Christmas issues are one of the main sources for the Victorian ghost story.

Much of this Victorian publication, however, was impossibly ephemeral, and has now nearly or wholly disappeared. In some cases this is no real loss, since filler material was used to stuff the signatures, and it had served its purpose when it was tossed aside by the contemporary reader. But many of these publications can still convey an evening's entertainment to a modern, and deserve a better fate than merely being listed in scant bibliographies.

The worst sufferers of all have been the short novels, such as Mrs. Riddell's *Uninhabited House*, which formed *Routledge's Christmas Annual* for 1875. Such short novels are not long enough to be reprinted as individual books, and they are too long to be included in most anthologies. This is lamentable, since the Victorian short novel is usually superior to the long supernatural novel (which is normally poor), and often permits a development beyond the short story of the period.

The present collection contains five short novels, ranging in time from 1846 to 1897. They have been selected for their typicality as well as for their quality: they show trends in Victorian fiction, in some cases displaying influences from extra-literary sources which deserve comment. None is currently available elsewhere. *The Amber Witch* has been sporadically reissued over the past generation, but is currently out of print. The other four novels have never been republished since their first book appearance, and are practically impossible to find. Mrs. Riddell's

Uninhabited House, for example, is not recorded for any library in the United States.

II

Mrs. Charlotte E. Riddell (1832–1906), who wrote under the names F. G. Trafford and Mrs. J. H. Riddell, was in many ways the Victorian ghost novelist par excellence. In her works are to be found the full typology of a High Victorian story: a novel of everyday middle-class life, with realistic detail predominant, usually domestic; a restrained, mildly sentimental plot; a simple concept of supernaturalism (usually an unquiet ghost who cannot rest until his *raison d'être* has been discovered); a full awareness that the story is fiction, without personal meaning. Her characters are middle-class Englishmen and women of town and country, and her environment is usually the England of her day, with recognizable countrysides or townscapes.

Born in Ireland of impoverished gentry, Mrs. Riddell (then Miss Cowan) removed to London in 1855, with the intention of gaining a living as a writer. After several early novels under the pen name F. G. Trafford, she gained critical approval and some financial success with *George Geith of Fen Court* (1864), which has been called the first successful English novel of business life. Mrs. Riddell's work often points out, inversely, the paradox that George Orwell developed: despite its external circumstances the Victorian novel is often vague on matters of making a living. Mrs. Riddell, however, who was forced to support herself because of a disastrous husband, was well aware of economics. It is an interesting touch in *The Uninhabited House* that her characters work as law clerks, pensioners, real estate speculators with detailed plans, and developers. There is a note of exactness that conveys conviction.

Mrs. Riddell's work, apart from a travel book and a few miscellaneous matters, consists of some fifty novels and short story collections, largely reprinted from periodicals. About one-third of her titles are supernatural; the remainder fall into the unclassifiable social novel that was the mainstay of Victorian publishing. All her work is quite readable, since she was the master of a clear style and could impart touches of imagination to situations that in another hand might have been hackneyed. At her best she had great skill in conveying atmosphere through background.

In addition to *The Uninhabited House* Mrs. Riddell wrote three other short novels of the supernatural: *Fairy Water* (1873), which is about a conventional haunted house; *The Haunted River* (1877), set on one of the branches of the Thames, at her own house; and *The Disappearance of Mr. Jeremiah Redworth* (1878), which has both a more extended course of supernatural manifestations and deeper character analysis than most of her other work. A fourth novel, *The Nun's Curse* (1888), is longer. It is concerned with an ancestral curse in Ireland, and in some ways is suggestive of LeFanu's work.

As a short story writer Mrs. Riddell was one of the most successful practitioners in the Victorian assembly. Her collection *Weird Stories* (1884) contains six excellent ghost stories, in which the impingement of the "rational" supernatural on everyday life is admirably depicted. "Nut Bush Farm," for example, would be a credit to any period of supernatural writing. Most of her other collections of short stories contain at least one or two ghost stories of varying quality. Some are conventional and were probably hastily written; others, like "The Last of Squire Ennismore," are well worth reading.

In other ways besides her writing aesthetics Mrs. Riddell was a typical Victorian female novelist. Her marriage was unfortunate and she was forced to support an ineffectual husband, whose speculations eventually brought them near to ruin. Mrs. Riddell spent most of her later life repaying her husband's debts as a point of honor, even though she was not legally bound to. Even when she was dying of cancer, she continued to pay off creditors. She died in poverty in 1906, one of the first recipients of a government pension for poverty-stricken authors. Today, even though her work at its best almost reached the level of the great Victorians, she is forgotten by all but specialists.

III

Johannes Wilhelm Meinhold (1797–1851) presents the curious circumstance of a German author who was more important in England and America than in his own country. After a small amount of public attention in Germany, he became involved in a hoax and a series of literary feuds, and was soon forgotten. In the English-speaking world, however, his major work, *The Amber Witch* (*Die Bernsteinhexe*), was translated twice, and went through edition after edition. It was one of the favorite works of the Victorian reader, the Pre-Raphaelites being particularly enthusiastic about it. Philip Burne-Jones prepared illustrations for it (reproduced in the present volume), while William Morris, at his Kelmscott Press, produced a fine edition of its sister work, *Sidonia the Sorceress*. The Irish musician William Vincent Wallace turned it into an opera (*The Amber Witch*) with libretto by Henry Fothergill Chorley, the eminent critic. All in all, in the excellent Duff Gordon translation, *The Amber Witch* (1846) became acclimated as an English novel.

Meinhold's environment probably had much to do with his later development as a writer. His family was native to the barren, pine-spattered sand islands of the Baltic—Swinemünde, Peenemünde, Usedom, etc.—on the last of which his father, an eccentric, was Lutheran pastor. Meinhold grew up almost in isolation among the neolithic natives, for whom witchcraft was a living, unhidden force. There were "weather-men" who controlled the rains and storms for the farmers and sailors, "wise men" who cured sick horses and cows by spells. Also common were love spells and charms, death magic, and a whole universe of patterned omens, fetches, and supernatural impositions.

After a brief period of education, entry into Lutheran orders, and a parsonage, Meinhold started his frustrated literary career. His first tragedy, based on an episode of Pomeranian history, was praised in manuscript by Jean Paul Richter, while his collection of poetry, *Gemischte Gedichte* (1824), received commendations from Goethe. Other literary work followed, none of which would have permitted him more than a paragraph or two in a history of local literature.

A hoax gained literary attention for Meinhold. In 1841–2, in a minor magazine of the day, *Christoterpe*, there appeared several fragments of a seventeenth-century manuscript chronicle. These fragments were obviously important, since they mirrored not only great events but a wealth of living detail during the Thirty Years' War, particularly the persecution of witches.

The King of Prussia, Frederick William IV, asked the editor of the chronicle, who was Meinhold, for the full text. Meinhold sent it to him with a confidential letter admitting that the story was a hoax. Not too long afterwards, he in turn was surprised to receive bound copies of his book, *Die Bernsteinhexe*, which the king had published at his own expense.

The book was received with some enthusiasm, which enthusiasm soon diminished when Meinhold claimed to be the author, not just the editor. He was not believed, and had to show his original working papers (together with proof that he had submitted an earlier version to a Viennese publisher some fifteen years before, as frank fiction) before his authorship was accepted. Meinhold's tactics left a sour taste in the mouths of the critics, but worse was yet to come.

The "chronicle" had been taken seriously by church and lay historians, who were using it as ammunition in a controversy about the role of the church in the witch persecutions. Meinhold now revealed that he had written the novel as a chronicle to demonstrate the follies of historian-critics. How seriously should one take a critic who cannot distinguish a novel from a chronicle? How much value is there in rationalistic Bible studies that use the same techniques as literary men? David Friedrich Strauss was included in the controversy. Meinhold was devastating, not only to his critics, but to himself. His novel, which had been adapted to the stage and seemed to be on its way to being an accepted modern classic, now fell into a well of silence, and Meinhold vegetated on his sandy island.

After *The Amber Witch* Meinhold tried his hand at other work, in the years 1846–8 issuing his collected writings. In Volumes Five through Seven appeared his second major novel, *Sidonia von Bork*, a fairly long historical novel about another Pomeranian witch, characterized by the same remarkable verisimilitude as *The Amber Witch*. *Sidonia*, which was translated into English within a year or two by Oscar Wilde's mother, received little attention in Germany.

Meinhold survived for a few more years, increasingly bothered by religious doubts. He gradually worked his way around to the philosophical mysticism of the Catholic author Johann von Goerres, although it is not true, as is sometimes stated, that he became a convert to Catholicism. He resigned his pastorate, and died in 1851, leaving a third novel unfinished.

The Amber Witch is factual in part at least. According to the old chronicles that Meinhold worked with, there was a Pastor Schweidler who lived in seventeenth-century Usedom, although somewhat later than Meinhold's character. In documents written by this historical Schweidler there is a reference to one of his predecessors, whose daughter was burned as a witch during the period of the Thirty Years' War. Many of the other personalities, too, are either historical or semi-historical, as are many of the events described. Even such minor details as the appearance of Gustavus Adolphus's procession through the island have been verified in the chronicles. Meinhold also drew extensively on the folklore of his fellow islanders for many of the supernatural incidents described, while for details of the witch process he used trial records as well as Renaissance witch-hunting manuals. Those who are interested in Meinhold's meticulous use of such material may consult Josef Rysan's monograph, *Wilhelm Meinhold's Bernsteinhexe, A Study in Witchcraft and Cultural History*.

Since documents are not available, it is almost pointless to discuss Meinhold's literary antecedents in any but the larger sense, but it would seem that his predecessors were more in English literature than in German. Sir Walter Scott's novels are obvious prototypes, while the work of James Hogg stands even closer to Meinhold. Hogg's *Confessions of a Justified Sinner* (1824—a year before the first version of *The Amber Witch*) bears marked resemblances to Meinhold's novel. Hogg's work was known in Germany, and, lacking documentary evidence, it is a reasonable guess that Meinhold had read it. Regardless of literary prototypes, however, Meinhold's work was markedly original in form.

He considered himself the creator of a new genre, the "chronicle-novel," and while he was not entirely correct, he did compose the first important novel masquerading as a primary document.

In England Meinhold was fortunate in acquiring a remarkable translator, Lady Lucy Duff Gordon (1821–1869), who is also remembered for her *Letters from the Cape*. Mrs. Duff Gordon succeeded admirably in conveying the archaic Latinate style of the foolish preacher and in creating a unified work, rather than a mere translation. Meinhold recognized her qualities in dedicating to her his second novel, *Sidonia von Bork*. Less successful was an earlier translator, E. A. Friedlaender, whose work appeared in 1844, two years before Mrs. Duff Gordon's.

The English version of *The Amber Witch* remains the most important witch novel in the nineteenth-century English-speaking world. Yet despite its popularity, it did little to influence Victorian popular fiction. It probably provided the impetus for W. Harrison Ainsworth's *Lancashire Witches* (1848), which, while not a chronicle in form, is based on historical witch trials. It may also have suggested Miss E. Lynn Linton's collection of data, *Witch Stories*. However, when witch literature became more plentiful at the turn of the nineteenth and twentieth centuries, as in the work of Fiona MacLeod and J. Brodie Innes, the roots were mostly in Celtic literary folklore.

IV

Miss Amelia B. Edwards (1831–1892) lived through two reputations: she was a popular journalist-novelist of the 1860's, whose works occasionally remained in print up through the 1890's, and she was also a serious Egyptologist—one of the founders and the first Secretary of the important Egypt Exploration Fund.

Precocious as a writer, she sold her first poem, "The Knights of Old," when she was seven years old, and had her first story published in the *New England Magazine* at the age of twelve. It was only natural that she should become a journalist, and for years she was a regular contributor to Dickens's magazines, where she often provided the ghost story for the Christmas issue. She was also on the staff of the *Saturday Review*. Among her many publications were a two-volume history of France, two collections of poetry, eight novels in book form, and three collections of short stories. Most of her fiction is now very difficult to find.

Miss Edwards was an enthusiastic traveler, and a turning point in her life came on a trip up the Nile, in 1873–4, where she reached the Second Cataract. She was both aroused to enthusiasm by remains of ancient

Egypt, and appalled by the systematic looting and destruction of priceless archeological remains for commercial purposes. Her most famous book, *A Thousand Miles up the Nile* (1876) was a result of this trip, a very entertaining combination of travel and popular archeology, with reproductions of many inscriptions and monuments. It is still remembered as the finest travel account into the world of ancient Egypt.

Upon returning to England Miss Edwards started an intensive study of ancient Egyptian, and began her second career of publicizing archeological preservation. Through her efforts, mostly, the Egypt Exploration Fund was established, with the collaboration of the British Museum. As first Secretary, she devoted most of her remaining life to lecturing in Europe and America. Her second account of her Egyptian experiences, *Pharaohs, Fellahs and Explorers* (1891) was her last major publication. She died shortly afterwards, as a result of influenza contracted on a lecture tour.

Today Miss Edwards is remembered for her two travel books about Egypt, and for a handful of short supernatural stories which have been mainstays for most ghost story anthologies since the turn of the present century. Any reader who has read the earlier collections is certain to remember "The Four-Fifteen Express" or "The North Mail" ("The Phantom Coach"), "The History of Salome," or "Number Three" ("How the Third Floor Knew the Potteries"). All in all Miss Edwards wrote seventeen short stories about supernatural topics, most of which appeared anonymously in periodicals. They usually reflect her delight in strange climes and landscapes, alien cultural personalities and modes of life. No other Victorian author of ghost stories surpassed her in conveying in brief form the color and romantic atmosphere of the mountains of Italy, the ancient monasteries of Central Europe, or the hidden secrets of the forests of Germany. In addition to these stories Miss Edwards also wrote a single long supernatural story, the novelette "Monsieur Maurice," which first appeared in a three-volume collection of the same name in 1873. It has never before been republished.

V

Some sixty or seventy years ago "Vernon Lee" (born Violet Paget, 1856–1935) was a power in English letters. An expatriate in Italy for most of her life, she was preeminent in many fields. She wrote travel essays that are among the best in English, and succeed in conveying the *genius loci*, as opposed to mere physical description, as well as anything in the language. She was the pioneer scholar in the culture of eighteenth-century Italy, with unique sympathy for the late baroque art and music that was scorned elsewhere during her lifetime; for this she is still remembered by musicologists. She wrote a very perceptive study of the use of connotation in writing, *The Handling of Words*, which has never been surpassed. She attempted, unsuccessfully, a psychology of musical listening parallel to William James's *Varieties of Religious Experience*. And she also wrote a fair amount of biography, poetry, political philosophy, and fiction. Remarkable for both versatility and quality, she deserves recognition even in her few failures.

Vernon Lee wrote three collections of supernatural fiction, and a single short novel, altogether twelve stories, a somewhat small output for a writer who is generally regarded as one of the late Victorian masters.

Her first publication in this field was *A Phantom Lover*, which first appeared in 1886 as a book. It was reprinted some five years later (1890) in *Hauntings, Fantastic Stories*, under the new title "Oke of Okehurst," by which it is now generally known. One can speculate whether her title change affected the interpretation of the story. Yet in many ways *A Phantom Lover* is not typical of Miss Lee's work. It is longer than her other stories, British in setting and approach, and its calculated ambiguities and subtleties are more in the manner of the earlier Henry James than her later work.

Hauntings contains three other fine stories, while *Pope Jacynth and Other Fantastic Stories* (1904) and *For Maurice: Five Unlikely Tales* (1927) provide the remainder. These stories reveal the world of passionately vivified scholarship in which Miss Lee lived: the castrati singers and instrumentalists of eighteenth-century Italy, the chronicles of the Middle Ages, the small gods of ancient Greece. They contain such original conceits as a statue of Marsyas, which was misinterpreted as a crucifix, and a visit of the Olympian gods to the Wartburg to listen to Tanhuser. There is nothing exactly comparable to them in English, except for an occasional short story by Richard Garnett, the librarian of the British Museum.

VI

The Ghost of Guir House (1897), American in origin, reflects a very strong trend in later supernatural fiction: occultism. While there were earlier occult novels—*Sethos* by Terrasson, the *Comte de Gabalis* by Montfaucon de Villars, and *Zanoni* by E. Bulwer-Lytton, to name only three important examples—the great blossoming of the occult novel took place in the last decades of the nineteenth century, into the twentieth. Scores of occult novels were published in America and Great Britain, often semi-literate, often issued by vanity publishers. This development was probably due, first, to the emergence of Spiritualism as an international phenomenon (with novels based on it by Julian Hawthorne, W. D. Howells, and others), and most of all, to the Theosophical Society of Madame Blavatsky.

The story of Madame Blavatsky's rise and fall, and the history of her system, has been told in many places, particularly in *Priestess of the Occult* by Gertrude Williams. According to Blavatsky and her circle (including the Dr. Hartmann quoted in *The Ghost of Guir House*), above and beyond ordinary humans who live and sweat in cities and country, there exists a small body of supermen, the Mahatmas. These Mahatmas, who live for the most part in Tibet, are supernally good and are attempting to reclaim the world, which is currently in an evil period (the *kaliyug*). They have the power to work miracles: levitation, transmutation of substances, thought control, teleportation, telepathy, and much else. Certain students of the Mysteries, including Madame Blavatsky, were in psychic communication with these Mahatmas, and received secret teachings, which they then passed on to a select group (for a fee)—the Theosophical Society.

Madame Blavatsky had a remarkable gift for publicity, and the impact of her ideas, which were also associated with a detailed pseudoscience, was overwhelming in the borderland thought of the late nineteenth century and later. To name only a few of the better-known authors who made use of them: A. Conan Doyle, in *The Mystery of Cloomber*, which also has suggestions of *The Moonstone*; F. Anstey, in his spoof, *A Fallen Idol*, where Western occultism proves to be a match for an evil Mahatma; the novels of Dion Fortune; the Jimgrim sequence of novels by Talbot Mundy, and many others.

The author of *The Ghost of Guir House*, Charles Willing Beale (1845–1932), led a life worthy of a biographical novel. After graduating from the University of Pennsylvania at the age of sixteen as a civil engineer, he surveyed for the Pacific Railroad for several years. He left reminiscences of many scrapes with hostile Indians, particularly in the Black Hills. In 1869 he settled in western North Carolina, and tried his hand at various business ventures: a railroad line, a sheep ranch, and a cigar factory. Eventually he built a successful hotel-resort, which numbered among its guests Woodrow Wilson, Theodore Roosevelt, Mark Twain, and other notables. Beale seems to have been a very charming host, and one of his "duties" was telling ghost stories, on the veranda, evenings, to his guests.

Even today Beale's feats of strength and endurance are remembered in western North Carolina, in the Asheville region, near which he lived. There are stories of his lifting enormous weights, such as the instance when he carried a two-horse plow three miles in the hills. And there is also Beale's Run. According to his descendants, he was once accused of mistreating a horse, by making the horse run too fast on a hot day. Beale scoffed at the charge, and claimed that he had driven the horse no faster than he could run himself, ten miles in an hour, the distance between Asheville and Arden. To settle the argument, he raced over the distance himself, ten miles in 55 minutes, which is not far from an Olympic record.

C. W. Beale also wrote considerably, contributing many pieces to periodicals in the late nineteenth century. He had only two published books, however, *The Ghost of Guir House* (1895; second edition 1897) and *The Secret of the Earth* (1898). The latter book is a juvenile account of a trip inside the hollow earth, a good thriller with reminiscences of Jules Verne.

As can be seen from *The Ghost of Guir House*, C. W. Beale was strongly interested in occult ideas. He studied the literature of his day, practiced hypnosis considerably, and spent hours in silent meditation. The basic idea of his story, of course, is an old one, but Mr. Beale's treatment reveals excellent local color, firmness of characterization that is enviable, and personal charm. Beale's wife, Maria Beale, drew the frontispiece (reproduced in the present volume).

VII

It would have been interesting to include in this collection an example of the "blood," or adventure novel of the Victorians, Mrs. Braddon, Malcolm Rymer, G. W. M. Reynolds and Thomas P. Prest being the foremost practitioners. This, however, turned out to be impracticable. Most bloods are now unreadable curiosities. The few that have claim to even the minor virtues of fast motion and extravagant incident are too long, and could not be excerpted.

I would also have liked to include a work by the greatest Victorian writer of ghost stories, the Irish novelist J. S. LeFanu. Only two or three of his stories would qualify in length, however, and all are so readily available that it would seem unfair to the reader to include them, despite their high quality.

New York, N.Y.
1970   E. F. BLEILER

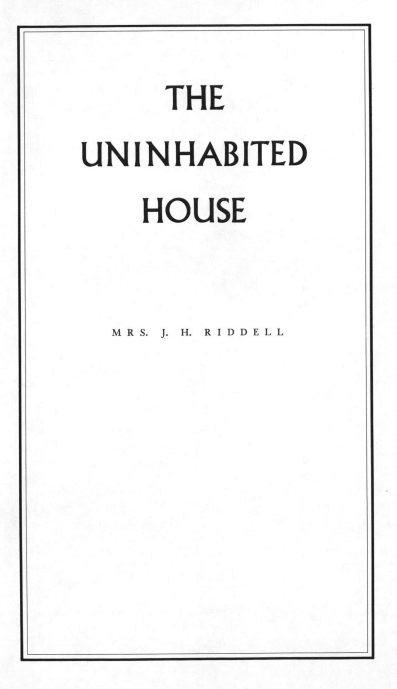

THE
UNINHABITED
HOUSE

MRS. J. H. RIDDELL

1.   Miss Blake—from Memory

If ever a residence, "suitable in every respect for a family of position," haunted a lawyer's offices, the "Uninhabited House," about which I have a story to tell, haunted those of Messrs. Craven and Son, No. 200, Buckingham Street, Strand.

It did not matter in the least whether it happened to be let or unlet: in either case, it never allowed Mr. Craven or his clerks, of whom I was one, to forget its existence.

When let, we were in perpetual hot water with the tenant; when unlet, we had to endeavour to find some tenant to take that unlucky house.

Happy were we when we could get an agreement signed for a couple of years—although we always had misgivings that the war waged with the last occupant would probably have to be renewed with his successor.

Still, when we were able to let the desirable residence to a solvent individual, even for twelve months, Mr. Craven rejoiced.

He knew how to proceed with the tenants who came blustering, or threatening, or complaining, or bemoaning; but he did not know what to do with Miss Blake and her letters, when no person was liable for the rent.

All lawyers—I am one myself, and can speak from a long and varied experience—all lawyers, even the very hardest, have one client, at all events, towards whom they exhibit much forbearance, for whom they feel a certain sympathy, and in whose interests they take a vast deal of trouble for very little pecuniary profit.

A client of this kind favours me with his business—he has favoured me with it for many years past. Each first of January I register a vow he shall cost me no more time or money. On each last day of December I find he is deeper in my debt than he was on the same date a twelvemonth previous.

I often wonder how this is—why we, so fierce to one human being, possibly honest and well-meaning enough, should be as wax in the hand of the moulder, when another individual, perhaps utterly disreputable, refuses to take "No" for an answer.

Do we purchase our indulgences in this way? Do we square our accounts with our own consciences by remembering that, if we have been as stone to Dick, Tom, and Harry, we have melted at the first appeal of Jack?

My principal, Mr. Craven—than whom a better man never breathed—had an unprofitable client, for whom he entertained feelings of the profoundest pity, whom he treated with a rare courtesy. That lady was Miss Blake; and when the old house on the Thames stood tenantless, Mr. Craven's bed did not prove one of roses.

In our firm there was no son—Mr. Craven had been the son; but the old father was dead, and our chief's wife had brought him only daughters.

Still the title of the firm remained the same, and Mr. Craven's own signature also.

He had been junior for such a number of years, that, when Death sent a royal invitation to his senior, he was so accustomed to the old form, that he, and all in his employment, tacitly agreed it was only fitting he should remain junior to the end.

A good man. I, of all human beings, have reason to speak well of him. Even putting the undoubted fact of all lawyers keeping one unprofitable client into the scales, if he had not been very good he must have washed his hands of Miss Blake and her niece's house long before the period at which this story opens.

The house did not belong to Miss Blake. It was the property of her niece, a certain Miss Helena Elmsdale, of whom Mr. Craven always spoke as that "poor child."

She was not of age, and Miss Blake managed her few pecuniary affairs.

Besides the "desirable residence, suitable," etcetera, aunt and niece had property producing about sixty-five pounds a year. When we could let the desirable residence, handsomely furnished, and with every convenience that could be named in the space of a half-guinea advertisement, to a family from the country, or an officer just returned from India, or to an invalid who desired a beautiful and quiet abode within an easy drive of the West End—when we could do this, I say, the income of aunt and niece rose to two hundred and sixty-five pounds a year, which made a very material difference to Miss Blake.

When we could not let the house, or when the payment of the rent was in dispute, Mr. Craven advanced the lady various five and ten pound notes, which, it is to be hoped, were entered duly to his credit in the Eternal Books. In the mundane records kept in our offices, they always appeared as debits to William Craven's private account.

As for the young men about our establishment, of whom I was one, we anathematised that house. I do not intend to reproduce the language we used concerning it at one period of our experience, because eventually the evil wore itself out, as most evils do, and at last we came to look upon the desirable residence as an institution of our firm—as a sort of cause célèbre, with which it was creditable to be associated—as a species of remarkable criminal always on its trial, and always certain to be defended by Messrs. Craven and Son.

In fact, the Uninhabited House—for uninhabited it usually was, whether anyone was answerable for the rent or not—finally became an object of as keen interest to all Mr. Craven's clerks as it became a source of annoyance to him.

So the beam goes up and down. While Mr. Craven pooh-poohed the complaints of tenants, and laughed at the idea of a man being afraid of a ghost, we did not laugh, but swore. When, however, Mr. Craven began to look serious about the matter, and hoped some evil-disposed persons were not trying to keep the place tenantless, our interest in the old house became absorbing. And as our interest in the residence grew, so, likewise, did our appreciation of Miss Blake.

We missed her when she went abroad—which she always did the day a fresh agreement was signed—and we welcomed her return to England and our offices with effusion. Safely I can say no millionaire ever received such an ovation as fell to the lot of Miss Blake when, after a foreign tour, she returned to those lodgings near Brunswick Square, which her residence ought, I think, to have rendered classic.

She never lost an hour in coming to us. With the dust of travel upon her, with the heat and burden of quarrels with railway porters, and encounters with cabmen, visible to anyone who chose to read the signs of the times, Miss Blake came pounding up our stairs, wanting to see Mr. Craven.

If that gentleman was engaged, she would sit down in the general office, and relate her latest grievance to a posse of sympathising clerks.

"And he says he won't pay the rent," was always the refrain of these lamentations.

"It is in Ireland he thinks he is, poor soul!" she was wont to declare.

"We'll teach him different, Miss Blake," the spokesman of the party would declare; whilst another ostentatiously mended a pen, and a third brought down a ream of foolscap and laid it with a thump before him on the desk.

"And, indeed, you're all decent lads, though full of your tricks," Miss Blake would sometimes remark, in a tone of gentle reproof. "But if you had a niece just dying with grief, and a house nobody will live in on your hands, you would not have as much heart for fun, I can tell you that."

Hearing which, the young rascals tried to look sorrowful, and failed.

In the way of my profession I have met with many singular persons, but I can safely declare I never met with any person so singular as Miss Blake.

She was—I speak of her in the past tense, not because she is dead, but because times and circumstances have changed since the period when we both had to do with the Uninhabited House, and she has altered in consequence—one of the most original people who ever crossed my path.

Born in the north of Ireland, the child of a Scottish-Ulster mother and a Connaught father, she had ingeniously contrived to combine in her own person the vices of two distinct races, and exclude the virtues of both.

Her accent was the most fearful which could be imagined. She had the brogue of the West grafted on the accent of the North. And yet there was a variety about her even in this respect. One never could tell, from visit to visit, whether she proposed to pronounce "written" as "wrutten" or "wretten";* whether she would elect to style her parents, to whom she made frequent reference, her "pawpaw and mawmaw," or her "pepai and memai."

It all depended with whom Miss Blake had lately been most intimate. If she had been "hand and glove" with a "nob" from her own country—she was in no way reticent about thus styling her grander acquaintances, only she wrote the word "knob"—who thought to conceal his nationality by "awing" and "hawing," she spoke about people being "married" and wearing "sockcloth and oshes." If, on the contrary, she had been thrown into the society of a lady who so far honoured England as to talk as some people do in England, we had every A turned into E, and every U into O, while she minced her words as if she had been saying "niminy piminy" since she first began to talk, and honestly believed no human being could ever have told she had been born west of St. George's Channel.

But not merely in accent did Miss Blake evidence the fact that her birth had been the result of an injudicious cross; the more one knew of her, the more clearly one saw the wrong points she threw out.

Extravagant to a fault, like her Connaught father, she was in no respect generous, either from impulse or calculation.

Mean about minor details, a turn of character probably inherited from the Ulster mother, she was utterly destitute of that careful and honest economy which is an admirable trait in the natives of the north of Ireland, and which enables them so frequently, after being strictly just, to be much more than liberal.

Honest, Miss Blake was not—or, for that matter, honourable either. Her indebtedness to our firm could not be considered other than a matter of honour, and yet she never dreamt of paying her debt to Mr. Craven.

---

* The wife of a celebrated Indian officer stated that she once, in the north of Ireland, heard Job's utterance thus rendered—"Oh! that my words were wrutten, that they were prented in a buke."

Indeed, to do Miss Blake strict justice, she never thought of paying the debts she owed to anyone, unless she was obliged to do so.

Nowadays, I fear it would fare hard with her were she to try her old tactics with the British tradesman; but, in the time of which I am writing, co-operative societies were not, and then the British tradesman had no objection, I fancy, to be gulled.

Perhaps, like the lawyer and the unprofitable client, he set-off being gulled on one side his ledger against being fleeced on the other.

Be this as it may, we were always compounding some liability for Miss Blake, as well as letting her house and fighting with the tenants.

At first, as I have said, we found Miss Blake an awful bore, but we generally ended by deciding we could better spare a better man. Indeed, the months when she did not come to our office seemed to want flavour.

Of gratitude—popularly supposed to be essentially characteristic of the Irish—Miss Blake was utterly destitute. I never did know—I have never known since, so ungrateful a woman.

Not merely did she take everything Mr. Craven did for her as a right, but she absolutely turned the tables, and brought him in her debtor.

Once, only once, that I can remember, he ventured to ask when it would be convenient for her to repay some of the money he had from time to time advanced.

Miss Blake was taken by surprise, but she rose equal to the occasion. "You are joking, Mr. Craven," she said. "You mean, when will I want to ask you to give me a share of the profits you have made out of the estate of my poor sister's husband. Why, that house has been as good as an annuity to you. For six long years it has stood empty, or next to empty, and never been out of law all the time."

"But, you know, Miss Blake, that not a shilling of profit has accrued to me from the house being in law," he pleaded. "I have always been too glad to get the rent for you, to insist upon my costs, and, really——."

"Now, do not try to impose upon me," she interrupted, "because it is of no use. Didn't you make thousands of the dead man, and now haven't you got the house? Why, if you never had a penny of costs, instead of all you have pocketed, that house and the name it has brought to you, and the fame which has spread abroad in consequence, can't be reckoned as less than hundreds a year to your firm. And yet you ask me for the return of a trumpery four or five sovereigns—I am ashamed of you! But I won't imitate your bad example. Let me have five more to-day, and you can stop ten out of the Colonel's first payment."

"I am very sorry," said my employer, "but I really have not five pounds to spare."

"Hear him," remarked Miss Blake, turning towards me. "Young

man"—Miss Blake steadily refused to recognise the possibility of any clerk being even by accident a gentleman—"will you hand me over the newspaper?"

I had not the faintest idea what she wanted with the newspaper, and neither had Mr. Craven, till she sat down again deliberately—the latter part of this conversation having taken place after she rose, preparatory to saying farewell—opened the sheet out to its full width, and commenced to read the debates.

"My dear Miss Blake," began Mr. Craven, after a minute's pause, "you know my time, when it is mine, is always at your disposal, but at the present moment several clients are waiting to see me, and——"

"Let them wait," said Miss Blake, as he hesitated a little. "Your time and their time is no more valuable than mine, and I mean to stay *here*," emphasising the word, "till you let me have that five pounds. Why, look, now, that house is taken on a two years' agreement, and you won't see me again for that time—likely as not, never; for who can tell what may happen to anybody in foreign parts? Only one charge I lay upon you, Mr. Craven: don't let me be buried in a strange country. It is bad enough to be so far as this from my father and my mother's remains, but I daresay I'll manage to rest in the same grave as my sister, though Robert Elmsdale lies between. He separated us in life—not that she ever cared for him; but it won't matter much when we are all bones and dust together——"

"If I let you have that five pounds," here broke in Mr. Craven, "do I clearly understand that I am to recoup myself out of Colonel Morris' first payment?"

"I said so as plain as I could speak," agreed Miss Blake; and her speech was very plain indeed.

Mr. Craven lifted his eyebrows and shrugged his shoulders, while he drew his cheque-book towards him.

"How is Helena?" he asked, as he wrote the final legendary flourish after Craven and Son.

"Helena is but middling, poor dear," answered Miss Blake—on that occasion she called her niece Hallana. "She frets, the creature, as is natural; but she will get better when we leave England. England is a hard country for anyone who is all nairves like Halana."

"Why do you never bring her to see me?" asked Mr. Craven, folding up the cheque.

"Bring her to be stared at by a parcel of clerks!" exclaimed Miss Blake, in a tone which really caused my hair to bristle. "Well-mannered, decent young fellows in their own rank, no doubt, but not fit to look at my sister's child. Now, now, Mr. Craven, ought Kathleen Blake's—or, rather, Kathleen Elmsdale's daughter to serve as a fifth of November guy for London lads? You know she is handsome enough to be a duchess, like her mother."

"Yes, yes, I know," agreed Mr. Craven, and handed over the cheque.

After I had held the door open for Miss Blake to pass out, and closed it securely and resumed my seat, Miss Blake turned the handle and treated us to another sight of her bonnet.

"Good-bye, William Craven, for two years at any rate; and if I never see you again, God bless you, for you've been a true friend to me and that poor child who has nobody else to look to," and then, before Mr. Craven could cross the room, she was gone.

"I wonder," said I, "if it will be two years before we see her again?"

"No, nor the fourth of two years," answered my employer. "There is something queer about that house."

"You don't think it is haunted, sir, do you?" I ventured.

"Of course not," said Mr. Craven, irritably; "but I do think some one wants to keep the place vacant, and is succeeding admirably."

The question I next put seemed irrelevant, but really resulted from a long train of thought. This was it:

"Is Miss Elmsdale very handsome, sir?"

"She is very beautiful," was the answer; "but not so beautiful as her mother was."

Ah me! two old, old stories in a sentence. He had loved the mother, and he did not love the daughter. He had seen the mother in his bright, hopeful youth, and there was no light of morning left for him in which he could behold the child.

To other eyes she might, in her bright spring-time, seem lovely as an angel from heaven, but to him no more such visions were to be vouchsafed.

If beauty really went on decaying, as the ancients say, by this time there could be no beauty left. But oh! greybeard, the beauty remains, though our eyes may be too dim to see it; the beauty, the grace, the rippling laughter, and the saucy smiles, which once had power to stir to their very depths our hearts, friend—our hearts, yours and mine, comrade, feeble, and cold, and pulseless now.

2. THE CORONER'S INQUEST

The story was told to me afterwards, but I may as well weave it in with mine at this juncture.

From the maternal ancestress, the Demoiselles Blake inherited a certain amount of money. It was through no fault of the paternal Blake— through no want of endeavours on his part to make ducks and drakes of all fortune which came in his way, that their small inheritance remained intact; but the fortune was so willed that neither the girls nor he could divert the peaceful tenure of its half-yearly dividends.

The mother died first, and the father followed her ere long, and then the young ladies found themselves orphans, and the possessors of a fixed income of one hundred and thirty pounds a year.

A modest income, and yet, as I have been given to understand, they might have married well for the money.

In those days, particularly in Ireland, men went very cheap, and the Misses Blake, one and both, could, before they left off mourning, have wedded, respectively, a curate, a doctor, a constabulary officer, and the captain of a government schooner.

The Misses Blake looked higher, however, and came to England, where rich husbands are presumably procurable. Came, but missed their market. Miss Kathleen found only one lover, William Craven, whose honest affection she flouted; and Miss Susannah found no lover at all.

Miss Kathleen wanted a duke, or an earl—a prince of the blood royal being about that time unprocurable; and an attorney, to her Irish ideas, seemed a very poor sort of substitute. For which reason she rejected the attorney with scorn, and remained single, the while dukes and earls were marrying and intermarrying with their peers or their inferiors.

Then suddenly there came a frightful day when Kathleen and Susannah learned they were penniless, when they understood their trustee had robbed them, as he had robbed others, and had been paying their interest out of what was left of their principal.

They tried teaching, but they really had nothing to teach. They tried letting lodgings. Even lodgers rebelled against their untidiness and want of punctuality.

The eldest was very energetic and very determined, and the youngest very pretty and very conciliatory. Nevertheless, business is business, and lodgings are lodgings, and the Misses Blake were on the verge of beggary, when Mr. Elmsdale proposed for Miss Kathleen and was accepted.

Mr. Craven, by that time a family man, gave the bride away, and secured Mr. Elmsdale's business.

Possibly, had Mrs. Elmsdale's marriage proved happy, Mr. Craven might have soon lost sight of his former love. In matrimony, as in other matters, we are rarely so sympathetic with fulfilment as with disappointment. The pretty Miss Blake was a disappointed woman after she had secured Mr. Elmsdale. She then understood that the best life could offer her was something very different indeed from the ideal duke her beauty should have won, and she did not take much trouble to conceal her dissatisfaction with the arrangements of Providence.

Mr. Craven, seeing what Mr. Elmsdale was towards men, pitied her. Perhaps, had he seen what Mrs. Elmsdale was towards her husband, he might have pitied him; but, then, he did not see, for women are wonderful dissemblers.

There was Elmsdale, bluff in manner, short in person, red in the face, cumbersome in figure, addicted to naughty words, not nice about driving fearfully hard bargains, a man whom men hated, not undeservedly; and yet, nevertheless, a man capable of loving a woman with all the veins of his heart, and who might, had any woman been found to love him, have compassed earthly salvation.

There were those who said he never could compass eternal; but they chanced to be his debtors—and, after all, that question lay between himself and God. The other lay between himself and his wife, and it must be confessed, except so far as his passionate, disinterested love for an utterly selfish woman tended to redeem and humanise his nature, she never helped him one step along the better path.

But, then, the world could not know this, and Mr. Craven, of whom I am speaking at the moment, was likely, naturally, to think Mr. Elmsdale all in the wrong.

On the one hand he saw the man as he appeared to men: on the other he saw the woman as she appeared to men, beautiful to the last; fragile, with the low voice, so beautiful in any woman, so more especially beautiful in an Irish woman; with a languid face which insured compassion while never asking for it; with the appearance of a martyr, and the tone and the manner of a suffering saint.

Everyone who beheld the pair together, remarked, "What a pity it was such a sweet creature should be married to such a bear!" but Mr. Elmsdale was no bear to his wife: he adored her. The selfishness, the discontent, the ill-health, as much the consequence of a peevish, petted temper, as of disease, which might well have exhausted the patience and tired out the love of a different man, only endeared her the more to him.

She made him feel how inferior he was to her in all respects; how tremendously she had condescended, when she agreed to become his wife; and he quietly accepted her estimation of him, and said with a humility which was touching from its simplicity:

"I know I am not worthy of you, Kathleen, but I do my best to make you happy."

For her sake, not being a liberal man, he spent money freely; for her sake he endured Miss Blake; for her sake he bought the place which afterwards caused us so much trouble; for her sake, he, who had always scoffed at the folly of people turning their houses into stores for "useless timber," as he styled the upholsterer's greatest triumphs, furnished his rooms with a lavish disregard of cost; for her sake, he, who hated society, smiled on visitors, and entertained the guests she invited, with no grudging hospitality. For her sake he dressed well, and did many other things which were equally antagonistic to his original nature; and he might just as well have gone his own way, and pleased himself only, for all the pleasure he gave her, or all the thanks she gave him.

If Mr. Elmsdale had come home drunk five evenings a week, and beaten his wife, and denied her the necessaries of life, and kept her purse in a chronic state of emptiness, she might very possibly have been extremely grateful for an occasional kind word or smile; but, as matters stood, Mrs. Elmsdale was not in the least grateful for a devotion, as beautiful as it was extraordinary, and posed herself on the domestic sofa in the character of a martyr.

Most people accepted the representation as true, and pitied her. Miss Blake, blissfully forgetful of that state of impecuniosity from which Mr. Elmsdale's proposal had extricated herself and her sister, never wearied of stating that "Katty had thrown herself away, and that Mr. Elmsdale was not fit to tie her shoe-string."

She generously admitted the poor creature did his best; but, according to Blake, the poor creature's best was very bad indeed.

"It's not his fault, but his misfortune," the lady was wont to remark, "that he's like dirt beside her. He can't help his birth, and his dragging-up, and his disreputable trade, or business, or whatever he likes to call it; he can't help never having had a father nor mother to speak of, and not a lady or gentleman belonging to the family since it came into existence. I'm not blaming him, but it is hard for Kathleen, and she reared as she was, and accustomed to the best society in Ireland,—which is very different, let me tell you, from the best anybody ever saw in England."

There were some who thought, if Mrs. Elmsdale could tolerate her sister's company, she might without difficulty have condoned her husband's want of acquaintance with some points of grammar and etiquette; and who said, amongst themselves, that whereas he only maltreated, Miss Blake mangled every letter in the alphabet; but these carping critics were in the minority.

Mrs. Elmsdale was a beauty, and a martyr; Mr. Elmsdale a rough beast, who had no capacity of ever developing into a prince. Miss Blake was a model of sisterly affection, and if eccentric in her manner, and bewildering in the vagaries of her accent, well, most Irish people, the highest in rank not excepted, were the same. Why, there was Lord So-and-so, who stated at a public meeting that "roight and moight were not always convartible tarms"; and accepted the cheers and laughter which greeted his utterance as evidence that he had said something rather neat.

Miss Blake's accent was a very different affair indeed from those wrestles with his foe in which her brother-in-law always came off worsted.

He endured agonies in trying to call himself Elmsdale, and rarely succeeded in styling his wife anything except Mrs. HE. I am told Miss Blake's mimicry of this peculiarity was delicious: but I never was privileged to hear her delineation, for, long before the period when this story opens, Mr. Elmsdale had departed to that land where no confusion of tongues can much signify, and where Helmsdale no doubt served his purpose just as well as Miss Blake's more refined pronunciation of his name.

Further, Miss Helena Elmsdale would not allow a word in depreciation of her father to be uttered when she was near, and as Miss Helena could on occasion develop a very pretty little temper, as well as considerable power of satire, Miss Blake dropped out of the habit of ridiculing Mr. Elmsdale's sins of omission and commission, and contented herself by generally asserting that, as his manner of living had broken her poor sister's heart, so his manner of dying had broken her—Miss Blake's—heart.

"It is only for the sake of the orphan child I am able to hold up at all," she would tell us. "I would not have blamed him so much for leaving us poor, but it was hard and cruel to leave us disgraced into the bargain"; and then Miss Blake would weep, and the wag of the office would take out his handkerchief and ostentatiously wipe his eyes.

She often threatened to complain of that boy—a merry, mischievous young imp—to Mr. Craven; but she never did so. Perhaps because the clerks always gave her rapt attention; and an interested audience was very pleasant to Miss Blake.

Considering the nature of Mr. Elmsdale's profession, Miss Blake had possibly some reason to complain of the extremely unprofitable manner in which he cut up. He was what the lady described as "a dirty money-lender."

Heaven only knows how he drifted into his occupation; few men, I imagine, select such a trade, though it is one which seems to exercise an enormous fascination for those who have adopted it.

The only son of a very small builder who managed to leave a few hundred pounds behind him for the benefit of Elmsdale, then clerk in a contractor's office, he had seen enough of the anxieties connected with his father's business to wash his hands of bricks and mortar.

Experience, perhaps, had taught him also that people who advanced money to builders made a very nice little income out of the capital so employed; and it is quite possible that some of his father's acquaintances, always in want of ready cash, as speculative folks usually are, offered such terms for temporary accommodation as tempted him to enter into the business of which Miss Blake spoke so contemptuously.

Be this as it may, one thing is certain—by the time Elmsdale was thirty he had established a very nice little connection amongst needy men: whole streets were mortgaged to him; terraces, nominally the property of some well-to-do builder, were virtually his, since he only waited the well-to-do builder's inevitable bankruptcy to enter into possession. He was not a sixty per cent. man, always requiring some very much better security than "a name" before parting with his money; but still even twenty per cent. usually means ruin, and, as a matter of course, most of Mr. Elmsdale's clients reached that pleasant goal.

They could have managed to do so, no doubt, had Mr. Elmsdale never existed; but as he was in existence, he served the purpose for which it seemed his mother had borne him; and sooner or later—as a rule, sooner than later—assumed the shape of Nemesis to most of those who "did business" with him.

There were exceptions, of course. Some men, by the help of exceptional good fortune, roguery, or genius, managed to get out of Mr. Elmsdale's hands by other paths than those leading through Basinghall or Portugal Streets; but they merely proved the rule.

Notably amongst these fortunate persons may be mentioned a Mr. Harrison and a Mr. Harringford—'Arrison and 'Arringford, as Mr. Elmsdale called them, when he did not refer to them as the two Haitches.

Of these, the first-named, after a few transactions, shook the dust of Mr. Elmsdale's office off his shoes, sent him the money he owed by his lawyer, and ever after referred to Mr. Elmsdale as "that thief," "that scoundrel," that "swindling old vagabond," and so forth; but, then, hard words break no bones, and Mr. Harrison was not very well thought of himself.

His remarks, therefore, did Mr. Elmsdale very little harm—a money-lender is not usually spoken of in much pleasanter terms by those who once have been thankful enough for his cheque; and the world in general does not attach a vast amount of importance to the opinions of a former borrower. Mr. Harrison did not, therefore, hurt or benefit his quondam friend to any appreciable extent; but with Mr. Harringford the case was different.

He and Elmsdale had been doing business together for years, "everything he possessed in the world," he stated to an admiring coroner's jury summoned to sit on Mr. Elmsdale's body and inquire into the cause of that gentleman's death—"everything he possessed in the world, he owed to the deceased. Some people spoke hardly of him, but his experience of Mr. Elmsdale enabled him to say that a kinder-hearted, juster, honester, or better-principled man never existed. He charged high interest, certainly, and he expected to be paid his rate; but, then, there was no deception about the matter: if it was worth a borrower's while to take money at twenty per cent., why, there was an end of the matter. Business men are not children," remarked Mr. Harringford, "and ought not to borrow money at twenty per cent. unless they can make thirty per cent. out of it." Personally, he had never paid Mr. Elmsdale more than twelve and a half or fifteen per cent.; but, then, their transactions were on a large scale. Only the day before Mr. Elmsdale's death—he hesitated a little over that word, and became, as the reporters said, "affected"—he had paid him twenty thousand pounds. The deceased told him he had urgent need of the money, and at considerable inconvenience he raised the amount. If the question were pressed as to whether he guessed for what purpose that sum was so urgently needed, he would answer it, of course; but he suggested that it should not be pressed, as likely to give pain to those who were already in terrible affliction.

Hearing which, the jury pricked up their ears, and the coroner's curiosity became so intense that he experienced some difficulty in saying, calmly, that, "as the object of his sitting there was to elicit the truth, however much he should regret causing distress to anyone, he must request that Mr. Harringford, whose scruples did him honour, would keep back no fact tending to throw light upon so sad an affair."

Having no alternative after this but to unburden himself of his secret, Mr. Harringford stated that he feared the deceased had been a heavy loser at Ascot. Mr. Harringford, having gone to that place with some friends, met Mr. Elmsdale on the race-course. Expressing astonishment at meeting him there, Mr. Elmsdale stated he had run down to look after a client of his who he feared was going wrong. He said he did not much care to do business with a betting man. In the course of subsequent conversation, however, he told the witness he had some money on the favourite.

As frequently proves the case, the favourite failed to come in first: that was all Mr. Harringford knew about the matter. Mr. Elmsdale never mentioned how much he had lost—in fact, he never referred again, except in general terms, to their meeting. He stated, however, that he must have money, and that immediately; if not the whole amount, half, at all events. The witness found, however, he could more easily raise the larger than the smaller sum. There had been a little unpleasantness between him and Mr. Elmsdale with reference to the demand for money made so suddenly and so peremptorily, and he bitterly regretted having even for a moment forgotten what was due to so kind a friend.

He knew of no reason in the world why Mr. Elmsdale should have committed suicide. He was, in business, eminently a cautious man, and Mr. Harringford had always supposed him to be wealthy; in fact, he believed him to be a man of large property. Since the death of his wife, he had, however, noticed a change in him; but still it never crossed the witness's mind that his brain was in any way affected.

Miss Blake, who had to this point postponed giving her evidence, on account of the "way she was upset," was now able to tell a sympathetic jury and a polite coroner all she knew of the matter.

"Indeed," she began, "Robert Elmsdale had never been the same man since her poor sister's death; he mooned about, and would sit for half an hour at a time, doing nothing but looking at a faded bit of the dining-room carpet."

He took no interest in anything; if he was asked any questions about the garden, he would say, "What does it matter? *she* cannot see it now."

"Indeed, my lord," said Miss Blake, in her agitation probably confounding the coroner with the chief justice, "it was just pitiful to see the creature; I am sure his ways got to be heart-breaking."

"After my sister's death," Miss Blake resumed, after a pause, devoted by herself, the jury, and the coroner to sentiment, "Robert Elmsdale gave up his office in London, and brought his business home. I do not know why he did this. He would not, had she been living, because he always kept his trade well out of her sight, poor man. Being what she was, she could not endure the name of it, naturally. It was not my place to say he shouldn't do what he liked in his own house, and I thought the excitement of building a new room, and quarrelling with the builder, and swearing at the men, was good for him. He made a fireproof place for his papers, and he fitted up the office like a library, and bought a beautiful large table, covered with leather; and nobody to have gone in would have thought the room was used for business. He had a Turkey carpet on the floor, and chairs that slipped about on castors; and he planned a covered way out into the road, with a separate entrance for itself, so that none of us ever knew who went out or who came in. He kept his affairs secret as the grave."

"No," in answer to the coroner, who began to think Miss Blake's narrative would never come to an end. "I heard no shot: none of us did: we all slept away from that part of the house; but I was restless that night, and could not sleep, and I got up and looked out at the river, and saw a flare of light on it. I thought it odd he was not gone to bed, but took little notice of the matter for a couple of hours more, when it was just getting gray in the morning, and I looked out again, and still seeing the light, slipped on a dressing-wrapper and my slippers, and ran downstairs to tell him he would ruin his health if he did not go to his bed.

"When I opened the door I could see nothing; the table stood between me and him; but the gas was flaring away, and as I went round to put it out, I came across him lying on the floor. It never occurred to me he was dead; I thought he was in a fit, and knelt down to unloose his cravat, then I found he had gone.

"The pistol lay on the carpet beside him—and that," finished Miss Blake, "is all I have to tell."

When asked if she had ever known of his losing money by betting, she answered it was not likely he would tell her anything of that kind.

"He always kept his business to himself," she affirmed, "as is the way of most men."

In answer to other questions, she stated she never heard of any losses in business; there was plenty of money always to be had for the asking. He was liberal enough, though perhaps not so liberal latterly, as before his wife's death; she didn't know anything of the state of his affairs. Likely, Mr. Craven could tell them all about that."

Mr. Craven, however, proved unable to do so. To the best of his belief, Mr. Elmsdale was in very easy circumstances. He had transacted a large amount of business for him, but never any involving pecuniary loss or anxiety; he should have thought him the last man in the world to run into such folly as betting; he had no doubt Mrs. Elmsdale's death had affected him disastrously. He said more than once to witness, if it were not for the sake of his child, he should not care if he died that night.

All of which, justifying the jury in returning a verdict of "suicide while of unsound mind," they expressed their unanimous opinion to that effect—thus "saving the family the condemnation of *felo de se*," remarked Miss Blake.

The dead man was buried, the church service read over his remains, the household was put into mourning, the blinds were drawn up, the windows flung open, and the business of life taken up once more by the survivors.

3.   OUR LAST TENANT

It is quite competent for a person so to manage his affairs, that, whilst understanding all about them himself, another finds it next to impossible to make head or tail of his position.

Mr. Craven found that Mr. Elmsdale had effected this feat; entries there were in his books, intelligible enough, perhaps, to the man who made them, but as so much Hebrew to a stranger.

He had never kept a business banking account; he had no regular journal or ledger; he seemed to have depended on memoranda, and vague and uncertain writings in his diary, both for memory and accuracy; and as most of his business had been conducted *viva voce*, there were few letters to assist in throwing the slightest light on his transactions.

Even from the receipts, however, one thing was clear, viz., that he had, since his marriage, spent a very large sum of money; spent it lavishly, not to say foolishly. Indeed, the more closely Mr. Craven looked into affairs, the more satisfied he felt that Mr. Elmsdale had committed suicide simply because he was well-nigh ruined.

Mortgage-deeds Mr. Craven himself had drawn up, were nowhere to be found; neither could one sovereign of the money Mr. Harringford paid be discovered.

Miss Blake said she believed "that Harringford had never paid at all"; but this was clearly proved to be an error of judgment on the part of that impulsive lady. Not merely did Harringford hold the receipt for the money and the mortgage-deeds cancelled, but the cheque he had given to the mortgagee bore the endorsement—"Robert Elmsdale"; while the clerk who cashed it stated that Mr. Elmsdale presented the order in person, and that to him he handed the notes.

Whatever he had done with the money, no notes were to be found; a diligent search of the strong room produced nothing more important than the discovery of a cash-box containing three hundred pounds; the title-deeds of River Hall—such being the modest name by which Mr. Elmsdale had elected to have his residence distinguished; the leases relating to some small cottages near Barnes; all the letters his wife had ever written to him; two locks of her hair, one given before marriage, the other cut after her death; a curl severed from the head of my "baby daughter"; quantities of receipts—and nothing more.

"I wonder he can rest in his grave," said Miss Blake, when at last she began to realize, in a dim sort of way, the position of affairs.

According to the River Hall servants' version, Mr. Elmsdale did anything rather than rest in his grave. About the time the new mourning had been altered to fit perfectly, a nervous housemaid, who began perhaps to find the house dull, mooted the question as to whether "master walked."

Within a fortnight it was decided in solemn conclave that master did; and further, that the place was not what it had been; and moreover, that in the future it was likely to be still less like what it had been.

There is a wonderful instinct in the lower classes, which enables them to comprehend, without actual knowledge, when misfortune is coming upon a house: and in this instance that instinct was not at fault.

Long before Mr. Craven had satisfied himself that his client's estate was a very poor one, the River Hall servants, one after another, had given notice to leave—indeed, to speak more accurately, they did not give notice, for they left; and before they left they took care to baptize the house with such an exceedingly bad name, that neither for love nor money could Miss Blake get a fresh "help" to stay in it for more than twenty-four hours.

First one housemaid was taken with "the shivers"; then the cook had "the trembles"; then the coachman was prepared to take his solemn affidavit, that, one night long after everyone in the house *to his knowledge* was in bed, he "see from his room above the stables, a light a-shining on the Thames, and the figures of one or more a passing and a repassing across the blind." More than this, a new page-boy declared that, on a certain evening, before he had been told there was anything strange about the house, he heard the door of the passage leading from the library into the side-road slam violently, and looking to see who had gone out by that unused entrance, failed to perceive sign of man, woman, or child, by the bright moonlight.

Moved by some feeling which he professed himself unable to "put a name on," he proceeded to the door in question, and found it barred, chained, and bolted. While he was standing wondering what it meant, he noticed the light as of gas shining from underneath the library door; but when he softly turned the handle and peeped in, the room was dark as the grave, and "like cold water seemed running down his back."

Further, he averred, as he stole away into the hall, there was a sound followed him as between a groan and a cry. Hearing which statement, an impressionable charwoman went into hysterics, and had to be recalled to her senses by a dose of gin, suggested and taken strictly as a medicine.

But no supply of spirituous liquors, even had Miss Blake been disposed to distribute anything of the sort, could induce servants after a time to remain in, or charwomen to come to, the house. It had received a bad name, and that goes even further in disfavour of a residence than it does against a man or woman.

Finally, Miss Blake's establishment was limited to an old creature almost doting and totally deaf, the advantages of whose presence might have been considered problematical; but, then, as Miss Blake remarked, "she was somebody."

"And now she has taken fright," proceeded the lady. "How anyone could make her hear their story, the Lord in heaven alone knows; and if there was anything to see, I am sure she is far too blind to see it; but she says she daren't stay. She does not want to see poor master again till she is dead herself."

"I have got a tenant for the house the moment you like to say you will leave it," said Mr. Craven, in reply. "He cares for no ghost that ever was manufactured. He has a wife with a splendid digestion, and several grown-up sons and daughters. They will soon clear out the shadows; and their father is willing to pay two hundred and fifty pounds a year."

"And you think there is really nothing more of any use amongst the papers?"

"I am afraid not—I am afraid you must face the worst."

"And my sister's child left no better off than a street beggar," suggested Miss Blake.

"Come, come," remonstrated Mr. Craven; "matters are not so bad as all that comes to. Upon three hundred a year, you can live very comfortable on the Continent; and——"

"We'll go," interrupted Miss Blake; "but it is hard lines—not that anything better could have been expected from Robert Elmsdale."

"Ah! dear Miss Blake, the poor fellow is dead. Remember only his virtues, and let his faults rest."

"I sha'n't have much to burden my memory with, then," retorted Miss Blake, and departed.

Her next letter to my principal was dated from Rouen; but before that reached Buckingham Street, our troubles had begun.

For some reason best known to himself, Mr. Treseby, the good-natured country squire possessed of a wife with an excellent digestion, at the end of two months handed us half a year's rent, and requested we should try to let the house for the remainder of his term, he, in case of our failure, continuing amenable for the rent. In the course of the three years we secured eight tenants, and as from each a profit in the way of forfeit accrued, we had not to trouble Mr. Treseby for any more money, and were also enabled to remit some small bonuses—which came to her, Miss Blake assured us, as godsends—to the Continent.

After that the place stood vacant for a time. Various care-takers were eager to obtain the charge of it, but I only remember one who was not eager to leave.

That was a night-watchman, who never went home except in the day-time, and then to sleep, and he failed to understand why his wife, who was a pretty, delicate little creature, and the mother of four small children, should quarrel with her bread and butter, and want to leave so fine a place.

He argued the matter with her in so practical a fashion, that the nearest magistrate had to be elected umpire between them.

The whole story of the place was repeated in court, and the night-watchman's wife, who sobbed during the entire time she stood in the witness-box, made light of her black eye and numerous bruises, but said, "Not if Tim murdered her, could she stay alone in the house another night."

To prevent him murdering her, he was sent to gaol for two months, and Mr. Craven allowed her eight shillings a week till Tim was once more a free man, when he absconded, leaving wife and children chargeable to the parish.

"A poor, nervous creature," said Mr. Craven, who would not believe that where gas was, any house could be ghost-ridden. "We must really try to let the house in earnest."

And we did try, and we did let, over, and over, and over again, always with a like result, till at length Mr. Craven said to me: "Do you know, Patterson, I really am growing very uneasy about that house on the Thames. I am afraid some evil-disposed person is trying to keep it vacant."

"It certainly is very strange," was the only remark I felt capable of making.

We had joked so much about the house amongst ourselves, and ridiculed Miss Blake and her troubles to such an extent, that the matter bore no serious aspect for any of us juniors.

"If we are not soon able to let it," went on Mr. Craven, "I shall advise Miss Blake to auction off the furniture and sell the place. We must not always have an uninhabited house haunting our offices, Patterson."

I shook my head in grave assent, but all the time I was thinking the day when that house ceased to haunt our offices, would be a very dreary one for the wags amongst our clerks.

"Yes, I certainly shall advise Miss Blake to sell," repeated Mr. Craven, slowly.

Although a hard-working man, he was eminently slow in his ideas and actions.

There was nothing express about our dear governor; upon no special mental train did he go careering through life. Eminently he preferred the parliamentary pace: and I am bound to say the life-journey so performed was beautiful exceedingly, with waits not devoid of interest at little stations utterly outside his profession, with kindly talk to little children, and timid women, and feeble men; with a pleasant smile for most with whom he came in contact, and time for words of kindly advice which did not fall perpetually on stony ground, but which sometimes grew to maturity, and produced rich grain of which himself beheld the garnering.

Nevertheless, to my younger and quicker nature, he did seem often very tardy.

"Why not advise her now?" I asked.

"Ah! my boy," he answered, "life is very short, yet it is long enough to have no need in it for hurry."

The same day, Colonel Morris appeared in our office. Within a fortnight, that gallant officer was our tenant; within a month, Mrs. Morris, an exceedingly fine lady, with grown-up children, with very young children also, with ayahs, with native servants, with English servants, with a list of acquaintances such as one may read of in the papers the day after a Queen's drawing-room, took possession of the Uninhabited House, and, for about three months, peace reigned in our dominions.

Buckingham Street, as represented by us, stank in the nostrils of no human being.

So far we were innocent of offence, we were simply ordinary solicitors and clerks, doing as fully and truly as we knew how, an extremely good business at rates which yielded a very fair return to our principal.

The Colonel was delighted with the place, he kindly called to say; so was Mrs. Morris; so were the grown-up sons and daughters of Colonel and Mrs. Morris; and so, it is to be presumed, were the infant branches of the family.

The native servants liked the place because Mr. Elmsdale, in view of his wife's delicate health, had made the house "like an oven," to quote Miss Blake. "It was bad for her, I know," proceeded that lady, "but she would have her own way, poor soul, and he—well, he'd have had the top brick of the chimney of a ten-story house off, if she had taken a fancy for that article."

Those stoves and pipes were a great bait to Colonel Morris, as well as a source of physical enjoyment to his servants.

He, too, had married a woman who was not always easy to please; but River Hall did please her, as was natural, with its luxuries of heat, ease, convenience, large rooms opening one out of another, wide verandahs overlooking the Thames, staircases easy of ascent; baths, hot, cold, and shower; a sweet, pretty garden, conservatory with a door leading into it from the spacious hall, all exceedingly cheap at two hundred pounds a year.

Accordingly, at first, the Colonel was delighted with the place, and not the less so because Mrs. Morris was delighted with it, and because it was also so far from town, that he had a remarkably good excuse for frequently visiting his club.

Before the new-comers, local tradesmen bowed down and did worship.

Visitors came and visitors went, carriages appeared in shoals, and double-knocks were plentiful as blackberries. A fresh leaf had evidently been turned over at River Hall, and the place meant to give no more trouble for ever to Miss Blake, or Mr. Craven, or anybody. So, as I have said, three months passed. We had got well into the dog-days by that time; there was very little to do in the office. Mr. Craven had left for his annual holiday, which he always took in the company of his wife and daughters—a correct, but possibly a depressing, way of spending a vacation which must have been intended to furnish some social variety in a man's life; and we were all very idle, and all very much inclined to grumble at the heat, and length, and general slowness of the days, when one morning, as I was going out in order to send a parcel off to Mrs. Craven, who should I meet coming panting up the stairs but Miss Blake!

"Is that you, Patterson?" she gasped. I assured her it was I in the flesh, and intimated my astonishment at seeing her in hers.

"Why, I thought you were in France, Miss Blake," I suggested.

"That's where I have just come from," she said. "Is Mr. Craven in?"
I told her he was out of town.

"Ay—that's where everybody can be but me," she remarked, plain-
tively. "They can go out and stay out, while I am at the beck and call of
all the scum of the earth. Well, well, I suppose there will be quiet for me
sometime, if only in my coffin."

As I failed to see that any consolatory answer was possible, I made
no reply. I only asked:

"Won't you walk into Mr. Craven's office, Miss Blake?"

"Now, I wonder," she said, "what good you think walking into his
office will do me!"

Nevertheless, she accepted the invitation. I have, in the course of
years, seen many persons suffering from heat, but I never did see any
human being in such a state as Miss Blake was that day.

Her face was a pure, rich red, from temple to chin; it resembled
nothing so much as a brick which had been out for a long time, first in
the sun and the wind, and then in a succession of heavy showers of rain.
She looked weather-beaten, and sun-burnt, and sprayed with salt-water,
all at once. Her eyes were a lighter blue than I previously thought eyes
could be. Her cheek-bones stood out more prominently than I had
thought cheek-bones capable of doing. Her mouth—not quite a bad one,
by the way—opened wider than any within my experience; and her
teeth, white and exposed, were suggestive of a set of tombstones planted
outside a stonemason's shop, or an upper and lower set exhibited at the
entrance to a dentist's operating-room. Poor dear Miss Blake, she and
those pronounced teeth parted company long ago, and a much more
becoming set—which she got exceedingly cheap, by agreeing with the
maker to "send the whole of the city of London to her, if he liked"—
now occupy their place.

But on that especial morning they were very prominent. Everything,
in fact, about the lady, or belonging to her, seemed exaggerated, as if the
heat of the weather had induced a tropical growth of her mental and
bodily peculiarities. Her bonnet was crooked beyond even the ordinary
capacity of Miss Blake's head-gear; the strings were rolled up till they
looked like ropes which had been knotted under her chin. A veil, as large,
and black as a pirate's flag, floated down her back; her shawl was at sixes
and sevens; one side of her dress had got torn from the bodice, and
trailed on the ground leaving a broadly-marked line of dust on the carpet.
She looked as if she had no petticoats on; and her boots—those were the
days ere side-springs and buttons obtained—were one laced unevenly,
and the other tied on with a piece of ribbon.

As for her gloves, they were in the state we always beheld them;
if she ever bought a new pair (which I do not believe), she never treated

us to a sight of them till they had been long past decent service. They never were buttoned, to begin with; they had a wrinkled and haggard appearance, as if from extreme old age. If their colour had originally been lavender, they were always black with dirt; if black, they were white with wear.

As a bad job, she had, apparently, years before, given up putting a stitch in the ends of the fingers, when a stitch gave way; and the consequence was that we were perfectly familiar with Miss Blake's nails—and those nails looked as if, at an early period of her life, a hammer had been brought heavily down upon them. Mrs. Elmsdale might well be a beauty, for she had taken not only her own share of the good looks of the family, but her sister's also.

We used often, at the office, to marvel why Miss Blake ever wore a collar, or a tucker, or a frill, or a pair of cuffs. So far as clean linen was concerned, she would have appeared infinitely brighter and fresher had she and female frippery at once parted company. Her laces were always in tatters, her collars soiled, her cuffs torn, and her frills limp. I wonder what the natives thought of her in France! In London, we decided—and accurately, I believe—that Miss Blake, in the solitude of her own chamber, washed and got-up her cambrics and fine linen—and it was a "get-up" and a "put-on" as well.

Had any other woman, dressed like Miss Blake, come to our office, I fear the clerks would not have been over-civil to her. But Miss Blake was our own, our very own. She had grown to be as our very flesh and blood. We did not love her, but she was associated with us by the closest ties that can subsist between lawyer and client. Had anything happened to Miss Blake, we should, in the event of her death, have gone in a body to her funeral, and felt a want in our lives for ever after.

But Miss Blake had not the slightest intention of dying: we were not afraid of that calamity. The only thing we really did dread was that some day she might insist upon laying the blame of River Hall remaining uninhabited on our shoulders, and demand that Mr. Craven should pay her the rent out of his own pocket.

We knew if she took that, or any other pecuniary matter, seriously in hand, she would carry it through; and, between jest and earnest, we were wont to speculate whether, in the end, it might not prove cheaper to our firm if Mr. Craven were to farm that place, and pay Miss Blake's niece an annuity of say one hundred a year.

Ultimately we decided that it would, but that such a scheme was impracticable, because Miss Blake would always think we were making a fortune out of River Hall, and give us no peace till she had a share of the profit.

For a time, Miss Blake—after unfastening her bonnet-strings, and taking out her brooch and throwing back her shawl—sat fanning herself with a dilapidated glove, and saying, "Oh dear! oh dear! what is to become of me I cannot imagine." But, at length, finding I was not to be betrayed into questioning, she observed:

"If William Craven knew the distress I am in, he would not be out of town enjoying himself, I'll be bound."

"I am quite certain he would not," I answered, boldly. "But as he is away, is there nothing we can do for you?"

She shook her head mournfully. "You're all a parcel of boys and children together," was her comprehensive answer.

"But there is our manager, Mr. Taylor," I suggested.

"Him!" she exclaimed. "Now, if you don't want me to walk out of the office and never set foot in it again, don't talk to me about Taylor."

"Has Mr. Taylor offended you?" I ventured to inquire.

"Lads of your age should not ask too many questions," she replied. "What I have against Taylor is nothing to you; only don't make me desperate by mentioning his name."

I hastened to assure her that it should never be uttered by me again in her presence, and there ensued a pause, which she filled by looking round the office and taking a mental inventory of everything it contained.

Eventually, her survey ended in this remark, "And he can go out of town as well, and keep a brougham for his wife, and draw them daughters of his out like figures in a fashion-book, and my poor sister's child living in a two-pair lodging."

"I fear, Miss Blake," I ventured, "that something is the matter at River Hall."

"You fear, do you, young man?" she returned. "You ought to get a first prize for guessing. As if anything else could ever bring me back to London."

"Can I be of no service to you in the matter?"

"I don't think you can, but you may as well see his letter." And diving into the depths of her pocket, she produced Colonel Morris' communication, which was very short, but very much to the purpose.

"Not wishing," he said, "to behave in any unhandsome manner, I send you herewith" (herewith meant the keys of River Hall and his letter) "a cheque for one half-year's rent. You must know that, had I been aware of the antecedents of the place, I should never have become your tenant; and I must say, considering I have a wife in delicate health, and young children, the deception practised by your lawyers in concealing the fact that no previous occupant has been able to remain in the house, seems most unpardonable. I am a soldier, and, to me, these trade tricks appear dishonourable. Still, as I understand your position is an exceptional one, I am willing to forgive the wrong which has been done, and to pay six months' rent for a house I shall no longer occupy. In the event of these concessions appearing insufficient, I beg to enclose the names of my solicitors, and have the honour, madam, to remain

"Your most obedient servant,

"HERCULES MORRIS."

In order to gain time, I read this letter twice over; then, diplomatically, as I thought, I said:

"What are you going to do, Miss Blake?"

"What are *you* going to do, is much nearer the point, I am thinking!" retorted that lady. "Do you imagine there is so much pleasure or profit in keeping a lawyer, that people want to do lawyer's work for themselves?"

Which really was hard upon us all, considering that so long as she could do her work for herself, Miss Blake ignored both Mr. Craven and his clerks.

Not a shilling of money would she ever, if she could help it, permit to pass through our hands—not the slightest chance did she ever voluntarily give Mr. Craven of recouping himself those costs or loans in which her acquaintance involved her sister's former suitor.

Had he felt any inclination—which I am quite certain he never did—to deduct Miss Helena's indebtedness, as represented by her aunt, out of Miss Helena's income, he could not have done it. The tenant's money usually went straight into Miss Blake's hands.

What she did with it, Heaven only knows. I know she did not buy herself gloves!

Twirling the Colonel's letter about, I thought the position over.

"What, then," I asked, "do you wish us to do?"

Habited as I have attempted to describe, Miss Blake sat at one side of a library-table. In, I flatter myself, a decent suit of clothes, washed, brushed, shaved, I sat on the other. To ordinary observers, I know I must have seemed much the best man of the two—yet Miss Blake got the better of me.

She, that dilapidated, red-hot, crumpled-collared, fingerless-gloved woman, looked me over from head to foot, as I conceived, though my boots were hidden away under the table, and I declare—I swear—she put me out of countenance. I felt small under the stare of a person with whom I would not then have walked through Hyde Park in the afternoon for almost any amount of money which could have been offered to me.

"Though you are only a clerk," she said at length, apparently quite unconscious of the effect she had produced, "you seem a very decent sort of young man. As Mr. Craven is out of the way, suppose you go and see that Morris man, and ask him what he means by his impudent letter."

I rose to the bait. Being in Mr. Craven's employment, it is unnecessary to say I, in common with every other person about the place, thought I could manage his business for him very much better than he could manage it for himself; and it had always been my own personal conviction that if the letting of the Uninhabited House were entrusted to me, the place would not stand long empty.

Miss Blake's proposition was, therefore, most agreeable; but still, I did not at once swallow her hook. Mr. Craven, I felt, might scarcely approve of my taking it upon myself to call upon Colonel Morris while Mr. Taylor was able and willing to venture upon such a step, and I therefore suggested to our client the advisability of first asking Mr. Craven's opinion about the affair.

"And keep me in suspense while you are writing and answering and running up a bill as long as Midsummer Day," she retorted. "No, thank you. If you don't think my business worth your attention, I'll go to somebody that may be glad of it." And she began tying her strings and feeling after her shawl in a manner which looked very much indeed like carrying out her threat.

At that moment I made up my mind to consult Taylor as to what ought to be done. So I appeased Miss Blake by assuring her, in a diplomatic manner, that Colonel Morris should be visited, and promising to communicate the result of the interview by letter.

"That you won't," she answered. "I'll be here to-morrow to know what he has to say for himself. He is just tired of the house, like the rest of them, and wants to be rid of his bargain."

"I am not quite sure of that," I said, remembering my principal's suggestion. "It is strange, if there really is nothing objectionable about the house, that *no one* can be found to stay in it. Mr. Craven has hinted that he fancies some evil-disposed person must be playing tricks, in order to frighten tenants away."

"It is likely enough," she agreed. "Robert Elmsdale had plenty of enemies and few friends; but that is no reason why we should starve, is it?"

I failed to see the logical sequence of Miss Blake's remark, nevertheless I did not dare to tell her so; and agreed it was no reason why she and her niece should be driven into that workhouse which she frequently declared they "must come to."

"Remember," were her parting words, "I shall be here to-morrow morning early, and expect you to have good news for me."

Inwardly resolving not to be in the way, I said I hoped there would be good news for her, and went in search of Taylor.

"Miss Blake has been here," I began. "THE HOUSE is empty again. Colonel Morris has sent her half a year's rent, the keys, and the address of his solicitors. He says we have acted disgracefully in the matter, and she wants me to go and see him, and declares she will be back here first thing to-morrow morning to know what he has to say for himself. What ought I to do?"

Before Mr. Taylor answered my question, he delivered himself of a comprehensive anathema which included Miss Blake, River Hall, the late owner, and ourselves. He further wished he might be essentially etceteraed if he believed there was another solicitor, besides Mr. Craven, in London who would allow such a hag to haunt his offices.

"Talk about River Hall being haunted," he finished; "it is we who are witch-ridden, I call it, by that old Irishwoman. She ought to be burnt at Smithfield. I'd be at the expense of the faggots!"

"What have you and Miss Blake quarrelled about?" I inquired.

"You say she is a witch, and she has made me take a solemn oath never to mention your name again in her presence."

"I'd keep her presence out of these offices, if I was Mr. Craven," he answered. "She has cost us more than the whole freehold of River Hall is worth."

Something in his manner, more than in his words, made me comprehend that Miss Blake had borrowed money from him, and not repaid it, so I did not press for further explanation, but only asked him once again what I ought to do about calling upon Colonel Morris.

"Call, and be hanged, if you like!" was the reply; and as Mr. Taylor was not usually a man given to violent language, I understood that Miss Blake's name acted upon his temper with the same magical effect as a red rag does upon that of a turkey-cock.

4.   MYSELF AND MISS BLAKE

Colonel Morris, after leaving River Hall, had migrated temporarily to a fashionable West End hotel, and was, when I called to see him, partaking of tiffin in the bosom of his family, instead of at his club.

As it was notorious that he and Mrs. Morris failed to lead the most harmonious of lives, I did not feel surprised to find him in an extremely bad temper.

In person, short, dapper, wiry, thin, and precise, his manner matched his appearance. He had martinet written on every square foot of his figure. His moustache was fiercely waxed, his shirt-collar inflexible, his backbone stiff, while his shoulder-blades met flat and even behind. He held his chin a little up in the air, and his walk was less a march than a strut.

He came into the room where I had been waiting for him, as I fancied he might have come on a wet, cold morning to meet an awkward-squad.

He held the card I sent for his inspection in his hand, and referred to it, after he had looked me over with a supercilious glance.

"Mr. Patterson, from Messrs. Craven and Son," he read slowly out loud, and then added:

"May I inquire what Mr. Patterson from Messrs. Craven and Son wants with me?"

"I come from Miss Blake, sir," I remarked.

"It is here written that you come from Messrs. Craven and Son," he said.

"So I do, sir—upon Miss Blake's business. She is a client of ours, as you may remember."

"I do remember. Go on."

He would not sit down himself or ask me to be seated, so we stood throughout the interview. I with my hat in my hand, he twirling his moustache or scrutinising his nails while he talked.

"Miss Blake has received a letter from you, sir, and has requested me to ask you for an explanation of it."

"I have no further explanation to give," he replied.

"But as you took the house for two years, we cannot advise Miss Blake to allow you to relinquish possession in consideration of your having paid her six months' rent."

"Very well. Then you can advise her to fight the matter, as I suppose you will. *I* am prepared to fight it."

"We never like fighting, if a matter can be arranged amicably," I answered. "Mr. Craven is at present out of town; but I know I am only speaking his words, when I say we shall be glad to advise Miss Blake to accept any reasonable proposition which you may feel inclined to make."

"I have sent her half a year's rent," was his reply; "and I have refrained from prosecuting you all for conspiracy, as I am told I might have done. Lawyers, I am aware, admit they have no consciences, and I can make some allowance for a person in Miss Blake's position, otherwise——"

"Yes, sir?" I said, interrogatively.

"I should never have paid one penny. It has, I find, been a well-known fact to Mr. Craven, as well as to Miss Blake, that no tenant can remain in River Hall. When my wife was first taken ill there—in consequence of the frightful shock she received—I sent for the nearest medical man, and he refused to come; absolutely sent me a note, saying, 'he was very sorry, but he must decline to attend Mrs. Morris. Doubtless, she had her own physician, who would be happy to devote himself to the case.'"

"And what did you do?" I asked, my pulses tingling with awakened curiosity.

"Do!" he repeated, pleased, perhaps, to find so appreciative a listener. "I sent, of course, for the best advice to be had in London, and I went to the local doctor—a man who keeps a surgery and dispenses medicines—myself, to ask what he meant by returning such an insolent message in answer to my summons. And what do you suppose he said by way of apology?"

"I cannot imagine," I replied.

"He said he would not for ten times over the value of all the River Hall patients, attend a case in the house again. 'No person can live in it,' he went on, 'and keep his, her, or its health. Whether it is the river, or the drains, or the late owner, or the devil, I have not an idea. I can only tell you no one has been able to remain in it since Mr. Elmsdale's death, and if I attend a case there, of course I say, Get out of this at once. Then comes Miss Blake and threatens me with assault and battery—swears she will bring an action against me for libelling the place; declares I wish to drive her and her niece to the workhouse, and asserts I am in league with some one who wants to keep the house vacant, and I am sick of it. Get what doctor you choose, but don't send for me.'"

"Well, sir?" I suggested.

"Well! I don't consider it well at all. Here am I, a man returning to his native country—and a beastly country it is!—after nearly thirty years' absence, and the first transaction upon which I engage proves a swindle. Yes, a swindle, Mr. Patterson. I went to you in all good faith, took that house at your own rent, thought I had got a desirable home, and believed I was dealing with respectable people, and now I find I was utterly deceived, both as regards the place and your probity. You knew the house was uninhabitable, and yet you let it to me."

"I give you my word," I said, "that we really do not know yet in what way the house is uninhabitable. It is a good house, as you know; it is well furnished; the drainage is perfect; so far as we are concerned, we do not believe a fault can be found with the place. Still, it has been a fact that tenants will not stay in it, and we were therefore glad to let it to a gentleman like yourself, who would, we expected, prove above subscribing to that which can only be a vulgar prejudice."

"What is a vulgar prejudice?" he asked.

"The idea that River Hall is haunted," I replied.

"River Hall is haunted, young man," he said, solemnly.

"By what?" I asked.

"By some one who cannot rest in his grave," was the answer.

"Colonel Morris," I said, "some one *must* be playing tricks in the house."

"If so, that some one does not belong to this world," he remarked.

"Do you mean really and seriously to tell me you believe in ghosts?" I asked, perhaps a little scornfully.

"I do, and if you had lived in River Hall, you would believe in them too," he replied. "I will tell you," he went on, "what I saw in the house myself. You know the library?"

I nodded in assent. We did know the library. There our trouble seemed to have taken up its abode.

"Are you aware lights have frequently been reflected from that room, when no light has actually been in it?"

I could only admit this had occasionally proved a ground of what we considered unreasonable complaint.

"One evening," went on the Colonel, "I determined to test the matter for myself. Long before dusk I entered the room and examined it thoroughly—saw to the fastenings of the windows, drew up the blinds, locked the door, and put the key in my pocket. After dinner I took a cigar and walked up and down the grass path beside the river, until dark. There was no light—not a sign of light of any kind, as I turned once more and walked up the path again; but as I was retracing my steps I saw that the room was brilliantly illuminated. I rushed to the nearest window and looked in. The gas was all ablaze, the door of the strong room open, the table strewed with papers, while in an office-chair drawn close up to the largest drawer, a man was seated counting over bank-notes. He had a pile of them before him, and I distinctly saw that he wetted his fingers in order to separate them."

"Most extraordinary!" I exclaimed. I could not decently have said anything less; but I confess that I had in my recollection the fact of Colonel Morris having dined.

"The most extraordinary part of the story is still to come," he remarked. "I hurried at once into the house, unlocked the door, found the library in pitch darkness, and when I lit the gas the strong room was closed; there was no office-chair in the room, no papers were on the table—everything, in fact, was precisely in the same condition as I had left it a few hours before. Now, no person in the flesh could have performed such a feat as that."

"I cannot agree with you there," I ventured. "It seems to me less difficult to believe the whole thing a trick, than to attribute the occurrence to supernatural agency. In fact, while I do not say it is impossible for ghosts to be, I cannot accept the fact of their existence."

"Well, I can, then," retorted the Colonel. "Why, sir, once at the Cape of Good Hope——" but there he paused. Apparently he recollected just in time that the Cape of Good Hope was a long way from River Hall.

"And Mrs. Morris," I suggested, leading him back to the banks of the Thames. "You mentioned some shock——"

"Yes," he said, frankly. "She met the same person on the staircase I saw in the library. He carried in one hand a lighted candle, and in the other a bundle of bank-notes. He never looked at her as he passed— never turned his head to the spot where she stood gazing after him in a perfect access of terror, but walked quietly downstairs, crossed the hall, and went straight into the library without opening the door. She fainted dead away, and has never known an hour's good health since."

"According to all accounts, she had not before, or good temper either," I thought; but I only said, "You had told Mrs. Morris, I presume, of your adventure in the library?"

"No," he answered; "I had not; I did not mention it to anyone except a brother officer, who dined with me the next evening."

"Your conversation with him might have been overheard, I suppose," I urged.

"It is possible, but scarcely probable," he replied. "At all events, I am quite certain it never reached my wife's ears, or she would not have stayed another night in the house."

I stood for a few moments irresolute, but then I spoke. I told him how much we—meaning Messrs. Craven and Son—his manager and his cashier, and his clerks, regretted the inconvenience to which he had been put; delicately I touched upon the concern we felt at hearing of Mrs. Morris' illness. But, I added, I feared his explanation, courteous and ample as it had been, would not satisfy Miss Blake, and trusted he might, upon consideration, feel disposed to compromise the matter. "We," I added, "will be only too happy to recommend our client to accept any reasonable proposal you may think it well to make."

Whereupon it suddenly dawned upon the Colonel that he had been showing me all his hand, and forthwith he adopted a very natural course. He ordered me to leave the room and the hotel, and not to show my face before him again at my peril. And I obeyed his instructions to the letter.

On the same evening of that day I took a long walk round by the Uninhabited House.

There it was, just as I had seen it last, with high brick walls dividing it from the road; with its belt of forest-trees separating it from the next residence, with its long frontage to the river, with its closed gates and shuttered postern-door.

The entrance to it was not from the main highway, but from a lane which led right down to the Thames; and I went to the very bottom of that lane and swung myself by means of a post right over the river, so that I might get a view of the windows of the room with which so ghostly a character was associated. The blinds were all down and the whole place looked innocent enough.

The strong, sweet, subtle smell of mignonette came wafted to my senses, the odours of jessamine, roses, and myrtle floated to me on the evening breeze. I could just catch a glimpse of the flower-gardens, radiant with colour, full of leaf and bloom.

"No haunted look there," I thought. "The house is right enough, but some one must have determined to keep it empty." And then I swung myself back into the lane again, and the shadow of the high brick wall projected itself across my mind as it did across my body.

"Is this place to let again, do you know?" said a voice in my ear, as I stood looking at the private door which gave a separate entrance to that evil-reputed library.

The question was a natural one, and the voice not unpleasant, yet I started, having noticed no one near me.

"I beg your pardon," said the owner of the voice. "Nervous, I fear!"

"No, not at all, only my thoughts were wandering. I beg your pardon —I do not know whether the place is to let or not."

"A good house?" This might have been interrogative, or uttered as an assertion, but I took it as the former, and answered accordingly.

"Yes, a good house—a very good house, indeed," I said.

"It is often vacant, though," he said, with a light laugh.

"Through no fault of the house," I added.

"Oh! it is the fault of the tenants, is it?" he remarked, laughing once more. "The owners, I should think, must be rather tired of their property by this time."

"I do not know that," I replied. "They live in hope of finding a good and sensible tenant willing to take it."

"And equally willing to keep it, eh?" he remarked. "Well, I, perhaps, am not much of a judge in the matter, but I should say they will have to wait a long time first."

"You know something about the house?" I said, interrogatively.

"Yes," he answered, "most people about here do, I fancy—but least said soonest mended"; and as by this time we had reached the top of the lane, he bade me a civil good-evening, and struck off in a westerly direction.

Though the light of the setting sun shone full in my face, and I had to shade my eyes in order to enable me to see at all, moved by some feeling impossible to analyse, I stood watching that retreating figure. Afterwards I could have sworn to the man among ten thousand.

A man of about fifty, well and plainly dressed, who did not appear to be in ill-health, yet whose complexion had a blanched look, like forced sea-kale; a man of under, rather than over middle height, not of slight make, but lean as if the flesh had been all worn off his bones; a man with sad, anxious, outlooking, abstracted eyes, with a nose slightly hooked, without a trace of whisker, with hair thin and straight and flaked with white, active and lithe in his movements, a swift walker, though he had a slight halt. While looking at him thrown up in relief against the glowing western sky, I noticed, what had previously escaped my attention, that he was a little deformed. His right shoulder was rather higher than the other. A man with a story in his memory, I imagined; a man who had been jilted by the girl he loved, or who had lost her by death, or whose wife had proved faithless; whose life, at all events, had been marred by a great trouble. So, in my folly, I decided; for I was young then, and romantic, and had experienced some sorrow myself connected with pecuniary matters.

For the latter reason, it never perhaps occurred to me to associate the trouble of my new acquaintance, if he could be so called, with money annoyances. I knew, or thought I knew, at all events, the expression loss of fortune stamps on a man's face; and the look which haunted me for days after had nothing in it of discontent, or self-assertion, or struggling gentility, or vehement protest against the decrees of fortune. Still less was it submissive. As I have said, it haunted me for days, then the memory grew less vivid, then I forgot the man altogether. Indeed, we shortly became so absorbed in the fight between Miss Blake and Colonel Morris, that we had little time to devote to the consideration of other matters.

True to her promise, Miss Blake appeared next morning in Buckingham Street. Without bestowing upon me even the courtesy of "good morning," she plunged into the subject next her heart.

"Did you see him?" she asked.

I told her I had. I repeated much of what he said; I assured her he was determined to fight the matter, and that although I did really not think any jury would give a verdict in his favour, still I believed, if the matter came into court, it would prevent our ever letting the house again.

"I should strongly recommend you, Miss Blake," I finished, "to keep what he offers, and let us try and find another tenant."

"And who asked you to recommend anything, you fast young man?" she demanded. "I am sure I did not, and I am very sure Mr. Craven would not be best pleased to know his clerks were setting themselves up higher than their master. You would never find William Craven giving himself airs such as you young whipper-snappers think make you seem of some consequence. I just tell him what I want done, and he does it, and you will please to do the same, and serve a writ on that villain without an hour's delay."

I asked on what grounds we were to serve the writ. I pointed out that Colonel Morris did not owe her a penny, and would not owe her a penny for some months to come; and in reply she said she would merely inquire if I meant that she and her poor niece were to go to the work-house.

To this I answered that the amount already remitted by Colonel Morris would prevent such a calamity, but she stopped my attempt at consolation by telling me not to talk about things I did not understand.

"Give me William Craven's address," she added, "and I will write to him direct. I wonder what he means by leaving a parcel of ignorant boys to attend to his clients while he is away enjoying himself! Give me his address, and some paper and an envelope, and I can write my letter here."

I handed her the paper and the envelope, and placed pen and ink conveniently before her, but I declined to give her Mr. Craven's address. We would forward the letter, I said; but when Mr. Craven went away for his holiday, he was naturally anxious to leave business behind as much as possible.

Then Miss Blake took steady aim, and fired at me. Broadside after broadside did she pour into my unprotected ears; she opened the vials of her wrath and overwhelmed me with reproaches; she raked up all the grievances she had for years been cherishing against England, and by some sort of verbal legerdemain made me responsible for every evil she could recollect as ever having happened to her. Her sister's marriage, her death, Mr. Elmsdale's suicide, the unsatisfactory state of his affairs, the prejudice against River Hall, the defection of Colonel Morris—all these things she laid at my door, and insisted on making me responsible for them.

"And now," she finished, pushing back her bonnet and pulling off her gloves, "I'll just write my opinion of you to Mr. Craven, and I'll wait till you direct the envelope, and I'll go with you to the post, and I'll see you put the letter in the box. If you and your fine Colonel Morris think you can frighten or flatter me, you are both much mistaken, I can tell you that!"

I did not answer her. I was too greatly affronted to express what I felt in words. I sat on the other side of the table—for I would not leave her alone in Mr. Craven's office—sulking, while she wrote her letter, which she did in a great, fat, splashing sort of hand, with every other word underlined; and when she had done, and tossed the missive over to me, I directed it, took my hat, and prepared to accompany her to the Charing Cross office.

We went down the staircase together in silence, up Buckingham Street, across the Strand, and so to Charing Cross, where she saw me drop the letter into the box. All this time we did not exchange a syllable, but when, after raising my hat, I was about to turn away, she seized hold of my arm, and said, "Don't let us part in bad blood. Though you are only a clerk, you have got your feelings, no doubt, and if in my temper I hurt them, I am sorry. Can I say more? You are a decent lad enough, as times go in England, and my bark is worse than my bite. I didn't write a word about you to William Craven. Shake hands, and don't bear malice to a poor lonely woman."

Thus exhorted, I took her hand and shook it, and then, in token of entire amity, she told me she had forgotten to bring her purse with her and could I let her have a sovereign. She would pay me, she declared solemnly, the first day she came again to the office.

This of course I did not believe in the least, nevertheless I gave her what she required—and Heaven knows, sovereigns were scarce enough with me then—thankfully, and felt sincerely obliged to her for making herself my debtor. Miss Blake did sometimes ruffle one's feathers most confoundedly, and yet I knew it would have grieved me had we parted in enmity.

Sometimes, now, when I look upon her quiet and utterly respectable old age—when I contemplate her pathetic grey hair and conventional lace cap—when I view her clothed like other people and in her right mind, I am very glad indeed to remember I had no second thought about that sovereign, but gave it to her—with all the veins of my heart, as she would have emphasised the proceeding.

"Though you have no name to speak of," observed Miss Blake as she pocketed the coin, "I think there must be some sort of blood in you. I knew Pattersons once who were connected by marriage with a great duke in the west of Ireland. Can you say if by chance you can trace relationship to any of them?"

"I can say most certainly not, Miss Blake," I replied. "We are Pattersons of nowhere and relations of no one."

"Well, well," remarked the lady, pityingly, "you can't help that, poor lad. And if you attend to your duties, you may yet be a rich City alderman."

With which comfort she left me, and wended her homeward way through St. Martin's Lane and the Seven Dials.

5.   THE TRIAL

Next day but one Mr. Craven astonished us all by walking into the office about ten o'clock. He looked stout and well, sunburnt to a degree, and all the better physically for his trip to the seaside. We were unfeignedly glad to see him. Given a good employer, and it must be an extremely bad employé who rejoices in his absence. If we were not saints, we were none of us very black sheep, and accordingly, from the porter to the managing clerk, our faces brightened at sight of our principal.

But after the first genial "how are you" and "good morning," Mr. Craven's face told tales: he had come back out of sorts. He was vexed about Miss Blake's letter, and, astonishing to relate, he was angry with me for having called upon Colonel Morris.

"You take too much upon you, Patterson," he remarked. "It is a growing habit with you, and you must try to check it."

I did not answer him by a word; my heart seemed in my mouth; I felt as if I was choking. I only inclined my head in token that I heard and understood, and assented; then, having, fortunately, work to attend to out of doors, I seized an early opportunity of slipping down the staircase and walking off to Chancery Lane. When I returned, after hours, to Buckingham Street, one of the small boys in the outer office told me I was to go to Mr. Craven's room directly.

"You'll catch it," remarked the young fiend. "He has asked for you a dozen times, at least."

"What can be wrong now?" I thought, as I walked straight along the passage to Mr. Craven's office.

"Patterson," he said, as I announced my return.

"Yes, sir?"

"I spoke hastily to you this morning, and I regret having done so."

"Oh! sir," I cried. And that was all. We were better friends than ever. Do you wonder that I liked my principal? If so, it is only because I am unable to portray him as he really was. The age of chivalry is past; but still it is no exaggeration to say I would have died cheerfully if my dying could have served Mr. Craven.

Life holds me now by many and many a nearer and dearer tie than was the case in those days so far and far away; nevertheless, I would run any risk, encounter any peril, if by so doing I could serve the man who in my youth treated me with a kindness far beyond my deserts.

He did not, when he came suddenly to town in this manner, stop at his own house, which was, on such occasions, given over to charwomen and tradespeople of all descriptions; but he put up at an old-fashioned family hotel where, on that especial evening, he asked me to dine with him.

Over dessert he opened his mind to me on the subject of the "Uninhabited House." He said the evil was becoming one of serious magnitude. He declared he could not imagine what the result might prove. "With all the will in the world," he said, "to assist Miss Blake and that poor child, I cannot undertake to provide for them. Something must be done in the affair, and I am sure I cannot see what that something is to be. Since Mr. Elmsdale bought the place, the neighbourhood has gone down. If we sold the freehold as it stands, I fear we should not get more than a thousand pounds for it, and a thousand pounds would not last Miss Blake three years; as for supposing she could live on the interest, that is out of the question. The ground might be cut up and let for business purposes, of course, but that would be a work of time. I confess, I do not know what to think about the matter or how to act in it."

"Do you suppose the place really is haunted?" I ventured to inquire.

"Haunted?—pooh! nonsense," answered Mr. Craven, pettishly. "Do I suppose this room is haunted; do I believe my offices are haunted? No sane man has faith in any folly of the kind; but the place has got a bad name; I suspect it is unhealthy, and the tenants, when they find that out, seize on the first excuse which offers. It is known we have compromised a good many tenancies, and I am afraid we shall have to fight this case, if only to show we do not intend being patient for ever. Besides, we shall exhaust the matter: we shall hear what the ghost-seers have to say for themselves on oath. There is little doubt of our getting a verdict, for the British juryman is, as a rule, not imaginative."

"I think we shall get a verdict," I agreed; "but I fancy we shall never get another tenant."

"There are surely as good fish in the sea as ever came out of it," he answered, with a smile; "and we shall come across some worthy country squire, possessed of pretty daughters, who will be delighted to find so cheap and sweet a nest for his birds, when they want to be near London."

"I wish sir," I said, "you would see Colonel Morris yourself. I am quite certain that every statement he made to me is true in his belief. I do not say, I believe him; I only say, what he told me justifies the inference that some one is playing a clever game in River Hall," and then I repeated in detail all the circumstances Colonel Morris had communicated to me, not excepting the wonderful phenomenon witnessed by Mr. Morris, of a man walking through a closed door.

Mr. Craven listened to me in silence, then he said, "I will not see Colonel Morris. What you tell me only confirms my opinion that we must fight this question. If he and his witnesses adhere to the story you repeat, on oath, I shall then have some tangible ground upon which to stand with Miss Blake. If they do not—and, personally, I feel satisfied no one who told such a tale could stand the test of cross-examination— we shall then have defeated the hidden enemy who, as I believe, lurks behind all this. Miss Blake is right in what she said to you: Robert Elmsdale must have had many a good hater. Whether he ever inspired that different sort of dislike which leads a man to carry on a war in secret, and try to injure this opponent's family after death, I have no means of knowing. But we must test the matter now, Patterson, and I think you had better call upon Colonel Morris and tell him so."

This service, however, to Mr. Craven's intense astonishment, I utterly declined.

I told him—respectfully, of course: under no possible conditions of life could I have spoken other than respectfully to a master I loved so well—that if a message were to be delivered *viva voce* from our office, it could not be so delivered by me.

I mentioned the fact that I felt no desire to be kicked downstairs. I declared that I should consider it an unseemly thing for me to engage in personal conflict with a gentleman of Colonel Morris's years and social position, and, as a final argument, I stated solemnly that I believed no number of interviews would change the opinions of our late tenant or induce him to alter his determination.

"He says he will fight," I remarked, as a finish to my speech, "and I am confident he will till he drops."

"Well, well," said Mr. Craven, "I suppose he must do so then; but meantime it is all very hard upon me."

And, indeed, so it proved; what with Miss Blake, who, of course, required frequent advances to sustain her strength during the approaching ordeal; what with policemen, who could not "undertake to be always a-watching River Hall"; what with watchmen, who kept their vigils in the nearest public-house as long as it was open, and then peacefully returned home to sleep; what with possible tenants, who came to us imagining the place was to let, and whom we referred to Colonel Morris, who dismissed them, each and all, with a tale which disenchanted them with the "desirable residence"—it was all exceeding hard upon Mr. Craven and his clerks till the quarter turned when we could take action about the matter.

Before the new year was well commenced, we were in the heat of the battle. We had written to Colonel Morris, applying for one quarter's rent of River Hall. A disreputable blackguard of a solicitor would have served him with a writ; but we were eminently respectable: not at the bidding of her most gracious Majesty, whose name we invoked on many and many of our papers, would Mr. Craven have dispensed with the preliminary letter; and I feel bound to say I follow in his footsteps in that respect.

To this notice, Colonel Morris replied, referring us to his solicitors.

We wrote to them, eliciting a reply to the effect that they would receive service of a writ. We served that writ, and then, as Colonel Morris intended to fight, instructed counsel.

Meanwhile the "Uninhabited House," and the furniture it contained, was, as Mr. Taylor tersely expressed the matter, "Going to the devil."

We could not help that, however—war was put upon us, and go to war we felt we must.

Which was all extremely hard upon Mr. Craven. To my knowledge, he had already, in three months, advanced thirty pounds to Miss Blake, besides allowing her to get into his debt for counsel's fees, and costs out of pocket, and cab hire, and Heaven knows what besides—with a problematical result also. Colonel Morris' solicitors were sparing no expenses to crush us. Clearly they, in a blessed vision, beheld an enormous bill, paid without difficulty or question. Fifty guineas here or there did not signify to their client, whilst to us—well, really, let a lawyer be as kind and disinterested as he will, fifty guineas disbursed upon the suit of an utterly insolvent, or persistently insolvent, client means something eminently disagreeable to him.

Nevertheless, we were all heartily glad to know the day of war was come. Body and soul, we all went in for Miss Blake, and Helena, and the "Uninhabited House." Even Mr. Taylor relented, and was to be seen rushing about with papers in hand relating to the impending suit of Blake *v.* Morris.

"She is a blank, blank woman," he remarked to me; "but still the case is interesting. I don't think ghosts have ever before come into court in my experience."

And we were all of the same mind. We girt up our loins for the fight. Each of us, I think, on the strength of her celebrity, lent Miss Blake a few shillings, and one or two of our number franked her to luncheon.

She patronized us all, I know, and said she should like to tell our mothers they had reason to be proud of their sons. And then came a dreadfully solemn morning, when we went to Westminster and championed Miss Blake.

Never in our memory of the lady had she appeared to such advantage as when we met her in Edward the Confessor's Hall. She looked a little paler than usual, and we felt her general get-up was a credit to our establishment. She wore an immense fur tippet, which, though then of an obsolete fashion, made her look like a three-per-cent. annuitant going to receive her dividends. Her throat was covered with a fine white lawn handkerchief; her dress was mercifully long enough to conceal her boots; her bonnet was perfectly straight, and the strings tied by some one who understood that bows should be pulled out and otherwise fancifully manipulated. As she carried a muff as large as a big drum, she had conceived the happy idea of dispensing altogether with gloves, and I saw that one of the fingers she gave me to shake was adorned with a diamond ring.

"Miss Elmsdale's," whispered Taylor to me. "It belonged to her mother."

Hearing which, I understood Helena had superintended her aunt's toilet.

"Did you ever see Miss Elmsdale?" I inquired of our manager.

"Not for years," was the answer. "She bade fair to be pretty."

"Why does not Miss Blake bring her out with her sometimes?" I asked.

"I believe she is expecting the Queen to give her assent to her marrying the Prince of Wales," explained Taylor, "and she does not wish her to appear much in public until after the wedding."

The court was crammed. Somehow it had got into the papers—probably through Colonel Morris' gossips at the club—that ours was likely to prove a very interesting case, and though the morning was damp and wretched, ladies and gentlemen had turned out into the fog and drizzle, as ladies and gentlemen will when there seems the least chance of a new sensation being provided for them.

Further, there were lots of reporters.

"It will be in every paper throughout the kingdom," groaned Taylor. "We had better by far have left the Colonel alone."

That had always been my opinion, but I only said, "Well, it is of no use looking back now."

I glanced at Mr. Craven, and saw he was ill at ease. We had considerable faith in ourselves, our case, and our counsel; but, then, we could not be blind to the fact that Colonel Morris' counsel were men very much better known than our men—that a cloud of witnesses, thirsting to avenge themselves for the rent we had compelled them to pay for an uninhabitable house, were hovering about the court—(had we not seen and recognized them in the Hall?)—that, in fact, there were two very distinct sides to the question, one represented by Colonel Morris and his party, and the other by Miss Blake and ourselves.

Of course our case lay in a nutshell. We had let the place, and Colonel Morris had agreed to take it. Colonel Morris now wanted to be rid of his bargain, and we were determined to keep him to it. Colonel Morris said the house was haunted, and that no one could live in it. We said the house was not haunted, and that anybody could live in it; that River Hall was "in every respect suited for the residence of a family of position" —see advertisements in *Times* and *Morning Post*.

Now, if the reader will kindly consider the matter, it must be an extremely difficult thing to prove, in a court of law, that a house, by reason solely of being haunted, is unsuitable for the residence of a gentleman of position.

Smells, bad drainage, impure water, unhealthiness of situation, dampness, the absence of advantages mentioned, the presence of small game—more odious to tenants of furnished houses than ground game to farmers—all these things had, we knew, been made pretexts for repudiation of contracts, and often successfully, but we could find no precedent for ghosts being held as just pleas upon which to relinquish a tenancy; and we made sure of a favourable verdict accordingly.

To this day, I believe that our hopes would have been justified by the result, had some demon of mischief not put it into the head of Taylor —who had the management of the case—that it would be a good thing to get Miss Blake into the witness-box.

"She will amuse the jury," he said, "and juries have always a kindly feeling for any person who can amuse them."

Which was all very well, and might be very true in a general way, but Miss Blake proved the exception to his rule.

Of course she amused the jury, in fact, she amused everyone. To get her to give a straightforward answer to any question was simply impossible.

Over and over again the judge explained to her that "yes" or "no" would be amply sufficient; but all in vain. She launched out at large in reply to our counsel, who, nevertheless, when he sat down, had gained his point.

Miss Blake declared upon oath she had never seen anything worse than herself at River Hall, and did not believe anybody else ever had.

She had never been there during Colonel Morris' tenancy, or she must certainly have seen something worse than a ghost, a man ready and anxious to "rob the orphan," and she was going to add the "widow" when peals of laughter stopped her utterance. Miss Blake had no faith in ghosts resident at River Hall, and if anybody was playing tricks about the house, she should have thought a "fighting gentleman by profession" capable of getting rid of them.

"Unless he was afraid," added Miss Blake, with withering irony.

Then up rose the opposition counsel, who approached her in an easy, conversational manner.

"And so you do not believe in ghosts, Miss Blake?" he began.

"Indeed and I don't," she answered.

"But if we have not ghosts, what is to become of the literature of your country?" he inquired.

"I don't know what you mean, by talking about my country," said Miss Blake, who was always proclaiming her nationality, and quarrelling with those who discovered it without such proclamation.

"I mean," he explained, "that all the fanciful legends and beautiful stories for which Ireland is celebrated have their origin in the supernatural. There are, for instance, several old families who have their traditional banshee."

"For that matter, we have one ourselves," agreed Miss Blake, with conscious pride.

At this junction our counsel interposed with a suggestion that there was no insinuation about any banshee residing at River Hall.

"No, the question is about a ghost, and I am coming to that. Different countries have different usages. In Ireland, as Miss Blake admits, there exists a very ladylike spirit, who announces the coming death of any member of certain families. In England, we have ghosts, who appear after the death of some members of some families. Now, Miss Blake, I want you to exercise your memory. Do you remember a night in the November after Mr. Elmsdale's death?"

"I remember many nights in many months that I passed broken-hearted in that house," she answered, composedly; but she grew very pale; and feeling there was something unexpected behind both question and answer, our counsel looked at us, and we looked back at him, dismayed.

"Your niece, being nervous, slept in the same room as that occupied by you?" continued the learned gentleman.

"She did," said Miss Blake. Her answer was short enough, and direct enough, at last.

"Now, on the particular November night to which I refer, do you recollect being awakened by Miss'Elmsdale?"

"She wakened me many a time," answered Miss Blake, and I noticed that she looked away from her questioner, and towards the gallery.

"Exactly so; but on one especial night she woke you, saying, her father was walking along the passage; that she knew his step, and that she heard his keys strike against the wall?"

"Yes, I remember that," said Miss Blake, with suspicious alacrity. "She kept me up till daybreak. She was always thinking about him, poor child."

"Very natural indeed," commented our adversary. "And you told her not to be foolish, I daresay, and very probably tried to reassure her by saying one of the servants must have passed; and no doubt, being a lady possessed of energy and courage, you opened your bedroom door, and looked up and down the corridor?"

"Certainly I did," agreed Miss Blake.

"And saw nothing—and no one?"

"I saw nothing."

"And then, possibly, in order to convince Miss Elmsdale of the full extent of her delusion, you lit a candle, and went downstairs."

"Of course—why wouldn't I?" said Miss Blake, defiantly.

"Why not, indeed?" repeated the learned gentleman, pensively. "Why not?—Miss Blake being brave as she is witty. Well, you went downstairs, and, as was the admirable custom of the house—a custom worthy of all commendation—you found the doors opening from the hall bolted and locked?"

"I did."

"And no sign of a human being about?"

"Except myself," supplemented Miss Blake.

"And rather wishing to find that some human being besides yourself was about, you retraced your steps, and visited the servants' apartments?"

"You might have been with me," said Miss Blake, with an angry sneer.

"I wish I had," he answered. "I can never sufficiently deplore the fact of my absence. And you found the servants asleep?"

"Well, they seemed asleep," said the lady; "but that does not prove that they were so."

"Doubtless," he agreed. "Nevertheless, so far as you could judge, none of them looked as if they had been wandering up and down the corridors?"

"I could not judge one way or another," said Miss Blake: "for the tricks of English servants, it is impossible for anyone to be up to."

"Still, it did not occur to you at the time that any of them was feigning slumber?"

"I can't say it did. You see, I am naturally unsuspicious," explained Miss Blake, naïvely.

"Precisely so. And thus it happened that you were unable to confute Miss Elmsdale's fancy?"

"I told her she must have been dreaming," retorted Miss Blake. "People who wake all of a sudden often confound dreams with realities."

"And people who are not in the habit of awaking suddenly often do the same thing," agreed her questioner; "and so, Miss Blake, we will pass out of dreamland, and into daylight—or rather foglight. Do you recollect a particularly foggy day, when your niece, hearing a favourite dog moaning piteously, opened the door of the room where her father died, in order to let it out?"

Miss Blake set her lips tight, and looked up at the gallery. There was a little stir in that part of the court, a shuffling of feet, and suppressed whispering. In vain the crier shouted, "Silence! silence, there!" The bustle continued for about a minute, and then all became quiet again. A policeman stated "a female had fainted," and our curiosity being satisfied, we all with one accord turned towards our learned friend, who, one hand under his gown, holding it back, and the other raised to emphasise his question, had stood in this picturesque attitude during the time occupied in carrying the female out, as if done in stone.

"Miss Blake, will you kindly answer my question?" he said, when order once again reigned in court.

"You're worse than a heathen," remarked the lady, irrelevantly.

"I am sorry you do not like me," he replied, "for I admire you very much; but my imperfections are beside the matter in point. What I want you to tell us is, did Miss Elmsdale open that door?"

"She did—the creature, she did," was the answer; "her heart was always tender to dumb brutes."

"I have no doubt the young lady's heart was everything it ought to be," was the reply; "and for that reason, though she had an intense repugnance to enter the room, she opened the door to let the dog out."

"She said so: I was not there," answered Miss Blake.

Whereupon ensued a brisk skirmish between counsel as to whether Miss Blake could give evidence about a matter of mere hearsay. And after they had fought for ten minutes over the legal bone, our adversary said he would put the question differently, which he did, thus:

"You were sitting in the dining-room, when you were startled by hearing a piercing shriek."

"I heard a screech—you can call it what you like," said Miss Blake, feeling an utter contempt for English phraseology.

"I stand corrected; thank you, Miss Blake. You heard a screech, in short, and you hurried across the hall, and found Miss Elmsdale in a fainting condition, on the floor of the library. Was that so?"

"She often fainted: she is all nairves," explained poor Miss Blake.

"No doubt. And when she regained consciousness, she entreated to be taken out of that dreadful room."

"She never liked the room after her father's death: it was natural, poor child."

"Quite natural. And so you took her into the dining-room, and there, curled upon the hearthrug, fast asleep, was the little dog she fancied she heard whining in the library."

"Yes, he had been away for two or three days, and came home hungry and sleepy."

"Exactly. And you have, therefore, no reason to believe *he* was shamming slumber."

"I believe I am getting very tired of your questions and cross-questions," she said, irritably.

"Now, what a pity!" remarked her tormentor; "for I could never tire of your answers. At all events, Miss Elmsdale could not have heard him whining in the library—so called."

"She might have heard some other dog," said Miss Blake.

"As a matter of fact, however, she stated to you there was no dog in the room."

"She did. But I don't think she knew whether there was or not."

"In any case, she did not see a dog; you did not see one; and the servants did not."

"I did not," replied Miss Blake; "as to the servants, I would not believe them on their oath."

"Hush! hush! Miss Blake," entreated our opponent. "I am afraid you must not be quite so frank. Now to return to business. When Miss Elmsdale recovered consciousness, which she did in that very comfortable easy-chair in the dining-room—what did she tell you?"

"Do you think I am going to repeat her half-silly words?" demanded Miss Blake, angrily. "Poor dear, she was out of her mind half the time, after her father's death."

"No doubt; but still, I must just ask you to tell us what passed. Was it anything like this? Did she say, 'I have seen my father. He was coming out of the strong-room when I lifted my head after looking for Juan, and he was wringing his hands, and seemed in some terrible distress'?"

"God forgive them that told you her words," remarked Miss Blake; "but she did say just those, and I hope they'll do you and her as played eavesdropper all the good I wish."

"Really, Miss Blake," interposed the judge.

"I have no more questions to ask, my lord," said Colonel Morris' counsel, serenely triumphant. "Miss Blake can go down now."

And Miss Blake did go down; and Taylor whispered in my ear: "She had done for us."

6.   WE AGREE TO COMPROMISE

Colonel Morris' side of the case was now to be heard, and heads were bending eagerly forward to catch each word of wisdom that should fall from the lips of Serjeant Playfire, when I felt a hand, cold as ice, laid on mine, and turning, beheld Miss Blake at my elbow.

She was as white as the nature of her complexion would permit, and her voice shook as she whispered:

"Take me away from this place, will you?"

I cleared a way for her out of the court, and when we reached Westminster Hall, seeing how upset she seemed, asked if I could get anything for her—"a glass of water, or wine," I suggested, in my extremity.

"Neither water nor wine will mend a broken heart," she answered, solemnly; "and mine has been broken in there"—with a nod she indicated the court we had just left.

Not remembering at the moment an approved recipe for the cure of such a fracture, I was cudgelling my brains to think of some form of reply not likely to give offence, when, to my unspeakable relief, Mr. Craven came up to where we stood.

"I will take charge of Miss Blake now, Patterson," he said, gravely

—very gravely; and accepting this as an intimation that he desired my absence, I was turning away, when I heard Miss Blake say:

"Where is she—the creature? What have they done with her at all?"

"I have sent her home," was Mr. Craven's reply. "How could you be so foolish as to mislead me as you have done?"

"Come," thought I, smelling the battle afar off, "we shall soon have Craven *v.* Blake tried privately in our office," I knew Mr. Craven pretty well, and understood he would not readily forgive Miss Blake for having kept Miss Helena's experiences a secret from him.

Over and over I had heard Miss Blake state there was not a thing really against the house, and that Helena, poor dear, only hated the place because she had there lost her father.

"Not much of a loss either, if she could be brought to think so," finished Miss Blake, sometimes.

Consequently, to Mr. Craven, as well as to all the rest of those connected with the firm, the facts elicited by Serjeant Playfire were new as unwelcome.

If the daughter of the house dreamed dreams and beheld visions, why should strangers be denied a like privilege? If Miss Elmsdale believed her father could not rest in his grave, how were we to compel belief as to calm repose on the part of yearly tenants?

"Playfire has been pitching into us pretty strong," remarked Taylor, when I at length elbowed my way back to where our manager sat. "Where is Mr. Craven?"

"I left him with Miss Blake."

"It is just as well he has not heard all the civil remarks Playfire made about our connection with the business. Hush! he is going to call his witnesses. No, the court is about to adjourn for luncheon."

Once again I went out into Westminster Hall, and was sauntering idly up and down over its stones when Mr. Craven joined me.

"A bad business this, Patterson," he remarked.

"We shall never get another tenant for that house," I answered.

"Certainly no tenant will ever again be got through me," he said, irritably; and then Taylor came to him, all in a hurry, and explaining he was wanted, carried him away.

"They are going to compromise," I thought, and followed slowly in the direction taken by my principal.

How I knew they were thinking of anything of the kind, I cannot say, but intuitively I understood the course events were taking.

Our counsel had mentally decided that, although the jury might feel inclined to uphold contracts and to repudiate ghosts, still, it would be impossible for them to overlook the fact that Colonel Morris had rented the place in utter ignorance of its antecedents, and that we had, so far, taken a perhaps undue advantage of him; moreover, the gallant officer had witnesses in court able to prove, and desirous of proving, that we had over and over again compromised matters with dissatisfied tenants, and cancelled agreements, not once or twice, but many, times; further, on no single occasion had Miss Blake and her niece ever slept a single night in the uninhabited house from the day when they left it; no matter how scarce of money they chanced to be, they went into lodgings rather than reside at River Hall. This was beyond dispute, and Miss Blake's evidence supplied the reason for conduct so extraordinary.

For some reason the house was uninhabitable. The very owners could not live in it; and yet—so in imagination we heard Serjeant Playfire declaim—"The lady from whom the TRUTH had that day been reluctantly wrung had the audacity to insist that delicate women and tender children should continue to inhabit a dwelling over which a CURSE seemed brooding —a dwelling where the dead were always striving for mastery with the living; or else pay Miss Blake a sum of money which should enable her and the daughter of the suicide to live in ease and luxury on the profits of DECEPTION."

And looking at the matter candidly, our counsel did not believe the jury could return a verdict. He felt satisfied, he said, there was not a landlord in the box, that they were all tenants, who would consider the three months' rent paid over and above the actual occupation rent, ample, and more than ample, remuneration.

On the other hand, Serjeant Playfire, whose experience of juries was large, and calculated to make him feel some contempt for the judgment of "twelve honest men" in any case from pocket-picking to manslaughter, had a prevision that, when the judge had explained to Mr. Foreman and gentlemen of the jury, the nature of a contract, and told them super-natural appearances, however disagreeable, were not recognized in law as a sufficient cause for breaking an agreement, a verdict would be found for Miss Blake.

"There must be one landlord amongst them," he considered; "and if there is, he will wind the rest round his finger. Besides, they will take the side of the women, naturally; and Miss Blake made them laugh, and the way she spoke of her niece touched them; while, as for the Colonel, he won't like cross-examination, and I can see my learned friend means to make him appear ridiculous. Enough has been done for honour— let us think of safety."

"For my part," said Colonel Morris, when the question was referred to him, "I am not a vindictive man, nor, I hope, an ungenerous foe; I do not like to be victimized, and I have vindicated my principles. The victory was mine in fact, if not in law, when that old Irishwoman's confession was wrung out of her. So, therefore, gentlemen, settle the matter as you please—I shall be satisfied."

And all the time he was inwardly praying some arrangement might be come to. He was brave enough in his own way, but it is one thing to go into battle, and another to stand legal fire without the chance of sending a single bullet in return. Ridicule is the vulnerable spot in the heel of many a modern Achilles; and while the rest of the court was "convulsed with laughter" over Miss Blake's cross-examination, the gallant Colonel felt himself alternately turning hot and cold when he thought that through even such an ordeal he might have to pass. And, accordingly, to cut short this part of my story, amongst them the lawyers agreed to compromise the matter thus—

Colonel Morris to give Miss Blake a third quarter's rent—in other words, fifty pounds more, and each side to pay its own costs.

When this decision was finally arrived at, Mr. Craven's face was a study. Full well he knew on whom would fall the costs of one side. He saw in prophetic vision the fifty pounds passing out of his hands into those of Miss Blake, but no revelation was vouchsafed on the subject of loans unpaid, of costs out of pocket, or costs at all. After we left court he employed himself, I fancy, for the remainder of the afternoon in making mental calculations of how much poorer a man Mrs. Elmsdale's memory, and the Uninhabited House had left him; and, upon the whole, the arithmetical problem could not have proved satisfactory when solved.

The judge complimented everyone upon the compromise effected. It was honourable in every way, and creditable to all parties concerned, but the jury evidently were somewhat dissatisfied at the turn affairs had taken, while the witnesses were like to rend Colonel Morris asunder.

"They had come, at great inconvenience to themselves, to expose the tactics of that Blake woman and her solicitor," so they said; "and they thought the affair ought not to have been hushed up."

As for the audience, they murmured openly. They received the statement that the case was over, with groans, hisses, and other marks of disapproval, and we heard comments on the matter uttered by disappointed spectators all the way up Parliament Street, till we arrived at that point where we left the main thoroughfare, in order to strike across to Buckingham Street.

There—where Pepys once lived—we betook ourselves to our books and papers, with a sense of unusual depression in the atmosphere. It was a gray, dull, cheerless afternoon, and more than one of us, looking out at the mud bank, which, at low water, then occupied the space now laid out as gardens, wondered how River Hall, desolate, tenantless, uninhabited, looked under that sullen sky, with the murky river flowing onward, day and night, day and night, leaving, unheeding, an unsolved mystery on its banks.

For a week we saw nothing of Miss Blake, but at the end of that time, in consequence of a somewhat imperative summons from Mr. Craven, she called at the office late one afternoon. We comprehended she had selected that, for her, unusual time of day for a visit, hoping our principal might have left ere she arrived; but in this hope she was disappointed: Mr. Craven was in, at leisure, and anxious to see her.

I shall never forget that interview. Miss Blake arrived about five o'clock, when it was quite dark out of doors, and when, in all our offices except Mr. Craven's, the gas was flaring away triumphantly. In his apartment he kept the light always subdued, but between the fire and the lamp there was plenty of light to see that Miss Blake looked ill and depressed, and that Mr. Craven had assumed a peculiar expression, which, to those who knew him best, implied he had made up his mind to pursue a particular course of action, and meant to adhere to his determination.

"You wanted to see me," said our client, breaking the ice.

"Yes; I wanted to tell you that our connection with the River Hall property must be considered at an end."

"Well, well, that is the way of men, I suppose—in England."

"I do not think any man, whether in England or Ireland, could have done more for a client than I have tried to do for you, Miss Blake," was the offended answer.

"I am sure I have never found fault with you," remarked Miss Blake, deprecatingly.

"And I do not think," continued Mr. Craven, unheeding her remark, "any lawyer ever met with a worse return for all his trouble than I have received from you."

"Dear, dear," said Miss Blake, with comic disbelief in her tone, "that is very bad."

"There are two classes of men who ought to be treated with entire confidence," persisted Mr. Craven, "lawyers and doctors. It is as foolish to keep back anything from one as from another."

"I daresay," argued Miss Blake; "but we are not all wise alike, you know."

"No," remarked my principal, who was indeed no match for the lady, "or you would never have allowed me to take your case into court in ignorance of Helena having seen her father."

"Come, come," retorted Miss Blake; "you do not mean to say you believe she ever did see her father since he was buried, and had the stone-work put all right and neat again, about him? And, indeed, it went to my heart to have a man who had fallen into such bad ways laid in the same grave with my dear sister, but I thought it would be un-christian——"

"We need not go over all that ground once more, surely," interrupted Mr. Craven. "I have heard your opinions concerning Mr. Elmsdale frequently expressed ere now. That which I never did hear, however, until it proved too late, was the fact of Helena having fancied she saw her father after his death."

"And what good would it have done you, if I had repeated all the child's foolish notions?"

"This, that I should not have tried to let a house believed by the owner herself to be uninhabitable."

"And so you would have kept us without bread to put in our mouths, or a roof over our heads."

"I should have asked you to do at first what I must ask you to do at last. If you decline to sell the place, or let it unfurnished, on a long lease, to some one willing to take it, spite of its bad character, I must say the house will never again be let thróugh my instrumentality, and I must beg you to advertise River Hall yourself, or place it in the hands of an agent."

"Do you mean to say, William Craven," asked Miss Blake, solemnly, "that you believe that house to be haunted?"

"I do not," he answered. "I do not believe in ghosts, but I believe the place has somehow got a bad name—perhaps through Helena's fancies, and that people imagine it is haunted, and get frightened probably at sight of their own shadows. Come, Miss Blake, I see a way out of this difficulty; you go and take up your abode at River Hall for six months, and at the end of that time the evil charm will be broken."

"And Helena dead," she observed.

"You need not take Helena with you."

"Nor anybody else, I suppose you mean," she remarked. "Thank you, Mr. Craven; but though my life is none too happy, I should like to die a natural death, and God only knows whether those who have been peeping and spying about the place might not murder me in my bed, if I ever went to bed in the house; that is——"

"Then, in a word, you do believe the place is haunted."

"I do nothing of the kind," she answered, angrily; "but though I have courage enough, thank Heaven, I should not like to stay all alone in any house, and I know there is not a servant in England would stay there with me, unless she meant to take my life. But I tell you what, William Craven, there are lots of poor creatures in the world even poorer than we are—tutors and starved curates, and the like. Get one of them to stay at the Hall till he finds out where the trick is, and I won't mind saying he shall have fifty pounds down for his pains; that is, I mean, of course, when he has discovered the secret of all these strange lights, and such-like."

And feeling she had by this proposition struck Mr. Craven under the fifth rib, Miss Blake rose to depart.

"You will kindly think over what I have said," observed Mr. Craven.

"I'll do that if you will kindly think over what I have said," she retorted, with the utmost composure; and then, after a curt good-evening, she passed through the door I held open, nodding to me, as though she would have remarked, "I'm more than a match for your master still, young man."

"What a woman that is!" exclaimed Mr. Craven, as I resumed my seat.

"Do you think she really means what she says about the fifty pounds?" I inquired.

"I do not know," he answered, "but I know I would cheerfully pay that sum to anyone who could unravel the mystery of River Hall."

"Are you in earnest, sir?" I asked, in some surprise.

"Certainly I am," he replied.

"Then let me go and stay at River Hall," I said. "I will undertake to run the ghost to earth for half the money."

7.   My Own Story

It is necessary now that I should tell the readers something about my own antecedents.

Aware of how uninteresting the subject must prove, I shall make that something as short as possible.

Already it will have been clearly understood, both from my own hints, and from Miss Blake's far from reticent remarks on my position, that I was a clerk at a salary in Mr. Craven's office.

But this had not always been the case. When I went first to Buckingham Street, I was duly articled to Mr. Craven, and my mother and sister, who were of aspiring dispositions, lamented that my choice of a profession had fallen on law rather than soldiering.

They would have been proud of a young fellow in uniform; but they did not feel at all elated at the idea of being so closely connected with a "musty attorney."

As for my father, he told me to make my own choice, and found the money to enable me to do so. He was an easy-going soul, who was in the miserable position of having a sufficient income to live on without exerting either mind or body; and yet whose income was insufficient to enable him to have superior hobbies, or to gratify any particular taste.

We resided in the country, and belonged to the middle class of comfort-able, well-to-do English people. In our way, we were somewhat exclusive as to our associates—and as the Hall and Castle residents were, in their way, exclusive also, we lived almost out of society.

Indeed, we were very intimate with only one family in our neigh-bourhood; and I think it was the example of the son of that house which first induced me to think of leading a different existence from that in which my father had grown as green and mossy as a felled tree.

Ned Munro, the eldest hope of a proud but reduced stock, elected to study for the medical profession.

"The life here," he remarked, vaguely indicating the distant houses occupied by our respective sires, "may suit the old folks, but it does not suit me." And he went out into the wilderness of the world.

After his departure I found that the life at home did not suit me either, and so I followed his lead, and went, duly articled, to Mr. Craven, of Buckingham Street, Strand. Mr. Craven and my father were old friends. To this hour I thank Heaven for giving my father such a friend.

After I had been for a considerable time with Mr. Craven, there came a dreadful day, when tidings arrived that my father was ruined, and my immediate presence required at home. What followed was that which is usual enough in all such cases, with this difference—the loss of his fortune killed my father.

From what I have seen since, I believe when he took to his bed and quietly gave up living altogether, he did the wisest and best thing possible under the circumstances. Dear, simple, kindly old man, I cannot fancy how his feeble nature might have endured the years which followed; filled by my mother and sister with lamentations, though we knew no actual want—thanks to Mr. Craven.

My father had been dabbling in shares, and when the natural con-sequence—ruin, utter ruin, came to our pretty country home, Mr. Craven returned me the money paid to him, and offered me a salary.

Think of what this kindness was, and we penniless; while all the time relations stood aloof, holding out nor hand nor purse, till they saw whether we could weather the storm without their help.

Amongst those relations chanced to be a certain Admiral Patterson, an uncle of my father. When we were well-to-do he had not disdained to visit us in our quiet home, but when poverty came he tied up his purse-strings and ignored our existence, till at length, hearing by a mere chance that I was supporting my mother and sister by my own exertions (always helped by Mr. Craven's goodness), he said, audibly, that the "young jackanapes must have more in him than he thought," and wrote to beg that I would spend my next holiday at his house.

I was anxious to accept the invitation, as a friend told me he felt

certain the old gentleman would forward my views; but I did not choose
to visit my relative in shabby clothes and with empty pockets; therefore,
it fell out that I jumped at Miss Blake's suggestion, and closed with Mr.
Craven's offer on the spot.

Half fifty—twenty-five—pounds would replenish my wardrobe, pay
my travelling expenses, and leave me with money in my pocket, as well.

I told Mr. Craven all this in a breath. When I had done so he laughed,
and said:

"You have worked hard, Patterson. Here is ten pounds. Go and see
your uncle; but leave River Hall alone."

Then, almost with tears, I entreated him not to baulk my purpose.
If I could rid River Hall of its ghost, I would take money from him, not
otherwise. I told him I had set my heart on unravelling the mystery
attached to that place, and I could have told him another mystery at the
same time, had shame not tied my tongue. I was in love—for the first
time in my life—hopelessly, senselessly, with a face of which I thought
all day and dreamed all night, that had made itself in a moment part and
parcel of my story, thus:

I had been at Kentish Town to see one of our clients, and having
finished my business, walked on as far as Camden Town, intending to
take an omnibus which might set me down somewhere near Chancery
Lane.

Whilst standing at the top of College Street, under shelter of my
umbrella, a drizzling rain falling and rendering the pavement dirty and
slippery, I noticed a young lady waiting to cross the road—a young
lady with, to my mind, the sweetest, fairest, most lovable face on which
my eyes had ever rested. I could look at her without causing annoyance,
because she was so completely occupied in watching lumbering vans,
fast carts, crawling cabs, and various other vehicles, which chanced at
that moment to be crowding the thoroughfare, that she had no leisure to
bestow even a glance on any pedestrian.

A governess, I decided: for her dress, though neat, and even elegant,
was by no means costly; moreover, there was an expression of settled
melancholy about her features, and further, she carried a roll, which
looked like music, in her hand. In less time than it has taken me to write
this paragraph, I had settled all about her to my own satisfaction.

Father bankrupt. Mother delicate. Young brothers and sisters, probably, all crying aloud for the pittance she was able to earn by giving
lessons at so much an hour.

She had not been long at her present occupation, I felt satisfied, for
she was evidently unaccustomed to being out in the streets alone on a
wet day.

I would have offered to see her across the road, but for two reasons:

one, because I felt shy about proffering my services; the other, because I was exceedingly doubtful whether I might not give offence by speaking.

After the fashion of so many of her sex, she made about half a dozen false starts, advancing as some friendly cabby made signs for her to venture the passage, retreating as she caught sight of some coming vehicle still yards distant.

At last, imagining the way clear, she made a sudden rush, and had just got well off the curb, when a mail phaeton turned the corner, and in one second she was down in the middle of the road, and I struggling with the horses and swearing at the driver, who, in his turn, very heartily anathematized me.

I do not remember all I said to the portly, well-fed, swaggering cockney upstart; but there was so much in it uncomplimentary to himself and his driving, that the crowd already assembled cheered, as all crowds will cheer profane and personal language; and he was glad enough to gather up his reins and touch his horses, and trot off, without having first gone through the ceremony of asking whether the girl he had so nearly driven over was living or dead.

Meantime she had been carried into the nearest shop, whither I followed her.

I do not know why all the people standing about imagined me to be her brother, but they certainly did so, and, under that impression, made way for me to enter the parlour behind the shop, where I found my poor beauty sitting, faint and frightened and draggled, whilst the woman of the house was trying to wipe the mud off her dress, and endeavouring to persuade her to swallow some wine-and-water.

As I entered, she lifted her eyes to mine, and said, "Thank you, sir. I trust you have not got hurt yourself," so frankly and so sweetly that the small amount of heart her face had left me passed into her keeping at once.

"Are you much hurt?" I replied by asking.

"My arm is, a little," she answered. "If I could only get home! Oh! I wish I were at home."

I went out and fetched a cab, and assisted her into it. Then I asked her where the man should drive, and she gave me the name of the street which Miss Blake, when in England, honoured by making her abode. Miss Blake's number was 110. My charmer's number was 15. Having obtained this information, I closed the cab-door, and taking my seat beside the driver, we rattled off in the direction of Brunswick Square.

Arrived at the house, I helped her—when, in answer to my knock, an elderly woman appeared, to ask my business—into the narrow hall of a dreary house. Oh! how my heart ached when I beheld her surroundings!

She did not bid me good-bye; but asking me into the parlour, went, as I understood, to get money to pay the cabman.

Seizing my opportunity, I told the woman, who still stood near the door, that I was in a hurry, and leaving the house, bade the driver take me to the top of Chancery Lane.

On the next Sunday I watched No. 15, till I beheld my lady-fair come forth, veiled, furred, dressed all in her dainty best, prayer-book in hand, going alone to St. Pancras Church—not the old, but the new— whither I followed her.

By some freak of fortune, the verger put me into the same pew as that in which he had just placed her.

When she saw me her face flushed crimson, and then she gave a little smile of recognition.

I fear I did not much heed the service on that particular Sunday; but I still felt shy, so shy that, after I had held the door open for her to pass out, I allowed others to come between us, and did not dare to follow and ask how she was.

During the course of the next week came Miss Blake and Mr. Craven's remark about the fifty pounds; and within four-and-twenty hours something still more astounding occurred—a visit from Miss Blake and her niece, who wanted "a good talking-to"—so Miss Blake stated.

It was a dull, foggy day, and when my eyes rested on the younger lady, I drew back closer into my accustomed corner, frightened and amazed.

"You were in such a passion yesterday," began Miss Blake, coming into the office, dragging her blushing niece after her, "that you put it out of my head to tell you three things—one, that we have moved from our old lodgings; the next, that I have not a penny to go on with; and the third, that Helena here has gone out of her mind. She won't have River Hall let again, if you please. She intends to go out as a gover- ness—what do you think of that?—and nothing I can say makes any impression upon her. I should have thought she had had enough of governessing the first day she went out to give a lesson: she got herself run over and nearly killed; was brought back in a cab by some gentleman, who had the decency to take the cab away again: for how we should have paid the fare, I don't know, I am sure. So I have just brought her to you to know if her mother's old friend thinks it is a right thing for Kathleen Elmsdale's daughter to put herself under the feet of a parcel of ignorant, purse-proud snobs?"

Mr. Craven looked at the girl kindly. "My dear," he said, "I think, I believe, there will be no necessity for you to do anything of that kind. We have found a person—have we not, Patterson?—willing to devote himself to solving the River Hall mystery. So, for the present at all events, Helena——"

He paused, for Helena had risen from her seat and crossed the room to where I sat.

"Aunt, aunt," she said, "this is the gentleman who stopped the horses," and before I could speak a word she held my hand in hers, and was thanking me once again with her beautiful eyes.

Miss Blake turned and glared upon me. "Oh! it was you, was it?" she said, ungraciously. "Well, it is just what I might have expected, and me hoping all the time it was a lord or a baronet, at the least."

We all laughed—even Miss Elmsdale laughed at this frank confession; but when the ladies were gone, Mr. Craven, looking at me pityingly, remarked:

"This is a most unfortunate business, Patterson. I hope—I do hope, you will not be so foolish as to fall in love with Miss Elmsdale."

To which I made no reply. The evil, if evil it were, was done. I had fallen in love with Miss Blake's niece ere those words of wisdom dropped from my employer's lips.

8. My First Night at River Hall

It was with a feeling of depression for which I could in no way account that, one cold evening, towards the end of February, I left Buckingham Street and wended my way to the Uninhabited House. I had been eager to engage in the enterprise; first, for the sake of the fifty pounds reward; and secondly, and much more, for the sake of Helena Elmsdale. I had tormented Mr. Craven until he gave a reluctant consent to my desire. I had brooded over the matter until I became eager to commence my investigations, as a young soldier may be to face the enemy; and yet, when the evening came, and darkness with it; when I set my back to the more crowded thoroughfares, and found myself plodding along a lonely suburban road, with a keen wind lashing my face, and a suspicion of rain at intervals wetting my cheeks, I confess I had no feeling of enjoyment in my self-imposed task.

After all, talking about a haunted house in broad daylight to one's fellow-clerks, in a large London office, is a very different thing from taking up one's residence in the same house, all alone, on a bleak winter's night, with never a soul within shouting distance. I had made up my mind to go through with the matter, and no amount of mental depression, no wintry blasts, no cheerless roads, no desolate goal, should daunt me; but still I did not like the adventure, and at every step I felt I liked it less.

Before leaving town I had fortified my inner man with a good dinner and some excellent wine, but by the time I reached River Hall I might have fasted for a week, so faint and spiritless did I feel.

"Come, this will never do," I thought, as I turned the key in the door, and crossed the threshold of the Uninhabited House. "I must not begin with being chicken-hearted, or I may as well give up the investigation at once."

The fires I had caused to be kindled in the morning, though almost out by the time I reached River Hall, had diffused a grateful warmth throughout the house; and when I put a match to the paper and wood laid ready in the grate of the room I meant to occupy, and lit the gas, in the hall, on the landing, and in my sleeping-apartment, I began to think things did not look so cheerless, after all.

The seals which, for precaution's sake, I had placed on the various locks, remained intact. I looked to the fastenings of the hall-door, examined the screws by which the bolts were attached to the wood, and having satisfied myself that everything of that kind was secure, went up to my room, where the fire was now crackling and blazing famously, put the kettle on the hob, drew a chair up close to the hearth, exchanged my boots for slippers, lit a pipe, pulled out my law-books, and began to read.

How long I had read, I cannot say; the kettle on the hob was boiling, at any rate, and the coals had burned themselves into a red-hot mass of glowing cinders, when my attention was attracted—or rather, I should say, distracted—by the sound of a tapping outside the window-pane. First I listened, and read on, then I laid down my book and listened more attentively. It was exactly the noise which a person would make tapping upon glass with one finger.

The wind had risen almost to a tempest, but, in the interval between each blast, I could hear the tapping as distinctly as if it had been inside my own skull—tap, tap, imperatively; tap, tap, tap, impatiently; and when I rose to approach the casement, it seemed as if three more fingers had joined in the summons, and were rapping for bare life.

"They have begun betimes," I thought; and taking my revolver in one hand, with the other I opened the shutters, and put aside the blind.

As I did so, it seemed as if some dark body occupied one side of the sash, while the tapping continued as madly as before.

It is as well to confess at once that I was for the moment frightened. Subsequently I saw many wonderful sights, and had some terrible experiences in the Uninhabited House; but I can honestly say, no sight or experience so completely cowed me for the time being, as that dull blackness to which I could assign no shape, that spirit-like rapping of fleshless fingers, which seemed to increase in vehemence as I obeyed its summons.

Doctors say it is not possible for the heart to stand still and a human being live, and, as I am not a doctor, I do not like to contradict their dogma, otherwise I could positively declare my heart did cease beating as I listened, looking out into the night with the shadow of that darkness projecting itself upon my mind, to the impatient tapping, which was now distinctly audible even above the raging of the storm.

How I gathered sufficient courage to do it, I cannot tell; but I put my face close to the glass, thus shutting out the gas and fire-light, and saw that the dark object which alarmed me was a mass of ivy the wind had detached from the wall, and that the invisible fingers were young branches straying from the main body of the plant, which, tossed by the air-king, kept striking the window incessantly, now one, now two, now three, tap, tap, tap; tap, tap; tap, tap; and sometimes, after a long silence, all together, tap-p-p, like the sound of clamming bells.

I stood for a minute or two, listening to the noise, so as to satisfy myself as to its cause, then I laid down the revolver, took out my pocket-knife, and opened the window. As I did so, a tremendous blast swept into the room, extinguishing the gas, causing the glowing coals to turn, for a moment, black on one side and to fiercest blaze on the other, scattering the dust lying on the hearth over the carpet, and dashing the ivy-sprays against my face with a force which caused my cheeks to smart and tingle long afterwards.

Taking my revenge, I cut them as far back as I could, and then, without closing the window, and keeping my breath as well as I could, I looked out across the garden over the Thames, away to the opposite bank, where a few lights glimmered at long intervals.

"An eerie, lonely place for a fellow to be in all by himself," I continued; "and yet, if the rest of the ghosts, bodiless or clothed with flesh, which frequent this house prove to be as readily laid as those ivy-twigs, I shall earn my money—and—my—thanks, easily enough."

So considering, I relit the gas, replenished the fire, refilled my pipe, reseated myself by the hearth, and with feet stretched out towards the genial blaze, attempted to resume my reading.

All in vain: I could not fix my attention on the page; I could not connect one sentence with another. When my mind ought to have concentrated its energies upon Justice That, and Vice-Chancellor This, and Lord Somebody Else, I felt it wandering away, trying to fit together all the odds and ends of evidence worthy or unworthy concerning the Uninhabited House. Which really was, as we had always stated, a good house, a remarkably good house, well furnished, suitable in every respect, &c.

Had I been a "family of respectability," or a gentleman of position, with a large number of servants, a nice wife, and a few children sprinkled about the domestic picture, I doubt not I should have enjoyed the contemplation of that glowing fire, and rejoiced in the idea of finding myself located in so desirable a residence, within an easy distance of the West End; but, as matters stood, I felt anything rather than elated.

In that large house there was no human inmate save myself, and I had an attack of nervousness upon me for which I found it impossible to account. Here was I, at length, under the very roof where my mistress had passed all her childish days, bound to solve the mystery which was making such havoc with her young life, permitted to essay a task, the accomplishment of which should cover me with glory, and perhaps restore peace and happiness to her heart; and yet I was *afraid*. I did not hesitate to utter that word to my own soul then, any more than I hesitate to write it now for those who list to read: for I can truly say I think there are few men whose courage such an adventure would not try were they to attempt it; and I am sure, had any one of those to whom I tell this story been half as much afraid as I, he would have left River Hall there and then, and allowed the ghosts said to be resident, to haunt it undisturbed for evermore.

If I could only have kept memory from running here and there in quest of evidence pro and con the house being haunted, I should have fared better: but I could not do this.

Let me try as I would to give my attention to those legal studies that ought to have engrossed my attention, I could not succeed in doing so: my thoughts, without any volition on my part, kept continually on the move; now with Miss Blake in Buckingham Street, again with Colonel Morris on the river walk, once more with Miss Elmsdale in the library; and went constantly flitting hither and thither, recalling the experiences of a frightened lad, or the terror of an ignorant woman; yet withal I had a feeling that in some way memory was playing me false, as if, when ostentatiously bringing out all her stores for me to make or mar as I could, she had really hidden away, in one of her remotest corners, some link, great or little as the case might be, but still, whether great or little, necessary to connect the unsatisfactory narratives together.

Till late in the night I sat trying to piece my puzzle together, but without success. There was a flaw in the story, a missing point in it, somewhere, I felt certain. I often imagined I was about to touch it, when, heigh! presto! it eluded my grasp.

"The whole affair will resolve itself into ivy-boughs," I finally, if not truthfully, decided. "I am satisfied it is all—ivy," and I went to bed.

Now, whether it was that I had thought too much of the ghostly narratives associated with River Hall, the storminess of the night, the fact of sleeping in a strange room, or the strength of a tumbler of brandy-and-water, in which brandy took an undue lead, I cannot tell; but during the morning hours I dreamed a dream which filled me with an unspeakable horror, from which I awoke struggling for breath, bathed in a cold perspiration, and with a dread upon me such as I never felt in any waking moment of my life.

I dreamt I was lying asleep in the room I actually occupied, when I was aroused from a profound slumber by the noise produced by some one tapping at the window-pane. On rising to ascertain the cause of this summons, I saw Colonel Morris standing outside and beckoning me to join him. With that disregard of space, time, distance, and attire which obtains in dreams, I at once stepped out into the garden. It was a pitch-dark night, and bitterly cold, and I shivered, I know, as I heard the sullen flow of the river, and listened to the moaning of the wind among the trees.

We walked on for some minutes in silence, then my companion asked me if I felt afraid, or if I would go on with him.

"I will go where you go," I answered.

Then suddenly he disappeared, and Playfire, who had been his counsel at the time of the trial, took my hand and led me onwards.

We passed through a doorway, and, still in darkness, utter darkness, began to descend some steps. We went down—down—hundreds of steps as it seemed to me, and in my sleep, I still remembered the old idea of its being unlucky to dream of going downstairs. But at length we came to the bottom, and then began winding along interminable passages, now so narrow only one could walk abreast, and again so low that we had to stoop our heads in order to avoid striking the roof.

After we had been walking along these for hours, as time reckons in such cases, we commenced ascending flight after flight of steep stone-steps. I laboured after Playfire till my limbs ached and grew weary, till, scarcely able to drag my feet from stair to stair, I entreated him to stop; but he only laughed and held on his course the more rapidly, while I, hurrying after, often stumbled and recovered myself, then stumbled again and lay prone.

The night air blew cold and chill upon me as I crawled out into an unaccustomed place and felt my way over heaps of uneven earth and stones that obstructed my progress in every direction. I called out for Playfire, but the wind alone answered me; I shouted for Colonel Morris; I entreated some one to tell me where I was; and in answer there was a dead and terrible silence. The wind died away; not a breath of air disturbed the heavy stillness which had fallen so suddenly around me. Instead of the veil of merciful blackness which had hidden everything hitherto from view, a gray light spread slowly over the objects around, revealing a burial-ground, with an old church standing in the midst—a burial-ground where grew rank nettles and coarse, tall grass; where brambles trailed over the graves, and weeds and decay consorted with the dead.

Moved by some impulse which I could not resist, I still held on my course, over mounds of earth, between rows of headstones, till I reached the other side of the church, under the shadow of which yawned an open pit. To the bottom of it I peered, and there beheld an empty coffin; the lid was laid against the side of the grave, and on a headstone, displaced from its upright position, sat the late occupant of the grave, looking at me with wistful, eager eyes. A stream of light from within the church fell across that one empty grave, that one dead watcher.

"So you have come at last," he said; and then the spell was broken, and I would have fled, but that, holding me with his left hand, he pointed with his right away to a shadowy distance, where the gray sky merged into deepest black.

I strained my eyes to discover the object he strove to indicate, but I failed to do so. I could just discern something flitting away into the darkness, but I could give it no shape or substance.

"Look—look!" the dead man said, rising, in his excitement, and clutching me more firmly with his clay-cold fingers.

I tried to fly, but I could not; my feet were chained to the spot. I fought to rid myself of the clasp of the skeleton hand, and then we fell together over the edge of the pit, and I awoke.

9.   A TEMPORARY PEACE

It was scarcely light when I jumped out of bed, and murmuring, "Thank God it was only a dream," dressed myself with all speed, and flinging open the window, looked out on a calm morning after the previous night's storm.

Muddily and angrily the Thames rolled onward to the sea. On the opposite side of the river I could see stretches of green, with here and there a house dotting the banks.

A fleet of barges lay waiting the turn of the tide to proceed to their destination. The voices of the men shouting to each other, and blaspheming for no particular reason, came quite clear and distinct over the water. The garden was strewed with twigs and branches blown off the trees during the night; amongst them the sprigs of ivy I had myself cut off.

An hour and a scene not calculated to encourage superstitious fancies, it may be, but still not likely to enliven any man's spirits—a quiet, dull, gray, listless, dispiriting morning, and, being country-bred, I felt its influence.

"I will walk into town, and ask Ned Munro to give me some breakfast," I thought, and found comfort in the idea.

Ned Munro was a doctor, but not a struggling doctor. He was not rich, but he "made enough for a beginner": so he said. He worked hard for little pay; "but I mean some day to have high pay, and take the world easy," he explained. He was blessed with great hopes and good courage; he had high spirits, and a splendid constitution. He neither starved himself nor his friends; his landlady "loved him as her son"; and there were several good-looking girls who were very fond of him, not as a brother.

But Ned had no notion of marrying, yet awhile. "Time enough for that," he told me once, "when I can furnish a good house, and set up a brougham, and choose my patients, and have a few hundreds lying idle in the bank."

Meantime, as no one of these items had yet been realized, he lived in lodgings, ate toasted haddocks with his morning coffee, and smoked and read novels far into the night.

Yes, I could go and breakfast with Munro. Just then it occurred to me that the gas I had left lighted when I went to bed was out; that the door I had left locked was open.

Straight downstairs I went. The gas in the hall was out, and every door I had myself closed and locked the previous morning stood ajar, with the seal, however, remaining intact.

I had borne as much as I could: my nerves were utterly unhinged. Snatching my hat and coat, I left the house, and fled, rather than walked, towards London.

With every step I took towards town came renewed courage; and when I reached Ned's lodgings, I felt ashamed of my pusillanimity.

"I have been sleep-walking, that is what it is," I decided. "I have opened the doors and turned off the gas myself, and been frightened at the work of my own hands. I will ask Munro what is the best thing to insure a quiet night."

Which I did accordingly, receiving for answer—

"Keep a quiet mind."

"Yes, but if one cannot keep a quiet mind; if one is anxious and excited, and——"

"In love," he finished, as I hesitated.

"Well, no; I did not mean that," I said; "though, of course, that might enter into the case also. Suppose one is uneasy about a certain amount of money, for instance?"

"Are you?" he asked, ignoring the general suggestiveness of my remark.

"Well, yes; I want to make some if I can."

"Don't want, then," he advised. "Take my word for it, no amount of money is worth the loss of a night's rest; and you have been tossing about all night, I can see. Come, Patterson, if it's forgery or embezzle-ment, out with it, man, and I will help you if I am able."

"If it were either one or the other, I should go to Mr. Craven," I answered, laughing.

"Then it must be love," remarked my host; "and you will want to take me into your confidence some day. The old story, I suppose: beautiful girl, stern parents, wealthy suitor, poor lover. I wonder if we could interest her in a case of small-pox. If she took it badly, you might have a chance; but I have a presentiment that she has been vaccinated."

"Ned," was my protest, "I shall certainly fling a plate at your head."

"All right, if you think the exertion would do you good," he answered. "Give me your hand, Patterson"; and before I knew what he wanted with it, he had his fingers on my wrist.

"Look here, old fellow," he said; "you will be laid up, if you don't take care of yourself. I thought so when you came in, and I am sure of it now. What have you been doing?"

"Nothing wrong, Munro," I answered, smiling in spite of myself. "I have not been picking, or stealing, or abducting any young woman, or courting my neighbour's wife; but I am worried and perplexed. When I sleep I have dreadful dreams—horrible dreams," I added, shuddering.

"Can you tell me what is worrying and perplexing you?" he asked, kindly, after a moment's thought.

"Not yet, Ned," I answered; "though I expect I shall have to tell you soon. Give me something to make me sleep quietly: that is all I want now."

"Can't you go out of town?" he inquired.

"I do not want to go out of town," I answered.

"I will make you up something to strengthen your nerves," he said, after a pause; "but if you are not better—well, before the end of the week, take my advice, and run down to Brighton over Sunday. Now, you ought to give me a guinea for that," he added, laughing. "I assure you, all the gold-headed cane, all the wonderful chronometer doctors who pocket thousands per annum at the West End, could make no more of your case than I have done."

"I am sure they could not," I said, gratefully; "and when I have the guinea to spare, be sure I shall not forget your fee."

Whether it was owing to his medicine, or his advice, or his cheery, health-giving manner, I have no idea; but that night, when I walked towards the Uninhabited House, I felt a different being.

On my way I called at a small corn-chandler's, and bought a quartern of flour done up in a thin and utterly insufficient bag. I told the man the wrapper would not bear its contents, and he said he could not help that.

I asked him if he had no stronger bags. He answered that he had, but he could not afford to give them away.

I laid down twopence extra, and inquired if that would cover the expense of a sheet of brown paper.

Ashamed, he turned aside and produced a substantial bag, into which he put the flour in its envelope of curling-tissue.

I thanked him, and pushed the twopence across the counter. With a grunt, he thrust the money back. I said good-night, leaving current coin of the realm to the amount indicated behind me.

Through the night be shouted, "Hi! sir, you've forgotten your change."

Through the night I shouted back, "Give your next customer its value in civility."

All of which did me good. Squabbling with flesh and blood is not a bad preliminary to entering a ghost-haunted house.

Once again I was at River Hall. Looking up at its cheerless portal, I was amazed at first to see the outside lamp flaring away in the darkness. Then I remembered that all the other gas being out, of course this, which I had not turned off, would blaze more brightly.

Purposely I had left my return till rather late. I had gone to one of the theatres, and remained until a third through the principal piece. Then I called at a supper-room, had half a dozen oysters and some stout; after which, like a giant refreshed, I wended my way westward.

Utterly false would it be for me to say I liked the idea of entering the Uninhabited House; but still, I meant to do it, and I did.

No law-books for me that night; no seductive fire; no shining lights all over the house. Like a householder of twenty years' standing, I struck a match, and turned the gas on to a single hall-lamp. I did not trouble myself even about shutting the doors opening into the hall; I only strewed flour copiously over the marble pavement, and on the first flight of stairs, and then, by the servant's passages, crept into the upper story, and so to bed.

That night I slept dreamlessly. I awoke in broad daylight, wondering why I had not been called sooner, and then remembered there was no one to call, and that if I required hot water, I must boil it for myself.

With that light heart which comes after a good night's rest, I put on some part of my clothing, and was commencing to descend the principal staircase, when my proceedings of the previous night flashed across my mind; and pausing, I looked down into the hall. No sign of a foot on the flour. The white powder lay there innocent of human pressure as the untrodden snow; and yet, and yet, was I dreaming—could I have been drunk without my own knowledge, before I went to bed? The gas was ablaze in the hall and on the staircase, and every door left open over-night was close shut.

Curiously enough, at that moment fear fell from me like a garment which has served its turn, and in the strength of my manhood, I felt able to face anything the Uninhabited House might have to show.

Over the latter part of that week, as being utterly unimportant in its events or consequences, I pass rapidly, only saying that, when Saturday came, I followed Munro's advice, and ran down to Brighton, under the idea that by so doing I should thoroughly strengthen myself for the next five days' ordeal. But the idea was a mistaken one. The Uninhabited House took its ticket for Brighton by the same express; it got into the compartment with me; it sat beside me at dinner; it hob-nobbed to me over my own wine; uninvited it came out to walk with me; and when I stood still, listening to the band, it stood still too. It went with me to the pier, and when the wind blew, as the wind did, it said, "We were quite as well off on the Thames."

When I woke, through the night, it seemed to shout, "Are you any better off here?" And when I went to church the next day it crept close up to me in the pew, and said, "Come, now, it is all very well to say you are a Christian; but if you were really one you would not be afraid of the place you and I wot of."

Finally, I was so goaded and maddened that I shook my fist at the sea, and started off by the evening train for the Uninhabited House.

This time I travelled alone. The Uninhabited House preceded me.

There, in its old position, looking gloomy and mysterious in the shadows of night, I found it on my return to town; and, as if tired of playing tricks with one who had become indifferent to their vagaries, all the doors remained precisely as I had left them; and if there were ghosts in the house that night, they did not interfere with me or the chamber I occupied.

Next morning, while I was dressing, a most remarkable thing occurred; a thing for which I was in no wise prepared. Spirits, and sights and sounds supposed appropriate to spirithood, I had expected; but for a modest knock at the front door I was not prepared.

When, after hurriedly completing my toilet, I undrew the bolts and undid the chain, and opened the door wide, there came rushing into the house a keen easterly wind, behind which I beheld a sad-faced woman, dressed in black, who dropped me a curtsey, and said:

"If you please, sir—I suppose you are the gentleman?"

Now, I could make nothing out of this, so I asked her to be good enough to explain.

Then it all came out: "Did I want a person to char?"

This was remarkable—very. Her question amazed me to such an extent that I had to ask her in, and request her to seat herself on one of the hall chairs, and go upstairs myself, and think the matter over before I answered her.

It had been so impressed upon me that no one in the neighbourhood would come near River Hall, that I should as soon have thought of Victoria by the grace of God paying me a friendly visit, as of being waited on by a charwoman.

I went downstairs again.

At sight of me my new acquaintance rose from her seat, and began curling up the corner of her apron.

"Do you know," I said, "that this house bears the reputation of being haunted?"

"I have heard people say it is, sir," she answered.

"And do you know that servants will not stay in it—that tenants will not occupy it?"

"I have heard so, sir," she answered once again.

"Then what do you mean by offering to come?" I inquired.

She looked up into my face, and I saw the tears come softly stealing into her eyes, and her mouth began to pucker, ere, drooping her head, she replied:

"Sir, just three months ago, come the twentieth, I was a happy woman. I had a good husband and a tidy home. There was not a lady in the land I would have changed places with. But that night, my man, coming home in a fog, fell into the river and was drowned. It was a week before they found him, and all the time—while I had been hoping to hear his step every minute in the day—I was a widow."

"Poor soul!" I said, involuntarily.

"Well, sir, when a man goes, all goes. I have done my best, but still I have not been able to feed my children—his children—properly, and the sight of their poor pinched faces breaks my heart, it do, sir," and she burst out sobbing.

"And so, I suppose," I remarked, "you thought you would face this house rather than poverty?"

"Yes, sir. I heard the neighbours talking about this place, and you, sir, and I made up my mind to come and ask if I mightn't tidy up things a bit for you, sir. I was a servant, sir, before I married, and I'd be so thankful."

Well, to cut the affair shorter for the reader than I was able to do for myself, I gave her half a crown, and told her I would think over her proposal, and let her hear from me—which I did. I told her she might come for a couple of hours each morning, and a couple each evening, and she could bring one of the children with her if she thought she was likely to find the place lonely.

I would not let her come in the day-time, because, in the quest I had set myself, it was needful I should feel assured no person could have an opportunity of elaborating any scheme for frightening me, on the premises.

"Real ghosts," said I to Mr. Craven, "I do not mind; but the physical agencies which may produce ghosts, I would rather avoid." Acting on which principle I always remained in the house while Mrs. Stott—my charwoman was so named—cleaned, and cooked, and boiled, and put things straight.

No one can imagine what a revolution this woman effected in my ways and habits, and in the ways and habits of the Uninhabited House.

Tradesmen called for orders. The butcher's boy came whistling down the lane to deliver the rump-steak or mutton-chop I had decided on for dinner; the greengrocer delivered his vegetables; the cheesemonger took solemn affidavit concerning the freshness of his stale eggs and the superior quality of a curious article which he called country butter, and declared came from a particular dairy famed for the excellence of its produce; the milkman's yahoo sounded cheerfully in the morning hours; and the letter-box was filled with cards from all sorts and descriptions of people—from laundresses to wine merchants, from gardeners to undertakers.

The doors now never shut nor opened of their own accord. A great peace seemed to have settled over River Hall.

It was all too peaceful, in fact. I had gone to the place to hunt a ghost, and not even the ghost of a ghost seemed inclined to reveal itself to me.

10.   THE WATCHER IS WATCHED

I have never been able exactly to satisfy my own mind as to the precise period during my occupation of the Uninhabited House when it occurred to me that I was being watched. Hazily I must have had some consciousness of the fact long before I began seriously to entertain the idea.

I felt, even when I was walking through London, that I was being often kept in sight by some person. I had that vague notion of a stranger being interested in my movements which it is so impossible to define to a friend, and which one is chary of seriously discussing with oneself. Frequently, when the corner of a street was reached, I found myself involuntarily turning to look back; and, prompted by instinct, I suppose, for there was no reason about the matter, I varied my route to and from the Uninhabited House, as much as the nature of the roads permitted. Further, I ceased to be punctual as to my hours of business, sometimes arriving at the office late, and, if Mr. Craven had anything for me to do

Cityward, returning direct from thence to River Hall without touching Buckingham Street.

By this time February had drawn to a close, and better weather might therefore have been expected; instead of which, one evening as I paced westward, snow began to fall, and continued coming down till somewhere about midnight.

Next morning Mrs. Stott drew my attention to certain footmarks on the walks, and beneath the library and drawing-room windows—the footmarks, evidently, of a man whose feet were not a pair. With the keenest interest, I examined these traces of a human pursuer. Clearly the footprints had been made by only one person, and that person deformed in some way. Not merely was the right foot-track different from that of the left, but the way in which its owner put it to the ground must have been different also. The one mark was clear and distinct, cut out in the snow with a firm tread, while the other left a little broken bank at its right edge, and scarcely any impression of the heel.

"Slightly lame," I decided. "Eases his right foot, and has his boots made to order."

"It is very odd," I remarked aloud to Mrs. Stott.

"That it is, sir," she answered; adding, "I hope to gracious none of them mobsmen are going to come burglaring here!"

"Pooh!" I replied; "there is nothing for them to steal, except chairs and tables, and I don't think one man could carry many of them away."

The whole of that day I found my thoughts reverting to those footmarks in the snow. What purpose anyone proposed to serve by prowling about River Hall I could not imagine. Before taking up my residence in the Uninhabited House, I had a theory that some malicious person or persons was trying to keep the place unoccupied—nay, further, imagination suggested the idea that, owing to its proximity to the river, Mr. Elmsdale's Hall might have taken the fancy of a gang of smugglers, who had provided for themselves means of ingress and egress unknown to the outside world. But all notions of this kind now seemed preposterous.

Slowly, but surely, the conviction had been gaining upon me that, let the mystery of River Hall be what it would, no ordinary explanation could account for the phenomena which it had presented to tenant after tenant; and my own experiences in the house, slight though they were, tended to satisfy me there was something beyond malice or interest at work about the place.

The very peace vouchsafed to me seemed another element of mystery, since it would certainly have been natural for any evil-disposed person to inaugurate a series of ghostly spectacles for the benefit of an investigator like myself; and yet, somehow, the absence of supernatural appearances, and the presence of that shadowy human being who thought it worth while to track my movements, and who had at last left tangible proof of his reality behind him in the snow, linked themselves together in my mind.

"If there is really anyone watching me," I finally decided, "there must be a deeper mystery attached to River Hall than has yet been suspected. Now, the first thing is to make sure that some one is watching me, and the next to guard against danger from him."

In the course of the day, I made a, for me, curious purchase. In a little shop, situated in a back street, I bought half a dozen reels of black sewing-cotton.

This cotton, on my return home, I attached to the trellis-work outside the drawing-room window, and wound across the walk and round such trees and shrubs as grew in positions convenient for my purpose.

"If these threads are broken to-morrow morning, I shall know I have a flesh-and-blood foe to encounter," I thought.

Next morning I found all the threads fastened across the walks leading round by the library and drawing-room snapped in two.

It was, then, flesh and blood I had come out to fight, and I decided that night to keep watch.

As usual, I went up to my bedroom, and, after keeping the gas burning for about the time I ordinarily spent in undressing, put out the light, softly turned the handle of the door, stole, still silently, along the passage, and so into a large apartment with windows which overlooked both the library and drawing-room.

It was here, I knew, that Miss Elmsdale must have heard her father walking past the door, and I am obliged to confess that, as I stepped across the room, a nervous chill seemed for the moment to take my courage captive.

If any reader will consider the matter, mine was not an enviable position. Alone in a desolate house, reputed to be haunted, watching for some one who had sufficient interest in the place to watch it and me closely.

It was still early—not later than half-past ten. I had concluded to keep my vigil until after midnight, and tried to while away the time with thoughts foreign to the matter in hand.

All in vain, however. Let me force what subject I pleased upon my mind, it reverted persistently to Mr. Elmsdale and the circumstances of his death.

"Why did he commit suicide?" I speculated. "If he had lost money, was that any reason why he should shoot himself?"

People had done so, I was aware; and people, probably, would continue to do so; but not hard-headed, hard-hearted men, such as Robert Elmsdale was reputed to have been. He was not so old that the achievement of a second success should have seemed impossible. His credit was good, his actual position unsuspected. River Hall, unhaunted, was not a bad property, and in those days he could have sold it advantageously.

I could not understand the motive of his suicide, unless, indeed, he was mad or drunk at the time. And then I began to wonder whether anything about his life had come out on the inquest—anything concerning habits, associates, and connections. Had there been any other under-current, besides betting, in his life brought out in evidence, which might help me to a solution of the mystery?

"I will ask Mr. Craven to-morrow," I thought, "whether he has a copy of the *Times*, containing a report of the inquest. Perhaps——"

What possibility I was about to suggest to my own mind I shall never now know, for at that moment there flamed out upon the garden a broad, strong flame of light—a flame which came so swiftly and suddenly, that a man, creeping along the River Walk, had not time to step out of its influence before I had caught full sight of him. There was not much to see, however. A man about the middle height, muffled in a cloak, wearing a cap, the peak of which was drawn down over his forehead: that was all I could discern, ere, cowering back from the light, he stole away into the darkness.

Had I yielded to my first impulse, I should have rushed after him in pursuit; but an instant's reflection told me how worse than futile such a wild-goose chase must prove. Cunning must be met with cunning, watching with watching.

If I could discover who he was, I should have taken the first step towards solving the mystery of River Hall; but I should never do so by putting him on his guard. The immediate business lying at that mo-ment to my hand was to discover whence came the flare of light which, streaming across the walk, had revealed the intruder's presence to me. For that business I can truthfully say I felt little inclination.

Nevertheless, it had to be undertaken. So, walking downstairs, I unlocked and opened the library-door, and found, as I anticipated, the room in utter darkness. I examined the fastenings of the shutters—they were secure as I had left them; I looked into the strong-room—not even a rat lay concealed there; I turned the cocks of the gas lights—but no gas whistled through the pipes, for the service to the library was separate from that of the rest of the house, and capable of being shut off at pleasure. I, mindful of the lights said to have been seen emanating from that room, had taken away the key from the internal tap, so that gas could not be used without my knowledge or the possession of a second key. Therefore, as I have said, it was no surprise to me to find the library in darkness. Nor could I say the fact of the light flaring, apparently, from a closely-shut-up room surprised me either. For a long time I had been expecting to see this phenomenon: now, when I did see it, I involuntarily connected the light, the apartment, and the stranger together.

For he was no ghost. Ghosts do not leave footmarks behind them in the snow. Ghosts do not break threads of cotton. It was a man I had seen in the garden, and it was my business to trace out the connection between him and the appearances at River Hall.

Thinking thus, I left the library, extinguished the candle by the aid of which I had made the investigations stated above, and after lowering the gaslight I always kept burning in the hall, began ascending the broad, handsome staircase, when I was met by the figure of a man descending the steps. I say advisedly, the figure; because, to all external appearance, he was as much a living man as myself.

And yet I knew the thing which came towards me was not flesh and blood. Knew it when I stood still, too much stupefied to feel afraid. Knew it, as the figure descended swiftly, noiselessly. Knew it, as, for one instant, we were side by side. Knew it, when I put out my hand to stop its progress, and my hand, encountering nothing, passed through the phantom as through air. Knew, it, when I saw the figure pass through the door I had just locked, and which opened to admit the ghostly visitor —opened wide, and then closed again, without the help of mortal hand.

After that I knew nothing more till I came to my senses again and found myself half lying, half sitting on the staircase, with my head resting against the banisters. I had fainted; but if any man thinks I saw in a vision what I have described, let him wait till he reaches the end of this story before expressing too positive an opinion about the matter.

How I passed the remainder of that night, I could scarely tell. Towards morning, however, I fell asleep, and it was quite late when I awoke: so late, in fact, that Mrs. Stott had rung for admittance before I was out of bed.

That morning two curious things occurred: one, the postman brought a letter for the late owner of River Hall, and dropped it in the box; another, Mrs. Stott asked me if I would allow her and two of the children to take up their residence at the Uninhabited House. She could not manage to pay her rent, she explained, and some kind friends had offered to maintain the elder children if she could keep the two youngest.

"And I thought, sir, seeing how many spare rooms there are here, and the furniture wanting cleaning, and the windows opening when the sun is out, that perhaps you would not object to my staying here altogether. I should not want any more wages, sir, and I would do my best to give satisfaction."

For about five minutes I considered this proposition, made to me whilst sitting at breakfast, and decided in favour of granting her request. I felt satisfied she was not in league with the person or persons engaged in watching my movements; it would be well to have some one in care of the premises during my absence, and it would clearly be to her interest to keep her place at River Hall, if possible.

Accordingly, when she brought in my boots, I told her she could remove at once if she liked.

"Only remember one thing, Mrs. Stott," I said. "If you find any ghosts in the dark corners, you must not come to me with any complaints."

"I sleep sound, sir," she answered, "and I don't think any ghosts will trouble me in the daytime. So thank you, sir; I will bring over a few things and stay here, if you please."

"Very good; here is the key of the back door," I answered; and in five minutes more I was trudging Londonward.

As I walked along I decided not to say anything to Mr. Craven concerning the previous night's adventures; first, because I felt reluctant to mention the apparition, and secondly, because instinct told me I should do better to keep my own counsel, and confide in no one, till I had obtained some clue to the mystery of that midnight watcher.

"Now here's a very curious thing!" said Mr. Craven, after he had opened and read the letter left at River Hall that morning. "This is from a man who has evidently not heard of Mr. Elmsdale's death, and who writes to say how much he regrets having been obliged to leave England without paying his I O U held by my client. To show that, though he may have seemed dishonest, he never meant to cheat Mr. Elmsdale, he encloses a draft on London for the principal and interest of the amount due."

"Very creditable to him," I remarked. "What is the amount, sir?"

"Oh! the total is under a hundred pounds," answered Mr. Craven; "but what I meant by saying the affair seemed curious is this: amongst Mr. Elmsdale's papers there was not an I O U of any description."

"Well, that is singular," I observed; then asked, "Do you think Mr. Elmsdale had any other office besides the library at River Hall?"

"No," was the reply, "none whatever. When he gave up his offices in town, he moved every one of his papers to River Hall. He was a reserved, but not a secret man; not a man, for instance, at all likely to lead a double life of any sort."

"And yet he betted," I suggested.

"Certainly that does puzzle me," said Mr. Craven. "And it is all against my statement, for I am certain no human being, unless it might be Mr. Harringford, who knew him in business, was aware of the fact."

"And what is your theory about the absence of all-important documents?" I inquired.

"I think he must have raised money on them," answered Mr. Craven.

"Are you aware whether anyone else ever produced them?" I asked.

"I am not; I never heard of their being produced: but, then, I should not have been likely to hear." Which was very true, but very unsatisfactory. Could we succeed in tracing even one of those papers, a clue might be found to the mystery of Mr. Elmsdale's suicide.

That afternoon I repaired to the house of one of our clients, who had, I knew, a file of the *Times* newspapers, and asked him to allow me to look at it.

I could, of course, have seen a file at many places in the city, but I preferred pursuing my investigations where no one was likely to watch the proceeding.

"*Times!* bless my soul, yes; only too happy to be able to oblige Mr. Craven. Walk into the study, there is a good fire, make yourself quite at home, I beg, and let me send you a glass of wine."

All of which I did, greatly to the satisfaction of the dear old gentleman.

Turning over the file for the especial year in which Mr. Elmsdale had elected to put a pistol to his head, I found at last the account of the inquest, which I copied out in shorthand, to be able to digest it more fully at leisure; and as it was growing dusk, wended my way back to Buckingham Street.

As I was walking slowly down one side of the street, I noticed a man standing within the open door of a house near Buckingham Gate.

At any other time I should not have given the fact a second thought, but life at River Hall seemed to have endowed me with the power of making mountains out of molehills, of regarding the commonest actions of my fellows with distrust and suspicion; and I was determined to know more of the gentleman who stood back in the shadow, peering out into the darkening twilight.

With this object I ran upstairs to the clerk's office, and then passed into Mr. Craven's room. He had gone, but his lamp was still burning, and I took care to move between it and the window, so as to show myself to any person who might be watching outside; then, without removing hat or top-coat, I left the room, and proceeded to Taylor's office, which I found in utter darkness. This was what I wanted; I wished to see without being seen; and across the way, standing now on the pavement, was the man I had noticed, looking up at our offices.

"All right," thought I, and running downstairs, I went out again, and walked steadily up Buckingham Street, along John Street, up Adam Street, as though *en route* to the Strand. Before, however, I reached that thoroughfare, I paused, hesitated, and then immediately and suddenly wheeled round and retraced my steps, meeting, as I did so, a man walking a few yards behind me and at about the same pace.

I did not slacken my speed for a moment as we came face to face;

I did not turn to look back after him; I retraced my steps to the office; affected to look out some paper, and once again pursued my former route, this time without meeting or being followed by anyone, and made my way into the City, where I really had business to transact.

I could have wished for a longer and a better look at the man who honoured me so far as to feel interested in my movements; but I did not wish to arouse his suspicions.

I had scored one trick; I had met him full, and seen his face distinctly —so distinctly that I was able to feel certain I had seen it before, but where, at the moment, I could not remember.

"Never mind," I continued: "that memory will come in due time; meanwhile the ground of inquiry narrows, and the plot begins to thicken."

11. MISS BLAKE ONCE MORE

Upon my return to River Hall I found in the letter-box an envelope addressed to—Patterson, Esq.

Thinking it probably contained some circular, I did not break the seal until after dinner; whereas, had I only known from whom the note came, should I not have devoured its contents before satisfying the pangs of physical hunger!

Thus ran the epistle:—

"DEAR SIR,—
"Until half an hour ago I was ignorant that you were the person who had undertaken to reside at River Hall. If you would add another obligation to that already conferred upon me, *leave that terrible house at once.* What I have seen in it, you know; what may happen to you, if you persist in remaining there, I tremble to think. For the sake of your widowed mother and only sister, you ought not to expose yourself to a risk which is *worse than useless.* I never wish to hear of River Hall being let again. Immediately I come of age, I shall sell the place; and if anything could give me happiness in this world, it would be to hear the house was razed to the ground. Pray! pray! listen to a warning, which, believe me, is not idly given, and leave a place which has already been the cause of so much misery to yours, gratefully and sincerely,
"HELENA ELMSDALE."

It is no part of this story to tell the rapture with which I gazed upon the writing of my "lady-love." Once I had heard Miss Blake remark, when Mr. Craven was remonstrating with her on her hieroglyphics, that "Halana wrote an 'unmaning hand,' like all the rest of the English," and, to tell the truth, there was nothing particularly original or characteristic about Miss Elmsdale's calligraphy.

But what did that signify to me? If she had strung pearls together, I should not have valued them one-half so much as I did the dear words which revealed her interest in me.

Over and over I read the note, at first rapturously, afterwards with a second feeling mingling with my joy. How did she know it was I who had taken up my residence at River Hall? Not a soul I knew in London, besides Mr. Craven, was aware of the fact, and he had promised faithfully to keep my secret.

Where, then, had Miss Elmsdale obtained her information? from whom had she learned that I was bent on solving the mystery of the "Uninhabited House"?

I puzzled myself over these questions till my brain grew uneasy with vain conjectures.

Let me imagine what I would—let me force my thoughts into what grooves I might—the moment the mental pressure was removed, my suspicions fluttered back to the man whose face seemed not unfamiliar.

"I am confident he wants to keep that house vacant," I decided. "Once let me discover who he is, and the mystery of the 'Uninhabited House' shall not long remain a mystery."

But then the trouble chanced to be how to find out who he was. I could not watch and be watched at the same time, and I did not wish to take anyone into my confidence, least of all a professional detective.

So far fortune had stood my friend; I had learnt something suspected by no one else, and I made up my mind to trust to the chapter of accidents for further information on the subject of my unknown friend.

When Mr. Craven and I were seated at our respective tables, I said to him:

"Could you make any excuse to send me to Miss Blake's to-day, sir?"

Mr. Craven looked up in utter amazement. "To Miss Blake's!" he repeated. "Why do you want to go there?"

"I want to see Miss Elmsdale," I answered, quietly enough, though I felt the colour rising in my face as I spoke.

"You had better put all that nonsense on one side, Patterson," he remarked. "What you have to do is to make your way in the world, and you will not do that so long as your head is running upon pretty girls. Helena Elmsdale is a good girl; but she would no more be a suitable wife for you, than you would be a suitable husband for her. Stick to law, my lad, for the present, and leave love for those who have nothing more important to think of."

"I did not want to see Miss Elmsdale for the purpose you imply," I said, smiling at the vehemence of Mr. Craven's advice. "I only wish to ask her one question."

"What is the question?"

"From whom she learned that I was in residence at River Hall," I answered, after a moment's hesitation.

"What makes you think she is aware of that fact?" he inquired.

"I received a note from her last night, entreating me to leave the place, and intimating that some vague peril menaced me if I persisted in remaining there."

"Poor child! poor Helena!" said Mr. Craven, thoughtfully; then spreading a sheet of note-paper on his blotting-pad, and drawing his cheque-book towards him, he proceeded:

"Now remember, Patterson, I trust to your honour implicitly. You must not make love to that girl; I think a man can scarcely act more dishonourably towards a woman, than to induce her to enter into what must be, under the best circumstances, a very long engagement."

"You may trust me, sir," I answered, earnestly. "Not," I added, "that I think it would be a very easy matter to make love to anyone with Miss Blake sitting by."

Mr. Craven laughed; he could not help doing so at the idea I had suggested. Then he said, "I had a letter from Miss Blake this morning asking me for money."

"And you are going to let her have some of that hundred pounds you intended yesterday to place against her indebtedness to you," I suggested.

"That is so," he replied. "Of course, when Miss Helena comes of age, we must turn over a new leaf—we really must."

To this I made no reply. It would be a most extraordinary leaf, I considered, in which Miss Blake did not appear as debtor to my employer but it scarcely fell within my province to influence Mr. Craven's actions.

"You had better ask Miss Blake to acknowledge receipt of this," said my principal, holding up a cheque for ten pounds as he spoke. "I am afraid I have not kept the account as I ought to have done."

Which was undeniably true, seeing we had never taken a receipt from her at all, and that loans had been debited to his private account instead of to that of Miss Blake. But true as it was, I only answered that I would get her acknowledgment; and taking my hat, I walked off to Hunter Street.

Arrived there, I found, to my unspeakable joy, that Miss Blake was out, and Miss Elmsdale at home.

When I entered the shabby sitting-room where her beauty was so grievously lodged, she rose and greeted me with kindly words, and sweet smiles, and vivid blushes.

"You have come to tell me you are not going ever again to that dreadful house," she said, after the first greeting and inquiries for Miss Blake were over. "You cannot tell the horror with which the mere mention of River Hall now fills me."

"I hope it will never be mentioned to you again till I have solved the mystery attached to it," I answered.

"Then you will not do what I ask," she cried, almost despairingly.

"I cannot," was my reply. "Miss Elmsdale, you would not have a soldier turn back from the battle. I have undertaken to find out the secret attached to your old home, and, please God, I shall succeed in my endeavours."

"But you are exposing yourself to danger, to——"

"I must take my chance of that. I cannot, if I would, turn back now, and I would not if I could. But I have come to you for information. How did you know it was I who had gone to River Hall?"

The colour flamed up in her face as I put the question.

"I—I was told so," she stammered out.

"May I ask by whom?"

"No, Mr. Patterson, you may not," she replied. "A—a friend—a kind friend, informed me of the fact, and spoke of the perils to which you were exposing yourself—living there all alone—all alone," she repeated. "I would not pass a night in the house again if the whole parish were there to keep me company, and what must it be to stay in that terrible, terrible place alone! You are here, perhaps, because you do not believe—because you have not seen."

"I do believe," I interrupted, "because I have seen; and yet I mean to go through with the matter to the end. Have you a likeness of your father in your possession, Miss Elmsdale?" I asked.

"I have a miniature copied from his portrait, which was of course too large to carry from place to place," she answered. "Why do you wish to know?"

"If you let me see it, I will reply to your question," I said.

Round her dear throat she wore a thin gold chain. Unfastening this, she handed to me the necklet, to which was attached a locket enamelled in black. It is no exaggeration to say, as I took this piece of personal property, my hand trembled so much that I could not open the case.

True love is always bashful, and I loved the girl, whose slender neck the chain had caressed, so madly and senselessly, if you will, that I felt as if the trinket were a living thing, a part and parcel of herself.

"Let me unfasten it," she said, unconscious that aught save awkwardness affected my manipulation of the spring. And she took the locket and handed it back to me open, wet with tears—her tears.

Judge how hard it was for me then to keep my promise to Mr. Craven and myself—how hard it was to refrain from telling her all my reasons for having ever undertaken to fight the dragon installed at River Hall.

I thank God I did refrain. Had I spoken then, had I presumed upon her sorrow and her simplicity, I should have lost something which constitutes the sweetest memory of my life.

But that is in the future of this story, and meantime I was looking at the face of her father.

I looked at it long and earnestly; then I closed the locket, softly pressing down the spring as I did so, and gave back miniature and chain into her hand.

"Well, Mr. Patterson?" she said, inquiringly.

"Can you bear what I have to tell?" I asked.

"I can, whatever it may be," she answered.

"I have seen that face at River Hall."

She threw up her arms with a gesture of despair.

"And," I went on, "I may be wrong, but I think I am destined to solve the mystery of its appearance."

She covered her eyes, and there was silence between us for a minute, when I said:

"Can you give me the name of the person who told you I was at River Hall?"

"I cannot," she repeated. "I promised not to mention it."

"He said I was in danger."

"Yes, living there all alone."

"And he wished you to warn me."

"No; he asked my aunt to do so, and she refused; and so I—I thought I would write to you without mentioning the matter to her."

"You have done me an incalculable service," I remarked, "and in return I will tell you something."

"What is that?" she asked.

"From to-night I shall not be alone in the house."

"Oh! how thankful I am!" she exclaimed; then instantly added, "Here is my aunt."

I rose as Miss Blake entered, and bowed.

"Oh! it is you, is it?" said the lady. "The girl told me some one was waiting."

Hot and swift ran the colour to my adored one's cheeks.

"Aunt," she observed, "I think you forget this gentleman comes from Mr. Craven."

"Oh, no! my dear, I don't forget Mr. Craven, or his clerks either," responded Miss Blake, as, still cloaked and bonneted, she tore open Mr. Craven's envelope.

"I am to take back an answer, I think," said I.

"You are, I see," she answered. "He's getting mighty particular, is William Craven. I suppose he thinks I am going to cheat him out of his paltry ten pounds. Ten pounds, indeed! and what is that, I should like to know, to us in our present straits! Why, I had more than twice ten yesterday from a man on whom we have no claim—none whatever—who, without asking, offered it in our need."

"Aunt," said Miss Elmsdale, warningly.

"If you will kindly give me your acknowledgment, Miss Blake, I should like to be getting back to Buckingham Street," I said. "Mr. Craven will wonder at my absence."

"Not a bit of it," retorted Miss Blake. "You and Mr. Craven understand each other, or I am very much mistaken; but here is the receipt, and good day to you."

I should have merely bowed my farewell, but that Miss Elmsdale stood up valiantly.

"Good-bye, Mr. Patterson," she said, holding out her dainty hand, and letting it lie in mine while she spoke. "I am very much obliged to you. I can never forget what you have done and dared in our interests."

And I went out of the room, and descended the stairs, and opened the front door, she looking graciously over the balusters the while, happy, ay, and more than happy.

What would I not have done and dared at that moment for Helena Elmsdale? Ah! ye lovers, answer!

12.   HELP

"There has been a gentleman to look at the house, sir, this afternoon," said Mrs. Stott to me, when, wet and tired, I arrived, a few evenings after my interview with Miss Elmsdale, at River Hall.

"To look at the house!" I repeated. "Why, it is not to let."

"I know that, sir, but he brought an order from Mr. Craven's office to allow him to see over the place, and to show him all about. For a widow lady from the country, he said he wanted it. A very nice gentleman, sir; only he did ask a lot of questions, surely——"

"What sort of questions?" I inquired.

"Oh! as to why the tenants did not stop here, and if I thought there was anything queer about the place; and he asked how you liked it, and how long you were going to stay; and if you had ever seen aught strange in the house.

"He spoke about you, sir, as if he knew you quite well, and said you must be stout-hearted to come and fight the ghosts all by yourself. A mighty civil, talkative gentleman—asked me if I felt afraid of living here, and whether I had ever met any spirits walking about the stairs and passages by themselves."

"Did he leave the order you spoke of just now behind him?"

"Yes, sir. He wanted me to give it back to him; but I said I must keep it for you to see. So then he laughed, and made the remark that he supposed, if he brought the lady to see the place, I would let him in again. A pleasant-spoken gentleman, sir—gave me a shilling, though I told him I did not require it."

Meantime I was reading the order, written by Taylor, and dated two years back.

"What sort of looking man was he?" I asked.

"Well, sir, there was not anything particular about him in any way. Not a tall gentleman, not near so tall as you, sir; getting into years, but still very active and light-footed, though with something of a halt in his way of walking. I could not rightly make out what it was; nor what it was that caused him to look a little crooked when you saw him from behind.

"Very lean, sir; looked as if the dinners he had eaten done him no good. Seemed as if, for all his pleasant ways, he must have seen trouble, his face was so worn-like."

"Did he say if he thought the house would suit?" I inquired.

"He said it was a very nice house, sir, and that he imagined anybody not afraid of ghosts might spend two thousand a year in it very comfortably. He said he should bring the lady to see the place, and asked me particularly if I was always at hand, in case he should come tolerably early in the morning."

"Oh!" was my comment, and I walked into the dining-room, wondering what the meaning of this new move might be; for Mrs. Stott had described, to the best of her ability, the man who stood watching our offices in London; and—good heavens!—yes, the man I had encountered in the lane leading to River Hall, when I went to the Uninhabited House, after Colonel Morris' departure.

"That is the man," thought I, "and he has some close, and deep, and secret interest in the mystery associated with this place, the origin of which I must discover."

Having arrived at this conclusion, I went to bed, for I had caught a bad cold, and was aching from head to foot, and had been sleeping ill, and hoped to secure a good night's rest.

I slept, it is true, but as for rest, I might as well, or better, have been awake. I fell from one dream into another; found myself wandering through impossible places; started in an agony of fear, and then dozed again, only to plunge into some deeper quagmire of trouble; and through all there was a vague feeling I was pursuing a person who eluded all my efforts to find him; playing a terrible game of hide-and-seek with a man who always slipped away from my touch, panting up mountains and running down declivities after one who had better wind and faster legs than I; peering out into the darkness, to catch a sight of a vague figure standing somewhere in the shadow, and looking, with the sun streaming into my eyes and blinding me, adown long white roads filled with a multitude of people, straining my sight to catch a sight of the coming traveller, who yet never came.

When I awoke thoroughly, as I did long and long before daybreak, I knew I was ill. I had a bad sore throat and an oppression at my chest which made me feel as if I was breathing through a sponge. My limbs ached more than had been the case on the previous evening whilst my head felt heavier than a log of teak.

"What should I do if I were to have a bad illness in that house?" I wondered to myself, and for a few minutes I pondered over the expediency of returning home; but this idea was soon set aside.

Where could I go that the Uninhabited House would not be a haunting presence? I had tried running away from it once before, and found it more real to me in the King's Road, Brighton, than on the banks of the Thames. No!—ill or well, I would stay on; the very first night of my absence might be the night of possible explanation.

Having so decided, I dressed and proceeded to the office, remaining there, however, only long enough to write a note to Mr. Craven, saying I had a very bad cold, and begging him to excuse my attendance.

After that I turned my steps to Munro's lodgings. If it were possible to avert an illness, I had no desire to become invalided in Mr. Elmsdale's Hall.

Fortunately, Munro was at home and at dinner. "Just come in time, old fellow," he said, cheerily. "It is not one day in a dozen you would have found me here at this hour. Sit down, and have some steak. Can't eat—why, what's the matter, man? You don't mean to say you have got another nervous attack. If you have, I declare I shall lodge a complaint against you with Mr. Craven."

"I am not nervous," I answered; "but I have caught cold, and I want you to put me to rights."

"Wait till I have finished my dinner," he replied; and then he proceeded to cut himself another piece of steak—having demolished which, and seen cheese placed on the table, he said:

"Now, Harry, we'll get to business, if you please. Where is this cold you were talking about?"

I explained as well as I could, and he listened to me without interruption. When I had quite finished, he said:

"Hal Patterson, you are either becoming a hypochondriac, or you are treating me to half confidences. Your cold is not worth speaking about. Go home, and get to bed, and take a basin of gruel, or a glass of something hot, after you are in bed, and your cold will be well in the morning. But there is something more than a cold the matter with you. What has come to you, to make a few rheumatic pains and a slight sore throat seem of consequence in your eyes?"

"I am afraid of being ill," I answered.

"Why are you afraid of being ill? why do you imagine you are going to be ill? why should you fall ill any more than anybody else?"

I sat silent for a minute, then I said, "Ned, if I tell you, will you promise upon your honour not to laugh at me?"

"I won't, if I can help it. I don't fancy I shall feel inclined to laugh," he replied.

"And unless I give you permission, you will not repeat what I am going to tell you to anyone?"

"That I can safely promise," he said. "Go on."

And I went on. I began at the beginning and recited all the events chronicled in the preceding pages; and he listened, asking no questions, interposing no remark.

When I ceased speaking, he rose and said he must think over the statements I had made.

"I will come and look you up to-night, Patterson," he observed. "Go home to River Hall, and keep yourself quiet. Don't mention that you feel ill. Let matters go on as usual. I will be with you about nine. I have an appointment now that I must keep."

Before nine Munro appeared, hearty, healthy, vigorous as usual.

"If this place were in Russell Square," he said, after a hasty glance round the drawing-room, "I should not mind taking a twenty-one years' lease of it at forty pounds a year, even if ghosts were included in the fixtures."

"I see you place no credence in my story," I said, a little stiffly.

"I place every credence in your story," was the reply. "I believe you believe it, and that is saying more than most people could say nowadays about their friends' stories if they spoke the truth."

It was of no use for me to express any further opinion upon the matter. I felt if I talked for a thousand years I should still fail to convince my listener there was anything supernatural in the appearances beheld at River Hall. It is so easy to pooh-pooh another man's tale; it is pleasant to explain every phenomenon that the speaker has never witnessed; it is so hard to credit that anything absolutely unaccountable on natural grounds has been witnessed by your dearest friend, that, knowing my only chance of keeping my temper and preventing Munro gaining a victory over me was to maintain a discreet silence, I let him talk on and strive to account for the appearances I had witnessed in his own way.

"Your acquaintance of the halting gait and high shoulder may or might have some hand in the affair," he finished. "My own opinion is he has not. The notion that you are being watched, is, if my view of the matter be correct, only a further development of the nervous excitement which has played you all sort of fantastic tricks since you came to this house. If anyone does wander through the gardens, I should set him down as a monomaniac or an intending burglar, and in any case the very best thing you can do is to pack up your traps and leave River Hall to its fate."

I did not answer; indeed, I felt too sick at heart to do so. What he said was what other people would say. If I could not evolve some clearer theory than I had yet been able to hit on, I should be compelled to leave the mystery of River Hall just as I had found it. Miss Blake had, I knew, written to Mr. Craven that the house had better be let again, as there "was no use in his keeping a clerk there in free lodgings for ever": and now came Ned Munro, with his worldly wisdom, to assure me mine was a wild-goose chase, and that the only sensible course for me to pursue was to abandon it altogether. For the first time, I felt disheartened about the business, and I suppose I showed my disappointment, for Munro, drawing his chair nearer to me, laid a friendly hand on my shoulder and said:

"Cheer up, Harry! never look so downhearted because your nervous system has been playing you false. It was a plucky thing to do, and to carry out; but you have suffered enough for honour, and I should not continue the experiment of trying how much you can suffer, were I in your shoes."

"You are very kind, Munro," I answered; "but I cannot give up. If I had all the wish in the world to leave here to-night, a will stronger than my own would bring me back here to-morrow. The place haunts me. Believe me, I suffer less from its influence, seated in this room, than when I am in the office or walking along the Strand."

"Upon the same principle, I suppose, that a murderer always carries the memory of his victim's face about with him; though he may have felt callously indifferent whilst the body was an actual presence."

"Precisely," I agreed.

"But then, my dear fellow, you are not a murderer in any sense of the word. You did not create the ghosts supposed to be resident here."

"No; but I feel bound to find out who did," I answered.

"That is, if you can, I suppose?" he suggested.

"I feel certain I shall," was the answer. "I have an idea in my mind, but it wants shape. There is a mystery, I am convinced, to solve which, only the merest hint is needed."

"There are a good many things in this world in the same position, I should say," answered Munro. "However, Patterson, we won't argue about the matter; only there is one thing upon which I am determined—

after this evening, I will come and stay here every night. I can say I am going to sleep out of town. Then, if there are ghosts, we can hunt them together; if there are none, we shall rest all the better. Do you agree to that?" and he held out his hand, which I clasped in mine, with a feeling of gratitude and relief impossible to describe.

As he said, I had done enough for honour; but still I could not give up, and here was the support and help I required so urgently, ready for my need.

"I am so much obliged," I said at last.

"Pooh! nonsense!" he answered. "You would do as much or more for me any day. There, don't let us get sentimental. You must not come out, but, following the example of your gallant Colonel Morris, I will, if you please, smoke a cigar in the garden. The moon must be up by this time."

I drew back the curtains and unfastened the shutter, which offered egress to the grounds, then, having rung for Mrs. Stott to remove the supper-tray, I sat down by the fire to await Munro's return, and began musing concerning the hopelessness of my position, the gulf of poverty and prejudice and struggle that lay between Helena and myself.

I was determined to win her; but the prize seemed unattainable as the Lord Mayor's robes must have appeared to Whittington, when he stood at the foot of Highgate Hill; and, prostrated as I was by that subtle malady to which as yet Munro had given no name, the difficulties grew into mountains, the chances of success dwarfed themselves into molehills.

Whilst thus thinking vaguely, purposelessly, but still most miserably, I was aroused from reverie by the noise of a door being shut cautiously and carefully—an outer door, and yet one with the sound of which I was unacquainted.

Hurrying across the hall, I flung the hall-door wide, and looked out into the night. There was sufficient moonlight to have enabled me to discern any object moving up or down the lane, but not a creature was in sight, not a cat or dog even traversed the weird whiteness of that lonely thoroughfare.

Despite Munro's dictum, I passed out into the night air, and went down to the very banks of the Thames. There was not a boat within hail. The nearest barge lay a couple of hundred yards from the shore.

As I retraced my steps, I paused involuntarily beside the door, which led by a separate entrance to the library.

"That is the door which shut," I said to myself, pressing my hand gently along the lintel, and sweeping the hitherto unbroken cobwebs away as I did so. "If my nerves are playing me false this time, the sooner their tricks are stopped the better, for no human being opened this door, no living creature has passed through it."

Having made up my mind on which points, I re-entered the house, and walked into the drawing-room, where Munro, pale as death, stood draining a glass of neat brandy.

"What is the matter?" I cried, hurriedly. "What have you seen, what——"

"Let me alone for awhile," he interrupted, speaking in a thick, hoarse whisper; then immediately asked, "Is that the library with the windows nearest the river?"

"Yes," I answered.

"I want to go into that room," he said, still in the same tone.

"Not now," I entreated. "Sit down and compose yourself; we will go into it, if you like, before you leave."

"Now, now—this minute," he persisted. "I tell you, Patterson, I must see what is in it."

Attempting no further opposition, I lit a couple of candles, and giving one into his hand, led the way to the door of the library, which I unlocked and flung wide open.

To one particular part Munro directed his steps, casting the light from his candle on the carpet, peering around in search of something he hoped, and yet still feared, to see. Then he went to the shutters and examined the fastenings, and finding all well secured, made a sign for me to precede him out of the room. At the door he paused, and took one more look into the darkness of the apartment, after which he waited while I turned the key in the lock, accompanying me back across the hall.

When we were once more in the drawing-room, I renewed my inquiry as to what he had seen; but he bade me let him alone, and sat mopping great beads of perspiration off his forehead, till, unable to endure the mystery any longer, I said:

"Munro, whatever it may be that you have seen, tell me all, I entreat. Any certainty will be better than the possibilities I shall be conjuring up for myself."

He looked at me wearily, and then drawing his hand across his eyes, as if trying to clear his vision, he answered, with an uneasy laugh:

"It was nonsense, of course. I did not think I was so imaginative, but I declare I fancied I saw, looking through the windows of that now utterly dark room, a man lying dead on the floor."

"Did you hear a door shut?" I inquired.

"Distinctly," he answered; "and what is more, I saw a shadow flitting through the other door leading out of the library, which we found, if you remember, bolted on the inside."

"And what inference do you draw from all this?"

"Either that some one is, in a to me unintelligible way, playing a very clever game at River Hall, or else that I am mad."

"You are no more mad than other people who have lived in this house," I answered.

"I don't know how you have done it, Patterson," he went on, unheeding my remark. "I don't, upon my soul, know how you managed to stay on here. It would have driven many a fellow out of his mind. I do not like leaving you. I wish I had told my landlady I should not be back. I will, after this time; but to-night I am afraid some patient may be wanting me."

"My dear fellow," I answered, "the affair is new to you, but it is not new to me. I would rather sleep alone in the haunted house, than in a mansion filled from basement to garret, with the unsolved mystery of this place haunting me."

"I wish you had never heard of, nor seen, nor come near it," he exclaimed, bitterly; "but, however, let matters turn out as they will, I mean to stick to you, Patterson. There's my hand on it."

And he gave me his hand, which was cold as ice—cold as that of one dead.

"I am going to have some punch, Ned," I remarked. "That is, if you will stop and have some."

"All right," he answered. "Something 'hot and strong' will hurt neither of us, but you ought to have yours in bed. May I give it to you there?"

"Nonsense!" I exclaimed, and we drew our chairs close to the fire, and, under the influence of a decoction which Ned insisted upon making himself, and at making which, indeed, he was much more of an adept than I, we talked valiantly about ghosts and their doings, and about how our credit and happiness were bound up in finding out the reason why the Uninhabited House was haunted.

"Depend upon it, Hal," said Munro, putting on his coat and hat, preparatory to taking his departure, "depend upon it that unfortunate Robert Elmsdale must have been badly cheated by some one, and sorely exercised in spirit, before he blew out his brains."

To this remark, which, remembering what he had said in the middle of the day, showed the wonderful difference that exists between theory and practice, I made no reply.

Unconsciously, almost, a theory had been forming in my own mind, but I felt much corroboration of its possibility must be obtained before I dare give it expression.

Nevertheless, it had taken such hold of me that I could not shake off the impression, which was surely, though slowly, gaining ground, even against the dictates of my better judgment.

"I will just read over the account of the inquest once again," I decided, as I bolted and barred the chain after Munro's departure; and so, by way of ending the night pleasantly, I took out the report, and studied it till two, chiming from a neighbouring church, reminded me that the fire was out, that I had a bad cold, and that I ought to have been between the blankets and asleep hours previously.

13.   Light at Last

Now, whether it was owing to having gone out the evening before from a very warm room into the night air, and, afterwards, into that chilly library, or to having sat reading the report given about Mr. Elmsdale's death till I grew chilled to my very marrow, I cannot say, all I know is, that when I awoke next morning I felt very ill, and welcomed, with rejoicing of spirit, Ned Munro, who arrived about mid-day, and at once declared he had come to spend a fortnight with me in the Uninhabited House.

"I have arranged it all. Got a friend to take charge of my patients; stated that I am going to pay a visit in the country, and so forth. And now, how are you?"

I told him, very truthfully, that I did not feel at all well.

"Then you will have to get well, or else we shall never be able to fathom this business," he said. "The first thing, consequently, I shall do, is to write a prescription, and get it made up. After that, I mean to take a survey of the house and grounds."

"Do precisely what you like," I answered. "This is Liberty Hall to the living as well as to the dead," and I laid my head on the back of the easy-chair, and went off to sleep.

All that day Munro seemed to feel little need of my society. He examined every room in the house, and every square inch about the premises. He took short walks round the adjacent neighbourhood, and made, to his own satisfaction, a map of River Hall and the country and town thereunto adjoining. Then he had a great fire lighted in the library, and spent the afternoon tapping the walls, trying the floors, and trying to obtain enlightenment from the passage which led from the library direct to the door opening into the lane.

After dinner, he asked me to lend him the shorthand report I had made of the evidence given at the inquest. He made no comment upon it when he finished reading, but sat, for a few minutes, with one hand shading his eyes, and the other busily engaged in making some sort of a sketch on the back of an old letter.

"What are you doing, Munro?" I asked, at last.

"You shall see presently," he answered, without looking up, or pausing in his occupation.

At the expiration of a few minutes, he handed me over the paper, saying:

"Do you know anyone that resembles?"

I took the sketch, looked at it, and cried out incoherently in my surprise.

"Well," he went on, "who is it?"

"The man who follows me! The man I saw in this lane!"

"And what is his name?"

"That is precisely what I desire to find out," I answered. "When did you see him? How did you identify him? Why did——"

"I have something to tell you, if you will only be quiet, and let me speak," he interrupted. "It was, as you know, late last night before I left here, and for that reason, and also because I was perplexed and troubled, I walked fast—faster than even is my wont. The road was very lonely; I scarcely met a creature along the road, flooded with the moonlight. I never was out on a lovelier night; I had never, even in the country, felt I had it so entirely to myself.

"Every here and there I came within sight of the river, and it seemed, on each occasion, as though a great mirror had been put up to make every object on land—every house, every tree, bush, fern, more clearly visible than it had been before. I am coming to my story, Hal, so don't look so impatient.

"At last, as I came once again in view of the Thames, with the moon reflected in the water, and the dark arches of the bridge looking black and solemn contrasted against the silvery stream, I saw before me, a long way before me, a man whose figure stood out in relief against the white road—a man walking wearily and with evident difficulty—a man, too, slightly deformed.

"I walked on rapidly, till within about a score yards of him, then I slackened my speed, and taking care that my leisurely footsteps should be heard, overtook him by degrees, and then, when I was quite abreast, asked if he could oblige me with a light.

"He looked up in my face, and said, with a forced, painful smile and studied courtesy of manner:

"'I am sorry, sir, to say that I do not smoke.'

"I do not know exactly what reply I made. I know his countenance struck me so forcibly, it was with difficulty I could utter some commonplace remark concerning the beauty of the night.

"'I do not like moonlight,' he said, and as he said it, something, a connection of ideas, or a momentary speculation, came upon me so suddenly, that once again I failed to reply coherently, but asked if he could tell me the shortest way to the Brompton Road.

"'To which end?' he inquired.

"'That nearest Hyde Park Corner,' I answered.

"As it turned out, no question could have served my purpose better.

"'I am going part of the way there,' he said, 'and will show you the nearest route—that is,' he added, 'if you can accommodate your pace to mine,' and he pointed, as he spoke, to his right foot, which evidently was causing him considerable pain.

"Now, that was something quite in my way, and by degrees I got him to tell me about the accident which had caused his slight deformity. I told him I was a doctor, and had been to see a patient, and so led him on to talk about sickness and disease, till at length he touched upon diseases of a morbid character; asking me if it were true that in some special maladies the patient was haunted by an apparition which appeared at a particular hour.

"I told him it was quite true, and that such cases were peculiarly distressing, and generally proved most difficult to cure—mentioning several well-authenticated instances, which I do not mean to detail to you, Patterson, as I know you have an aversion to anything savouring of medical shop.

"'You doctors do not believe in the actual existence of any such apparitions, of course?' he remarked, after a pause.

"I told him we did not; that we knew they had their rise and origin solely in the malady of the patient.

"'And yet,' he said, 'some ghost stories—I am not now speaking of those associated with disease, are very extraordinary, unaccountable——'

"'Very extraordinary, no doubt,' I answered; 'but I should hesitate before saying unaccountable. Now, there is that River Hall place up the river. There must be some rational way of explaining the appearances in that house, though no one has yet found any clue to that enigma.'

"'River Hall—where is that?' he asked; then suddenly added, 'Oh! I remember now: you mean the Uninhabited House, as it is called. Yes, there is a curious story, if you like. May I ask if you are interested in any way in that matter?'

"'Not in any way, except that I have been spending the evening there with a friend of mine.'

"'Has he seen anything of the reputed ghost?' asked my companion, eagerly. 'Is he able to throw any light on the dark subject?'

"'I don't think he can,' I replied. 'He has seen the usual appearances which I believe it is correct to see at River Hall; but so far, they have added nothing to his previous knowledge.'

"'He has seen, you say?'

"'Yes; all the orthodox lions of that cheerful house.'

"'And still he is not daunted—he is not afraid?'

"'He is not afraid. Honestly, putting ghosts entirely on one side, I should not care to be in his shoes, all alone in a lonely house.'

"'And you would be right, sir,' was the answer. 'A man must be mad to run such a risk.'

"'So I told him,' I agreed.

"'Why, I would not stay in that house alone for any money which could be offered to me,' he went on, eagerly.

"'I cannot go so far as that,' I said; 'but still it must be a very large sum which could induce me to do so.'

"'It ought to be pulled down, sir,' he continued; 'the walls ought to be razed to the ground.'

"'I suppose they will,' I answered, 'when Miss Elmsdale, the owner, comes of age; unless, indeed, our modern Don Quixote runs the ghost to earth before that time.'

"'Did you say the young man was ill?' asked my companion.

"'He has got a cold,' I answered.

"'And colds are nasty things to get rid of,' he commented, 'particularly in those low-lying localities. That is a most unhealthy part; you ought to order your patient a thorough change of air.'

"'I have, but he won't take advice,' was my reply. 'He has nailed his colours to the mast, and means, I believe, to stay in River Hall till he kills the ghost, or the ghost kills him.'

"'What a foolish youth!'

"'Undoubtedly; but, then, youth is generally foolish, and we have all our crotchets.'

"We had reached the other side of the bridge by this time, and saying his road lay in an opposite direction to mine, the gentleman I have sketched told me the nearest way to take, and bade me a civil good night, adding, 'I suppose I ought to say good morning.'"

"And is that all?" I asked, as Munro paused.

"Bide a wee, as the Scotch say, my son. I strode off along the road he indicated, and then, instead of making the detour he had kindly sketched out for my benefit, chose the first turning to my left, and, quite convinced he would soon pass that way, took up my position in the portico of a house which lay well in shadow. It stood a little back from the side-path, and a poor little Arab sleeping on the stone step proved to me the policeman was not over and above vigilant in that neighbourhood.

"I waited, Heaven only knows how long, thinking all the time I must be mistaken, and that his home did lie in the direction he took; but at last, looking out between the pillars and the concealing shrubs, I saw him. He was looking eagerly into the distance, with such a drawn, worn, painful expression, that for a moment my heart relented, and I thought I would let the poor devil go in peace.

"It was only for a moment, however; touching the sleeping boy, I bade him awake, if he wanted to earn a shilling. 'Keep that gentleman in sight, and get to know for me where he lives, and come back here, and I will give you a shilling, and perhaps two, for your pains.'

"With his eyes still heavy with slumber, and his perceptions for the moment dulled, he sped after the figure, limping wearily on. I saw him ask my late companion for charity, and follow the gentleman for a few steps, when the latter, threatening him with his stick, the boy dodged to escape a blow, and then, by way of showing how lightly his bosom's lord sat upon him, began turning wheels down the middle of the street. He passed the place where I stood, and spun a hundred feet further on, then he gathered himself together, and seeing no one in sight, stealthily crept back to his porch again.

"'You young rascal,' I said, 'I told you to follow him home. I want to know his name and address particularly.'

"'Come along, then,' he answered, 'and I'll show you. Bless you, we all knows him—better than we do the police, or anybody hereabouts. He's a beak and a ward up at the church, whatever that is, and he has building-yards as big, oh! as big as two workhouses, and——'"

"His name, Munro—his name?" I gasped.

"Harringford."

I expected it. I knew then that for days and weeks my suspicions had been vaguely connecting Mr. Harringford with the mystery of the Uninhabited House.

This was the hiding figure in my dream, the link hitherto wanting in my reveries concerning River Hall. I had been looking for this—waiting for it; I understood at last; and yet, when Munro mentioned the name of the man who had thought it worth his while to watch my movements, I shrunk from the conclusion which forced itself upon me.

"Must we go on to the end with this affair?" I asked, after a pause, and my voice was so changed, it sounded like that of a stranger to me.

"We do not yet know what the end will prove," Munro answered; "but whatever it may be, we must not turn back now."

"How ought we to act, do you think?" I inquired.

"We ought not to act at all," he answered. "We had better wait and see what his next move will be. He is certain to take some step. He will try to get you out of this house by hook or by crook. He has already striven to effect his purpose through Miss Elmsdale, and failed. It will therefore be necessary for him to attempt some other scheme. It is not for me to decide on the course he is likely to pursue; but, if I were in your place, I should stay within doors at night. I should not sit in the dark near windows still unshuttered. I should not allow any strangers to enter the house, and I should have a couple of good dogs running loose about the premises. I have brought Brenda with me as a beginning, and I think I know where to lay my hand on a good old collie, who will stay near any house I am in, and let no one trespass about it with impunity."

"Good heavens! Munro, you don't mean to say you think the man would *murder* me!" I exclaimed.

"I don't know what he might, or might not do," he replied. "There is something about this house he is afraid may be found out, and he is afraid you will find it out. Unless I am greatly mistaken, a great deal depends upon the secret being preserved intact. At present we can only surmise its nature; but I mean, in the course of a few days, to know more of Mr. Harringford's antecedents than he might be willing to communicate to anyone. What is the matter with you, Hal? You look as white as a corpse."

"I was only thinking," I answered, "of one evening last week, when I fell asleep in the drawing-room, and woke in a fright, imagining I saw that horrid light streaming out from the library, and a face pressed up close to the glass of the window on my left hand peering into the room."

"I have no doubt the face was there," he said, gravely; "but I do not think it will come again, so long as Brenda is alive. Nevertheless, I should be careful. Desperate men are capable of desperate deeds."

The first post next morning brought me a letter from Mr. Craven, which proved Mr. Harringford entertained for the present no intention of proceeding to extremities with me.

He had been in Buckingham Street, so said my principal, and offered to buy the freehold of River Hall for twelve hundred pounds.

Mr. Craven thought he might be induced to increase his bid to fifteen hundred, and added: "Miss Blake has half consented to the arrangement, and Miss Elmsdale is eager for the matter to be pushed on, so that the transfer may take place directly she comes of age. I confess, now an actual offer has been made, I feel reluctant to sacrifice the property for such a sum, and doubt whether it might not be better to offer it for sale by auction—that is, if you think there is no chance of your discovering the reason why River Hall bears so bad a name. Have you obtained any clue to the mystery?"

To this I replied in a note, which Munro himself conveyed to the office.

"I have obtained an important clue; but that is all I can say for the present. Will you tell Mr. Harringford I am at River Hall, and that you think, being on the spot and knowing all about the place, I could negotiate the matter better than anyone else in the office? If he is desirous of purchasing, he will not object to calling some evening and discussing the matter with me. I have an idea that a large sum of money might be made out of this property by an enterprising man like Mr. Harringford; and it is just possible, after hearing what I have to say, he may find himself able to make a much better offer for the Uninhabited House than that mentioned in your note. At all events, the interview can do no harm. I am still suffering so much from cold that it would be imprudent for me to wait upon Mr. Harringford, which would otherwise be only courteous on my part."

"Capital!" said Munro, reading over my shoulder. "That will bring my gentleman to River Hall——. But what is wrong, Patterson? You are surely not going to turn chickenhearted now?"

"No," I answered; "but I wish it was over. I dread something, and I do not know what it is. Though nothing shall induce me to waver, I am afraid, Munro. I am not ashamed to say it: I am afraid, as I was the first night I stayed in this house. I am not a coward, but I am afraid."

He did not reply for a moment. He walked to the window and looked out over the Thames; then he came back, and, wringing my hand, said, in tones that tried unsuccessfully to be cheerful:

"I know what it is, old fellow. Do you think I have not had the feeling myself, since I came here? But remember, it has to be done, and I will stand by you. I will see you through it."

"It won't do for you to be in the room, though," I suggested.

"No; but I will stay within earshot," he answered.

We did not talk much more about the matter. Men rarely do talk much about anything which seems to them very serious, and I may candidly say that I had never felt anything in my life to be much more serious than that impending interview with Mr. Harringford.

That he would come we never doubted for a moment, and we were right. As soon as it was possible for him to appoint an interview, Mr. Harringford did so.

"Nine o'clock on to-morrow (Thursday) evening," was the hour he named, apologizing at the same time for being unable to call at an earlier period of the day.

"Humph!" said Munro, turning the note over. "You will receive him in the library, of course, Hal?"

I replied such was my intention.

"And that will be a move for which he is in no way prepared," commented my friend.

From the night when Munro walked and talked with Mr. Harringford, no person came spying round and about the Uninhabited House. Of this fact we were satisfied, for Brenda, who gave tongue at the slightest murmur wafted over the river from the barges lying waiting for the tide, never barked as though she were on the track of living being; whilst the collie—a tawny-black, unkempt, ill-conditioned, savage-natured, but yet most true and faithful brute, which Munro insisted on keeping within doors, never raised his voice from the day he arrived at River Hall, till the night Mr. Harringford rang the visitor's-bell, when the animal, who had been sleeping with his nose resting on his paws, lifted his head and indulged in a prolonged howl.

Not a nice beginning to an interview which I dreaded.

14. A TERRIBLE INTERVIEW

I was in the library, waiting to receive Mr. Harringford. A bright fire blazed on the hearth, the table was strewn with papers Munro had brought to me from the office, the gas was all ablaze, and the room looked bright and cheerful—as bright and as cheerful as if no ghost had been ever heard of in connection with it.

At a few minutes past nine my visitor arrived. Mrs. Stott ushered him into the library, and he entered the room evidently intending to shake hands with me, which civility I affected not to notice.

After the first words of greeting were exchanged, I asked if he would have tea, or coffee, or wine; and finding he rejected all offers of refreshment, I rang the bell and told Mrs. Stott I could dispense with her attendance for the night.

"Do you mean to tell me you stay in this house entirely alone?" asked my visitor.

"Until Mrs. Stott came I was quite alone," I answered.

"I would not have done it for any consideration," he remarked.

"Possibly not," I replied. "People are differently constituted."

It was not long before we got to business. His offer of twelve hundred pounds I pooh-poohed as ridiculous.

"Well," he said—by this time I knew I had a keen man of business to deal with—"put the place up to auction, and see whether you will get as much."

"There are two, or rather, three ways of dealing with the property, which have occurred to me, Mr. Harringford," I explained. "One is letting or selling this house for a reformatory, or school. Ghosts in that case won't trouble the inmates, we may be quite certain; another is utilizing the buildings for a manufactory; and the third is laying the ground out for building purposes, thus——"

As I spoke, I laid before him a plan for a tri-sided square of building, the south side being formed by the river. I had taken great pains with the drawing of this plan: the future houses, the future square, the future river-walk with seats at intervals, were all to be found in the roll which

I unfolded and laid before him, and the effect my sketch produced surprised me.

"In Heaven's name, Mr. Patterson," he asked, "where did you get this? You never drew it out of your own head!"

I hastened to assure him I had certainly not got it out of any other person's head; but he smiled incredulously.

"Probably," he suggested, "Mr. Elmsdale left some such sketch behind him—something, at all events, which suggested the idea to you."

"If he did, I never saw nor heard of it," I answered.

"You may have forgotten the circumstance," he persisted; "but I feel confident you must have seen something like this before. Perhaps amongst the papers in Mr. Craven's office."

"May I inquire why you have formed such an opinion?" I said, a little stiffly.

"Simply because this tri-sided square was a favourite project of the late owner of River Hall," he replied. "After the death of his wife, the place grew distasteful to him, and I have often heard him say he would convert the ground into one of the handsomest squares in the neighbourhood of London. All he wanted was a piece of additional land lying to the west, which piece is, I believe, now to be had at a price——"

I sat like one stricken dumb. By no mental process, for which I could ever account, had that idea been evolved. It sprang into life at a bound. It came to me in my sleep, and I wakened at once with the whole plan clear and distinct before my mind's eye, as it now lay clear and distinct before Mr. Harringford.

"It is very extraordinary," I managed at last to stammer out; "for I can honestly say I never heard even a suggestion of Mr. Elmsdale's design; indeed, I did not know he had ever thought of building upon the ground."

"Such was the fact, however," replied my visitor. "He was a speculative man in many ways. Yes, very speculative, and full of plans and projects. However, Mr. Patterson," he proceeded, "all this only proves the truth of the old remark, that 'great wits and little wits sometimes jump together.'"

There was a ring of sarcasm in his voice, as in his words, but I did not give much heed to it. The design, then, was not mine. It had come to me in sleep, it had been forced upon me, it had been explained to me in a word, and as I asked myself, By whom? I was unable to repress a shudder.

"You are not well, I fear," said Mr. Harringford; "this place seems to have affected your health. Surely you have acted imprudently in risking so much to gain so little."

"I do not agree with you," I replied. "However, time will show whether I have been right or wrong in coming here. I have learned many things of which I was previously in ignorance, and I think I hold a clue in my hands which, properly followed, may lead me to the hidden mystery of River Hall."

"Indeed!" he exclaimed. "May I ask the nature of that clue?"

"It would be premature for me to say more than this, that I am inclined to doubt whether Mr. Elmsdale committed suicide."

"Do you think his death was the result of accident, then?" he inquired, his face blanching to a ghastly whiteness.

"No, I do not," I answered, bluntly. "But my thoughts can have little interest for anyone, at present. What we want to talk about is the sale and purchase of this place. The offer you made to Mr. Craven, I consider ridiculous. Let on building lease, the land alone would bring in a handsome income, and the house ought to sell for about as much as you offer for the whole property."

"Perhaps it might, if you could find a purchaser," he answered; "and the land might return an income, if you could let it as you suggest; but, in the meantime, while the grass grows, the steed starves; and while you are waiting for your buyer and your speculative builder, Miss Blake and Miss Elmsdale will have to walk barefoot, waiting for shoes you may never be able to provide for them."

There was truth in this, but only a half-truth, I felt, so I said:

"When examined at the inquest, Mr. Harringford, you stated, I think, that you were under considerable obligations to Mr. Elmsdale?"

"Did I?" he remarked. "Possibly, he had given me a helping-hand once or twice, and probably I mentioned the fact. It is a long time ago, though."

"Not so very long," I answered; "not long enough, I should imagine, to enable you to forget any benefits you may have received from Mr. Elmsdale."

"Mr. Patterson," he interrupted, "are we talking business or sentiment? If the former, please understand I have my own interests to attend to, and that I mean to attend to them. If the latter, I am willing, if you say Miss Elmsdale has pressing need for the money, to send her my cheque for fifty or a hundred pounds. Charity is one thing, trade another, and I do not care to mix them. I should never have attained to my present position, had I allowed fine feelings to interfere with the driving of a bargain. I don't want River Hall. I would not give that," and he snapped his fingers, "to have the title-deeds in my hands to-morrow; but as Miss Elmsdale wishes to sell, and as no one else will buy, I offer what I consider a fair price for the place. If you think you can do better, well and good. If——"

He stopped suddenly in his sentence, then rising, he cried, "It is a trick—a vile, infamous, disgraceful trick!" while his utterance grew thick, and his face began to work like that of a person in convulsions.

"What do you mean?" I asked, rising also, and turning to look in the direction he indicated with outstretched arm and dilated eyes.

Then I saw—no need for him to answer. Standing in the entrance to the strong room was Robert Elmsdale himself, darkness for a background, the light of the gas falling full upon his face.

Slowly, sternly, he came forward, step by step. With footfalls that fell noiselessly, he advanced across the carpet, moving steadily forward towards Mr. Harringford, who, beating the air with his hands, screamed, "Keep him off! don't let him touch me!" and fell full length on the floor.

Next instant, Munro was in the room. "Hullo, what is the matter?" he asked. "What have you done to him—what has he been doing to you?"

I could not answer. Looking in my face, I think Munro understood we had both seen that which no man can behold unappalled.

"Come, Hal," he said, "bestir yourself. Whatever has happened, don't sink under it like a woman. Help me to lift him. Merciful Heaven!" he added, as he raised the prostrate figure. "He is dead!"

To this hour, I do not know how we managed to carry him into the drawing-room. I cannot imagine how our trembling hands bore that inert body out of the library and across the hall. It seems like a dream to me calling up Mrs. Stott, and then tearing away from the house in quest of further medical help, haunted, every step I took, by the memory of that awful presence, the mere sight of which had stricken down one of us in the midst of his buying, and bargaining, and boasting.

I had done it—I had raised that ghost—I had brought the man to his death; and as I fled through the night, innocent as I had been of the thought of such a catastrophe, I understood what Cain must have felt when he went out to live his life with the brand of murderer upon him.

But the man was not dead; though he lay for hours like one from whom life had departed, he did not die then. We had all the genius, and knowledge, and skill of London at his service. If doctors could have saved him, he had lived. If nursing could have availed him, he had recovered, for I never left him.

When the end came I was almost worn out myself.

And the end came very soon.

"No more doctors," whispered the sick man; "they cannot cure me. Send for a clergyman, and a lawyer, Mr. Craven as well as any other. It is all over now; and better so; life is but a long fever. Perhaps he will sleep now, and let me sleep too. Yes, I killed him. Why, I will tell you. Give me some wine.

"What I said at the inquest about owing my worldly prosperity to him was true. I trace my pecuniary success to Mr. Elmsdale; but I trace also hours, months, and years of anguish to his agency. My God! the nights that man has made me spend when he was living, the nights I have spent in consequence of his death——"

He stopped; he had mentally gone back over a long journey. He was retracing the road he had travelled, from youth to old age. For he was old, if not in years, in sorrow. Lying on his death-bed, he understood for what a game he had burnt his candle to the socket; comprehended how the agony, and the suspense, and the suffering, and the long, long fever of life, which with him never knew a remittent moment, had robbed him of that which every man has a right to expect, some pleasure in the course of his existence.

"When I first met Elmsdale," he went on, "I was a young man, and an ambitious one. I was a clerk in the City. I had been married a couple of years to a wife I loved dearly. She was possessed of only a small dot; and after furnishing our house, and paying for all the expenses incident on the coming of a first child, we thought ourselves fortunate in knowing there was still a deposit standing in our name at the Joint-Stock Bank, for something over two hundred pounds.

"Nevertheless, I was anxious. So far, we had lived within our income; but with an annual advance of salary only amounting to ten pounds, or thereabouts, I did not see how we were to manage when more children came, particularly as the cost of living increased day by day. It was a dear year that of which I am speaking.

"I do not precisely remember on what occasion it was I first saw Mr. Elmsdale; but I knew afterwards he picked me out as a person likely to be useful to him.

"He was on good terms with my employers, and asked them to allow me to bid for some houses he wanted to purchase at a sale.

"To this hour I do not know why he did not bid for them himself. He gave me a five-pound note for my services; and that was the beginning of our connection. Off and on, I did many things for him of one sort or another, and made rather a nice addition to my salary out of doing them, till the devil, or he, or both, put it into my head to start as builder and speculator on my own account.

"I had two hundred pounds and my furniture: that was the whole of my capital; but Elmsdale found me money. I thought my fortune was made, the day he advanced me my first five hundred pounds. If I had known—if I had known——"

"Don't talk any more," I entreated. "What can it avail to speak of such matters now?"

He turned towards me impatiently.

"Not talk," he repeated, "when I have for years been as one dumb, and at length the string of my tongue is loosened! Not talk, when, if I keep silence now, he will haunt me in eternity, as he has haunted me in time!"

I did not answer, I only moistened his parched lips, and bathed his burning forehead as tenderly as my unaccustomed hands understood how to perform such offices.

"Lift me up a little, please," he said; and I put the pillows in position as deftly as I could.

"You are not a bad fellow," he remarked, "but I am not going to leave you anything."

"God forbid!" I exclaimed, involuntarily.

"Are not you in want of money?" he asked.

"Not of yours," I answered.

"Mine," he said; "it is not mine, it is his. He thought a great deal of money, and he has come back for it. He can't rest, and he won't let me rest till I have paid him principal and interest—compound interest. Yes—well, I am able to do even that."

We sat silent for a few minutes, then he spoke again.

"When I first went into business with my borrowed capital, nothing I touched really succeeded. I found myself going back—back. Far better was my position as clerk; then at least I slept sound at nights, and relished my meals. But I had tasted of so-called independence, and I could not go back to be at the beck and call of an employer. Ah! no employer ever made me work so hard as Mr. Elmsdale; no beck and call were ever so imperative as his.

"I pass over a long time of anxiety, struggle, and hardship. The world thought me a prosperous man; probably no human being, save Mr. Elmsdale, understood my real position, and he made my position almost unendurable.

"How I came first to bet on races, would be a long story, longer than I have time to tell; but my betting began upon a very small scale, and I always won—always in the beginning. I won so certainly and so continuously, that finally I began to hope for deliverance from Mr. Elmsdale's clutches.

"I don't know how"—the narrative was not recited straight on as I am writing it, but by starts, as strength served him—"Mr. Elmsdale ascertained I was devoting myself to the turf: all I can say is, he did ascertain the fact, and followed me down to Ascot to make sure there was no mistake in his information.

"At the previous Derby my luck had begun to turn. I had lost then—lost heavily for me, and he taxed me with having done so.

"In equity, and at law, he had then the power of foreclosing on every house and rood of ground I owned. I was in his power—in the power of Robert Elmsdale. Think of it——. But you never knew him. Young man, you ought to kneel down and thank God you were never so placed as to be in the power of such a devil——

"If ever you should get into the power of a man like Robert Elmsdale, don't offend him. It is bad enough to owe him money; but it is worse for him to owe you a grudge. I had offended him. He was always worrying me about his wife—lamenting her ill-health, extolling her beauty, glorifying himself on having married a woman of birth and breeding; just as if his were the only wife in the world, as if other men had not at home women twice as good, if not as handsome as Miss Blake's sister.

"Under Miss Blake's insolence I had writhed; and once, when my usual prudence deserted me, I told Mr. Elmsdale I had been in Ireland and seen the paternal Blake's ancestral cabin, and ascertained none of the family had ever mixed amongst the upper thousand, or whatever the number may be which goes to make up society in the Isle of Saints.

"It was foolish, and it was wrong; but I could not help saying what I did, and from that hour he was my enemy. Hitherto, he had merely been my creditor. My own imprudent speech transformed him into a man lying in wait to ruin me.

"He bided his time. He was a man who could wait for years before he struck, but who would never strike till he could make sure of inflicting a mortal wound. He drew me into his power more and more, and then he told me he did not intend to continue trusting anyone who betted—that he must have his money. If he had not it by a certain date, which he named, he would foreclose.

"That meant he would beggar me, and I with an ailing wife and a large family!

"I appealed to him. I don't remember now what I said, but I do recollect I might as well have talked to stone.

"What I endured during the time which followed, I could not describe, were I to talk for ever. Till a man in extremity tries to raise money, he never understands the difficulty of doing so. I had been short of money every hour since I first engaged in business, and yet I never comprehended the meaning of a dead-lock till then.

"One day, in the City, when I was almost mad with anxiety, I met Mr. Elmsdale.

"'Shall you be ready for me, Harringford?' he asked.

"'I do not know—I hope so,' I answered.

"'Well, remember, if you are not prepared with the money, I shall be prepared to act,' he said, with an evil smile.

"As I walked home that evening, an idea flashed into my mind. I had tried all honest means of raising the money; I would try dishonest. My credit was good. I had large transactions with first-rate houses. I was in the habit of discounting largely, and I—well, I signed names to paper that I ought not to have done. I had the bills put through. I had four months and three days in which to turn round, and I might, by that time, be able to raise sufficient to retire the acceptances.

"In the meantime, I could face Mr. Elmsdale, and so I wrote, appointing an evening when I would call with the money, and take his release for all claims upon me.

"When I arrived at River Hall he had all the necessary documents ready, but refused to give them up in exchange for my cheque.

"He could not trust me, he said, and he had, moreover, no banking account. If I liked to bring the amount in notes, well and good; if not, he would instruct his solicitors.

"The next day I had important business to attend to, so a stormy interview ended in my writing 'pay cash' on the cheque, and his consenting to take it to my bankers himself.

"My business on the following day, which happened to be out of town, detained me much longer than I anticipated, and it was late before I could reach River Hall. Late though it was, however, I determined to go after my papers. I held Mr. Elmsdale's receipt for the cheque, certainly; but I knew I had not an hour to lose in putting matters in train for another loan, if I was to retire the forged acceptances. By experience, I knew how the months slipped away when money had to be provided at the end of them, and I was feverishly anxious to hold my leases and title-deeds once more.

"I arrived at the door leading to the library. Mr. Elmsdale opened it as wide as the chain would permit, and asked who was there. I told him, and, grumbling a little at the unconscionable hour at which I had elected to pay my visit, he admitted me.

"He was out of temper. He had hoped and expected, I knew, to find payment of the cheque refused, and he could not submit with equanimity to seeing me slip out of his hands.

"Evidently, he did not expect me to come that night, for his table was strewed with deeds and notes, which he had been reckoning up, no doubt, as a miser counts his gold.

"A pair of pistols lay beside his desk—close to my hand, as I took the seat he indicated.

"We talked long and bitterly. It does not matter now what he said or I said. We fenced round and about a quarrel during the whole interview. I was meek, because I wanted him to let me have part of the money at all events on loan again; and he was blatant and insolent because he fancied I cringed to him—and I did cringe.

"I prayed for help that night from Man as I have never since prayed for help from God.

"You are still young, Mr. Patterson, and life, as yet, is new to you, or else I would ask whether, in going into an entirely strange office, you have not, if agitated in mind, picked up from the table a letter or card, and kept twisting it about, utterly unconscious for the time being of the social solecism you were committing.

"In precisely the same spirit—God is my witness, as I am a dying man, with no object to serve in speaking falsehoods—while we talked, I took up one of the pistols and commenced handling it.

"'Take care,' he said; 'that is loaded'; hearing which I laid it down again.

"For a time we went on talking; he trying to ascertain how I had obtained the money, I striving to mislead him.

"'Come, Mr. Elmsdale,' I remarked at last, 'you see I have been able to raise the money; now be friendly, and consent to advance me a few thousands, at a fair rate, on a property I am negotiating for. There is no occasion, surely, for us to quarrel, after all the years we have done business together. Say you will give me a helping-hand once more, and—'

"Then he interrupted me, and swore, with a great oath, he would never have another transaction with me.

"'Though you have paid _me_,' he said, 'I know you are hopelessly insolvent. I cannot tell where or how you have managed to raise that money, but certain am I it has been by deceiving some one; and so sure as I stand here I will know all about the transaction within a month.'

"While we talked, he had been, at intervals, passing to and from his strong room, putting away the notes and papers previously lying about on the table; and, as he made this last observation, he was standing just within the door, placing something on the shelf.

"'It is of no use talking to me any more,' he went on. 'If you talked from now to eternity you could not alter my decision. There are your deeds; take them, and never let me see you in my house again.'

"He came out of the darkness into the light at that moment, looking burly, and insolent, and braggart, as was his wont.

"Something in his face, in the tone of his voice, in the vulgar assumption of his manner, maddened me. I do not know, I have never been able to tell, what made me long at that moment to kill him—but I did long. With an impulse I could not resist, I rose as he returned towards the table, and snatching a pistol from the table—fired.

"Before he could realize my intention, the bullet was in his brain. He was dead, and I a murderer.

"You can understand pretty well what followed. I ran into the passage and opened the door; then, finding no one seemed to have heard the report of the pistol, my senses came back to me. I was not sorry for what I had done. All I cared for was to avert suspicion from myself, and to secure some advantage from his death.

"Stealing back into the room, I took all the money I could find, as well as deeds and other securities. These last I destroyed next day, and in doing so I felt a savage satisfaction.

"'He would have served them the same as me,' I thought. All the rest you know pretty well.

"From the hour I left him lying dead in the library every worldly plan prospered with me. If I invested in land, it trebled in value. Did I speculate in houses, they were sought after as investments. I grew rich, respected, a man of standing. I had sold my soul to the devil, and he paid me even higher wages than those for which I engaged—but there was a balance.

"One after another, wife and children died; and while my heart was breaking by reason of my home left desolate, there came to me the first rumour of this place being haunted.

"I would not believe it—I did not—I fought against the truth as men fight with despair.

"I used to come here at night and wander as near to the house as I safely could. The place dogged me, sleeping and waking. That library was an ever-present memory. I have sat in my lonely rooms till I could endure the horrors of imagination no longer, and been forced to come from London that I might look at this terrible house, with the silent river flowing sullenly past its desolate gardens.

"Life seemed ebbing away from me. I saw that day by day the blood left my cheeks. I looked at my hands, and beheld they were becoming like those of some one very aged. My lameness grew perceptible to others as well as to me, and I could distinguish, as I walked in the sunshine, the shadow my figure threw was that of one deformed. I grew weak, and worn, and tired, yet I never thoroughly lost heart till I knew you had come here to unravel the secret.

"'And it will be revealed to him,' I thought, 'if I do not kill him too.'

"You have been within an ace of death often and often since you set yourself this task, but at the last instant my heart always failed me.

"Well, you are to live, and I to die. It was to be so, I suppose; but you will never be nearer your last moment, till you lie a corpse, than you have been twice, at any rate."

Then I understood how accurately Munro had judged when he warned me to be on my guard against this man—now harmless and dying, but so recently desperate and all-powerful for evil; and as I recalled the nights I had spent in that desolate house, I shivered.

Even now, though the years have come and the years have gone since I kept my lonely watch in River Hall, I start sometimes from sleep with a great horror of darkness upon me, and a feeling that stealthily some one is creeping through the silence to take my life!

15. CONCLUSION

I can remember the day and the hour as if it had all happened yesterday. I can recall the view from the windows distinctly, as though time had stood still ever since. There are no gardens under our windows in Buckingham Street. Buckingham Gate stands the entrance to a desert of mud, on which the young Arabs—shoeless, stockingless—are disporting themselves. It is low water, and the river steamers keep towards the middle arches of Waterloo. Up aloft the Hungerford Suspension rears itself in mid air, and that spick-and-span new bridge, across which trains run now ceaselessly, has not yet been projected. It is a bright spring day. The sunshine falls upon the buildings on the Surrey side, and lights them with a picturesque beauty to which they have not the slightest title. A barge, laden with hay, is lying almost motionless in the middle of the Thames.

There is, even in London, a great promise and hope about that pleasant spring day, but for me life has held no promise, and the future no hope, since that night when the mystery of River Hall was solved in my presence, and out of his own mouth the murderer uttered his condemnation.

How the weeks and the months had passed with me is soon told. Ill when I left River Hall, shortly after my return home I fell sick unto death, and lay like one who had already entered the Valley of the Shadow.

I was too weak to move; I was too faint to think; and when at length I was brought slowly back to the recollection of life and its cares, of all I had experienced and suffered in the Uninhabited House, the time spent in it seemed to me like the memory of some frightful dream.

I had lost my health there, and my love too. Helena was now further removed from me than ever. She was a great heiress. Mr. Harringford had left her all his money absolutely, and already Miss Blake was considering which of the suitors, who now came rushing to woo, it would be best for her niece to wed.

As for me, Taylor repeated, by way of a good joke, that her aunt referred to me as a "decent sort of young man" who "seemed to be but weakly," and, ignoring the fact of ever having stated "she would not mind giving fifty pounds," remarked to Mr. Craven, that, if I was in poor circumstances, he might pay me five or ten sovereigns, and charge the amount to her account.

Of all this Mr. Craven said nothing to me. He only came perpetually to my sick-bed, and told my mother that whenever I was able to leave town I must get away, drawing upon him for whatever sums I might require. I did not need to encroach on his kindness, however, for my uncle, hearing of my illness, sent me a cordial invitation to spend some time with him.

In his cottage, far away from London, strength at last returned to me, and by the autumn my old place in Mr. Craven's office was no longer vacant. I sat in my accustomed corner, pursuing former avocations, a changed man.

I was hard-working as ever, but hope lightened my road no longer.

To a penny I knew the amount of my lady's fortune, and understood Mr. Harringford's bequest had set her as far above me as the stars are above the earth.

I had the conduct of most of Miss Elmsdale's business. As a compliment, perhaps, Mr. Craven entrusted all the work connected with Mr. Harringford's estate to me, and I accepted that trust as I should have done any other which he might choose to place in my hands.

But I could have dispensed with his well-meant kindness. Every visit I paid to Miss Blake filled my soul with bitterness. Had I been a porter, a crossing-sweeper, or a potman, she might, I suppose, have treated me with some sort of courtesy; but, as matters stood, her every tone, word, and look, said, plainly as possible, "If you do not know your station, I will teach it to you."

As for Helena, she was always the same—sweet, and kind, and grateful, and gracious; but she had her friends about her: new lovers waiting for her smiles. And, after a time, the shadow cast across her youth would, I understood, be altogether removed, and leave her free to begin a new and beautiful life, unalloyed by that hideous, haunting memory of suicide, which had changed into melancholy the gay cheerfulness of her lovely girlhood.

Yes; it was the old story of the streamlet and the snow, of the rose and the wind. To others my love might not have seemed hopeless, but to me it was dead as the flowers I had seen blooming a year before.

Not for any earthly consideration would I have made a claim upon her affection.

What I had done had been done freely and loyally. I gave it all to her as utterly as I had previously given my heart, and now I could make no bargain with my dear. I never for a moment thought she owed me anything for my pains and trouble. Her kindly glances, her sweet words, her little, thoughtful turns of manner, were free gifts of her goodness, but in no sense payment for my services.

She understood I could not presume upon them, and was, perhaps, better satisfied it should be so.

But nothing satisfied Miss Blake, and at length between her and Mr. Craven there ensued a serious disagreement. She insisted he should not "send that clerk of his" to the house again, and suggested if Mr. Craven were too high and mighty to attend to the concerns of Miss Elmsdale himself, Miss Blake must look out for another solicitor.

"The sooner the better, madam," said Mr. Craven, with great state; and Miss Blake left in a huff, and actually did go off to a rival attorney, who, however, firmly declined to undertake her business.

Then Helena came as peacemaker. She smoothed down Mr. Craven's ruffled feathers and talked him into a good temper, and effected a reconciliation with her aunt, and then nearly spoilt everything by adding:

"But indeed I think Mr. Patterson had better not come to see us for the present, at all events."

"You ungrateful girl!" exclaimed Mr. Craven; but she answered, with a little sob, that she was not ungrateful, only—only she thought it would be better if I stayed away.

And so Taylor took my duties on him, and, as a natural consequence, some very pretty disputes between him and Miss Blake had to be arranged by Mr. Craven.

Thus the winter passed, and it was spring again—that spring day of which I have spoken. Mr. Craven and I were alone in the office. He had come late into town and was reading his letters; whilst I, seated by a window overlooking the Thames, gave about equal attention to the river outside and a tedious document lying on my table.

We had not spoken a word, I think, for ten minutes, when a slip of paper was brought in, on which was written a name.

"Ask her to walk in," said Mr. Craven, and, going to the door, he greeted the visitor, and led Miss Elmsdale into the room.

I rose, irresolute; but she came forward, and, with a charming blush, held out her hand, and asked me some commonplace question about my health.

Then I was going, but she entreated me not to leave the room on her account.

"This is my birthday, Mr. Craven," she went on, "and I have come to ask you to wish me many happy returns of the day, and to do something for me—will you?"

"I wish you every happiness, my dear," he answered, with a tenderness born, perhaps, of olden memories and of loving-kindness towards one so sweet, and beautiful, and lonely. "And if there is anything I can do for you on your birthday, why, it is done, that is all I can say."

She clasped her dear hands round his arm, and led him towards a further window. I could see her downcast eyes—the long lashes lying on her cheeks, the soft colour flitting and coming, making her alternately pale and rosy, and I was jealous. Heaven forgive me! If she had hung so trustfully about one of the patriarchs, I should have been jealous, though he reckoned his years by centuries.

What she had to say was said quickly. She spoke in a whisper, bringing her lips close to his ear, and lifting her eyes imploringly to his when she had finished.

"Upon my word, miss," he exclaimed, aloud, and he held her from him and looked at her till the colour rushed in beautiful blushes even to her temples, and her lashes were wet with tears, and her cheeks dimpled with smiles. "Upon my word—and you make such a request to me—to me, who have a character to maintain, and who have daughters of my own to whom I am bound to set a good example! Patterson, come here. Can you imagine what this young lady wants me to do for her now? She is twenty-one to-day, she tells me, and she wants me to ask you to marry her. She says she will never marry anyone else." Then, as I hung back a little, dazed, fearful, and unable to credit the evidence of my senses, he added:

"Take her; she means it every word, and you deserve to have her. If she had chosen anybody else I would never have drawn out her settlements."

But I would not take her, not then. Standing there with the spring landscape blurred for the moment before me, I tried to tell them both what I felt. At first, my words were low and broken, for the change from misery to happiness affected me almost as though I had been suddenly plunged from happiness into despair. But by degrees I recovered my senses, and told my darling and Mr. Craven it was not fit she should, out of very generosity, give herself to me—a man utterly destitute of fortune—a man who, though he loved her better than life, was only a clerk at a clerk's salary.

"If I were a duke," I went on, breaking ground at last, "with a duke's revenue and a duke's rank, I should only value what I had for her sake. I would carry my money, and my birth, and my position to her, and ask her to take all, if she would only take me with them; but, as matters stand, Mr. Craven——"

"I owe everything worth having in life to you," she said, impetuously, taking my hand in hers. "I should not like you at all if you were a duke, and had a ducal revenue."

"I think you are too strait-laced, Patterson," agreed Mr. Craven. "She does owe everything she has to your determination, remember."

"But I undertook to solve the mystery for fifty pounds," I remarked, smiling in spite of myself.

"Which has never been paid," remarked my employer. "But," he went on, "you young people come here and sit down, and let us talk the affair over all together." And so he put us in chairs as if we had been clients, while he took his professional seat, and, after a pause, began:

"My dear Helena, I think the young man has reason. A woman should marry her equal. He will, in a worldly sense, be more than your equal some day; but that is nothing. A man should be head of the household.

"It is good, and nice, and loving of you, my child, to wish to endow your husband with all your worldly goods; but your husband ought, before he takes you, to have goods of his own wherewith to endow you. Now, now, now, don't purse up your pretty mouth, and try to controvert a lawyer's wisdom. You are both young: you have plenty of time before you.

"He ought to be given an opportunity of showing what he can do, and you ought to mix in society and see whether you meet anyone you think you can like better. There is no worse time for finding out a mistake of that sort, than after marriage." And so the kind soul prosed on, and would, possibly, have gone on prosing for a few hours more, had I not interrupted one of his sentences by saying I would not have Miss Elmsdale bound by any engagement, or consider herself other than free as air.

"Well, well," he answered, testily, "we understand that thoroughly. But I suppose you do not intend to cast the young lady's affections from you as if they were of no value?"

At this juncture her eyes and mine met. She smiled, and I could not help smiling too.

"Suppose we leave it in this way," Mr. Craven said, addressing apparently some independent stranger. "If, at the end of a year, Miss Elmsdale is of the same mind, let her write to me and say so. That course will leave her free enough, and it will give us twelve months in which to turn round, and see what we can do in the way of making his fortune. I do not imagine he will ever be able to count down guineas against her guineas, or that he wants to do anything so absurd. But he is right in saying an heiress should not marry a struggling clerk. He ought to be earning a good income before he is much older, and he shall, or my name is not William Craven."

I got up and shook his hand, and Helena kissed him.

"Tut, tut! fie, fie! what's all this?" he exclaimed, searching sedulously for his double eyeglass—which all the while he held between his finger and thumb. "Now, young people, you must not occupy my time any longer. Harry, see this self-willed little lady into a cab; and you need not return until the afternoon. If you are in time to find me before I leave, that will do quite well. Good-bye, Miss Helena."

I did not take his hint, though. Failing to find a cab—perhaps for want of looking for one—I ventured to walk with my beautiful companion up Regent Street as far as Oxford Circus.

Through what enchanted ground we passed in that short distance, how can I ever hope to tell! It was all like a story of fairyland, with Helena for Queen of Unreality. But it was real enough. Ah! my dear, you knew your own mind, as I, after years and years of wedded happiness, can testify.

Next day, Mr. Craven started off to the west of England. He did not tell me where he was going; indeed, I never knew he had been to see my uncle until long afterwards.

What he told that gentleman, what he said of me and Helena, of my poor talents and her beauty, may be gathered from the fact that the old admiral agreed first to buy me a partnership in some established firm, and then swore a mighty oath, that if the heiress was, at the end of twelve months, willing to marry his nephew, he would make him his heir.

"I should like to have you with me, Patterson," said Mr. Craven, when we were discussing my uncle's proposal, which a few weeks after took me greatly by surprise; "but, if you remain here, Miss Blake will always regard you as a clerk. I know of a good opening; trust me to arrange everything satisfactorily for you."

Whether Miss Blake, even with my altered fortunes, would ever have become reconciled to the match, is extremely doubtful, had the *beau monde* not turned a very decided cold-shoulder to the Irish patriot.

Helena, of course, everyone wanted, but Miss Blake no one wanted; and the fact was made very patent to that lady.

"They'll be for parting you and me, my dear," said the poor creature one day, when society had proved more than usually cruel. "If ever I am let see you after your marriage, I suppose I shall have to creep in at the area-door, and make believe I am some faithful old nurse wanting to have a look at my dear child's sweet face."

"No one shall ever separate me from you, dear, silly aunt," said my charmer, kissing first one of her relative's high cheek-bones, and then the other.

"We'll have to jog on, two old spinsters together, then, I am thinking," replied Miss Blake.

"No," was the answer, very distinctly spoken. "I am going to marry Mr. Henry Patterson, and he will not ask me to part from my ridiculous, foolish aunt."

"Patterson! that conceited clerk of William Craven's? Why, he has not darkened our doors for fifteen months and more."

"Quite true," agreed her niece; "but, nevertheless, I am going to marry him. I asked him to marry me a year ago."

"You don't mane that, Halana!" said poor Miss Blake. "You should not talk like an infant in arms."

"We are only waiting for your consent," went on my lady fair.

"Then that you will never have. While I retain my powers of speech you shall not marry a pauper who has only asked you for the sake of your money."

"He did not ask me; I asked him," said Helena, mischievously; "and he is not a beggar. His uncle has bought him a partnership, and is going to leave him his money; and he will be here himself to-morrow, to tell you all about his prospects."

At first, Miss Blake refused to see me; but after a time she relented, and, thankful, perhaps, to have once again anyone over whom she could tyrannise, treated her niece's future husband—as Helena declared—most shamefully.

"But you two must learn to agree, for there shall be no quarrelling in our house," added the pretty autocrat.

"You needn't trouble yourself about that, Halana," said her aunt. "He'll be just like all the rest. If he's civil to me before marriage, he won't be after. He will soon find out there is no place in the house, or, for that matter, in the world, for Susan Blake"; and my enemy, for the first time in my memory, fairly broke down and began to whimper.

"Miss Blake," I said, "how can I convince you that I never dreamt, never could dream of asking you and Helena to separate?"

"See that, now, and he calls you Helena already," said the lady, reproachfully.

"Well, he must begin sometime. And that reminds me the sooner he begins to call you aunt, the better."

I did not begin to do so then, of that the reader may be quite certain; but there came a day when the word fell quite naturally from my lips.

For a long period ours was a hollow truce, but, as time passed on, and I resolutely refused to quarrel with Miss Blake, she gradually ceased trying to pick quarrels with me.

Our home is very dear to her. All the household management Helena from the first hour took into her own hands; but in the nursery Miss Blake reigns supreme.

She has always a grievance, but she is thoroughly happy. She dresses now like other people, and wears over her gray hair caps of Helena's selection.

Time has softened some of her prejudices, and age renders her eccentricities less noticeable; but she is still, after her fashion, unique, and we feel in our home, as we used to feel in the office—that we could better spare a better man.

The old house was pulled down, and not a square, but a fine terrace occupied its site. Munro lives in one of those desirable tenements, and is growing rich and famous day by day. Mr. Craven has retired from practice, and taken a place in the country, where he is bored to death though he professes himself charmed with the quiet.

Helena and I have always been town-dwellers. Though the Uninhabited House is never mentioned by either of us, she knows I have still a shuddering horror of lonely places.

My experiences in the Uninhabited House have made me somewhat nervous. Why, it was only the other night—

"What are you doing, making all that spluttering on your paper?" says an interrupting voice at this juncture, and, looking up, I see Miss Blake seated by the window, clothed and in her right mind.

"You had better put by that writing," she proceeds, with the manner of one having authority, and I am so amazed, when I contrast Miss Blake as she is, with what she was, that I at once obey!

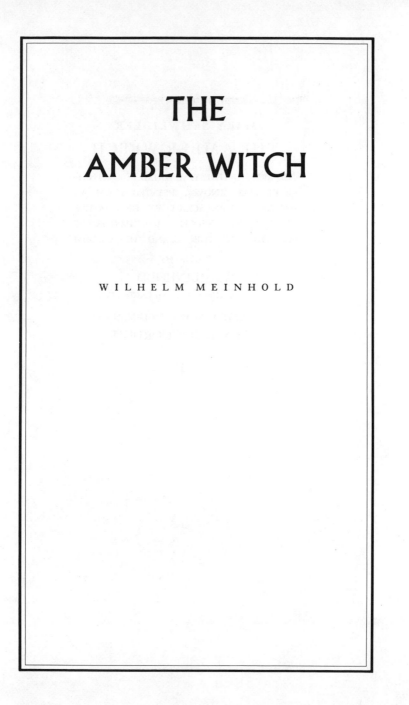

THE
AMBER WITCH

WILHELM MEINHOLD

MARY SCHWEIDLER

THE AMBER WITCH

THE MOST INTERESTING TRIAL FOR WITCH-
CRAFT EVER KNOWN. PRINTED FROM AN
IMPERFECT MANUSCRIPT BY HER FATHER
ABRAHAM SCHWEIDLER, THE PASTOR OF
COSEROW, IN THE ISLAND OF USEDOM

EDITED BY

W. MEINHOLD

DOCTOR OF THEOLOGY, AND PASTOR, ETC.

TRANSLATED FROM THE GERMAN BY

LADY DUFF GORDON

—

1846

PREFACE

In laying before the public this deeply affecting and romantic trial, which I have not without reason called on the title-page the most interesting of all trials for witchcraft ever known, I will first give some account of the history of the manuscript.

At Coserow, in the Island of Usedom, my former cure, the same which was held by our worthy author some two hundred years ago, there existed under a seat in the choir of the church a sort of niche, nearly on a level with the floor. I had, indeed, often seen a heap of various writings in this recess; but owing to my short sight, and the darkness of the place, I had taken them for antiquated hymn-books, which were lying about in great numbers. But one day, while I was teaching in the church, I looked for a paper mark in the Catechism of one of the boys, which I could not immediately find; and my old sexton, who was past eighty (and who, although called Appelmann, was thoroughly unlike his namesake in our story, being a very worthy, although a most ignorant man), stooped down to the said niche, and took from it a folio volume which I had never before observed, out of which he, without the slightest hesitation, tore a strip of paper suited to my purpose, and reached it to me. I immediately seized upon the book, and, after a few minutes' perusal, I know not which was greater, my astonishment or my vexation at this costly prize. The manuscript, which was bound in vellum, was not only defective both at the beginning and at the end, but several leaves had even been torn out here and there in the middle. I scolded the old man as I had never done during the whole course of my life; but he excused himself, saying that one of my predecessors had given him the manuscript for waste paper, as it had lain about there ever since the memory of man, and he had often been in want of paper to twist round the altar candles, etc. The aged and half-blind pastor had mistaken the folio for old parochial accounts which could be of no more use to any one.*

No sooner had I reached home than I fell to work upon my new acquisition, and after reading a bit here and there with considerable trouble, my interest was powerfully excited by the contents.

---

* The original manuscript does indeed contain several accounts which at first sight may have led to this mistake; besides, the handwriting is extremely difficult to read, and in several places the paper is discoloured and decayed.

I soon felt the necessity of making myself better acquainted with the nature and conduct of these witch trials, with the proceedings, nay, even with the history of the whole period in which these events occur. But the more I read of these extraordinary stories, the more was I confounded; and neither the trivial Beeker (*die bezauberte Welt*, the enchanted world), nor the more careful Horst (*Zauberbibliothek*, the library of magic), to which, as well as to several other works on the same subject, I had flown for information, could resolve my doubts, but rather served to increase them.

Not alone is the demoniacal character, which pervades nearly all these fearful stories, so deeply marked, as to fill the attentive reader with feelings of alternate horror and dismay, but the eternal and unchangeable laws of human feeling and action are often arrested in a manner so violent and unforeseen, that the understanding is entirely baffled. For instance, one of the original trials which a friend of mine, a lawyer, discovered in our province, contains the account of a mother, who, after she had suffered the torture, and received the holy Sacrament, and was on the point of going to the stake, so utterly lost all maternal feeling, that her conscience obliged her to accuse as a witch her only dearly-loved daughter, a girl of fifteen, against whom no one had ever entertained a suspicion, in order, as she said, to save her poor soul. The court, justly amazed at an event which probably has never since been paralleled, caused the state of the mother's mind to be examined both by clergymen and physicians, whose original testimonies are still appended to the records, and are all highly favourable to her soundness of mind. The unfortunate daughter, whose name was Elizabeth Hegel, was actually executed on the strength of her mother's accusation.*

The explanation commonly received at the present day, that these phenomena were produced by means of animal magnetism, is utterly insufficient. How, for instance, could this account for the deeply demoniacal nature of old Lizzie Kolken as exhibited in the following pages? It is utterly incomprehensible, and perfectly explains why the old pastor, notwithstanding the horrible deceits practised on him in the person of his daughter, retained as firm a faith in the truth of witchcraft as in that of the Gospel.

During the earlier centuries of the middle ages little was known of witchcraft. The crime of magic, when it did occur, was leniently punished. For instance, the Council of Ancyra (314) ordained the whole punishment of witches to consist in expulsion from the Christian community. The Visigoths punished them with stripes, and Charlemagne, by advice of his bishops, confined them in prison until such time as they should

---

* It is my intention to publish this trial also, as it possesses very great psychological interest.

sincerely repent.* It was not until very soon before the Reformation, that Innocent VIII. lamented that the complaints of universal Christendom against the evil practices of these women had become so general and so loud, that the most vigorous measures must be taken against them; and towards the end of the year 1489, he caused the notorious Hammer for Witches (*Malleus Maleficarum*) to be published, according to which proceedings were set on foot with the most fanatical zeal, not only in Catholic, but, strange to say, even in Protestant Christendom, which in other respects abhorred everything belonging to Catholicism. Indeed, the Protestants far outdid the Catholics in cruelty, until, among the latter, the noble-minded Jesuit, J. Spee, and among the former, but not until seventy years later, the excellent Thomasius, by degrees put a stop to these horrors.

After careful examination into the nature and characteristics of witchcraft, I soon perceived that among all these strange and often romantic stories, not one surpassed my 'amber witch' in lively interest; and I determined to throw her adventures into the form of a romance. Fortunately, however, I was soon convinced that her story was already in itself the most interesting of all romances; and that I should do far better to leave it in its original antiquated form, omitting whatever would be uninteresting to modern readers, or so universally known as to need no repetition. I have therefore attempted, not indeed to supply what is missing at the beginning and end, but to restore those leaves which have been torn out of the middle, imitating, as accurately as I was able, the language and manner of the old biographer, in order that the difference between the original narrative and my own interpolations might not be too evident.

This I have done with much trouble, and after many ineffectual attempts; but I refrain from pointing out the particular passages which I have supplied, so as not to disturb the historical interest of the greater part of my readers. For modern criticism, which has now attained to a degree of acuteness never before equalled, such a confession would be entirely superfluous, as critics will easily distinguish the passages where Pastor Schweidler speaks from those written by Pastor Meinhold.

I am, nevertheless, bound to give the public some account of what I have omitted, namely,—

1st. Such long prayers as were not very remarkable for Christian unction.

2d. Well-known stories out of the Thirty Years' War.

* Horst, *Zauberbibliothek*, vi. p. 231.

3d. Signs and wonders in the heavens, which were seen here and there, and which are recorded by other Pomeranian writers of these fearful times; for instance, by Micrælius.* But when these events formed part of the tale itself, as, for instance, the cross on the Streckelberg, I, of course, allowed them to stand.

4th. The specification of the whole income of the church at Coserow, before and during the terrible times of the Thirty Years' War.

5th. The enumeration of the dwellings left standing, after the devastations made by the enemy in every village throughout the parish.

6th. The names of the districts to which this or that member of the congregation had emigrated.

7th. A ground plan and description of the old Manse.

I have likewise here and there ventured to make a few changes in the language, as my author is not always consistent in the use of his words or in his orthography. The latter I have, however, with very few exceptions, retained.

And thus I lay before the gracious reader a work, glowing with the fire of heaven, as well as with that of hell.

MEINHOLD.

* *Vom Alten Pommerlande* (of old Pomerania), book v.

INTRODUCTION

The origin of our biographer cannot be traced with any degree of certainty, owing to the loss of the first part of his manuscript. It is, however, pretty clear that he was not a Pomeranian, as he says he was in Silesia in his youth, and mentions relations scattered far and wide, not only at Hamburg and Cologne, but even at Antwerp; above all, his south German language betrays a foreign origin, and he makes use of words which are, I believe, peculiar to Swabia. He must, however, have been living for a long time in Pomerania at the time he wrote, as he even more frequently uses Low-German expressions, such as occur in contemporary native Pomeranian writers.

Since he sprang from an ancient noble family, as he says on several occasions, it is possible that some particulars relating to the Schweidlers might be discovered in the family records of the seventeenth century which would give a clew to his native country; but I have sought for that name in all the sources of information accessible to me, in vain, and am led to suspect that our author, like many of his contemporaries, laid aside his nobility and changed his name when he took holy orders.

I will not, however, venture on any further conjectures; the manuscript, of which six chapters are missing, begins with the words "Imperialists plundered," and evidently the previous pages must have contained an account of the breaking out of the Thirty Years' War in the island of Usedom. It goes on as follows:—

"Coffers, chests, and closets were all plundered and broken to pieces, and my surplice also was torn, so that I remained in great distress and tribulation. But my poor little daughter they did not find, seeing that I had hidden her in the stable, which was dark, without which I doubt not they would have made my heart heavy indeed. The lewd dogs would even have been rude to my old maid Ilse, a woman hard upon fifty, if an old cornet had not forbidden them. Wherefore I gave thanks to my Maker when the wild guests were gone, that I had first saved my child from their clutches, although not one dust of flour, nor one grain of corn, one morsel of meat even of a finger's length was left, and I knew not how I should any longer support my own life, and my poor child's. *Item*, I thanked God that I had likewise secured the *vasa sacra*, which I had forthwith buried in the church in front of the altar, in presence of the two churchwardens, Hinrich Seden and Claus Bulken, of Uekeritze, commending them to the care of God. And now because, as I have already said, I

was suffering the pangs of hunger, I wrote to his lordship the Sheriff
Wittich v. Appelmann, at Pudgla, that for the love of God and his holy
Gospel he should send me that which his highness' grace Philippus Julius
had allowed me as *præstanda* from the convent at Pudgla, to wit, thirty
bushels of barley and twenty-five marks of silver, which, howbeit his
lordship had always withheld from me hitherto (for he was a very hard
inhuman man, inasmuch as he despised the holy Gospel and the preaching
of the Word, and openly, without shame, reviled the servants of God,
saying that they were useless feeders, and that Luther had but half
cleansed the pigstye of the Church—God mend it!). But he answered
me nothing, and I should have perished for want if Hinrich Seden
had not begged for me in the parish. May God reward the honest fellow
for it in eternity! Moreover, he was then growing old, and was sorely
plagued by his wicked wife Lizzie Kolken. Methought when I married
them that it would not turn out over well, seeing that she was in common
report of having long lived in unchastity with Wittich Appelmann,
who had ever been an arch-rogue, and especially an arrant whoremaster,
and such the Lord never blesses. This same Seden now brought me five
loaves, two sausages, and a goose, which old goodwife Paal, at Loddin,
had given him; also a flitch of bacon from the farmer Jack Tewert. But he
said I must shield him from his wife, who would have had half for herself,
and when he denied her she cursed him, and wished him gout in his head,
whereupon he straightway felt a pain in his right cheek, and it was quite
hard and heavy already. At such shocking news I was affrighted, as became
a good pastor, and asked whether peradventure he believed that she stood
in evil communication with Satan, and could bewitch folks? But he said
nothing, and shrugged his shoulders. So I sent for old Lizzie to come to
me, who was a tall, meagre woman of about sixty, with squinting eyes,
so that she could not look any one in the face; likewise with quite red
hair, and indeed her goodman had the same. But though I diligently
admonished her out of God's Word, she made no answer until at last I
said, 'Wilt thou unbewitch thy goodman (for I saw from the window how
that he was raving in the street like a madman), or wilt thou that I should
inform the magistrate of thy deeds?' Then, indeed, she gave in, and
promised that he should soon be better (and so he was); moreover she
begged that I would give her some bread and some bacon, inasmuch as it
was three days since she had a bit of anything to put between her lips,
saving always her tongue. So my daughter gave her half a loaf, and a piece
of bacon about two handsbreadths large; but she did not think it enough,
and muttered between her teeth; whereupon my daughter said, 'If thou
art not content, thou old witch, go thy ways and help thy goodman; see
how he has laid his head on Zabel's fence, and stamps with his feet for
pain.' Whereupon she went away, but still kept muttering between her
teeth, 'Yea, forsooth, I will help him and thee too.'"

The Seventh Chapter

How the Imperialists Robbed Me of All That Was
Left, and Likewise Broke into the Church and Stole
the *Vasa Sacra*; Also What More Befell Us

After a few days, when we had eaten almost all our food, my last cow
fell down dead (the wolves had already devoured the others, as mentioned above), not without a strong suspicion that Lizzie had a hand in it,
seeing that the poor beast had eaten heartily the day before; but I leave
that to a higher judge, seeing that I would not willingly calumniate any
one; and it may have been the will of God, whose wrath I have well
deserved. *Summa*, I was once more in great need, and my daughter
Mary pierced my heart with her sighs, when the cry was raised that
another troop of Imperialists was come to Uekeritze, and was marauding
there more cruelly than ever, and, moreover, had burnt half the village.
Wherefore I no longer thought myself safe in my cottage; and after I
had commended everything to the Lord in a fervent prayer, I went up
with my daughter and old Ilse into the Streckelberg, where I already
had looked out for ourselves a hole like a cavern, well grown over with
brambles, against the time when the troubles should drive us thither.
We therefore took with us all we had left to us for the support of our
bodies, and fled into the woods, sighing and weeping, whither we soon
were followed by the old men, and the women and children; these raised
a great cry of hunger when they saw my daughter sitting on a log and
eating a bit of bread and meat, and the little things came with their tiny
hands stretched out and cried "Have some too, have some too." Therefore, being justly moved by such great distress, I hindered not my daughter from sharing all the bread and meat that remained among the hungry
children. But first I made them pray—"The eyes of all wait upon thee";
upon which words I then spake comfortably to the people, telling them
that the Lord, who had now fed their little children, would find means
to fill their own bellies, and that they must not be weary of trusting in
him.

This comfort did not, however, last long; for after we had rested within
and around the cavern for about two hours, the bells in the village began
to ring so dolefully that it went nigh to break all our hearts, the more as
loud firing was heard between-whiles; *item*, the cries of men and the
barking of dogs resounded, so that we could easily guess that the enemy
was in the village. I had enough to do to keep the women quiet, that they
might not by their senseless lamentations betray our hiding-place to the
cruel enemy; and more still when it began to smell smoky, and presently
the bright flames gleamed through the trees. I therefore sent old Paasch
up to the top of the hill, that he might look around and see how matters

stood, but told him to take good care that they did not see him from the village, seeing that the twilight had but just begun.

This he promised, and soon returned with the news that about twenty horsemen had galloped out of the village towards the Damerow, but that half the village was in flames. *Item*, he told us that by a wonderful dispensation of God a great number of birds had appeared in the juniper-bushes and elsewhere, and that if we could catch them they would be excellent food for us. I therefore climbed up the hill myself, and having found everything as he had said, and also perceived that the fire had, by the help of God's mercy, abated in the village; *item*, that my cottage was left standing, far beyond my merits and deserts; I came down again and comforted the people, saying, "The Lord hath given us a sign, and he will feed us, as he fed the people of Israel in the wilderness; for he has sent us a fine flight of fieldfares across the barren sea, so that they whirr out of every bush as ye come near it. Who will now run down into the village, and cut off the mane and tail of my dead cow which lies out behind on the common?" (for there was no horsehair in all the village, seeing that the enemy had long since carried off or stabbed all the horses). But no one would go, for fear was stronger even than hunger, till my old Ilse spoke, and said, "I will go, for I fear nothing, when I walk in the ways of God; only give me a good stick." When old Paasch had lent her his staff, she began to sing, "God the Father be with us," and was soon out of sight among the bushes. Meanwhile I exhorted the people to set to work directly, and to cut little wands for springes, and to gather berries while the moon still shone; there were a great quantity of mountain-ash and elder-bushes all about the mountain. I myself and my daughter Mary stayed to guard the little children, because it was not safe there from wolves. We therefore made a blazing fire, sat ourselves around it, and heard the little folks say the Ten Commandments, when there was a rustling and crackling behind us, and my daughter jumped up and ran into the cavern, crying, "*Proh dolor hostis!*" But it was only some of the able-bodied men who had stayed behind in the village, and who now came to bring us word how things stood there. I therefore called to her directly, "*Emergas amici*," whereupon she came skipping joyously out, and sat down again by the fire, and forthwith my warden Hinrich Seden related all that had happened, and how his life had only been saved by means of his wife Lizzie Kolken; but that Jurgen Flatow, Chim Burse, Claus Peer, and Chim Seideritz were killed, and the last named of them left lying on the church steps. The wicked incendiaries had burned down twelve sheds, and it was not their fault that the whole village was not destroyed, but only in consequence of the wind not being in the quarter that suited their purpose. Meanwhile they tolled the bells in mockery and scorn, to see whether any one would come and quench the fire; and that when he and the three other young fellows came forward they fired off their muskets at them, but, by God's help, none of them were hit. Hereupon his three comrades jumped over the paling and escaped; but him they caught, and had already taken aim at him with their firelocks, when his wife Lizzie Kolken came out of the church with another troop and beckoned to them to leave him in peace. But they stabbed Lene Hebers as she lay in childbed, speared the child, and flung it over Claus Peer's hedge among the nettles, where it was yet lying when they came away. There was not a living soul left in the village, and still less a morsel of bread, so that unless the Lord took pity on their need they must all die miserably of hunger.

(Now who is to believe that such people can call themselves Christians!)

I next inquired, when he had done speaking (but with many sighs, as any one may guess), after my cottage; but of that they knew nought save that it was still standing. I thanked the Lord therefore with a quiet sigh; and having asked old Seden what his wife had been doing in the church, I thought I should have died for grief when I heard that the villains came out of it with both the chalices and patens in their hands. I therefore spoke very sharply to old Lizzie, who now came slinking through the bushes; but she answered insolently that the strange soldiers had forced her to open the church, as her goodman had crept behind the hedge, and nobody else was there; that they had gone straight up to the altar, and seeing that one of the stones was not well fitted (which, truly, was an arch-lie), had begun to dig with their swords till they found the chalices and patens; or somebody else might have betrayed the spot to them, so I need not always to lay the blame on her, and rate her so hardly.

Meanwhile the old men and the women came with a good store of berries; *item*, my old maid, with the cow's tail and mane, who brought word that the whole house was turned upside down, the windows all broken, and the books and writings trampled in the dirt in the midst of the street, and the doors torn off their hinges. This, however, was a less sorrow to me than the chalices; and I only bade the people make springes and snares, in order next morning to begin our fowling, with the help of Almighty God. I therefore scraped the rods myself until near midnight; and when we had made ready a good quantity, I told old Seden to repeat the evening blessing, which we all heard on our knees; after which I wound up with a prayer, and then admonished the people to creep in under the bushes to keep them from the cold (seeing that it was now about the end of September, and the wind blew very fresh from the sea), the men apart, and the women also apart by themselves. I myself went up with my daughter and my maid into the cavern, where I had not slept long before I heard old Seden moaning bitterly because, as he said, he was seized with the colic. I therefore got up and gave him

my place, and sat down again by the fire to cut springes, till I fell asleep
for half an hour; and then morning broke, and by that time he had got
better, and I woke the people to morning prayer. This time old Paasch
had to say it, but could not get through with it properly, so that I had
to help him. Whether he had forgot it, or whether he was frightened, I
cannot say. *Summa.* After we had all prayed most devoutly, we presently
set to work, wedging the springes into the trees, and hanging berries all
around them; while my daughter took care of the children, and looked
for blackberries for their breakfast. Now we wedged the snares right
across the wood along the road to Uekeritze; and mark what a wondrous
act of mercy befell from gracious God! As I stepped into the road with
the hatchet in my hand (it was Seden his hatchet, which he had fetched
out of the village early in the morning), I caught sight of a loaf as long
as my arm, which a raven was pecking, and which doubtless one of the
Imperial troopers had dropped out of his knapsack the day before, for
there were fresh hoofmarks in the sand by it. So I secretly buttoned the
breast of my coat over it, so that none should perceive anything, although
the aforesaid Paasch was close behind me; *item*, all the rest followed at
no great distance. Now, having set the springes so very early, towards
noon we found such a great number of birds taken in them that Katy
Berow, who went beside me while I took them out, scarce could hold
them all in her apron; and at the other end old Pagels pulled nearly as
many out of his doublet and coat pockets. My daughter then sat down
with the rest of the womankind to pluck the birds; and as there was no
salt (indeed it was long since most of us had tasted any), she desired two
men to go down to the sea, and to fetch a little salt-water in an iron pot
borrowed from Staffer Zuter; and so they did. In this water we first
dipped the birds, and then roasted them at a large fire, while our mouths
watered only at the sweet savour of them, seeing it was so long since we
had tasted any food.

And now when all was ready, and the people seated on the earth, I
said, "Behold how the Lord still feeds his people Israel in the wilderness
with fresh quails: if now he did yet more, and sent us a piece of manna
bread from heaven, what think ye? Would ye then ever weary of believing
in him, and not rather willingly endure all want, tribulation, hunger and
thirst, which he may hereafter lay upon you according to his gracious
will?" Whereupon they all answered and said, "Yea, surely!" *Ego*:
"Will you then promise me this in truth?" And they said again, "Yea,
that will we!" Then with tears I drew forth the loaf from my breast, held
it on high, and cried, "Behold, then, thou poor believing little flock,
how sweet a manna loaf your faithful Redeemer hath sent ye through
me!" Whereupon they all wept, sobbed and groaned; and the little
children again came running up and held out their hands, crying, "See,

bread, bread!" But as I myself could not pray for heaviness of soul, I bade Paasch his little girl say the *Gratias* the while my Mary cut up the loaf and gave to each his share. And now we all joyfully began to eat our meat from God in the wilderness.

Meanwhile I had to tell in what manner I had found the blessed manna bread, wherein I neglected not again to exhort them to lay to heart this great sign and wonder, how that God in his mercy had done to them as of old to the prophet Elijah, to whom a raven brought bread in his great need in the wilderness; as likewise this bread had been given to me by means of a raven, which showed it to me, when otherwise I might have passed it by in my heaviness without ever seeing it.

When we were satisfied with food, I said the thanksgiving from Luke xii. 24, where the Lord saith, "Consider the ravens: for they neither sow nor reap; which neither have storehouse nor barn; and God feedeth them: how much more are ye better than the fowls?" But our sins stank before the Lord. For old Lizzie, as I afterwards heard, would not eat her birds because she thought them unsavoury, but threw them among the juniper-bushes; whereupon the wrath of the Lord was kindled against us as of old against the people of Israel, and at night we found but seven birds in the snares, and next morning but two. Neither did any raven come again to give us bread. Wherefore I rebuked old Lizzie, and admonished the people to take upon themselves willingly the righteous chastisement of the Most High God, to pray without ceasing, to return to their desolate dwellings, and to see whether the all-merciful God would peradventure give them more on the sea. That I also would call upon him with prayer night and day, remaining for a time in the cavern with my daughter and the maid to watch the springes, and see whether his wrath might be turned from us. That they should meanwhile put my manse to rights to the best of their power, seeing that the cold was become very irksome to me. This they promised me, and departed with many sighs. What a little flock! I counted but twenty-five souls where there used to be above eighty: all the rest had been slain by hunger, pestilence, or the sword. I then abode a while alone and sorrowing in the cave, praying to God, and sent my daughter with the maid into the village to see how things stood at the manse; *item*, to gather together the books and papers, and also to bring me word whether Hinze the carpenter, whom I had straightway sent back to the village, had knocked together some coffins for the poor corpses, so that I might bury them next day. I then went to look at the springes, but found only one single little bird, whereby I saw that the wrath of God had not yet passed away. Howbeit, I found a fine blackberry bush, from which I gathered nearly a pint of berries, and put them, together with the bird, in Staffer Zuter his pot, which the honest fellow had left with us for a while, and set them on the fire for supper against my child and the maid should return. It was not long before they came through the coppice and told me of the fearful devastation which Satan had made in the village and manse by the permission of all-righteous God. My child had gathered together a few books, which she brought with her, above all, a *Virgilius* and a Greek Bible. And after she had told me that the carpenter would not have done till next day, and we had satisfied the cravings of hunger, I made her read to me again, for the greater strengthening of my faith, the *locus* about the blessed raven from the Greek of Luke, at the twelfth chapter; also, the beautiful *locus parallelus*, Matt. vi. After which the maid said the evening blessing, and we all went into the cave to rest for the night. When I awoke next morning, just as the blessed sun rose out the sea and peeped over the mountain, I heard my poor hungry child already standing outside the cave reciting the beautiful verses about the joys of paradise which St. Augustine wrote and I had taught her. She sobbed for grief as she spoke the words:—

> Uno pane vivunt cives utriusque patriæ;
> Avidi et semper pleni, quod habent desiderant.
> Non sacietas fastidit, neque fames cruciat;
> Inhiantes semper edunt, et edentes inhiant.
> Flos perpetuus rosarum ver agit perpetuum;
> Candent lilia, rubescit crocus, sudat balsamum,
> Virent prata, vernant sata, rivi mellis influunt;
> Pigmentorum spirat odor liquor et aromatum,
> Pendent poma floridorum non lapsura nemorum.
> Non alternat luna vices, sol vel cursus syderum.
> Agnus est fælicis urbis lumen inocciduum.

At these words my own heart was melted; and when she ceased from speaking, I asked, "What art thou doing, my child?" Whereupon she answered, "Father, I am eating." Thereat my tears now indeed began to flow, and I praised her for feeding her soul, as she had no meat for her body. I had not, however, spoken long, before she cried to me to come and look at the great wonder that had risen out of the sea, and already appeared over the cave. For behold a cloud, in shape just like a cross, came over us, and let great heavy drops, as big or bigger than large peas, fall on our heads, after which it sank behind the coppice. I presently arose and ran up the mountain with my daughter to look after it. It floated on towards the Achterwater, where it spread itself out into a long blue streak, whereon the sun shone so brightly that it seemed like a golden bridge on which, as my child said, the blessed angels danced. I fell on my knees with her and thanked the Lord that our cross had passed away from us; but, alas! our cross was yet to come, as will be told hereafter.

The Eighth Chapter

HOW OUR NEED WAXED SORER AND SORER, AND HOW I
SENT OLD ILSE WITH ANOTHER LETTER TO PUDGLA, AND
HOW HEAVY A MISFORTUNE THIS BROUGHT UPON ME

Next day, when I had buried the poor corpses amid the lamentations of
the whole village (by the same token that they were all buried under
where the lime-tree overhangs the wall), I heard with many sighs that
neither the sea nor the Achterwater would yield anything. It was now
ten days since the poor people had caught a single fish. I therefore went
out into the field, musing how the wrath of the just God might be turned
from us, seeing that the cruel winter was now at hand, and neither corn,
apples, fish nor flesh to be found in the village, nor even throughout all
the parish. There was indeed plenty of game in the forests of Coserow
and Uekeritze; but the old forest ranger, Zabel Nehring, had died last
year of the plague, and there was no new one in his place. Nor was there
a musket nor a grain of powder to be found in all the parish; the enemy
had robbed and broken everything: we were therefore forced, day after
day, to see how the stags and the roes, the hares and the wild boars, *et cet.*,
ran past us, when we would so gladly have had them in our bellies, but
had no means of getting at them: for they were too cunning to let themselves be caught in pit-falls. Nevertheless, Claus Peer succeeded in
trapping a roe, and gave me a piece of it, for which may God reward
him. *Item*, of domestic cattle there was not a head left; neither was there
a dog, nor a cat, which the people had not either eaten in their extreme
hunger, or knocked on the head or drowned long since. Albeit old farmer
Paasch still owned two cows; *item*, an old man in Uekeritze was said
to have one little pig:—this was all. Thus, then, nearly all the people
lived on blackberries and other wild fruits: the which also soon grew
to be scarce, as may easily be guessed. Besides all this, a boy of fourteen
was missing (old Labahn his son) and was never more heard of, so that
I shrewdly think that the wolves devoured him.

And now let any Christian judge by his own heart in what sorrow and
heaviness I took my staff in my hand, seeing that my child fell away
like a shadow from pinching hunger; although I myself, being old, did
not, by the help of God's mercy, find any great failing in my strength.
While I thus went continually weeping before the Lord, on the way to
Uekeritze, I fell in with an old beggar with his wallet, sitting on a stone,
and eating a piece of God's rare gift, to wit, a bit of bread. Then truly
did my poor mouth so fill with water that I was forced to bow my head
and let it run upon the earth before I could ask, "Who art thou? and
whence comest thou? seeing that thou hast bread." Whereupon he
answered that he was a poor man of Bannemin, from whom the enemy

had taken all; and as he had heard that the Lieper Winkel had long been in peace, he had travelled thither to beg. I straightway answered him, "Oh, poor beggar-man, spare to me, a sorrowful servant of Christ, who is poorer even than thyself, one little slice of bread for his wretched child; for thou must know that I am the pastor of this village, and that my daughter is dying of hunger. I beseech thee by the living God not to let me depart without taking pity on me, as pity also hath been shown to thee!" But the beggar-man would give me none, saying that he himself had a wife and four children, who were likewise staggering towards death's door under the bitter pangs of hunger; that the famine was sorer far in Bannemin than here, where we still had berries; whether I had not heard that but a few days ago a woman (he told me her name, but horror made me forget it) had there killed her own child, and devoured it from hunger? That he could not therefore help me, and I might go to the Lieper Winkel myself.

I was horror-stricken at his tale, as is easy to guess, for we in our own trouble had not yet heard of it, there being little or no traffic between one village and another; and thinking on Jerusalem, and sheer despairing because the Lord had visited us, as of old that ungodly city, although we had not betrayed or crucified him, I almost forgot all my necessities, and took my staff in my hand to depart. But I had not gone more than a few yards when the beggar called me to stop, and when I turned myself round he came towards me with a good hunch of bread which he had taken out of his wallet, and said, "There! but pray for me also, so that I may reach my home; for if on the road they smell that I have bread, my own brother would strike me dead, I believe." This I promised with joy, and instantly turned back to take to my child the gift hidden in my pocket. And behold, when I came to the road which leads to Loddin, I could scarce trust my eyes (before I had overlooked it in my distress) when I saw my glebe, which could produce seven bushels, ploughed, sown, and in stalk; the blessed crop of rye had already shot lustily out of the earth a finger's length in height. I could not choose but think that the Evil One had deceived me with a false show, yet, however hard I rubbed my eyes, rye it was and rye it remained. And seeing that old Paasch his piece of land which joined mine was in like manner sown, and that the blades had shot up to the same height, I soon guessed that the good fellow had done this deed, seeing that all the other land lay waste. Wherefore, I readily forgave him for not knowing the morning prayer; and thanking the Lord for so much love from my flock, and earnestly beseeching him to grant me strength and faith to bear with them steadfastly and patiently all the troubles and adversities which it might please him henceforward to lay upon us, according to his divine pleasure, I ran rather than walked back into the village to old Paasch his farm, where I found him just about to kill his cow, which he was slaughtering from grim hunger. "God bless thee," said I, "worthy friend, for sowing my field; how shall I reward thee?" But the old man answered, "Let that be, and do you pray for us"; and when I gladly promised this and asked him how he had kept his corn safe from the savage enemy, he told me that he had hidden it secretly in the caves of the Streckelberg, but that now all his store was used up. Meanwhile he cut a fine large piece of meat from the top of the loin, and said, "There is something for you, and when that is gone you can come again for more." As I was then about to go with many thanks, his little Mary, a child nearly seven years old, the same who had said the *Gratias* on the Streckelberg, seized me by the hand and wanted to go to school to my daughter; for since my *Custos*, as above mentioned, departed this life in the plague, she had to teach the few little ones there were in the village; this, however, had long been abandoned. I could not, therefore, deny her, although I feared that my child would share her bread with her, seeing that she dearly loved the little maid, who was her godchild; and so indeed it happened; for when the child saw me take out the bread, she shrieked for joy, and began to scramble up on the bench. Thus she also got a piece of the slice, our maid got another, and my child put the third piece into her own mouth, as I wished for none, but said that I felt no signs of hunger and would wait until the meat was boiled, the which I now threw upon the bench. It was a goodly sight to see the joy which my poor child felt when I then also told her about the rye. She fell upon my neck, wept, sobbed, then took the little one up in her arms, danced about the room with her, and recited as she was wont, all manner of Latin *versus*, which she knew by heart. Then she would prepare a right good supper for us, as a little salt was still left in the bottom of a barrel of meat which the Imperialists had broken up. I let her take her own way, and having scraped some soot from the chimney and mixed it with water, I tore a blank leaf out of *Virgilius*, and wrote to the *Pastor Liepensis*, his reverence Abraham Tiburtius, praying that for God his sake he would take our necessities to heart, and would exhort his parishioners to save us from dying of grim hunger, and charitably to spare to us some meat and drink, according as the all-merciful God had still left some to them, seeing that a beggar had told me that they had long been in peace from the terrible enemy. I knew not, however, wherewithal to seal the letter, until I found in the church a little wax still sticking to a wooden altar-candlestick, which the Imperialists had not thought it worth their while to steal, for they had only taken the brass ones. I sent three fellows in a boat with Hinrich Seden, the churchwarden, with this letter to Liepe.

First, however, I asked my old Ilse, who was born in Liepe, whether she would not rather return home, seeing how matters stood, and that I, for the present at least, could not give her a stiver of her wages (mark that she had already saved up a small sum, seeing that she had lived in my service above twenty years, but the soldiers had taken it all). Howbeit, I could nowise persuade her to this, but she wept bitterly, and besought me only to let her stay with the good damsel whom she had rocked in her cradle. She would cheerfully hunger with us if it needs must be, so that she were not turned away. Whereupon I yielded to her, and the others went alone.

Meanwhile the broth was ready, but scarce had we said the *Gratias*, and were about to begin our meal, when all the children of the village, seven in number, came to the door, and wanted bread, as they had heard we had some from my daughter her little godchild. Her heart again melted, and notwithstanding I besought her to harden herself against them, she comforted me with the message to Liepe, and poured out for each child a portion of broth on a wooden platter (for these also had been despised by the enemy), and put into their little hands a bit of meat, so that all our store was eaten up at once. We were, therefore, left fasting next morning, till towards mid-day, when the whole village gathered together in a meadow on the banks of the river to see the boat return. But, God be merciful to us, we had cherished vain hopes! six loaves and a sheep, *item*, a quarter of apples, was all they had brought. His reverence Abraham Tiburtius wrote to me that after the cry of their wealth had spread throughout the island, so many beggars had flocked thither that it was impossible to be just to all, seeing that they themselves did not know how it might fare with them in these heavy troublous times. Meanwhile he would see whether he could raise any more. I therefore with many sighs had the small pittance carried to the manse, and though two loaves were, as *Pastor Liepensis* said in his letter, for me alone, I gave them up to be shared among all alike, whereat all were content save Seden his squint-eyed wife, who would have had somewhat *extra* on the score of her husband's journey, which, however, as may be easily guessed, she did not get; wherefore she again muttered certain words between her teeth as she went away, which, however, no one understood. Truly she was an ill woman, and not to be moved by the word of God.

Any one may judge for himself that such a store could not last long; and as all my parishioners felt an ardent longing after spiritual food, and as I and the churchwardens could only get together about sixteen farthings in the whole parish, which was not enough to buy bread and wine, the thought struck me once more to inform my lord the Sheriff of our need. With how heavy a heart I did this may be easily guessed, but necessity knows no law. I therefore tore the last blank leaf out of *Virgilius*, and begged that, for the sake of the Holy Trinity, his lordship would mercifully consider mine own distress and that of the whole parish, and bestow a little money to enable me to administer the holy sacrament for the comfort of afflicted souls; also, if possible, to buy a cup, were it only of tin, since the enemy had plundered us of ours, and I should otherwise be forced to consecrate the sacred elements in an earthen vessel. *Item*, I besought him to have pity on our bodily wants, and at last to send me the first-fruits which had stood over for so many years. That I did not want it for myself alone, but would willingly share it with my parishioners, until such time as God in his mercy should give us more.

Here a huge blot fell upon my paper; for the windows being boarded up, the room was dark, and but little light came through two small panes of glass which I had broken out of the church, and stuck in between the boards; this, perhaps, was the reason why I did not see better. However, as I could not anywhere get another piece of paper, I let it pass, and ordered the maid, whom I sent with the letter to Pudgla, to excuse the same to his lordship the Sheriff, the which she promised to do, seeing that I could not add a word more on the paper, as it was written all over. I then sealed it as I had done before.

But the poor creature came back trembling for fear and bitterly weeping, and said that his lordship had kicked her out of the castle-gate, and had threatened to set her in the stocks if she ever came before him again. "Did the parson think that he was as free with his money as I seemed to be with my ink? I surely had water enough to celebrate the Lord's supper wherewithal. For if the Son of God had once changed the water into wine, he could surely do the like again. If I had no cup, I might water my flock out of a bucket, as he did himself"; with many more blasphemies, such as he afterwards wrote to me, and by which, as may easily be guessed, I was filled with horror. Touching the first-fruits, as she told me he said nothing at all. In such great spiritual and bodily need the blessed Sunday came round, when nearly all the congregation would have come to the Lord's table, but could not. I therefore spoke on the words of St. Augustine, *crede et manducasti*, and represented that the blame was not mine, and truly told what had happened to my poor maid at Pudgla, passing over much in silence, and only praying God to awaken the hearts of magistrates for our good. Peradventure I may have spoken more harshly than I meant. I know not, only that I spoke that which was in my heart. At the end I made all the congregation stay on their knees for nearly an hour, and call upon the Lord for his holy sacrament; *item*, for the relief of their bodily wants, as had been done every Sunday, and at all the daily prayers I had been used to read ever since the heavy time of the plague. Last of all I led the glorious hymn, "When in greatest need we be," which was no sooner finished than my new churchwarden, Claus Bulk of Uekeritze, who had formerly been a groom with his lordship, and whom he had now put into a farm, ran off to Pudgla, and told him all that had taken place in the church. Whereat his lordship was greatly angered, insomuch that he summoned the whole parish, which still numbered about 150 souls, without counting the children, and dictated *ad protocollum* whatsoever they could remember of the sermon, seeing that he meant to inform his princely grace the Duke of Pomerania of the blasphemous lies which I had vomited against him, and which must sorely offend every Christian heart. *Item*, what an avaricious wretch I must be to be always wanting something of him, and to be daily, so to say, pestering him in these hard times with my filthy letters, when he had not enough to eat himself. This he said should break the parson his neck, since his princely grace did all that he asked of him, and that no one in the parish need give me anything more, but only let me go my ways. He would soon take care that they should have quite a different sort of parson from what I was.

(Now I would like to see the man who could make up his mind to come into the midst of such wretchedness at all.)

This news was brought to me in the selfsame night, and gave me a great fright, as I now saw that I should not have a gracious master in his lordship, but should all the time of my miserable life, even if I could anyhow support it, find in him an ungracious lord. But I soon felt some comfort, when Chim Krüger from Uekeritze, who brought me the news, took a little bit of his sucking-pig out of his pocket and gave it to me. Meanwhile old Paasch came in and said the same, and likewise brought me a piece of his old cow; *item*, my other warden, Hinrich Seden, with a slice of bread, and a fish which he had taken in his net, all saying they wished for no better priest than me, and that I was only to pray to the merciful Lord to bestow more upon them, whereupon I should want for nothing. Meanwhile I must be quiet and not betray them. All this I promised, and my daughter Mary took the blessed gifts of God off the table and carried them into the inner chamber. But, alas! next morning, when she would have put the meat into the caldron, it was all gone. I know not who prepared this new sorrow for me, but much believe it was Hinrich Seden his wicked wife, seeing he can never hold his tongue, and most likely told her everything. Moreover, Paasch his little daughter saw that she had meat in her pot next day; *item*, that she had quarrelled with her husband, and had flung the fish-board at him, whereon some fresh fish-scales were sticking: she had, however, presently recollected herself when she saw the child. (Shame on thee, thou old witch, it is true enough, I dare say!) Hereupon nought was left us but to feed our poor souls with the word of God. But even our souls were so cast down that they could receive nought, any more than our bellies; my poor child, especially, from day to day grew paler, greyer, and yellower, and always threw up all her food, seeing she ate it without salt or bread. I had long

wondered that the bread from Liepe was not yet done, but that every da,
at dinner I still had a morsel. I had often asked, "Whence comes all
this blessed bread? I believe, after all, you save the whole for me, and
take none for yourself or the maid." But they both then lifted to their
mouths a piece of fir-tree bark, which they had cut to look like bread, and
laid by their plates; and as the room was dark, I did not find out their
deceit, but thought that they, too, were eating bread. But at last the maid
told me of it, so that I should allow it no longer, as my daughter would
not listen to her. It is not hard to guess how my heart was wrung when I
saw my poor child lying on her bed of moss struggling with grim hunger.
But things were to go yet harder with me, for the Lord in his anger would
break me in pieces like a potter's vessel. For behold, on the evening of the
same day, old Paasch came running to me, complaining that all his and
my corn in the field had been pulled up and miserably destroyed, and that
it must have been done by Satan himself, as there was not a trace either
of oxen or horses. At these words my poor child screamed aloud and
fainted. I would have run to help her, but could not reach her bed,
and fell on the ground myself for bitter grief. The loud cries of the maid
and old Paasch soon brought us both to our senses. But I could not rise
from the ground alone, for the Lord had bruised all my bones. I besought
them, therefore, when they would have helped me, to leave me where
I was; and when they would not, I cried out that I must again fall on the
ground to pray, and begged them all save my daughter to depart out of
the room. This they did, but the prayer would not come. I fell into heavy
doubting and despair, and murmured against the Lord that he plagued
me more sorely than Lazarus or Job. Wretch that I was, I cried, "Thou
didst leave to Lazarus at least the crumbs and the pitiful dogs, but to
me thou hast left nothing, and I myself am less in thy sight even than a
dog; and Job thou didst not afflict until thou hadst mercifully taken away
his children, but to me thou hast left my poor little daughter, that her
torments may increase mine own a thousandfold. Behold, then, I can
only pray that thou wilt take her from the earth, so that my grey head
may gladly follow her to the grave! Woe is me, ruthless father, what have
I done? I have eaten bread, and suffered my child to hunger! Oh,
Lord Jesu, who hast said, 'What man is there of you, whom if his son
ask bread will he give him a stone?' Behold I am that man!—behold I
am that ruthless father! I have eaten bread and have given wood to my
child! Punish me; I will bear it and lie still. Oh, righteous Jesu, I have
eaten bread, and have given wood to my child!" As I did not speak,
but rather shrieked these words, wringing my hands the while, my
child fell upon my neck, sobbing, and chid me for murmuring against
the Lord, seeing that even she, a weak and frail woman, had never
doubted his mercy, so that with shame and repentance I presently

elf, and humbled myself before the Lord for such heavy

he maid had run into the village with loud cries to see if
nything for her poor young mistress, but the people had
aten their noontide meal, and most of them were gone to sea to
seek their blessed supper; thus she could find nothing, seeing that old
wife Seden, who alone had any victuals, would give her none, although
she prayed her by Jesu's wounds.

She was telling us this when we heard a noise in the chamber, and
presently Lizzie her worthy old husband, who had got in at the window
by stealth, brought us a pot of good broth, which he had taken off the fire
whilst his wife was gone for a moment into the garden. He well knew
that his wife would make him pay for it, but that he did not mind, so the
young mistress would but drink it, and she would find it salted and all.
He would make haste out of the window again, and see that he got home
before his wife, that she might not find out where he had been. But my
daughter would not touch the broth, which sorely vexed him, so that he
set it down on the ground cursing, and ran out of the room. It was not
long before his squint-eyed wife came in at the front door, and when she
saw the pot still steaming on the ground, she cried out, "Thou thief,
thou cursed thieving carcass!" and would have flown at the face of my
maid. But I threatened her, and told her all that had happened, and that
if she would not believe me she might go into the chamber and look out
of the window, whence she might still, belike, see her good man running
home. This she did, and presently we heard her calling after him,
"Wait, and the devil shall tear off thine arms; only wait till thou art
home again!" After this she came back, and, muttering something, took
the pot off the ground. I begged her, for the love of God, to spare a little
to my child; but she mocked at me and said, "You can preach to her, as
you did to me," and walked towards the door with the pot. My child
indeed besought me to let her go, but I could not help calling after her,
"For the love of God, one good sup, or my poor child must give up the
ghost: wilt thou that at the day of judgment God should have mercy
on thee, so show mercy this day to me and mine!" But she scoffed at us
again, and cried out, "Let her cook herself some bacon," and went out
at the door. I then sent the maid after her with the hour-glass which
stood before me on the table, to offer it to her for a good sup out of the pot;
but the maid brought it back, saying that she would not have it. Alas,
how I wept and sobbed, as my poor dying child with a loud sigh buried
her head again in the moss! Yet the merciful God was more gracious to
me than my unbelief had deserved; for when the hard-hearted woman
bestowed a little broth on her neighbour, old Paasch, he presently
brought it to my child, having heard from the maid how it stood with

her; and I believe that this broth, under God, alone saved her life, for she raised her head as soon as she had supped it, and was able to go about the house again in an hour. May God reward the good fellow for it! Thus I had some joy in the midst of my trouble. But while I sat by the fireside in the evening musing on my fate, my grief again broke forth, and I made up my mind to leave my house, and even my cure, and to wander through the wide world with my daughter as a beggar. God knows I had cause enough for it; for now that all my hopes were dashed, seeing that my field was quite ruined, and that the Sheriff had become my bitter enemy; moreover, that it was five years since I had had a wedding, *item*, but two christenings during the past year, I saw my own and my daughter's death staring me in the face, and no prospect of better times at hand. Our want was increased by the great fears of the congregation; for although by God's wondrous mercy they had already begun to take good draughts of fish both in the sea and the Achterwater, and many of the people in the other villages had already gotten bread, salt, oatmeal, etc., from the Polters and Quatzners, of Anklam and Lassan in exchange for their fish; nevertheless, they brought me nothing, fearing lest it might be told at Pudgla, and make his lordship ungracious to them. I therefore beckoned my daughter to me, and told her what was in my thoughts, saying that God in his mercy could any day bestow on me another cure if I was found worthy in his sight of such a favour, seeing that these terrible days of pestilence and war had called away many of the servants of his word, and that I had not fled like a hireling from his flock, but on the contrary, till *datum* shared sorrow and death with it. Whether she were able to walk five or ten miles a day; for that then we would beg our way to Hamburg, to my departed wife her step-brother, Martin Behring, who is a great merchant in that city.

This at first sounded strange to her, seeing that she had very seldom been out of our parish, and that her departed mother and her little brother lay in our churchyard. She asked, "Who was to make up their graves and plant flowers on them? *Item*, as the Lord had given her a smooth face, what I should do if in these wild and cruel times she were attacked on the highways by marauding soldiers or other villains, seeing that I was a weak old man and unable to defend her; *item*, wherewithal should we shield ourselves from the frost, as the winter was setting in and the enemy had robbed us of our clothes, so that we had scarce enough left to cover our nakedness?" All this I had not considered, and was forced to own that she was right; so after much discussion we determined to leave it this night to the Lord, and to do whatever he should put into our hearts next morning. At any rate, we saw that we could in nowise keep the old maid any longer; I therefore called her out of the kitchen, and told her she had better go early next morning to Liepe, as there still was food there, whereas here she must starve, seeing that perhaps we ourselves might leave the parish and the country to-morrow. I thanked her for the love and faith she had shown us, and begged her at last, amid the loud sobs of my poor daughter, to depart forthwith privately, and not to make our hearts still heavier by leave-taking; that old Paasch was going a-fishing to-night on the Achterwater, as he had told me, and no doubt would readily set her on shore at Grüssow, where she had friends, and could eat her fill even to-day. She could not say a word for weeping, but when she saw that I was really in earnest she went out of the room. Not long after we heard the house-door shut to, whereupon my daughter moaned, "She is gone already," and ran straight to the window to look after her. "Yes," cried she, as she saw her through the little panes, "she is really gone"; and she wrung her hands and would not be comforted. At last, however, she was quieted when I spoke of the maid Hagar, whom Abraham had likewise cast off, but on whom the Lord had nevertheless shown mercy in the wilderness; and hereupon we commended ourselves to the Lord, and stretched ourselves on our couches of moss.

The Ninth Chapter

HOW THE OLD MAID-SERVANT HUMBLED ME BY HER FAITH, AND THE LORD YET BLESSED ME HIS UNWORTHY SERVANT

"Bless the Lord, O my soul; and all that is within me, bless his holy name. Bless the Lord, O my soul, and forget not all his benefits. Who forgiveth all thine iniquities; who healeth all thy diseases; who redeemeth thy life from destruction; who crowneth thee with loving kindness and tender mercies" (Psalm ciii.).

Alas! wretched man that I am, how shall I understand all the benefits and mercies which the Lord bestowed upon me the very next day? I now wept for joy, as of late I had done for sorrow; and my child danced about the room like a young roe, and would not go to bed, but only cry and dance, and between-whiles repeat the 103rd Psalm, then dance and cry again until morning broke. But as she was still very weak, I rebuked her presumption, seeing that this was tempting the Lord; and now mark what had happened.

After we had both woke in the morning with deep sighs, and called upon the Lord to manifest to us in our hearts what we should do, we still could not make up our minds. I therefore called to my child, if she felt strong enough, to leave her bed and light a fire in the stove herself, as our maid was gone; that we would then consider the matter further. She accordingly got up, but came back in an instant with cries of joy, because the maid had privately stolen back into the house, and had already made a fire. Hereupon I sent for her to my bedside, and wondered at her disobedience, and asked what she now wanted here but to torment me and my daughter still more, and why she did not go yesterday with old Paasch? But she lamented and wept so sore that she scarce could speak, and I understood only thus much—that she had eaten with us, and would likewise starve with us, for that she could never part from her young mistress, whom she had known from her cradle. Such faithful love moved me so, that I said almost with tears, "But hast thou not heard that my daughter and I have determined to wander as beggars about the country; where, then, wilt thou remain?" To this she answered that neither would she stay behind, seeing it was more fitting for her to beg than for us; but that she could not yet see why I wished to go out into the wide world; whether I had already forgotten that I had said in my induction sermon that I would abide with my flock in affliction and in death? That I should stay yet a little longer where I was, and send her to Liepe, as she hoped to get something worth having for us there from her friends and others. These words, especially those about my induction sermon, fell heavy on my conscience, and I was ashamed of my want of faith, since not my daughter only, but yet more even my maid, had stronger faith than I, who nevertheless professed to be a servant of God's word. I believed that the Lord—to keep me, poor fearful hireling, and at the same time to humble me—had awakened the spirit of this poor maidservant to prove me, as the maid in the palace of the high-priest had also proved the fearful St. Peter. Wherefore I turned my face towards the wall, like Hezekiah, and humbled myself before the Lord, which scarce had I done before my child ran into the room again, with a cry of joy; for behold, some Christian heart had stolen quietly into the house in the night, and had laid in the chamber two loaves, a good piece of meat, a bag of oatmeal, *item*, a bag of salt, holding near a pint. Any one may guess what shouts of joy we all raised. Neither was I ashamed to confess my sins before my maid; and in our common morning prayer, which we said on our knees, I made fresh vows to the Lord of obedience and faith. Thus we had that morning a grand breakfast, and sent something to old Paasch besides; *item*, my daughter again sent for all the little children to come, and kindly fed them with our store before they said their tasks; and when in my heart of little faith I sighed thereat, although I said nought, she smiled, and said, "Take therefore no thought for the morrow, for the morrow shall take thought for the things of itself."

The Holy Ghost spoke by her, as I cannot but believe, nor thou either, beloved reader: for mark what happened. In the afternoon she (I mean my child) went up the Streckelberg to seek for blackberries, as old Paasch had told her, through the maid, that a few bushes were still left. The maid was chopping wood in the yard, to which end she had borrowed old Paasch his axe, for the Imperialist thieves had thrown away mine, so that it could nowhere be found; and I myself was pacing up and down in the room, meditating my sermon; when my child, with her apron full, came quickly in at the door, quite red and with beaming eyes, and scarce able for joy to say more than "Father, father, what have I got?" "Well," quoth I, "what hast thou got, my child?" Whereupon she opened her apron, and I scarce trusted my eyes when I saw, instead of the blackberries which she had gone to seek, two shining pieces of amber, each nearly as big as a man's head, not to mention the small pieces, some of which were as large as my hand, and that, God knows, is no small one. "Child of my heart," cried I, "how camest thou by this blessing from God?" As soon as she could fetch her breath, she told me as follows:—

That while she was seeking for blackberries in a dell near the shore she saw somewhat glistening in the sun, and on coming near she found this wondrous godsend, seeing that the wind had blown the sand away from off a black vein of amber. That she straightway had broken off these pieces with a stick, and that there was plenty more to be got, seeing that it rattled about under the stick when she thrust it into the sand, neither could she force it farther than, at most, a foot deep into the ground; *item*, she told me that she had covered the place all over again with sand, and swept it smooth with her apron, so as to leave no traces.

Moreover, that no stranger was at all likely to go thither, seeing that no blackberries grew very near, and she had gone to the spot, moved by curiosity and a wish to look upon the sea, rather than from any need; but that she could easily find the place again herself, inasmuch as she had marked it with three little stones. What was our first act after the all-merciful God had rescued us out of such misery, nay, even, as it seemed, endowed us with great riches, any one may guess. When we at length got up off our knees, my child would straightway have run to tell the maid our joyful news. But I forbade her, seeing that we could not be sure that the maid might not tell it again to her friends, albeit in all other things she was a faithful woman and feared God; but that if she did that, the Sheriff would be sure to hear of it, and to seize upon our treasure for his princely highness the Duke—that is to say, for himself; and that nought would be left to us but the sight thereof, and our want would begin all over again; that we therefore would say, when folks asked about the luck that had befallen us, that my deceased brother, who was a councillor at Rotterdam, had left us a good lump of money; and, indeed, it was true that I had inherited near two hundred florins from him a year ago, which, however, the soldiery (as mentioned above) cruelly robbed me of; *item*, that I would go to Wolgast myself next day and sell the little bits as best I might, saying that thou hadst picked them up by the seaside; thou mayest tell the maid the same, if thou wilt, but show the larger pieces to no one, and I will send them to thy uncle at Hamburg to be turned into money for us; perchance I may be able to sell one of them at Wolgast, if I find occasion, so as to buy clothes enough for the winter for thee and for me, wherefore thou, too, mayst go with me. We will take the few farthings which the congregation have brought together to pay the ferry, and thou canst order the maid to wait for us till eventide at the water-side to carry home the victuals. She agreed to all this, but said we had better first break off some more amber, so that we might get a good round sum for it at Hamburg; and I thought so too, wherefore we stopped at home next day, seeing that we did not want for food, and that my child, as well as myself, both wished to refresh ourselves a little before we set out on our journey; *item*, we likewise bethought us that old Master Rothoog, of Loddin, who is a cabinetmaker, might knock together a little box for us to put the amber in, wherefore I sent the maid to him in the afternoon. Meanwhile we ourselves went up the Streckelberg, where I cut a young fir-tree with my pocket-knife, which I had saved from the enemy, and shaped it like a spade, so that I might be better able to dig deep therewith. First, however, we looked about us well on the mountain, and, seeing nobody, my daughter walked on to the place, which she straightway found again. Great God! what a mass of amber was there! The vein was hard upon twenty feet long, as near as I could feel, and the depth of it I could not sound. Nevertheless, save four good-sized pieces, none, however, so big as those of yesterday, we this day only broke out little splinters, such as the apothecaries bruise for incense. After we had most carefully covered and smoothed over the place, a great mishap was very near befalling us; for we met Witthan her little girl, who was seeking blackberries, and she asked what my daughter carried in her apron, who straightway grew red, and stammered so that our secret would have been betrayed if I had not presently said, "What is that to thee? She has got fir-apples for firing," which the child believed. Wherefore we resolved in future only to go up the mountain at night by moonlight, and we went home and got there before the maid, and hid our treasure in the bedstead, so that she should not see it.

The Tenth Chapter

HOW WE JOURNEYED TO WOLGAST, AND MADE GOOD BARTER THERE

Two days after, so says my daughter, but old Ilse thinks it was three (and I myself know not which is true), we at last went to the town, seeing

that Master Rothoog had not got the box ready before. My daughter
covered it over with a piece of my departed wife her wedding-gown,
which the Imperialists had indeed torn to pieces, but as they had left it
lying outside, the wind had blown it into the orchard, where we found it.
It was very shabby before, otherwise I doubt not they would have carried
it off with them. On account of the box, we took old Ilse with us, who had
to carry it, and, as amber is very light ware, she readily believed that the
box held nothing but eatables. At daybreak, then, we took our staves in
our hands and set out with God. Near Zitze, a hare ran across the road
before us, which they say bodes no good. Well-a-day! When we came
near Bannemin I asked a fellow if it was true that here a mother had
slaughtered her own child from hunger, as I had heard. He said it was,
and that the old woman's name was Zisse; but that God had been wroth at
such a horrid deed, and she had got no good by it, seeing that she vomited
so much upon eating it that she forthwith gave up the ghost. On the whole,
he thought things were already going rather better with the parish, as
Almighty God had richly blessed them with fish, both out of the sea and
the Achterwater. Nevertheless a great number of people had died of
hunger here also. He told us that their vicar, his reverence Johannes
Lampius, had had his house burnt down by the Imperialists, and was
lying in a hovel near the church. I sent him my greeting, desiring that he
would soon come to visit me (which the fellow promised he would take
care to deliver to him), for the reverend Johannes is a pious and learned
man, and has also composed sundry Latin *Chronosticha* on these wretched
times, in *metrum heroicum*, which, I must say, please me greatly. When
we had crossed the ferry we went in at Sehms his house, on the Castle
Green, who keeps an ale-house; he told us that the pestilence had not yet
altogether ceased in the town; whereat I was much afraid, more especially
as he described to us so many other horrors and miseries of these fearful
times, both here and in other places, *e.g.* of the great famine in the island
of Rügen, where a number of people had grown as black as Moors from
hunger; a wondrous thing if it be true, and one might almost gather
therefrom how the first blackamoors came about. But be that as it may.
Summa. When Master Sehms had told us all the news he had heard, and
we had thus learnt, to our great comfort, that the Lord had not visited us
only in these times of heavy need, I called him aside into a chamber and
asked him whether I could not here find means to get money for a piece
of amber which my daughter had found by the sea. At first he said
"No"; but then recollecting, he began, "Stay, let me see, at Nicolas
Graeke's, the inn at the castle, there are two great Dutch merchants—
Dieterich von Pehnen and Jacob Kiekebusch—who are come to buy
pitch and boards, *item* timber for ships and beams; perchance they may
like to cheapen your amber too; but you had better go up to the castle

yourself, for I do not know for certain whether they still are there." This I did, although I had not yet eaten anything in the man's house, seeing that I wanted to know first what sort of bargain I might make, and to save the farthings belonging to the church until then. So I went into the castle-yard. Gracious God! what a desert had even his Princely Highness' house become within a short time! The Danes had ruined the stables and hunting-lodge, Anno 1628; *item*, destroyed several rooms in the castle; and in the *locamentum* of his Princely Highness Duke Philippus, where, Anno 22, he so graciously entertained me and my child, as will be told further on, now dwelt the innkeeper Nicolas Graeke; and all the fair tapestries, whereon was represented the pilgrimage to Jerusalem of his Princely Highness Bogislaus x, were torn down and the walls left grey and bare. At this sight my heart was sorely grieved; but I presently inquired for the merchants, who sat at the table drinking their parting cup, with their travelling equipments already lying by them, seeing that they were just going to set out on their way to Stettin; straightway one of them jumped up from his liquor—a little fellow with a right noble paunch and a black plaster on his nose—and asked me what I would of them? I took him aside into a window, and told him I had some fine amber, if he had a mind to buy it of me, which he straightway agreed to do. And when he had whispered somewhat into the ear of his fellow, he began to look very pleasant, and reached me the pitcher before we went to my inn. I drank to him right heartily, seeing that (as I have already said) I was still fasting, so that I felt my very heart warmed by it in an instant. (Gracious God, what can go beyond a good draught of wine taken within measure!) After this we went to my inn, and told the maid to carry the box on one side into a small chamber. I had scarce opened it and taken away the gown, when the man (whose name was Dieterich von Pehnen, as he had told me by the way) held up both hands for joy, and said he had never seen such wealth of amber, and how had I come by it? I answered that my child had found it on the sea-shore; whereat he wondered greatly that we had so much amber here, and offered me three hundred florins for the whole box. I was quite beside myself for joy at such an offer, but took care not to let him see it, and bargained with him till I got five hundred florins, and I was to go with him to the castle and take the money forthwith. Hereupon I ordered mine host to make ready at once a mug of beer and a good dinner for my child, and went back to the castle with the man and the maid, who carried the box, begging him, in order to avoid common talk, to say nothing of my good fortune to mine host, nor, indeed, to any one else in the town, and to count out the money to me privately, seeing that I could not be sure that the thieves might not lay in wait for me on the road home if they heard of it, and this the man did; for he whispered something into the ear of his fellow, who straightway opened his leathern surcoat, *item* his doublet and hose, and unbuckled from his paunch a well-filled purse, which he gave to him. *Summa.* Before long I had my riches in my pocket, and, moreover, the man begged me to write to him at Amsterdam whenever I found any more amber, the which I promised to do. But the worthy fellow (as I have since heard) died of the plague at Stettin, together with his companion—truly I wish it had happened otherwise. Shortly after I was very near getting into great trouble; for, as I had an extreme longing to fall on my knees, so that I could not wait until such time as I should have got back to my inn, I went up three or four steps of the castle stairs and entered into a small chamber, where I humbled myself before the Lord. But the host, Nicolas Graeke, followed me, thinking I was a thief, and would have stopped me, so that I knew not how to excuse myself by saying that I had been made drunken by the wine which the strange merchants had given to me (for he had seen what a good pull I had made at it), seeing I had not broken my fast that morning, and that I was looking for a chamber wherein I might sleep a while, which lie he believed (if, in truth, it were a lie, for I was really drunken, though not with wine, but with love and gratitude to my Maker), and accordingly he let me go.

But I must now tell my story of his Princely Highness, as I promised above. Anno 22, as I chanced to walk with my daughter, who was then a child of about twelve years old, in the castle-garden at Wolgast, and was showing her the beautiful flowers that grew there, it chanced that as we came round from behind some bushes we espied my gracious lord the Duke Philippus Julius, with his Princely Highness the Duke Bogislaff, who lay here on a visit, standing on a mount and conversing, wherefore we were about to return. But as my gracious lords presently walked on toward the drawbridge, we went to look at the mount where they had stood; of a sudden my little girl shouted loudly for joy, seeing that she found on the earth a costly signet-ring, which one of their Princely Highnesses doubtless had dropped. I therefore said, "Come and we will follow our gracious lords with all speed, and thou shalt say to them in Latin, '*Serenissimi principes, quis vestrum hunc annulum deperdidit?*' (for, as I have mentioned above, I had instructed her in the Latin tongue ever since her seventh year); and if one of them says '*Ego*,' give to him the ring. *Item.*—Should he ask thee in Latin to whom thou belongest, be not abashed, and say '*Ego sum filia pastoris Coserowiensis*'; for thou wilt thus find favour in the eyes of their Princely Highnesses, for they are both gracious gentlemen, more especially the taller one, who is our gracious ruler, Philippus Julius himself." This she promised to do; but as she trembled sorely as she went, I encouraged her yet more and promised her a new gown if she did it, seeing that even as a little child she would have given a great deal for fine clothes. As soon, then, as we

THE AMBER WITCH 143

were come into the courtyard, I stood by the statue of his Princely Highness Ernest Ludewig, and whispered her to run boldly after them, as their Princely Highnesses were only a few steps before us, and had already turned toward the great entrance. This she did, but of a sudden she stood still, and would have turned back, because she was frightened by the spurs of their Princely Highnesses, as she afterwards told me, seeing that they rattled and jingled very loudly.

But my gracious lady the Duchess Agnes saw her from the open window wherein she lay, and called to his Princely Highness, "My lord, there is a little maiden behind you, who, it seems, would speak with you," whereupon his Princely Highness straightway turned him round, smiling pleasantly, so that my little maid presently took courage, and, holding up the ring, spoke in Latin as I had told her. Hereat both the princes wondered beyond measure, and after my gracious Duke Philippus had felt his finger, he answered, "*Dulcissima puella, ego perdidi*"; whereupon she gave it to him. Then he patted her cheek, and again asked, "*Sed quœnam es, et unde venis?*" whereupon she boldly gave her answer, and at the same time pointed with her finger to where I stood by the statue; whereupon his Princely Highness motioned me to draw near. My gracious lady saw all that passed from the window, but but all at once she left it. She, however, came back to it again before I had time even humbly to draw near to my gracious lord, and beckoned to my child, and held a cake out of the window for her. On my telling her, she ran up to the window, but her Princely Highness could not reach so low nor she so high above her as to take it, wherefore my gracious lady commanded her to come up into the castle, and as she looked anxiously round after me, motioned me also, as did my gracious lord himself, who presently took the timid little maid by the hand and went up with his Princely Highness the Duke Bogislaff. My gracious lady came to meet us at the door, and caressed and embraced my little daughter, so that she soon grew quite bold and ate the cake. When my gracious lord had asked me my name, *item*, why I had in so singular a manner taught my daughter the Latin tongue, I answered that I had heard much from a cousin at Cologne of Maria Schurman, and as I had observed a very excellent *ingenium* in my child, and also had time enough in my lonely cure, I did not hesitate to take her in hand, and teach her from her youth up, seeing I had no boy alive. Hereat their Princely Highnesses marvelled greatly, and put some more questions to her in Latin, which she answered without any prompting from me. Whereupon my gracious lord Duke Philippus said in the vulgar tongue, "When thou art grown up and art one day to be married, tell it to me, and thou shalt then have another ring from me, and whatsoever else pertains to a bride, for thou hast this day done me good service, seeing that this ring is a precious jewel to me, as I had it from my wife." Hereupon I whispered her to kiss his Princely Highness' hand for such a promise, and so she did.

(But alas! most gracious God, it is one thing to promise, and quite another to hold. Where is his Princely Highness at this time? Wherefore let me ever keep in mind that "thou only art faithful, and that which thou hast promised thou wilt surely hold." Psalm xxxiii. 4. Amen.)

Item. When his Princely Highness had also inquired concerning myself and my cure, and heard that I was of ancient and noble family, and my *salarium* very small, he called from the window to his chancellor, D. Rungius, who stood without, looking at the sun-dial, and told him that I was to have an addition from the convent at Pudgla, *item* from the crown-lands at Ernsthoff, as I mentioned above; but, more's the pity, I never have received the same, although the *instrumentum donationis* was sent me soon after by his Princely Highness' chancellor.

Then cakes were brought for me also, *item*, a glass of foreign wine in a glass painted with armorial bearings, whereupon I humbly took my leave, together with my daughter.

However, to come back to my bargain, anybody may guess what joy my child felt when I showed her the fair ducats and florins I had gotten for the amber. To the maid, however, we said that we had inherited such riches from my brother in Holland; and after we had again given thanks to the Lord on our knees, and eaten our dinner, we bought in a great store of bread, salt, meat, and stock-fish: *item*, of clothes, seeing that I provided what was needful for us three throughout the winter from the cloth-merchant. Moreover, for my daughter I bought a hair-net and a scarlet silk bodice, with a black apron and white petticoat, *item*, a fine pair of earrings, as she begged hard for them; and as soon as I had ordered the needful from the cordwainer we set out on our way homewards, as it began to grow very dark; but we could not carry nearly all we had bought. Wherefore we were forced to get a peasant from Bannemin to help us, who likewise was come into the town; and as I found out from him that the fellow who gave me the piece of bread was a poor cotter called Panter-mehl, who dwelt in the village by the roadside, I shoved a couple of loaves in at his house-door without his knowing it, and we went on our way by the bright moonlight, so that by the help of God we got home about ten o'clock at night. I likewise gave a loaf to the other fellow, though truly he deserved it not, seeing that he would go with us no further than to Zitze. But I let him go, for I, too, had not deserved that the Lord should so greatly bless me.

The Eleventh Chapter

HOW I FED ALL THE CONGREGATION: *ITEM*, HOW I JOUR-
NEYED TO THE HORSE FAIR AT GÜTZKOW, AND WHAT BEFELL
ME THERE

Next morning my daughter cut up the blessed bread, and sent to every
one in the village a good large piece. But as we saw that our store would
soon run low, we sent the maid with a truck, which we bought of Adam
Lempken, to Wolgast to buy more bread, which she did. *Item*, I gave
notice throughout the parish that on Sunday next I should administer
the blessed sacrament, and in the meantime I bought up all the large
fish that the people of the village had caught. And when the blessed
Sunday was come I first heard the confessions of the whole parish, and
after that I preached a sermon on Matt. xv. 32—"I have compassion
on the multitude . . . for they have nothing to eat." I first applied the
same to spiritual food only, and there arose a great sighing from both the
men and the women, when, at the end, I pointed to the altar, whereon
stood the blessed food for the soul, and repeated the words, "I have
compassion on the multitude . . . for they have nothing to eat." (N.B.—
The pewter cup I had borrowed at Wolgast, and bought there a little
earthenware plate for a paten till such time as Master Bloom should have
made ready the silver cup and paten I had bespoke.) Thereupon as soon
as I had consecrated and administered the blessed sacrament, *item*, led
the closing hymn, and every one had silently prayed his "Our Father"
before going out of church, I came out of the confessional again, and
motioned the people to stay yet a while, as the blessed Saviour would
feed not only their souls, but their bodies also, seeing that he still had
the same compassion on his people as of old on the people at the Sea of
Galilee, as they should presently see. Then I went into the tower and
fetched out two baskets which the maid had bought at Wolgast, and
which I had hidden there in good time; set them down in front of the
altar, and took off the napkins with which they were covered, whereupon
a very loud shout arose, inasmuch as they saw one filled with broiled
fish and the other with bread, which we had put into them privately.
Hereupon, like our Saviour, I gave thanks and brake it, and gave it to the
churchwarden Hinrich Seden, that he might distribute it among the
men, and to my daughter for the women. Whereupon I made application
of the text, "I have compassion on the multitude . . . for they have
nothing to eat," to the food of the body also; and walking up and down
in the church, amid great outcries from all, I exhorted them alway to
trust in God's mercy, to pray without ceasing, to work diligently, and to
consent to no sin. What was left I made them gather up for their children
and the old people who were left at home.

After church, when I had scarce put off my surplice, Hinrich Seden his squint-eyed wife came and impudently asked for more for her husband's journey to Liepe; neither had she had anything for herself, seeing she had not come to church. This angered me sore, and I said to her, "Why wast thou not at church? Nevertheless, if thou hadst come humbly to me thou shouldst have gotten somewhat even now, but as thou comest impudently, I will give thee nought: think on what thou didst to me and to my child." But she stood at the door and glowered impudently about the room till my daughter took her by the arm and led her out, saying, "Hear'st thou, thou shalt come back humbly before thou gett'st anything, but when thou comest thus, thou also shalt have thy share, for we will no longer reckon with thee an eye for an eye, and a tooth for a tooth; let the Lord do that if such be his will, but we will gladly forgive thee!" Hereupon she at last went out at the door, muttering to herself as she was wont; but she spat several times in the street, as we saw from the window.

Soon after I made up my mind to take into my service a lad, near upon twenty years of age, called Claus Neels, seeing that his father, old Neels of Loddin, begged hard that I would do so, besides which the lad pleased me well in manners and otherwise. Then, as we had a good harvest this year, I resolved to buy me a couple of horses forthwith, and to sow my field again; for although it was now late in the year, I thought that the most merciful God might bless the crop with increase if it seemed good to him.

Neither did I feel much care with respect to food for them, inasmuch as there was a great plenty of hay in the neighbourhood, seeing that all the cattle had been killed or driven away (as related above). I therefore made up my mind to go in God's name with my new ploughman to Gützkow, whither a great many Mecklenburg horses were brought to the fair, seeing that times were not yet so bad there as with us. Meanwhile I went a few more times up the Streckelberg with my daughter at night, and by moonlight, but found very little; so that we began to think our luck had come to an end, when, on the third night, we broke off some pieces of amber bigger even than those the two Dutchmen had bought. These I resolved to send to my wife's brother, Martin Behring, at Hamburg, seeing that the schipper Wulff of Wolgast intends, as I am told, to sail thither this very autumn, with pitch and wood for shipbuilding. I accordingly packed it all up in a strong chest, which I carried with me to Wolgast when I started with my man on my journey to Gützkow. Of this journey I will only relate thus much, that there were plenty of horses and very few buyers in the market. Wherefore I bought a pair of fine black horses for twenty florins apiece; *item*, a cart for five florins; *item*, twenty-five bushels of rye, which also came from Mecklenburg, at one florin the bushel, whereas it is hardly to be had now at Wolgast for love or money, and costs three florins or more the bushel. I might therefore have made a good bargain in rye at Gützkow if it had become my office, and had I not, moreover, been afraid lest the robbers, who swarm in these evil times, should take away my corn, and ill-use and perchance murder me into the bargain, as has happened to sundry people already.

For, at this time especially, such robberies were carried on after a strange and frightful fashion on Strellin heath at Gützkow; but by God's help it all came to light just as I journeyed thither with my man-servant to the fair, and I will here tell how it happened. Some months before a man had been broken on the wheel at Gützkow, because, being tempted of Satan, he murdered a travelling workman. The man, however, straightway began to walk after so fearful a fashion, that in the evening and night-season he sprang down from the wheel in his gallows' dress whenever a cart passed by the gallows, which stands hard by the road to Wolgast, and jumped up behind the people, who in horror and dismay flogged on their horses, and thereby made a great rattling on the log embankment which leads beside the gallows into a little wood called the Kraulin. And it was a strange thing that on the same night the travellers were almost always robbed or murdered on Strellin heath. Hereupon the magistrates had the man taken down from the wheel and buried under the gallows, in hopes of laying his ghost. But it went on just as before, sitting at night snow-white on the wheel, so that none durst any longer travel the road to Wolgast. Until at last it happened that, at the time of the above-named fair, young Rüdiger von Nienkerken of Mellenthin, in Usedom, who had been studying at Wittenberg and elsewhere, and was now on his way home, came this road by night with his carriage. Just before, at the inn, I myself had tried to persuade him to stop the night at Gützkow on account of the ghost, and to go on his journey with me next morning, but he would not. Now as soon as this young lord drove along the road, he also espied the apparition sitting on the wheel, and scarcely had he passed the gallows when the ghost jumped down and ran after him. The driver was horribly afraid, and lashed on the horses, as everybody else had done before, and they, taking fright, galloped away over the log-road with a marvellous clatter. Meanwhile, however, the young nobleman saw by the light of the moon how that the apparition flattened a ball of horse-dung whereon it trod, and straightway felt sure within himself that it was no ghost. Whereupon he called to the driver to stop; and as the man would not hearken to him, he sprang out of the carriage, drew his rapier, and hastened to attack the ghost. When the ghost saw this he would have turned and fled, but the young nobleman gave him such a blow on the head with his fist that he fell upon the ground with a loud wailing. *Summa*: the young lord, having called back his driver, dragged the ghost into the town again, where he turned out to be a shoemaker called Schwelm.

I also, on seeing such a great crowd, ran thither with many others to look at the fellow. He trembled like an aspen leaf; and when he was roughly told to make a clean breast, whereby he might peradventure save his own life, if it appeared that he had murdered no one, he confessed that he had got his wife to make him a gallows' dress, which he had put on, and had sat on the wheel before the dead man, when, from the darkness and the distance, no one could see that the two were sitting there together; and this he did more especially when he knew that a cart was going from the town to Wolgast. When the cart came by, and he jumped down and ran after it, all the people were so affrighted that they no longer kept their eyes upon the gallows, but only on him, flogged the horses, and galloped with much noise and clatter over the log embankment. This was heard by his fellows in Strellin and Dammbecke (two villages which are about three-fourths on the way), who held themselves ready to unyoke the horses and to plunder the travellers when they came up with them. That after the dead man was buried he could play the ghost more easily still, etc. That this was the whole truth, and that he himself had never in his life robbed, still less murdered, any one; wherefore he begged to be forgiven: that all the robberies and murders which had happened had been done by his fellows alone. Ah, thou cunning knave! But I heard afterwards that he and his fellows were broken on the wheel together, as was but fair.

And now to come back to my journey. The young nobleman abode that night with me at the inn, and early next morning we both set forth; and as we had grown into good-fellowship together, I got into his coach with him, as he offered me, so as to talk by the way, and my Claus drove behind us. I soon found that he was a well-bred, honest, and learned gentleman, seeing that he despised the wild student life, and was glad that he had now done with their scandalous drinking-bouts: moreover, he talked his Latin readily. I had therefore much pleasure with him in the coach. However, at Wolgast the rope of the ferry-boat broke, so that we were carried down the stream to Zeuzin, and at length we only got ashore with great trouble. Meanwhile it grew late, and we did not get into Coserow till nine, when I asked the young lord to abide the night with me, which he agreed to do. We found my child sitting in the chimney-corner, making a petticoat for her little god-daughter out of her own old clothes. She was greatly frighted, and changed colour when she saw the young lord come in with me, and heard that he was to lie there that night, seeing that as yet we had no more beds than we had bought for our own need from old Zabel Nehring the forest ranger his widow, at Uekeritze. Wherefore she took me aside: What was to be done? My bed

The Gallows Ghost

was in an ill plight, her little god-child having lain on it that morning; and she could nowise put the young nobleman into hers, although she would willingly creep in by the maid herself. And when I asked her why not? she blushed scarlet and began to cry, and would not show herself again the whole evening, so that the maid had to see to everything, even to the putting white sheets on my child's bed for the young lord, as she would not do it herself. I only tell this to show how maidens are. For next morning she came into the room with her red silk bodice, and the net on her hair, and the apron; *summa*, dressed in all the things I had bought her at Wolgast, so that the young lord was amazed, and talked much with her over the morning meal. Whereupon he took his leave, and desired me to visit him at his castle.

The Twelfth Chapter
WHAT FURTHER JOY AND SORROW BEFELL US: *ITEM*, HOW WITTICH APPELMANN RODE TO DAMEROW TO THE WOLF-HUNT, AND WHAT HE PROPOSED TO MY DAUGHTER

The Lord blessed my parish wonderfully this winter, inasmuch as not only a great quantity of fish were caught and sold in all the villages, but in Coserow they even killed four seals: *item*, the great storm of the 12th of December threw a goodly quantity of amber on the shore, so that many found amber, although no very large pieces, and they began to buy cows and sheep from Liepe and other places, as I myself also bought two cows; *item*, my grain which I had sown, half on my own field and half on old Paasch's, sprang up bravely and gladly, as the Lord had till *datum* bestowed on us an open winter; but so soon as it had shot up a finger's length, we found it one morning again torn up and ruined, and this time also by the devil's doings, since now, as before, not the smallest trace of oxen or of horses was to be seen in the field. May the righteous God, however, reward it, as indeed he already has done. Amen.

Meanwhile, however, something uncommon happened. For one morning, as I have heard, when Lord Wittich saw out of the window that the daughter of his fisherman, a child of sixteen, whom he had diligently pursued, went into the coppice to gather dry sticks, he went thither too; wherefore, I will not say, but every one may guess for himself. When he had gone some way along the convent mound, and was come to the first bridge, where the mountain-ash stands, he saw two wolves coming towards him; and as he had no weapon with him, save a staff, he climbed up into a tree; whereupon the wolves trotted round it, blinked at him with their eyes, licked their lips, and at last jumped with their fore-paws up against the tree, snapping at him; he then saw that one was a he-wolf, a great fat brute with only one eye. Hereupon in his fright he began to scream, and the long-suffering of God was again shown to him, without, however, making him wiser; for the maiden, who had crept behind a juniper-bush in the field when she saw the Sheriff coming, ran back again to the castle and called together a number of people, who came and drove away the wolves, and rescued his lordship. He then ordered a great wolf-hunt to be held next day in the convent wood, and he who brought the one-eyed monster, dead or alive, was to have a barrel of beer for his pains. Still they could not catch him, albeit they that day took four wolves in their nets, and killed them. He therefore straightway ordered a wolf-hunt to be held in my parish. But when the fellow came to toll the bell for a wolf-hunt, he did not stop a while, as is the wont for wolf-hunts, but loudly rang the bell on, *sine morâ*, so that all the folk thought a fire had broken out, and ran screaming out of their houses. My child also came running out (I myself had driven to visit a sick person at Zempin, seeing that walking began to be wearisome to me, and that I could now afford to be more at mine ease); but she had not stood long, and was asking the reason of the ringing, when the Sheriff himself, on his grey charger, with three cart-loads of toils and nets following him, galloped up and ordered the people straightway to go into the forest and to drive the wolves with rattles. Hereupon he, with his hunters and a few men whom he had picked out of the crowd, were to ride on and spread the nets behind Damerow, seeing that the island is wondrous narrow there, and the wolf dreads the water. When he saw my daughter he turned his horse round, chucked her under the chin, and graciously asked her who she was, and whence she came? When he had heard it, he said she was as fair as an angel, and that he had not known till now that the parson here had so beauteous a girl. He then rode off, looking round at her two or three times. At the first beating they found the one-eyed wolf, who lay in the rushes near the water. Hereat his lordship rejoiced greatly, and made the grooms drag him out of the net with long iron hooks, and hold him there for near an hour, while my lord slowly and cruelly tortured him to death, laughing heartily the while, which is a *prognosticon* of what he afterwards did with my poor child, for wolf or lamb is all one to this villain. Just God! But I will not be beforehand with my tale.

Next day came old Seden his squint-eyed wife, limping like a lame dog, and put it to my daughter whether she would not go into the service of the Sheriff; praised him as a good and pious man; and vowed that all the world said of him were foul lies, as she herself could bear witness, seeing that she had lived in his service for above ten years. *Item*, she praised the good cheer they had there, and the handsome beer-money that the great lords who often lay there gave the servants which waited upon them; that she herself had more than once received a rose-noble from his Princely Highness Duke Ernest Ludewig; moreover, many pretty fellows came there, which might make her fortune, inasmuch as she was a fair woman, and might take her choice of a husband; whereas here in Coserow, where nobody ever came, she might wait till she was old and ugly before she got a curch on her head, etc. Hereat my daughter was beyond measure angered, and answered, "Ah! thou old witch, and who has told thee that I wish to go into service to get a curch on my head? Go thy ways, and never enter the house again, for I have nought to do with thee." Whereupon she walked away again, muttering between her teeth.

Scarce had a few days passed, and I was standing in the chamber with the glazier, who was putting in new windows, when I heard my daughter scream in the kitchen. Whereupon I straightway ran in thither, and was shocked and affrighted when I saw the Sheriff himself standing in the corner with his arm round my child her neck; he, however, presently let her go, and said: "Aha, reverend Abraham, what a coy little fool you have for a daughter! I wanted to greet her with a kiss, as I always use to do, and she struggled and cried out as if I had been some young fellow who had stolen in upon her, whereas I might be her father twice over." As I answered nought, he went on to say that he had done it to encourage her, seeing that he desired to take her into his service, as indeed I knew, with more excuses of the same kind which I have forgot. Hereupon I pressed him to come into the room, seeing that after all he was the ruler set over me by God, and humbly asked what his lordship desired of me. Whereupon he answered me graciously that it was true he had just cause for anger against me, seeing that I had preached at him before the whole congregation, but that he was ready to forgive me, and to have the complaint he had sent in *contra me* to his Princely Highness at Stettin, and which might easily cost me my place, returned to him if I would but do his will. And when I asked what his Lordship's will might be, and excused myself as best I might with regard to the sermon, he answered that he stood in great need of a faithful housekeeper whom he could set over the other women-folk; and as he had learnt that my daughter was a faithful and trustworthy person, he would that I should send her into his service. "See there," said he to her, and pinched her cheek the while, "I want to lead you to honour, though you are such a young creature, and yet you cry out as if I were going to bring you to dishonour. Fie upon you!" (My child still remembers all this *verbotenus*; I myself should have forgot it a hundred times over in all the wretchedness I since underwent.) But she was offended at his words, and, jumping up from her seat, she answered shortly, "I thank your lordship for the honour, but will only keep house for my papa, which is a better honour for me";

whereupon he turned to me and asked what I said to that. I must own that I was not a little affrighted, inasmuch as I thought of the future and of the credit in which the Sheriff stood with his Princely Highness. I therefore answered with all humility that I could not force my child, and that I loved to have her about me, seeing that my dear huswife had departed this life during the heavy pestilence, and I had no child but only her. That I hoped therefore his lordship would not be displeased with me that I could not send her into his lordship's service. This angered him sore, and after disputing some time longer in vain he took leave, not without threats that he would make me pay for it. *Item*, my man, who was standing in the stable, heard him say as he went round the corner, "I will have her yet, in spite of him!"

I was already quite disheartened by all this, when, on the Sunday following, there came his huntsman Johannes Kurt, a tall, handsome fellow, and smartly dressed. He brought a roebuck tied before him on his horse, and said that his lordship had sent it to me for a present, in hopes that I would think better of his offer, seeing that he had been ever since seeking on all sides for a housekeeper in vain. Moreover, that if I changed my mind about it his lordship would speak for me to his Princely Highness, so that the dotation of Duke Philippus Julius should be paid to me out of the princely *ærarium*, etc. But the young fellow got the same answer as his master had done, and I desired him to take the roebuck away with him again. But this he refused to do; and as I had by chance told him at first that game was my favourite meat, he promised to supply me with it abundantly, seeing that there was plenty of game in the forest, and that he often went a-hunting on the Streckelberg; moreover, that I (he meant my daughter) pleased him uncommonly, the more because I would not do his master's will, who, as he told me in confidence, would never leave any girl in peace, and certainly would not let my damsel alone. Although I had rejected his game, he brought it notwithstanding, and in the course of three weeks he was sure to come four or five times, and grew more and more sweet upon my daughter. He talked a vast deal about his good place, and how he was in search of a good huswife, whence we soon guessed what quarter the wind blew from. *Ergo*, my daughter told him that if he was seeking for a huswife she wondered that he lost his time in riding to Coserow to no purpose, for that she knew of no huswife for him there, which vexed him so sore that he never came again.

And now any one would think that the grapes were sour even for the Sheriff; nevertheless he came riding to us soon after, and without more ado asked my daughter in marriage for his huntsman. Moreover, he promised to build him a house of his own in the forest; *item*, to give him pots and kettles, crockery, bedding, etc., seeing that he had stood godfather to the young fellow, who, moreover, had ever borne himself well during seven years he had been in his service. Hereupon my daughter answered that his lordship had already heard that she would keep house for nobody but her papa, and that she was still much too young to become a huswife.

This, however, did not seem to anger him, but after he had talked a long time to no purpose, he took leave quite kindly, like a cat which pretends to let a mouse go, and creeps behind the corners, but she is not in earnest, and presently springs out upon it again. For doubtless he saw that he had set to work stupidly; wherefore he went away in order to begin his attack again after a better fashion, and Satan went with him, as whilom with Judas Iscariot.

The Thirteenth Chapter

WHAT MORE HAPPENED DURING THE WINTER: *ITEM*, HOW IN THE SPRING WITCHCRAFT BEGAN IN THE VILLAGE

Nothing else of note happened during the winter, save that the merciful God bestowed a great plenty of fish, both from the Achterwater and the sea, and the parish again had good food; so that it might be said of us, as it is written, "For a small moment have I forsaken thee; but with great mercies will I gather thee." Wherefore we were not weary of praising the Lord; and the whole congregation did much for the church, buying new pulpit and altar cloths, seeing that the enemy had stolen the old ones. *Item*, they desired to make good to me the money I had paid for the new cups, which, however, I would not take.

There were still, however, about ten peasants in the parish who had not been able to buy their seed-corn for the spring, inasmuch as they had spent all their earnings on cattle and corn for bread. I therefore made an agreement with them that I would lend them the money for it, and that if they could not repay me this year, they might the next, which offer they thankfully took; and we sent seven waggons to Friedland, in Mecklenburg, to fetch seed-corn for us all. For my beloved brother-in-law, Martin Behring, in Hamburg, had already sent me by the schipper Wulf, who had sailed home by Christmas, 700 florins for the amber: may the Lord prosper it with him!

Old Thiemcke died this winter in Loddin, who used to be the midwife in the parish, and had also brought my child into the world. Of late, however, she had had but little to do, seeing that in this year I only baptized two children, namely, Jung his son in Uekeritze, and Lene Hebers her little daughter, the same whom the Imperialists afterwards speared. *Item*, it was now full five years since I had married the last couple. Hence any one may guess that I might have starved to death had not the righteous God so mercifully considered and blessed me in other ways. Wherefore to him alone be all honour and glory. Amen.

Meanwhile, however, it so happened that, not long after the Sheriff had last been here, witchcraft began in the village. I sat reading with my child the second book of *Virgilius* of the fearful destruction of the city of Troy, which was more terrible even than that of our own village, when a cry arose that our old neighbour Zabel his red cow, which he had bought only a few days before, had stretched out all-fours and seemed about to die; and this was the more strange as she had fed heartily but half an hour before. My child was therefore begged to go and pluck three hairs from its tail, and bury them under the threshold of the stall; for it was well known that if this was done by a pure maid the cow would get better. My child then did as they would have her, seeing that she is the only maid in the whole village (for the others are still children); and the cow got better from that very hour, whereat all the folks were amazed. But it was not long before the same thing befell Witthahn her pig, whilst it was feeding heartily. She too came running to beg my child for God's sake to take compassion on her, and to do something for her pig, as ill men had bewitched it. Hereupon she had pity on her also, and it did as much good as it had done before. But the woman, who was *gravida*, was straightway taken in labour from the fright; and my child was scarce out of the pigsty when the woman went into her cottage, wailing and holding by the wall, and called together all the woman of the neighbourhood, seeing that the proper midwife was dead, as mentioned above; and before long something shot to the ground from under her; and when the women stooped down to pick it up, the devil's imp, which had wings like a bat, flew up off the ground, whizzed and buzzed about the room, and then shot out of the window with a great noise, so that the glass clattered down into the street. When they looked after it nothing was to be found. Any one may judge for himself what a great noise this made in all the neighbourhood; and the whole village believed that it was no one but old Seden his squint-eyed wife that had brought forth such a devil's brat.

But the people soon knew not what to believe. For that woman her cow got the same thing as all the other cows; wherefore she too came lamenting, and begged my daughter to take pity on her, as on the rest, and to cure her poor cow for the love of God. That if she had taken it ill of her that she had said anything about going into service with the Sheriff, she could only say she had done it for the best, etc. *Summa*, she talked over my unhappy child to go and cure her cow.

Meanwhile I was on my knees every Sunday before the Lord with the whole congregation, praying that he would not allow the Evil One to take from us that which his mercy had once more bestowed upon us after such extreme want. *Item*, that he would bring to light the *auctor* of such devilish works, so that he might receive the punishment he deserved.

But all was of no avail. For a very few days had passed when the mischief befell Stoffer Zuter his spotted cow, and he, too, like all the rest, came running to fetch my daughter; she accordingly went with him, but could do no good, and the beast died under her hands.

Item, Katy Berow had bought a little pig with the money my daughter had paid her in the winter for spinning, and the poor woman kept it like a child, and let it run about her room. This little pig got the mischief, like all the rest, in the twinkling of an eye; and when my daughter was called it grew no better, but also died under her hands; whereupon the poor woman made a great outcry and tore her hair for grief, so that my child was moved to pity her, and promised her another pig next time my sow should litter. Meantime another week passed over, during which I went on, together with the whole congregation, to call upon the Lord for his merciful help, but all in vain, when the same thing happened to old wife Seden her little pig. Whereupon she again came running for my daughter with loud outcries, and although my child told her that she must have seen herself that nothing she could do for the cattle cured them any longer, she ceased not to beg and pray her and to lament till she went forth to do what she could for her with the help of God. But it was all to no purpose, inasmuch as the little pig died before she left the sty. What think you this devil's whore then did? After she had run screaming through the village she said that any one might see that my daughter was no longer a maid, else why could she now do no good to the cattle, whereas she had formerly cured them? She supposed my child had lost her maiden honour on the Streckelberg, whither she went so often this spring, and that God only knew who had taken it! But she said no more then, and we did not hear the whole until afterwards. And it is indeed true that my child had often walked on the Streckelberg this spring, both with me and also alone, in order to seek for flowers and to look upon the blessed sea, while she recited aloud, as she was wont, such verses out of *Virgilius* as pleased her best (for whatever she read a few times, that she remembered).

Neither did I forbid her to take these walks, for there were no wolves now left on the Streckelberg, and even if there had been they always fly before a human creature in the summer season. Howbeit, I forbade her to dig for amber. For as it now lay deep, and we knew not what to do with the earth we threw up, I resolved to tempt the Lord no further, but to wait till my store of money grew very scant before we would dig any more.

But my child did not do as I had bidden her, although she had promised she would, and of this her disobedience came all our misery. (Oh, blessed Lord, how grave a matter is thy holy fourth commandment!) For as his reverence Johannes Lampius, of Crummin, who visited me this spring, had told me that the Cantor of Wolgast wanted to sell the *Opp. St. Augustini*, and I had said before her that I desired above all things to buy that book, but had not money enough left, she got up in the night without my knowledge to dig for amber, meaning to sell it as best she might at Wolgast, in order secretly to present me with the *Opp. St. Augustini* on my birthday, which falls on the 28th *mensis Augusti*. She had always covered over the earth she cast up with twigs of fir, whereof there were plenty in the forest, so that no one should perceive anything of it.

Meanwhile, however, it befell that the young *nobilis* Rüdiger of Nienkerken came riding one day to gather news of the terrible witchcraft that went on in the village. When I had told him all about it he shook his head doubtingly, and said he believed that all witchcraft was nothing but lies and deceit; whereat I was struck with great horror, inasmuch as I had hitherto held the young lord to be a wiser man, and now could not but see that he was an Atheist. He guessed what my thoughts were, and with a smile he answered me by asking whether I had ever read Johannes Wierus, who would hear nothing of witchcraft, and who argued that all witches were melancholy persons who only imagined to themselves that they had a *pactum* with the devil; and that to him they seemed more worthy of pity than of punishment? Hereupon I answered that I had not indeed read any such book (for say, who can read all that fools write?), but that the appearances here and in all other places proved that it was a monstrous error to deny the reality of witchcraft, inasmuch as people might then likewise deny that there were such things as murder, adultery, and theft.

But he called my *argumentum* a *dilemma*, and after he had discoursed a great deal of the devil, all of which I have forgotten, seeing it savoured strangely of heresy, he said he would relate to me a piece of witchcraft which he himself had seen at Wittenberg.

It seems that one morning, as an Imperial captain mounted his good charger at the Elstergate in order to review his company, the horse presently began to rage furiously, reared, tossed his head, snorted, kicked, and roared, not as horses used to neigh, but with a sound as though the voice came from a human throat, so that all the folks were amazed, and thought the horse bewitched. It presently threw the captain, and crushed his head with its hoof, so that he lay writhing on the ground, and straightway set off at full speed. Hereupon a trooper fired his carabine at the bewitched horse, which fell in the midst of the road, and presently died. That he, Rüdiger, had then drawn near, together with many others, seeing that the colonel had forthwith given orders to the surgeon of the regiment to cut open the horse and see in what state it was inwardly. However, that everything was quite right, and both the surgeon and army physician testified that the horse was thoroughly sound; whereupon all the people cried out more than ever about witchcraft. Meanwhile he himself (I mean the young *nobilis*) saw a thin smoke coming out from the horse's nostrils, and on stooping down to look what it might be, he drew out a match as long as my finger, which still smouldered, and which some wicked fellow had privately thrust into its nose with a pin. Hereupon all thoughts of witchcraft were at an end, and search was made for the culprit, who was presently found to be no other than the captain's own groom. For one day that his master had dusted his jacket for him he swore an oath that he would have his revenge, which indeed the provost-marshal himself had heard as he chanced to be standing in the stable. *Item*, another soldier bore witness that he had seen the fellow cut a piece off the fuse not long before he led out his master's horse. And thus thought the young lord, would it be with all witchcraft if it were sifted to the bottom; like as I myself had seen at Gützkow, where the devil's apparition turned out to be a cordwainer, and that one day I should own that it was the same sort of thing here in our village. By reason of this speech I liked not the young nobleman from that hour forward, believing him to be an Atheist. Though, indeed, afterwards, I have had cause to see that he was in the right, more's the pity; for had it not been for him what would have become of my daughter?

But I will say nothing beforehand.—*Summa*: I walked about the room in great displeasure at his words, while the young lord began to argue with my daughter upon witchcraft, now in Latin, and now in the vulgar tongue, as the words came into his mouth, and wanted to hear her mind about it. But she answered that she was a foolish thing, and could have no opinion on the matter; but that, nevertheless, she believed that what happened in the village could not be by natural means. Hereupon the maid called me out of the room (I forget what she wanted of me); but when I came back again my daughter was as red as scarlet, and the nobleman stood close before her. I therefore asked her, as soon as he had ridden off, whether anything had happened, which she at first denied, but afterwards owned that he had said to her while I was gone that he knew but one person who could bewitch; and when she asked him who that person was, he caught hold of her hand and said, "It is yourself, sweet maid; for you have thrown a spell upon my heart, as I feel right well!" But that he said nothing further, but only gazed on her face with eager eyes, and this it was that made her so red.

But this is the way with maidens; they ever have their secrets if one's back is turned but for a minute; and the proverb

> To drive a goose and watch a maid
> Needs the devil himself to aid

is but too true, as will be shown hereafter, more's the pity!

The Fourteenth Chapter

How Old Seden Disappeared All on a Sudden; *Item*, How the Great Gustavus Adolphus Came to Pomerania, and Took the Fort at Peenemünde

We were now left for some time in peace from witchcraft; unless, indeed, I reckon the caterpillars, which miserably destroyed my orchard, and which truly were a strange thing; for the trees blossomed so fair and sweetly that one day as we were walking under them, and praising the almighty power of the most merciful God, my child said, "If the Lord goes on to bless us so abundantly, it will be Christmas Eve with us every night of next winter!" But things soon fell out far otherwise; for all in a moment the trees were covered with such swarms of caterpillars (great and small, and of every shape and colour) that one might have measured them by the bushel, and before long my poor trees looked like brooms, and the blessed fruit—which was so well set—all fell off, and was scarce good enough for the pigs. I do not choose to lay this to any one, though I had my own private thoughts upon the matter, and have them yet. However, my barley, whereof I had sown about three bushels out on the common, shot up bravely. On my field I had sown nothing, seeing that I dreaded the malice of Satan. Neither was corn at all plentiful throughout the parish—in part because they had sown no winter crops, and in part because the summer crops did not prosper. However, in all the villages a great supply of fish was caught by the mercy of God, especially herring; but they were very low in price. Moreover, they killed many seals; and at Whitsuntide I myself killed one as I walked by the sea with my daughter. The creature lay on a rock close to the water, snoring like a Christian. Thereupon I pulled off my shoes and drew near him softly, so that he heard me not, and then struck him over his nose with my staff (for a seal cannot bear much on his nose), so that he tumbled over into the water; but he was quite stunned, and I could easily kill him outright. It was a fat beast, though not very large; and we melted forty pots of train-oil out of his fat, which we put by for a winter store.

Meanwhile, however, something seized old Seden all at once, so that he wished to receive the holy sacrament. When I went to him he could give no reason for it; or perhaps he would give none for fear of his old Lizzie, who was always watching him with her squinting eyes, and would not leave the room. However, Zuter his little girl, a child near twelve years old, said that a few days before, while she was plucking grass for the cattle under the garden-hedge by the road, she heard the husband and wife quarrelling violently again, and that the goodman threw in her teeth that he now knew of a certainty that she had a familiar spirit, and that he would straightway go and tell it to the priest. Albeit this is only a child's tale, it may be true for all that, seeing that children and fools, they say, speak the truth.

But be that as it may. *Summa*, my old warden grew worse and worse; and though I visited him every morning and evening—as I use to do to my sick—in order to pray with him, and often observed that he had somewhat on his mind, nevertheless he could not disburthen himself of it, seeing that old Lizzie never left her post.

This went on for a while, when at last one day, about noon, he sent to beg me to scrape a little silver off the new sacramental cup, because he had been told that he should get better if he took it mixed with the dung of fowls. For some time I would not consent, seeing that I straightway suspected that there was some devilish mischief behind it; but he begged and prayed, till I did as he would have me.

And lo and behold, he mended from that very hour; so that when I went to pray with him at evening, I found him already sitting on the bench with a bowl between his knees, out of which he was supping broth. However, he would not pray (which was strange, seeing that he used to pray so gladly, and often could not wait patiently for my coming, insomuch that he sent after me two or three times if I was not at hand, or elsewhere employed); but he told me he had prayed already, and that he would give me the cock whose dung he had taken for my trouble, as it was a fine large cock, and he had nothing better to offer for my Sunday's dinner. And as the poultry was by this time gone to roost, he went up to the perch which was behind the stove, and reached down the cock, and put it under the arm of the maid, who was just come to call me away.

Not for all the world, however, would I have eaten the cock, but I turned it out to breed. I went to him once more, and asked whether I should give thanks to the Lord next Sunday for his recovery; whereupon he answered that I might do as I pleased in the matter. Hereat I shook my head, and left the house, resolving to send for him as soon as ever I should hear that his old Lizzie was from home (for she often went to fetch flax to spin from the Sheriff). But mark what befell within a few days! We heard an outcry that old Seden was missing, and that no one could tell what had become of him. His wife thought he had gone up into the Streckelberg, whereupon the accursed witch ran howling to our house and asked my daughter whether she had not seen anything of her goodman, seeing that she went up the mountain every day. My daughter said she had not; but, woe is me, she was soon to hear enough of him; for one morning, before sunrise, as she came down into the wood on her way back from her forbidden digging after amber, she heard a woodpecker (which no doubt was old Lizzie herself) crying so dolefully, close beside her, that she went in among the bushes to see what was the matter. There was the woodpecker sitting on the ground before a bunch of hair, which was red, and just like what old Seden's had been, and as soon as it espied her it flew up, with its beak full of the hair and slipped into a hollow tree. While my daughter still stood looking at this devil's work, up came old Paasch—who also had heard the cries of the wood-pecker, as he was cutting roofing shingles on the mountain, with his boy —and was likewise struck with horror when he saw the hair on the ground. At first they thought a wolf must have eaten him, and searched all about, but could not find a single bone. On looking up they fancied they saw something red at the very top of the tree, so they made the boy climb up, and he forthwith cried out that here, too, there was a great bunch of red hair stuck to some leaves as if with pitch, but that it was not pitch, but something speckled red and white, like fishguts; *item*, that the leaves all around, even where there was no hair, were stained and spotted, and had a very ill smell. Hereupon the lad, at his master's bidding, threw down the clotted branch, and they two below straightway judged that this was the hair and brains of old Seden, and that the devil had carried him óff bodily, because he would not pray nor give thanks to the Lord for his recovery. I myself believed the same, and told it on the Sunday as a warning to the congregation. But further on it will be seen that the Lord had yet greater cause for giving him into the hands of Satan, inasmuch as he had been talked over by his wicked wife to renounce his Maker in the hopes of getting better. Now, however, this devil's whore did as if her heart was broken, tearing out her red hair by whole handsful when she heard about the woodpecker from my child and old Paasch, and bewailing that she was now a poor widow, and who was to take care of her for the future, etc.

Meanwhile we celebrated on this barren shore, as best we could and might, together with the whole Protestant Church, the 25th day *mensis Junii*, whereon, one hundred years ago, the Estates of the holy Roman Empire laid their confession before the most high and mighty Emperor Carolus V., at Augsburg; and I preached a sermon on Matt. x. 32, of the right confession of our Lord and Saviour Jesus Christ, whereupon the whole congregation came to the Sacrament. Now, towards the evening of the selfsame day, as I walked with my daughter by the sea-shore, we saw several hundred sail of ships, both great and small, round about Ruden, and plainly heard firing, whereupon we judged forthwith that this must be the most high and mighty King Gustavus Adolphus, who was now coming, as he had promised, to the aid of poor persecuted Christendom. While we were still debating, a boat sailed towards us from Oie wherein was Kate Berow her son, who is a farmer there, and was coming to see his old mother. The same told us that it really was the king, who had this morning run before Ruden with his fleet from Rügen; that a few men of Oie were fishing there at the time, and saw how he went ashore with his officers, and straightway bared his head and fell upon his knees.

Thus, then, most gracious God, did I thy unworthy servant enjoy a still greater happiness and delight that blessed evening than I had done on the blessed morn; and any one may think that I delayed not for a moment to fall on my knees with my child, and to follow the example of the king. And God knows I never in my life prayed so fervently as that evening, whereon the Lord showed such a wondrous sign upon us as to cause the deliverer of his poor Christian people to come among them on the very day when they had everywhere called upon him, on their knees, for his gracious help against the murderous wiles of the Pope and the devil. That night I could not sleep for joy, but went quite early in the morning to Damerow, where something had befallen Vithe his boy. I supposed that he, too, was bewitched; but this time it was not witchcraft, seeing that the boy had eaten something unwholesome in the forest. He could not tell what kind of berries they were; but the *malum*, which turned all his skin bright scarlet, soon passed over. As I therefore was returning home shortly after, I met a messenger from Peenemünde, whom his Majesty the high and mighty King Gustavus Adolphus had sent to tell the Sheriff that on the 29th of June, at ten o'clock in the morning, he was to send three guides to meet his Majesty at Coserow, and to guide him through the woods to Swine, where the Imperialists were encamped. *Item*, he related how his Majesty had taken the fort at Peenemünde yesterday (doubtless the cause of the firing we heard last evening), and that the Imperialists had run away as fast as they could, and played the bushranger properly; for after setting their camp on fire they all fled into the woods and coppices, and part escaped to Wolgast and part to Swine.

Straightway I resolved in my joy to invent a *carmen gratulatorium* to his Majesty, whom, by the grace of Almighty God, I was to see, the which my little daughter might present to him.

I accordingly proposed it to her as soon as I got home, and she straightway fell on my neck for joy, and then began to dance about the room. But when she had considered a little, she thought her clothes were not good enough to wear before his Majesty, and that I should buy her a blue silk gown, with a yellow apron, seeing that these were the Swedish colours, and would please his Majesty right well. For a long time I would not, seeing that I hate this kind of pride; but she teased me with her kisses and coaxing words, till I, like an old fool, said yes, and ordered my ploughman to drive her over to Wolgast to-day to buy the stuff. Wherefore I think that the just God, who hateth the proud, and showeth mercy on the humble, did rightly chastise me for such pride. For I myself felt a sinful pleasure when she came back with two women who were to help her to sew, and laid the stuff before me. Next day she set to work at sunrise to sew, and I composed my *carmen* the while. I had not got very far in it when the young Lord Rüdiger of Nienkerken came riding up, in order, as he said, to inquire whether his Majesty were indeed going to march through Coserow. And when I told him all I knew of the matter, *item* informed him of our plan, he praised it exceedingly, and instructed my daughter (who looked more kindly upon him to-day than I altogether liked) how the Swedes use to pronounce the Latin, as *ratscho* pro *ratio*, *uet* pro *ut*, *schis* pro *scis*, etc., so that she might be able to answer his Majesty with all due readiness. He said, moreover, that he had held much converse with Swedes at Wittenberg, as well as at Griepswald, wherefore if she pleased they might act a short *colloquium*, wherein he would play the king. Hereupon he sat down on the bench before her, and they both began chattering together, which vexed me sore, especially when I saw that she made but small haste with her needle the while. But say, dear reader, what was I to do? Wherefore I went my ways, and let them chatter till near noon, when the young lord at last took leave. But he promised to come again on Tuesday, when the king was here, and believed that the whole island would flock together at Coserow. As soon as he was gone, seeing that my *vena poetica* (as may be easily guessed) was still stopped up, I had the horses put to and drove all over the parish, exhorting the people in every village to be at the Giant's Stone by Coserow at nine o'clock on Tuesday, and that they were all to fall on their knees as soon as they should see the king coming and that I knelt down; *item*, to join at once in singing the Ambrosian hymn of praise, which I should lead off as soon as the bells began to ring. This they all promised to do; and after I had again exhorted them to it on Sunday in church, and prayed to the Lord for his Majesty out of the fulness of my heart, we scarce could await the blessed Tuesday for joyful impatience.

The Fifteenth Chapter

OF THE ARRIVAL OF THE HIGH AND MIGHTY KING GUSTAVUS ADOLPHUS AND WHAT BEFELL THEREAT

Meanwhile I finished my *carmen* in *metrum elegiacum*, which my daughter transcribed (seeing that her handwriting is fairer than mine) and diligently learned, so that she might say it to his Majesty. *Item*, her clothes were gotten ready, and became her purely; and on Monday she went up to the Streckelberg, although the heat was such that the crows gasped on the hedges; for she wanted to gather flowers for a garland she designed to wear, and which was also to be blue and yellow. Towards evening she came home with her apron filled with all manner of flowers; but her hair was quite wet, and hung all matted about her shoulders. (My God, my God, was everything to come together to destroy me, wretched man that I am!) I asked, therefore, where she had been that her hair was so wet and matted: whereupon she answered that she had gathered flowers round the Kölpin, and from thence she had gone down to the sea-shore, where she had bathed in the sea, seeing that it was very hot and no one could see her. Thus, said she, jesting, she should appear before his Majesty to-morrow doubly a clean maid. This displeased me at the time, and I looked grave, although I said nought.

Next morning at six o'clock all the people were already at the Giant's Stone, men, women, and children. *Summa*, everybody that was able to walk was there. At eight o'clock my daughter was already dressed in all her bravery, namely, a blue silken gown, with a yellow apron and kerchief, and a yellow hair-net, with a garland of blue and yellow flowers round her head. It was not long before my young lord arrived, finely dressed, as became a nobleman. He wanted to inquire, as he said, by which road I should go up to the Stone with my daughter, seeing that his father, Hans von Nienkerken, *item* Wittich Appelmann and the Lepels of Gnitze, were also going, and that there was much people on all the high roads, as though a fair was being held. But I straightway perceived that all he wanted was to see my daughter, inasmuch as he presently occupied himself about her, and began chattering with her in the Latin again. He made her repeat to him the *carmen* to his Majesty; whereupon he, in the person of the king, answered her: "*Dulcissima et venustissima puella, quœ mihi in coloribus cœli, ut angelus Domini appares utinam semper mecum esses, nunquam mihi male caderet*"; whereupon she grew red, as likewise did I, but from vexation, as may be easily guessed. I therefore begged that his lordship would but go forward toward the Stone, seeing that my daughter had yet to help me on with my surplice; whereupon, however, he answered that he would wait for us the while in the chamber, and that we might then go together. *Summa*, I blessed myself from this young lord; but what could I do? As he would not go, I was forced to wink at it all; and before long we went up to the Stone, where I straightway chose three sturdy fellows from the crowd, and sent them up the steeple, that they might begin to ring the bells as soon as they should see me get up upon the Stone and wave my napkin. This they promised to do, and straightway departed; whereupon I sat down on the Stone with my daughter, thinking that the young lord would surely stand apart, as became his dignity; albeit he did not, but sat down with us on the Stone. And we three sat there all alone, and all the folk looked at us, but none drew near to see my child's fine clothes, not even the young lasses, as is their wont to do; but this I did not observe till afterwards, when I heard how matters stood with us even then. Towards nine o'clock Hans von Nienkerken and Wittich Appelmann galloped up, and old Nienkerken called to his son in an angry voice: and seeing that the young lord heard him not, he rode up to the Stone, and cried out so loud that all the folk might hear, "Canst thou not hearken, boy, when thy father calls thee?" Whereupon Rüdiger followed him in much displeasure, and we saw from a distance how the old lord seemed to threaten his son, and spat out before him; but knew not what this might signify: we were to learn it soon enough, though, more's the pity! Soon after the two Lepels of Gnitze came from the Damerow; and the noblemen saluted one other on the green sward close beside us, but without looking on us. And I heard the Lepels say that nought could yet be seen of his Majesty, but that the coastguard fleet around Ruden was in motion, and that several hundred ships were sailing this way. As soon as this news was known, all the folk ran to the sea-shore (which is but a step from the Stone); and the noblemen rode thither too, all save Wittich, who had dismounted, and who, when he saw that I sent old Paasch his boy up into a tall oak-tree to look out for the king, straightway busied himself about my daughter again, who now sat all alone upon the Stone: "Why had she not taken his huntsman? and whether she would not change her mind on the matter and have him now, or else come into service with him (the Sheriff) himself? for that if she would not, he believed she might be sorry for it one day." Whereupon she answered him (as she told me), that there was but one thing she was sorry for, namely, that his lordship would take so much useless pains upon her; whereupon she rose with all haste and came to where I stood under the tree, looking after the lad who was climbing up it. But our old Ilse said that he swore a great curse when my daughter turned her back upon him, and went straightway into the alder-grove close by the high road, where stood the old witch Lizzie Kolken.

Meanwhile I went with my daughter to the sea-shore, and found it quite true that the whole fleet was sailing over from Ruden and Oie towards Wollin, and several ships passed so close before us that we could see the soldiers standing upon them and the flashing of their arms. *Item*, we heard the horses neigh and the soldiery laugh. On one ship, too, they were drumming, and on another cattle lowed and sheep bleated. Whilst we yet gazed we saw smoke come out from one of the ships, followed by a great noise, and presently we were aware of the ball bounding over the water, which foamed and splashed on either side, and coming straight towards us. Hereupon the crowd ran away on every side with loud cries, and we plainly heard the soldiery in the ships laugh thereat. But the ball flew up and struck into the midst of an oak hard by Paasch his boy, so that nearly two cartloads of boughs fell to the earth with a great crash, and covered all the road by which his Majesty was to come. Hereupon the boy would stop no longer in the tree, however much I exhorted him thereto, but cried out to us as he came down that a great troop of soldiers was marching out of the forest by Damerow, and that likely enough the king was among them. Hereupon the Sheriff ordered the road to be cleared forthwith, and this was some time a-doing, seeing that the thick boughs were stuck fast in the trees all around; the nobles, as soon as all was made ready, would have ridden to meet his Majesty, but stayed still on the little green sward, because we already heard the noise of horses, carriages, and voices close to us in the forest.

It was not long before the cannons broke through the brushwood with the three guides seated upon them. And seeing that one of them was known to me (it was Stoffer Krauthahn of Peenemünde), I drew near and begged him that he would tell me when the king should come. But he answered that he was going forward with the cannon to Coserow, and that I was only to watch for a tall dark man, with a hat and feather and a gold chain round his neck, for that that was the king, and that he rode next after the great standard whereon was a yellow lion.

Wherefore I narrowly watched the procession as it wound out of the forest. And next after the artillery came the Finnish and Lapland bow-men, who went clothed all in furs, although it was now the height of summer, whereat I greatly wondered. After these there came much people, but I know not what they were. Presently I espied over the hazel-tree which stood in my way so that I could not see everything as soon as it came forth out of the coppice, the great flag with the lion on it, and behind that the head of a very dark man with a golden chain round his neck, whereupon straightway I judged this must be the king. I there-fore waved my napkin toward the steeple, whereupon the bells forthwith rang out, and while the dark man rode nearer to us, I pulled off my skull-cap, fell upon my knees, and led the Ambrosian hymn of praise, and all the people plucked their hats from their heads and knelt down on the ground all around, singing after me; men, women, and children, save only the nobles, who stood still on the green sward, and did not take off their hats and behave with attention until they saw that his Majesty drew in his horse. (It was a coal-black charger, and stopped with its two fore-feet right upon my field, which I took as a sign of good fortune.) When we had finished, the Sheriff quickly got off his horse, and would have approached the king with his three guides, who followed after him; *item*, I had taken my child by the hand, and would also have drawn near to the king. Howbeit, his Majesty motioned away the Sheriff and beck-oned us to approach, whereupon I wished his Majesty joy in the Latin tongue, and extolled his magnanimous heart, seeing that he had deigned to visit German ground for the protection and aid of poor persecuted Christendom; and praised it as a sign from God that such had happened on this the high festival of our poor church, and I prayed his Majesty graciously to receive what my daughter desired to present to him; whereupon his Majesty looked on her and smiled pleasantly. Such gracious bearing made her bold again, albeit she trembled visibly just before, and she reached him a blue and yellow wreath, whereon lay the *carmen*, saying, "*Accipe hanc vilem coronam et hæc*," whereupon she began to recite the *carmen*. Meanwhile his Majesty grew more and more gracious, looking now on her and now on the *carmen*, and nodded with especial kindness towards the end, which was as follows:—

> Tempus erit, quo tu reversus ab hostibus ultor
> Intrabis patriæ libera regna meæ;
> Tunc meliora student nostræ tibi carmina musæ,
> Tunc tua, maxime rex, Martia facta canam.
> Tu modo versiculis ne spernas vilibus ausum
> Auguror et res est ista futura brevi!
> Sis fœlix, fortisque diu, vive optime princeps,
> Omnia, et ut possis vincere, dura.   Vale!

As soon as she held her peace, his Majesty said, "*Propius accedas, patria virgo, ut te osculer*"; whereupon she drew near to his horse, blushing deeply. I thought he would only have kissed her forehead, as potentates commonly use to do, but not at all! he kissed her lips with a loud smack, and the long feathers on his hat drooped over her neck, so that I was quite afraid for her again. But he soon raised up his head, and taking off his gold chain, whereon dangled his own effigy, he hung it round my child's neck with these words: "*Hocce tuæ pulchritudini! et si favente Deo redux fuero victor, promissum carmen et præterea duo oscula exspecto.*"

Hereupon the Sheriff with his three men again came forward and bowed down to the ground before his Majesty. But as he knew no Latin, *item* no Italian nor French, I had to act as interpreter. For his Majesty inquired how far it was to Swine, and whether there was still much foreign soldiery there: And the Sheriff thought there were still about 200 Croats in the camp; whereupon his Majesty spurred on his horse, and nodding graciously, cried "*Valete!*" And now came the rest of the troops, about 3000 strong, out of the coppice, which likewise had a valiant bearing, and attempted no fooleries, as troops are wont to do, when they passed by us and the women, but marched on in honest quietness, and we followed the train until the forest beyond Coserow, where we commended it to the care of the Almighty, and every one went on his way home.

The Sixteenth Chapter

HOW LITTLE MARY PAASCH WAS SORELY PLAGUED OF THE
DEVIL, AND THE WHOLE PARISH FELL OFF FROM ME

Before I proceed any further I will first mark that the illustrious King
Gustavus Adolphus, as we presently heard, had cut down the 300
Croats at Swine, and was thence gone by sea to Stettin. May God be for
ever gracious to him! Amen.

But my sorrows increased from day to day, seeing that the devil now
played pranks such as he never had played before. I had begun to think
that the ears of God had hearkened to our ardent prayers, but it pleased
him to try us yet more hardly than ever. For, a few days after the arrival
of the most illustrious King Gustavus Adolphus, it was bruited about that
my child her little god-daughter was possessed of the Evil One, and
tumbled about most piteously on her bed, insomuch that no one was
able to hold her. My child straightway went to see her little god-daughter,
but presently came weeping home. Old Paasch would not suffer her even
to come near her, but railed at her very angrily, and said that she should
never come within his doors again, as his child had got the mischief
from the white roll which she had given her that morning. It was true
that my child had given her a roll, seeing that the maid had been the day
before to Wolgast and had brought back a napkin full of them.

Such news vexed me sore, and after putting on my cassock I went to
old Paasch his house to exorcise the foul fiend and to remove such disgrace from my child. I found the old man standing on the floor by the
cockloft steps weeping; and after I had spoken "The peace of God," I
asked him first of all whether he really believed that his little Mary had
been bewitched by means of the roll which my child had given her?
He said, "Yes!" And when I answered that in that case I also must have
been bewitched, *item* Pagel his little girl, seeing that we both had eaten
of the rolls, he was silent, and asked me with a sigh, whether I would not
go into the room and see for myself how matters stood. I then entered
with "The peace of God," and found six people standing round little
Mary her bed; her eyes were shut, and she was as stiff as a board;
wherefore Kit Wells (who was a young and sturdy fellow) seized the
little child by one leg and held her out like a hedgestake, so that I might
see how the devil plagued her. I now said a prayer, and Satan, perceiving
that a servant of Christ was come, began to tear the child so fearfully that
it was pitiful to behold; for she flung about her hands and feet so that
four strong men were scarce able to hold her: *item* she was afflicted with
extraordinary risings and fallings of her belly, as if a living creature were
therein, so that at last the old witch Lizzie Kolken sat herself upon her
belly, whereupon the child seemed to be somewhat better, and I told

her to repeat the Apostles' Creed, so as to see whether it really were the devil who possessed her. She straightway grew worse than before, and began to gnash her teeth, to roll her eyes, and to strike so hard with her hands and feet that she flung her father, who held one of her legs, right into the middle of the room, and then struck her foot so hard against the bedstead that the blood flowed, and Lizzie Kolken was thrown about on her belly as though she had been in a swing. And as I ceased not, but exorcised Satan that he should leave her, she began to howl and to bark like a dog, *item* to laugh, and spoke at last, with a gruff bass voice, like an old man's, "I will not depart." But he should soon have been forced to depart out of her, had not both father and mother besought me by God's holy Sacrament to leave their poor child in peace, seeing that nothing did her any good, but rather made her worse. I was therefore forced to desist, and only admonished the parents to seek for help, like the Canaanitish woman, in true repentance and incessant prayer, and with her to sigh in constant faith, "Have mercy upon me, O Lord, Thou Son of David, my daughter is grievously vexed of a devil," Matthew xv.; that the heart of our Lord would then melt, so that he would have mercy on their child, and command Satan to depart from her. *Item*, I promised to pray for the little child on the following Sunday with the whole congregation, and told them to bring her, if it were any ways possible, to the church, seeing that the ardent prayer of the whole congregation has power to rise beyond the clouds. This they promised to do, and I then went home sorely troubled, where I soon learned that she was somewhat better; thus it still is sure that Satan hates nothing so much, after the Lord Jesus, as the servants of the Gospel. But wait, and I shall even yet "bruise thy head with my heel" (Genesis, chap. iii.); nought shall avail thee.

Howbeit before the blessed Sunday came, 1 perceived that many of my people went out of my way, both in the village and elsewhere in the parish, where I went to visit sundry sick folks. When I went to Uekeritze to see young Tittlewitz, there even befell me as follows:—Claus Pieper the peasant stood in his yard chopping wood, and on seeing me he flung the axe out of his hand so hastily that it stuck in the ground, and he ran towards the pigsty, making the sign of the cross. I motioned him to stop, and asked why he thus ran from me, his confessor? Whether, peradventure, he also believed that my daughter had bewitched her little god-child? "*Ille*. Yes, he believed it, because the whole parish did. *Ego.* Why, then, had she been so kind to her formerly, and kept her like a sister through the worst of the famine? *Ille.* This was not the only mischief she had done. *Ego.* What, then, had she done besides? *Ille.* That was all one to me. *Ego.* He should tell me, or I would complain to the magistrate. *Ille.* That I might do, if I pleased." Whereupon he went his way insolently. Any one may guess that I was not slow to inquire everywhere what people thought my daughter had done; but no one would tell me anything, and I might have grieved to death at such evil reports. Moreover not one child came during this whole week to school to my daughter; and when I sent out the maid to ask the reason she brought back word that the children were ill, or that the parents wanted them for their work. I thought and thought, but all to no purpose, until the blessed Sunday came round when I meant to have held a great Sacrament, seeing that many people had made known their intention to come to the Lord's table. It seemed strange to me that I saw no one standing (as was their wont) about the church door; I thought, however, that they might have gone into the houses. But when I went into the church with my daughter, there were not more than six people assembled, among whom was old Lizzie Kolken; and the accursed witch no sooner saw my daughter follow me than she made the sign of the cross and ran out of the door under the steeple; whereupon the five others, among them mine own church-warden Claus Bulken (I had not appointed any one in the room of old Seden), followed her. I was so horror-struck that my blood curdled, and I began to tremble, so that I fell with my shoulder against the confessional. My child, to whom I had as yet told nothing, in order to spare her, then asked me, "Father, what is the matter with all the people; are they, too, bewitched?" Whereupon I came to myself again and went into the churchyard to look after them. But all were gone save my churchwarden, Claus Bulken, who stood under the lime-tree, whistling to himself. I stepped up to him and asked what had come to the people? Whereupon he answered he could not tell; and when I asked him again why, then, he himself had left the church, he said, What was he to do there alone, seeing that no collection could be made? I then implored him to tell me the truth, and what horrid suspicion had arisen against me in the parish? But he answered, I should very soon find it out for myself; and he jumped over the wall and went into old Lizzie her house, which stands close by the churchyard.

My child had made ready some veal broth for dinner, for which I mostly use to leave everything else; but I could not swallow one spoonful, but sat resting my head on my hand, and doubted whether I should tell her or no. Meanwhile the old maid came in ready for a journey, and with a bundle in her hand, and begged me with tears to give her leave to go. My poor child turned pale as a corpse, and asked in amaze what had come to her? but she merely answered, "Nothing!" and wiped her eyes with her apron. When I recovered my speech, which had well-nigh left me at seeing that this faithful old creature was also about to forsake me, I began to question her why she wished to go; she who had dwelt with me so long, and who would not forsake us even in the great famine, but had faithfully borne up against it, and, indeed, had humbled me by her faith, and had exhorted me to stand out gallantly to the last, for which I should be grateful to her as long as I lived. Hereupon she merely wept and sobbed yet more, and at length brought out that she still had an old mother of eighty living in Liepe, and that she wished to go and nurse her till her end. Hereupon my daughter jumped up and answered with tears, "Alas, old Ilse, why wilt thou leave us, for thy mother is with thy brother? Do but tell me why thou wilt forsake me, and what harm have I done thee, that I may make it good to thee again." But she hid her face in her apron and sobbed and could not get out a single word; whereupon my child drew away the apron from her face, and would have stroked her cheeks to make her speak. But when Ilse saw this she struck my poor child's hand and cried, "Ugh!" spat out before her, and straightway went out at the door. Such a thing she had never done even when my child was a little girl, and we were both so shocked that we could neither of us say a word.

Before long my poor child gave a loud cry, and cast herself upon the bench, weeping and wailing, "What has happened, what has happened?" I therefore thought I ought to tell her what I had heard—namely, that she was looked upon as a witch. Whereat she began to smile instead of weeping any more, and ran out of the door to overtake the maid, who had already left the house, as we had seen. She returned after an hour, crying out that all the people in the village had run away from her when she would have asked them whither the maid was gone. *Item*, the little children, for whom she had kept school, had screamed, and had hidden themselves from her; also no one would answer her a single word, but all spat out before her, as the maid had done. On her way home she had seen a boat on the water, and had run as fast as she could to the shore, and called with might and main after old Ilse, who was in the boat. But she had taken no notice of her, not even once to look round after her, but had motioned her to be gone. And now she went on to weep and to sob the whole day and the whole night, so that I was more miserable than even in the time of the great famine. But the worst was yet to come, as will be shown in the following chapter.

The Seventeenth Chapter

HOW MY POOR CHILD WAS TAKEN UP FOR A WITCH, AND CARRIED TO PUDGLA

The next day, Monday, the 12th July, at about eight in the morning, while we sat in our grief, wondering who could have prepared such great sorrow for us, and speedily agreed that it could be none other than the accursed witch Lizzie Kolken, a coach with four horses drove quickly up to the door, wherein sat six fellows, who straightway all jumped out. Two went and stood at the front, two at the back door, and two more, one of whom was the constable Jacob Knake, came into the room, and handed me a warrant from the Sheriff for the arrest of my daughter, as in common repute of being a wicked witch, and for her examination before the criminal court. Any one may guess how my heart sank within me when I read this. I dropped to the earth like a felled tree, and when I came to myself my child had thrown herself upon me with loud cries, and her hot tears ran down over my face. When she saw that I came to myself, she began to praise God therefor with a loud voice, and essayed to comfort me, saying that she was innocent, and should appear with a clean conscience before her judges. *Item*, she repeated to me the beautiful text from Matthew, chap. v.: "Blessed are ye when men shall revile you, and persecute you, and shall say all manner of evil against you falsely for my sake."

And she begged me to rise and to throw my cassock over my doublet, and go with her, for that without me she would not suffer herself to be carried before the Sheriff. Meanwhile, however, all the village—men, women, and children—had thronged together before my door; but they remained quiet, and only peeped in at the windows, as though they would have looked right through the house. When we had both made us ready, and the constable, who at first would not take me with them, had thought better of it, by reason of a good fee which my daughter gave him, we walked to the coach; but I was so helpless that I could not get up into it.

Old Paasch, when he saw this, came and helped me up into the coach, saying, "God comfort ye! Alas, that you should ever see your child to come to this!" and he kissed my hand to take leave.

A few others came up to the coach, and would have done likewise; but I besought them not to make my heart still heavier, and to take Christian charge of my house and my affairs until I should return. Also to pray diligently for me and my daughter, so that the Evil One, who had long gone about our village like a roaring lion, and who now threatened to devour me, might not prevail against us, but might be forced to depart from me and from my child as from our guileless Saviour in the wilderness. But to this none answered a word; and I heard right well, as we drove away, that many spat out after us, and one said (my child thought it was Berow her voice), "We would far sooner lay fire under thy coats than pray for thee." We were still sighing over such words as these when we came near to the churchyard, and there sat the accursed witch Lizzie Kolken at the door of her house with her hymn-book in her lap, screeching out at the top of her voice, "God the Father, dwell with us," as we drove past her; the which vexed my poor child so sore that she swounded, and fell like one dead upon me. I begged the driver to stop, and called to old Lizzie to bring us a pitcher of water; but she did as though she had not heard me, and went on to sing so that it rang again. Whereupon the constable jumped down, and at my request ran back to my house to fetch a pitcher of water; and he presently came back with it, and the people after him, who began to say aloud that my child's bad conscience had stricken her, and that she had now betrayed herself. Wherefore I thanked God when she came to life again, and we could leave the village. But at Uekeritze it was just the same, for all the people had flocked together, and were standing on the green before Labahn his house when we went by.

Nevertheless, they were quiet enough as we drove past, albeit some few cried, "How can it be, how can it be?" I heard nothing else. But in the forest near the watermill the miller and all his men ran out and shouted, laughing, "Look at the witch, look at the witch!" Whereupon one of the men struck at my poor child with the sack which he held in his hand, so that she turned quite white, and the flour flew all about the coach like a cloud. When I rebuked him, the wicked rogue laughed and said, that if no other smoke than that ever came under her nose, so much the better for her. *Item*, it was worse in Pudgla than even at the mill. The people stood so thick on the hill, before the castle, that we could scarce force our way through, and the Sheriff caused the death-bell in the castle-tower to toll as an *avisum*. Whereupon more and more people came running out of the ale-houses and cottages. Some cried out, "Is that the witch?" Others, again, "Look at the parson's witch! the parson's witch!" and much more, which for very shame I may not write. They scraped up the mud out of the gutter which ran from the castle-kitchen and threw it upon us; *item*, a great stone, the which struck one of the horses so that it shied, and belike would have upset the coach had not a man sprung forward and held it in. All this happened before the castle-gates, where the Sheriff stood smiling and looking on, with a heron's feather stuck in his grey hat. But so soon as the horse was quiet again, he came to the coach and mocked at my child, saying, "See, young maid, thou wouldst not come to me, and here thou art nevertheless!" Whereupon she answered, "Yea, I come; and may you one day come before your judge as I come before you"; whereunto I said, Amen, and asked him how his lordship could answer before God and man for what he had done to a wretched man like myself and to my child? But he answered, saying, Why had I come with her? And when I told him of the rude people here, *item*, of the churlish miller's man, he said that it was not his fault, and threatened the people all around with his fist, for they were making a great noise. Thereupon he commanded my child to get down and to follow him, and went before her into the castle; motioned the constable, who would have gone with them, to stay at the foot of the steps, and began to mount the winding staircase to the upper rooms alone with my child.

But she whispered me privately, "Do not leave me, father"; and I presently followed softly after them. Hearing by their voices in which chamber they were, I laid my ear against the door to listen. And the villain offered to her that if she would love him nought should harm her, saying he had power to save her from the people; but that if she would not, she should go before the court next day, and she might guess herself how it would fare with her, seeing that he had many witnesses to prove that she had played the wanton with Satan, and had suffered him to kiss her. Hereupon she was silent, and only sobbed, which the arch-rogue took as a good sign, and went on: "If you have had Satan himself for a sweetheart, you surely may love me." And he went to her and would have taken her in his arms, as I perceived; for she gave a loud scream, and flew to the door; but he held her fast, and begged and threatened as the devil prompted him. I was about to go in when I heard her strike him in the face, saying, "Get thee behind me, Satan," so that he let her go. Whereupon she ran out at the door so suddenly that she threw me on the ground, and fell upon me with a loud cry. Hereat the Sheriff, who had followed her, started, but presently cried out, "Wait, thou prying parson, I will teach thee to listen!" and ran out and beckoned to the constable who stood on the steps below. He bade him first shut me up in one dungeon, seeing that I was an eavesdropper, and then return and thrust my child into another. But he thought better of it when we had come half-way down the winding-stair, and said he would excuse me this time, and that the constable might let me go, and only lock up my child very fast, and bring the key to him, seeing she was a stubborn person, as he had seen at the very first hearing which he had given her.

Hereupon my poor child was torn from me, and I fell in a swound upon the steps. I know not how I got down them; but when I came to myself, I was in the constable his room, and his wife was throwing water in my face. There I passed the night sitting in a chair, and sorrowed more than I prayed, seeing that my faith was greatly shaken, and the Lord came not to strengthen it.

The Eighteenth Chapter
OF THE FIRST TRIAL, AND WHAT CAME THEREOF

Next morning, as I walked up and down in the court, seeing that I had many times asked the constable in vain to lead me to my child (he would not even tell me where she lay), and for very disquietude I had at last begun to wander about there; about six o'clock there came a coach from Uzdom, wherein sat his worship, Master Samuel Pieper, *consul dirigens*, *item*, the *camerarius* Gebhard Wenzel, and a *scriba*, whose name, indeed, I heard, but have forgotten it again; and my daughter forgot it too, albeit in other things she has an excellent memory, and, indeed, told me most of what follows, for my old head well-nigh burst, so that I myself could remember but little. I straightway went up to the coach, and begged that the worshipful court would suffer me to be present at the trial, seeing that my daughter was yet in her nonage, but which the Sheriff, who meanwhile had stepped up to the coach from the terrace, whence he had seen all, had denied me. But his worship Master Samuel Pieper, who was a little round man, with a fat paunch, and a beard mingled with grey hanging down to his middle, reached me his hand, and condoled with me like a Christian in my trouble: I might come into court in God's name; and he wished with all his heart that all whereof my daughter was filed might prove to be foul lies. Nevertheless I had still to wait two hours before their worships came down the winding stair again. At last towards nine o'clock I heard the constable moving about the chairs and benches in the judgment-chamber; and as I conceived that the time was now come, I went in and sat myself down on a bench. No one, however, was yet there, save the constable and his young daughter, who was wiping the table, and held a rosebud between her lips. I was fain to beg her to give it me, so that I might have it to smell to; and I believe that I should have been carried dead out of the room that day if I had not had it. God is thus able to preserve our lives even by means of a poor flower, if so he wills it!

At length their worships came in and sat round the table, whereupon *Dom. Consul* motioned the constable to fetch in my child. Meanwhile he asked the Sheriff whether he had put *Rea* in chains, and when he said No, he gave him such a reprimand that it went through my very marrow. But the Sheriff excused himself, saying that he had not done so from regard to her quality, but had locked her up in so fast a dungeon that she could not possibly escape therefrom. Whereupon *Dom. Consul* answered that much is possible to the devil, and that they would have to answer for it should *Rea* escape. This angered the Sheriff, and he replied that if the devil could convey her through walls seven feet thick, and through three doors, he could very easily break her chains too. Whereupon *Dom. Consul* said that hereafter he would look at the prison himself; and I think that the Sheriff had been so kind only because he yet hoped (as, indeed, will hereafter be shown) to talk over my daughter to let him have his will of her.

And now the door opened, and my poor child came in with the constable, but walking backwards, and without her shoes, the which she was forced to leave without. The fellow had seized her by her long hair, and thus dragged her up to the table, when first she was to turn round and look upon her judges. He had a vast deal to say in the matter, and was in every way a bold and impudent rogue, as will soon be shown. After *Dom. Consul* had heaved a deep sigh, and gazed at her from head to foot, he first asked her her name, and how old she was; *item*, if she knew why she was summoned before them? On the last point she answered that the Sheriff had already told her father the reason; that she wished not to wrong any one, but thought that the Sheriff himself had brought upon her the repute of a witch, in order to gain her to his wicked will. Hereupon she told all his ways with her, from the very first, and how he would by all means have had her for his housekeeper; and that when she would not (although he had many times come himself to her father his house), one day, as he went out of the door, he had muttered in his beard, "I will have her, despite of all!" which their servant Claus Neels had heard, as he stood in the stable; and he had also sought to gain his ends by means of an ungodly woman, one Lizzie Kolken, who had formerly been in his service; that this woman, belike, had contrived the spells which they laid to her charge: she herself knew nothing of witchcraft; *item*, she related what the Sheriff had done to her the evening before, when she had just come, and when he for the first time spoke out plainly, thinking that she was then altogether in his power: nay, more, that he had come to her that very night again, in her dungeon, and had made her the same offers, saying that he would set her free if she would let him have his will of her; and that when she denied him, he had struggled with her, whereupon she had screamed aloud, and had scratched him across the nose, as might yet be seen, whereupon he had left her; wherefore she would not acknowledge the Sheriff as her judge, and trusted in God to save her from the hand of her enemies, as of old he had saved the chaste Susannah.—

When she now held her peace amid loud sobs, *Dom. Consul* started up after he had looked, as we all did, at the Sheriff's nose, and had in truth espied the scar upon it, and cried out in amaze, "Speak, for God his sake, speak, what is this that I hear of your lordship?" Whereupon the Sheriff, without changing colour, answered that although, indeed, he was not called upon to say anything to their worships, seeing that he was the head of the court, and that *Rea*, as appeared from numberless *indicia*, was a wicked witch, and therefore could not bear witness against him or any one else; he, nevertheless, would speak, so as to give no cause of scandal to the court; that all the charges brought against him by this person were foul lies; it was, indeed, true, that he would have hired her for a housekeeper, whereof he stood greatly in need, seeing that his old Dorothy was already growing infirm; it was also true that he had yesterday questioned her in private, hoping to get her to confess by fair means, whereby her sentence would be softened, inasmuch as he had pity on her great youth; but that he had not said one naughty word to her, nor had he been to her in the night; and that it was his little lap-dog, called Below, which had scratched him, while he played with it that very morning; that his old Dorothy could bear witness to this, and that the cunning witch had only made use of this wile to divide the court against itself, thereby and with the devil's help, to gain her own advantage, inasmuch as she was a most cunning creature, as the court would soon find out.

Hereupon I plucked up a heart, and declared that all my daughter had said was true, and that the evening before I myself had heard, through the door, how his lordship had made offers to her, and would have done wantonness with her; *item*, that he had already sought to kiss her once at Coserow; *item*, the troubles which his lordship had formerly brought upon me in the matter of the first-fruits.

Howbeit the Sheriff presently talked me down, saying, that if I had slandered him, an innocent man, in church, from the pulpit, as the whole congregation could bear witness, I should doubtless find it easy to do as much here, before the court; not to mention that a father could, in no case, be a witness for his own child.

But *Dom. Consul* seemed quite confounded, and was silent, and leaned his head on the table, as in deep thought. Meanwhile the impudent constable began to finger his beard from under his arm; and *Dom. Consul* thinking it was a fly, struck at him with his hand, without even looking up; but when he felt the constable his hand, he jumped up and asked him what he wanted? Whereupon the fellow answered, "Oh, only a louse was creeping there, and I would have caught it."

At such impudence his worship was so exceeding wroth that he struck the constable on the mouth, and ordered him, on pain of heavy punishment, to leave the room.

Hereupon he turned to the Sheriff, and cried, angrily, "Why, in the name of all the ten devils, is it thus your lordship keeps the constable in order? and truly, in this whole matter, there is something which passes my understanding." But the Sheriff answered, "Not so; should you not understand it all when you think upon the eels?"

Hereat *Dom. Consul* of a sudden turned ghastly pale, and began to tremble, as it appeared to me, and called the Sheriff aside into another chamber. I have never been able to learn what that about the eels could mean.—

Meanwhile *Dominus Camerarius* Gebhard Wenzel sat biting his pen, and looking furiously—now at me, and now at my child, but said not a word; neither did he answer *Scriba*, who often whispered somewhat into his ear, save by a growl. At length both their worships came back into the chamber together, and *Dom. Consul*, after he and the Sheriff had seated themselves, began to reproach my poor child violently, saying that she had sought to make a disturbance in the worshipful court; that his lordship had shown him the very dog which had scratched his nose, and that, moreover, the fact had been sworn to by the old housekeeper.

(Truly *she* was not likely to betray him, for the old harlot had lived with him for years, and she had a good big boy by him, as will be seen hereafter.)

Item, he said that so many *indicia* of her guilt had come to light, that it was impossible to believe anything she might say; she was therefore to give glory to God, and openly to confess everything, so as to soften her punishment; whereby she might perchance, in pity for her youth, escape with life, etc.

Hereupon he put his spectacles on his nose, and began to cross-question her, during near four hours, from a paper which he held in his hand. These were the main articles, as far as we both can remember:

Quæstio. Whether she could bewitch?—*Responsio.* No; she knew nothing of witchcraft.

Q. Whether she could charm?—*R.* Of that she knew as little.

Q. Whether she had ever been on the Blocksberg?—*R.* That was too far off for her; she knew few hills save the Streckelberg, where she had been very often.

Q. What had she done there?—*R.* She had looked out over the sea, or gathered flowers; *item*, at times carried home an apronful of dry brush-wood.

Q. Whether she had ever called upon the devil there?—*R.* That had never come into her mind.

Q. Whether, then, the devil had appeared to her there, uncalled?—*R.* God defend her from such a thing.

Q. So she could not bewitch?—*R.* No.

Q. What, then, befell Kit Zuter his spotted cow, that it suddenly died in her presence?—*R.* She did not know; and that was a strange question.

Q. Then it would be as strange a question, why Katie Berow her little pig had died?—*R.* Assuredly; she wondered what they would lay to her charge.

Q. Then she had not bewitched them?—*R.* No; God forbid it.

Q. Why, then, if she were innocent, had she promised old Katie another little pig, when her sow should litter?—*R.* She did that out of kind-heartedness. (And hereupon she began to weep bitterly, and said she plainly saw that she had to thank old Lizzie Kolken for all this, inasmuch as she had often threatened her when she would not fulfil all her greedy desires, for she wanted everything that came in her way;

moreover, that Lizzie had gone all about the village when the cattle were bewitched, persuading the people that if only a pure maid pulled a few hairs out of the beasts' tails they would get better. That she pitied them, and knowing herself to be a maid, went to help them; and indeed, at first it cured them, but latterly not.)

Q. What cattle had she cured?—*R.* Zabel his red cow; *item*, Witthan her pig, and old Lizzie's own cow.

Q. Why could she afterwards cure them no more?—*R.* She did not know, but thought—albeit she had no wish to fyle any one—that old Lizzie Kolken, who for many a long year had been in common repute as a witch, had done it all, and bewitched the cows in her name and then charmed them back again, as she pleased, only to bring her to misfortune.

Q. Why, then, had old Lizzie bewitched her own cow, *item*, suffered her own pig to die, if it was she that had made all the disturbance in the village, and could really charm?—*R.* She did not know; but belike there was some one (and here she looked at the Sheriff) who paid her double for it all.

Q. It was in vain that she sought to shift the guilt from off herself; had she not bewitched old Paasch his crop, nay, even her own father's, and caused it to be trodden down by the devil, *item*, conjured all the caterpillars into her father's orchard?—*R.* The question was almost as monstrous as the deed would have been. There sat her father, and his worship might ask him whether she ever had shown herself an undutiful child to him. (Hereupon I would have risen to speak, but *Dom. Consul* suffered me not to open my mouth, but went on with his examination; whereupon I remained silent and downcast.)

Q. Whether she did likewise deny that it was through her malice that the woman Witthan had given birth to a devil's imp, which straightway started up and flew out at the window, so that when the midwife sought for it it had disappeared?—*R.* Truly she did; and indeed she had all the days of her life done good to the people instead of harm, for during the terrible famine she had often taken the bread out of her own mouth to share it among the others, especially the little children. To this the whole parish must needs bear witness, if they were asked; whereas witches and warlocks always did evil and no good to men, as our Lord Jesus taught (Matt. xii.), when the Pharisees blasphemed him, saying that he cast out devils by Beelzebub the prince of the devils; hence his worship might see whether she could in truth be a witch.

Q. He would soon teach her to talk of blasphemies; he saw that her tongue was well hung; but she must answer the questions he asked her, and say nothing more. The question was not *what* good she had done to the poor, but *wherewithal* she had done it; she must now show how she and her father had of a sudden grown so rich that she could go pranking about in silken raiment, whereas she used to be so very poor?

Hereupon she looked towards me, and said, "Father, shall I tell?" Whereupon I answered, "Yes, my child, now thou must openly tell all, even though we thereby become beggars." She accordingly told how, when our need was sorest, she had found the amber, and how much we had gotten for it from the Dutch merchants.

Q. What were the names of these merchants?—*R.* Dieterich von Pehnen and Jakob Kiekebusch; but, as we have heard from a schipper, they since died of the plague at Stettin.

Q. Why had we said nothing of such a godsend?—*R.* Out of fear of our enemy the Sheriff, who, as it seemed, had condemned us to die of hunger, inasmuch as he forbade the parishioners, under pain of heavy displeasure, to supply us with anything, saying, that he would send them a better parson.

Hereupon *Dom. Consul* again looked the Sheriff sharply in the face, who answered that it was true he had said this, seeing that the parson had preached at him in the most scandalous manner from the pulpit; but that he knew very well, at the time, that they were far enough from dying of hunger.

Q. How came so much amber on the Streckelberg? She had best confess at once that the devil had brought it to her.—*R.* She knew nothing about that. But there was a great vein of amber there, as she could show to them all that very day; and she had broken out the amber, and covered the hole well over with fir-twigs, so that none should find it.

Q. When had she gone up the Streckelberg; by day or by night?—*R.* Hereupon she blushed, and for a moment held her peace; but presently made answer, "Sometimes by day, and sometimes by night,"

Q. Why did she hesitate? She had better make a full confession of all, so that her punishment might be less heavy. Had she not there given over old Seden to Satan, who had carried him off through the air, and left only a part of his hair and brains sticking to the top of an oak?—*R.* She did not know whether that was his hair and brains at all, nor how it came there. She went to the tree one morning because she heard a woodpecker cry so dolefully. *Item*, old Paasch, who also had heard the cries, came up with his axe in his hand.

Q. Whether the woodpecker was not the devil himself, who had carried off old Seden?—*R.* She did not know: but he must have been dead some time, seeing that the blood and brains which the lad fetched down out of the tree were quite dried up.

Q. How and when, then, had he come by his death?—*R.* That Almighty God only knew. But Zuter his little girl had said, that one day, while she gathered nettles for the cows under Seden his hedge, she heard the goodman threaten his squint-eyed wife that he would tell the parson that he now knew of a certainty that she had a familiar spirit; whereupon the goodman had presently disappeared. But that this was a child's tale, and she would fyle no one on the strength of it.

Hereupon *Dom. Consul* again looked the Sheriff steadily in the face, and said, "Old Lizzie Kolken must be brought before us this very day": whereto the Sheriff made no answer; and he went on to ask,—

Q. Whether, then, she still maintained that she knew nothing of the devil?—*R*. She maintained it now, and would maintain it until her life's end.

Q. And nevertheless, as had been seen by witnesses, she had been re-baptized by him in the sea in broad daylight.—Here again she blushed, and for a moment was silent.

Q. Why did she blush again? She should for God his sake think on her salvation, and confess the truth.—*R*. She had bathed herself in the sea, seeing that the day was very hot; that was the whole truth.

Q. What chaste maiden would ever bathe in the sea? Thou liest; or wilt thou even yet deny that thou didst bewitch old Paasch his little girl with a white roll?—*R*. Alas! alas! she loved the child as though it were her own little sister; not only had she taught her as well as all the other children without reward, but during the heavy famine she had often taken the bit from her own mouth to put it into the little child's. How, then, could she have wished to do her such grievous harm?

Q. Wilt thou even yet deny?—Reverend Abraham, how stubborn is your child! See here, is this no witches' salve, which the constable fetched out of thy coffer last night? Is this no witches' salve, eh?—*R*. It was a salve for the skin, which would make it soft and white, as the apothecary at Wolgast had told her, of whom she bought it.

Q. Hereupon he shook his head, and went on: How! wilt thou then lastly deny that on this last Saturday the 10th July, at twelve o'clock at night, thou didst on the Streckelberg call upon thy paramour the devil in dreadful words, whereupon he appeared to thee in the shape of a great hairy giant, and clipped thee and toyed with thee?

At these words she grew more pale than a corpse, and tottered so that she was forced to hold by a chair: and I, wretched man, who would readily have sworn away my life for her, when I saw and heard this, my senses forsook me, so that I fell down from the bench, and *Dom. Consul* had to call in the constable to help me up.

When I had come to myself a little, and the impudent varlet saw our common consternation, he cried out, grinning at the court the while, 'Is it all out? is it all out? has she confessed?' Whereupon *Dom. Consul* again showed him the door with a sharp rebuke, as might have been expected; and it is said that this knave played the pimp for the Sheriff, and indeed I think he would not otherwise have been so bold.

Summa: I should well-nigh have perished in my distress, but for the

The Apparition on the Streckelberg

little rose, which by the help of God's mercy kept me up bravely; and now the whole court rose and exhorted my poor fainting child, by the living God, and as she would save her soul, to deny no longer, but in pity to herself and her father to confess the truth.

Hereupon she heaved a deep sigh, and grew as red as she had been pale before, insomuch that even her hand upon the chair was like scarlet, and she did not raise her eyes from the ground.

R. She would now then confess the simple truth, as she saw right well that wicked people had stolen after and watched her at nights. That she had been to seek for amber on the mountain, and that to drive away fear she had, as she was wont to do at her work, recited the Latin *carmen* which her father had made on the illustrious King Gustavus Adolphus: when young Rüdiger of Nienkerken, who had ofttimes been at her father's house and talked of love to her, came out of the coppice, and when she cried out for fear, spoke to her in Latin, and clasped her in his arms. That he wore a great wolf's-skin coat, so that folks should not know him if they met him, and tell the lord his father that he had been on the mountain by night.

At this her confession I fell into sheer despair, and cried in great wrath, "O thou ungodly and undutiful child, after all, then, thou hast a paramour! Did not I forbid thee to go up the mountain by night? What didst thou want on the mountain by night?" and I began to moan and weep and wring my hands, so that *Dom. Consul* even had pity on me, and drew near to comfort me. Meanwhile she herself came towards me, and began to defend herself, saying, with many tears, that she had gone up the mountain by night, against my commands, to get so much amber that she might secretly buy for me, against my birthday, the *Opera Sancti Augustini*, which the Cantor at Wolgast wanted to sell. That it was not her fault that the young lord lay in wait for her one night; and that she would swear to me, by the living God, that nought that was unseemly had happened between them there, and that she was still a maid.

And herewith the first hearing was at end, for after *Dom. Consul* had whispered somewhat into the ear of the Sheriff, he called in the constable again, and bade him keep good watch over *Rea*; *item*, not to leave her at large in her dungeon any longer, but to put her in chains. These words pierced my very heart, and I besought his worship to consider my sacred office, and my ancient noble birth, and not to do me such dishonour as to put my daughter in chains. That I would answer for her to the worshipful court with my own head that she would not escape. Whereupon *Dom. Consul*, after he had gone to look at the dungeon himself, granted me my request, and commanded the constable to leave her as she had been hitherto.

The Nineteenth Chapter

HOW SATAN, BY THE PERMISSION OF THE MOST RIGHTEOUS
GOD, SOUGHT ALTOGETHER TO RUIN US, AND HOW WE LOST
ALL HOPE

The same day, at about three in the afternoon, when I was gone to
Conrad Seep his alehouse to eat something, seeing that it was now nearly
two days since I had tasted aught save my tears, and he had placed
before me some bread and sausage, together with a mug of beer, the
constable came into the room and greeted me from the Sheriff, without,
however, so much as touching his cap, asking whether I would not dine
with his lordship; that his lordship had not remembered till now that I
belike was still fasting, seeing the trial had lasted so long. Hereupon I
made answer to the constable that I already had my dinner before me, as
he saw himself, and desired that his lordship would hold me excused.
Hereat the fellow wondered greatly, and answered; did I not see that
his lordship wished me well, albeit I had preached at him as though he
were a Jew? I should think on my daughter, and be somewhat more
ready to do his lordship's will, whereby peradventure all would yet end
well. For his lordship was not such a rough ass as *Dom. Consul*, and
meant well by my child and me, as beseemed a righteous magistrate.

After I had with some trouble rid myself of this impudent fox, I tried
to eat a bit, but nothing would go down save the beer. I therefore soon
sat and thought again whether I would not lodge with Conrad Seep, so as
to be always near my child; *item*, whether I should not hand over my
poor misguided flock to M. Vigelius, the pastor of Benz, for such time as
the Lord still should prove me. In about an hour I saw through the
window how that an empty coach drove to the castle, and the Sheriff
and *Dom. Consul* straightway stepped thereinto with my child; *item*,
the constable climbed up behind. Hereupon I left everything on the
table and ran to the coach, asking humbly whither they were about to
take my poor child; and when I heard they were going to the Streckelberg
to look after the amber, I begged them to take me also, and to suffer me
to sit by my child, for who could tell how much longer I might yet sit
by her! This was granted to me, and on the way the Sheriff ordered me
to take up my abode in the castle and to dine at his table as often as I
pleased, and that he would, moreover, send my child her meat from his
own table. For that he had a Christian heart, and well knew that we were
to forgive our enemies. But I refused his kindness with humble thanks,
as my child did also, seeing we were not yet so poor that we could not
maintain ourselves. As we passed by the watermill the ungodly varlet
there again thrust his head out of a hole and pulled wry faces at my child;
but, dear reader, he got something to remember it by; for the Sheriff

beckoned to the constable to fetch the fellow out, and after he had reproached him with the tricks he had twice played my child, the constable had to take the coachman his new whip and to give him fifty lashes, which, God knows, were not laid on with a feather. He bellowed like a bull, which, however, no one heard for the noise of the mill-wheels, and when at last he did as though he could not stir, we left him lying on the ground and went on our way.

As we drove through Uekeritze a number of people flocked together, but were quiet enough, save one fellow who, *salvâ veniâ*, mocked at us with unseemly gestures in the midst of the road when he saw us coming. The constable had to jump down again, but could not catch him, and the others would not give him up, but pretended that they had only looked at our coach and had not marked him. May be this was true! And I am therefore inclined to think that it was Satan himself who did it to mock at us; for mark, for God's sake, what happened to us on the Streckelberg! Alas! through the delusions of the foul fiend, we could not find the spot where we had dug for the amber. For when we came to where we thought it must be, a huge hill of sand had been heaped up as by a whirlwind, and the fir-twigs which my child had covered over it were gone. She was near falling in a swound when she saw this, and wrung her hands and cried out with her Saviour, "My God, my God! why hast thou forsaken me!"

Howbeit, the constable and the coachman were ordered to dig, but not one bit of amber was to be found, even so big as a grain of corn, whereupon *Dom. Consul* shook his head and violently upbraided my child. And when I answered that Satan himself, as it seemed, had filled up the hollow in order to bring us altogether into his power, the constable was ordered to fetch a long stake out of the coppice which we might thrust still deeper into the sand. But no hard *objectum* was anywhere to be felt, notwithstanding the Sheriff, *Dom. Consul*, and myself in my anguish did try everywhere with the stake.

Hereupon my child besought her judges to go with her to Coserow, where she still had much amber in her coffer which she had found here, and that if it were the gift of the devil it would all be changed, since it was well known that all the presents the devil makes to witches straightway turn to mud and ashes.

But, God be merciful to us, God be merciful to us! when we returned to Coserow, amid the wonderment of all the village, and my daughter went to her coffer, the things therein were all tossed about, and the amber gone. Hereupon she shrieked so loud that it would have softened a stone, and cried out: "The wicked constable hath done this! when he fetched the salve out of my coffer, he stole the amber from me, unhappy maid." But the constable, who stood by, would have torn her hair, and cried out, "Thou witch, thou damned witch, is it not enough that thou hast belied my lord, but thou must now belie me too?" But *Dom. Consul* forbade him, so that he did not dare lay hands upon her. *Item*, all the money was gone which she had hoarded up from the amber she had privately sold, and which she thought already came to about ten florins.

But the gown which she had worn at the arrival of the most illustrious King Gustavus Adolphus, as well as the golden chain with his effigy which he had given her, I had locked up, as though it were a relic, in the chest in the vestry, among the altar and pulpit cloths, and there we found them still; and when I excused myself therefore, saying that I had thought to have saved them up for her there against her bridal day, she gazed with fixed and glazed eyes into the box, and cried out, "Yes, against the day when I shall be burnt; O Jesu, Jesu, Jesu!" Hereat *Dom. Consul* shuddered and said, "See how thou still dost smite thyself with thine own words! For the sake of God and thy salvation,' confess, for if thou knowest thyself to be innocent, how, then, canst thou think that thou wilt be burnt?" But she still looked him fixedly in the face, and cried aloud in Latin, "*Innocentia, quid est innocentia? Ubi libido dominatur, innocentia leve præsidium est.*"

Hereupon *Dom. Consul* again shuddered, so that his beard wagged, and said, "What, dost thou indeed know Latin? Where didst thou learn the Latin?" And when I answered this question as well as I was able for sobbing, he shook his head and said, "I never in my life heard of a woman that knew Latin." Upon this he knelt down before her coffer, and turned over everything therein, drew it away from the wall, and when he found nothing he bade us show him her bed, and did the same with that. This, at length, vexed the Sheriff, who asked him whether they should not drive back again, seeing that night was coming on. But he answered, "Nay, I must first have the written paction which Satan has given her"; and he went on with his search until it was almost dark. But they found nothing at all, although *Dom. Consul*, together with the constable, passed over no hole or corner, even in the kitchen and cellar. Hereupon he got up again into the coach, muttering to himself, and bade my daughter sit so that she should not look upon him.

And now we once more had the same *spectaculum* with the accursed old witch Lizzie Kolken, seeing that she again sat at her door as we drove by, and began to sing at the top of her voice, "We praise thee, O Lord." But she screeched like a stuck pig, so that *Dom. Consul* was amazed thereat, and when he had heard who she was, he asked the Sheriff whether he would not that she should be seized by the constable and be tied behind the coach to run after it, as we had no room for her elsewhere; for that he had often been told that all old women who had red squinting eyes and sharp voices were witches, not to mention the suspicious things which *Rea* had declared against her. But he answered that he could not do this, seeing that old Lizzie was a woman in good repute and fearing God as *Dom. Consul* might learn for himself; but that, nevertheless, he had had her summoned for the morrow, together with the other witnesses.

Yea, in truth, an excellently devout and worthy woman!—for scarcely were we out of the village, when so fearful a storm of thunder, lightning, wind, and hail burst over our heads, that the corn all around us was beaten down as with a flail, and the horses before the coach were quite maddened; however, it did not last long. But my poor child had to bear all the blame again, inasmuch as *Dom. Consul* thought that it was not old Lizzie, which, nevertheless, was as clear as the sun at noonday! but my poor daughter who brewed the storm;—for, beloved reader, what could it have profited her, even if she had known the black art? This, however, did not strike *Dom. Consul*, and Satan, by the permission of the all-righteous God, was presently to use us still worse; for just as we got to the Master's Dam, he came flying over us in the shape of a stork, and dropped a frog so exactly over us that it fell into my daughter her lap: she gave a shrill scream, but I whispered her to sit still, and that I would secretly throw the frog away by one leg.

But the constable had seen it, and cried out, "Hey, sirs! hey, look at the cursed witch! what has the devil just thrown into her lap?" Whereupon the Sheriff and *Dom. Consul* looked round and saw the frog, which crawled in her lap, and the constable after he had blown upon it three times, took it up and showed it to their lordships. Hereat *Dom. Consul* began to spew, and when he had done, he ordered the coachman to stop, got down from the coach, and said we might drive home, that he felt qualmish, and would go afoot and see if he got better. But first he privately whispered to the constable, which, howbeit, we heard right well, that when he got home he should lay my poor child in chains, but not so as to hurt her much; to which neither she nor I could answer save by tears and sobs. But the Sheriff had heard it too, and when his worship was out of sight he began to stroke my child her cheeks from behind her back, telling her to be easy, as he also had a word to say in the matter, and that the constable should not lay her in chains. But that she must leave off being so hard to him as she had been hitherto, and come and sit on the seat beside him, that he might privately give her some good advice as to what was to be done. To this she answered, with many tears, that she wished to sit only by her father, as she knew not how much longer she might sit by him at all; and she begged for nothing more save that his lordship would leave her in peace. But this he would not do, but pinched her back and sides with his knees; and as she bore with this, seeing that there was no help for it, he waxed bolder, taking it for a good sign.

Meanwhile *Dom. Consul* called out close behind us (for being frightened he ran just after the coach), "Constable, constable, come here quick; here lies a hedgehog in the midst of the road!" whereupon the constable jumped down from the coach.

This made the Sheriff still bolder; and at last my child rose up and said, "Father, let us also go afoot; I can no longer guard myself from him here behind!" But he pulled her down again by her clothes, and cried out angrily, "Wait, thou wicked witch, I will help thee to go afoot if thou art so wilful; thou shalt be chained to the block this very night." Whereupon she answered, "Do you do that which you cannot help doing; the righteous God, it is to be hoped, will one day do unto you what He cannot help doing."

Meanwhile we had reached the castle, and scarcely were we got out of the coach, when *Dom. Consul*, who had run till he was all of a sweat, came up together with the constable, and straightway gave over my child into his charge, so that I had scarce time to bid her farewell. I was left standing on the floor below, wringing my hands in the dark, and hearkened whither they were leading her, inasmuch as I had not the heart to follow, when *Dom. Consul*, who had stepped into a room with the Sheriff, looked out at the door again, and called after the constable to bring *Rea* once more before them. And when he had done so, and I went into the room with them, *Dom. Consul* held a letter in his hand, and, after spitting thrice, he began thus: "Wilt thou still deny, thou stubborn witch? Hear what the old knight, Hans von Nienkerken, writes to the court!" Whereupon he read out to us that his son was so disturbed by the tale the accursed witch had told of him that he had fallen sick from that very hour, and that he, the father, was not much better. That his son Rüdiger had indeed at times, when he went that way, been to see Pastor Schweidler, whom he had first known upon a journey; but that he swore that he wished he might turn black if he had ever used any folly or jesting with the cursed devil's whore his daughter; much less ever been with her by night on the Streckelberg, or embraced her there.

At this dreadful news we both (I mean my child and I) fell down in a swound together, seeing that we had rested our last hopes on the young lord; and I know not what further happened. For when I came to myself, my host, Conrad Seep, was standing over me, holding a funnel between my teeth, through which he ladled some warm beer down my throat, and I never felt more wretched in all my life; insomuch that Master Seep had to undress me like a little child, and to help me into bed.

The Twentieth Chapter

OF THE MALICE OF THE GOVERNOR AND OF OLD LIZZIE:
ITEM, OF THE EXAMINATION OF WITNESSES

The next morning my hairs, which till *datum* had been mingled with grey, were white as snow, albeit the Lord otherwise blessed me wondrously. For near daybreak a nightingale flew into the elder-bush beneath my window, and sang so sweetly that straightway I thought it must be a good angel. For after I had hearkened a while to it, I was all at once able again to pray, which since last Sunday I could not do; and the spirit of our Lord Jesus Christ began to speak within me, "Abba, Father"; and straightway I was of good cheer, trusting that God would once more be gracious unto me his wretched child; and when I had given him thanks for such great mercy, I fell into a refreshing slumber, and slept so long that the blessed sun stood high in the heavens when I awoke.

And seeing that my heart was still of good cheer, I sat up in my bed, and sang with a loud voice, "Be not dismayed, thou little flock": whereupon Master Seep came into the room, thinking I had called him. But he stood reverently waiting till I had done; and after marvelling at my snow-white hair, he told me it was already seven; *item*, that half my congregation, among others my ploughman, Claus Neels, were already assembled in his house to bear witness that day. When I heard this, I bade mine host forthwith send Claus to the castle, to ask when the court would open, and he brought word back that no one knew, seeing that *Dom. Consul* was already gone that morning to Mellenthin to see old Nienkerken, and was not yet come back. This message gave me good courage, and I asked the fellow whether he also had come to bear witness against my poor child? To which he answered, "Nay, I know nought save good of her, and I would give the fellows their due, only——"

These words surprised me, and I vehemently urged him to open his heart to me. But he began to weep, and at last said that he knew nothing. Alas! he knew but too much, and could then have saved my poor child if he had willed. But from fear of the torture he held his peace, as he since owned; and I will here relate what had befallen him that very morning.

He had set out betimes that morning, so as to be alone with his sweetheart, who was to go along with him (she is Steffen of Zempin his daughter, not farmer Steffen, but the lame gouty Steffen), and had got to Pudgla about five, where he found no one in the ale-house save old Lizzie Kolken, who straightway hobbled up to the castle; and when his sweetheart was gone home again, time hung heavy on his hands, and he climbed over the wall into the castle garden, where he threw himself on his face behind a hedge to sleep. But before long the Sheriff came with old Lizzie, and after they had looked all round and seen no one, they went into an arbour close by him, and conversed as follows:—

Ille. Now that they were alone together, what did she want of him?

Illa. She came to get the money for the witchcraft she had contrived in the village.

Ille. Of what use had all this witchcraft been to him? My child, so far from being frightened, defied him more and more; and he doubted whether he should ever have his will of her.

Illa. He should only have patience; when she was laid upon the rack she would soon learn to be fond.

Ille. That might be, but till then she (Lizzie) should get no money.

Illa. What! Must she then do his cattle a mischief?

Ille. Yes, if she felt chilly, and wanted a burning fagot to warm her *podex*, she had better. Moreover, he thought that she had bewitched him, seeing that his desire for the parson's daughter was such as he had never felt before.

Illa. (Laughing.) He had said the same thing some thirty years ago, when he first came after her.

Ille. Ugh! thou old baggage, don't remind me of such things, but see to it that you get three witnesses, as I told you before, or else methinks they will rack your old joints for you after all.

Illa. She had the three witnesses ready, and would leave the rest to him. But that if she were racked she would reveal all she knew.

Ille. She should hold her ugly tongue, and go to the devil.

Illa. So she would, but first she must have her money.

Ille. She should have no money till he had had his will of my daughter.

Illa. He might at least pay her for her little pig which she herself had bewitched to death, in order that she might not get into evil repute.

Ille. She might choose one when his pigs were driven by, and say she had paid for it. Hereupon, said my Claus, the pigs were driven by, and one ran into the garden, the door being open, and as the swineherd followed it, they parted; but the witch muttered to herself, "Now help, devil, help, that I may—" but he heard no further.

The cowardly fellow, however, hid all this from me, as I have said above, and only said, with tears, that he knew nothing. I believed him, and sat down at the window to see when *Dom. Consul* should return; and when I saw him I rose and went to the castle, where the constable, who was already there with my child, met me before the judgment-chamber. Alas! she looked more joyful than I had seen her for a long time, and smiled at me with her sweet little mouth: but when she saw my snow-white hair, she gave a cry, which made *Dom. Consul* throw open the door of the judgment-chamber, and say, "Ha, ha! thou knowest well what news I have brought thee; come in, thou stubborn devil's brat!" Whereupon we stepped into the chamber to him, and he lift up his voice and spake to me, after he had sat down with the Sheriff, who was by.

He said that yestereven, after he had caused me to be carried like one dead to Master Seep his ale-house, and that my stubborn child had been brought to life again, he had once more adjured her, to the utmost of his power, no longer to lie before the face of the living God, but to confess the truth; whereupon she had borne herself very unruly, and had wrung her hands and wept and sobbed, and at last answered that the young *nobilis* never could have said such things, but that his father must have written them, who hated her, as she had plainly seen when the Swedish king was at Coserow. That he, *Dom. Consul*, had indeed doubted the truth of this at the time, but as a just judge had gone that morning right early with the *scriba* to Mellenthin, to question the young lord himself.

That I might now see myself what horrible malice was in my daughter. For that the old knight had led him to his son's bedside, who still lay sick from vexation, and that he had confirmed all his father had written, and had cursed the scandalous she-devil (as he called my daughter) for seeking to rob him of his knightly honour. "What sayest thou now?" he continued; "wilt thou still deny thy great wickedness? See here the *protocollum* which the young lord hath signed *manu propriâ!*" But the wretched maid had meanwhile fallen on the ground again, and the constable had no sooner seen this than he ran into the kitchen, and came back with a burning brimstone match, which he was about to hold under her nose.

But I hindered him, and sprinkled her face with water, so that she opened her eyes, and raised herself up by a table. She then stood a while, without saying a word or regarding my sorrow. At last she smiled sadly, and spake thus: That she clearly saw how true was that spoken by the Holy Ghost, "Cursed be the man that trusteth in man"; and that the faithlessness of the young lord had surely broken her poor heart if the all-merciful God had not graciously prevented him, and sent her a dream that night, which she would tell, not hoping to persuade the judges, but to raise up the white head of her poor father.

"After I had sat and watched all the night," quoth she, "towards morning I heard a nightingale sing in the castle-garden so sweetly that my eyes closed, and I slept. Then methought I was a lamb, grazing quietly in my meadow at Coserow. Suddenly the Sheriff jumped over the hedge and turned into a wolf, who seized me in his jaws, and ran with me towards the Streckelberg, where he had his lair. I, poor little lamb, trembled and bleated in vain, and saw death before my eyes, when he laid me down before his lair, where lay the she-wolf and her young. But behold a hand, like the hand of a man, straightway came out of the bushes and touched the wolves, each one with one finger, and crushed them so that nought was left of them save a grey powder. Hereupon the hand took me up, and carried me back to my meadow."

Only think, beloved reader, how I felt when I heard all this, and about the dear nightingale too, which no one can doubt to have been the servant of God. I clasped my child with many tears, and told her what had happened to me, and we both won such courage and confidence as we had never yet felt, to the wonderment of *Dom. Consul*, as it seemed; but the Sheriff turned as pale as a sheet when she stepped towards their worships and said, "And now do with me as you will, the lamb fears not, for she is in the hands of the Good Shepherd!" Meanwhile *Dom Camerarius* came in with the *scriba*, but was terrified as he chanced to touch my daughter's apron with the skirts of his coat; and stood and scraped at his coat as a woman scrapes a fish. At last, after he had spat out thrice, he asked the court whether it would not begin to examine witnesses, seeing that all the people had been waiting some time both in the castle and at the ale-house. Hereunto they agreed, and the constable was ordered to guard my child in his room, until it should please the court to summon her. I therefore went with her, but, we had to endure much from the impudent rogue, seeing he was not ashamed to lay his arm round my child her shoulders and to ask for a kiss *in meâ presentiâ*. But, before I could get out a word, she tore herself from him, and said, "Ah, thou wicked knave, must I complain of thee to the court; hast thou forgotten what thou hast already done to me?" To which, he answered, laughing, "See, see! how coy"; and still sought to persuade her to be more willing, and not to forget her own interest; for that he meant as well by her as his master; she might believe it or not; with many other scandalous words besides which I have forgot; for I took my child upon my knees and laid my head on her neck, and we sat and wept.

The Twenty-first Chapter

DE CONFRONTATIONE TESTIUM

When we were summoned before the court again, the whole court was full of people, and some shuddered when they saw us, but others wept; my child told the same tale as before. But when our old Ilse was called, who sat on a bench behind, so that we had not seen her, the strength wherewith the Lord had gifted her was again at an end, and she repeated the words of our Saviour, "He that eateth bread with me hath lift up his heel against me": and she held fast by my chair. Old Ilse, too, could not walk straight for very grief, nor could she speak for tears, but she twisted and wound herself about before the court like a woman in travail. But when *Dom. Consul* threatened that the constable should presently help her to her words, she testified that my child had very often got up in the night and called aloud upon the foul fiend.

Q. Whether she had ever heard Satan answer her?—*R.* She never had heard him at all.

Q. Whether she had perceived that *Rea* had a familiar spirit, and in what shape? She should think upon her oath, and speak the truth.—*R.* She had never seen one.

Q. Whether she had ever heard her fly up the chimney?—*R.* Nay, she had always gone softly out at the door.

Q. Whether she never at mornings had missed her broom or pitch-fork?—*R.* Once the broom was gone, but she had found it again behind the stove, and may be left it there herself by mistake.

Q. Whether she had never heard *Rea* cast a spell or wish harm to this or that person?—*R.* No, never; she had always wished her neighbours nothing but good, and even in the time of bitter famine had taken the bread out of her own mouth to give it to others.

Q. Whether she did not know the salve which had been found in *Rea* her coffer?—*R.* Oh, yes! her young mistress had brought it back from Wolgast for her skin, and had once given her some when she had chapped hands, and it had done her a vast deal of good.

Q. Whether she had anything further to say?—*R.* No, nothing but good.

Hereupon my man Claus Neels was called up. He also came forward in tears, but answered every question with a "Nay," and at last testified that he had never seen nor heard anything bad of my child, and knew nought of her doings by night, seeing that he slept in the stable with the horses; and that he firmly believed that evil folks—and here he looked at old Lizzie—had brought this misfortune upon her, and that she was quite innocent.

When it came to the turn of this old limb of Satan, who was to be the chief witness, my child again declared that she would not accept old Lizzie's testimony against her, and called upon the court for justice, for that she had hated her from her youth up, and had been longer by habit and repute a witch than she herself.

But the old hag cried out, "God forgive thee thy sins; the whole village knows that I am a devout woman, and one serving the Lord in all things"; whereupon she called up old Zuter Witthahn and my church-warden Claus Bulk, who bore witness hereto. But old Paasch stood and shook his head; nevertheless when my child said, "Paasch, wherefore dost thou shake thy head?" he started, and answered, "Oh, nothing!"

Howbeit, *Dom. Consul* likewise perceived this, and asked him, whether he had any charge to bring against old Lizzie; if so, he should give glory to God, and state the same; *item*, it was competent to every one so to do; indeed the court required of him to speak out all he knew.

But from fear of the old dragon, all were still as mice, so that you might have heard the flies buzz about the inkstand. I then stood up, wretched as I was, and stretched out my arms over my amazed and faint-hearted people and spake, "Can ye thus crucify me together with my poor child? Have I deserved this at your hands? Speak, then; alas, will none speak?" I heard, indeed, how several wept aloud, but not one spake; and hereupon my poor child was forced to submit.

And the malice of the old hag was such that she not only accused my child of the most horrible witchcraft, but also reckoned to a day when she had given herself up to Satan to rob her of her maiden honour; and she said that Satan had, without doubt, then defiled her when she could no longer heal the cattle, and when they all died. Hereupon my child said nought, save that she cast down her eyes and blushed deep, for shame at such filthiness; and to the other blasphemous slander which the old hag uttered with many tears, namely, that my daughter had given up her (Lizzie's) husband, body and soul, to Satan, she answered as she had done before. But when the old hag came to her re-baptism in the sea, and gave out that while seeking for strawberries in the coppice she had recognised my child's voice, and stolen towards her, and perceived these devil's doings, my child fell in smiling, and answered, "Oh, thou evil woman! how couldst thou hear my voice speaking down by the sea, being thyself in the forest upon the mountain? surely thou liest, seeing that the murmur of the waves would make that impossible." This angered the old dragon, and seeking to get out of the blunder she fell still deeper into it, for she said, "I saw thee move thy lips, and from that I knew that thou didst call upon thy paramour the devil!" for my child straight-way replied, "Oh, thou ungodly woman! thou saidst thou wert in the forest when thou didst hear my voice; how then up in the forest couldst thou see whether I, who was below by the water, moved my lips or not?"——

Such contradictions amazed even *Dom. Consul*, and he began to threaten the old hag with the rack if she told such lies; whereupon she answered and said, "List, then, whether I lie! When she went naked into the water she had no mark on her body, but when she came out again I saw that she had between her breasts a mark the size of a silver penny, whence I perceived that the devil had given it her, although I had not seen him about her, nor, indeed, had I seen any one, either spirit or child of man, for she seemed to be quite alone."

Hereupon the Sheriff jumped up from his seat, and cried, "Search must straightway be made for this mark"; whereupon *Dom. Consul* answered, "Yea, but not by us, but by two women of good repute," for he would not hearken to what my child said, that it was a mole, and that she had had it from her youth up, wherefore the constable his wife was sent for, and *Dom. Consul* muttered somewhat into her ear, and as prayers and tears were of no avail, my child was forced to go with her. Howbeit, she obtained this favour, that old Lizzie Kolken was not to follow her, as she would have done, but our old maid Ilse. I, too, went in my sorrow, seeing that I knew not what the women might do to her. She wept bitterly as they undressed her, and held her hands over her eyes for very shame.

Well-a-day, her body was just as white as my departed wife's; although in her childhood, as I remember, she was very yellow, and I saw with amazement the mole between her breasts, whereof I had never heard aught before. But she suddenly screamed violently and started back, seeing that the constable his wife, when nobody watched her, had run a needle into the mole, so deep that the red blood ran down over her breasts. I was sorely angered thereat, but the woman said that she had done it by order of the judge, which, indeed, was true; for when we came back into court, and the Sheriff asked how it was, she testified that there was a mark of the size of a silver penny, of a yellowish colour, but that it had feeling, seeing that *Rea* had screamed aloud when she had, unperceived, driven a needle therein. Meanwhile, however, *Dom. Camerarius* suddenly rose, and, stepping up to my child, drew her eyelids asunder, and cried out, beginning to tremble, "Behold the sign which never fails": whereupon the whole court started to their feet, and looked at the little spot under her right eyelid, which in truth had been left there by a stye, but this none would believe. *Dom. Consul* now said, "See, Satan hath marked thee on body and soul! and thou dost still continue to lie unto the Holy Ghost; but it shall not avail thee, and thy punishment will only be the heavier. Oh, thou shameless woman! thou hast refused to accept the testimony of old Lizzie; wilt thou also refuse that of these people, who have all heard thee on the mountain call upon the devil thy paramour, and seen him appear in the likeness of a hairy giant, and kiss and caress thee?"

Hereupon old Paasch, goodwife Witthahn, and Zuter came forward and bare witness, that they had seen this happen about midnight, and that on this declaration they would live and die; that old Lizzie had awakened them one Saturday night about eleven o'clock, had given them a can of beer, and persuaded them to follow the parson's daughter privately, and to see what she did upon the mountain. At first they refused but in order to get at the truth about the witchcraft in the village, they had at last, after a devout prayer, consented, and had followed her in God's name.

They had soon through the bushes seen the witch in the moonshine; she seemed to dig, and spake in some strange tongue the while, whereupon the grim arch-fiend suddenly appeared, and fell upon her neck. Hereupon they ran away in consternation, but, by the help of the Almighty God, on whom from the very first they had set their faith, they were preserved from the power of the Evil One. For, notwithstanding he had turned round on hearing a rustling in the bushes, he had had no power to harm them.

Finally, it was even charged to my child as a crime, that she had fainted on the road from Coserow to Pudgla, and none would believe that this had been caused by vexation at old Lizzie her singing, and not from a bad conscience, as stated by the judge.

When all the witnesses had been examined, *Dom. Consul* asked her whether she had brewed the storm, what was the meaning of the frog that dropped into her lap, *item*, the hedgehog which lay directly in his path? To all of which she answered, that she had caused the one as little as she knew of the other. Whereupon *Dom. Consul* shook his head, and asked her, last of all, whether she would have an advocate, or trust entirely in the good judgment of the court. To this she gave answer that she would by all means have an advocate. Wherefore I sent my ploughman, Claus Neels, the next day to Wolgast to fetch the *Syndicus* Michelsen, who is a worthy man, and in whose house I have been many times when I went to the town, seeing that he courteously invited me.

I must also note here that at this time my old Ilse came back to live with me; for after the witnesses were gone she stayed behind in the chamber, and came boldly up to me, and besought me to suffer her once more to serve her old master and her dear young mistress; for that now she had saved her poor soul, and confessed all she knew. Wherefore she could no longer bear to see her old masters in such woeful plight, without so much as a mouthful of victuals, seeing that she had heard that old wife Seep, who had till *datum* prepared the food for me and my child, often let the porridge burn; *item*, over-salted the fish and the meat. Moreover, that I was so weakened by age and misery, that I needed help and support, which she would faithfully give me, and was ready to sleep in the stable, if needs must be; that she wanted no wages for it, I was only not to turn her away. Such kindness made my daughter to weep, and she said to me, "Behold, father, the good folks come back to us again; think you, then, that the good angels will forsake us for ever? I thank thee, old Ilse; thou shalt indeed prepare my food for me, and always bring it as far as the prison-door, if thou mayest come no further; and mark, then, I pray thee, what the constable does therewith."

This the maid promised to do, and from this time forth took up her abode in the stable. May God repay her at the day of judgment for what she then did for me and for my poor child!

The Twenty-second Chapter

HOW THE SYNDICUS DOM. MICHELSEN ARRIVED, AND PREPARED HIS DEFENCE OF MY POOR CHILD

The next day, at about three o'clock P.M., *Dom. Syndicus* came driving up, and got out of his coach at my inn. He had a huge bag full of books with him, but was not so friendly in his manner as was usual with him, but very grave and silent. And after he had saluted me in my own room, and had asked how it was possible for my child to have come to such misfortune, I related to him the whole affair, whereat, however, he only shook his head. On my asking him whether he would not see my child that same day, he answered, "Nay"; he would rather first study the *acta*. And after he had eaten of some wild duck which my old Ilse had roasted for him, he would tarry no longer, but straightway went up to the castle, whence he did not return till the following afternoon. His manner was not more friendly now than at his first coming, and I followed him with sighs when he asked me to lead him to my daughter. As we went in with the constable, and I, for the first time, saw my child in chains before me—she who in her whole life had never hurt a worm—I again felt as though I should die for very grief. But she smiled and cried out to *Dom. Syndicus*, "Are you indeed the good angel who will cause my chains to fall from my hands, as was done of yore to St. Peter?" To which he replied, with a sigh, "May the Almighty God grant it"; and as, save the chair whereon my child sat against the wall, there was none other in the dungeon (which was a filthy and stinking hole, wherein were more wood-lice than ever I saw in my life), *Dom. Syndicus* and I sat down on her bed, which had been left for her at my prayer; and he ordered the constable to go his ways until he should call him back. Hereupon he asked my child what she had to say in her justification; and she had not gone far in her defence when I perceived, from the shadow at the door, that some one must be standing without. I therefore went quickly to the door, which was half open, and found the impudent constable, who stood there to listen. This so angered *Dom. Syndicus* that he snatched up his staff in order to hasten his going, but the arch-rogue took to his heels as soon as he saw this. My child took this opportunity to tell her worshipful *defensor* what she had suffered from the impudence of this fellow, and to beg that some other constable might be set over her, seeing that this one had come to her last night again with evil designs, so that she at last had shrieked aloud and beaten him on the head with her chains; whereupon he had left her. This *Dom. Syndicus* promised to obtain for her; but with regard to the *defensio*, wherewith she now went on, he thought it would be better to make no further mention of the *impetus* which the Sheriff had made on her chastity. "For," said he, "as the princely central court at Wolgast has to give sentence upon thee, this statement would do thee far more harm than good, seeing that the *præses* thereof is a cousin of the Sheriff, and ofttimes goes a-hunting with him. Besides, thou being charged with a capital crime hast no *fides*, especially as thou canst bring no witnesses against him. Thou couldst, therefore, gain no belief even if thou didst confirm the charge on the rack, wherefrom, moreover, I am come hither to save thee by my *defensio*." These reasons seemed sufficient to us both, and we resolved to leave vengeance to Almighty God, who seeth in secret, and to complain of our wrongs to him, as we might not complain to men. But all my daughter said about old Lizzie—*item*, of the good report wherein she herself had, till now, stood with everybody—he said he would write down, and add thereunto as much and as well of his own as he was able, so as, by the help of Almighty God, to save her from the torture. That she was to make herself easy and commend herself to God; within two days he hoped to have his *defensio* ready and to read it to her. And now, when he called the constable back again, the fellow did not come, but sent his wife to lock the prison, and I took leave of my child with many tears: *Dom. Syndicus* told the woman the while what her impudent rogue of a husband had done, that she might let him hear more of it. Then he sent the woman away again and came back to my daughter, saying that he had forgotten to ascertain whether she really knew the Latin tongue, and that she was to say her *defensio* over again in Latin, if she was able. Hereupon she began and went on therewith for a quarter of an hour or more, in such wise that not only *Dom. Syndicus* but I myself also was amazed, seeing that she did not stop for a single word, save the word "hedgehog," which we both had forgotten at the moment when she asked us what it was.—*Summa. Dom. Syndicus* grew far more gracious when she had finished her oration, and took leave of her, promising that he would set to work forthwith.

After this I did not see him again till the morning of the third day at ten o'clock, seeing that he sat at work in a room at the castle, which the Sheriff had given him, and also ate there, as he sent me word by old Ilse when she carried him his breakfast next day.

At the above-named time he sent the new constable for me, who, meanwhile, had been fetched from Uzdom at his desire. For the Sheriff was exceeding wroth when he heard that the impudent fellow had attempted my child in the prison, and cried out in a rage, "S'death, and 'ouns, I'll mend thy coaxing!" Whereupon he gave him a sound thrashing with a dog-whip he held in his hand, to make sure that she should be at peace from him.

But, alas! the new constable was even worse than the old, as will be shown hereafter. His name was Master Köppner, and he was a tall fellow with a grim face, and a mouth so wide that at every word he said the spittle ran out at the corners, and stuck in his long beard like soap-suds, so that my child had an especial fear and loathing of him. Moreover, on all occasions he seemed to laugh in mockery and scorn, as he did when he opened the prison-door to us, and saw my poor child sitting in her grief and distress. But he straightway left us without waiting to be told, whereupon *Dom. Syndicus* drew his defence out of his pocket, and read it to us; we have remembered the main points thereof, and I will recount them here, but most of the *auctores* we have forgotten.

1. He began by saying that my daughter had ever till now stood in good repute, as not only the whole village, but even my servants bore witness; *ergo*, she could not be a witch, inasmuch as the Saviour hath said, "A good tree cannot bring forth evil fruit, neither can a corrupt tree bring forth good fruit" (Matt. vii.).

2. With regard to the witchcraft in the village, that belike was the contrivance of old Lizzie, seeing that she bore a great hatred towards *Rea*, and had long been in evil repute, for that the parishioners dared not to speak out, only from fear of the old witch; wherefore Zuter, her little girl, must be examined, who had heard old Lizzie her goodman tell her she had a familiar spirit, and that he would tell it to the parson; for that notwithstanding the above-named was but a child, still it was written in Psalm viii., "Out of the mouth of babes and sucklings hast thou ordained strength . . ."; and the Saviour himself appealed (Matt. xxi.) to the testimony of little children.

3. Furthermore, old Lizzie might have bewitched the crops, *item*, the fruit-trees, inasmuch as none could believe that *Rea*, who had ever shown herself a dutiful child, would have bewitched her own father's corn, or made caterpillars come on his trees; for no one, according to Scripture, can serve two masters.

Item, she (old Lizzie) might very well have been the woodpecker that was seen by *Rea* and old Paasch on the Streckelberg, and herself have given over her goodman to the Evil One for fear of the parson, inasmuch as Spitzel *De Expugnatione Orci* asserts; *item*, the *Malleus Maleficarum* proves beyond doubt that the wicked children of Satan ofttimes change themselves into all manner of beasts, as the foul fiend himself likewise seduced our first parents in the shape of a serpent (Gen. iii.).

5. That old Lizzie had most likely made the wild weather when *Dom. Consul* was coming home with *Rea* from the Streckelberg, seeing

it was impossible that *Rea* could have done it, as she was sitting in the coach, whereas witches when they raise storms always stand in the water, and throw it over their heads backwards; *item*, beat the stones soundly with a stick, as Hannold relates. Wherefore she too, may be, knew best about the frog and the hedgehog.

6. That *Rea* was erroneòusly charged with that as a *crimen* which ought rather to serve as her justification, namely, her sudden riches. For the *Malleus Maleficarum* expressly says that a witch can never grow rich, seeing that Satan, to do dishonour to God, always buys them for a vile price, so that they should not betray themselves by their riches. Wherefore that as *Rea* had grown rich, she could not have got her wealth from the foul fiend, but it must be true that she had found amber on the mountain; that the spells of old Lizzie might have been the cause why they could not find the vein of amber again, or that the sea might have washed away the cliff below, as often happens, whereupon the top had slipped down, so that only a *miraculum naturale* had taken place. The proof which he brought forward from Scripture we have quite forgotten, seeing it was but middling.

7. With regard to her re-baptism, the old hag had said herself that she had not seen the devil or any other spirit or man about *Rea*, wherefore she might in truth have been only naturally bathing, in order to greet the King of Sweden next day, seeing that the weather was hot, and that bathing was not of itself sufficient to impair the modesty of a maiden. For that she had as little thought any would see her as Bathsheba the daughter of Eliam, and wife of Uriah the Hittite, who in like manner did bathe herself, as is written (2 Sam. xi. 2), without knowing that David could see her. Neither could her mark be a mark given by Satan, inasmuch as there was feeling therein; *ergo*, it must be a natural mole, and it was a lie that she had it not before bathing. Moreover, that on this point the old harlot was nowise to be believed, seeing that she had fallen from one contradiction into another about it, as stated in the *acta*.

8. Neither was it just to accuse *Rea* of having bewitched Paasch his little daughter; for as old Lizzie was going in and out of the room, nay, even sat herself down on the little girl her belly when the pastor went to see her, it most likely was that wicked woman (who was known to have a great spite against *Rea*) that contrived the spell through the power of the foul fiend, and by permission of the all-just God; for that Satan was "a liar and the father of it," as our Lord Christ says (John viii.).

9. With regard to the appearance of the foul fiend on the mountain in the shape of a hairy giant, that indeed was the heaviest *gravamen*, inasmuch as not only old Lizzie, but likewise three trustworthy witnesses, had seen him. But who could tell whether it was not old Lizzie herself who had contrived this devilish apparition in order to ruin her enemy

altogether; for that notwithstanding the apparition was not the young nobleman, as *Rea* had declared it to be, it still was very likely that she had not lied, but had mistaken Satan for the young lord, as he appeared in his shape; *exemplum*, for this was to be found even in Scripture: for that all *Theologi* of the whole Protestant Church were agreed that the vision which the witch of Endor showed to King Saul was not Samuel himself, but the arch-fiend; nevertheless, Saul had taken it for Samuel. In like manner the old harlot might have conjured up the devil before *Rea*, who did not perceive that it was not the young lord, but Satan, who had put on that shape in order to seduce her; for as *Rea* was a fair woman, none could wonder that the devil gave himself more trouble for her than for an old withered hag, seeing he has ever sought after fair women to lie with them.

Lastly, he argued that *Rea* was in nowise marked as a witch, for that she neither had bleared and squinting eyes nor a hooked nose, whereas old Lizzie had both, which Theophrastus Paracelsus declares to be an unfailing mark of a witch, saying, "Nature marketh none thus unless by abortion, for these are the chiefest signs whereby witches be known whom the spirit *Asiendens* hath subdued unto himself."

When *Dom. Syndicus* had read his *defensio*, my daughter was so rejoiced thereat that she would have kissed his hand, but he snatched it from her and breathed upon it thrice, whereby we could easily see that he himself was nowise in earnest with his *defensio*. Soon after he took leave in an ill-humour, after commending her to the care of the Most High, and begged that I would make my farewell as short as might be, seeing that he purposed to return home that very day, the which, alas! I very unwillingly did.

The Twenty-third Chapter
How My Poor Child Was Sentenced to Be Put to the Question

After *acta* had been sent to the honourable the central court, about fourteen days passed over before any answer was received. My lord the Sheriff was especially gracious toward me the while, and allowed me to see my daughter as often as I would (seeing that the rest of the court were gone home), wherefore I was with her nearly all day. And when the constable grew impatient of keeping watch over me, I gave him a fee to lock me in together with my child. And the all-merciful God was gracious unto us, and caused us often and gladly to pray, for we had a steadfast hope, believing that the cross we had seen in the heavens would now soon pass away from us, and that the ravening wolf would receive his reward when the honourable high court had read through the *acta*, and should come to the excellent *defensio* which *Dom. Syndicus* had constructed for my child. Wherefore I began to be of good cheer again, especially when I saw my daughter her cheeks growing of a right lovely red. But on Thursday, 25th *mensis Augusti*, at noon, the worshipful court drove into the castle-yard again as I sat in the prison with my child, as I was wont; and old Ilse brought us our food, but could not tell us the news for weeping. But the tall constable peeped in at the door, grinning, and cried, "Oh, ho! they are come, they are come, they are come; now the tickling will begin": whereat my poor child shuddered, but less at the news than at sight of the fellow himself. Scarce was he gone than he came back again to take off her chains and to fetch her away. So I followed her into the judgment-chamber, where *Dom. Consul* read out the sentence of the honourable high court as follows:— That she should once more be questioned in kindness touching the articles contained in the indictment; and if she then continued stubborn she should be subjected to the *peine forte et dure*, for that the *defensio* she had set up did not suffice, and that there were *indicia legitima prægnantia et sufficientia ad torturam ipsam*; to wit—

1. *Mala fama.*
2. *Maleficium, publicè commissum.*
3. *Apparitio dæmonis in monte.*

Whereupon the most honourable central court cited about 20 *auctores*, whereof, howbeit, we remember but little. When *Dom. Consul* had read out this to my child, he once more lift up his voice and admonished her with many words to confess of her own free-will, for that the truth must now come to light.

Hereupon she steadfastly replied, that after the *defensio* of *Dom. Syndicus* she had indeed hoped for a better sentence; but that, as it was the will of God to try her yet more hardly, she resigned herself altogether into His gracious hands, and could not confess aught save what she had said before, namely, that she was innocent, and that evil men had brought this misery upon her. Hereupon *Dom. Consul* motioned the constable, who straightway opened the door of the next room, and admitted *Pastor Benzensis* in his surplice, who had been sent for by the court to admonish her still better out of the word of God. He heaved a deep sigh, and said, "Mary, Mary, is it thus I must meet thee again?" Whereupon she began to weep bitterly, and to protest her innocence afresh. But he heeded not her distress, and as soon as he had heard her pray, "Our Father," "The eyes of all wait upon thee," and "God the Father dwell with us," he lift up his voice and declared to her the hatred of the living God to all witches and warlocks, seeing that not only is the punishment of fire awarded to them in the Old Testament, but that the Holy Ghost expressly saith in the New Testament (Gal. v.), "That they which do such things shall not inherit the kingdom of God"; but "shall have their part in the lake which burneth with fire and brimstone, which is the second death" (Apocal. xxi.). Wherefore she must not be stubborn nor murmur against the court when she was tormented, seeing that it was all done out of Christian love, and to save her poor soul. That, for the sake of God and her salvation, she should no longer delay repentance, and thereby cause her body to be tormented, and give over her wretched soul to Satan, who certainly would not fulfil those promises in hell which he had made her here upon earth; seeing that "He was a murderer from the beginning—a liar and the father of it" (John viii.). "Oh!" cried he, "Mary, my child, who so oft hast sat upon my knees, and for whom I now cry every morning and every night unto my God, if thou wilt have no pity upon thee and me, have pity at least upon thy worthy father, whom I cannot look upon without tears, seeing that his hairs have turned snow-white within a few days, and save thy soul, my child, and confess! Behold, thy Heavenly Father grieveth over thee no less than thy fleshly father, and the holy angels veil their faces for sorrow that thou, who wert once their darling sister, art now become the sister and bride of the devil. Return therefore, and repent! This day thy Saviour calleth thee, poor stray lamb, back into His flock, 'And ought not this woman, being a daughter of Abraham, whom Satan hath bound . . . be loosed from this bond?' Such are His merciful words (Luke xiii.); *item*, 'Return, thou backsliding Israel, saith the Lord, and I will not cause mine anger to fall upon you, for I am merciful' (Jer. iii.). Return then, thou backsliding soul, unto the Lord thy God! He who heard the prayer of the idolatrous Manasseh when 'he besought the Lord his God and humbled himself' (2 Chron. xxxiii.); who, through Paul, accepted the repentance of the sorcerers at Ephesus (Acts xix.), the same merciful God now crieth unto thee as unto the angel of the church of Ephesus, 'Remember, therefore, from whence thou art fallen, and repent' (Apocal. ii.). Oh, Mary, Mary, remember, my child, from whence thou art fallen, and repent!"

Hereupon he held his peace, and it was some time before she could say a word for tears and sobs; but at last she answered, "If lies are no less hateful to God than witchcraft, I may not lie, but must rather declare, to the glory of God, as I have ever declared, that I am innocent."

Hereupon *Dom. Consul* was exceeding wroth, and frowned and asked the tall constable if all was ready, *item*, whether the women were at hand to undress *Rea*; whereupon he answered with a grin, as he was wont, "Ho, ho, I have never been wanting in my duty, nor will I be wanting to-day; I will tickle her in such wise that she shall soon confess."

When he had said this, *Dom. Consul* turned to my daughter, and said,

"Thou art a foolish thing, and knowest not the torment which awaits thee, and therefore is it that thou still art stubborn. Now, then, follow me to the torture-chamber, where the executioner shall show thee the *instrumenta*; and thou mayest yet think better of it when thou hast seen what the question is like."

Hereupon he went into another room, and the constable followed him with my child. And when I would have gone after them, *Pastor Benzensis* held me back, with many tears, and conjured me not to do so, but to tarry where I was. But I hearkened not unto him, and tore myself from him, and swore that so long as a single vein should beat in my wretched body I would never forsake my child. I therefore went into the next room, and from thence down into a vault, where was the torture-chamber, wherein were no windows, so that those without might not hear the cries of the tormented. Two torches were already burning there when I went in, and although *Dom. Consul* would at first have sent me away, after a while he had pity upon me, so that he suffered me to stay.

And now that hell-hound the constable stepped forward, and first showed my poor child the ladder, saying with savage glee, "See here! first of all thou wilt be laid on that, and thy hands and feet will be tied. Next, the thumb-screw here will be put upon thee, which straightway will make the blood to spirt out at the tips of thy fingers; thou mayest see that they are still red with the blood of old Gussy Biehlke, who was burnt last year, and who, like thee, would not confess at first. If thou still wilt not confess, I shall next put these Spanish boots on thee, and should they be too large, I shall just drive in a wedge, so that the calf, which is now at the back of thy leg, will be driven to the front, and the blood will shoot out of thy feet, as when thou squeezest blackberries in a bag.

"Again, if thou wilt not yet confess—holla!" shouted he, and kicked open a door behind him, so that the whole vault shook, and my poor child fell upon her knees for fright. Before long two women brought in a bubbling caldron, full of boiling pitch and brimstone. This caldron the hell-hound ordered them to set down on the ground, and drew forth, from under the red cloak he wore, a goose's wing, wherefrom he plucked five or six quills, which he dipped into the boiling brimstone. After he had held them a while in the caldron he threw them upon the earth, where they twisted about and spirted the brimstone on all sides. And then he called to my poor child again, "See! these quills I shall throw upon thy white loins, and the burning brimstone will presently eat into thy flesh down to the very bones, so that thou wilt thereby have a foretaste of the joys which await thee in hell."

When he had spoken thus far, amid sneers and laughter, I was so overcome with rage that I sprang forth out of the corner where I stood leaning my trembling joints against an old barrel, and cried, "O, thou

The Torture Chamber

hellish dog! sayest thou this of thyself, or have others bidden thee?" Whereupon, however, the fellow gave me such a blow upon the breast that I fell backwards against the wall, and *Dom. Consul* called out in great wrath, "You old fool, if you needs must stay here, at any rate leave the constable in peace, for if not I will have you thrust out of the chamber forthwith. The constable has said no more than is his duty; and it will thus happen to thy child if she confess not, and if it appear that the foul fiend have given her some charm against the torture." Hereupon this hell-hound went on to speak to my poor child, without heeding me, save that he laughed in my face: "Look here! when thou hast thus been well shorn, ho, ho, ho! I shall pull thee up by means of these two rings in the floor and the roof, stretch thy arms above thy head, and bind them fast to the ceiling; whereupon I shall take these two torches, and hold them under thy shoulders, till thy skin will presently become like the rind of a smoked ham. Then thy hellish paramour will help thee no longer, and thou wilt confess the truth. And now thou hast seen and heard all that I shall do to thee, in the name of God, and by order of the magistrates."

And now *Dom. Consul* once more came forward and admonished her to confess the truth. But she abode by what she had said from the first; whereupon he delivered her over to the two women who had brought in the caldron, to strip her naked as she was born, and to clothe her in the black torture-shift; after which they were once more to lead her barefooted up the steps before the worshipful court. But one of these women was the Sheriff his housekeeper (the other was the impudent constable his wife), and my daughter said that she would not suffer herself to be touched save by honest women, and assuredly not by the housekeeper, and begged *Dom. Consul* to send for her maid, who was sitting in her prison reading the Bible, if he knew of no other decent woman at hand. Hereupon the housekeeper began to pour forth a wondrous deal of railing and ill words, but *Dom. Consul* rebuked her, and answered my daughter that he would let her have her wish in this matter too, and bade the impudent constable his wife call the maid hither from out of the prison. After he had said this, he took me by the arm, and prayed me so long to go up with him, for that no harm would happen to my daughter as yet, that I did as he would have me.

Before long she herself came up, led between the two women, barefooted, and in the black torture-shift, but so pale that I myself should scarce have known her. The hateful constable, who followed close behind, seized her by the hand, and led her before the worshipful court.

Hereupon the admonitions began all over again, and *Dom. Consul* bade her look upon the brown spots that were upon the black shift, for that they were the blood of old wife Biehlke, and to consider that within a few minutes it would in like manner be stained with her own blood.

Hereupon she answered, "I have considered that right well, but I hope that my faithful Saviour, who hath laid this torment upon me, being innocent, will likewise help me to bear it, as he helped the holy martyrs of old; for if these, through God's help, overcame by faith the torments inflicted on them by blind heathens, I also can overcome the torture inflicted on me by blind heathens, who, indeed, call themselves Christians, but who are more cruel than those of yore; for the old heathens only caused the holy virgins to be torn of savage beasts, but ye which have received the new commandment, 'That ye love one another; as your Saviour hath loved you, that ye also love one another. By this shall all men know that ye are his disciples' (St. John xiii.); yourselves will act the part of savage beasts, and tear with your own hands the body of an innocent maiden, your sister, who has never done aught to harm you. Do, then, as ye list, but have a care how ye will answer it to the highest Judge of all. Again, I say, the lamb feareth nought, for it is in the hand of the good Shepherd."

When my matchless child had thus spoken, *Dom. Consul* rose, pulled off the black skull-cap which he ever wore, because the top of his head was already bald, bowed to the court, and said, "We hereby make known to the worshipful court that the question ordinary and extraordinary of the stubborn and blaspheming witch, Mary Schweidler, is about to begin, in the name of the Father, and of the Son, and of the Holy Ghost. Amen."

Hereupon all the court rose save the Sheriff, who had got up before, and was walking uneasily up and down in the room. But of all that now follows, and of what I myself did, I remember not one word, but will relate it all as I have received it from my daughter and other *testes*, and they have told me as follows:—

That when *Dom. Consul* after these words had taken up the hour-glass which stood upon the table, and walked on before, I would go with him, whereupon *Pastor Benzensis* first prayed me with many words and tears to desist from my purpose, and when that was of no avail my child herself stroked my cheeks, saying, "Father, have you ever read that the Blessed Virgin stood by when her guileless Son was scourged? Depart, therefore, from me. You shall stand by the pile whereon I am burned, that I promise you; for in like manner did the Blessed Virgin stand at the foot of the cross. But, now, go; go, I pray you, for you will not be able to bear it, neither shall I."

And when this also failed, *Dom. Consul* bade the constable seize me, and by main force lock me into another room; whereupon, however, I tore myself away, and fell at his feet, conjuring him by the wounds of Christ not to tear me from my child; that I would never forget his kindness and mercy, but pray for him day and night; nay, that at the day of judgment I would be his intercessor with God and the holy angels if that he would but let me go with my child; that I would be quite quiet, and not speak one single word, but that I must go with my child, etc. This so moved the worthy man that he burst into tears, and so trembled with pity for me that the hour-glass fell from his hands and rolled right before the feet of the Sheriff, as though God himself would signify to him that his glass was soon to run out; and, indeed, he understood it right well, for he grew white as any chalk when he picked it up and gave it back to *Dom. Consul.* The latter at last gave way, saying that this day would make him ten years older; but he bade the impudent constable (who also went with us) lead me away if I made any *rumor* during the torture. And hereupon the whole court went below, save the Sheriff, who said his head ached, and that he believed his old *malum*, the gout, was coming upon him again, wherefore he went into another chamber; *item, Pastor Benzensis* likewise departed.

Down in the vault the constable first brought in tables and chairs, whereon the court sat, and *Dom. Consul* also pushed a chair toward me, but I sat not thereon, but threw myself upon my knees in a corner. When this was done they began again with their vile admonitions, and as my child, like her guileless Saviour before His unrighteous judges, answered not a word, *Dom. Consul* rose up and bade the tall constable lay her on the torture-bench.

She shook like an aspen leaf when he bound her hands and feet; and when he was about to bind over her sweet eyes a nasty old filthy clout wherein my maid had seen him carry fish but the day before, and which was still all over shining scales, I perceived it, and pulled off my silken neckerchief, begging him to use that instead, which he did. Hereupon the thumb-screw was put on her, and she was once more asked whether she would confess freely, but she only shook her poor blinded head and sighed with her dying Saviour, "Eli, Eli, lama sabachthani?" and then in Greek, "Θεέ μου, Θεέ μου, ἱνατί με ἐγκατέλιπες"; Whereat *Dom. Consul* started back, and made the sign of the cross (for inasmuch as he knew no Greek, he believed, as he afterwards said himself, that she was calling upon the devil to help her), and then called to the constable with a loud voice, "Screw!"

But when I heard this I gave such a cry that the whole vault shook; and when my poor child, who was dying of terror and despair, had heard my voice she first struggled with her bound hands and feet like a lamb that lies dying in the slaughter-house, and then cried out, "Loose me, and I will confess whatsoe'er you will." Hereat *Dom. Consul* so greatly rejoiced, that while the constable unbound her, he fell on his knees, and thanked God for having spared him this anguish. But no sooner was my poor desperate child unbound, and had laid aside her crown of thorns

(I mean my silken neckerchief), than she jumped off the ladder, and flung herself upon me, who lay for dead in a corner in a deep swound.

This greatly angered the worshipful court, and when the constable had borne me away, *Rea* was admonished to make her confession according to promise. But seeing she was too weak to stand upon her feet, *Dom. Consul* gave her a chair to sit upon, although *Dom. Camerarius* grumbled thereat, and these were the chief questions which were put to her by order of the most honourable high central court, as *Dom. Consul* said, and which were registered *ad protocollum*.

Q. Whether she could bewitch?—*R.* Yes, she could bewitch.

Q. Who taught her to do so?—*R.* Satan himself.

Q. How many devils had she?—*R.* One devil was enough for her.

Q. What was this devil called?—*Illa* (considering). His name was *Disidæmonia*.

Hereat *Dom. Consul* shuddered, and said that that must be a very terrible devil indeed, for that he had never heard such a name before, and that she must spell it, so that *Scriba* might make no *error*; which she did, and he then went on as follows:—

Q. In what shape had he appeared to her?—*R.* In the shape of the Sheriff, and sometimes as a goat with terrible horns.

Q. Whether Satan had re-baptized her, and where?—*R.* In the sea.

Q. What name had he given her?—*R.*—.

Q. Whether any of the neighbors had been by when she was re-baptized, and which of them?—*R.* Hereupon my matchless child cast up her eyes towards heaven, as though doubting whether she should file old Lizzie or not, but at last she said, "No."

Q. She must have had sponsors; who were they? and what gift had they given her as christening money?—*R.* There were none there save spirits; wherefore old Lizzie could see no one when she came and looked on at her re-baptism.

Q. Whether she had ever lived with the devil?—*R.* She never had lived anywhere save in her father's house.

Q. She did not choose to understand. He meant whether she had ever played the wanton with Satan, and known him carnally? Hereupon she blushed, and was so ashamed that she covered her face with her hands, and presently began to weep and to sob: and as, after many questions, she gave no answer, she was again admonished to speak the truth, or that the executioner should lift her up on the ladder again. At last she said, "No!" which, howbeit, the worshipful court would not believe, and bade the executioner seize her again, whereupon she answered, "Yes!"

Q. Whether she had found the devil hot or cold?—*R.* She did not remember which.

Q. Whether she had ever conceived by Satan, and given birth to a changeling, and of what shape?—*R.* No, never.

_Q_. Whether the foul fiend had given her any sign or mark about her body, and in what part thereof?—_R_. That the mark had already been seen by the worshipful court.

She was next charged with all the witchcraft done in the village, and owned to it all, save that she still said that she knew nought of old Seden his death, _item_, of little Paasch her sickness, nor, lastly, would she confess that she had, by the help of the foul fiend, raked up my crop or conjured the caterpillars into my orchard. And albeit they again threatened her with the question, and even ordered the executioner to lay her on the bench and put on the thumb-screw to frighten her, she remained firm and said, "Why should you torture me, seeing that I have confessed far heavier crimes than these, which it will not save my life to deny?"

Hereupon the worshipful court at last were satisfied, and suffered her to be lifted off the torture-bench, especially as she confessed the _articulus principalis_; to wit, that Satan had really appeared to her on the mountain in the shape of a hairy giant. Of the storm and the frog, _item_, of the hedgehog, nothing was said, inasmuch as the worshipful court had by this time seen the folly of supposing that she could have brewed a storm while she quietly sat in the coach. Lastly, she prayed that it might be granted to her to suffer death clothed in the garments which she had worn when she went to greet the King of Sweden; _item_, that they would suffer her wretched father to be driven with her to the stake, and to stand by while she was burned, seeing that she had promised him this in the presence of the worshipful court.

Hereupon she was once more given into the charge of the tall constable, who was ordered to put her into a stronger and severer prison. But he had not led her out of the chamber before the Sheriff his bastard, whom he had had by the housekeeper, came into the vault with a drum, and kept drumming and crying out, "Come to the roast goose! come to the roast goose!" whereat _Dom. Consul_ was exceeding wroth, and ran after him, but he could not catch him, seeing that the young varlet knew all the ins and outs of the vault. Without doubt it was the Lord who sent me the swound, so that I should be spared this fresh grief; wherefore to Him alone be honour and glory. Amen.

The Twenty-fourth Chapter
HOW IN MY PRESENCE THE DEVIL FETCHED OLD LIZZIE KOLKEN

When I recovered from my above-mentioned swound, I found my host, his wife, and my old maid standing over me, and pouring warm beer down my throat. The faithful old creature shrieked for joy when I opened my eyes again, and then told me that my daughter had not suffered herself to be racked, but had freely confessed her crimes and filed herself as a witch. This seemed pleasant news to me in my misery, inasmuch as I deemed the death by fire to be a less heavy punishment than the torture. Howbeit when I would have prayed I could not, whereat I again fell into heavy grief and despair, fearing that the Holy Ghost had altogether turned away His face from me, wretched man that I was. And albeit the old maid, when she had seen this, came and stood before my bed and began to pray aloud to me; it was all in vain, and I remained a hardened sinner. But the Lord had pity upon me, although I deserved it not, insomuch that I presently fell into a deep sleep, and did not awake until next morning when the prayer-bell rang; and then I was once more able to pray, whereat I greatly rejoiced, and still thanked God in my heart, when my ploughman Claus Neels came in and told me that he had come yesterday to tell me about my oats, seeing that he had gotten them all in; and that the constable came with him who had been to fetch old Lizzie Kolken, inasmuch as the honourable high court had ordered her to be brought up for trial. Hereat the whole village rejoiced, but *Rea* herself laughed, and shouted, and sang, and told him and the constable by the way (for the constable had let her get up behind for a short time), that this should bring great luck to the Sheriff. They need only bring her up before the court, and in good sooth she would not hold her tongue within her teeth, but that all men should marvel at her confession; that such a court as that was a laughing-stock to her, and that she spat, *salvâ veniâ*, upon the whole brotherhood, *et cet.*

Upon hearing this I once more felt a strong hope, and rose to go to old Lizzie. But I was not quite dressed before she sent the impudent constable to beg that I would go to her with all speed and give her the sacrament, seeing that she had become very weak during the night. I had my own thoughts on the matter, and followed the constable as fast as I could, though not to give her the sacrament, as indeed anybody may suppose. But in my haste, I, weak old man that I was, forgot to take my witnesses with me; for all the misery I had hitherto suffered had so clouded my senses that it never once came into my head. None followed me save the impudent constable; and it will soon appear how that this villain had given himself over body and soul to Satan to destroy my child, whereas he might have saved her. For when he had opened the prison (it was the same cell wherein my child had first been shut up), we found old Lizzie lying on the ground on a truss of straw, with a broom for a pillow (as though she were to fly to hell upon it, as she no longer could fly to Blockula), so that I shuddered when I caught sight of her.

Scarce was I come in when she cried out fearfully, "I'm a witch, I'm a witch! Have pity upon me, and give me the sacrament quick, and

I will confess everything to you!" And when I said to her, "Confess, then!" she owned that she, with the help of the Sheriff, had contrived all the witchcraft in the village, and that my child was as innocent thereof as the blessed sun in heaven. Howbeit that the Sheriff had the greatest guilt, inasmuch as he was a warlock and a witch's priest, and had a spirit far stronger than hers, called Dudaim, which spirit had given her such a blow on the head in the night as she should never recover. This same Dudaim it was that had raked up the crops, heaped sand over the amber, made the storm, and dropped the frog into my daughter her lap; *item*, carried off her old goodman through the air.

And when I asked her how that could be, seeing that her goodman had been a child of God until very near his end, and much given to prayer; albeit I had indeed marvelled why he had other thoughts in his last illness; she answered that one day he had seen her spirit, which she kept in a chest, in the shape of a black cat, and whose name was Kit, and had threatened that he would tell me of it; whereupon she, being frightened, had caused her spirit to make him so ill that he despaired of ever getting over it. Thereupon she had comforted him, saying that she would presently heal him if he would deny God, who, as he well saw, could not help him. This he promised to do; and when she had straightway made him quite hearty again, they took the silver which I had scraped off the new sacrament cup, and went by night down to the seashore, where he had to throw it into the sea with these words: "When this silver returns again to the chalice, then shall my soul return to God." Whereupon the Sheriff, who was by, re-baptized him in the name of Satan, and called him Jack. He had had no sponsors save only herself, old Lizzie. Moreover, that on St. John's Eve, when he went with them to Blockula for the first time (the Herrenberg was their Blockula), they had talked of my daughter, and Satan himself had sworn to the Sheriff that he should have her. For that he would show the old one (wherewith the villain meant God) what he could do, and that he would make the carpenter's son sweat for vexation (fie upon thee, thou arch villain, that thou couldst thus speak of my blessed Saviour!). Whereupon her old goodman had grumbled, and as they had never rightly trusted him, the spirit Dudaim one day flew off with him through the air by the Sheriff's order, seeing that her own spirit, called Kit, was too weak to carry him. That the same Dudaim had also been the woodpecker who afterwards 'ticed my daughter and old Paasch to the spot with his cries, in order to ruin her. But that the giant who had appeared on the Streckelberg was not a devil, but the young lord of Mellenthin himself, as her spirit, Kit, had told her.

And this she said was nothing but the truth, whereby she would live and die; and she begged me, for the love of God, to take pity upon her, and, after her repentant confession, to speak forgiveness of her sins, and to give her the Lord's Supper; for that her spirit stood there behind the stove, grinning like a rogue, because he saw that it was all up with her now. But I answered, "I would sooner give the sacrament to an old sow than to thee, thou accursed witch, who not only didst give over thine own husband to Satan, but hast likewise tortured me and my poor child almost unto death with pains like those of hell." Before she could make any answer, a loathsome insect, about as long as my finger, and with a yellow tail, crawled in under the door of the prison. When she espied it she gave a yell, such as I never before heard, and never wish to hear again. For once, when I was in Silesia, in my youth, I saw one of the enemy's soldiers spear a child before its mother's face, and I thought *that* a fearful shriek which the mother gave; but her cry was child's play to the cry of old Lizzie. All my hair stood on end, and her own red hair grew so stiff that it was like the twigs of the broom whereon she lay; and then she howled, "That is the spirit Dudaim, whom the accursed Sheriff has sent to me—the sacrament, for the love of God, the sacrament!—I will confess a great deal more—I have been a witch these thirty years!— the sacrament, the sacrament!" While she thus bellowed and flung about her arms and legs, the loathsome insect rose into the air, and buzzed and whizzed about her where she lay, insomuch that it was fearful to see and to hear. And this she-devil called by turns on God, on her spirit Kit, and on me, to help her, till the insect all of a sudden darted into her open jaws, whereupon she straightway gave up the ghost, and turned all black and blue like a blackberry.

I heard nothing more save that the window rattled, not very loud, but as though one had thrown a pea against it, whereby I straightway perceived that Satan had just flown through it with her soul. May the all-merciful God keep every mother's child from such an end, for the sake of Jesus Christ our blessed Lord and Saviour! Amen.

As soon as I was somewhat recovered, which, however, was not for a long time, inasmuch as my blood had turned to ice, and my feet were as stiff as a stake; I began to call out after the impudent constable, but he was no longer in the prison. Thereat I greatly marvelled, seeing that I had seen him there but just before the vermin crawled in, and straightway I suspected no good, as, indeed, it turned out; for when at last he came upon my calling him, and I told him to let this carrion be carted out which had just died in the name of the devil, he did as though he was amazed; and when I desired him that he would bear witness to the innocence of my daughter, which the old hag had confessed on her death-bed, he pretended to be yet more amazed, and said that he had heard nothing. This went through my heart like a sword, and I leaned against a pillar without, where I stood for a long time: but as soon as I was come to myself I went to *Dom. Consul,* who was about to go to Usedom and already sat in his coach. At my humble prayer he went back into the judgment-chamber with the *Camerarius* and the *Scriba,* whereupon I told all that had taken place, and how the wicked constable denied that he had heard the same. But they say that I talked a great deal of nonsense beside; among other things, that all the little fishes had swam into the vault to release my daughter. Nevertheless, *Dom. Consul,* who often shook his head, sent for the impudent constable, and asked him for his testimony. But the fellow pretended that as soon as he saw that old Lizzie wished to confess, he had gone away, so as not to get any more hard words, wherefore he had heard nothing. Hereupon I, as *Dom. Consul* afterwards told the pastor of Benz, clenched my fists and answered, "What, thou arch-rogue, didst thou not crawl about the room in the shape of a reptile?" whereupon he would hearken to me no longer, thinking me distraught, nor would he make the constable take an oath, but left me standing in the midst of the room, and got into his coach again.

Neither do I know how I got out of the room; but next morning when the sun rose, and I found myself lying in bed at Master Seep his ale-house, the whole *casus* seemed to me like a dream; neither was I able to rise, but lay a-bed all the blessed Saturday and Sunday, talking all manner of *allotria.* It was not till towards evening on Sunday, when I began to vomit and threw up green bile (no wonder!), that I got somewhat better. About this time *Pastor Benzensis* came to my bedside, and told me how distractedly I had borne myself, but so comforted me from the word of God, that I was once more able to pray from my heart. May the merciful God reward my dear gossip, therefore, at the day of judgment! For prayer is almost as brave a comforter as the Holy Ghost himself, from whom it comes; and I shall ever consider that so long as a man can still pray, his misfortunes are not unbearable, even though in all else "his flesh and his heart faileth" (Psalm lxxiii.).

The Twenty-fifth Chapter

HOW SATAN SIFTED ME LIKE WHEAT, WHEREAS MY DAUGHTER WITHSTOOD HIM RIGHT BRAVELY

On Monday I left my bed betimes, and as I felt in passable good case, I went up to the castle to see whether I might peradventure get to my daughter, but I could not find either constable, albeit I had brought a few groats with me to give them as beer-money; neither would the folks that I met tell me where they were; *item,* the impudent constable his wife, who was in the kitchen making brimstone matches. And when I asked her when her husband would come back, she said not before to-morrow morning early; *item*, that the other constable would not be here any sooner. Hereupon I begged her to lead me to my daughter herself, at the same time showing her the two groats; but she answered that she had not the keys, and knew not how to get at them: moreover, she said she did not know where my child was now shut up, seeing that I would have spoken to her through the door; *item*, the cook, the huntsman, and whomsoever else I met in my sorrow, said they knew not in what hole the witch might lie.

Hereupon I went all round about the castle, and laid my ear against every little window that looked as though it might be her window, and cried, "Mary, my child, where art thou?" *Item*, at every grating I found I kneeled down, bowed my head, and called in like manner into the vault below. But all in vain; I got no answer anywhere. The Sheriff at length saw what I was about, and came down out of the castle to me with a very gracious air, and, taking me by the hand, he asked me what I sought? But when I answered him that I had not seen my only child since last Thursday, and prayed him to show pity upon me, and let me be led to her, he said that could not be, but that I was to come up into his chamber, and talk further of the matter. By the way he said, "Well, so the old witch told you fine things about me, but you see how Almighty God has sent his righteous judgment upon her. She has long been ripe for the fire; but my great long-suffering, wherein a good magistrate should ever strive to be like unto the Lord, has made me overlook it till *datum*, and in return for my goodness she raises this outcry against me." And when I replied, "How does your Lordship know that the witch raised such an outcry against you?" he first began to stammer, and then said, "Why, you yourself charged me thereon before the judge. But I bear you no anger therefor, and God knows that I pity you, who are a poor, weak old man, and would gladly help you if I were able." Meanwhile he led me up four or five flights of stairs, so that I, old man that I am, could follow him no further, and stood still gasping for breath. But he took me by the hand and said, "Come, I must first show you how matters really stand, or I fear you will not accept my help, but will plunge yourself into destruction." Hereupon we stepped out upon a terrace at the top of the castle, which looked toward the water; and the villain went on to say, "Reverend Abraham, can you see well afar off?" and when I answered that I once could see very well, but that the many tears I had shed had now peradventure dimmed my eyes, he pointed to the Streckelberg, and said, "Do you, then, see nothing there?" *Ego.* "Nought save a black speck, which I cannot make out." *Ille.* "Know, then, that that is the pile whereon your daughter is to burn at ten o'clock to-morrow morning, and which the constables are now raising." When this hellhound had thus spoken, I gave a loud cry and swounded. Oh, blessed

Lord! I know not how I lived through such distress; thou alone didst strengthen me beyond nature, in order, "after so much weeping and wailing, to heap joys and blessings upon me; without thee I never could have lived through such misery: therefore to thy name ever be all honour and glory, O thou God of Israel!"

When I came again to myself I lay on a bed in a fine room, and perceived a taste in my mouth like wine. But as I saw none near me save the Sheriff, who held a pitcher in his hand, I shuddered and closed mine eyes, considering what I should say or do. This he presently observed, and said, "Do not shudder thus; I mean well by you, and only wish to put a question to you, which you must answer me on your conscience as a priest. Say, reverend Abraham, which is the greater sin, to commit whoredom, or to take the lives of two persons?" and when I answered him, "To take the lives of two persons," he went on, "Well, then, is not that what your stubborn child is about to do? Rather than give herself up to me, who have ever desired to save her, and who can even yet save her, albeit her pile is now being raised, she will take away her own life and that of her wretched father, for I scarcely think that you, poor man, will outlive this sorrow. Wherefore do you, for God his sake, persuade her to think better of it while I am yet able to save her. For know that about ten miles from hence I have a small house in the midst of the forest, where no human being ever goes; thither will I send her this very night, and you may dwell there with her all the days of your life, if so it please you. You shall live as well as you can possibly desire, and to-morrow morning I will spread a report betimes that the witch and her father have run away together during the night, and that nobody knows whither they are gone." Thus spake the serpent to me, as whilom to our mother Eve; and, wretched sinner that I am, the tree of death which he showed me seemed to me also to be a tree of life, so pleasant was it to the eye. Nevertheless I answered, "My child will never save her miserable life by doing aught to peril the salvation of her soul." But now, too, the serpent was more cunning than all the beasts of the field (especially such an old fool as I), and spake thus: "Why, who would have her peril the salvation of her soul? Reverend Abraham, must I teach you Scripture? Did not our Lord Christ pardon Mary Magdalene, who lived in open whoredom? and did he not speak forgiveness to the poor adulteress who had committed a still greater *crimen*? nay, more, doth not St. Paul expressly say that the harlot Rahab was saved, Hebrews xi.? *item*, St. James ii. says the same. But where have ye read that any one was saved who had wantonly taken her own life and that of her father? Wherefore, for the love of God, persuade your child not to give herself up, body and soul, to the devil, by her stubbornness, but to suffer herself to be saved while it is yet time. You can abide with her, and pray away all the sins she may commit, and likewise aid me with your prayers, who freely own that I am a miserable sinner, and have done you much evil, though not so much evil by far, reverend Abraham, as David did to Uriah, and he was saved, notwithstanding he put the man to a shameful death, and afterwards lay with his wife. Wherefore I, poor man, likewise hope to be saved, seeing that my desire for your daughter is still greater than that which this David felt for Bathsheba; and I will gladly make it all up to you twofold as soon as we are in my cottage."

When the tempter had thus spoken, methought his words were sweeter than honey, and I answered, "Alas, my lord, I am ashamed to appear before her face with such a proposal." Whereupon he straightway said, "Then do you write it to her; come, here is pen, ink, and paper."

And now, like Eve, I took the fruit and ate, and gave it to my child that she might eat also; that is to say, that I recapitulated on paper all that Satan had prompted, but in the Latin tongue, for I was ashamed to write it in mine own; and lastly I conjured her not to take away her own life and mine, but to submit to the wondrous will of God. Neither were mine eyes opened when I had eaten (that is, written), nor did I perceive that the ink was gall instead of honey, and I translated my letter to the Sheriff (seeing that he understood no Latin), smiling like a drunken man the while; whereupon he clapped me on the shoulder, and after I had made fast the letter with his signet, he called his huntsman, and gave it to him to carry to my daughter; *item*, he sent her pen, ink, and paper, together with his signet, in order that she might answer it forthwith.

Meanwhile he talked with me right graciously, praising my child and me, and made me drink to him many times from his great pitcher, wherein was most goodly wine; moreover, he went to a cupboard and brought out cakes for me to eat, saying that I should now have such every day. But when the huntsman came back in about half an hour with her answer, and I had read the same, then, first, were mine eyes opened, and I knew good and evil; had I had a fig-leaf, I should have covered them therewith for shame; but as it was, I held my hand over them and wept so bitterly that the Sheriff waxed very wroth, and cursing bade me tell him what she had written. Thereupon I interpreted the letter to him, the which I likewise place here, in order that all may see my folly, and the wisdom of my child. It was as follows:—

"IESVS!

"Pater infelix!

"Ego cras non magis pallebo rogum aspectura, et rogus non magis erubescet, me suscipiens, quam pallui et iterum erubescui, literas tuas legens. Quid? et te, pium patrem, pium servum Domini, ita Satanas sollicitavit, ut communionem facias cum inimicis meis, et non intelligas: in tali vitâ esse mortem, et in tali morte vitam? Scilicet si clementissimus

Deus Mariæ Magdalenæ aliisque ignovit, ignovit, quia resipiscerent ob carnis debilitatem, et non iterum peccarent. Et ego peccarem cum quavis detestatione carnis, et non semel, sed iterum atque iterum sine reversione usque ad mortem? Quomodo clementissimus Deus hæc sceleratissima ignoscere posset? infelix pater! recordare quid mihi dixisti de sanctis martyribus et virginibus Domini, quæ omnes mallent vitam quam pudicitiam perdere. His et ego sequar, et sponsus meus, Jesus Christus, et mihi miseræ, ut spero, coronam æternam dabit, quamvis eum non minus offendi ob debilitatem carnis ut Maria, et me sontem declaravi, cum insons sum. Fac igitur, ut valeas et ora pro me apud Deum et non apud Satanam, ut et ego mox coram Deo pro te orare possim.

MARIA S., captiva."

When the Sheriff heard this, he flung the pitcher which he held in his hand to the ground, so that it flew in pieces, and cried, "The cursed devil's whore! the constable shall make her squeak for this a good hour longer"; with many more such things beside, which he said in his malice, and which I have now forgotten; but he soon became quite gracious again, and said, "She is foolish; do you go to her and see whether you cannot persuade her to her own good as well as yours; the huntsman shall let you in, and should the fellow listen, give him a good box on the ears in my name; do you hear, reverend Abraham? Go now forthwith and bring me back an answer as quickly as possible!" I therefore followed the huntsman, who led me into a vault where was no light save what fell through a hole no bigger than a crown-piece; and here my daughter sat upon her bed and wept. Any one may guess that I straightway began to weep too, and was no better able to speak than she. We thus lay mute in each other's arms for a long time, until I at last begged her to forgive me for my letter, but of the Sheriff his message I said nought, although I had purposed so to do. But before long we heard the Sheriff himself call down into the vault from above, "What (and here he gave me a heavy curse) are you doing there so long? Come up this moment, reverend Johannes!" Thus I had scarce time to give her one kiss before the huntsman came back with the keys and forced us to part; albeit we had as yet scarcely spoken, save that I had told her in a few words what had happened with old Lizzie. It would be hard to believe into what grievous anger the Sheriff fell when I told him that my daughter remained firm and would not hearken unto him; he struck me on the breast, and said, "Go to the devil then, thou infamous parson!" and when I turned myself away and would have gone, he pulled me back, and said, "If thou breathest but one word of all that has passed, I will have thee burnt too, thou grey-headed old father of a witch; so look to it!" Hereupon I plucked up a heart, and answered that that would be the greatest joy to me, especially if I could be burnt to-morrow with my child. Hereunto he made no answer, but clapped to the door behind me. Well, clap the door as thou wilt, I greatly fear that the just God will one day clap the doors of heaven in thy face!

The Twenty-sixth Chapter

HOW I RECEIVED THE HOLY SACRAMENT WITH MY DAUGHTER AND THE OLD MAIDSERVANT, AND HOW SHE WAS THEN LED FOR THE LAST TIME BEFORE THE COURT, WITH THE DRAWN SWORD AND THE OUTCRY, TO RECEIVE SENTENCE

Now any one would think that during that heavy Tuesday night I should not have been able to close mine eyes; but know, dear reader, that the Lord can do more than we can ask or understand, and that his mercy is new every morning. For toward daybreak I fell asleep as quietly as though I had had no care upon my heart; and when I awoke I was able to pray more heartily than I had done for a long time; so that, in the midst of my tribulation, I wept for joy at such great mercy from the Lord. But I prayed for nought save that he would endow my child with strength and courage to suffer the martyrdom he had laid upon her with Christian patience, and to send his angel to me, woeful man, so to pierce my heart with grief when I should see my child burn that it might straightway cease to beat, and I might presently follow her. And thus I still prayed when the maid came in all dressed in black, and with the silken raiment of my sweet lamb hanging over her arm; and she told me, with many tears, that the dead-bell had already tolled from the castle tower, for the first time, and that my child had sent for her to dress her, seeing that the court was already come from Usedom, and that in about two hours she was to set out on her last journey. Moreover, she had sent her word that she was to take her some blue and yellow flowers for a garland; wherefore she asked me what flowers she should take; and seeing that a jar filled with fire lilies and forget-me-nots stood in my window, which she had placed there yesterday, I said, "Thou canst gather no better flowers for her than these, wherefore do thou carry them to her, and tell her that I will follow thee in about half an hour, in order to receive the sacrament with her." Hereupon the faithful old creature prayed me to suffer her to go to the sacrament with us, the which I promised her. And scarce had I dressed myself and put on my surplice when *Pastor Benzensis* came in at the door and fell upon my neck, weeping, and as mute as a fish. As soon as he came to his speech again he told me of the great *miraculum* (*dæmonis* I mean) which had befallen at the burial of old Lizzie. For that, just as the bearers were about to lower the coffin into the grave, a noise was heard therein, as though of a carpenter boring through a deal board; wherefore they thought the old hag must be come to life again, and opened the coffin. But there she lay as before, all black and blue in the face, and as cold as ice; but her eyes had started wide open, so that all were horror-stricken, and expected some devilish apparition; and, indeed, a live rat presently jumped out of the coffin and ran into a skull which lay beside the grave. Thereupon they all ran away, seeing that old Lizzie had ever been in evil repute as a witch. Howbeit at last he himself went near the grave again, whereupon the rat disappeared, and all the others took courage and followed him. This the man told me, and any one may guess that this was in fact Satan, who had flown down the hag her throat as an insect, whereas his proper shape was that of a rat: albeit I wonder what he could so long have been about in the carrion; unless indeed it were that the evil spirits are as fond of all that is loathsome as the angels of God are of all that is fair and lovely. Be that as it may; *Summa*: I was not a little shocked at what he told me, and asked him what he now thought of the Sheriff? whereupon he shrugged his shoulders, and said that he had indeed been a wicked fellow as long as he could remember him, and that it was full ten years since he had given him any first-fruits; but that he did not believe that he was a warlock, as old Lizzie had said. For although he had indeed never been to the table of the Lord in his church, he had heard that he often went at Stettin, with his Princely Highness the Duke, and that the pastor at the castle church had shown him the entry in his communion-book. Wherefore he likewise could not believe that he had brought this misery upon my daughter, if she were innocent, as the hag had said; besides, that my daughter had freely confessed herself a witch. Hereupon I answered, that she had done that for fear of the torture; but that she was not afraid of death; whereupon I told him, with many sighs, how the sheriff had yesterday tempted me, miserable and unfaithful servant, to evil, insomuch that I had been willing to sell my only child to him and to Satan, and was not worthy to receive the sacrament to-day. Likewise how much more steadfast a faith my daughter had than I, as he might see from her letter, which I still carried in my pocket; herewith I gave it into his hand, and when he had read it, he sighed as though he had been himself a father, and said, "Were this true, I should sink into the earth for sorrow; but come, brother, come, that I may prove her faith myself."

Hereupon we went up to the castle, and on our way we found the greensward before the hunting-lodge, *item*, the whole space in front of the castle, already crowded with people, who, nevertheless, were quite quiet as we went by: we gave our names again to the huntsman. (I have never been able to remember his name, seeing that he was a Polak; he was not, however, the same fellow who wooed my child, and whom the Sheriff had therefore turned off.) The man presently ushered us into a fine large room, whither my child had been led when taken out of her prison.

The maid had already dressed her, and she looked lovely as an angel. She wore the chain of gold with the effigy round her neck again, *item*, the garland in her hair, and she smiled as we entered, saying, "I am ready!" Whereat the reverend Martinus was sorely angered and shocked, saying, "Ah, thou ungodly woman, let no one tell me further of thine innocence! Thou art about to go to the holy sacrament, and from thence to death, and thou flauntest as a child of this world about to go to the dancing-room." Whereupon she answered and said, "Be not wroth with me, dear godfather, because that I would go into the presence of my good King of Heaven in the same garments wherein I appeared some time since before the good King of Sweden. For it strengthens my weak and trembling flesh, seeing I hope that my righteous Saviour will in like manner take me to his heart, and will also hand his effigy upon my neck when I stretch out my hands to him in all humility, and recite my *carmen*, saying, 'O Lamb of God, innocently slain upon the cross, give my thy peace, O Jesu!'" These words softened my dear gossip, and he spoke, saying, "Ah, child, child, I thought to have reproached thee, but thou hast constrained me to weep with thee: art thou, then, indeed innocent?" "Verily," said she, "to you, my honoured godfather, I may now own that I am innocent, as truly as I trust that God will aid me in my last hour through Jesus Christ. Amen."

When the maid heard this, she made such outcries that I repented that I had suffered her to be present, and we all had enough to do to comfort her from the word of God till she became somewhat more tranquil; and when this was done, my dear gossip thus spake to my child: "If, indeed, thou dost so steadfastly maintain thine innocence, it is my duty, according to my conscience as a priest, to inform the worshipful court thereof"; and he was about to leave the room. But she withheld him, and fell upon the ground and clasped his knees, saying, "I beseech you, by the wounds of Jesus, to be silent. They would stretch me on the rack again, and uncover my nakedness, and I, wretched weak woman, would in such torture confess all that they would have me, especially if my father again be there, whereby both my soul and my body are tortured at once: wherefore stay, I pray you, stay; is it, then, a misfortune to die innocent, and is it not better to die innocent than guilty?"

My good gossip at last gave way, and after standing awhile and praying to himself, he wiped away his tears, and then spake the exhortation to confession, in the words of Isaiah xliii. 1, 2, "But now thus saith the Lord that created thee, O Jacob, and he that formed thee, O Israel, Fear not; for I have redeemed thee, I have called thee by thy name; thou art mine. When thou passest through the waters, I will be with thee; and through the rivers, they shall not overflow thee: when thou walkest through the fire, thou shalt not be burned, neither shall the flame kindle upon thee. For I am the Lord thy God, the Holy One of Israel, thy Saviour."

And when he had ended this comfortable address, and asked her whether she would willingly bear until her last hour that cross which the most merciful God according to his unsearchable will had laid upon her, she spake such beautiful words that my gossip afterwards said he should not forget them so long as he should live, seeing that he had never witnessed a bearing at once so full of faith and joy, and withal so deeply sorrowful. She spake after this manner: "Oh, holy cross, which my Jesus hath sanctified by his innocent suffering; oh, dear cross, which is laid upon me by the hand of a merciful Father; oh, blessed cross, whereby I am made like unto my Lord Jesus, and am called unto eternal glory and blessedness: how! shall I not willingly bear thee, thou sweet cross of my bridegroom, of my brother?" The reverend Johannes had scarce given us absolution, and after this, with many tears, the holy sacrament, when we heard a loud trampling upon the floor, and presently the impudent constable looked into the room and asked whether we were ready, seeing that the worshipful court was now waiting for us; and when he had been told that we were ready, my child would have first taken leave of me, but I forbade her, saying, "Not so; thou knowest that which thou hast promised me; . . . 'and whither thou goest I will go, and where thou lodgest I will lodge: . . . where thou diest will I die . . .' if that the Lord, as I hope, will hear the ardent sighs of my poor soul." Hereupon she let me go, and embraced only the old maid-servant, thanking her for all the kindness she had shown her from her youth up, and begging her not to go with her to make her death yet more bitter by her cries. The faithful old creature was unable for a long time to say a word for tears. Howbeit at last she begged forgiveness of my child for that she unwittingly accused her, and said, that out of her wages she had bought five pounds' weight of flax to hasten her death; that the shepherd of Pudgla had that very morning taken it with him to Coserow, and that she should wind it closely round her body; for that she had seen how old wife Schurne, who was burnt in Liepe, had suffered great torments before she came to her death, by reason of the damp wood.

But ere my child could thank her for this, the dreadful outcry of blood began in the judgment-chamber; for a voice cried as loudly as might be, "Woe upon the accursed witch, Mary Schweidler, because that she hath fallen off from the living God!" Then all the folk without cried, "Woe upon the accursed witch!" When I heard this I fell back against the wall, but my sweet child stroked my cheeks with her darling hands, and said, "Father, father, do but remember that the people likewise cried out against the innocent Jesus, 'Crucify him, crucify him!' Shall not we then drink of the cup which our Heavenly Father hath prepared for us?"

Hereupon the door opened, and the constable walked in, amid a great tumult among the people, holding a drawn sword in his hand, which he bowed thrice before my child, and cried, "Woe upon the accursed witch, Mary Schweidler, because that she hath fallen off from the living God!" and all the folks in the hall and without the castle cried as loud as they could, "Woe upon the accursed witch!"

Hereupon he said, "Mary Schweidler, come before the high and worshipful court to hear sentence of death passed upon thee!" Whereupon she followed him with us two miserable men (for *Pastor Benzensis* was no less cast down than myself). As for the old maid-servant, she lay on the ground for dead.

After we had with great pains pushed our way through all the people, the constable stood still before the open judgment-chamber, and once more bowed his sword before my child and cried for the third time, "Woe upon the accursed witch, Mary Schweidler, because that she hath fallen off from the living God!" And all the people, as well as the cruel judges themselves, cried as loud as they could, "Woe upon the accursed witch!"

When we had entered the room, *Dom. Consul* first asked my worthy gossip whether the witch had abode by her free avowal in confession; whereupon, after considering a short time, he answered, that he had best ask herself, for there she stood. According, taking up a paper which lay before him on the table, he spake as follows:—"Mary Schweidler, now that thou hast confessed, and received the holy and most honourable sacrament of the Lord's Supper, answer me once again these following questions:—

"1. Is it true that thou hast fallen off from the living God and given thyself up to Satan?

"2. Is it true that thou hadst a spirit called *Disidœmonia*, who re-baptized thee and carnally knew thee?

"3. Is it true that thou hast done all manner of mischief to the cattle?

"4. Is it true that Satan appeared to thee on the Streckelberg in the likeness of a hairy giant?"

When she had with many sighs said "Yes" to all these questions, he rose, took a wand in one hand and a second paper in the other, put his spectacles on his nose, and said, "Now, then, hear thy sentence." (This sentence I since copied: he would not let me see the other *Acta*, but pretended that they were at Wolgast. The sentence, however, was word for word as follows.)

"We, the Sheriff and the Justices appointed to serve the high and worshipful criminal court. Inasmuch as Mary Schweidler, the daughter of Abraham Schweidlerus, the pastor of Coserow, hath, after the appointed inquisition, repeatedly made free confession that she hath a devil named *Disidæmonia*, the which did re-baptize her in the sea, and did also know her carnally; *item*, that she by his help did mischief to the cattle; that he also appeared to her on the Streckelberg in the likeness of a hairy giant. We do therefore by these presents make known and direct that *Rea* be first duly torn four times on each breast with red-hot iron pincers, and after that be burned to death by fire, as a rightful punishment to herself and a warning to others. Nevertheless we, in pity for her youth, are pleased of our mercy to spare her the tearing with red-hot pincers, so that she shall only suffer death by the simple punishment of fire. Wherefore she is hereby condemned and judged accordingly on the part of the criminal court.

"*Publicatum* at the castle of Pudgla, the 30th day *mensis Augusti, anno Salutis* 1630."

As he spake the last word he brake his wand in two and threw the pieces before the feet of my innocent lamb, saying to the constable, "Now, do your duty!" But so many folks, both men and women, threw themselves on the ground to seize the pieces of the wand (seeing they are said to be good for the gout in the joints, *item*, for cattle when troubled with lice), that the constable fell to the earth over a woman who was on her knees before him, and his approaching death was thus foreshadowed to him by the righteous God. Something of the same sort likewise befell the Sheriff now for the second time; for when the worshipful court rose, throwing down tables, stools, and benches, a table, under which two boys were fighting for the pieces of the wand, fell right upon his foot, whereupon he flew into a violent rage, and threatened the people with his fist, saying that they should have fifty right good lashes a-piece, both men and women, if they were not quiet forthwith, and did not depart peaceably out of the room. This frighted them, and after the people were gone out into the street, the constable took a rope out of his pocket, wherewith he bound my lamb her hands so tightly behind her back that she cried aloud; but when she saw how this wrung my heart, she straightway constrained herself and said, "Oh, father, remember that it fared no better with the blessed Saviour!" Howbeit, when my dear gossip, who stood behind her, saw that her little hands, and more especially her nails, had turned black and blue, he spoke for her to the worshipful court, whereupon the abominable Sheriff only said, "Oh, let her be; let her feel what it is to fall off from the living God." But *Dom. Consul* was more merciful, inasmuch as, after feeling the cords, he bade the constable bind her hands less cruelly and slacken the rope a little, which accordingly he was forced to do. But my dear gossip was not content herewith, and begged that she might sit in the cart without being bound, so that she should be able to hold her hymn-book, for he had summoned the school to sing a hymn by the way for her comfort, and he was ready to answer for it with his own head that she should not escape out of the cart. Moreover; it is the custom for fellows with pitchforks always to go with the carts wherein condemned criminals, and more especially witches, are carried to execution. But this the cruel Sheriff would not suffer, and the rope was left upon her hands, and the impudent constable seized her by the arm and led her from the judgment-chamber. But in the hall we saw a great *scandalum*, which again pierced my very heart. For the housekeeper and the impudent constable his wife were fighting for my child her bed, and her linen, and wearing apparel, which the housekeeper had taken for herself, and which the other woman wanted to have. The latter now called to her husband to help her, whereupon he straightway let go my daughter and struck the housekeeper on her mouth with his fist, so that the blood ran out therefrom, and she shrieked and wailed fearfully to the Sheriff, who followed us with the court. He threatened them both in vain, and said that when he came back he would inquire into the matter and give to each her due share. But they would not hearken to this, until my daughter asked *Dom. Consul* whether every dying person, even a condemned criminal, had power to leave his goods and chattels to whomsoever he would? and when he answered, "Yes, all but the clothes, which belong of right to the executioner," she said, "Well, then, the constable may take my clothes, but none shall have my bed save my faithful old maid-servant Ilse!" Hereupon the housekeeper began to curse and revile my child loudly, who heeded her not, but stepped out at the door toward the cart, where there stood so many people that nought could be seen save head against head. The folks crowded about us so tumultuously that the Sheriff, who, meanwhile, had mounted his grey horse, constantly smote them right and left across their eyes with his riding-whip, but they nevertheless would scarce fall back. Howbeit, at length he cleared the way, and when about ten fellows with long pitchforks, who for the most part also had rapiers at their sides, had placed themselves round about our cart, the constable lifted my daughter up into it, and bound her fast to the rail. Old Paasch, who stood by, lifted me up, and my dear gossip was likewise forced to be lifted in, so weak had he become from all the distress. He motioned his sexton, Master Krekow, to walk before the cart with the school, and bade him from time to time lead a verse of the goodly hymn, "On God alone I rest my fate," which he promised to do. And here I will also note, that I myself sat down upon the straw by my daughter, and that our dear confessor the reverend Martinus sat backwards. The constable was perched up behind with his drawn sword. When all this was done, *item*, the court mounted up into another carriage, the Sheriff gave the order to set out.

The Twenty-seventh Chapter

OF THAT WHICH BEFELL US BY THE WAY: *ITEM*, OF THE
FEARFUL DEATH OF THE SHERIFF AT THE MILL

We met with many wonders by the way, and with great sorrow; for hard
by the bridge, over the brook which runs into the Schmolle, stood the
housekeeper her hateful boy, who beat a drum and cried aloud, "Come
to the roast goose! come to the roast goose!" whereupon the crowd set
up a loud laugh, and called out after him, "Yes, indeed, to the roast
goose! to the roast goose!" Howbeit, when Master Krekow led the
second verse the folks became somewhat quieter again, and most of them
joined in singing it from their books, which they had brought with them.
But when he ceased singing awhile the noise began again as bad as before.
Some cried out, "The devil hath given her these clothes, and hath adorned
her after that fashion"; and seeing the Sheriff had ridden on before,
they came close round the cart, and felt her garments, more especially
the women and young maidens. Others, again, called loudly, as the young
varlet had done, "Come to the roast goose! come to the roast goose!"
whereupon one fellow answered, "She will not let herself be roasted
yet; mind ye that: she will quench the fire!" This, and much filthiness
beside, which I may not for very shame write down, we were forced to
hear, and it especially cut me to the heart to hear a fellow swear that he
would have some of her ashes, seeing he had not been able to get any
of the wand, and that nought was better for the fever and the gout than
the ashes of a witch. I motioned the *Custos* to begin singing again,
whereupon the folks were once more quiet for a while—*i.e.*, for so long
as the verse lasted; but afterwards they rioted worse than before. But we
were now come among the meadows, and when my child saw the beauteous
flowers which grew along the sides of the ditches, she fell into deep
thought, and began again to recite aloud the sweet song of St. Augustinus
as follows:—

> Flos perpetuus rosarum ver agit perpetuum,
> Candent lilia, rubescit crocus, sudat balsamum,
> Virent prata, vernant sata, rivi mellis influunt,
> Pigmentorum spirat odor liquor et aromatum,
> Pendent poma floridorum non lapsura nemorum,
> Non alternat luna vices, sol vel cursus syderum,
> Agnus est fælicis urbis lumen inocciduum.

By this *Casus* we gained that all the folk ran cursing away from the
cart, and followed us at the distance of a good musket-shot, thinking
that my child was calling on Satan to help her. Only one lad, of about
five-and-twenty, whom, however, I did not know, tarried a few paces
behind the cart, until his father came, and seeing he would not go away

willingly, pushed him into the ditch, so that he sank up to his loins in the water. Thereat even my poor child smiled, and asked me whether I did not know any more Latin hymns wherewith to keep the stupid and foul-mouthed people still further from us. But, dear reader, how could I then have been able to recite Latin hymns, even had I known any? But my *confrater*, the reverend Martinus, knew such an one; albeit it is indeed heretical; nevertheless, seeing that it above measure pleased my child, and that she made him repeat to her sundry verses thereof three and four times, until she could say them after him, I said nought; otherwise I have ever been very severe against aught that is heretical. Howbeit I comforted myself therewith that our Lord God would forgive her in consideration of her ignorance. And the first line ran as follows: —*Dies iræ, dies illa*. But these two verses pleased her more than all the rest, and she recited them many times with great edification, wherefore I will insert them here.

> Judex ergo cum sedebit
> Quidquid latet apparebit,
> Nil inultum remanebit:
>
> *Item,*
> Rex tremendæ majestatis!
> Qui salvandos salvas gratis,
> Salva me, fons pietatis!

When the men with the pitchforks, who were round about the cart, heard this, and at the same time saw a heavy storm coming up from the Achterwater, they straightway thought no other but that my child had made it; and, moreover, the folk behind cried out, "The witch hath done this; the damned witch hath done this!" and all the ten, save one, who stayed behind, jumped over the ditch, and ran away. But *Dom. Consul*, who, together with the worshipful court, drove behind us, no sooner saw this than he called to the constable, "What is the meaning of all this?" Whereupon the constable cried aloud to the Sheriff, who was a little way on before us, but who straightway turned him about, and when he had heard the cause, called after the fellows that he would hang them all up on the first tree, and feed his falcons with their flesh, if they did not return forthwith. This threat had its effect; and when they came back he gave each of them about half a dozen strokes with his riding-whip, whereupon they tarried in their places, but as far off from the cart as they could for the ditch.

Meanwhile, however, the storm came up from the southward, with thunder, lightning, hail, and such a wind, as though the all-righteous God would manifest his wrath against these ruthless murderers; and the tops of the lofty beeches around us were beaten together like besoms, so that our cart was covered with leaves as with hail, and no one could hear his own voice for the noise. This happened just as we were entering the forest from the convent dam, and the Sheriff now rode close behind us, beside the coach wherein was *Dom. Consul*. Moreover, just as we were crossing the bridge over the mill-race, we were seized by the blast, which swept up a hollow from the Achterwater with such force that we conceived it must drive our cart down the abyss, which was at least forty feet deep or more; and seeing that, at the same time, the horses did as though they were upon ice, and could not stand, the driver halted to let the storm pass over, the which the Sheriff no sooner perceived than he galloped up and bade him go on forthwith. Whereupon the man flogged on the horses, but they slipped about after so strange a fashion that our guards with the pitchforks fell back, and my child cried aloud for fear; and when we were come to the place where the great water-wheel turned just below us, the driver fell with his horse, which broke one of its legs. Then the constable jumped down from the cart, but straightway fell too on the slippery ground; *item*, the driver, after getting on his legs again, fell a second time. Hereupon the Sheriff, with a curse, spurred on his grey charger, which likewise began to slip as our horses had also done. Nevertheless, he came sliding towards us, without, however, falling down; and when he saw that the horse with the broken leg still tried to get up, but always straightway fell again on the slippery ground, he hallooed and beckoned the fellows with pitchforks to come and unharness the mare; *item*, to push the cart over the bridge, lest it should be carried down the precipice. Presently a long flash of lightning shot into the water below us, followed by a clap of thunder so sudden and so awful that the whole bridge shook, and the Sheriff his horse (our horses stood quite still) started back a few paces, lost its footing, and, together with its rider, shot headlong down upon the great mill-wheel below, whereupon a fearful cry arose from all those that stood behind us on the bridge. For a while nought could be seen for the white foam, until the Sheriff his legs and body were borne up into the air by the wheel, his head being stuck fast between the fellies; and thus, fearful to behold, he went round and round upon the wheel. Naught ailed the grey charger, which swam about in the mill-pond below. When I saw this I seized the hand of my innocent lamb, and cried, "Behold, Mary, our Lord God yet liveth! 'and he rode upon a cherub, and did fly; yea, he did fly upon the wings of the wind. Then did he beat them small as the dust before the wind; he did cast them out as the dirt in the streets.' Look down, and see what the Almighty God hath done." While she hereupon raised her eyes towards heaven with a sigh, we heard *Dom. Consul* calling out behind us as loudly as he could: and seeing that none could understand his words for the fearful storm and the tumult of the waters, he jumped down from the coach, and would have crossed the bridge on foot, but straightway he fell upon his nose, so that it bled, and he crept back again on his hands and feet, and held a long talk with *Dom. Camerarius*, who, howbeit, did not stir out of the coach. Meanwhile the driver and the constable had unyoked the maimed horse, bound it, and dragged it off the bridge, and now they came back to the cart and bade us get down therefrom and cross the bridge on foot, the which we did after the constable had unbound my child with many curses and ill words, threatening that, in return for her malice, he would keep her roasting till late in the evening. (I could not blame him much therefore; for truly this was a strange thing!) But albeit my child herself got safe across, we two—I mean reverend Martinus and myself—like all the others, fell two or three times to the ground. At length we all, by God his grace, got safe and sound to the miller's house, where the constable delivered my child into the miller his hands, to guard her on forfeit of his life, while he ran down to the mill-pond to save the Sheriff his grey charger. The driver was bidden the while to get the cart and the other horses off the bewitched bridge. We had, however, stood but a short time with the miller, under the great oak before his door, when *Dom. Consul*, with the worshipful court, and all the folks, came over the little bridge, which is but a couple of musket-shots off from the first one, and he could scarce prevent the crowd from falling upon my child and tearing her in pieces, seeing that they all, as well as *Dom. Consul* himself, imagined that none other but she had brewed the storm and bewitched the bridge (especially as she herself had not fallen thereon), and had likewise caused the Sheriff his death; all of which, nevertheless, were foul lies, as ye shall hereafter hear. He, therefore, railed at her for a cursed she-devil, who, even after having confessed and received the holy Sacrament, had not yet renounced Satan; but that nought should save her, and she should, nevertheless, receive her reward. And, seeing that she kept silence, I hereupon answered, "Did he not see that the all-righteous God had so ordered it, that the Sheriff, who would have robbed my innocent child of her honour and her life, had here forfeited his own life as a fearful example to others?" But *Dom. Consul* would not see this, and said that a child might perceive that our Lord God had not made this storm, or did I peradventure believe that our Lord God had likewise bewitched the bridge? I had better cease to justify my wicked child, and rather begin to exhort her to repent, seeing that this was the second time that she had brewed a storm, and that no man with a grain of sense could believe what I said, etc.

Meanwhile the miller had already stopped the mill, *item*, turned off the water, and some four or five fellows had gone with the constable down to the great water-wheel to take the Sheriff out of the fellies, wherein he had till *datum* still been carried round and round. This they could not

The Doom of the Wheel

do until they had first sawn out one of the fellies; and when at last they brought him to the bank, his neck was found to be broken, and he was as blue as a corn-flower. Moreover, his throat was frightfully torn, and the blood ran out of his nose and mouth. If the people had not reviled my child before, they reviled her doubly now, and would have thrown dirt and stones at her, had not the worshipful court interfered with might and main, saying that she would presently receive her well-deserved punishment.

Also, my dear gossip, the Reverend Martinus, climbed up into the cart again, and admonished the people not to forestall the law; and seeing that the storm had somewhat abated, he could now be heard. And when they had become somewhat more quiet, *Dom. Consul* left the corpse of the Sheriff in charge with the miller, until such time as, by God's help, he should return. *Item,* he caused the grey charger to be tied up to the oak-tree till the same time, seeing that the miller swore that he had no room in the mill, inasmuch as his stable was filled with straw; but that he would give the grey horse some hay, and keep good watch over him. And now were we wretched creatures forced to get into the cart again, after that the unsearchable will of God had once more dashed all our hopes. The constable gnashed his teeth with rage, while he took the cords out of his pocket to bind my poor child to the rail withal. As I saw right well what he was about to do, I pulled a few groats out of my pocket, and whispered into his ear, "Be merciful, for she cannot possibly run away, and do you hereafter help her to die quickly, and you shall get ten groats more from me!" This worked well, and albeit he pretended before the people to pull the ropes tight, seeing they all cried out with might and main, "Haul hard, haul hard!" in truth he bound her hands more gently than before, and even without making her fast to the rail; but he sat up behind us again with the naked sword, and after that *Dom. Consul* had prayed aloud, "God the Father, dwell with us," likewise the *Custos* had led another hymn (I know not what he sang, neither does my child), we went on our way, according to the unfathomable will of God, after this fashion: the worshipful court went before, whereas all the folks, to our great joy, fell back, and the fellows with the pitchforks lingered a good way behind us, now that the Sheriff was dead.

The Twenty-eighth Chapter
HOW MY DAUGHTER WAS AT LENGTH SAVED BY THE HELP OF THE ALL-MERCIFUL, YEA, OF THE ALL-MERCIFUL GOD

Meanwhile, by reason of my unbelief, wherewith Satan again tempted me, I had become so weak that I was forced to lean my back against the constable his knees, and expected not to live till even we should come to the mountain; for the last hope I had cherished was now gone, and I saw that my innocent lamb was in the same plight. Moreover, the reverend Martinus began to upbraid her, saying that he, too, now saw that all her oaths were lies, and that she really could brew storms. Hereupon, she answered with a smile, although, indeed, she was as white as a sheet, "Alas, reverend godfather, do you then really believe that the weather and the storms no longer obey our Lord God? Are storms, then, so rare at this season of the year, that none save the foul fiend can cause them? Nay, I have never broken the baptismal vow you once made in my name, nor will I ever break it, as I hope that God will be merciful to me in my last hour, which is now at hand." But the reverend Martinus shook his head doubtingly, and said, "The Evil One must have promised thee much, seeing thou remainest so stubborn even unto thy life's end, and blasphemest the Lord thy God; but wait, and thou wilt soon learn with horror that the devil 'is a liar, and the father of it'" (St. John viii.). Whilst he yet spake this, and more of a like kind, we came to Uekeritze, where all the people, both great and small, rushed out of their doors, also Jacob Schwarten his wife, who, as we afterwards heard, had only been brought to bed the night before, and her goodman came running after her to fetch her back, in vain. She told him he was a fool, and had been one for many a weary day, and that if she had to crawl up the mountain on her bare knees, she would go to see the parson's witch burned; that she had reckoned upon it for so long, and if he did not let her go, she would give him a thump on the chaps, etc.

Thus did the coarse and foul-mouthed people riot around the cart wherein we sat, and as they knew not what had befallen, they ran so near us that the wheel went over the foot of a boy. Nevertheless, they all crowded up again, more especially the lasses, and felt my daughter her clothes, and would even see her shoes and stockings, and asked her how she felt. *Item*, one fellow asked whether she would drink somewhat, with many more fooleries besides, till at last, when several came and asked her for her garland and her golden chain, she turned towards me and smiled, saying, "Father, I must begin to speak some Latin again, otherwise the folks will leave me no peace." But it was not wanted this time; for our guards, with the pitchforks, had now reached the hindmost, and, doubtless, told them what had happened, as we presently heard a great shouting behind us, for the love of God to turn back before the witch did them a mischief; and as Jacob Schwarten his wife heeded it not, but still plagued my child to give her her apron to make a christening coat for her baby, for that it was pity to let it be burnt, her goodman gave her such a thump on her back with a knotted stick which he had pulled out of the hedge that she fell down with loud shrieks; and when he went to help her up she pulled him down by his hair, and, as reverend Martinus said, now executed what she had threatened; inasmuch as she struck him on the nose with her fist with might and main, until the other people came running up to them, and held her back. Meanwhile, however, the storm had almost passed over, and sank down toward the sea.

And when we had gone through the little wood, we suddenly saw the Streckelberg before us, covered with people, and the pile and stake upon the top, upon the which the tall constable jumped up when he saw us coming, and beckoned with his cap with all his might. Thereat my senses left me, and my sweet lamb was not much better; for she bent to and fro like a reed, and stretching her bound hands towards heaven, she once more cried out:

> Rex tremendæ majestatis!
> Qui salvandos salvas gratis,
> Salva me, fons pietatis!

And, behold, scarce had she spoken these words, when the sun came out and formed a rainbow right over the mountain most pleasant to behold; and it is clear that this was a sign from the merciful God, such as he often gives us, but which we blind and unbelieving men do not rightly mark. Neither did my child heed it; for albeit she thought upon that first rainbow which shadowed forth our troubles, yet it seemed to her impossible that she could now be saved, wherefore she grew so faint, that she no longer heeded the blessed sign of mercy, and her head fell forward (for she could no longer lean it upon me, seeing that I lay my length at the bottom of the cart), till her garland almost touched my worthy gossip his knees. Thereupon he bade the driver stop for a moment, and pulled out a small flask filled with wine, which he always carries in his pocket when witches are to be burnt, in order to comfort them therewith in their terror. (Henceforth, I myself will ever do the like, for this fashion of my dear gossip pleases me well.) He first poured some of this wine down my throat, and afterwards down my child's; and we had scarce come to ourselves again, when a fearful noise and tumult arose among the people behind us, and they not only cried out in deadly fear, "The Sheriff is come back! the Sheriff is come again!" but as they could neither run away forwards or backwards (being afraid of the ghost behind and of my child before them), they ran on either side, some rushing into the coppice, and others wading into the Achterwater up to their necks. *Item*, as soon as *Dom. Camerarius* saw the ghost come out of the coppice with a grey hat and a grey feather, such as the Sheriff wore, riding on the grey charger, he crept under a bundle of straw in the cart: and *Dom. Consul* cursed my child again, and bade the coachman drive on as madly as they could, even should all the horses die of it, when the impudent constable behind us called to him, "It is not the

Sheriff, but the young lord of Nienkerken, who will surely seek to save the
witch: shall I, then, cut her throat with my sword?" At these fearful
words my child and I came to ourselves again, and the fellow had already
lift up his naked sword to smite her, seeing *Dom. Consul* had made him
a sign with his hand, when my dear gossip, who saw it, pulled my child
with all his strength back into his lap. (May God reward him on the day
of judgment, for I never can.) The villain would have stabbed her as she
lay in his lap; but the young lord was already there, and seeing what he
was about to do, thrust the boarspear, which he held in his hand, in
between the constable's shoulders, so that he fell headlong on the earth,
and his own sword, by the guidance of the most righteous God, went
into his ribs on one side, and out again at the other. He lay there and
bellowed, but the young lord heeded him not, but said to my child,
"Sweet maid, God be praised that you are safe!" When, however, he
saw her bound hands, he gnashed his teeth, and, cursing her judges,
he jumped off his horse, and cut the rope with his sword, which he held
in his right hand, took her hand in his, and said, "Alas, sweet maid, how
have I sorrowed for you! but I could not save you, as I myself also lay
in chains, which you may see from my looks."

But my child could answer him never a word, and fell into a swound
again for joy; howbeit, she soon came to herself again, seeing my dear
gossip still had a little wine by him. Meanwhile the dear young lord did
me some injustice, which, however, I freely forgive him; for he railed
at me and called me an old woman, who could do nought save weep and
wail. Why had I not journeyed after the Swedish king, or why had I
not gone to Mellenthin myself to fetch his testimony, as I knew right well
what he thought about witchcraft? (But, blessed God, how could I do
otherwise than believe the judge, who had been there? Others, besides
old women, would have done the same; and I never once thought of the
Swedish king; and say, dear reader, how could I have journeyed after
him, and left my own child? But young folks do not think of these things
seeing they know not what a father feels.)

Meanwhile, however, *Dom. Camerarius*, having heard that it was the
young lord, had again crept out from beneath the straw, *item*, *Dom.
Consul* had jumped down from the coach and ran towards us, railing at
him loudly, and asking him by what power and authority he acted thus,
seeing that he himself had heretofore denounced the ungodly witch?
But the young lord pointed with his sword to his people, who now came
riding out of the coppice, about eighteen strong, armed with sabres,
pikes, and muskets, and said, "There is my authority, and I would let
you feel it on your back if I did not know that you were but a stupid ass.
When did you hear any testimony from me against this virtuous maiden?
You lie in your throat if you say you did." And as *Dom. Consul* stood and

straightway forswore himself, the young lord, to the astonishment of all, related as follows:—That as soon as he heard of the misfortune which had befallen me and my child, he ordered his horse to be saddled forthwith, in order to ride to Pudgla to bear witness to our innocence: this, however, his old father would nowise suffer, thinking that his nobility would receive a stain if it came to be known that his son had conversed with a reputed witch by night on the Streckelberg. He had caused him therefore, as prayers and threats were of no avail, to be bound hand and foot, and confined in the donjon-keep, where till *datum* an old servant had watched him, who refused to let him escape, notwithstanding he offered him any sum of money; whereupon he fell into the greatest anguish and despair at the thought that innocent blood would be shed on his account; but that the all-righteous God had graciously spared him this sorrow; for his father had fallen sick from vexation, and lay a-bed all this time, and it so happened that this very morning about prayer-time the huntsman, in shooting at a wild duck in the moat, had by chance sorely wounded his father's favourite dog, called Packan, which had crept howling to his father's bedside, and had died there; whereupon the old man, who was weak, was so angered that he was presently seized with a fit and gave up the ghost too. Hereupon his people released him, and after he had closed his father's eyes and prayed an "Our Father" over him, he straightway set out with all the people he could find in the castle in order to save the innocent maiden. For he testified here himself before all, on the word and honour of a knight, nay, more, by his hopes of salvation, that he himself was that devil which had appeared to the maiden on the mountain in the shape of a hairy giant; for having heard by common report that she ofttimes went thither, he greatly desired to know what she did there, and that from fear of his hard father he disguised himself in a wolf's skin, so that none might know him, and he had already spent two nights there, when on the third the maiden came, and he then saw her dig for amber on the mountain, and that she did not call upon Satan, but recited a Latin *carmen* aloud to herself. This he would have testified at Pudgla, but, from the cause aforesaid, he had not been able: moreover, his father had laid his cousin, Claus von Nienkerken, who was there on a visit, in his bed, and made him bear false witness; for as *Dom. Consul* had not seen him (I mean the young lord) for many a long year, seeing he had studied in foreign parts, his father thought that he might easily be deceived, which accordingly happened.

When the worthy young lord had stated this before *Dom. Consul* and all the people, which flocked together on hearing that the young lord was no ghost, I felt as though a millstone had been taken off my heart; and seeing that the people (who had already pulled the constable from under the cart, and crowded round him, like a swarm of bees) cried to me that he was dying, but desired first to confess somewhat to me, I jumped from the cart as lightly as a young bachelor, and called to *Dom. Consul* and the young lord to go with me, seeing that I could easily guess what he had on his mind. He sat upon a stone, and the blood gushed from his side like a fountain (now that they had drawn out the sword); he whimpered on seeing me, and said that he had in truth hearkened behind the door to all that old Lizzie had confessed to me, namely, that she herself, together with the Sheriff, had worked all the witchcraft on man and beast, to frighten my poor child, and force her to play the wanton. That he had hidden this, seeing that the Sheriff had promised him a great reward for so doing; but that he would now confess it freely, since God had brought my child her innocence to light. Wherefore he besought my child and myself to forgive him. And when *Dom. Consul* shook his head, and asked whether he would live and die on the truth of this confession, he answered, "Yes!" and straightway fell on his side to the earth and gave up the ghost.

Meanwhile time hung heavy with the people on the mountain, who had come from Coserow, from Zitze, from Gnitze, etc., to see my child burnt, and they all came running down the hill in long rows like geese, one after the other, to see what had happened. And among them was my ploughman, Claus Neels. When the worthy fellow saw and heard what had befallen us, he began to weep aloud for joy; and straightway he too told what he had heard the Sheriff say to old Lizzie in the garden, and how he had promised a pig in the room of her own little pig, which she had herself bewitched to death in order to bring my child into evil repute. *Summa*: all that I have noted above, and which till *datum* he had kept to himself for fear of the question. Hereat all the people marvelled, and gently bewailed her misfortunes; and many came, among them old Paasch, and would have kissed my daughter her hands and feet, as also mine own, and praised us now as much as they had before reviled us. But thus it ever is with the people. Wherefore my departed father used to say:

> The people's hate is death,
> Their love a passing breath!

My dear gossip ceased not from fondling my child, holding her in his lap, and weeping over her like a father (for I could not have wept more myself than he wept). Howbeit she herself wept not, but begged the young lord to send one of his horsemen to her faithful old maid-servant at Pudgla, to tell her what had befallen us, which he straightway did to please her. But the worshipful court (for *Dom. Camerarius* and the *scriba* had now plucked up a heart, and had come down from the coach) was not yet satisfied, and *Dom. Consul* began to tell the young lord about the bewitched bridge, which none other save my daughter could have bewitched. Hereto the young lord gave answer that this was indeed a strange thing, inasmuch as his own horse had also broken a leg thereon, whereupon he had taken the Sheriff his horse, which he saw tied up at the mill; but he did not think that this could be laid to the charge of the maiden, but that it came about by natural means, as he had half discovered already, although he had not had time to search the matter thoroughly. Wherefore he besought the worshipful court and all the people, together with my child herself, to return back thither, where, with God's help, he would clear her from this suspicion also, and prove her perfect innocence before them all.

Thereunto the worshipful court agreed; and the young lord, having given the Sheriff his grey charger to my ploughman to carry the corpse, which had been laid across the horse's neck, to Coserow, the young lord got into the cart by us, but did not seat himself beside my child, but backward by my dear gossip: moreover, he bade one of his own people drive us instead of the old coachman, and thus we turned back in God his name. *Custos Benzensis*, who, with the children, had run in among the vetches by the wayside (my defunct *Custos* would not have done so, he had more courage), went on before again with the young folks, and by command of his reverence the pastor led the Ambrosian *Te Deum*, which deeply moved us all, more especially my child, insomuch that her book was wetted with her tears, and she at length laid it down and said, at the same time giving her hand to the young lord, "How can I thank God and you for that which you have done for me this day?" Whereupon the young lord answered, saying, "I have greater cause to thank God than yourself, sweet maid, seeing that you have suffered in your dungeon unjustly, but I justly, inasmuch as by my thoughtlessness I brought this misery upon you. Believe me that this morning when, in my donjon-keep, I first heard the sound of the dead-bell, I thought to have died; and when it tolled for the third time, I should have gone distraught in my grief, had not the Almighty God at that moment taken the life of my strange father, so that your innocent life should be saved by me. Wherefore I have vowed a new tower, and whatsoe'er beside may be needful, to the blessed house of God; for nought more bitter could have befallen me on earth than your death, sweet maid, and nought more sweet than your life!"

But at these words my child only wept and sighed; and when he looked on her, she cast down her eyes and trembled, so that I straightway perceived that my sorrows were not yet come to an end, but that another barrel of tears was just tapped for me, and so indeed it was. Moreover, the ass of a *Custos*, having finished the *Te Deum* before we were come to the bridge, straightway struck up the next following hymn, which was a funeral one, beginning, "The body let us now inter." (God be praised that no harm has come of it till *datum*.) My beloved gossip rated him not a little, and threatened him that for his stupidity he should not get the money for the shoes which he had promised him out of the Church-dues. But my child comforted him, and promised him a pair of shoes at her own charges, seeing that peradventure a funeral hymn was better for her than a song of gladness.

And when this vexed the young lord, and he said, "How now, sweet maid, you know not how enough to thank God and me for your rescue, and yet you speak thus?" She answered, smiling sadly, that she had only spoken thus to comfort the poor *Custos*. But I straightway saw that she was in earnest, for that she felt that although she had escaped one fire, she already burned in another.

Meanwhile we were come to the bridge again, and all the folks stood still, and gazed open-mouthed, when the young lord jumped down from the cart, and after stabbing his horse, which still lay kicking on the bridge, went on his knees, and felt here and there with his hand. At length he called to the worshipful court to draw near, for that he had found out the witchcraft. But none save *Dom. Consul* and a few fellows out of the crowd, among whom was old Paasch, would follow him; *item*, my dear gossip and myself, and the young lord, showed us a lump of tallow about the size of a large walnut, which lay on the ground, and wherewith the whole bridge had been smeared, so that it looked quite white, but, which all the folks in their fright had taken for flour out of the mill; *item*, with some other *materia*, which stunk like fitchock's dung, but what it was we could not find out. Soon after a fellow found another bit of tallow, and showed it to the people; whereupon I cried, "Aha! none hath done this but that ungodly miller's man, in revenge for the stripes which the Sheriff gave him for reviling my child." Whereupon I told what he had done, and *Dom. Consul*, who also had heard thereof, straightway sent for the miller.

He, however, did as though he knew nought of the matter, and only said that his man had left his service about an hour ago. But a young lass, the miller's maid-servant, said that that very morning, before daybreak, when she had got up to let out the cattle, she had seen the man scouring the bridge. But that she had given it no further heed, and had gone to sleep for another hour; and she pretended to know no more than the miller whither the rascal was gone. When the young lord had heard this news, he got up into the cart, and began to address the people, seeking to persuade them no longer to believe in witchcraft, now that they had seen what it really was. When I heard this, I was horror-stricken (as was but right) in my conscience, as a priest, and I got upon the cart-wheel, and whispered into his ear, for God his sake, to leave this *materia*, seeing that if the people no longer feared the devil, neither would they fear our Lord God.

The dear young lord forthwith did as I would have him, and only asked the people whether they now held my child to be perfectly innocent? and when they had answered, "Yes!" he begged them to go quietly home, and to thank God that he had saved innocent blood. That he, too, would now return home, and that he hoped that none would molest me and my child if he let us return to Coserow alone. Hereupon he turned hastily towards her, took her hand and said: "Farewell, sweet maid, I trust that I shall soon clear your honour before the world, but do you thank God therefor, not me." He then did the like to me and to my dear gossip, whereupon he jumped down from the cart, and went and sat beside *Dom. Consul* in his coach. The latter also spake a few words to the people, and likewise begged my child and me to forgive him (and I must say it to his honour, that the tears ran down his cheeks the while), but he was so hurried by the young lord that he brake short his discourse, and they drove off over the little bridge, without so much as looking back. Only *Dom. Consul* looked round once, and called out to me, that in his hurry he had forgotten to tell the executioner that no one was to be burned to-day: I was therefore to send the churchwarden of Uekeritze up the mountain, to say so in his name; the which I did. And the blood-hound was still on the mountain, albeit he had long since heard what had befallen; and when the bailiff gave him the orders of the worshipful court, he began to curse so fearfully that it might have awakened the dead; moreover, he plucked off his cap, and trampled it under foot, so that any one might have guessed what he felt.

But to return to ourselves, my child sat as still and as white as a pillar of salt, after the young lord had left her so suddenly and so unawares, but she was somewhat comforted when the old maid-servant came running with her coats tucked up to her knees, and carrying her shoes and stockings in her hands. We heard her afar off, as the mill had stopped, blubbering for joy, and she fell at least three times on the bridge, but at last she got over safe, and kissed now mine and now my child her hands and feet; begging us only not to turn her away, but to keep her until her life's end; the which we promised to do. She had to climb up behind where the impudent constable had sat, seeing that my dear gossip would not leave me until I should be back in mine own manse. And as the young lord his servant had got up behind the coach, old Paasch drove us home, and all the folks who had waited till *datum* ran beside the cart, praising and pitying as much as they had before scorned and reviled us. Scarce, however, had we passed through Uekeritze, when we again heard cries of "Here comes the young lord, here comes the young lord!" so that my child started up for joy, and became as red as a rose; but some of the folks ran into the buckwheat, by the road, again, thinking it was another ghost. It was, however, in truth, the young lord who galloped up on a black horse, calling out as he drew near us, "Notwithstanding the haste I am in, sweet maid, I must return and give you safe-conduct home, seeing that I have just heard that the filthy people reviled you by the way, and I know not whether you are yet safe." Hereupon he urged old Paasch to mend his pace, and as his kicking and trampling did not even make the horses trot, the young lord struck the saddle-horse from time to time with the flat of his sword, so that we soon reached the village and the manse. Howbeit, when I prayed him to dismount a while, he would not, but excused himself, saying that he must still ride through Usedom to Anclam, but charged old Paasch, who was our bailiff, to watch over my child as the apple of his eye, and should anything unusual happen he was straightway to inform the town-clerk at Pudgla, or *Dom. Consul* at Usedom, thereof, and when Paasch had promised to do this, he waved his hand to us, and galloped off as fast as he could.

But before he got round the corner by Pagel his house, he turned back for the third time: and when we wondered thereat, he said we must forgive him, seeing his thoughts wandered to-day.

That I had formerly told him that I still had my patent of nobility, the which he begged me to lend him for a time. Hereupon I answered that I must first seek for it, and that he had best dismount the while. But he would not, and again excused himself, saying he had no time. He therefore stayed without the door, until I brought him the patent, whereupon he thanked me and said, "Do not wonder hereat, you will soon see what my purpose is." Whereupon he struck his spurs into his horse's sides and did not come back again.

The Twenty-ninth Chapter
OF OUR NEXT GREAT SORROW, AND FINAL JOY

And now might we have been at rest, and have thanked God on our knees by day and night. For, besides mercifully saving us out of such great tribulation, he turned the hearts of my beloved flock, so that they knew not how to do enough for us. Every day they brought us fish, meat, eggs, sausages, and whatsoe'er besides they could give me, and which I have since forgotten. Moreover they, every one of them, came to church the next Sunday, great and small (except goodwife Kliene of Zempin, who had just got a boy, and still kept her bed), and I preached a thanksgiving sermon on Job v. 17, 18, and 19 verses, "Behold, happy is the man whom God correcteth; therefore despise not thou the chastening of the Almighty: for he maketh sore, and bindeth up; and his hands make whole.

He shall deliver thee in six troubles, yea, in seven there shall no evil touch thee." And during my sermon I was ofttimes forced to stop by reason of all the weeping, and to let them blow their noses. And I might truly have compared myself to Job, after that the Lord had mercifully released him from his troubles, had it not been for my child, who prepared much fresh grief for me.

She had wept when the young lord would not dismount, and now that he came not again, she grew more uneasy from day to day. She sat and read first the Bible, then the hymn-book, *item*, the history of Dido in *Virgilius*, or she climbed up the mountain to fetch flowers (likewise sought after the vein of amber there, but found it not, which shows the cunning and malice of Satan). I saw this for a while with many sighs, but spake not a word (for, dear reader, what could I say?) until it grew worse and worse; and as she now recited her *carmina* more than ever both at home and abroad, I feared lest the people should again repute her a witch, and one day I followed her up the mountain. Well-a-day, she sat on the pile, which still stood there, but with her face turned towards the sea, reciting the *versus* where Dido mounts the funeral pile in order to stab herself for love of Æneas:—

> At trepida et cœptis immanibus effera Dido
> Sanguineam volvens aciem, maculisque trementes
> Interfusa genas, et pallida morte futurâ
> Interiora domus irrumpit limina et altos
> Conscendit furibunda rogos . . . .

When I saw this, and heard how things really stood with her, I was affrighted beyond measure, and cried, "Mary, my child, what art thou doing?" She started when she heard my voice, but sat still on the pile, and answered, as she covered her face with her apron, "Father, I am burning my heart." I drew near to her and pulled the apron from her face, saying, "Wilt thou, then, again kill me with grief?" whereupon she covered her face with her hands, and moaned, "Alas, father, wherefore was I not burned here? My torment would then have endured but for a moment, but now it will last as long as I live!" I still did as though I had seen nought, and said, "Wherefore, dear child, dost thou suffer such torment?" whereupon she answered, "I have long been ashamed to tell you; for the young lord, the young lord, my father, do I suffer this torment! He no longer thinks of me; and albeit he saved my life he scorns me, or he would surely have dismounted and come in a while; but we are of far too low degree for him!" Hereupon I indeed began to comfort her and to persuade her to think no more of the young lord; but the more I comforted her, the worse she grew. Nevertheless I saw that she did yet in secret cherish a strong hope by reason of the patent of nobility which he had made me give him. I would not take this hope from her, seeing that I felt the same myself, and to comfort her I flattered her hopes, whereupon she was more quiet for some days, and did not go up the mountain, the which I had forbidden her. Moreover, she began again to teach little Paasch her god-daughter, out of whom, by the help of the all-righteous God, Satan was now altogether departed. But she still pined, and was as white as a sheet; and when soon after a report came that none in the castle at Mellenthin knew what was become of the young lord, and that they thought he had been killed, her grief became so great that I had to send my ploughman on horseback to Mellenthin to gain tidings of him. And she looked at least twenty times out of the door and over the paling to watch for his return; and when she saw him coming she ran out to meet him as far as the corner by Pagels. But, blessed God! he brought us even worse news than we had heard before, saying, that the people at the castle had told him that their young master had ridden away the self-same day whereon he had rescued the maiden. That he had, indeed, returned after three days to his father's funeral, but had straightway ridden off again, and that for five weeks they had heard nothing further of him, and knew not whither he was gone, but supposed that some wicked ruffians had killed him.

And now my grief was greater than ever it had been before; so patient and resigned to the will of God as my child had shown herself heretofore, and no martyr could have met her last hour stronger in God and Christ, so impatient and despairing was she now. She gave up all hope, and took it into her head that in these heavy times of war the young lord had been killed by robbers. Nought availed with her, not even prayer, for when I called upon God with her, on my knees, she straightway began so grievously to bewail that the Lord had cast her off, and that she was condemned to nought save misfortunes in this world; that it pierced through my heart like a knife, and my thoughts forsook me at her words. She lay also at night, and "like a crane or a swallow so did she chatter; she did mourn like a dove; her eyes did fail with looking upward," because no sleep came upon her eyelids. I called to her from my bed, "Dear child, wilt thou, then, never cease? sleep, I pray thee!" and she answered and said, "Do you sleep, dearest father; I cannot sleep until I sleep the sleep of death. Alas, my father; that I was not burned!" But how could I sleep when she could not? I indeed said, each morning, that I had slept a while, in order to content her; but it was not so; but, like David, "all the night made I my bed to swim; I watered my couch with my tears." Moreover I again fell into heavy unbelief, so that I neither could nor would pray. Nevertheless the Lord "did not deal with me after my sins, nor reward me according to mine iniquities. For as the heaven is high above the earth, so great was his mercy toward" me, miserable sinner!

For mark what happened on the very next Saturday! Behold, our old maid-servant came running in at the door, quite out of breath, saying that a horseman was coming over the Master's Mount, with a tall plume waving on his hat, and that she believed it was the young lord. When my child, who sat upon the bench combing her hair, heard this, she gave a shriek of joy, which would have moved a stone under the earth, and straightway ran out of the room to look over the paling. She presently came running in again, fell upon my neck, and cried without ceasing, "The young lord! the young lord!" whereupon she would have run out to meet him, but I forbade her, saying she had better first bind up her hair, which she then remembered, and laughing, weeping, and praying, all at once, she bound up her long hair. And now the young lord came galloping round the corner, attired in a green velvet doublet with red silk sleeves, and a grey hat with a heron's feather therein; *summa*, gaily dressed as beseems a wooer. And when we now ran out at the door, he called aloud to my child in the Latin, from afar off, " *Quomodo stat dulcissima virgo?*" Whereupon she gave answer, saying, "*Bene te aspecto.*" He then sprang smiling off his horse, and gave it into the charge of my ploughman, who meanwhile had come up together with the maid; but he was affrighted when he saw my child so pale, and taking her hand spake in the vulgar tongue, "My God! what is it ails you, sweet maid? you look more pale than when about to go to the stake." Whereupon she answered, "I have been at the stake daily since you left us, good my lord, without coming into our house, or so much as sending us tidings of whither you were gone."

This pleased him well, and he said, "Let us first of all go into the chamber, and you shall hear all." And when he had wiped the sweat from his brow, and sat down on the bench beside my child, he spake as follows:—That he had straightway promised her that he would clear her honour before the whole world, and the self-same day whereon he left us he made the worshipful court draw up an authentic record of all that had taken place, more especially the confession of the impudent constable, *item*, that of my ploughboy, Claus Neels; wherewith he rode throughout the same night, as he had promised, to Anclam, and next day to Stettin, to our gracious sovereign Duke Bogislaw: who marvelled greatly when he heard of the wickedness of his Sheriff, and of that which he had done to my child: moreover, he asked whether she were the pastor's daughter who once upon a time had found the signet-ring of his Princely Highness Philippus Julius of most Christian memory in the castle garden at Wolgast? and as he did not know thereof, the Duke asked, whether she knew Latin? And he, the young lord, answered yes, that she knew the Latin better than he did himself. His Princely Highness said, "Then, indeed, it must be the same," and straightway he put on his spectacles, and read the *acta* himself. Hereupon, and after his Princely Highness had read the record of the worshipful court, shaking his head the while, the young lord humbly besought his Princely Highness to give him an *amende honorable* for my child, *item, literas commendatitias* for himself to our most gracious Emperor at Vienna, to beg for a renewal of my patent of nobility, seeing that he was determined to marry none other maiden than my daughter so long as he lived.

When my child heard this, she gave a cry of joy, and fell back in a swound with her head against the wall. But the young lord caught her in his arms, and gave her three kisses (which I could not then deny him, seeing, as I did with joy, how matters went), and when she came to herself again, he asked her, whether she would not have him, seeing that she had given a cry at his words? Whereupon she said, "Whether I will not have you, my lord! Alas! I love you as dearly as my God and my Saviour! You first saved my life, and now you have snatched my heart from the stake, whereon, without you, it would have burned all the days of my life!" Hereupon I wept for joy, when he drew her into his lap, and she clasped his neck with her little hands.

They thus sat and toyed a while, till the young lord again perceived me, and said, "What say you thereto; I trust it is also your will, reverend Abraham?" Now, dear reader, what could I say, save my hearty good-will? seeing that I wept for very joy, as did my child, and I answered, how should it not be my will, seeing that it was the will of God? But whether the worthy, good young lord had likewise considered that he would stain his noble name if he took to wife my child, who had been habit and repute a witch, and had been well-nigh bound to the stake?

Hereupon he said, By no means; for that he had long since prevented this, and he proceeded to tell us how he had done it, namely, his Princely Highness had promised him to make ready all the *scripta* which he required, within four days, when he hoped to be back from his father's burial. He therefore rode straightway back to Mellenthin, and after paying the last honour to my lord his father, he presently set forth on his way again, and found that his Princely Highness had kept his word meanwhile. With these *scripta* he rode to Vienna, and albeit he met with many pains, troubles, and dangers by the way (which he would relate to us at some other time), he nevertheless reached the city safely. There he by chance met with a Jesuit with whom he had once upon a time had his *locamentum* for a few days at Prague, while he was yet a *studiosus*, and this man, having heard his business, bade him be of good cheer, seeing that his Imperial Majesty stood sorely in need of money in these hard times of war, and that he, the Jesuit, would manage it all for him. This he really did, and his Imperial Majesty not only renewed my patent of nobility, but likewise confirmed the *amende honorable* to my child granted by his Princely Highness the Duke, so that he might now maintain the honour of his betrothed bride against all the world, as also hereafter that of his wife.

Hereupon he drew forth the *acta* from his bosom, and put them into my hand, saying, "And now, reverend Abraham, you must also do me a pleasure, to wit, tomorrow morning, when I hope to go with my betrothed bride to the Lord's table, you must publish the banns between me and your daughter, and on the day after you must marry us. Do not say nay thereto, for my pastor, the reverend Philippus, says that this is no uncommon custom among the nobles in Pomerania, and I have already given notice of the wedding for Monday at mine own castle, whither we will then go, and where I purpose to bed my bride." I should have found much to say against this request, more especially that in honour of the Holy Trinity he should suffer himself to be called three times in church according to custom, and that he should delay a while the espousals; but when I perceived that my child would gladly have the marriage held right soon, for she sighed and grew red as scarlet, I had not the heart to refuse them, but promised all they asked. Whereupon I exhorted them both to prayer, and when I had laid my hands upon their heads, I thanked the Lord more deeply than I had ever yet thanked him, so that at last I could no longer speak for tears, seeing that they drowned my voice.

Meanwhile the young lord his coach had driven up to the door, filled with chests and coffers: and he said, "Now, sweet maid, you shall see what I have brought you," and he bade them bring all the things into the room. Dear reader, what fine things were there, such as I had never seen in all my life! All that women can use was there, especially of clothes, to wit, bodices, plaited gowns, long robes, some of them bordered with fur, veils, aprons, *item*, the bridal shift with gold fringes, whereon the merry lord had laid some six or seven bunches of myrtle to make herself a wreath withal. *Item*, there was no end to the rings, neck-chains, ear-drops, etc., the which I have in part forgotten. Neither did the young lord leave me without a gift, seeing he had brought me a new surplice (the enemy had robbed me of my old one), also doublets, hosen, and shoes, *summa*, whatsoever appertains to a man's attire; wherefore I secretly besought the Lord not to punish us again in his sore displeasure for such pomps and vanities. When my child beheld all these things she was grieved that she could bestow upon him nought save her heart alone, and the chain of the Swedish king, the which she hung round his neck, and begged him, weeping the while, to take it as a bridal gift. This he at length promised to do, and likewise to carry it with him into the grave: but that my child must first wear it at her wedding, as well as the blue silken gown, for that this and no other should be her bridal dress, and this he made her promise to do.

And now a merry chance befell with the old maid, the which I will here note. For when the faithful old soul had heard what had taken place, she was beside herself for joy, danced and clapped her hands, and at last said to my child, "Now to be sure you will not weep when the young lord is to lie in your bed," whereat my child blushed scarlet for shame, and ran out of the room; and when the young lord would know what she meant therewith, she told him that he had already once slept in my child her bed when he came from Gützkow with me, whereupon he bantered her all the evening after that she was come back again. Moreover, he promised the maid that as she had once made my child her bed for him, she should make it again, and that on the day after to-morrow she and the ploughman too should go with us to Mellenthin, so that masters and servants should all rejoice together after such great distress.

And seeing that the dear young lord would stop the night under my roof, I made him lie in the small closet together with me (for I could not know what might happen). He soon slept like a top, but no sleep came into my eyes, for very joy, and I prayed the livelong blessed night, or thought over my sermon. Only near morning I dozed a little; and when I rose the young lord already sat in the next room with my child, who wore the black silken gown which he had brought her, and, strange to say, she looked fresher than even when the Swedish king came, so that I never in all my life saw her look fresher or fairer. *Item*, the young lord wore his black doublet, and picked out for her the best bits of myrtle for the wreath she was twisting. But when she saw me, she straightway laid the wreath beside her on the bench, folded her little hands, and said the morning prayer, as she was ever wont to do, which humility pleased the young lord right well, and he begged her that in future she would ever do the like with him, the which she promised.

Soon after we went to the blessed church to confession, and all the folk stood gaping open-mouthed because the young lord led my child on his arm. But they wondered far more when, after the sermon, I first read to them in the vulgar tongue the *amende honorable* to my child from his Princely Highness, together with the confirmation of the same by his Imperial Majesty, and after that my patent of nobility; and, lastly, began to publish the banns between my child and the young lord. Dear reader, there arose a murmur throughout the church like the buzzing of a swarm of bees. (N.B. These *scripta* were burnt in the fire which broke out in the castle a year ago, as I shall hereafter relate, wherefore I cannot insert them here *in origine*.)

Hereupon my dear children went together with much people to the Lord's table, and after church nearly all the folks crowded round them and wished them joy. *Item*, old Paasch came to our house again that afternoon, and once more besought my daughter's forgiveness because

The Bridal Gifts

that he had unwittingly offended her; that he would gladly give her a marriage-gift, but that he now had nothing at all; howbeit that his wife should set one of her hens in the spring, and he would take the chickens to her at Mellenthin himself. This made us all to laugh, more especially the young lord, who at last said: "As thou wilt bring me a marriage-gift, thou must also be asked to the wedding, wherefore thou mayest come to-morrow with the rest."

Whereupon my child said: "And your little Mary, my god-child, shall come too, and be my bridemaiden, if my lord allows it." Whereupon she began to tell the young lord all that that had befallen the child by the malice of Satan, and how they laid it to her charge until such time as the all-righteous God brought her innocence to light; and she begged that since her dear lord had commanded her to wear the same garments at her wedding which she had worn to salute the Swedish king, and afterwards to go to the stake, he would likewise suffer her to take for her bridemaiden her little god-child, as *indicium secundum* of her sorrows.

And when he had promised her this, she told old Paasch to send hither his child to her, that she might fit a new gown upon her which she had cut out for her a week ago, and which the maid would finish sewing this very day. This so went to the heart of the good old fellow that he began to weep aloud, and at last said, she should not do all this for nothing, for instead of the one hen his wife should set three for her in the spring.

When he was gone, and the young lord did nought save talk with his betrothed bride, both in the vulgar and in the Latin tongue, I did better —namely, went up the mountain to pray, wherein, moreover, I followed my child's example, and clomb up upon the pile, there in loneliness to offer up my whole heart to the Lord as an offering of thanksgiving, seeing that with this sacrifice he is well pleased, as in Ps. li. 19, "The sacrifice of God is a troubled spirit; a broken and contrite heart, O God, shalt thou not despise."

That night the young lord again lay in my room, but next morning, when the sun had scarce risen——

———————

Here end these interesting communications, which I do not intend to dilute with any additions of my own. My readers, more especially those of the fair sex, can picture to themselves at pleasure the future happiness of this excellent pair.

All further historical traces of their existence, as well as that of the pastor, have disappeared, and nothing remains but a tablet fixed in the wall of the church at Mellenthin, on which the incomparable lord, and his yet more incomparable wife, are represented. On his faithful breast still hangs "the golden chain, with the effigy of the Swedish King."

They both seem to have died within a short time of each other, and to have been buried in the same coffin. For in the vault under the church there is still a large double coffin, in which, according to tradition, lies a chain of gold of incalculable value. Some twenty years ago, the owner of Mellenthin, whose unequalled extravagance had reduced him to the verge of beggary, attempted to open the coffin in order to take out this precious relic, but he was not able. It appeared as if some powerful spell held it firmly together; and it has remained unopened down to the present time. May it remain so until the last awful day, and may the impious hand of avarice or curiosity never desecrate these holy ashes of holy beings!

FINIS

MONSIEUR
MAURICE

AMELIA B. EDWARDS

The events I am about to relate took place more than fifty years ago. I am a white-haired old woman now, and I was then a little girl scarce ten years of age; but those times, and the places and people associated with them, seem, in truth, to lie nearer my memory than the times and people of to-day. Trivial incidents which, if they had happened yesterday, would be forgotten, come back upon me sometimes with all the vivid detail of a photograph; and words unheeded many a year ago start out, like the handwriting on the wall, in sudden characters of fire.

But this is no new experience. As age creeps on, we all have the same tale to tell. The days of our youth are those we remember best and most fondly, and even the sorrows of that bygone time become pleasures in the retrospect. Of my own solitary childhood I retain the keenest recollection, as the following pages will show.

My father's name was Bernhard—Johann Ludwig Bernhard; and he was a native of Coblentz on the Rhine. Having grown grey in the Prussian service, fought his way slowly and laboriously from the ranks upward, been seven times wounded and twice promoted on the field, he was made colonel of his regiment in 1814, when the Allies entered Paris. In 1819, being no longer fit for active service, he retired on a pension, and was appointed King's steward of the Château of Augustenburg at Brühl—a sort of military curatorship to which few duties and certain contingent emoluments were attached. Of these last, a suite of rooms in the Château, a couple of acres of private garden, and the revenue accruing from a small local impost, formed the most important part. It was towards the latter half of this year (1819) that, having now for the first time in his life a settled home in which to receive me, my father fetched me from Nuremberg where I was living with my aunt, Martha Baur, and took me to reside with him at Brühl.

Now my aunt, Martha Baur, was an exemplary person in her way; a rigid Lutheran, a strict disciplinarian, and the widow of a wealthy wool-stapler. She lived in a gloomy old house near the Frauen-Kirche, where she received no society, and led a life as varied and lively on the whole as that of a Trappist. Every Wednesday afternoon we paid a visit to the grave of her "blessed man" in the Protestant cemetery outside the walls, and on Sundays we went three times to church. These were the only breaks in the long monotony of our daily life. On market-days we never went out of doors at all; and when the great annual fair-time came round, we drew down all the front blinds and inhabited the rooms at the back.

As for the pleasures of childhood, I cannot say that I knew many of them in those old Nuremberg days. Still I was not unhappy, nor even very dull. It may be that, knowing nothing pleasanter, I was not even conscious of the dreariness of the atmosphere I breathed. There was, at all events, a big old-fashioned garden full of vegetables and cottage-flowers, at the back of the house, in which I almost lived in Spring and Summer-time, and from which I managed to extract a great deal of enjoyment; while for companions and playmates I had old Karl, my aunt's gardener, a pigeon-house full of pigeons, three staid elderly cats, and a tortoise. In the way of education I fared scantily enough, learning just as little as it pleased my aunt to teach me, and having that little presented to me under its driest and most unattractive aspect.

Such was my life till I went away with my father in the Autumn of 1819. I was then between nine and ten years of age—having lost my mother in earliest infancy, and lived with aunt Martha Baur ever since I could remember.

The change from Nuremberg to Brühl was for me like the transition from Purgatory to Paradise. I enjoyed for the first time all the delights of liberty. I had no lessons to learn; no stern aunt to obey; but, which was infinitely pleasanter, a kind-hearted Rhenish Mädchen, with a silver arrow in her hair, to wait upon me; and an indulgent father whose only orders were that I should be allowed to have my own way in everything.

And my way was to revel in the air and the sunshine; to roam about the park and pleasure-grounds; to watch the soldiers at drill, and hear the band play every day, and wander at will about the deserted state-apartments of the great empty Château.

Looking back upon it from this distance of time, I should pronounce the Electoral Residenz at Brühl to be a miracle of bad taste; but not Aladdin's palace if planted amid the gardens of Armida could then have seemed lovelier in my eyes. The building, a heavy many-windowed pile in the worst style of the worst Renaissance period, stood, and still stands, in a fat, flat country about ten miles from Cologne, to which city it bears much the same relation that Hampton Court bears to London, or Versailles to Paris. Stucco and whitewash had been lavished upon it inside and out, and pallid scagliola did duty everywhere for marble. A grand staircase supported by agonised colossi, grinning and writhing in vain efforts to look as if they didn't mind the weight, led from the great hall to the state apartments; and in these rooms the bad taste of the building may be said to have culminated. Here were mirrors framed in meaningless arabesques, cornices painted to represent bas-reliefs, consoles and pilasters of mock marble, and long generations of Electors in the tawdriest style of portraiture, all at full length, all in their robes of office, and all too evidently by one and the same hand. To me, however, they were all majestic and beautiful. I believed in themselves, their wigs, their armour, their ermine, their high-heeled shoes and their stereotyped smirk, from the earliest to the latest.

But the gardens and grounds were my chief delight, as indeed they were the main attraction of the place, making it the focus of a holiday resort for the townsfolk of Cologne and Bonn, and a point of interest for travellers. First came a great gravelled terrace upon which the ground-floor windows opened—a terrace where the sun shone more fiercely than elsewhere, and orange-trees in tubs bore golden fruit, and great green, yellow, and striped pumpkins, alternating with beds of brilliant white and scarlet geraniums, lay lazily sprawling in the sunshine as if they enjoyed it. Beyond this terrace came vast flats of rich green sward laid out in formal walks, flower-beds and fountains; and beyond these again stretched some two or three miles of finely wooded park, pierced by long avenues that radiated from a common centre and framed in exquisite little far-off views of Falkenlust and the blue hills of the Vorgebirge.

We were lodged at the back, where the private gardens and offices abutted on the village. Our own rooms looked upon our own garden, and upon the church and Franciscan convent beyond. In the warm dusk, when all was still, and my father used to sit smoking his meerschaum by the open window, we could hear the low pealing of the chapel-organ, and the monks chanting their evening litanies.

A happy time—a pleasant, peaceful place! Ah me! how long ago!

2

A whole delightful Summer and Autumn went by thus, and my new home seemed more charming with every change of season. First came the gathering of the golden harvest; then the joyous vintage-time, when the wine-press creaked all day in every open cellar along the village street, and long files of country carts came down from the hills in the dusk evenings, laden with baskets and barrels full of white and purple grapes. And then the long avenues and all the woods of Brühl put on their Autumn robes of crimson, and flame-colour, and golden brown; and the berries reddened in the hedges; and the Autumn burned itself away like a gorgeous sunset; and November came in grey and cold, like the night-time of the year.

I was so happy, however, that I enjoyed even the dull November. I loved the bare avenues carpeted with dead and rustling leaves—the solitary gardens—the long, silent afternoons and evenings when the big logs crackled on the hearth, and my father smoked his pipe in the chimney corner. We had no such wood-fires at Aunt Martha Baur's in those dreary old Nuremberg days, now almost forgotten; but then, to be sure, Aunt Martha Baur, who was a sparing woman and looked after every groschen, had to pay for her own logs, whereas ours were cut from the Crown Woods, and cost not a pfennig.

It was, as well as I can remember, just about this time, when the days were almost at their briefest, that my father received an official communication from Berlin desiring him to make ready a couple of rooms for the immediate reception of a state-prisoner, for whose safe-keeping he would be held responsible till further notice. The letter—(I have it in my desk now)—was folded square, sealed with five seals, and signed in the King's name by the Minister of War; and it was brought, as I well remember, by a mounted orderly from Cologne.

So a couple of empty rooms were chosen on the second story, just over one of the State apartments at the end of the east wing; and my father, who was by no means well pleased with his office, set to work to ransack the Château for furniture.

"Since it is the King's pleasure to make a gaoler of me," said he, "I'll try to give my poor devil of a prisoner all the comforts I can. Come with me, my little Gretchen, and let's see what chairs and tables we can find up in the garrets."

Now I had been longing to explore the top rooms ever since I came to live at Brühl—those top rooms under the roof, of which the shutters were always closed, and the doors always locked, and where not even the housemaids were admitted oftener than twice a year. So at this welcome invitation I sprang up, joyfully enough, and ran before my father all the way. But when he unlocked the first door, and all beyond was dark, and the air that met us on the threshold had a faint and dead odour, like the atmosphere of a tomb, I shrank back trembling, and dared not venture in. Nor did my courage altogether come back when the shutters were thrown open, and the wintry sunlight streamed in upon dusty floors, and cobwebbed ceilings, and piles of mysterious objects covered in a ghostly way with large white sheets, looking like heaps of slain upon a funeral pyre.

The slain, however, turned out to be the very things of which we were in search; old-fashioned furniture in all kinds of incongruous styles, and of all epochs—Louis Quatorze cabinets in cracked tortoise-shell and blackened buhl—antique carved chairs emblazoned elaborately with coats of arms, as old as the time of Albert Dürer—slender-legged tables in battered marqueterie—time-pieces in lack-lustre ormolu, still pointing to the hour at which they had stopped, who could tell how many years ago? bundles of moth-eaten tapestries and faded silken hangings—exquisite oval mirrors framed in chipped wreaths of delicate Dresden china—mouldering old portraits of dead-and-gone court beauties in powder and patches, warriors in wigs, and prelates in point-lace—whole suites of furniture in old stamped leather and worm-eaten Utrecht velvet; broken toilette services in pink and blue Sèvres; screens, wardrobes, cornices—in short, all kinds of luxurious lumber going fast to dust, like those who once upon a time enjoyed and owned it.

And now, going from room to room, we chose a chair here, a table there, and so on, till we had enough to furnish a bedroom and sitting-room.

"He must have a writing-table," said my father, thoughtfully, "and a book-case."

Saying which, he stopped in front of a ricketty-looking gilded çabinet with empty red-velvet shelves, and tapped it with his cane.

"But supposing he has no books!" suggested I, with the precocious wisdom of nine years of age.

"Then we must beg some, or borrow some, my little Mädchen," replied my father, gravely; "for books are the main solace of the captive, and he who hath them not lies in a twofold prison."

"He shall have my picture-book of Hartz legends!" said I, in a sudden impulse of compassion. Whereupon my father took me up in his arms, kissed me on both cheeks, and bade me choose some knicknacks for the prisoner's sitting-room.

"For though we have gotten together all the necessaries for comfort, we have taken nothing for adornment," said he, "and 'twere pity the prison were duller than it need be. Choose thou a pretty face or two from among these old pictures, my little Gretchen, and an ornament for his mantelshelf. Young as thou art, thou hast the woman's wit in thee."

So I picked out a couple of Sèvres candlesticks; a painted Chinese screen, all pagodas and parrots; two portraits of patched and powdered beauties in the Watteau style; and a queer old clock surmounted by a gilt Cupid in a chariot drawn by doves. If these failed to make him happy, thought I, he must indeed be hard to please.

That afternoon, the things having been well dusted, and the rooms thoroughly cleaned, we set to work to arrange the furniture, and so quickly was this done that before we sat down to supper the place was ready for occupation, even to the logs upon the hearth and the oil-lamp upon the table.

All night my dreams were of the prisoner. I was seeking him in the gloom of the upper rooms, or amid the dusky mazes of the leafless plantations—always seeing him afar off, never overtaking him, and trying in vain to catch a glimpse of his features. But his face was always turned from me.

My first words on waking, were to ask if he had yet come. All day long I was waiting, and watching, and listening for him, starting up at every sound, and continually running to the window. Would he be young and handsome? Or would he be old, and white-haired, and world-forgotten, like some of those Bastille prisoners I had heard my father speak of? Would his chains rattle when he walked about? I asked myself these questions, and answered them as my childish imagination prompted, a hundred times a day; and still he came not.

So another twenty-four hours went by, and my impatience was almost beginning to wear itself out, when at last, about five o'clock in the afternoon of the third day, it being already quite dark, there came a sudden clanging of the gates, followed by a rattle of wheels in the courtyard, and a hurrying to and fro of feet upon the stairs.

Then, listening with a beating heart, but seeing nothing, I knew that he was come.

I had to sleep that night with my curiosity ungratified; for my father had hurried away at the first sounds from without, nor came back till long after I had been carried off to bed by my Rhenish handmaiden.

3

He was neither old nor white-haired. He was, as well as I, in my childish way could judge, about thirty-five years of age, pale, slight, dark-eyed, delicate-looking. His chains did not rattle as he walked, for the simple reason that, being a prisoner on parole, he suffered no kind of restraint, but was as free as myself of the Château and grounds. He wore his hair long, tied behind with a narrow black ribbon, and very slightly powdered; and he dressed always in deep mourning—black, all black, from head to foot, even to his shoe-buckles. He was a Frenchman, and he went by the name of Monsieur Maurice.

I cannot tell how I knew that this was only his Christian name; but so it was, and I knew him by no other, neither did my father. I have, indeed, evidence among our private papers to show that neither by those in authority at Berlin, nor by the prisoner himself, was he at any time informed either of the family name of Monsieur Maurice, or of the nature of the offence, whether military or political, for which that gentleman was consigned to his keeping at Brühl.

"Of one thing at least I am certain," said my father, holding out his pipe for me to fill it. "He is a soldier."

It was just after dinner, the second day following our prisoner's arrival, and I was sitting on my father's knee before the fire, as was our pleasant custom of an afternoon.

"I see it in his eye," my father went on to say. "I see it in his walk. I see it in the way he arranges his papers on the table. Everything in order. Everything put away into the smallest possible compass. All this bespeaketh the camp."

"I don't believe he is a soldier, for all that," said I, thoughtfully. "He is too gentle."

"The bravest soldiers, my little Gretchen, are ofttimes the gentlest," replied my father. "The great French hero, Bayard, and the great English hero, Sir Philip Sidney, about whom thou wert reading 'tother day, were both as tender and gentle as women."

"But he neither smokes, nor swears, nor talks loud," said I, persisting in my opinion.

My father smiled, and pinched my ear.

"Nay, little one," said he, "Monsieur Maurice is not like thy father— a rough German Dragoon risen from the ranks. He is a gentleman, and a Frenchman; and he hath all the polish of what the Frenchman calls the *vieille école*. And there again he puzzles me with his court-manners and his powdered hair! He's no Bonapartist, I'll be sworn—yet if he be o' the King's side, what doth he here, with the usurper at Saint Helena, and Louis the Eighteenth come to his own again?"

"But he *is* a Bonapartist, father," said I, "for he carries the Emperor's portrait on his snuff-box."

My father laid down his pipe, and drew a long breath expressive of astonishment.

"He showed thee his snuff-box!" exclaimed he.

"Ay—and told me it was the Emperor's own gift."

"Thunder and Mars! And when was this, my little Gretchen?"

"Yesterday morning, on the terrace. And he asked my name; and told me I should go up some day to his room and see his sketches; and he kissed me when he said good-bye; and—and I like Monsieur Maurice very much, father, and I'm sure it's very wicked of the King to keep him here in prison!"

My father looked at me, shook his head, and twirled his long grey moustache.

"Bonapartist or Legitimist, again I say what doth he here?" muttered he presently, more to himself than to me. "If Legitimist, why not with his King? If Bonapartist—then he is his King's prisoner; not ours. It passeth my comprehension how we should hold him at Brühl."

"Let him run away, father dear, and don't run after him!" whispered I, putting my arms coaxingly about his neck.

"But 'tis some cursed mess of politics at bottom, depend on't!" continued my father, still talking to himself. "Ah, you don't know what politics are, my little Gretchen!—so much the better for you!"

"I do know what politics are," replied I, with great dignity. "They are the *chef-d'œuvre* of Satan. I heard you say so the other day."

My father burst into a Titanic roar of laughter.

"Said I so?" shouted he. "Thunder and Mars! I did not remember that I had ever said anything half so epigrammatic!"

Now from this it will be seen that the prisoner and I were already acquainted. We had, indeed, taken to each other from the first, and our mutual liking ripened so rapidly that before a week was gone by we had become the fastest friends in the world.

Our first meeting, as I have already said, took place upon the terrace. Our second, which befell on the afternoon of the same day when my father and I had held the conversation just recorded, happened on the stairs. Monsieur Maurice was coming up with his hat on; I was running down. He stopped, and held out both his hands.

"*Bonjour, petite,*" he said, smiling. "Whither away so fast?"

The hoar frost was clinging to his coat, where he had brushed against the trees in his walk, and he looked pale and tired.

"I am going home," I replied.

"Home? Did you not tell me you lived in the Château?"

"So I do, Monsieur; but at the other side, up the other staircase. This is the side of the state-apartments."

Then, seeing in his face a look half of surprise, half of curiosity, I added:—

"I often go there in the afternoon, when it is too cold, or too late for out-of-doors. They are such beautiful rooms, and full of such beautiful pictures! Would you like to see them?"

He smiled, and shook his head.

"Thanks, petite," he said, "I am too cold now, and too tired; but you shall show them to me some other day. Meanwhile, suppose you come up and pay me that promised visit?"

I assented joyfully, and slipping my hand into his with the ready confidence of childhood, turned back at once and went with him to his rooms on the second floor.

Here, finding the fire in the salon nearly out, we went down upon our knees and blew the embers with our breath, and laughed so merrily over our work that by the time the new logs had caught, I was as much at home as if I had known Monsieur Maurice all my life.

"*Tiens!*" he said, taking me presently upon his knee and brushing the specks of white ash from my clothes and hair, "what a little Cinderella I have made of my guest! This must not happen again,

Gretchen. Did you not tell me yesterday that your name was Gretchen?"

"Yes, but Gretchen, you know, is not my real name," said I, "my real name is Marguerite. Gretchen is only my pet name."

"Then you will always be Gretchen for me," said Monsieur Maurice, with the sweetest smile in the world.

There were books upon the table; there was a thing like a telescope on a brass stand in the window; there was a guitar lying on the couch. The fire, too, was burning brightly now, and the room altogether wore a cheerful air of habitation.

"It looks more like a lady's boudoir than a prison," said Monsieur Maurice, reading my thoughts. "I wonder whose rooms they were before I came here!"

"They were nobody's rooms," said I. "They were quite empty."

And then I told him where we had found the furniture, and how the ornamental part thereof had been of my choosing.

"I don't know who the ladies are," I said, referring to the portraits. "I only chose them for their pretty faces."

"Their lovers probably did the same, petite, a hundred years ago," replied Monsieur Maurice. "And the clock—did you choose that also?"

"Yes; but the clock doesn't go."

"So much the better. I would that time might stand still also—till I am free! till I am free!"

The tears rushed to my eyes. It was the tone more than the words that touched my heart. He stooped and kissed me on the forehead.

"Come to the window, little one," said he, "and I will show you something very beautiful. Do you know what this is?"

"A telescope!"

"No; a solar microscope. Now look down into this tube, and tell me what you see. A piece of Persian carpet? No—a butterfly's wing magnified hundreds and hundreds of times. And this which looks like an aigrette of jewels? Will you believe that it is just the tiny plume which waves on the head of every little gnat that buzzes round you on a Summer's evening?"

I uttered exclamation after exclamation of delight. Every fresh object seemed more wonderful and beautiful than the last, and I felt as if I could go on looking down that magic tube for ever. Meanwhile Monsieur Maurice, whose good-nature was at least as inexhaustible as my curiosity, went on changing the slides till we had gone through a whole boxful.

By this time it was getting rapidly dusk, and I could see no longer.

"You will show me some more another day?" said I, giving up reluctantly.

"That I will, petite, I have at least a dozen more boxes full of slides."

"And—and you said I should see your sketches, Monsieur Maurice."

"All in good time, little Gretchen," he said, smiling. "All in good time. See—those are the sketches, in yonder folio; that mahogany case under the couch contains a collection of gems in glass and paste; those red books in the bookcase are full of pictures. You shall see them all by degrees; but only by degrees. For if I did not keep something back to tempt my little guest, she would not care to visit the solitary prisoner."

I felt myself colour crimson.

"But—but indeed I would care to come, Monsieur Maurice, if you had nothing at all to show me," I said, half hurt, half angry.

He gave me a strange look that I could not understand, and stroked my hair caressingly.

"Come often, then, little one," he said. "Come very often; and when we are tired of pictures and microscopes, we will sit upon the floor, and tell sad stories of the deaths of kings."

Then, seeing my look puzzled, he laughed and added:—

"'Tis a great English poet says that, Gretchen, in one of his plays."

Here a shrill trumpet-call in the court-yard, followed by the prolonged roll of many drums, warned me that evening parade was called, and that as soon as it was over my father would be home and looking for me. So I started up, and put out my hand to say good-bye.

Monsieur Maurice took it between both his own.

"I don't like parting from you so soon, little Mädchen," he said. "Will you come again to-morrow?"

"Every day, if you like!" I replied eagerly.

"Then every day it shall be; and—let me see—you shall improve my bad German, and I will teach you French."

I could have clapped my hands for joy. I was longing to learn French, and I knew how much it would also please my father; so I thanked Monsieur Maurice again and again, and ran home with a light heart to tell of all the wonders I had seen.

4

From this time forth, I saw him always once, and sometimes twice a day—in the afternoons, when he regularly gave me the promised French lesson; and occasionally in the mornings, provided the weather was neither too cold nor too damp for him to join me in the grounds. For Monsieur Maurice was not strong. He could not with impunity face snow, and rain, and our keen Rhenish north-east winds; and it was only when the wintry sun shone out at noon and the air came tempered from the south, that he dared venture from his own fire-side. When, however, there shone a sunny day, with what delight I used to summon him for a walk, take him to my favourite points of view, and show him the woodland nooks that had been my chosen haunts in summer! Then, too, the unwonted colour would come back to his pale cheek, and the smile to his lips, and while the ramble and the sunshine lasted he would be all jest and gaiety, pelting me with dead leaves, chasing me in and out of the plantations, and telling me strange stories, half pathetic, half grotesque, of Dryads, and Fauns, and Satyrs—of Bacchus, and Pan, and Poly-phemus—of nymphs who became trees, and shepherds who were trans-formed to fountains, and all kinds of beautiful wild myths of antique Greece—far more beautiful and far more wild than all the tales of gnomes and witches in my book of Hartz legends.

At other times, when the weather was cold or rainy, he would take down his "Musée Napoléon," a noble work in eight or ten volumes, and show me engravings after pictures by great masters in the Louvre, explaining them to me as we went along, painting in words the glow and glory of the absent colour, and steeping my childish imagination in golden dreams of Raphael and Titian, and Paulo Veronese.

And sometimes, too, as the dusk came on and the firelight brightened in the gathering gloom, he would take up his guitar, and to the accom-paniment of a few slight chords sing me a quaint old French chanson of the feudal times; or an Arab chant picked up in the tent or the Nile boat; or a Spanish ballad, half love-song, half litany, learned from the lips of a muleteer on the Pyrenean border.

For Monsieur Maurice, whatever his present adversities, had travelled far and wide at some foregone period of his life—in Syria, and Persia; in northernmost Tartary and the Siberian steppes; in Egypt and the Nubian desert, and among the perilous wilds of central Arabia. He spoke and wrote with facility some ten or twelve languages. He drew admirably, and had a profound knowledge of the Italian schools of art; and his memory was a rich storehouse of adventure and anecdote, legend and song.

I am an old woman now, and Monsieur Maurice must have passed away many a year ago upon his last long journey; but even at this distance of time, my eyes are dimmed with tears when I remember how he used to unlock that storehouse for my pleasure, and ransack his memory for stories either of his own personal perils by flood and field, or of the hair-breadth 'scapes of earlier travellers. For it was his amusement to amuse me; his happiness to make me happy. And I in return loved him with all my childish heart. Nay, with something deeper and more romantic than a childish love—say rather with that kind of passionate hero-worship which is an attribute more of youth than of childhood, and, like the quality of mercy, blesseth him that gives even more than him that takes.

"What dreadful places you have travelled in, Monsieur Maurice!" I exclaimed one day. "What dangers you have seen!"

He had been showing me a little sketchbook full of Eastern jottings, and had just explained how a certain boat therein depicted had upset with him on a part of the Upper Nile so swarming with alligators that he had to swim for his life, and even so, barely scrambled up the slimy bank in time.

"He who travels far courts many kinds of death," replied Monsieur Maurice; "but he escapes that which is worst—death from ennui."

"Suppose they had dragged you back, when you were half way up the bank!" said I, shuddering.

And as I spoke, I felt myself turn pale; for I could see the brown monsters crowding to shore, and the red glitter of their cruel eyes and the hot breath steaming from their open jaws.

"Then they would have eaten me up as easily as you might swallow an oyster," laughed Monsieur Maurice. "Nay, my child, why that serious face? I should have escaped a world of trouble, and been missed by no one—except poor Ali."

"Who was Ali?" I asked quickly.

"Ali was my Nubian servant—my only friend, then; as you, little Gretchen, are my only friend, now," replied Monsieur Maurice, sadly. "Aye, my only little friend in the wide world—and I think a true one."

I did not know what to say; but I nestled closer to his side; and pressed my cheek up fondly against his shoulder.

"Tell me more about him, Monsieur Maurice," I whispered. "I am so glad he loved you dearly."

"He loved me very dearly," said Monsieur Maurice "so dearly that he gave his life for me."

"But is Ali dead?"

"Ay—Ali is dead. Nay, his story is brief enough, petite. I bought him in the slave market at Cairo—a poor, sickly, soulless lad, half stupid from ill-treatment. I gave him good food, good clothes, and liberty. I taught him to read. I made him my own servant; and his soul and his strength came back to him as if by a miracle. He became stalwart and intelligent, and so faithful that he was ten times more my slave than if I had held him to his bondage. I took him with me through all my Eastern pilgrimage. He was my body-guard; my cook; my dragoman; everything. He slept on a mat at the foot of my bed every night, like a dog. So he lived with me for nearly four years—till I lost him."

He paused.

I did not dare to ask, "what more?" but waited breathlessly.

"The rest is soon told," he said presently; but in an altered voice. "It happened in Ceylon. Our way lay along a bridle-path overhanging a steep gorge on the one hand and skirting the jungle on the other. Do you know what the jungle is, little Gretchen? Fancy an untrodden wilderness where huge trees, matted together by trailing creepers of gigantic size, shut out the sun and make a green roof of inextricable shade—where the very grass grows taller than the tallest man—where apes chatter, and parrots scream, and deadly reptiles swarm; and where nature has run wild since ever the world began. Well, so we went—I on my horse; Ali at my bridle; two porters following with food and baggage; the precipice below; the forest above; the morning sun just risen over all. On a sudden, Ali held his breath and listened. His practised ear had caught a sound that mine could not detect. He seized my rein—forced my horse back upon his haunches—drew his hunting knife, and ran forward to reconnoitre. The turn of the road hid him for a moment from my sight. The next instant, I had sprung from the saddle, pistol in hand, and run after him to share the sport or the danger. My little Gretchen—he was gone."

"Gone!" I echoed.

Monsieur Maurice shook his head, and turned his face away.

"I heard a crashing and crackling of the underwood," he said; "a faint moan dying on the sultry air. I saw a space of dusty road trampled over with prints of an enormous paw—a tiny trail of blood—a shred of silken fringe—and nothing more. He was gone."

"What was it?" I asked presently, in an awestruck whisper.

Monsieur Maurice, instead of answering my question, opened the sketch-book at a page full of little outlines of animals and birds, and laid his finger silently on the figure of a sleeping tiger.

I shuddered.

"*Pauvre petite!*" he said, shutting up the book, "it is too terrible a story. I ought not to have told it to you. Try to forget it."

"Ah, no!" I said. "I shall never forget it, Monsieur Maurice. Poor Ali! Have you still the piece of fringe you found lying in the road?"

He unlocked his desk and touched a secret spring; whereupon a small drawer flew out from a recess just under the lock.

"Here it is," he said, taking out a piece of folded paper.

It contained the thing he had described—a scrap of fringe composed of crimson and yellow twist, about two inches in length.

"And those other things?" I said, peering into the secret drawer with a child's inquisitiveness. "Have they a history, too?"

Monsieur Maurice hesitated—took them out—sighed—and said, somewhat reluctantly:—

"You may see them, little Gretchen, if you will. Yes; they, too, have

their history—but let it be. We have had enough sad stories for to-
day."

Those other things, as I had called them, were a withered rose in a
little cardboard box, and a miniature of a lady in a purple morocco case.

5

It so happened that the Winter this year was unusually severe, not only
at Brühl and the parts about Cologne, but throughout all the Rhine
country. Heavy snows fell at Christmas and lay unmelted for weeks upon
the ground. Long forgotten sleighs were dragged out from their hiding
places and put upon the road, not only for the transport of goods, but for
the conveyance of passengers. The ponds in every direction and all the
smaller streams were fast frozen. Great masses of dirty ice, too, came
floating down the Rhine, and there were rumours of the great river
being quite frozen over somewhere up in Switzerland, many hundred
miles nearer its source.

For myself, I enjoyed it all—the bitter cold, the short days, the rapid
exercise, the blazing fires within, and the glittering snow without. I
made snow-men and snow-castles to my heart's content. I learned to
skate with my father on the frozen ponds. I was never weary of admiring
the wintry landscape—the wide plains sheeted with silver; the purple
mountains peeping through brown vistas of bare forest; the nearer trees
standing out in featherlike tracery against the blue-green sky. To me
it was all beautiful; even more beautiful than in the radiant summer-
time.

Not so, however, was it with Monsieur Maurice. Racked by a severe
cough and unable to leave the house for weeks together, he suffered
intensely all the winter through. He suffered in body, and he suffered
also in mind. I could see that he was very sad, and that there were times
when the burden of life was almost more than he knew how to bear. He
had brought with him, as I have shown, certain things wherewith to
alleviate the weariness of captivity—books, music, drawing materials,
and the like; but I soon discovered that the books were his only solace,
and that he never took up pencil or guitar, unless for my amusement.

He wrote a great deal, however, and so consumed many a weary hour
of the twenty-four. He used a thick yellowish paper cut quite square, and
wrote a very small, neat, upright hand, as clear and legible as print.
Every time I found him at his desk and saw those closely covered
pages multiplying under his hand, I used to wonder what he could have
to write about, and for whose eyes that elaborate manuscript was
intended.

"How cold you are, Monsieur Maurice!" I used to say. "You are as cold as my snow-man in the court-yard! Won't you come out to-day for half-an-hour?"

And his hands, in truth, were always ice-like, even though the hearth was heaped with blazing logs.

"Not to-day, petite," he would reply. "It is too bleak for me—and besides, you see, I am writing."

It was his invariable reply. He was always writing—or if not writing, reading; or brooding listlessly over the fire. And so he grew paler every day.

"But the writing can wait, Monsieur Maurice," I urged one morning, "and you can't always be reading the same old books over and over again!"

"Some books never grow old, little Gretchen," he replied. "This, for instance, is quite new; and yet it was written by one Horatius Flaccus somewhere about eighteen hundred years ago."

"But the sun is really shining this morning, Monsieur Maurice!"

"*Comment!*" he said, smiling. "Do you think to persuade me that yonder is the sun—the great, golden, glorious, bountiful sun? No, no, my child! Where I come from, we have the only true sun, and believe in no other!"

"But you come from France, don't you, Monsieur Maurice?" I asked quickly.

"From the South of France, petite—from the France of palms, and orange-groves, and olives; where the myrtle flowers at Christmas, and the roses bloom all the year round!"

"But that must be where Paradise was, Monsieur Maurice!" I exclaimed.

"Ay; it was Paradise once—for me," he said, with a sigh.

Thus, after a moment's pause, he went on:—

"The house in which I was born stands on a low cliff above the sea. It is an old, old house, with all kinds of quaint little turrets, and gable ends, and picturesque nooks and corners about it—such as one sees in most French Châteaux of that period; and it lies back somewhat, with a great rambling garden stretching out between it and the edge of the cliff. Three *berceaux* of orange-trees lead straight away from the paved terrace on which the salon windows open, to another terrace overhanging the beach and the sea. The cliff is overgrown from top to bottom with shrubs and wild flowers, and a flight of steps cut in the living rock leads down to a little cove and a strip of yellow sand a hundred feet below. Ah, petite, I fancy I can see myself scrambling up and down those steps—a child younger than yourself; watching the sun go down into that purple sea; counting the sails in the offing at early morn; and building castles with that yellow sand, just as you build castles out yonder with the snow!"

I clasped my hands and listened breathlessly.

"Oh, Monsieur Maurice," I said, "I did not think there was such a beautiful place in the world! It sounds like a fairy tale."

He smiled, sighed, and—being seated at his desk with the pen in his hand—took up a blank sheet of paper, and began sketching the Château and the cliff.

"Tell me more about it, Monsieur Maurice," I pleaded coaxingly.

"What more can I tell you, little one? See—this window in the turret to the left was my bed-room window, and here, just below, was my study, where as a boy I prepared my lessons for my tutor. That large gothic window under the gable was the window of the library."

"And is it all just like that still?" I asked.

"I don't know," he said dreamily. "I suppose so."

He was now putting in the rocks, and the rough steps leading down to the beach.

"Had you any little brothers and sisters, Monsieur Maurice?" I asked next; for my interest and curiosity were unbounded.

He shook his head.

"None," he said, "none whatever. I was an only child; and I am the last of my name."

I longed to question him further, but did not dare to do so.

"You will go back there some day, Monsieur Maurice," I said hesitatingly, "when—when—"

"When I am free, little Gretchen? Ah! who can tell? Besides the old place is no longer mine. They have taken it from me, and given it to a stranger."

"Taken it from you, Monsieur Maurice!" I exclaimed indignantly.

"Ay; but—who knows? We see strange changes. Where a king reigns to-day, an emperor, or a mob, may rule to-morrow."

He spoke more to himself than to me, but I had some dim understanding, nevertheless, of what he meant.

He had by this time drawn the cliff, and the strip of sand, and the waste of sea beyond; and now he was blotting in some boats and figures —figures of men wading through the surf and dragging the boats in shore; and other figures making for the steps. Last of all, close under the cliff, in advance of all the rest, he drew a tiny man standing alone—a tiny man scarce an eighth of an inch in height, struck out with three or four touches of the pen, and yet so full of character that one knew at a glance he was the leader of the others. I saw the outstretched arm in act of command—I recognised the well-known cocked hat—the general outline of a figure already familiar to me in a hundred prints, and I exclaimed, almost involuntarily:—

"Bonaparte!"

Monsieur Maurice started; shot a quick, half apprehensive glance at me; crumpled the drawing up in his hand, and flung it into the fire.

"Oh, Monsieur Maurice!" I cried, "what have you done?"

"It was a mere scrawl," he said impatiently.

"No, no—it was beautiful. I would have given anything for it!"

Monsieur Maurice laughed, and patted me on the cheek.

"Nonsense, petite, nonsense!" he said. "It was only fit for the fire. I will make you a better drawing, if you remind me of it, to-morrow."

When I told this to my father—and I used to prattle to him a good deal about Monsieur Maurice at supper, in those days—he tugged at his moustache, and shook his head, and looked very grave indeed.

"The South of France!" he muttered, "the South of France! *Sacré cœur d'une bombe!* Why, the usurper, when he came from Elba, landed on that coast somewhere near Cannes!"

"And went to Monsieur Maurice's house, father!" I cried, "and that is why the King of France has taken Monsieur Maurice's house away from him, and given it to a stranger! I am sure that's it! I see it all now!"

But my father only shook his head again, and looked still more grave.

"No, no, no," he said, "neither all—nor half—nor a quarter! There's more behind. I don't understand it—I don't understand it. Thunder and Mars! Why don't we hand him over to the French Government? That's what puzzles me."

6

The severity of the Winter had, I think, in some degree abated, and the snowdrops were already above ground, when again a mounted orderly rode in from Cologne, bringing another official letter for the Governor of Brühl.

Now my father's duties as Governor of Brühl were very light—so light that he had not found it necessary to set apart any special room, or bureau, for the transaction of such business as might be connected therewith. When, therefore, letters had to be written or accounts made up, he wrote those letters and made up those accounts at a certain large writing-table, fitted with drawers, pigeon-holes, and a shelf for account-books, that stood in a corner of our sitting-room. Here also, if any persons had to be received, he received them. To this day, whenever I go back in imagination to those bygone times, I seem to see my father sitting at that writing-table nibbling the end of his pen, and one of the sergeants off guard perched on the edge of a chair close against the door, with his hat on his knees, waiting for orders.

There being, as I have said, no especial room set apart for business purposes, the orderly was shown straight to our own room, and there delivered his despatch. It was about a quarter past one. We had dined, and my father had just brought out his pipe. The door leading into our little dining-room was, indeed, standing wide open, and the dishes were still upon the table.

My father took the despatch, turned it over, broke the seals one by one (there were five of them, as before), and read it slowly through. As he read, a dark cloud seemed to settle on his brow.

Then he looked up frowning—seemed about to speak—checked himself—and read the despatch over again.

"From whose hands did you receive this?" he said abruptly.

"From General Berndorf, Excellency," stammered the orderly, carrying his hand to his cap.

"Is his Excellency the Baron von Bulow at Cologne?"

"I have not heard so, Excellency."

"Then this despatch came direct from Berlin, and has been forwarded from Cologne?"

"Yes, Excellency."

"How did it come from Berlin? By mail, or by special messenger?"

"By special messenger, Excellency."

Now General Berndorf was the officer in command of the garrison at Cologne, and the Baron von Bulow, as I well knew, was His Majesty's Minister of War at Berlin.

Having received these answers, my father stood silent, as if revolving some difficult matter in his thoughts. Then, his mind being made up, he turned again to the orderly and said:—

"Dine—feed your horse—and come back in an hour for the answer."

Thankful to be dismissed, the man saluted and vanished. My father had a rapid, stern way of speaking to subordinates, that had in general the effect of making them glad to get out of his presence as quickly as possible.

Then he read the despatch for the third time; turned to his writing-table; dropped into his chair; and prepared to write.

But the task, apparently, was not easy. Watching him from the fireside corner where I was sitting on a low stool with an open story-book upon my lap, I saw him begin and tear up three separate attempts. The fourth, however, seemed to be more successful. Once written, he read it over, copied it carefully, called to me for a light, sealed his letter, and addressed it to "His Excellency the Baron von Bulow."

This done, he enclosed it under cover to "General Berndorf, Cologne";

and had just sealed the outer cover when the orderly came back. My father gave it to him with scarcely a word, and two minutes after, we heard him clattering out of the courtyard at a hand-gallop.

Then my father came back to his chair by the fireside, lit his pipe, and sat thinking silently. I looked up in his face, but felt, somehow, that I must not speak to him; for the cloud was still there, and his thoughts were far away. Presently his pipe went out; but he held it still, unconscious and absorbed. In all the months we had been living at Brühl I had never seen him look so troubled.

So he sat, and so he looked for a long time—for perhaps the greater part of an hour—during which I could think of nothing but the despatch, and Monsieur Maurice, and the Minister of War; for that it all had to do with Monsieur Maurice I never doubted for an instant.

By just such another despatch, sealed and sent in precisely the same way, and from the same person, his coming hither had been heralded. How, then, should not this one concern him? And in what way would he be affected by it? Seeing that dark look in my father's face, I knew not what to think or what to fear.

At length, after what had seemed to me an interval of interminable silence, the time-piece in the corner struck half-past three—the hour at which Monsieur Maurice was accustomed to give me the daily French lesson; so I got up quietly and stole towards the door, knowing that I was expected upstairs.

"Where are you going, Gretchen?" said my father, sharply.

It was the first time he had opened his lips since the orderly had clattered out of the courtyard.

"I am going up to Monsieur Maurice," I replied.

My father shook his head.

"Not to-day, my child," he said, "not to-day. I have business with Monsieur Maurice this afternoon. Stay here till I come back."

And with this he got up, took his hat and went quickly out of the room.

So I waited and waited—as it seemed to me for hours. The waning day-light faded and became dusk; the dusk thickened into dark; the fire burned red and dull; and still I crouched there in the chimney-corner. I had no heart to read, work, or fan the logs into a blaze. I just watched the clock, and waited. When the room became so dark that I could see the hands no longer, I counted the strokes of the pendulum, and told the quarters off upon my fingers.

When at length my father came back, it was past five o'clock, and dark as midnight.

"Quick, quick, little Gretchen," he said, pulling off his hat and gloves, and unbuckling his sword. "A glass of kirsch, and more logs on the fire! I am cold through and through, and wet into the bargain."

"But—but, father, have you not been with Monsieur Maurice?" I said, anxiously.

"Yes, of course; but that was an hour ago, and more. I have been over to Kierberg since then, in the rain."

He had left Monsieur Maurice an hour ago—a whole, wretched, dismal hour, during which I might have been so happy!

"You told me to stay here till you came back," I said, scarce able to keep down the tears that started to my eyes.

"Well, my little Mädchen?"

"And—and I might have gone up to Monsieur Maurice, after all?"

My father looked at me gravely—poured out a second glass of kirsch—drew his chair to the front of the fire, and said:—

"I don't know about that, Gretchen."

I had felt all along that there was something wrong, and now I was certain of it.

"What do you mean, father?" I said, my heart beating so that I could scarcely speak. "What is the matter?"

"May the devil make broth of my bones, if I know!" said my father, tugging savagely at his moustache.

"But there is something!"

He nodded, grimly.

"Monsieur Maurice, it seems, is not to have so much liberty," he said, after a moment. "He is not to walk in the grounds oftener than twice a week; and then only with a soldier at his heels. And he is not to go beyond half a mile from the Château in any direction. And he is to hold no communication whatever with any person, or persons, either in-doors or out-of-doors, except such as are in direct charge of his rooms or his person. And—and heaven knows what other confounded regulations besides! I wish the Baron von Bulow had been in Spitzbergen before he put it into the King's head to send him here at all!"

"But—but he is not to be locked up?" I faltered, almost in a whisper.

"Well, no—not exactly that; but I am to post a sentry in the corridor, outside his door."

"Then the King is afraid that Monsieur Maurice will run away!"

"I don't know—I suppose so," groaned my father.

I sat silent for a moment, and then burst into a flood of tears.

"Poor Monsieur Maurice!" I cried. "He has coughed so all the Winter, and he was longing for the Spring! We were to have gathered primroses in the woods when the warm days came back again—and—and—and I suppose the King doesn't mean that I am not to speak to him any more!"

My sobs choked me, and I could say no more.

My father took me on his knee, and tried to comfort me.

"Don't cry, my little Gretchen," he said tenderly; "don't cry! Tears can help neither the prisoner nor thee."

"But I may go to him all the same, father?" I pleaded.

"By my sword, I don't know," stammered my father. "If it were a breach of orders . . . and yet for a baby like thee . . . thou'rt no more than a mouse about the room, after all!"

"I have read of a poor prisoner who broke his heart because the gaoler killed a spider he loved," said I, through my tears.

My father's features relaxed into a smile.

"But do you flatter yourself that Monsieur Maurice loves my little Mädchen as much as that poor prisoner loved his spider?" he said, taking me by the ear.

"Of course he does—and a hundred thousand times better!" I exclaimed, not without a touch of indignation.

My father laughed outright.

"Thunder and Mars!" said he, "is the case so serious? Then Monsieur Maurice, I suppose, must be allowed sometimes to see his little pet spider."

He took me up himself next morning to the prisoner's room, and then for the first time I found a sentry in occupation of the corridor. He grounded his musket and saluted as we passed.

"I bring you a visitor, Monsieur Maurice," said my father.

He was leaning over the fire in a moody attitude when we went in, with his arms on the chimney-piece, but turned at the first sound of my father's voice.

"Colonel Bernhard," he said, with a look of glad surprise, "this is kind, I—I had scarcely dared to hope" . . .

He said no more, but took me by both hands, and kissed me on the forehead.

"I trust I'm not doing wrong," said my father gruffly. "I hope it's not a breach of orders."

"I am sure it is not," replied Monsieur Maurice, still holding my hands. "Were your instructions twice as strict, they could not be supposed to apply to this little maiden."

"They are strict enough, Monsieur Maurice," said my father, drily.

A faint flush rose to the prisoner's cheek.

"I know it," he said. "And they are as unnecessary as they are strict. I had given you my parole, Colonel Bernhard."

My father pulled at his moustache, and looked uncomfortable.

"I'm sure you would have kept it, Monsieur Maurice," he said.

Monsieur Maurice bowed.

"I wish it, however, to be distinctly understood," he said, "that I withdrew that parole from the moment when a sentry was stationed at my door."

"Naturally—naturally."

"And, for my papers" . . .

"I wish to heaven they had said nothing about them!" interrupted my father, impatiently.

"Thanks. 'Tis a petty tyranny; but it cannot be helped. Since, however, you are instructed to seize them, here they are. They contain neither political nor private matter—as you will see."

"I shall see nothing of the kind, Monsieur Maurice," said my father. "I would not read a line of them for a marshal's bâton. The King must make a gaoler of me, if it so pleases him; but not a spy. I shall seal up the papers and send them to Berlin."

"And I shall never see my manuscript again!" said Monsieur Maurice, with a sigh. "Well—it was my first attempt at authorship—perhaps, my last—and there is an end to it!"

My father ground some new and tremendous oath between his teeth.

"I hate to take it, Monsieur Maurice," he said. "'Tis an odious office."

"The office alone is yours, Colonel Bernhard," said the prisoner, with all a Frenchman's grace. "The odium rests with those who impose it on you."

Hereupon they exchanged formal salutations; and my father, having warned me not to be late for our mid-day meal, put the papers in his pocket, and left me to take my daily French lesson.

7

The Winter lingered long, but the Spring came at last in a burst of sunshine. The grey mists were rent away, as if by magic. The cold hues vanished from the landscape. The earth became all freshness; the air all warmth; the sky all light. The hedgerows caught a tint of tender green. The crocuses came up in a single night. The woods which till now had remained bare and brown, flushed suddenly, as if the coming Summer were imprisoned in their glowing buds. The birds began to try their little voices here and there. Never once, in all the years that have gone by since then, have I seen so startling a transition. It was as if the Prince in the dear old fairy tale had just kissed the Sleeping Beauty, and all that enchanted world had sprung into life at the meeting of their lips.

But the Spring, with its sudden beauty and brightness, seems to have no charm for Monsieur Maurice. He has permission to walk in the grounds twice a week—with a sentry at his heels; but of that permission he sternly refuses to take advantage. It was not wonderful that he preferred his fireside and his books, while the sleet, and snow, and bitter east winds lasted; but it seems too cruel that he should stay there now, cutting himself off from all the warmth and sweetness of the opening season. In vain I come to him with my hands full of dewy crocuses. In vain I hang about him, pleading for just a turn or two on the terrace where the sunshine falls hottest. He shakes his head, and is immoveable.

"No, petite," he says. "Not to-day."

"That is just what you said yesterday, Monsieur Maurice."

"And it is just what I shall say to-morrow, Gretchen, if you ask me again."

"But you won't stay in for ever, Monsieur Maurice!"

"Nay—'for ever' is a big word, little Gretchen."

"I don't believe you know how brightly the sun is shining!" I say coaxingly. "Just come to the window, and see."

Unwillingly enough, he lets himself be dragged across the room—unwillingly he looks out upon the glittering slopes and budding avenues beyond.

"Yes, yes—I see it," he replies with an impatient sigh; "but the shadow of that fellow in the corridor would hide the brightest sun that ever shone! I am not a galley-slave, that I should walk about with a garde-chiourme behind me."

"What do you mean, Monsieur Maurice?" I ask, startled by his unusual vehemence.

"I mean that I go free, petite—or not at all."

"Then—then you will fall ill!" I falter, amid fast-gathering tears.

"No, no—not I, Gretchen. What can have put that idea into your wise little head?"

"It was papa, Monsieur Maurice . . . he said you were" . . .

Then, thinking suddenly how pale and wasted he had become of late, I hesitated.

"He said I was—What?"

"I—I don't like to tell!"

"But if I insist on being told? Come, Gretchen, I must know what Colonel Bernhard said."

"He said it was wrong to stay in like this week after week, and month after month. He—he said you were killing yourself by inches, Monsieur Maurice."

Monsieur Maurice laughed a short bitter laugh.

"Killing myself!" he repeated. "Well, I hope not; for weary as I am of it, I would sooner go on bearing the burden of life than do my enemies the favour of dying out of their way."

The words, the look, the accent made me tremble. I never forgot them.

How could I forget that Monsieur Maurice had enemies—enemies who longed for his death?

So the first blush of early Spring went by; and the crocuses lived their little life and passed away, and the primroses came in their turn, yellowing every shady nook in the scented woods; and the larches put on their crimson tassels, and the laburnum its mantle of golden fringe, and the almond-tree burst into a leafless bloom of pink—and still Monsieur Maurice, adhering to his resolve, refused to stir one step beyond the threshold of his rooms.

Sad and monotonous now to the last degree, his life dragged heavily on. He wrote no more. He read, or seemed to read, nearly the whole day through; but I often observed that his eyes ceased travelling along the lines, and that sometimes, for an hour and more together, he never turned a page.

"My little Gretchen," he said to me one day, "you are too much in these close rooms with me, and too little in the open air and sunshine."

"I had rather be here, Monsieur Maurice," I replied.

"But it is not good for you. You are losing all your roses."

"I don't think it is good for me to be out when you are always in-doors," I said, simply. "I don't care to run about, and—and I don't enjoy it."

He looked at me—opened his lips as if about to speak—then checked himself; walked to the window; and looked out silently.

The next morning, as soon as I made my appearance, he said:—

"The French lesson can wait awhile, petite. Shall we go out for a walk instead?"

I clapped my hands for joy.

"Oh, Monsieur Maurice!" I cried, "are you in earnest?"

For in truth it seemed almost too good to be true. But Monsieur Maurice was in earnest, and we went—closely followed by the sentry.

It was a beautiful, sunny April day. We went down the terraces and slopes; and in and out of the flower-beds, now gaudy with Spring flowers; and on to the great central point whence the three avenues diverged. Here we rested on a bench under a lime-tree, not far from the huge stone basin where the fountain played every Sunday throughout the Summer, and the sleepy water-lilies rocked to and fro in the sunshine.

All was very quiet. A gardener went by now and then, with his wheel-barrow, or a gamekeeper followed by his dogs; a blackbird whistled low in the bushes; a cow-bell tinkled in the far distance; the wood-pigeons murmured softly in the plantations. Other passers-by, other sounds there were none—save when a noisy party of flaxen-haired, bare-footed children came whooping and racing along, but turned sud-denly shy and silent at sight of Monsieur Maurice sitting under the lime-tree.

The sentry, meanwhile, took up his position against the pedestal of a mutilated statue close by, and leaned upon his musket.

Monsieur Maurice was at first very silent. Once or twice he closed his eyes, as if listening to the gentle sounds upon the air—once or twice he cast an uneasy glance in the direction of the sentry; but for a long time he scarcely moved or spoke.

At length, as if following up a train of previous thought, he said suddenly:—

"There is no liberty. There are comparative degrees of captivity, and comparative degrees of slavery; but of liberty, our social system knows nothing but the name. That sentry, if you asked him, would tell you that he is free. He pities me, perhaps, for being a prisoner. Yet he is even less free than myself. He is the slave of discipline. He must walk, hold up his head, wear his hair, dress, eat, and sleep according to the will of his superiors. If he disobeys, he is flogged. If he runs away, he is shot. At the present moment, he dares not lose sight of me for his life. I have done him no wrong; yet if I try to escape, it is his duty to shoot me. What is there in my captivity to equal the slavery of his condition? I cannot, it is true, go where I please; but, at least, I am not obliged to walk up and down a certain corridor, or in front of a certain sentry-box, for so many hours a day; and no power on earth could compel me to kill an innocent man who had never harmed me in his life."

In an instant I had the whole scene before my eyes—Monsieur Maurice flying—pursued—shot down—brought back to die!

"But—but you won't try to run away, Monsieur Maurice!" I cried, terrified at the picture my own fancy had drawn.

He darted a scrutinising glance at me, and said, after a moment's hesitation:—

"If I intended to do so, petite, I should hardly tell Colonel Bernhard's little daughter beforehand. Besides, why should I care now for liberty? What should I do with it? Have I not lost all that made it worth possessing —the Hero I worshipped, the Cause I honoured, the home I loved, the woman I adored? What better place for me than a prison . . . unless the grave?"

He roused himself. He had been thinking aloud, unconscious of my presence; but seeing my startled eyes fixed full upon his face, he smiled, and said with a sudden change of voice and manner:—

"Go pluck me that namesake of yours over yonder—the big white Marguerite on the edge of the grass plat. Thanks, petite. Now I'll be sworn you guess what I am going to do with it! No? Well, I am going to question these little sibylline leaves, and make the Marguerite tell me whether I am destined to a prison all the days of my life. What! you never heard of the old flower sortilége? Why, Gretchen, I thought every little German maiden learned it in the cradle with her mother tongue!"

"But how can the Marguerite answer you, Monsieur Maurice?" I exclaimed.

"You shall see—but I must tell you first that the flower is not used to pronounce upon such serious matters. She is the oracle of village lads and lasses—not of grave prisoners like myself."

And with this, half sadly, half playfully, he began stripping the leaves off one by one, and repeating over and over again:—

"Tell me, sweet Marguerite, shall I be free? Soon—in time—perhaps —never! Soon—in time—perhaps—never! Soon—in time—perhaps—"

It was the last leaf.

"Pshaw!" he said, tossing away the stalk with an impatient laugh. "You could have given me as good an answer as that, little Gretchen. Let us go in."

8

It was about a week after this when I was startled out of my deepest midnight sleep by a rush of many feet, and a fierce and sudden knocking at my father's bed-room door—the door opposite my own.

I sat up, trembling. A bright blaze gleamed along the threshold, and high above the clamour of tongues outside, I recognised my father's voice, quick, sharp, imperative. Then a door was opened and banged. Then came the rush of feet again—then silence.

It was a strange, wild hubbub; and it had all come, and gone, and was over in less than a minute. But what was it?

Seeing that fiery line along the threshold, I had thought for a moment that the Château was on fire; but the light vanished with those who brought it, and all was darkness again.

"Bertha!" I cried tremulously. "Bertha!"

Now Bertha was my Rhenish hand-maiden, and she slept in a closet opening off my room; but Bertha was as deaf to my voice as one of the Seven Sleepers.

Suddenly a shrill trumpet-call rang out in the courtyard.

I sprang out of bed, flew to Bertha, and shook her with all my strength till she woke.

"Bertha! Bertha!" I cried. "Wake up—strike a light—dress me quickly! I must know what is the matter!"

In vain Bertha yawns, rubs her eyes, protests that I have had a bad dream, and that nothing is the matter. Get up she must; dress herself and me in the twinkling of an eye; and go upon whatsoever dance I choose to lead her.

My father is gone, and his door stands wide open. We turn to the stairs, and a cold wind rushes up in our faces. We go down, and find the side-door that leads to the courtyard unfastened and ajar. There is not a soul in the courtyard. There is not the faintest glimmer of light from the guard-house windows. The sentry who walks perpetually to and fro in front of the gate is not at his post; and the gate is wide open!

Even Bertha sees by this time that something strange is afoot, and stares at me with a face of foolish wonder.

"Ach, Herr Gott!" she cries, clapping her hands together, "what's that?"

It is very faint, very distant; but quite audible in the dead silence of the night. In an instant I know what it is that has happened!

"It is the report of a musket!" I exclaim, seizing her by the hand, and dragging her across the courtyard. "Quick! quick! Oh, Monsieur Maurice! Monsieur Maurice!"

The night is very dark. There is no moon, and the stars, glimmering through a veil of haze, give little light. But we run as recklessly as if it were bright day, past the barracks, past the parade-ground, and round to the great gates on the garden side of the Château. These, however, are closed, and the sentry, standing watchful and motionless, with his musket made ready, refuses to let us through.

In vain I remind him that I am privileged, and that none of these gates are ever closed against me. The man is inexorable.

"No, Fräulein Gretchen," he says, "I dare not. This is not a fit hour for you to be out. Pray go home."

"But Gaspar, good Gaspar," I plead, clinging to the gate with both hands, "tell me if he has escaped! Hark; oh, hark! there it is again!"

And another, and another shot rings through the still night-air.

The sentry almost stamps with impatience.

"Go home, dear little Fräulein! Go home at once," he says. "There is danger abroad to-night. I cannot leave my post, or I would take you home myself. . . . Holy Saint Christopher! they are coming this way! Go—go—what would his Excellency the Governor say, if he found you here?"

I see quick gleams of wandering lights among the trees—I hear a distant shout! Then, seized by a sudden panic, I turn and fly, with Bertha at my heels—fly back the way I came, never pausing till I find myself once more at the courtyard gate. Here—breathless, trembling, panting—I stop to listen and look back. All is silent;—as silent as before.

"But, liebe Gretchen," says Bertha, as breathless as myself, "what is to do to-night?"

There is a coming murmur on the air. There is a red glow reflected on the barrack windows . . . they are coming! I turn suddenly cold and giddy.

"Hush, Bertha!" I whisper, "we must not stay here. Papa will be angry! Let us go up to the corridor window."

So we go back into the house, upstairs the way we came, and station ourselves at the corridor window, which looks into the courtyard.

Slowly the glow broadens; slowly the sound resolves itself into an irregular tramp of many feet and a murmur of many voices.

Then suddenly the courtyard is filled with soldiers and lighted torches, and . . . and I clasp my hands over my eyes in an agony of terror, lest the picture I drew a few days since should be coming true.

"What do you see, Bertha?" I falter. "Do you—do you see Monsieur Maurice?"

"No, but I see Gottlieb Kolb, and Corporal Fritz, and . . . yes—here is Monsieur Maurice between two soldiers, and his Excellency the Colonel walking beside them!"

I looked up, and my heart gave a leap of gladness. He was not dead—he was not even wounded! He had been pursued and captured; but àt least he was safe!

They stopped just under the corridor window. The torchlight fell full upon their faces. Monsieur Maurice looked pale and composed; perhaps just a shade haughtier than usual. My father had his drawn sword in his hand.

"Corporal Fritz," he said, turning to a soldier near him, "conduct the prisoner to his room, and post two sentries at his door, and one under his windows." Then turning to Monsieur Maurice, "I thank God, Sir," he said gravely, "that you have not paid for your imprudence with your life. I have the honour to wish you good night."

Monsieur Maurice ceremoniously took off his hat.

"Good night, Colonel Bernhard," he said. "I beg you, however, to remember that I had withdrawn my parole."

"I remember it, Monsieur Maurice," replied my father, drawing himself up, and returning the salutation.

Monsieur Maurice then crossed the courtyard with his guards, and entered the Château by the door leading to the state apartments. My father, after standing for a moment as if lost in thought, turned away and went over to the guard-house.

The soldiers then dispersed, or gathered into little knots of twos and threes, and talked in low voices of the events of the night.

"Accomplices!" said one, just close against the window where Bertha and I still lingered. "Liebe Mutter! I'll take my oath he had one! Why, it was I who first caught sight of the prisoner gliding through the trees—I saw him as plainly as I see you now—I covered him with my musket—I wouldn't have given a copper pfennig for his life, when paff! at the very moment I pulled the trigger, out steps a fellow from behind my shoulder, knocks up my musket, and disappears like a flash of lightning—Heaven only knows where, for I never laid eyes on him again!"

"What was he like?" asks another soldier, incredulously.

"Like? How should I know? It was as dark as pitch. I just caught a glimpse of him in the flash of the powder—an ugly, brown-looking devil he seemed! but he was gone in a breath, and I had no time to look for him."

The soldiers round about burst out laughing.

"Hold, Karl!" says one, slapping him boisterously on the shoulder. "You are a good shot, but you missed aim for once. No need to conjure up a brown devil to account for that, old comrade!"

Karl, finding his story discredited, retorted angrily; and a quarrel was fast brewing, when the sergeant on guard came up and ordered the men to their several quarters.

"Holy Saint Bridget!" said Bertha, shivering, "how cold it is!—and there, I declare, is the Convent clock striking half after one! Liebe Gretchen, you really must go to bed—what would your father say?"

So we both crept back to bed. Bertha was asleep again almost before she had laid her head upon her pillow; but I lay awake till dawn of day.

9

It was in my father's disposition to be both strict and indulgent—that is to say, as a father he was all tenderness, and as a soldier all discipline. His men both loved and feared him; but I, who never had cause to fear him in my life, loved him with all my heart, and never thought of him except as the fondest of parents. Chiefly, perhaps, for my sake, he had up to this time been extremely indulgent in all that regarded Monsieur Maurice. Now, however, he conceived that it was his duty to be indulgent no longer. He was responsible for the person of Monsieur Maurice, and Monsieur Maurice had attempted to escape; from this moment, therefore, Monsieur Maurice must be guarded, hedged in, isolated, like any other prisoner under similar circumstances—at all events until further instructions should arrive from Berlin. So my father, as it was his duty to do, wrote straightway to the Minister of War, doubled all previous precautions, and forbade me to go near the prisoner's rooms on any pretext whatever.

I neither coaxed nor pleaded. I had an instinctive feeling that the thing was inevitable, and that I had nothing to do but to suffer and obey. And I did suffer bitterly. Day after day, I hung about the terraces under his windows, watching for the glimpse that hardly ever came. Night after night I sobbed till I was tired, and fell asleep with his name upon my lips. It was a childish grief; but not therefore the less poignant. It was a childish love, too; necessarily transient and irrational, as such child- ish passions are; but not therefore the less real. The dull web of my later life has not been without its one golden thread of romance (alas! how long since tarnished!), but not even that dream has left a deeper scar upon my memory than did the hero-worship of my first youth. It was something more than love; it was adoration. To be with him was measureless content—to be banished from him was something akin to despair.

So Monsieur Maurice and his little Gretchen were parted. No more happy French lessons—no more walks—no more stories told by the firelight in the gloaming! All was over; all was blank. But for how long? Surely not for ever!

"Perhaps the king will think fit to hand him over to some other gaoler," said my father one day; "and, by Heaven! I'd thank him more heartily for that boon than for the order of the Red Eagle!"

My heart sank at the thought. Many and many a time had I pictured to myself what it would be if he were set at liberty, and with what mingled joy and grief I should bid him good-bye; but it had never occurred to me as a possibility that he might be transferred to another prison-house.

Thus a week—ten days—a fortnight went by, and still there came nothing from Berlin. I began to hope at last that nothing would come, and that matters would settle down in time, and be as they were before. But of such vain hopes I was speedily and roughly disabused; and in this wise.

It was a gloomy afternoon—one of those dun-coloured afternoons that seem all the more dismal for coming in the midst of Spring. I had been out of the way somewhere (wandering to and fro, I believe, like a dreary little ghost, among the grim galleries of the state apartments), and was going home at dusk to be in readiness for my father, who always came in after the afternoon parade. Coming up the passage out of which our rooms opened, I heard voices—my father's and another. Concluding that he had Corporal Fritz with him, I went in unhesitatingly. To my surprise, I found the lamp lighted, and a strange officer sitting face to face with my father at the table.

The stranger was in the act of speaking; my father listening, with a grave, intent look upon his face.

... "and if he had been shot, Colonel Bernhard, the State would have been well rid of a troublesome burden."

My father saw me in the doorway, put up his hand with a warning gesture, and said hastily:—

"You here, Gretchen! Go into the dining-room, my child, till I send for you."

The dining-room, as I have said elsewhere, opened out of the sitting-room which also served for my father's bureau. I had therefore to cross the room, and so caught a full view of the stranger's face. He was a sallow, dark man, with iron grey hair cut close to his head, a hard mouth, a cold grey eye, and a deep furrow between his brows. He wore a blue military frock buttoned to the chin; and a plain cocked hat lay beside his gloves upon the table.

I went into the dining-room and closed the door. It was half-door, half-window, the upper panels being made of ground glass, so as to let in a borrowed light; for the little room was at all times somewhat of the darkest. Such as it was, this borrowed light was now all I had; for the dining-room fire had gone out hours ago, and though there were candles on the chimney-piece, I had no means of lighting them. So I groped my way to the first chair I could find, and waited my father's summons.

"And if he had been shot, Colonel Bernhard, the State would have been well rid of a troublesome burden."

It was all I had heard; but it was enough to set me thinking. "If he had been shot" . . . If who had been shot? My fears answered that question but too readily. Who, then, was this new-comer? Was he from Berlin? And if from Berlin, what orders did he bring? A vague terror of coming evil fell upon me. I trembled—I held my breath. I tried to hear what was being said, but in vain. The voices in the next room went on in a low incessant murmur; but of that murmur I could not distinguish a word.

Then the sounds swelled a little, as if the speakers were becoming more earnest. And then, forgetting all I had ever heard or been taught about the heinousness of eavesdropping, I got up very softly and crept close against the door.

"That is to say, you dislike the responsibility, Colonel Bernhard."

These were the first words I heard.

"I dislike the office," said my father, bluntly. "I'd almost as soon be a hangman as a gaoler."

The stranger here said something that my ear failed to catch. Then my father spoke again.

"To tell you the truth, Herr Count, I only wish it would please His Excellency to transfer him elsewhere."

The stranger paused a moment, and then said in a low but very distinct voice:—

"Supposing, Colonel Bernhard, that you were yourself transferred—shall we say to Königsberg? Would you prefer it to Brühl?"

"Königsberg!" exclaimed my father in a tone of profound amazement.

"The appointment, I believe, is worth six hundred thalers a year more than Brühl," said the stranger.

"But it has never been offered to me," said my father, in his simple straightforward way. "Of course I should prefer it—but what of that? And what has Königsberg to do with Monsieur Maurice?"

"Ah, true—Monsieur Maurice! Well, to return then to Monsieur Maurice—how would it be, do you think, somewhat to relax the present vigilance?"

"To relax it?"

"To leave a door or a window unguarded now and then, for instance. In short, to—to provide certain facilities ... you understand?"

"Facilities?" exclaimed my father, incredulously. "Facilities for escape?"

"Well—yes; if you think fit to put it so plainly," replied the other, with a short little cough, followed by a snap like the opening and shutting of a snuff-box.

"But—but in the name of the Eleven Thousand Virgins, why wait for the man to run away? Why not give him his liberty, and get rid of him pleasantly?"

"Because—ahem!—because, you see, Colonel Bernhard, it would not then be possible to pursue him," said the stranger, drily.

"To pursue him?"

"Just so—and to shoot him."

I heard the sound of a chair pushed violently back; and my father's shadow, vague and menacing, started up with him, and fell across the door.

"What?" he shouted, in a terrible voice. "Are you taking me at my word? Are you offering me the hangman's office?"

Then, with a sudden change of tone and manner, he added:—

"But—I must have misunderstood you. It is impossible."

"We have both altogether misunderstood each other, Colonel Bernhard," said the stranger, stiffly. "I had supposed you would be willing to serve the State, even at the cost of some violence to your prejudices."

"Great God! then you did mean it!" said my father, with a strange horror in his voice.

"I meant—to serve the King. I also hoped to advance the interests of Colonel Bernhard," replied the other, haughtily.

"My sword is the King's—my blood is the King's, to the last drop," said my father in great agitation; "but my honour—my honour is my own!"

"Enough, Colonel Bernhard; enough. We will drop the subject."

And again I heard the little dry cough, and the snap of the snuff-box.

A long silence followed, my father walking to and fro with a quick, heavy step; the stranger, apparently, still sitting in his place at the table.

"Should you, on reflection, see cause to take a different view of your duty, Colonel Bernhard," he said at last, "you have but to say so before . . ."

"I can never take a different view of it, Herr Count!" interrupted my father, vehemently.

"—before I take my departure in the morning," continued the other, with studied composure; "in the meanwhile, be pleased to remember that you are answerable for the person of your prisoner. Either he must not escape, or he must not escape with life."

My father's shadow bent its head.

"And now, with your permission, I will go to my room."

My father rang the bell, and when Bertha came, bade her light the Count von Rettel to his chamber.

Hearing them leave the room, I opened the door very softly and hesitatingly, scarce knowing whether to come out or not. I saw my father standing with his back towards me and his face still turned in the direction by which they had gone out. I saw him throw up his clenched hands, and shake them wildly above his head.

"And it was for this!—for this!" he said fiercely. "A bribe! God of Heaven! He offered me Königsberg as a bribe! Oh, that I should have lived to be treated as an assassin!"

His voice broke into hoarse sobs. He dropped into a chair—he covered his face with his hands.

He had forgotten that I was in the next room, and now I dared not remind him of my presence. His emotion terrified me. It was the first time I had seen a man shed tears; and this alone, let the man be whom he might, would have seemed terrible to me at any time. How much more terrible when those tears were tears of outraged honour, and when the man who shed them was my father!

I trembled from head to foot. I had an instinctive feeling that I ought not to look upon his agony. I shrank back—closed the door—held my breath, and waited.

Presently the sound of sobbing ceased. Then he sighed heavily twice or thrice—got up abruptly—threw a couple of logs on the fire, and left the room. The next moment I heard him unlock the door under the stairs, and go into the cellar. I seized the opportunity to escape, and stole up to my own room as rapidly and noiselessly as my trembling knees would carry me.

I had my supper with Bertha that evening, and the Count ate at my father's table; but I afterwards learned that, though the Governor of Brühl himself waited ceremoniously upon his guest and served him with his best, he neither broke bread nor drank wine with him.

I saw that unwelcome guest no more. I heard his voice under the

window, and the clatter of his horse's hoofs as he rode away in the
early morning; but that was long enough before Bertha came to call me.

10

Weeks went by. Spring warmed, and ripened, and blossomed into
Summer. Gardens and terraces were ablaze once more with many-
coloured flowers; fountains played and sparkled in the sunshine; and
travellers bound for Cologne or Bonn put up again at Brühl in the midst
of the day's journey, to bait their horses and see the Château on their way.

For in these years just following the Peace of Paris, the Continent
was overrun by travellers, two thirds of whom were English. The diligence—the great, top-heavy, lumbering diligence of fifty years ago—
used then to come lurching and thundering down the main street five
times a week throughout the Summer season; and as many as three and
four travelling carriages a day would pass through in fine weather. The
landlord of the "Lion d'Or" kept fifty horses in his stables in those days,
and drove a thriving trade.

So the Summer came, and brought the stir of outer life into the precincts of our sleepy Château; but brought no better change in the
fortunes of Monsieur Maurice. Ever since that fatal night, the terms of
his imprisonment had been more rigorous than ever. Till then, he might,
if he would, walk twice a week in the grounds with a soldier at his heels;
but now he was placed in strict confinement in his own two rooms, with
one sentry always pacing the corridor outside his door, and another
under his windows. And across each of those windows might now be
seen a couple of bright new iron bars, thick as a man's wrist, forged and
fixed there by the village blacksmith.

I have no words to tell how the sight of those bars revolted me. If
instead of being a little helpless girl, I had been a man like my father,
and a servant of the State, I think they would have made a rebel of me.

Worse, however, than iron bars, locked doors, and guarded corridors,
was Hartmann—Herr Ludwig Hartmann, as he was styled in the despatch
that announced his coming—a pale, slight, silent man, with colourless
grey eyes and white eyelashes, who came direct from Berlin about a
month later, to act as Monsieur Maurice's "personal attendant."
Stealthy, watchful, secret, civil, he established himself in a room adjoining
the prisoner's apartment, and was as much at home in the course of a
couple of hours as if he had been settled there from the first.

He brought with him a paper of instructions, and, having on his
arrival submitted these instructions to my father, he at once took up a
certain routine of duties that never varied. He brushed Monsieur
Maurice's clothes, waited upon him at table, attended him in his bed-

room, was always within hearing, always on the alert, and haunted the prisoner like his shadow. Not even a housemaid could go in to sweep but he was present. Now the man's perpetual presence was intolerable to Monsieur Maurice. He had borne all else with patience, but this last tyranny was more than he could endure without murmuring. He appealed to my father; but my father, though Governor of Brühl, was powerless to help him. Hartmann had presented his instructions as a minister presents his credentials, and those instructions emanated from Berlin. So the new-comer, valet, gaoler, spy as he was, became an established fact, and was detested throughout the Château—by no one more heartily than myself.

I still, however, saw Monsieur Maurice now and then. My father often took me with him in his rounds, and always when he visited his prisoner. Sometimes, too, he would leave me for an hour with my friend, and call for me again on his way back; so that we were not wholly parted even now. But Hartmann took care never to leave us alone. Before my father's footsteps were out of hearing, he would be in the room; silent, unobtrusive, perfectly civil, but watchful as a lynx. We could not talk before him freely. Nothing was as it used to be. It was better than total banishments; it was better than never hearing his voice; but the constraint was hard to bear, and the pain of these meetings was almost greater than the pleasure.

And now, as I approach that part of my narrative which possesses the deepest interest for myself, I hesitate—hesitate and draw back before the great mystery in which it is involved. I ask myself what interpretation the world will put upon facts for which I can vouch; upon events which I myself witnessed? I cannot prove those events. They happened over fifty years ago; but they are as vividly present to my memory as if they had taken place yesterday. I can only relate them in their order, knowing them to be true, and leaving each reader to judge of them according to his convictions.

It was about the middle of the second week in June. Hartmann had been about six weeks at Brühl, and all was going on in the usual dull routine, when that routine was suddenly broken by the arrival of three mounted dragoons—an officer and two privates—whose errand, whatever it might be, had the effect of throwing the whole establishment into sudden and unwonted confusion.

I was out in the grounds when they arrived, and came back at midday to find no dinner on the table, no cook in the kitchen; but a full-dress parade going on in the courtyard, and all the interior of the Château in a state of wild commotion. Here were peasants bringing in wood, gardeners laden with vegetables and flowers, women running to and fro with baskets full of linen, and all to the accompaniment of such a hammering, bell-ringing, and clattering of tongues as I had never heard before.

I stood bewildered, not knowing what to do, or where to go.

"What is the matter? What has happened? What are you doing?" I asked, first of one and then of another; but they were all too busy to answer.

"Ach, lieber Gott!" said one, "I've no time for talking!"

"Don't ask me, little Fräulein," said another. "I have eight windows to clean up yonder, and only one pair of hands to do them with!"

"If you want to know what is to do," said a third impatiently, "you had better come and see."

The head-gardener's son came by with two pots of magnificent geraniums, one under each arm.

"Where are you going with those flowers, Wilhelm?" I asked, running after him.

"They are for the state salon, Fräulein Gretchen," he replied, and hurried on.

For the state salon! I ran round to the side of the grand entrance. There were soldiers putting up banners in the hall; others helping to carry furniture up stairs; carpenters with ladders; women with brooms and brushes; and Corporal Fritz bustling hither and thither, giving orders, and seeing after everything.

"But Corporal Fritz!" I exclaimed, "what are all these people about?"

"We are preparing the state apartments, dear little Fräulein," replied Corporal Fritz, rubbing his hands with an air of great enjoyment.

"But why? For whom?"

"For whom? Why, for the King, to be sure"; and Corporal Fritz clapped his hand to the side of his hat like a loyal soldier. "Don't you know, dear little Fräulein, that His Majesty sleeps here to-night, on his way to Ehrenbreitstein?"

This was news indeed! I ran up stairs—I was all excitement—I got in everybody's way—I tormented everybody with questions. I saw the table being laid in the grand salon where the King was to sup, and the bedstead being put up in the little salon where he was to sleep, and the ante-room being prepared for his officers. All was being made ready as rapidly, and decorated as tastefully, as the scanty resources of the Château would permit. I recognised much of the furniture from the attics above, and this, faded though it was, being helped out with flowers, flags, and greenery, made the great echoing rooms look gay and habitable.

By and by, my father came round to see how the work was going on, and finding me in the midst of it, took me by the hand and led me away.

"You are not wanted here, my little Gretchen," he said; "and, indeed, all the world is so busy to-day that I scarcely know what to do with thee."

"Take me to Monsieur Maurice!" I said, coaxingly.

"Ay—so I will," said my father; "with him, at all events, you will be out of the way."

So he took me round to Monsieur Maurice's rooms, and told me as we went along that the King had only given him six hours' notice, and that in order to furnish his Majesty's bed and his Majesty's supper, he had bought up all the poultry and eggs, and borrowed well-nigh all the silver, glass, and linen in the town.

By this time we were almost at Monsieur Maurice's door. A sudden thought flashed upon me. I pulled him back, out of the sentry's hearing.

"Oh, father!" I cried eagerly, "will you not ask the King to let Monsieur Maurice free?"

My father shook his head.

"Nay," he said, "I must not do that, my little Mädchen. And look you—not a word that the King is coming here to-night. It would only make the prisoner restless, and could avail nothing. Promise me to be silent."

So I promised, and he left me at the door without going in.

I spent all the afternoon with Monsieur Maurice. He divided his luncheon with me; he gave me a French lesson, he told me stories. I had not had such a happy day for months. Hartmann, it is true, was constantly in and out of the room, but even Hartmann was less in the way than usual. He seemed absent and preoccupied, and was therefore not so watchful as at other times. In the meanwhile I could still hear, though faintly, the noises in the rooms below; but all became quiet about five o'clock in the evening, and Monsieur Maurice, who had been told they were only cleaning the state apartments, asked no questions.

Meanwhile the afternoon waned, and the sun bent westward, and still no one came to fetch me away. My father knew where I was; Bertha was probably too busy to think about me; and I was only too glad to stay as long as Monsieur Maurice was willing to keep me. By and by, about half-past six o'clock, the sky became overclouded, and we heard a low muttering of very distant thunder. At seven, it rained heavily.

Now it was Monsieur Maurice's custom to dine late, and ours to dine early; but then, as his luncheon hour corresponded with our dinner-hour, and his dinner fell only a little later than our supper, it came to much the same thing, and did not therefore seem strange. So it happened that just as the storm came up, Hartmann began to prepare the table. Then, in the midst of the rain and the wind, my quick ear caught a sound of drums and bugles, and I knew the King was come. Monsieur Maurice evidently heard nothing; but I could see by Hartmann's face (he was laying the cloth and making a noise with the glasses) that he knew all, and was listening.

After this I heard no more. The wind raved; the rain pattered; the gloom thickened; and at half-past seven, when the soup was brought to table, it was so dark that Monsieur Maurice called for lights. He would not, however, allow the curtains to be drawn. He liked, he said, to sit and watch the storm.

A cover was laid for me at his right hand; but my supper hour was past, and what with the storm without, the heaviness in the air, and the excitement of the day, I was no longer hungry. So, having eaten a little soup and sipped some wine from Monsieur Maurice's glass, I went and curled myself up in an easy chair close to the window, and watched the driving mists as they swept across the park, and the tossing of the tree-tops against the sky.

It was a wild evening, lit by lurid gleams and openings in the clouds; and it seemed all the wilder by contrast with the quiet room and the dim radiance of the wax lights on the table. There was a soft halo round each little flame, and a dreamy haze in the atmosphere, from the midst of which Monsieur Maurice's pale face stood out against the shadowy background, like a head in a Dutch painting.

We were both very silent; partly because Hartmann was waiting, and partly, perhaps, because we had been talking all the afternoon. Monsieur Maurice ate slowly, and there were long intervals between the courses, during which he leaned his elbow on the table and his chin on his hand, looking across towards the window and the storm. Hartmann, meanwhile, seemed to be always listening. I could see that he was holding his breath, and trying to catch every faint echo from below.

It was a long, long dinner, and probably seemed all the longer to me because I did not partake of it. As for Monsieur Maurice, he tasted some dishes, and sent more away untouched.

"I think it is getting lighter," he said by and by. "Does it still rain?"

"Yes," I replied; "it is coming down steadily."

"We must open the window presently," he said. "I love the fresh smell that comes with the rain."

Here the conversation dropped again, and Hartmann, having been gone for a moment, came back with a dish of stewed fruit.

Then, for the first time, I observed there was a second attendant in the room.

"Will you not have some raspberries, Gretchen?" said Monsieur Maurice.

I shook my head. I was too much startled by the sight of the strange man, to answer him in words.

Who could he be? Where had he come from? He was standing be-hind Monsieur Maurice, far back in the gloom, near the door—a small, dark man, apparently; but so placed with regard to the table and the lights, that it was impossible to make out his features with distinctness.

Monsieur Maurice just tasted the raspberries and sent his plate away.

"How heavy the air of the room is!" he said. "Give me some Seltzer-water, and open that farthest window."

Hartmann reversed the order. He opened the window first; and as he did so, I saw that his hand shook upon the hasp, and that his face was deadly pale.

He then turned to the sideboard and opened a stone bottle that had been standing there since the beginning of dinner. He filled a tumbler with the sparkling water.

At the moment when he placed this tumbler on the salver—at the moment when he handed it to Monsieur Maurice—the other man glided quickly forward. I saw his bright eyes and his brown face in the full light. I saw *two hands* put out to take the glass; a brown hand and a white—his hand, and the hand of Monsieur Maurice. I saw—yes, before Heaven! as I live to remember and record it, I saw the brown hand grasp the tumbler and dash it to the ground!

"Pshaw!" said Monsieur Maurice, brushing the Seltzer-water impatiently from his sleeve, "how came you to upset it?"

But Hartmann, livid and trembling, stood speechless, staring at the door.

"It was the other man!" said I, starting up with a strange kind of breathless terror upon me. "He threw it on the ground—I saw him do it—where is he gone? what has become of him?"

"The other man! What other man?" said Monsieur Maurice. "My little Gretchen, you are dreaming."

"No, no, I am not dreaming. There was another man—a brown man! Hartmann saw him—"

"A brown man!" echoed Monsieur Maurice. Then catching sight of Hartmann's face, he pushed his chair back, looked at him steadily and sternly; and said, with a sudden change of voice and manner:—

"There is something wrong here. What does it mean? You saw a man—both of you? What was he like?"

"A brown man," I said again. "A brown man with bright eyes."

"And you?" said Monsieur Maurice, turning to Hartmann.

"I—I thought I saw something," stammered the attendant, with a violent effort at composure. "But it was nothing."

Monsieur Maurice looked at him as if he would look him through; got up, still looking at him; went to the sideboard, and, still looking at him, filled another tumbler with Seltzer-water.

"Drink that," he said, very quietly.

The man's lips moved, but he uttered never a word.

"Drink that," said Monsieur Maurice for the second time, and more sternly.

But Hartmann, instead of drinking it, instead of answering, threw up his hands in a wild way, and rushed out of the room.

Monsieur Maurice stood for a moment absorbed in thought; then wrote some words upon a card, and gave the card into my hand.

"For thy father, little one," he said. "Give it to no one but himself, and give it to him the first moment thou seest him. There's matter of life and death in it."

11

How the King supped, how the King slept, and what he thought of his Château of Augustenburg which he now saw for the first time, are matters respecting which I have no information. I only know that I had fallen asleep on Monsieur Maurice's sofa when Bertha came at ten o'clock that night to fetch me home; that I was very drowsy and unwilling to be moved; and that I woke in the morning dreaming of a brown man with bright eyes, and calling upon Monsieur Maurice to make haste and come before he should again have time to vanish away.

It was a lovely morning; bright and fresh, and sunshiny after the night's storm. My first thought was of Monsieur Maurice, and the card he had entrusted to my keeping. I had it still. My father was not at home when I came back last night. He was in attendance on the King, and did not return till long after I was asleep in my own little bed. This morning, early as I awoke, he was gone again, on the same duty.

I jumped up. I bade Bertha dress me quickly. "I must go to papa," I said. "I have a card for him from Monsieur Maurice."

"Nay, liebe Gretchen," said Bertha, "he is with the King."

But I told myself that I would find him, and see him, and give the card into his own hands, though a dozen kings were in the way. I could not read what was written on the card. I could read print easily and rapidly, but handwriting not at all. I knew, however, that it was urgent. Had he not said that it was matter of life or death?

I hurried to dress; I hurried to get out. I could not rest, I could not eat till I had given up the card. As good fortune would have it, the first person I met was Corporal Fritz. I asked him where I could find my father.

"Dear little Fräulein," said Corporal Fritz, "you cannot see him just yet. He is with the King."

"But I must see him," I said. "I must—indeed, I must. Go to him for me—please go to him, dear, good Corporal Fritz, and tell him his little Gretchen must speak to him, if only for one moment!"

"But dear little Fräulein".…

"Is the King at breakfast?" I interrupted.

"At breakfast! Eh, then, our gallant King hath a soldier's habits. His Majesty breakfasted at six this morning, and is gone out betimes to visit his hunting-lodge at Falkenlust."

"And my father?"

"His Excellency the Governor is in attendance upon the King."

"Then I will go to Falkenlust."

Corporal Fritz shook his head; shrugged his shoulders; took a pinch of snuff.

"'Tis a long road to Falkenlust, dear little Fräulein," said he; "and His Excellency, methinks, would be better pleased".…

I stayed to hear no more, but ran off at full speed down the terraces, straight to the Round Point and the fountain, and along the great avenue that led to Falkenlust. I ran till I was out of breath—then rested—then ran again, on, and on, and on, till the road lengthened and narrowed behind me, and the Château of Augustenburg looked almost as small in the distance at one end as the Falkenlust Lodge at the other.

Then all at once, far, far away, I saw a moving group of figures. They grew larger and more distinct—they were coming towards me! I had run till I could run no farther. Panting and breathless, I leaned against a tree, and waited.

And now, as they drew nearer, I saw that the group consisted of some eight or ten officers, two of whom were walking somewhat in advance of the rest. One of the two wore a plain cocked hat and an undress military frock; the other was in full uniform, and wore two or three glittering medals on his breast. This other was my father. I scarcely looked at the first. I never even asked myself whether he was, or was not the King. I had no eyes, no thought for any but my father.

So I stood, eager and breathless, on the verge of the gravel. So they every moment drew nearer the spot where I was standing. As they came close, my father's eyes met mine. He shook his head, and frowned. He thought I had come there to stare at the King.

Nothing daunted, I took two steps forward. I had Monsieur Maurice's card in my hand. I held it out to him.

"Read it," I said. "It is from Monsieur Maurice."

But he crushed it in his hand without looking at it, and waved me back authoritatively.

"At once!" I cried; "at once!"

The gentleman in the blue frock stopped and smiled.

"Is this your little girl, Colonel Bernhard?" he asked.

My father replied by a low bow.

The strange gentleman beckoned me to draw nearer.

"A golden-haired little Mädchen!" said he. "Come hither, pretty one, and tell me your name."

I knew then that he was the King. I trembled and blushed.

"My name is Gretchen," I said.

"And you have brought a letter for your father?"

"It is not a letter," I said. "It is a card. It is from Monsieur Maurice."

"And who is Monsieur Maurice?" asked the King.

"So please your Majesty," said my father, answering the question for me, "Monsieur Maurice is the prisoner I hold in charge."

The smile went out of the King's face.

"The prisoner!" he repeated, inquiringly. "What prisoner?"

"The state-prisoner whom I received, according to your Majesty's command, eight months ago—Monsieur Maurice."

"Monsieur Maurice!" echoed the King.

"I know the gentleman by no other name, please your Majesty," said my father.

The King looked grave.

"I never heard of Monsieur Maurice," he said, "I know of no state-prisoner here."

"The prisoner was consigned to my keeping by your Majesty's Minister of War," said my father.

"By von Bulow?"

My father bowed.

"Upon whose authority?"

"In your Majesty's name."

The King frowned.

"What papers did you receive with your prisoner, Colonel Bernhard?" he said.

"None, your Majesty—except a despatch from your Majesty's Minister of War, delivered a day or two before the prisoner arrived at Brühl."

"How did he come? and where did he come from?"

"He came in a close carriage, your Majesty, attended by two officers who left Brühl the same night and whose names and persons are unknown to me. I do not know where he came from. I only know that they had taken the last relay of horses from Cologne."

"You were not told his offence?"

"I was told nothing, your Majesty, except that Monsieur Maurice was an enemy to the state, and—"

"And what?"

My father's hand went up to his moustache, as it was wont to do in perplexity.

"I—so please your Majesty, I think there is some foul mystery in it at bottom," he said, bluntly. "There hath been that thing proposed to me that I am ashamed to repeat. I do beseech your Majesty that some investigation . . . ."

His eyes happened for a moment to rest upon the card. He stammered —changed colour—stopped short in his sentence—took off his hat—laid the card upon it—and so handed it to the King.

His Majesty Frederick William the Third of Prussia was, like most of the princes of his house, tanned, soldierly, and fresh-complexioned; but florid as he was, there came a darker flush into his face as he read what Monsieur Maurice had written.

"An attempt upon his life!" he exclaimed. "The thing is not possible."

My father was silent. The king looked at him keenly.

"*Is* it possible, Colonel Bernhard?" he said.

"I think it may be possible, your Majesty," replied my father in a low voice.

The King frowned.

"Colonel Bernhard," he said, "how can that be? You are responsible for the safety as well as the person of any prisoner committed to your charge."

"So long as the prisoner is left wholly to my charge I can answer for his safety with my head, so please your Majesty," said my father, reddening; "but not when he is provided with a special attendant over whom I have no control."

"What special attendant? Where did he come from? Who sent him?"

"I believe he came from Berlin, your Majesty. He was sent by your Majesty's Minister of War. His name is Hartmann."

The King stood thinking. His officers had fallen out of earshot, and were talking together in a little knot some four yards behind. I was still standing on the spot to which the King had called me. He looked round, and saw my anxious face.

"What, still there, little one?" he said. "You have not heard what we were saying?"

"Yes," I said; "I heard it."

"The child may have heard, your Majesty," interposed my father, hastily; "but she did not understand. Run home, Gretchen. Make thy obeisance to his Majesty, and run home quickly."

But I had understood every word. I knew that Monsieur Maurice's life had been in danger. I knew the King was all-powerful. Terrified at my own boldness—terrified at the thought of my father's anger—

trembling—sobbing—scarcely conscious of what I was saying, I fell at
the King's feet, and cried:—

"Save him—save him, Sire! Don't let them kill poor Monsieur
Maurice! Forgive him—please forgive him, and let him go home again!"

My father seized me by the hand, forced me to rise, and dragged me
back more roughly than he had ever touched me in his life.

"I beseech your Majesty's pardon for the child," he said. "She knows
no better."

But the King smiled, and called me back to him.

"Nay, nay," he said, laying his hand upon my head, "do not be vexed
with her. So, little one, you and Monsieur Maurice are friends?"

I nodded; for I was still crying, and too frightened at what I had done
to be able to speak.

"And you love him dearly?"

"Better than anyone—in the world—except Papa," I faltered, through
my tears.

"Not better than your brothers and sisters?"

"I have no brothers and sisters," I replied, my courage coming back
again by degrees. "I have no one but Papa, and Monsieur Maurice, and
Aunt Martha Baur—and I love Monsieur Maurice a thousand, thousand
times more than Aunt Martha Baur!"

There came a merry sparkle into the King's eyes, and my father
turned his face away to conceal a smile.

"But if Monsieur Maurice was free, he would go away and you would
never see him again. What would you do then?"

"I—should be very sorry," I faltered; "but" . . .

"But what?"

"I would rather he went away, and was happy."

The King stooped down and kissed me on the brow.

"That, my little Mädchen, is the answer of a true friend," he said,
gravely and kindly. "If your Monsieur Maurice deserves to go free, he
shall have his liberty. You have our royal word for it. Colonel Bernhard,
we will investigate this matter without the delay of an hour."

Saying thus, he turned from me to my father, and, followed by his
officers, passed on in the direction of the Château.

I stood there speechless, his gracious words yet ringing in my ears.
He had left me no time for thanks, if even I could have framed any. But
he had kissed me—he had promised me that Monsieur Maurice should
go free, "if he deserved it!" and who better than I knew how impossible
it was that he should not deserve it? It was all true. It was not a dream.
I had the King's royal word for it.

I had the King's royal word for it—and yet I could hardly believe
it!

12

I have told my story up to this point from my own personal experience, relating in their order, quite simply and faithfully, the things I myself heard and saw. I can do this, however, no longer. Respecting those matters that happened when I was not present, I can only repeat what was told me by others; and as regards certain foregone events in the life of Monsieur Maurice, I have but vague rumour; and still more vague conjecture upon which to base my conclusions.

The King had said that Monsieur Maurice's case should be investigated without the delay of an hour, and, so far as it could then and there be done, it was investigated immediately on his return to the Château. He first examined Baron von Bulow's original despatch, and all my father's minutes of matters relating to the prisoner, including a statement written immediately after the departure of a stranger calling himself the Count von Rettel, and detailing from memory, very circumstantially and fully, the substance of a certain conversation to which I had been accidentally a witness, and which I have myself recorded elsewhere.

The King, on reading this statement, was observed to be greatly disturbed. He questioned my father minutely as to the age, complexion, height, and general appearance of the said Count von Rettel, and with his own hand noted down my father's replies on the back of my father's manuscript. This done, His Majesty desired that the man Hartmann should be brought before him.

But Hartmann was nowhere to be found. His room was empty. His bed had not been slept in. He had disappeared, in short, as completely as if he had never dwelt within the precincts of the Château.

It was found, on more particular inquiry being made, that he had not been seen since the previous evening. Overwhelmed with terror, and perhaps with remorse, he had rushed out of Monsieur Maurice's presence, never to return. It was supposed that he had then immediately gathered together all that belonged to him, and had taken advantage of the bustle and confusion consequent on the King's arrival, to leave Brühl in one of the return carriages or fourgons that had brought the royal party from Cologne. I am not aware that anything more was ever seen or heard of him; or that any active search for him was judicially instituted either then, or at any other time. But he might easily have been pursued, and taken, and dealt with according to the law, without our being any the wiser at Brühl.

Hartmann being gone, the King then sent for the prisoner, and Monsieur Maurice, for the first time in many weeks, left his own rooms, and was brought round to the state-apartments. Seeing so many persons about; seeing also the flowers and flags upon the walls, he seemed surprised, but said nothing. Being brought into the royal presence, however, he appeared at once to recognise the King. He bowed profoundly, and a faint flush was seen to come into his face. He then cast a rapid glance round the room, as if to see who else was present; bowed also (but less profoundly) to my father, who was standing behind the King's chair; and waited to be spoken to.

"Vous êtes Français, Monsieur?" said the King, addressing him in French, of which language my father understood only a few words.

"Je suis Français, votre Majesté," replied Monsieur Maurice.

"Comment!" said the King, still in French. "Our person, then, is not unknown to you?"

"I have repeatedly enjoyed the honour of being in your Majesty's presence," replied Monsieur Maurice, respectfully.

Being then asked where, and on what occasion, my father understood him to say that he had seen his Majesty at Erfurt during the great meeting of the Sovereigns under Napoleon the First, and again at the Congress of Vienna; and also that he had, at that time, occupied some important office, such, perhaps, as military secretary, about the person of the Emperor. The King then proceeded to question him on matters relating to his imprisonment and his previous history, to all of which Monsieur Maurice seemed to reply at some length, and with great earnestness of manner. Of these explanations, however, my father's imperfect knowledge of the language enabled him to catch only a few words here and there.

Presently, in the midst of a somewhat lengthy statement, Monsieur Maurice pronounced the name of Baron von Bulow. Hereupon the King checked him by a gesture; desired all present to withdraw; caused the door to be closed; and carried on the rest of the examination in private. By and by, after the lapse of nearly three quarters of an hour, my father was recalled, and an officer in waiting was despatched to Monsieur Maurice's rooms to fetch what was left of the bottle of Seltzer-water, which Monsieur Maurice had himself locked up in the sideboard the night before.

The King then asked if there was any scientific man in Brühl capable of analysing the liquid; to which my father replied that no such person could be found nearer than Cologne or Bonn. Hereupon a dog was brought in from the stables, and, having been made to swallow about a quarter of a pint of the Seltzer-water, was presently taken with convulsions, and died on the spot.

The King then desired that the body of the dog, and all that yet remained in the bottle should be despatched to the Professor of Chemistry at Bonn, for immediate examination.

This done, he turned to Monsieur Maurice, and said in German, so that all present might hear and understand:—

"Monsieur, so far as we have the present means of judging, you have suffered an illegal and unjust imprisonment, and a base attempt has been made upon your life. You appear to be the victim of a foul conspiracy, and it will be our first care to sift that conspiracy to the bottom. In the meanwhile, we restore your liberty, requiring only your *parole d'honneur*, as a gentleman, a soldier, and a Frenchman, to present yourself at Berlin, if summoned, at any time required within the next three months."

Monsieur Maurice bowed, laid his hand upon his heart, and said:—

"I promise it, your Majesty, on my word of honour as a gentleman, a soldier, and a Frenchman."

"You are probably in need of present funds," the King then said; "and if so, our Secretary shall make you out an order on the Treasury for five hundred thalers."

"Believing myself to be beggared of all I once possessed, I gratefully accept your Majesty's bounty," replied Monsieur Maurice.

The King then held out his hand for Monsieur Maurice to kiss, which he did on bended knee, and so went out from the royal presence, a free man.

Half an hour later, he and I were strolling hand in hand under the trees. His step was slow, and the hand that held mine had grown sadly thin and transparent.

"Let us sit here awhile, and rest," he said, as we came to the bench by the fountain.

I reminded him that we had sat and rested in the same spot the very last time we walked together.

"Ay," he replied, with a sigh. "I was stronger then."

"You will get strong again, now that you are free," I said.

"Perhaps—if liberty, like most earthly blessings, has not come too late."

"Too late for what?"

"For enjoyment—for use—for everything. My friends believe me dead; my place in the life of the world is filled up; my very name is by this time forgotten. I am as one shipwrecked on the great ocean, and cast upon a foreign shore."

"Are you—are you going away soon?" I said, almost in a whisper.

"Yes," he said, "I go to-morrow."

"And you will—never—come back again?" I faltered.

"Heaven forbid!" he said quickly. Then, remembering how that answer would grieve me, he added; "but I will never forget thee, petite. Never, while I live."

"But—but if I never see you any more" . . . .

Monsieur Maurice drew my head to his shoulder, and kissed my wet eyes.

"Tush! that cannot, shall not be," he said, caressingly. "Some day, perhaps, I may win back that old home by the sea of which I have so often told thee, little one; and then thou shalt come and visit me."

"Shall I?" I said, wistfully. "Shall I indeed?"

And he said—"Ay, indeed."

But I felt, somehow, that it would never come to pass.

After this, we got up and walked on again, very silently; he thinking of the new life before him; I, of the sorrow of parting. By-and-by, a sudden recollection flashed upon me.

"But, Monsieur Maurice," I exclaimed, "who was the brown man that stood behind your chair last night, and what has become of him?"

Monsieur Maurice turned his face away.

"My dear little Gretchen," he said, hastily, "there was no brown man. He existed in your imagination only."

"But I saw him!"

"You fancied you saw him. The room was dark. You were half asleep in the easy chair—half asleep, and half dreaming."

"But Hartmann saw him!"

"A wicked man fears his own shadow," said Monsieur Maurice, gravely. "Hartmann saw nothing but the reflection of his crime upon the mirror of his conscience."

I was silenced, but not convinced. Some minutes later, having thought it over, I returned to the charge.

"But, Monsieur Maurice," I said, "it is not the first time he has been here."

"Who? The King?"

"No—the brown man."

Monsieur Maurice frowned.

"Nay, nay," he said, impatiently, "prithee, no more of the brown man. 'Tis a folly, and I dislike it."

"But he was here in the park the night you tried to run away," I said, persistently. "He saved your life by knocking up the musket that was pointed at your head!"

Pale as he always was, Monsieur Maurice turned paler still at these words of mine. His very lips whitened.

"What is that you say?" he asked, stopping short and laying his hand upon my shoulder.

And then I repeated, word for word, all that I had heard the soldiers saying that night under the corridor window. When I had done, he took off his hat and stood for a moment as if in prayer, silent and bare-headed.

"If it be so," he said presently, "if such fidelity can indeed survive the grave—then not once, but thrice .... Who knows? Who can tell?"

He was speaking to himself. I heard the words, and I remembered them; but I did not understand them till long after.

The King left Brühl that same afternoon *en route* for Ehrenbreitstein, and Monsieur Maurice went away the next morning in a post-chaise and pair, bound for Paris. He gave me, for a farewell gift, his precious microscope and all his boxes of slides, and he parted from me with many kisses; but there was a smile on his face as he got into the carriage, and something of triumph in the very wave of his hand as he drove away.

Alas! how could it be otherwise? A prisoner freed, an exile returning to his country, how should he not be glad to go, even though one little heart should be left to ache or break in the land of the stranger?

I never saw him again; never—never—never. He wrote now and then to my father, but only for a time; perhaps as many as six letters during three or four years—and then we heard from him no more. To these letters he gave us no opportunity of replying, for they contained no address; and although we had reason to believe that he was a man of family and title, he never signed himself by any other name than that by which we had known him.

We did hear, however, (I forget now through what channel) of the sudden disgrace and banishment of His Majesty's Minister of War, the Baron von Bulow. Respecting the causes of his fall there were many vague and contradictory rumours. He had starved to death a prisoner of war and forced his widow into a marriage with himself. He had sold State secrets to the French. He had been over to Elba in disguise, and had there held treasonable intercourse with the exiled Emperor, before his return to France in 1815. He had attempted to murder, or caused to be murdered, the witnesses of his treachery. He had forged the King's signature. He had tampered with the King's servants. He had been guilty, in short, of every crime, social and political, that could be laid to the charge of a fallen favourite.

Knowing what we knew, it was not difficult to disentangle a thread of truth here and there, or to detect under the most extravagant of these fictions, a substratum of fact. Among other significant circumstances, my father, chancing one day to see a portrait of the late minister in a shop-window at Cologne, discovered that his former visitor, the Count von Rettel, and the Baron von Bulow were one and the same person. He then understood why the King had questioned him so minutely with regard to this man's appearance, and shuddered to think how deadly that enmity must have been which could bring him in person upon so infamous an errand.

And here all ended. The guilty and the innocent vanished alike from the scene, and we at least, in our remote home on the Rhenish border, heard of them no more.

Monsieur Maurice never knew that I had been in any way instrumental in bringing his case before the King. He took his freedom as the fulfillment of a right, and dreamed not that his little Gretchen had pleaded for him. But that he should know it, mattered not at all. He had his liberty, and was not that enough?

Enough for me, for I loved him. Ay, child as I was, I loved him; loved him deeply and passionately—to my cost—to my loss—to my sorrow. An old, old wound; but I shall carry the scar to my grave!

And the brown man?

Hush! a strange feeling of awe and wonder creeps upon me to this day, when I remember those bright eyes glowing through the dusk, and the swift hand that seized the poisoned draught and dashed it on the ground. What of that faithful Ali, who went forward to meet the danger alone, and was snatched away to die horribly in the jungle? I can but repeat his master's words. I can but ask myself "Does such fidelity indeed survive the grave? Who knows? Who can tell?"

A
PHANTOM
LOVER

VERNON LEE

To COUNT PETER BOUTOURLINE,

AT TAGANTCHA,

GOVERNMENT OF KIEW, RUSSIA.

MY DEAR BOUTOURLINE,
   Do you remember my telling you, one afternoon that you sat upon the
hearthstool at Florence, the story of Mrs. Oke of Okehurst?
   You thought it a fantastic tale, you lover of fantastic things, and urged
me to write it out at once, although I protested that, in such matters, to
write is to exorcise, to dispel the charm; and that printers' ink chases
away the ghosts that may pleasantly haunt us, as efficaciously as gallons
of holy water.
   But if, as I suspect, you will now put down any charm that story may
have possessed to the way in which we had been working ourselves up,
that firelight evening, with all manner of fantastic stuff—if, as I fear, the
story of Mrs. Oke of Okehurst will strike you as stale and unprofitable—
the sight of this little book will serve at least to remind you, in the middle
of your Russian summer, that there is such a season as winter, such a
place as Florence, and such a person as your friend,
                                                    VERNON LEE
Kensington, *July* 1886.

                                    1

That sketch up there with the boy's cap? Yes; that's the same woman.
I wonder whether you could guess who she was. A singular being, is
she not? The most marvellous creature, quite, that I have ever met: a
wonderful elegance, exotic, far-fetched, poignant; an artificial perverse
sort of grace and research in every outline and movement and arrangement of head and neck, and hands and fingers. Here are a lot of pencil-
sketches I made while I was preparing to paint her portrait. Yes; there's
nothing but her in the whole sketch-book. Mere scratches, but they
may give some idea of her marvellous, fantastic kind of grace. Here she
is leaning over the staircase, and here sitting in the swing. Here she is
walking quickly out of the room. That's her head. You see she isn't

                                  299

really handsome; her forehead is too big, and her nose too short. This gives no idea of her. It was altogether a question of movement. Look at the strange cheeks, hollow and rather flat; well, when she smiled she had the most marvellous dimples here. There was something exquisite and uncanny about it. Yes; I began the picture, but it was never finished. I did the husband first. I wonder who has his likeness now? Help me to move these pictures away from the wall. Thanks. This is her portrait; a huge wreck. I don't suppose you can make much of it; it is merely blocked in, and seems quite mad. You see my idea was to make her leaning against a wall—there was one hung with yellow that seemed almost brown—so as to bring out the silhouette.

It was very singular I should have chosen that particular wall. It does look rather insane in this condition, but I like it; it has something of her. I would frame it and hang it up, only people would ask questions. Yes; you have guessed quite right—it is Mrs. Oke of Okehurst. I forgot you had relations in that part of the country; besides, I suppose the newspapers were full of it at the time. You didn't know that it all took place under my eyes? I can scarcely believe now that it did: it all seems so distant, vivid but unreal, like a thing of my own invention. It really was much stranger than any one guessed. People could no more understand it than they could understand her. I doubt whether any one ever understood Alice Oke besides myself. You mustn't think me unfeeling. She was a marvellous, weird, exquisite creature, but one couldn't feel sorry for her. I felt much sorrier for the wretched creature of a husband. It seemed such an appropriate end for her; I fancy she would have liked it could she have known. Ah! I shall never have another chance of painting such a portrait as I wanted. She seemed sent me from heaven or the other place. You have never heard the story in detail? Well, I don't usually mention it, because people are so brutally stupid or sentimental; but I'll tell it you. Let me see. It's too dark to paint any more to-day, so I can tell it you now. Wait; I must turn her face to the wall. Ah, she was a marvellous creature!

2

You remember, three years ago, my telling you I had let myself in for painting a couple of Kentish squireen? I really could not understand what had possessed me to say yes to that man. A friend of mine had brought him one day to my studio—Mr. Oke of Okehurst, that was the name on his card. He was a very tall, very well-made, very good-looking young man, with a beautiful fair complexion, beautiful fair moustache, and beautifully fitting clothes; absolutely like a hundred other young men you can see any day in the Park, and absolutely uninteresting from the crown of his head to the tip of his boots. Mr. Oke, who had been a lieutenant in the Blues before his marriage, was evidently extremely uncomfortable on finding himself in a studio. He felt misgivings about a man who could wear a velvet coat in town, but at the same time he was nervously anxious not to treat me in the very least like a tradesman. He walked round my place, looked at everything with the most scrupulous attention, stammered out a few complimentary phrases, and then, looking at his friend for assistance, tried to come to the point, but failed. The point, which the friend kindly explained, was that Mr. Oke was desirous to know whether my engagements would allow of my painting him and his wife, and what my terms would be. The poor man blushed perfectly crimson during this explanation, as if he had come with the most improper proposal; and I noticed—the only interesting thing about him—a very odd nervous frown between his eyebrows, a perfect double gash,—a thing which usually means something abnormal: a mad-doctor of my acquaintance calls it the maniac-frown. When I had answered, he suddenly burst out into rather confused explanations: his wife—Mrs. Oke—had seen some of my—pictures—paintings—portraits —at the—the—what d'you call it?—Academy. She had—in short, they had made a very great impression upon her. Mrs. Oke had a great taste for art; she was, in short, extremely desirous of having her portrait and his painted by me, *etcetera*.

"My wife," he suddenly added, "is a remarkable woman. I don't know whether you will think her handsome,—she isn't exactly, you know. But she's awfully strange," and Mr. Oke of Okehurst gave a little sigh and frowned that curious frown, as if so long a speech and so decided an expression of opinion had cost him a great deal.

It was a rather unfortunate moment in my career. A very influential sitter of mine—you remember the fat lady with the crimson curtain behind her?—had come to the conclusion or been persuaded that I had painted her old and vulgar, which, in fact, she was. Her whole clique had turned against me, the newspapers had taken up the matter, and for the moment I was considered as a painter to whose brushes no woman would trust her reputation. Things were going badly. So I snapped but too gladly at Mr. Oke's offer, and settled to go down to Okehurst at the end of a fortnight. But the door had scarcely closed upon my future sitter when I began to regret my rashness; and my disgust at the thought of wasting a whole summer upon the portrait of a totally uninteresting Kentish squire, and his doubtless equally uninteresting wife, grew greater and greater as the time for execution approached. I remember so well the frightful temper in which I got into the train for Kent, and the even more frightful temper in which I got out of it at the little station nearest to Okehurst. It was pouring floods. I felt a comfortable fury at the thought that my canvases would get nicely wetted before Mr. Oke's coachman had packed them on the top of the waggonette. It was just what served me right for coming to this confounded place to paint these confounded people. We drove off in the steady downpour. The roads were a mass of yellow mud; the endless flat grazing-grounds under the oak-trees, after having been burnt to cinders in a long drought, were turned into a hideous brown sop; the country seemed intolerably monotonous.

My spirits sank lower and lower. I began to meditate upon the modern Gothic country-house, with the usual amount of Morris furniture, Liberty rugs, and Mudie novels, to which I was doubtless being taken. My fancy pictured very vividly the five or six little Okes—that man certainly must have at least five children—the aunts, and sisters-in-law, and cousins; the eternal routine of afternoon tea and lawn-tennis; above all, it pictured Mrs. Oke, the bouncing, well-informed, model housekeeper, electioneering, charity-organising young lady, whom such an individual as Mr. Oke would regard in the light of a remarkable woman. And my spirit sank within me, and I cursed my avarice in accepting the commission, my spiritlessness in not throwing it over while yet there was time. We had meanwhile driven into a large park, or rather a long succession of grazing-grounds, dotted about with large oaks, under which the sheep were huddled together for shelter from the rain. In the distance, blurred by the sheets of rain, was a line of low hills, with a jagged fringe of bluish firs and a solitary windmill. It must be a good mile and a half since we had passed a house, and there was none to be seen in the distance —nothing but the undulation of sere grass, sopped brown beneath the huge blackish oak-trees, and whence arose, from all sides, a vague disconsolate bleating. At last the road made a sudden bend, and disclosed what was evidently the home of my sitter. It was not what I had expected. In a dip in the ground a large red-brick house, with the rounded gables and high chimney-stacks of the time of James I.,—a forlorn, vast place, set in the midst of the pasture-land, with no trace of garden before it, and only a few large trees indicating the possibility of one to the back; no lawn either, but on the other side of the sandy dip, which suggested a filled-up moat, a huge oak, short, hollow, with wreathing, blasted, black branches, upon which only a handful of leaves shook in the rain. It was not at all what I had pictured to myself the home of Mr. Oke of Okehurst.

My host received me in the hall, a large place, panelled and carved, hung round with portraits up to its curious ceiling—vaulted and ribbed like the inside of a ship's hull. He looked even more blond and pink and white, more absolutely mediocre in his tweed suit; and also, I thought,

even more good-natured and duller. He took me into his study, a room
hung round with whips and fishing-tackle in place of books, while my
things were being carried upstairs. It was very damp, and a fire was
smouldering. He gave the embers a nervous kick with his foot, and said,
as he offered me a cigar—

"You must excuse my not introducing you at once to Mrs. Oke.
My wife—in short, I believe my wife is asleep."

"Is Mrs. Oke unwell?" I asked, a sudden hope flashing across me that
I might be off the whole matter.

"Oh no! Alice is quite well; at least, quite as well as she usually is.
My wife," he added, after a minute, and in a very decided tone, "does
not enjoy very good health—a nervous constitution. Oh no! not at all
ill, nothing at all serious, you know. Only nervous, the doctors say;
mustn't be worried or excited, the doctors say; requires lots of repose,—
that sort of thing."

There was a dead pause. This man depressed me, I knew not why.
He had a listless, puzzled look, very much out of keeping with his evident
admirable health and strength.

"I suppose you are a great sportsman?" I asked from sheer despair,
nodding in the direction of the whips and guns and fishing-rods.

"Oh no! not now. I was once. I have given up all that," he answered,
standing with his back to the fire, and staring at the polar bear beneath
his feet. "I—I have no time for all that now," he added, as if an explanation were due. "A married man—you know. Would you like to come up
to your rooms?" he suddenly interrupted himself. "I have had one
arranged for you to paint in. My wife said you would prefer a north light.
If that one doesn't suit, you can have your choice of any other."

I followed him out of the study, through the vast entrance-hall. In
less than a minute I was no longer thinking of Mr. and Mrs. Oke and the
boredom of doing their likeness; I was simply overcome by the beauty
of this house, which I had pictured modern and philistine. It was,
without exception, the most perfect example of an old English manor-
house that I had ever seen; the most magnificent intrinsically, and the
most admirably preserved. Out of the huge hall, with its immense
fireplace of delicately carved and inlaid grey and black stone, and its
rows of family portraits, reaching from the wainscoting to the oaken
ceiling, vaulted and ribbed like a ship's hull, opened the wide, flat-
stepped staircase, the parapet surmounted at intervals by heraldic monsters, the wall covered with oak carvings of coats-of-arms, leafage, and
little mythological scenes, painted a faded red and blue, and picked out
with tarnished gold, which harmonised with the tarnished blue and
gold of the stamped leather that reached to the oak cornice, again delicately tinted and gilded. The beautifully damascened suits of court

armour looked, without being at all rusty, as if no modern hand had ever touched them; the very rugs under foot were of sixteenth-century Persian make; the only things of to-day were the big bunches of flowers and ferns, arranged in majolica dishes upon the landings. Everything was perfectly silent; only from below came the chimes, silvery like an Italian palace fountain, of an old-fashioned clock.

It seemed to me that I was being led through the palace of the Sleeping Beauty.

"What a magnificent house!" I exclaimed as I followed my host through a long corridor, also hung with leather, wainscoted with carvings, and furnished with big wedding coffers, and chairs that looked as if they came out of some Vandyck portrait. In my mind was the strong impression that all this was natural, spontaneous—that it had about it nothing of the picturesqueness which swell studios have taught to rich and æsthetic houses. Mr. Oke misunderstood me.

"It is a nice old place," he said, "but it's too large for us. You see, my wife's health does not allow of our having many guests; and there are no children."

I thought I noticed a vague complaint in his voice; and he evidently was afraid there might have seemed something of the kind, for he added immediately—

"I don't care for children one jackstraw, you know, myself; can't understand how any one can, for my part."

If ever a man went out of his way to tell a lie, I said to myself, Mr. Oke of Okehurst was doing so at the present moment.

When he had left me in one of the two enormous rooms that were allotted to me, I threw myself into an arm-chair and tried to focus the extraordinary imaginative impression which this house had given me.

I am very susceptible to such impressions; and besides the sort of spasm of imaginative interest sometimes given to me by certain rare and eccentric personalities, I know nothing more subduing than the charm, quieter and less analytic, of any sort of complete and out-of-the-common-run sort of house. To sit in a room like the one I was sitting in, with the figures of the tapestry glimmering grey and lilac and purple in the twilight, the great bed, columned and curtained, looming in the middle, and the embers reddening beneath the overhanging mantelpiece of inlaid Italian stonework, a vague scent of rose-leaves and spices, put into the china bowls by the hands of ladies long since dead, while the clock downstairs sent up, every now and then, its faint silvery tune of forgotten days, filled the room;—to do this is a special kind of volup-tuousness, peculiar and complex and indescribable, like the half-drunken-ness of opium or haschisch, and which, to be conveyed to others in any sense as I feel it, would require a genius, subtle and heady, like that of Baudelaire.

After I had dressed for dinner I resumed my place in the arm-chair, and resumed also my reverie, letting all these impressions of the past—which seemed faded like the figures in the arras, but still warm like the embers in the fireplace, still sweet and subtle like the perfume of the dead rose-leaves and broken spices in the china bowls—permeate me and go to my head. Of Oke and Oke's wife I did not think; I seemed quite alone, isolated from the world, separated from it in this exotic enjoyment.

Gradually the embers grew paler; the figures in the tapestry more shadowy; the columned and curtained bed loomed out vaguer; the room seemed to fill with greyness; and my eyes wandered to the mullioned bow-window, beyond whose panes, between whose heavy stone-work, stretched a greyish-brown expanse of sere and sodden park grass, dotted with big oaks; while far off, behind a jagged fringe of dark Scotch firs, the wet sky was suffused with the blood-red of the sunset. Between the falling of the raindrops from the ivy outside, there came, fainter or sharper, the recurring bleating of the lambs separated from their mothers, a forlorn, quavering, eerie little cry.

I started up at a sudden rap at my door.

"Haven't you heard the gong for dinner?" asked Mr. Oke's voice.

I had completely forgotten his existence.

3

I feel that I cannot possibly reconstruct my earliest impressions of Mrs. Oke. My recollection of them would be entirely coloured by my subsequent knowledge of her; whence I conclude that I could not at first have experienced the strange interest and admiration which that extraordinary woman very soon excited in me. Interest and admiration, be it well understood, of a very unusual kind, as she was herself a very unusual kind of woman; and I, if you choose, am a rather unusual kind of man. But I can explain that better anon.

This much is certain, that I must have been immeasurably surprised at finding my hostess and future sitter so completely unlike everything I had anticipated. Or no—now I come to think of it, I scarcely felt surprised at all; or if I did, that shock of surprise could have lasted but an infinitesimal part of a minute. The fact is, that, having once seen Alice Oke in the reality, it was quite impossible to remember that one could have fancied her at all different: there was something so complete, so completely unlike every one else, in her personality, that she seemed always to have been present in one's consciousness, although present, perhaps, as an enigma.

Let me try and give you some notion of her: not that first impression, whatever it may have been, but the absolute reality of her as I gradually learned to see it. To begin with, I must repeat and reiterate over and over again, that she was, beyond all comparison, the most graceful and exquisite woman I have ever seen, but with a grace and an exquisiteness that had nothing to do with any preconceived notion or previous experience of what goes by these names: grace and exquisiteness recognised at once as perfect, but which were seen in her for the first, and probably, I do believe, for the last time. It is conceivable, is it not, that once in a thousand years there may arise a combination of lines, a system of movements, an outline, a gesture, which is new, unprecedented, and yet hits off exactly our desires for beauty and rareness? She was very tall; and I suppose people would have called her thin. I don't know, for I never thought about her as a body—bones, flesh, that sort of thing; but merely as a wonderful series of lines, and a wonderful strangeness of personality. Tall and slender, certainly, and with not one item of what makes up our notion of a well-built woman. She was as straight—I mean she had as little of what people call figure—as a bamboo; her shoulders were a trifle high, and she had a decided stoop; her arms and her shoulders she never once wore uncovered. But this bamboo figure of hers had a suppleness and a stateliness, a play of outline with every step she took, that I can't compare to anything else; there was in it something of the peacock and something also of the stag; but, above all, it was her own. I wish I could describe her. I wish, alas!—I wish, I wish, I have wished a hundred thousand times—I could paint her, as I see her now, if I shut my eyes—even if it were only a silhouette. There! I see her so plainly, walking slowly up and down a room, the slight highness of her shoulders just completing the exquisite arrangement of lines made by the straight supple back, the long exquisite neck, the head, with the hair cropped in short pale curls, always drooping a little, except when she would suddenly throw it back, and smile, not at me, nor at any one, nor at anything that had been said, but as if she alone had suddenly seen or heard something, with the strange dimple in her thin, pale cheeks, and the strange whiteness in her full, wide-opened eyes: the moment when she had something of the stag in her movement. But where is the use of talking about her? I don't believe, you know, that even the greatest painter can show what is the real beauty of a very beautiful woman in the ordinary sense: Titian's and Tintoretto's women must have been miles handsomer than they have made them. Something—and that the very essence—always escapes, perhaps because real beauty is as much a thing in time—a thing like music, a succession, a series—as in space. Mind you, I am speaking of a woman beautiful in the conventional sense. Imagine, then, how much more so in the case of a woman like Alice Oke; and if the pencil and brush, imitating each line and tint, can't succeed, how is it possible to give even the vaguest notion with mere wretched words—words possessing only a wretched abstract meaning, an impotent conventional association? To make a long story short, Mrs. Oke of Okehurst was, in my opinion, to the highest degree exquisite and strange,—an exotic creature, whose charm you can no more describe than you could bring home the perfume of some newly discovered tropical flower by comparing it with the scent of a cabbage-rose or a lily.

That first dinner was gloomy enough. Mr. Oke—Oke of Okehurst, as the people down there called him—was horribly shy, consumed with a fear of making a fool of himself before me and his wife, I then thought. But that sort of shyness did not wear off; and I soon discovered that, although it was doubtless increased by the presence of a total stranger, it was inspired in Oke, not by me, but by his wife. He would look every now and then as if he were going to make a remark, and then evidently restrain himself, and remain silent. It was very curious to see this big, handsome, manly young fellow, who ought to have had any amount of success with women, suddenly stammer and grow crimson in the presence of his own wife. Nor was it the consciousness of stupidity; for when you got him alone, Oke, although always slow and timid, had a certain amount of ideas, and very defined political and social views, and a certain childlike earnestness and desire to attain certainty and truth which was rather touching. On the other hand, Oke's singular shyness was not, so far as I could see, the result of any kind of bullying on his wife's part. You can always detect, if you have any observation, the husband or the wife who is accustomed to be snubbed, to be corrected, by his or her better-half: there is a self-consciousness in both parties, a habit of watching and fault-finding, of being watched and found fault with. This was clearly not the case at Okehurst. Mrs. Oke evidently did not trouble herself about her husband in the very least; he might say or do any amount of silly things without rebuke or even notice; and he might have done so, had he chosen, ever since his wedding-day. You felt that at once. Mrs. Oke simply passed over his existence. I cannot say she paid much attention to any one's, even to mine. At first I thought it an affectation on her part —for there was something far-fetched in her whole appearance, something suggesting study, which might lead one to tax her with affectation at first; she was dressed in a strange way, not according to any established æsthetic eccentricity, but individually, strangely, as if in the clothes of an ancestress of the seventeenth century. Well, at first I thought it a kind of pose on her part, this mixture of extreme graciousness and utter indifference which she manifested towards me. She always seemed to be thinking of something else; and although she talked quite sufficiently, and with every sign of superior intelligence, she left the impression of having been as taciturn as her husband.

In the beginning, in the first few days of my stay at Okehurst, I imagined that Mrs. Oke was a highly superior sort of flirt; and that her absent manner, her look, while speaking to you, into an invisible distance, her curious irrelevant smile, were so many means of attracting and baffling adoration. I mistook it for the somewhat similar manners of certain foreign women—it is beyond English ones—which mean, to those who can understand, "pay court to me." But I soon found I was mistaken. Mrs. Oke had not the faintest desire that I should pay court to her; indeed she did not honour me with sufficient thought for that; and I, on my part, began to be too much interested in her from another point of view to dream of such a thing. I became aware, not merely that I had before me the most marvellously rare and exquisite and baffling subject for a portrait, but also one of the most peculiar and enigmatic of characters. Now that I look back upon it, I am tempted to think that the psychological peculiarity of that woman might be summed up in an exorbitant and absorbing interest in herself—a Narcissus attitude—curiously complicated with a fantastic imagination, a sort of morbid day-dreaming, all turned inwards, and with no outer characteristic save a certain restlessness, a perverse desire to surprise and shock, to surprise and shock more particularly her husband, and thus be revenged for the intense boredom which his want of appreciation inflicted upon her.

I got to understand this much little by little, yet I did not seem to have really penetrated the something mysterious about Mrs. Oke. There was a waywardness, a strangeness, which I felt but could not explain—a something as difficult to define as the peculiarity of her outward appearance, and perhaps very closely connected therewith. I became interested in Mrs. Oke as if I had been in love with her; and I was not in the least in love. I neither dreaded parting from her, nor felt any pleasure in her presence. I had not the smallest wish to please or to gain her notice. But I had her on the brain. I pursued her, her physical image, her psychological explanation, with a kind of passion which filled my days, and prevented my ever feeling dull. The Okes lived a remarkably solitary life. There were but few neighbours, of whom they saw but little; and they rarely had a guest in the house. Oke himself seemed every now and then seized with a sense of responsibility towards me. He would remark vaguely, during our walks and after-dinner chats, that I must find life at Okehurst horribly dull; his wife's health had accustomed him to solitude, and then also his wife thought the neighbours a bore. He never questioned his wife's judgment in these matters. He merely stated the case as if resignation were quite simple and inevitable; yet it seemed to me, sometimes, that this monotonous life of solitude, by the side of a woman who took no more heed of him than of a table or chair, was producing a vague depression and irritation in this young man, so evidently cut out for a cheerful, commonplace life. I often wondered how he could endure it at all, not having, as I had, the interest of a strange psychological riddle to solve, and of a great portrait to paint. He was, I found, extremely good,—the type of the perfectly conscientious young Englishman, the sort of man who ought to have been the Christian soldier kind of thing; devout, pure-minded, brave, incapable of any baseness, a little intellectually dense, and puzzled by all manner of moral scruples. The condition of his tenants and of his political party—he was a regular Kentish Tory— lay heavy on his mind. He spent hours every day in his study, doing the work of a land agent and a political whip, reading piles of reports and newspapers and agricultural treatises; and emerging for lunch with piles of letters in his hand, and that odd puzzled look in his good healthy face, that deep gash between his eyebrows, which my friend the mad-doctor calls the *maniac-frown*. It was with this expression of face that I should have liked to paint him; but I felt that he would not have liked it, that it was more fair to him to represent him in his mere wholesome pink and white and blond conventionality. I was perhaps rather unconscientious about the likeness of Mr. Oke; I felt satisfied to paint it no matter how, I mean as regards character, for my whole mind was swallowed up in thinking how I should paint Mrs. Oke, how I could best transport on to canvas that singular and enigmatic personality. I began with her husband, and told her frankly that I must have much longer to study her. Mr. Oke couldn't understand why it should be necessary to make a hundred and one pencil-sketches of his wife before even determining in what attitude to paint her; but I think he was rather pleased to have an opportunity of keeping me at Okehurst; my presence evidently broke the monotony of his life. Mrs. Oke seemed perfectly indifferent to my staying, as she was perfectly indifferent to my presence. Without being rude, I never saw a woman pay so little attention to a guest; she would talk with me sometimes by the hour, or rather let me talk to her, but she never seemed to be listening. She would lie back in a big seventeenth-century armchair while I played the piano, with that strange smile every now and then in her thin cheeks, that strange whiteness in her eyes; but it seemed a matter of indifference whether my music stopped or went on. In my portrait of her husband she did not take, or pretend to take, the very faintest interest; but that was nothing to me. I did not want Mrs. Oke to think me interesting; I merely wished to go on studying her.

The first time that Mrs. Oke seemed to become at all aware of my presence as distinguished from that of the chairs and tables, the dogs that lay in the porch, or the clergyman or lawyer or stray neighbour who was occasionally asked to dinner, was one day—I might have been there a week—when I chanced to remark to her upon the very singular resemblance that existed between herself and the portrait of a lady that hung in the hall with the ceiling like a ship's hull. The picture in question was a full length, neither very good nor very bad, probably done by some stray Italian of the early seventeenth century. It hung in a rather dark corner, facing the portrait, evidently painted to be its companion, of a dark man, with a somewhat unpleasant expression of resolution and efficiency, in a black Vandyck dress. The two were evidently man and wife; and in the corner of the woman's portrait were the words, "Alice Oke, daughter of Virgil Pomfret, Esq., and wife to Nicholas Oke of Okehurst," and the date 1626—"Nicholas Oke" being the name painted in the corner of the small portrait. The lady was really wonderfully like the present Mrs. Oke, at least so far as an indifferently painted portrait of the early days of Charles I. can be like a living woman of the nineteenth century. There were the same strange lines of figure and face, the same dimples in the thin cheeks, the same wide-opened eyes, the same vague eccentricity of expression, not destroyed even by the feeble painting and conventional manner of the time. One could fancy that this woman had the same walk, the same beautiful line of nape of the neck and stooping head as her descendant; for I found that Mr. and Mrs. Oke, who were first cousins, were both descended from that Nicholas Oke and that Alice, daughter of Virgil Pomfret. But the resemblance was heightened by the fact that, as I soon saw, the present Mrs. Oke distinctly made herself up to look like her ancestress, dressing in garments that had a seventeenth-century look; nay, that were sometimes absolutely copied from this portrait.

"You think I am like her," answered Mrs. Oke dreamily to my remark, and her eyes wandered off to that unseen something, and the faint smile dimpled her thin cheeks.

"You are like her, and you know it. I may even say you wish to be like her, Mrs. Oke," I answered, laughing.

"Perhaps I do."

And she looked in the direction of her husband. I noticed that he had an expression of distinct annoyance besides that frown of his.

"Isn't it true that Mrs. Oke tries to look like that portrait?" I asked, with a perverse curiosity.

"Oh, fudge!" he exclaimed, rising from his chair and walking nervously to the window. "It's all nonsense, mere nonsense. I wish you wouldn't, Alice."

"Wouldn't what?" asked Mrs. Oke, with a sort of contemptuous indifference. "If I am like that Alice Oke, why I am; and I am very pleased any one should think so. She and her husband are just about the only two members of our family—our most flat, stale, and unprofitable family—that ever were in the least degree interesting."

Oke grew crimson, and frowned as if in pain.

"I don't see why you should abuse our family, Alice," he said. "Thank God, our people have always been honourable and upright men and women!"

"Excepting always Nicholas Oke and Alice his wife, daughter of Virgil Pomfret, Esq.," she answered, laughing, as he strode out into the park.

"How childish he is!" she exclaimed when we were alone. "He really minds, really feels disgraced by what our ancestors did two centuries and a half ago. I do believe William would have those two portraits taken down and burned if he weren't afraid of me and ashamed of the neighbours. And as it is, these two people really are the only two members of our family that ever were in the least interesting. I will tell you the story some day."

As it was, the story was told to me by Oke himself. The next day, as we were taking our morning walk, he suddenly broke a long silence, laying about him all the time at the sere grasses with the hooked stick that he carried, like the conscientious Kentishman he was, for the purpose of cutting down his and other folk's thistles.

"I fear you must have thought me very ill-mannered towards my wife yesterday," he said shyly; "and indeed I know I was."

Oke was one of those chivalrous beings to whom every woman, every wife—and his own most of all—appeared in the light of something holy. "But—but—I have a prejudice which my wife does not enter into, about raking up ugly things in one's own family. I suppose Alice thinks that it is so long ago that it has really got no connection with us; she thinks of it merely as a picturesque story. I daresay many people feel like that; in short, I am sure they do, otherwise there wouldn't be such lots of discreditable family traditions afloat. But I feel as if it were all one whether it was long ago or not; when it's a question of one's own people, I would rather have it forgotten. I can't understand how people can talk about murders in their families, and ghosts, and so forth."

"Have you any ghosts at Okehurst, by the way?" I asked. The place seemed as if it required some to complete it.

"I hope not," answered Oke gravely.

His gravity made me smile.

"Why, would you dislike it if there were?" I asked.

"If there are such things as ghosts," he replied, "I don't think they should be taken lightly. God would not permit them to be, except as a warning or a punishment."

We walked on some time in silence, I wondering at the strange type of this commonplace young man, and half wishing I could put something into my portrait that should be the equivalent of this curious unimaginative earnestness. Then Oke told me the story of those two pictures—told it me about as badly and hesitatingly as was possible for mortal man.

He and his wife were, as I have said, cousins, and therefore descended from the same old Kentish stock. The Okes of Okehurst could trace back to Norman, almost to Saxon times, far longer than any of the titled or better-known families of the neighbourhood. I saw that William Oke, in his heart, thoroughly looked down upon all his neighbours. "We have never done anything particular, or been anything particular—never held any office," he said; "but we have always been here, and apparently always done our duty. An ancestor of ours was killed in the Scotch wars, another at Agincourt—mere honest captains." Well, early in the seventeenth century, the family had dwindled to a single member, Nicholas Oke, the same who had rebuilt Okehurst in its present shape. This Nicholas appears to have been somewhat different from the usual run of the family. He had, in his youth, sought adventures in America, and seems, generally speaking, to have been less of a nonentity than his ancestors. He married, when no longer very young, Alice, daughter of Virgil Pomfret, a beautiful young heiress from a neighbouring county. "It was the first time an Oke married a Pomfret," my host informed me, "and the last time. The Pomfrets were quite different sort of people—restless, self-seeking; one of them had been a favourite of Henry VIII." It was clear that William Oke had no feeling of having any Pomfret blood in his veins; he spoke of these people with an evident family dislike—the dislike of an Oke, one of the old, honourable, modest stock, which had quietly done its duty, for a family of fortune-seekers and Court minions. Well, there had come to live near Okehurst, in a little house recently inherited from an uncle, a certain Christopher Lovelock, a young gallant and poet, who was in momentary disgrace at Court for some love affair. This Lovelock had struck up a great friendship with his neighbours of Okehurst—too great a friendship, apparently, with the wife, either for her husband's taste or her own. Anyhow, one evening as he was riding home alone, Lovelock had been attacked and murdered, ostensibly by highwaymen, but as was afterwards rumoured, by Nicholas Oke, accompanied by his wife dressed as a groom. No legal evidence had been got, but the tradition had remained. "They used to tell it us when we were children," said my host, in a hoarse voice, "and to frighten my cousin—I mean my wife—and me with stories about Lovelock. It is merely a tradition, which I hope may die out, as I sincerely pray to heaven that it may be false." "Alice—Mrs. Oke—you see," he went on after some time, "doesn't feel about it as I do. Perhaps I am morbid. But I do dislike having the old story raked up."

And we said no more on the subject.

4

From that moment I began to assume a certain interest in the eyes of Mrs. Oke; or rather, I began to perceive that I had a means of securing her attention. Perhaps it was wrong of me to do so; and I have often reproached myself very seriously later on. But after all, how was I to guess that I was making mischief merely by chiming in, for the sake of the portrait I had undertaken, and of a very harmless psychological mania, with what was merely the fad, the little romantic affectation or eccentricity, of a scatter-brained and eccentric young woman? How in the world should I have dreamed that I was handling explosive substances? A man is surely not responsible if the people with whom he is forced to deal, and whom he deals with as with all the rest of the world, are quite different from all other human creatures.

So, if indeed I did at all conduce to mischief, I really cannot blame myself. I had met in Mrs. Oke an almost unique subject for a portrait-painter of my particular sort, and a most singular, *bizarre* personality. I could not possibly do my subject justice so long as I was kept at a distance, prevented from studying the real character of the woman. I required to put her into play. And I ask you whether any more innocent way of doing so could be found than talking to a woman, and letting her talk, about an absurd fancy she had for a couple of ancestors of hers of the time of Charles I., and a poet whom they had murdered?—particularly as I studiously respected the prejudices of my host, and refrained from mentioning the matter, and tried to restrain Mrs. Oke from doing so, in the presence of William Oke himself.

I had certainly guessed correctly. To resemble the Alice Oke of the year 1626 was the caprice, the mania, the pose, the whatever you may call it, of the Alice Oke of 1880; and to perceive this resemblance was the sure way of gaining her good graces. It was the most extraordinary craze, of all the extraordinary crazes of childless and idle women, that I had ever met; but it was more than that, it was admirably characteristic. It finished off the strange figure of Mrs. Oke, as I saw it in my imagination—this *bizarre* creature of enigmatic, far-fetched exquisiteness—that she should have no interest in the present, but only an eccentric passion in the past. It seemed to give the meaning to the absent look in her eyes, to her irrelevant and far-off smile. It was like the words to a weird piece of gipsy music, this that she, who was so different, so distant from all women of her own time, should try and identify herself with a woman of the past—that she should have a kind of flirtation—— But of this anon.

I told Mrs. Oke that I had learnt from her husband the outline of the tragedy, or mystery, whichever it was, of Alice Oke, daughter of Virgil Pomfret, and the poet Christopher Lovelock. That look of vague contempt, of a desire to shock, which I had noticed before, came into her beautiful, pale, diaphanous face.

"I suppose my husband was very shocked at the whole matter," she said—"told it you with as little detail as possible, and assured you very solemnly that he hoped the whole story might be a mere dreadful calumny? Poor Willie! I remember already when we were children, and I used to come with my mother to spend Christmas at Okehurst, and my cousin was down here for his holidays, how I used to horrify him by insisting upon dressing up in shawls and waterproofs, and playing the story of the wicked Mrs. Oke; and he always piously refused to do the part of Nicholas, when I wanted to have the scene on Cotes Common. I didn't know then that I was like the original Alice Oke; I found it out only after our marriage. You really think that I am?"

She certainly was, particularly at that moment, as she stood in a white Vandyck dress, with the green of the park-land rising up behind her, and the low sun catching her short locks and surrounding her head, her exquisitely bowed head, with a pale-yellow halo. But I confess I thought the original Alice Oke, siren and murderess though she might be, very uninteresting compared with this wayward and exquisite creature whom I had rashly promised myself to send down to posterity in all her unlikely wayward exquisiteness.

One morning while Mr. Oke was despatching his Saturday heap of Conservative manifestoes and rural decisions—he was justice of the peace in a most literal sense, penetrating into cottages and huts, defending the weak and admonishing the ill-conducted—one morning while I was making one of my many pencil-sketches (alas, they are all that remain to me now!) of my future sitter, Mrs. Oke gave me her version of the story of Alice Oke and Christopher Lovelock.

"Do you suppose there was anything between them?" I asked—"that she was ever in love with him? How do you explain the part which tradition ascribes to her in the supposed murder? One has heard of women and their lovers who have killed the husband; but a woman who combines with her husband to kill her lover, or at least the man who is in love with her—that is surely very singular." I was absorbed in my drawing, and really thinking very little of what I was saying.

"I don't know," she answered pensively, with that distant look in her eyes. "Alice Oke was very proud, I am sure. She may have loved the poet very much, and yet been indignant with him, hated having to love him. She may have felt that she had a right to rid herself of him, and to call upon her husband to help her to do so."

"Good heavens! what a fearful idea!" I exclaimed, half laughing. "Don't you think, after all, that Mr. Oke may be right in saying that it is easier and more comfortable to take the whole story as a pure invention?"

"I cannot take it as an invention," answered Mrs. Oke contemptuously, "because I happen to know that it is true."

"Indeed!" I answered, working away at my sketch, and enjoying putting this strange creature, as I said to myself, through her paces; "how is that?"

"How does one know that anything is true in this world?" she replied evasively; "because one does, because one feels it to be true, I suppose."

And, with that far-off look in her light eyes, she relapsed into silence.

"Have you ever read any of Lovelock's poetry?" she asked me suddenly the next day.

"Lovelock?" I answered, for I had forgotten the name. "Lovelock, who"—— But I stopped, remembering the prejudices of my host, who was seated next to me at table.

"Lovelock who was killed by Mr. Oke's and my ancestors."

And she looked full at her husband, as if in perverse enjoyment of the evident annoyance which it caused him.

"Alice," he entreated in a low voice, his whole face crimson, "for mercy's sake, don't talk about such things before the servants."

Mrs. Oke burst into a high, light, rather hysterical laugh, the laugh of a naughty child.

"The servants! Gracious heavens! do you suppose they haven't heard the story? Why, it's as well known as Okehurst itself in the neighbourhood. Don't they believe that Lovelock has been seen about the house? Haven't they all heard his footsteps in the big corridor? Haven't they, my dear Willie, noticed a thousand times that you never will stay a minute alone in the yellow drawing-room—that you run out of it, like a child, if I happen to leave you there for a minute?"

True! How was it I had not noticed that? or rather, that I only now remembered having noticed it? The yellow drawing-room was one of the most charming rooms in the house: a large, bright room, hung with yellow damask and panelled with carvings, that opened straight out on to the lawn, far superior to the room in which we habitually sat, which was comparatively gloomy. This time Mr. Oke struck me as really too childish. I felt an intense desire to badger him.

"The yellow drawing-room!" I exclaimed. "Does this interesting literary character haunt the yellow drawing-room? Do tell me about it. What happened there?"

Mr. Oke made a painful effort to laugh.

"Nothing ever happened there, so far as I know," he said, and rose from the table.

"Really?" I asked incredulously.

"Nothing did happen there," answered Mrs. Oke slowly, playing mechanically with a fork, and picking out the pattern of the tablecloth. "That is just the extraordinary circumstance, that, so far as any one knows, nothing ever did happen there; and yet that room has an evil reputation. No member of our family, they say, can bear to sit there alone for more than a minute. You see, William evidently cannot."

"Have you ever seen or heard anything strange there?" I asked of my host.

He shook his head. "Nothing," he answered curtly, and lit his cigar.

"I presume you have not," I asked, half laughing, of Mrs. Oke, "since you don't mind sitting in that room for hours alone? How do you explain this uncanny reputation, since nothing ever happened there?"

"Perhaps something is destined to happen there in the future," she answered, in her absent voice. And then she suddenly added, "Suppose you paint my portrait in that room?"

Mr. Oke suddenly turned round. He was very white, and looked as if he were going to say something, but desisted.

"Why do you worry Mr. Oke like that?" I asked, when he had gone into his smoking-room with his usual bundle of papers. "It is very cruel of you, Mrs. Oke. You ought to have more consideration for people who believe in such things, although you may not be able to put yourself in their frame of mind."

"Who tells you that I don't believe in *such things*, as you call them?" she answered abruptly.

"Come," she said, after a minute, "I want to show you why I believe in Christopher Lovelock. Come with me into the yellow room."

5

What Mrs. Oke showed me in the yellow room was a large bundle of papers, some printed and some manuscript, but all of them brown with age, which she took out of an old Italian ebony inlaid cabinet. It took her some time to get them, as a complicated arrangement of double locks and false drawers had to be put in play; and while she was doing so, I looked round the room, in which I had been only three or four times before. It was certainly the most beautiful room in this beautiful house, and, as it seemed to me now, the most strange. It was long and low, with something that made you think of the cabin of a ship, with a great mullioned window that let in, as it were, a perspective of the brownish green park-land, dotted with oaks, and sloping upwards to the distant line of bluish firs against the horizon. The walls were hung with flowered damask, whose yellow, faded to brown, united with the reddish colour of the carved wainscoting and the carved oaken beams. For the rest, it reminded me more of an Italian room than an English one. The furniture was Tuscan of the early seventeenth century, inlaid and carved; there were a couple of faded allegorical pictures, by some Bolognese master, on the walls; and in a corner, among a stack of dwarf orange-trees, a little Italian harpsichord of exquisite curve and slenderness, with flowers and landscapes painted upon its cover. In a recess was a shelf of old books, mainly English and Italian poets of the Elizabethan time; and close by it, placed upon a carved wedding-chest, a large and beautiful melon-shaped lute. The panes of the mullioned window were open, and yet the air seemed heavy, with an indescribable heady perfume, not that of any growing flower, but like that of old stuff that should have lain for years among spices.

"It is a beautiful room!" I exclaimed. "I should awfully like to paint you in it"; but I had scarcely spoken the words when I felt I had done wrong. This woman's husband could not bear the room, and it seemed to me vaguely as if he were right in detesting it.

Mrs. Oke took no notice of my exclamation, but beckoned me to the table where she was standing sorting the papers.

"Look!" she said, "these are all poems by Christopher Lovelock"; and touching the yellow papers with delicate and reverent fingers, she commenced reading some of them out loud in a slow, half-audible voice. They were songs in the style of those of Herrick, Waller, and Drayton, complaining for the most part of the cruelty of a lady called Dryope, in whose name was evidently concealed a reference to that of the mistress of Okehurst. The songs were graceful, and not without a certain faded passion: but I was thinking not of them, but of the woman who was reading them to me.

Mrs. Oke was standing with the brownish yellow wall as a background to her white brocade dress, which, in its stiff seventeenth-century make, seemed but to bring out more clearly the slightness, the exquisite suppleness, of her tall figure. She held the papers in one hand, and leaned the other, as if for support, on the inlaid cabinet by her side. Her voice, which was delicate, shadowy, like her person, had a curious throbbing cadence, as if she were reading the words of a melody, and restraining herself with difficulty from singing it; and as she read, her long slender throat throbbed slightly, and a faint redness came into her thin face. She evidently knew the verses by heart, and her eyes were mostly fixed

with that distant smile in them, with which harmonised a constant
tremulous little smile in her lips.

"That is how I would wish to paint her!" I exclaimed within myself;
and scarcely noticed, what struck me on thinking over the scene, that
this strange being read these verses as one might fancy a woman would
read love-verses addressed to herself.

"Those are all written for Alice Oke—Alice the daughter of Virgil
Pomfret," she said slowly, folding up the papers. "I found them at the
bottom of this cabinet. Can you doubt of the reality of Christopher
Lovelock now?"

The question was an illogical one, for to doubt of the existence of
Christopher Lovelock was one thing, and to doubt of the mode of his
death was another; but somehow I did feel convinced.

"Look!" she said, when she had replaced the poems, "I will show you
something else." Among the flowers that stood on the upper storey of her
writing-table—for I found that Mrs. Oke had a writing-table in the
yellow room—stood, as on an altar, a small black carved frame, with a
silk curtain drawn over it: the sort of thing behind which you would have
expected to find a head of Christ or of the Virgin Mary. She drew the
curtain and displayed a large-sized miniature, representing a young man,
with auburn curls and a peaked auburn beard, dressed in black, but with
lace about his neck, and large pear-shaped pearls in his ears: a wistful,
melancholy face. Mrs. Oke took the miniature religiously off its stand,
and showed me, written in faded characters upon the back, the name
"Christopher Lovelock," and the date 1626.

"I found this in the secret drawer of that cabinet, together with the
heap of poems," she said, taking the miniature out of my hand.

I was silent for a minute.

"Does—does Mr. Oke know that you have got it here?" I asked; and
then wondered what in the world had impelled me to put such a question.

Mrs. Oke smiled that smile of contemptuous indifference. "I have
never hidden it from any one. If my husband disliked my having it, he
might have taken it away, I suppose. It belongs to him, since it was
found in his house."

I did not answer, but walked mechanically towards the door. There
was something heady and oppressive in this beautiful room; something,
I thought, almost repulsive in this exquisite woman. She seemed to me,
suddenly, perverse and dangerous.

I scarcely know why, but I neglected Mrs. Oke that afternoon. I went
to Mr. Oke's study, and sat opposite to him smoking while he was
engrossed in his accounts, his reports, and electioneering papers. On the
table, above the heap of paper-bound volumes and pigeon-holed documents, was, as sole ornament of his den, a little photograph of his wife,

done some years before. I don't know why, but as I sat and watched him, with his florid, honest, manly beauty, working away conscientiously, with that little perplexed frown of his, I felt intensely sorry for this man. But this feeling did not last. There was no help for it: Oke was not as interesting as Mrs. Oke; and it required too great an effort to pump up sympathy for this normal, excellent, exemplary young squire, in the presence of so wonderful a creature as his wife. So I let myself go to the habit of allowing Mrs. Oke daily to talk over her strange craze, or rather of drawing her out about it. I confess that I derived a morbid and exquisite pleasure in doing so: it was so characteristic in her, so appropriate to the house! It completed her personality so perfectly, and made it so much easier to conceive a way of painting her. I made up my mind little by little, while working at William Oke's portrait (he proved a less easy subject than I had anticipated, and, despite his conscientious efforts, was a nervous, uncomfortable sitter, silent and brooding)—I made up my mind that I would paint Mrs. Oke standing by the cabinet in the yellow room, in the white Vandyck dress copied from the portrait of her ancestress. Mr. Oke might resent it, Mrs. Oke even might resent it; they might refuse to take the picture, to pay for it, to allow me to exhibit; they might force me to run my umbrella through the picture. No matter. That picture should be painted, if merely for the sake of having painted it; for I felt it was the only thing I could do, and that it would be far away my best work. I told neither of my resolution, but prepared sketch after sketch of Mrs. Oke, while continuing to paint her husband.

Mrs. Oke was a silent person, more silent even than her husband, for she did not feel bound, as he did, to attempt to entertain a guest or to show any interest in him. She seemed to spend her life—a curious, inactive, half-invalidish life, broken by sudden fits of childish cheerfulness—in an eternal day-dream, strolling about the house and grounds, arranging the quantities of flowers that always filled all the rooms, beginning to read and then throwing aside novels and books of poetry, of which she always had a large number; and, I believe, lying for hours, doing nothing, on a couch in that yellow drawing-room, which, with her sole exception, no member of the Oke family had ever been known to stay in alone. Little by little I began to suspect and to verify another eccentricity of this eccentric being, and to understand why there were stringent orders never to disturb her in that yellow room.

It had been a habit at Okehurst, as at one or two other English manor-houses, to keep a certain amount of the clothes of each generation, more particularly wedding-dresses. A certain carved oaken press, of which Mr. Oke once displayed the contents to me, was a perfect museum of costumes, male and female, from the early years of the seventeenth to the end of the eighteenth century—a thing to take away the breath of a *bric-a-brac* collector, an antiquary, or a *genre* painter. Mr. Oke was none of these, and therefore took but little interest in the collection, save in so far as it interested his family feeling. Still he seemed well acquainted with the contents of that press.

He was turning over the clothes for my benefit, when suddenly I noticed that he frowned. I know not what impelled me to say, "By the way, have you any dresses of that Mrs. Oke whom your wife resembles so much? Have you got that particular white dress she was painted in, perhaps?"

Oke of Okehurst flushed very red.

"We have it," he answered hesitatingly, "but—it isn't here at present —I can't find it. I suppose," he blurted out with an effort, "that Alice has got it. Mrs. Oke sometimes has the fancy of having some of these old things down. I suppose she takes ideas from them."

A sudden light dawned in my mind. The white dress in which I had seen Mrs. Oke in the yellow room, the day that she showed me Lovelock's verses, was not, as I had thought, a modern copy; it was the original dress of Alice Oke, the daughter of Virgil Pomfret—the dress in which, perhaps, Christopher Lovelock had seen her in that very room.

The idea gave me a delightful picturesque shudder. I said nothing. But I pictured to myself Mrs. Oke sitting in that yellow room—that room which no Oke of Okehurst save herself ventured to remain in alone, in the dress of her ancestress, confronting, as it were, that vague, haunting something that seemed to fill the place—that vague presence, it seemed to me, of the murdered cavalier poet.

Mrs. Oke, as I have said, was extremely silent, as a result of being extremely indifferent. She really did not care in the least about anything except her own ideas and day-dreams, except when, every now and then, she was seized with a sudden desire to shock the prejudices or superstitions of her husband. Very soon she got into the way of never talking to me at all, save about Alice and Nicholas Oke and Christopher Lovelock; and then, when the fit seized her, she would go on by the hour, never asking herself whether I was or was not equally interested in the strange craze that fascinated her. It so happened that I was. I loved to listen to her, going on discussing by the hour the merits of Lovelock's poems, and analysing her feelings and those of her two ancestors. It was quite wonderful to watch the exquisite, exotic creature in one of these moods, with the distant look in her grey eyes and the absent-looking smile in her thin cheeks, talking as if she had intimately known these people of the seventeenth century, discussing every minute mood of theirs, detailing every scene between them and their victim, talking of Alice, and Nicholas, and Lovelock as she might of her most intimate friends. Of Alice particularly, and of Lovelock. She seemed to know every word that Alice had spoken, every idea that had crossed her mind. It sometimes struck me as if she were telling me, speaking of herself in the third person, of her own feelings—as if I were listening to a woman's confidences, the recital of her doubts, scruples, and agonies about a living lover. For Mrs. Oke, who seemed the most self-absorbed of creatures in all other matters, and utterly incapable of understanding or sympathising with the feelings of other persons, entered completely and passionately into the feelings of this woman, this Alice, who, at some moments, seemed to be not another woman, but herself.

"But how could she do it—how could she kill the man she cared for?" I once asked her.

"Because she loved him more than the whole world!" she exclaimed, and rising suddenly from her chair, walked towards the window, covering her face with her hands.

I could see, from the movement of her neck, that she was sobbing. She did not turn round, but motioned me to go away.

"Don't let us talk any more about it," she said. "I am ill to-day, and silly."

I closed the door gently behind me. What mystery was there in this woman's life? This listlessness, this strange self-engrossment and stranger mania about people long dead, this indifference and desire to annoy towards her husband—did it all mean that Alice Oke had loved or still loved some one who was not the master of Okehurst? And his melancholy, his preoccupation, the something about him that told of a broken youth—did it mean that he knew it?

6

The following days Mrs. Oke was in a condition of quite unusual good spirits. Some visitors—distant relatives—were expected, and although she had expressed the utmost annoyance at the idea of their coming, she was now seized with a fit of housekeeping activity, and was perpetually about arranging things and giving orders, although all arrangements, as usual, had been made, and all orders given, by her husband.

William Oke was quite radiant.

"If only Alice were always well like this!" he exclaimed; "if only she would take, or could take, an interest in life, how different things would be! But," he added, as if fearful lest he should be supposed to accuse her in any way, "how can she, usually, with her wretched health? Still, it does make me awfully happy to see her like this."

I nodded. But I cannot say that I really acquiesced in his views. It seemed to me, particularly with the recollection of yesterday's extraordinary scene, that Mrs. Oke's high spirits were anything but normal. There was something in her unusual activity and still more unusual cheerfulness that was merely nervous and feverish; and I had, the whole day, the impression of dealing with a woman who was ill and who would very speedily collapse.

Mrs. Oke spent her day wandering from one room to another, and from the garden to the greenhouse, seeing whether all was in order, when, as a matter of fact, all was always in order at Okehurst. She did not give me any sitting, and not a word was spoken about Alice Oke or Christopher Lovelock. Indeed, to a casual observer, it might have seemed as if all that craze about Lovelock had completely departed, or never existed. About five o'clock, as I was strolling among the red-brick round-gabled out-houses—each with its armorial oak—and the old-fashioned spalliered kitchen and fruit garden, I saw Mrs. Oke standing, her hands full of York and Lancaster roses, upon the steps facing the stables. A groom was currycombing a horse, and outside the coach-house was Mr. Oke's little high-wheeled cart.

"Let us have a drive!" suddenly exclaimed Mrs. Oke, on seeing me. "Look what a beautiful evening—and look at that dear little cart! It is so long since I have driven, and I feel as if I must drive again. Come with me. And you, harness Jim at once and come round to the door."

I was quite amazed; and still more so when the cart drove up before the door, and Mrs. Oke called to me to accompany her. She sent away the groom, and in a minute we were rolling along, at a tremendous pace, along the yellow-sand road, with the sere pasture-lands, the big oaks, on either side.

I could scarcely believe my senses. This woman, in her mannish little coat and hat, driving a powerful young horse with the utmost skill, and chattering like a school-girl of sixteen, could not be the delicate, morbid, exotic, hot-house creature, unable to walk or to do anything, who spent her days lying about on couches in the heavy atmosphere, redolent with strange scents and associations, of the yellow drawing-room. The movement of the light carriage, the cool draught, the very grind of the wheels upon the gravel, seemed to go to her head like wine.

"It is so long since I have done this sort of thing," she kept repeating; "so long, so long. Oh, don't you think it delightful, going at this pace, with the idea that any moment the horse may come down and we two be killed?" and she laughed her childish laugh, and turned her face, no longer pale, but flushed with the movement and the excitement, towards me.

The cart rolled on quicker and quicker, one gate after another swinging to behind us, as we flew up and down the little hills, across the pasture lands, through the little red-brick gabled villages, where the people came out to see us pass, past the rows of willows along the streams, and the dark-green compact hop-fields, with the blue and hazy tree-tops of the horizon getting bluer and more hazy as the yellow light began to graze the ground. At last we got to an open space, a high-lying piece of common-land, such as is rare in that ruthlessly utilised country of grazing-grounds and hop-gardens. Among the low hills of the Weald, it seemed quite preternaturally high up, giving a sense that its extent of flat heather and gorse, bound by distant firs, was really on the top of the world. The sun was setting just opposite, and its lights lay flat on the ground, staining it with the red and black of the heather, or rather turning it into the surface of a purple sea, canopied over by a bank of dark-purple clouds—the jet-like sparkle of the dry ling and gorse tipping the purple like sunlit wavelets. A cold wind swept in our faces.

"What is the name of this place?" I asked. It was the only bit of impressive scenery that I had met in the neighbourhood of Okehurst.

"It is called Cotes Common," answered Mrs. Oke, who had slackened the pace of the horse, and let the reins hang loose about his neck. "It was here that Christopher Lovelock was killed."

There was a moment's pause; and then she proceeded, tickling the flies from the horse's ears with the end of her whip, and looking straight into the sunset, which now rolled, a deep purple stream, across the heath to our feet—

"Lovelock was riding home one summer evening from Appledore, when, as he had got half-way across Cotes Common, somewhere about here—for I have always heard them mention the pond in the old gravel-pits as about the place—he saw two men riding towards him, in whom he presently recognised Nicholas Oke of Okehurst accompanied by a groom. Oke of Okehurst hailed him; and Lovelock rode up to meet him. 'I am glad to have met you, Mr. Lovelock,' said Nicholas, 'because I have some important news for you'; and so saying, he brought his horse close to the one that Lovelock was riding, and suddenly turning round, fired off a pistol at his head. Lovelock had time to move, and the bullet, instead of striking him, went straight into the head of his horse, which fell beneath him. Lovelock, however, had fallen in such a way as to be able to extricate himself easily from his horse; and drawing his sword, he rushed upon Oke, and seized his horse by the bridle. Oke quickly jumped off and drew his sword; and in a minute, Lovelock, who was much the better swordsman of the two, was having the better of him. Lovelock had completely disarmed him, and got his sword at Oke's throat, crying out to him that if he would ask forgiveness he should be spared for the sake of their old friendship, when the groom suddenly rode up from behind and shot Lovelock through the back. Lovelock fell, and Oke immediately tried to finish him with his sword, while the groom drew up and held the bridle of Oke's horse. At that moment the sunlight fell upon the groom's face, and Lovelock recognised Mrs. Oke. He cried out, 'Alice, Alice! it is you who have murdered me!' and died. Then Nicholas Oke sprang into his saddle and rode off with his wife, leaving Lovelock dead by the side of his fallen horse. Nicholas Oke had taken the precaution of removing Lovelock's purse and throwing it into the pond, so the murder was put down to certain highwaymen who were about in that part of the country. Alice Oke died many years afterwards, quite an old woman, in the reign of Charles II.; but Nicholas did not live very long, and shortly before his death got into a very strange condition, always brooding, and sometimes threatening to kill his wife. They say that in one of these fits, just shortly before his death, he told the whole story of the murder, and made a prophecy that when the head of his house and master of Okehurst should marry another Alice Oke, descended from himself and his wife, there should be an end of the Okes of Okehurst. You see, it seems to be coming true. We have no children, and I don't suppose we shall ever have any. I, at least, have never wished for them."

Mrs. Oke paused, and turned her face towards me with the absent smile in her thin cheeks: her eyes no longer had that distant look; they were strangely eager and fixed. I did not know what to answer; this woman positively frightened me. We remained for a moment in that same place, with the sunlight dying away in crimson ripples on the heather, gilding the yellow banks, the black waters of the pond, surrounded by thin rushes, and the yellow gravel-pits; while the wind blew in our faces and bent the ragged warped bluish tops of the firs. Then Mrs. Oke touched the horse, and off we went at a furious pace. We did not exchange a single word, I think, on the way home. Mrs. Oke sat with her eyes fixed on the reins, breaking the silence now and then only by a word to the horse, urging him to an even more furious pace. The people we met along the roads must have thought that the horse was running away, unless they noticed Mrs. Oke's calm manner and the look of excited enjoyment in her face. To me it seemed that I was in the hands of a madwoman, and I quietly prepared myself for being upset or dashed against a cart. It had turned cold, and the draught was icy in our faces when we got within sight of the red gables and high chimney-stacks of Okehurst. Mr. Oke was standing before the door. On our approach I saw a look of relieved suspense, of keen pleasure come into his face.

He lifted his wife out of the cart in his strong arms with a kind of chivalrous tenderness.

"I am so glad to have you back, darling," he exclaimed—"so glad! I was delighted to hear you had gone out with the cart, but as you have not driven for so long, I was beginning to be frightfully anxious, dearest. Where have you been all this time?"

Mrs. Oke had quickly extricated herself from her husband, who had remained holding her, as one might hold a delicate child who has been causing anxiety. The gentleness and affection of the poor fellow had evidently not touched her—she seemed almost to recoil from it.

"I have taken him to Cotes Common," she said, with that perverse look which I had noticed before, as she pulled off her driving-gloves. "It is such a splendid old place."

Mr. Oke flushed as if he had bitten upon a sore tooth, and the double gash painted itself scarlet between his eyebrows.

Outside, the mists were beginning to rise, veiling the park-land dotted with big black oaks, and from which, in the watery moonlight, rose on all sides the eerie little cry of the lambs separated from their mothers. It was damp and cold, and I shivered.

7

The next day Okehurst was full of people, and Mrs. Oke, to my amazement, was doing the honours of it as if a house full of commonplace, noisy young creatures, bent upon flirting and tennis, were her usual idea of felicity.

The afternoon of the third day—they had come for an electioneering ball, and stayed three nights—the weather changed; it turned suddenly very cold and began to pour. Every one was sent indoors, and there was a general gloom suddenly over the company. Mrs. Oke seemed to have got sick of her guests, and was listlessly lying back on a couch, paying not the slightest attention to the chattering and piano-strumming in the room, when one of the guests suddenly proposed that they should play charades. He was a distant cousin of the Okes, a sort of fashionable artistic Bohemian, swelled out to intolerable conceit by the amateur-actor vogue of a season.

"It would be lovely in this marvellous old place," he cried, "just to dress up, and parade about, and feel as if we belonged to the past. I have heard you have a marvellous collection of old costumes, more or less ever since the days of Noah, somewhere, Cousin Bill."

The whole party exclaimed in joy at this proposal. William Oke looked puzzled for a moment, and glanced at his wife, who continued to lie listless on her sofa.

"There is a press full of clothes belonging to the family," he answered dubiously, apparently overwhelmed by the desire to please his guests;

"but—but—I don't know whether it's quite respectful to dress up in the clothes of dead people."

"Oh, fiddlestick!" cried the cousin. "What do the dead people know about it? Besides," he added, with mock seriousness, "I assure you we shall behave in the most reverent way and feel quite solemn about it all, if only you will give us the key, old man."

Again Mr. Oke looked towards his wife, and again met only her vague, absent glance.

"Very well," he said, and led his guests upstairs.

An hour later the house was filled with the strangest crew and the strangest noises. I had entered, to a certain extent, into William Oke's feeling of unwillingness to let his ancestors' clothes and personality be taken in vain; but when the masquerade was complete, I must say that the effect was quite magnificent. A dozen youngish men and women—those who were staying in the house and some neighbours who had come for lawn-tennis and dinner—were rigged out, under the direction of the theatrical cousin, in the contents of that oaken press: and I have never seen a more beautiful sight than the panelled corridors, the carved and escutcheoned staircase, the dim drawing-rooms with their faded tapestries, the great hall with its vaulted and ribbed ceiling, dotted about with groups or single figures that seemed to have come straight from the past. Even William Oke, who, besides myself and a few elderly people, was the only man not masqueraded, seemed delighted and fired by the sight. A certain schoolboy character suddenly came out in him; and finding that there was no costume left for him, he rushed upstairs and presently returned in the uniform he had worn before his marriage. I thought I had really never seen so magnificent a specimen of the handsome Englishman; he looked, despite all the modern associations of his costume, more genuinely old-world than all the rest, a knight for the Black Prince or Sidney, with his admirably regular features and beautiful fair hair and complexion. After a minute, even the elderly people had got costumes of some sort—dominoes arranged at the moment, and hoods and all manner of disguises made out of pieces of old embroidery and Oriental stuffs and furs; and very soon this rabble of masquers had become, so to speak, completely drunk with its own amusement—with the childishness, and, if I may say so, the barbarism, the vulgarity underlying the majority even of well-bred English men and women—Mr. Oke himself doing the mountebank like a schoolboy at Christmas.

"Where is Mrs. Oke? Where is Alice?" some one suddenly asked.

Mrs. Oke had vanished. I could fully understand that to this eccentric being, with her fantastic, imaginative, morbid passion for the past, such a carnival as this must be positively revolting; and, absolutely indifferent as she was to giving offence, I could imagine how she would have retired, disgusted and outraged, to dream her strange day-dreams in the yellow room.

But a moment later, as we were all noisily preparing to go in to dinner, the door opened and a strange figure entered, stranger than any of these others who were profaning the clothes of the dead: a boy, slight and tall, in a brown riding-coat, leathern belt, and big buff boots, a little grey cloak over one shoulder, a large grey hat slouched over the eyes, a dagger and pistol at the waist. It was Mrs. Oke, her eyes preternaturally bright, and her whole face lit up with a bold, perverse smile.

Every one exclaimed, and stood aside. Then there was a moment's silence, broken by faint applause. Even to a crew of noisy boys and girls playing the fool in the garments of men and women long dead and buried, there is something questionable in the sudden appearance of a young married woman, the mistress of the house, in a riding-coat and jack-boots; and Mrs. Oke's expression did not make the jest seem any less questionable.

"What is that costume?" asked the theatrical cousin, who, after a second, had come to the conclusion that Mrs. Oke was merely a woman of marvellous talent whom he must try and secure for his amateur troop next season.

"It is the dress in which an ancestress of ours, my namesake Alice Oke, used to go out riding with her husband in the days of Charles I.," she answered, and took her seat at the head of the table. Involuntarily my eyes sought those of Oke of Okehurst. He, who blushed as easily as a girl of sixteen, was now as white as ashes, and I noticed that he pressed his hand almost convulsively to his mouth.

"Don't you recognise my dress, William?" asked Mrs. Oke, fixing her eyes upon him with a cruel smile.

He did not answer, and there was a moment's silence, which the theatrical cousin had the happy thought of breaking by jumping upon his seat and emptying off his glass with the exclamation—

"To the health of the two Alice Okes, of the past and the present!"

Mrs. Oke nodded, and with an expression I had never seen in her face before, answered in a loud and aggressive tone—

"To the health of the poet, Mr. Christopher Lovelock, if his ghost be honouring this house with its presence!"

I felt suddenly as if I were in a madhouse. Across the table, in the midst of this room full of noisy wretches, tricked out red, blue, purple, and parti-coloured, as men and women of the sixteenth, seventeenth, and eighteenth centuries, as improvised Turks and Eskimos, and dominoes, and clowns, with faces painted and corked and floured over, I seemed to see that sanguine sunset, washing like a sea of blood over the heather, to where, by the black pond and the wind-warped firs, there lay the body of Christopher Lovelock, with his dead horse near him, the yellow gravel and lilac ling soaked crimson all around; and above emerged, as out of the redness, the pale blond head covered with the grey hat, the absent eyes, and strange smile of Mrs. Oke. It seemed to me horrible, vulgar, abominable, as if I had got inside a madhouse.

8

From that moment I noticed a change in William Oke; or rather, a change that had probably been coming on for some time got to the stage of being noticeable.

I don't know whether he had any words with his wife about her masquerade of that unlucky evening. On the whole I decidedly think not. Oke was with every one a diffident and reserved man, and most of all so with his wife; besides, I can fancy that he would experience a positive impossibility of putting into words any strong feeling of disapprobation towards her, that his disgust would necessarily be silent. But be this as it may, I perceived very soon that the relations between my host and hostess had become exceedingly strained. Mrs. Oke, indeed, had never paid much attention to her husband, and seemed merely a trifle more indifferent to his presence than she had been before. But Oke himself, although he affected to address her at meals from a desire to conceal his feeling, and a fear of making the position disagreeable to me, very clearly could scarcely bear to speak to or even see his wife. The poor fellow's honest soul was quite brimful of pain, which he was determined not to allow to overflow, and which seemed to filter into his whole nature and poison it. This woman had shocked and pained him more than was possible to say, and yet it was evident that he could neither cease loving her nor commence comprehending her real nature. I sometimes felt, as we took our long walks through the monotonous country, across the oak-dotted grazing-grounds, and by the brink of the dull-green, serried hop-rows, talking at rare intervals about the value of the crops, the drainage of the estate, the village schools, the Primrose League, and the iniquities of Mr. Gladstone, while Oke of Okehurst carefully cut down every tall thistle that caught his eye—I sometimes felt, I say, an intense and impotent desire to enlighten this man about his wife's character. I seemed to understand it so well, and to understand it well seemed to imply such a comfortable acquiescence; and it seemed so unfair that just he should be condemned to puzzle for ever over this enigma, and wear out his soul trying to comprehend what now seemed so plain to me. But how would it ever be possible to get this serious, conscientious, slow-brained representative of English simplicity and honesty and thoroughness to understand the mixture of self-engrossed vanity, of shallowness, of poetic vision, of love of morbid excitement, that walked this earth under the name of Alice Oke?

So Oke of Okehurst was condemned never to understand; but he was condemned also to suffer from his inability to do so. The poor fellow was constantly straining after an explanation of his wife's peculiarities; and although the effort was probably unconscious, it caused him a great deal of pain. The gash—the maniac-frown, as my friend calls it—between his eyebrows, seemed to have grown a permanent feature of his face.

Mrs. Oke, on her side, was making the very worst of the situation Perhaps she resented her husband's tacit reproval of that masquerade night's freak, and determined to make him swallow more of the same stuff, for she clearly thought that one of William's peculiarities, and one for which she despised him, was that he could never be goaded into an outspoken expression of disapprobation; that from her he would swallow any amount of bitterness without complaining. At any rate she now adopted a perfect policy of teasing and shocking her husband about the murder of Lovelock. She was perpetually alluding to it in her conversation, discussing in his presence what had or had not been the feelings of the various actors in the tragedy of 1626, and insisting upon her resemblance and almost identity with the original Alice Oke. Something had suggested to her eccentric mind that it would be delightful to perform in the garden at Okehurst, under the huge ilexes and elms, a little masque which she had discovered among Christopher Lovelock's works; and she began to scour the country and enter into vast correspondence for the purpose of effectuating this scheme. Letters arrived every other day from the theatrical cousin, whose only objection was that Okehurst was too remote a locality for an entertainment in which he foresaw great glory to himself. And every now and then there would arrive some young gentleman or lady, whom Alice Oke had sent for to see whether they would do.

I saw very plainly that the performance would never take place, and that Mrs. Oke herself had no intention that it ever should. She was one of those creatures to whom realisation of a project is nothing, and who enjoy plan-making almost the more for knowing that all will stop short at the plan. Meanwhile, this perpetual talk about the pastoral, about Lovelock, this continual attitudinising as the wife of Nicholas Oke, had the further attraction to Mrs. Oke of putting her husband into a condition of frightful though suppressed irritation, which she enjoyed with the enjoyment of a perverse child. You must not think that I looked on indifferent, although I admit that this was a perfect treat to an amateur student of character like myself. I really did feel most sorry for poor Oke, and frequently quite indignant with his wife. I was several times on the point of begging her to have more consideration for him, even of suggesting that this kind of behavior, particularly before a comparative stranger like me, was very poor taste. But there was something elusive about Mrs. Oke, which made it next to impossible to speak seriously with her; and besides, I was by no means sure that any interference on my part would not merely animate her perversity.

One evening a curious incident took place. We had just sat down to dinner, the Okes, the theatrical cousin, who was down for a couple of days, and three or four neighbours. It was dusk, and the yellow light of the candles mingled charmingly with the greyness of the evening. Mrs. Oke was not well, and had been remarkably quiet all day, more diaphanous, strange, and far-away than ever; and her husband seemed to have felt a sudden return of tenderness, almost of compassion, for this delicate, fragile creature. We had been talking of quite indifferent matters, when I saw Mr. Oke suddenly turn very white, and look fixedly for a moment at the window opposite to his seat.

"Who's that fellow looking in at the window, and making signs to you, Alice? Damn his impudence!" he cried, and jumping up, ran to the window, opened it, and passed out into the twilight. We all looked at each other in surprise; some of the party remarked upon the carelessness of servants in letting nasty-looking fellows hang about the kitchen, others told stories of tramps and burglars. Mrs. Oke did not speak; but I noticed the curious, distant-looking smile in her thin cheeks.

After a minute William Oke came in, his napkin in his hand. He shut the window behind him and silently resumed his place.

"Well, who was it?" we all asked.

"Nobody. I—I must have made a mistake," he answered, and turned crimson, while he busily peeled a pear.

"It was probably Lovelock," remarked Mrs. Oke, just as she might have said, "It was probably the gardener," but with that faint smile of pleasure still in her face. Except the theatrical cousin, who burst into a loud laugh, none of the company had ever heard Lovelock's name, and, doubtless imagining him to be some natural appanage of the Oke family, groom or farmer, said nothing, so the subject dropped.

From that evening onwards things began to assume a different aspect. That incident was the beginning of a perfect system—a system of what? I scarcely know how to call it. A system of grim jokes on the part of Mrs. Oke, of superstitious fancies on the part of her husband—a system of mysterious persecutions on the part of some less earthly tenant of Okehurst. Well, yes, after all, why not? We have all heard of ghosts, had uncles, cousins, grandmothers, nurses, who have seen them; we are all a bit afraid of them at the bottom of our soul; so why shouldn't they be? I am too sceptical to believe in the impossibility of anything, for my part!

Besides, when a man has lived throughout a summer in the same house with a woman like Mrs. Oke of Okehurst, he gets to believe in the possibility of a great many improbable things, I assure you, as a mere result of believing in her. And when you come to think of it, why not? That a weird creature, visibly not of this earth, a reincarnation of a woman who murdered her lover two centuries and a half ago, that such a creature should have the power of attracting about her (being altogether superior to earthly lovers) the man who loved her in that previous existence, whose love for her was his death—what is there astonishing in that? Mrs. Oke herself, I feel quite persuaded, believed or half believed it; indeed she very seriously admitted the possibility thereof, one day that I made the suggestion half in jest. At all events, it rather pleased me to think so; it fitted in so well with the woman's whole personality; it explained those hours and hours spent all alone in the yellow room, where the very air, with its scent of heady flowers and old perfumed stuffs, seemed redolent of ghosts. It explained that strange smile which was not for any of us, and yet was not merely for herself—that strange, far-off look in the wide pale eyes. I liked the idea, and I liked to tease, or rather to delight her with it. How should I know that the wretched husband would take such matters seriously?

He became day by day more silent and perplexed-looking; and, as a result, worked harder, and probably with less effect, at his land-improving schemes and political canvassing. It seemed to me that he was perpetually listening, watching, waiting for something to happen: a word spoken suddenly, the sharp opening of a door, would make him start, turn crimson, and almost tremble; the mention of Lovelock brought a helpless look, half a convulsion, like that of a man overcome by great heat, into his face. And his wife, so far from taking any interest in his altered looks, went on irritating him more and more. Every time that the poor fellow gave one of those starts of his, or turned crimson at the sudden sound of a footstep, Mrs. Oke would ask him, with her contemptuous indifference, whether he had seen Lovelock. I soon began to perceive that my host was getting perfectly ill. He would sit at meals never saying a word, with his eyes fixed scrutinisingly on his wife, as if vainly trying to solve some dreadful mystery; while his wife, ethereal, exquisite, went on talking in her listless way about the masque, about Lovelock, always about Lovelock. During our walks and rides, which we continued pretty regularly, he would start whenever in the roads or lanes surrounding Okehurst, or in its grounds, we perceived a figure in the distance. I have seen him tremble at what, on nearer approach, I could scarcely restrain my laughter on discovering to be some well-known farmer or neighbour or servant. Once, as we were returning home at dusk, he suddenly caught my arm and pointed across the oak-dotted pastures in the direction of the garden, then started off almost at a run, with his dog behind him, as if in pursuit of some intruder.

"Who was it?" I asked. And Mr. Oke merely shook his head mournfully. Sometimes in the early autumn twilights, when the white mists rose from the park-land, and the rooks formed long black lines on the palings, I almost fancied I saw him start at the very trees and bushes, the outlines of the distant oast-houses, with their conical roofs and projecting vanes, like gibing fingers in the half light.

"Your husband is ill," I once ventured to remark to Mrs. Oke, as she sat for the hundred-and-thirtieth of my preparatory sketches (I somehow could never get beyond preparatory sketches with her). She raised her beautiful, wide, pale eyes, making as she did so that exquisite curve of shoulders and neck and delicate pale head that I so vainly longed to reproduce.

"I don't see it," she answered quietly. "If he is, why doesn't he go up to town and see the doctor? It's merely one of his glum fits."

"You should not tease him about Lovelock," I added, very seriously. "He will get to believe in him."

"Why not? If he sees him, why he sees him. He would not be the only person that has done so"; and she smiled faintly and half perversely, as her eyes sought that usual distant indefinable something.

But Oke got worse. He was growing perfectly unstrung, like a hysterical woman. One evening that we were sitting alone in the smoking-room, he began unexpectedly a rambling discourse about his wife; how he had first known her when they were children, and they had gone to the same dancing-school near Portland Place; how her mother, his aunt-in-law, had brought her for Christmas to Okehurst while he was on his holidays; how finally, thirteen years ago, when he was twenty-three and she was eighteen, they had been married; how terribly he had suffered when they had been disappointed of their baby, and she had nearly died of the illness.

"I did not mind about the child, you know," he said in an excited voice; "although there will be an end of us now, and Okehurst will go to the Curtises. I minded only about Alice." It was next to inconceivable that this poor excited creature, speaking almost with tears in his voice and in his eyes, was the quiet, well-got-up, irreproachable young ex-Guardsman who had walked into my studio a couple of months before.

Oke was silent for a moment, looking fixedly at the rug at his feet, when he suddenly burst out in a scarce audible voice—

"If you knew how I cared for Alice—how I still care for her. I could kiss the ground she walks upon. I would give anything—my life any day—if only she would look for two minutes as if she liked me a little—as if she didn't utterly despise me"; and the poor fellow burst into a hysterical laugh, which was almost a sob. Then he suddenly began to laugh outright, exclaiming, with a sort of vulgarity of intonation which was extremely foreign to him—

"Damn it, old fellow, this *is* a queer world we live in!" and rang for more brandy and soda, which he was beginning, I noticed, to take pretty freely now, although he had been almost a blue-ribbon man—as much so as is possible for a hospitable country gentleman—when I first arrived.

<h2 style="text-align:center">9</h2>

It became clear to me now that, incredible as it might seem, the thing that ailed William Oke was jealousy. He was simply madly in love with his wife, and madly jealous of her. Jealous—but of whom? He himself would probably have been quite unable to say. In the first place—to clear off any possible suspicion—certainly not of me. Besides the fact that Mrs. Oke took only just a very little more interest in me than in the butler or the upper-housemaid, I think that Oke himself was the sort of man whose imagination would recoil from realising any definite object of jealousy, even though jealously might be killing him inch by inch. It remained a vague, permeating, continuous feeling—the feeling that he loved her, and she did not care a jackstraw about him, and that everything with which she came into contact was receiving some of that notice which was refused to him—every person, or thing, or tree, or stone: it was the recognition of that strange far-off look in Mrs. Oke's eyes, of that strange absent smile on Mrs. Oke's lips—eyes and lips that had no look and no smile for him.

Gradually his nervousness, his watchfulness, suspiciousness, tendency to start, took a definite shape. Mr. Oke was for ever alluding to steps or voices he had heard, to figures he had seen sneaking round the house. The sudden bark of one of the dogs would make him jump up. He cleaned and loaded very carefully all the guns and revolvers in his study, and even some of the old fowling-pieces and holster-pistols in the hall. The servants and tenants thought that Oke of Okehurst had been seized with a terror of tramps and burglars. Mrs. Oke smiled contemptuously at all these doings.

"My dear William," she said one day, "the persons who worry you have just as good a right to walk up and down the passages and staircase, and to hang about the house, as you or I. They were there, in all probability, long before either of us was born, and are greatly amused by your preposterous notions of privacy."

Mr. Oke laughed angrily. "I suppose you will tell me it is Lovelock— your eternal Lovelock—whose steps I hear on the gravel every night. I suppose he has as good a right to be here as you or I." And he strode out of the room.

"Lovelock—Lovelock! Why will she always go on like that about Lovelock?" Mr. Oke asked me that evening, suddenly staring me in the face.

I merely laughed.

"It's only because she has that play of his on the brain," I answered; "and because she thinks you superstitious, and likes to tease you."

"I don't understand," sighed Oke.

How could he? And if I had tried to make him do so, he would merely have thought I was insulting his wife, and have perhaps kicked me out of the room. So I made no attempt to explain psychological problems to him, and he asked me no more questions until once—— But I must first mention a curious incident that happened.

The incident was simply this. Returning one afternoon from our usual walk, Mr. Oke suddenly asked the servant whether any one had come. The answer was in the negative; but Oke did not seem satisfied. We had hardly sat down to dinner when he turned to his wife and asked, in a strange voice which I scarcely recognised as his own, who had called that afternoon.

"No one," answered Mrs. Oke; "at least to the best of my knowledge."

William Oke looked at her fixedly.

"No one?" he repeated, in a scrutinising tone; "no one, Alice?"

Mrs. Oke shook her head. "No one," she replied.

There was a pause.

"Who was it, then, that was walking with you near the pond, about five o'clock?" asked Oke slowly.

His wife lifted her eyes straight to his and answered contemptuously—

"No one was walking with me near the pond, at five o'clock or any other hour."

Mr. Oke turned purple, and made a curious hoarse noise like a man choking.

"I—I thought I saw you walking with a man this afternoon, Alice," he brought out with an effort; adding, for the sake of appearances before me, "I thought it might have been the curate come with that report for me."

Mrs. Oke smiled.

"I can only repeat that no living creature has been near me this afternoon," she said slowly. "If you saw any one with me, it must have been Lovelock, for there certainly was no one else."

And she gave a little sigh, like a person trying to reproduce in her mind some delightful but too evanescent impression.

I looked at my host; from crimson his face had turned perfectly livid, and he breathed as if some one were squeezing his windpipe.

No more was said about the matter. I vaguely felt that a great danger was threatening. To Oke or to Mrs. Oke? I could not tell which; but I was aware of an imperious inner call to avert some dreadful evil, to exert myself, to explain, to interpose. I determined to speak to Oke the following day, for I trusted him to give me a quiet hearing, and I did not trust Mrs. Oke. That woman would slip through my fingers like a snake if I attempted to grasp her elusive character.

I asked Oke whether he would take a walk with me the next afternoon, and he accepted to do so with a curious eagerness. We started about three o'clock. It was a stormy, chilly afternoon, with great balls of white clouds rolling rapidly in the cold blue sky, and occasional lurid gleams of sunlight, broad and yellow, which made the black ridge of the storm, gathered on the horizon, look blue-black like ink.

We walked quickly across the sere and sodden grass of the park, and on to the highroad that led over the low hills, I don't know why, in the direction of Cotes Common. Both of us were silent, for both of us had something to say, and did not know how to begin. For my part, I recognised the impossibility of starting the subject: an uncalled-for interference from me would merely indispose Mr. Oke, and make him doubly dense of comprehension. So, if Oke had something to say, which he evidently had, it was better to wait for him.

Oke, however, broke the silence only by pointing out to me the condition of the hops, as we passed one of his many hop-gardens. "It will be a poor year," he said, stopping short and looking intently before him— "no hops at all. No hops this autumn."

I looked at him. It was clear that he had no notion what he was saying. The dark-green bines were covered with fruit; and only yesterday he himself had informed me that he had not seen such a profusion of hops for many years.

I did not answer, and we walked on. A cart met us in a dip of the road, and the carter touched his hat and greeted Mr. Oke. But Oke took no heed; he did not seem to be aware of the man's presence.

The clouds were collecting all round; black domes, among which coursed the round grey masses of fleecy stuff.

"I think we shall be caught in a tremendous storm," I said; "hadn't we better be turning?" He nodded, and turned sharp round.

The sunlight lay in yellow patches under the oaks of the pasturelands, and burnished the green hedges. The air was heavy and yet cold, and everything seemed preparing for a great storm. The rooks whirled in black clouds round the trees and the conical red caps of the oast-houses which give that country the look of being studded with turreted castles; then they descended—a black line—upon the fields, with what seemed an unearthly loudness of caw. And all round there arose a shrill quavering bleating of lambs and calling of sheep, while the wind began to catch the topmost branches of the trees.

Suddenly Mr. Oke broke the silence.

"I don't know you very well," he began hurriedly, and without turning his face towards me; "but I think you are honest, and you have seen a good deal of the world—much more than I. I want you to tell me—but truly, please—what do you think a man should do if"—— and he stopped for some minutes.

"Imagine," he went on quickly, "that a man cares a great deal—a very great deal for his wife, and that he finds out that she—well, that—that she is deceiving him. No—don't misunderstand me; I mean—that she is constantly surrounded by some one else and will not admit it—some one whom she hides away. Do you understand? Perhaps she does not know all the risk she is running, you know, but she will not draw back—she will not avow it to her husband"——

"My dear Oke," I interrupted, attempting to take the matter lightly, "these are questions that can't be solved in the abstract, or by people to whom the thing has not happened. And it certainly has not happened to you or me."

Oke took no notice of my interruption. "You see," he went on, "the man doesn't expect his wife to care much about him. It's not that; he isn't merely jealous, you know. But he feels that she is on the brink of dishonouring herself—because I don't think a woman can really dishonour her husband; dishonour is in our own hands, and depends only on our own acts. He ought to save her, do you see? He must, must save her, in one way or another. But if she will not listen to him, what can he do? Must he seek out the other one, and try and get him out of the way? You see it's all the fault of the other—not hers, not hers. If only she would trust in her husband, she would be safe. But that other one won't let her."

"Look here, Oke," I said boldly, but feeling rather frightened; "I know quite well what you are talking about. And I see you don't understand the matter in the very least. I do. I have watched you and watched Mrs. Oke these six weeks, and I see what is the matter. Will you listen to me?"

And taking his arm, I tried to explain to him my view of the situation—that his wife was merely eccentric, and a little theatrical and imaginative, and that she took a pleasure in teasing him. That he, on the other hand, was letting himself get into a morbid state; that he was ill, and ought to see a good doctor. I even offered to take him to town with me.

I poured out volumes of psychological explanations. I dissected Mrs. Oke's character twenty times over, and tried to show him that there was absolutely nothing at the bottom of his suspicions beyond an imaginative *pose* and a garden-play on the brain. I adduced twenty instances, mostly invented for the nonce, of ladies of my acquaintance who had suffered from similar fads. I pointed out to him that his wife ought to have an outlet for her imaginative and theatrical over-energy. I advised him to take her to London and plunge her into some set where every one should be more or less in a similar condition. I laughed at the notion of there being any hidden individual about the house. I explained to Oke that he was suffering from delusions, and called upon so conscientious and religious a man to take every step to rid himself of them, adding innumerable examples of people who had cured themselves of seeing visions and of brooding over morbid fancies. I struggled and wrestled, like Jacob with the angel, and I really hoped I had made some impression. At first, indeed, I felt that not one of my words went into the man's brain—that, though silent, he was not listening. It seemed almost hopeless to present my views in such a light that he could grasp them. I felt as if I were expounding and arguing at a rock. But when I got on to the tack of his duty towards his wife and himself, and appealed to his moral and religious notions, I felt that I was making an impression.

"I daresay you are right," he said, taking my hand as we came in sight of the red gables of Okehurst, and speaking in a weak, tired, humble voice. "I don't understand you quite, but I am sure what you say is true. I daresay it is all that I'm seedy. I feel sometimes as if I were mad, and just fit to be locked up. But don't think I don't struggle against it. I do, I do continually, only sometimes it seems too strong for me. I pray God night and morning to give me the strength to overcome my suspicions, or to remove these dreadful thoughts from me. God knows, I know what a wretched creature I am, and how unfit to take care of that poor girl."

And Oke again pressed my hand. As we entered the garden, he turned to me once more.

"I am very, very grateful to you," he said, "and, indeed, I will do my best to try and be stronger. If only," he added, with a sigh, "if only Alice would give me a moment's breathing-time, and not go on day after day mocking me with her Lovelock."

10

I had begun Mrs. Oke's portrait, and she was giving me a sitting. She was unusually quiet that morning; but, it seemed to me, with the quietness of a woman who is expecting something, and she gave me the impression of being extremely happy. She had been reading, at my suggestion, the "Vita Nuova," which she did not know before, and the conversation came to roll upon that, and upon the question whether love so abstract and so enduring was a possibility. Such a discussion, which might have savoured of flirtation in the case of almost any other young and beautiful woman, became in the case of Mrs. Oke something quite different; it seemed distant, intangible, not of this earth, like her smile and the look in her eyes.

"Such love as that," she said, looking into the far distance of the oak-dotted park-land, "is very rare, but it can exist. It becomes a person's whole existence, his whole soul; and it can survive the death, not merely of the beloved, but of the lover. It is unextinguishable, and goes on in the spiritual world until it meet a reincarnation of the beloved; and when this happens, it jets out and draws to it all that may remain of that lover's soul, and takes shape and surrounds the beloved one once more."

Mrs. Oke was speaking slowly, almost to herself, and I had never, I think, seen her look so strange and so beautiful, the stiff white dress bringing out but the more the exotic exquisiteness and incorporealness of her person.

I did not know what to answer, so I said half in jest—

"I fear you have been reading too much Buddhist literature, Mrs. Oke. There is something dreadfully esoteric in all you say."

She smiled contemptuously.

"I know people can't understand such matters," she replied, and was silent for some time. But, through her quietness and silence, I felt, as it were, the throb of a strange excitement in this woman, almost as if I had been holding her pulse.

Still, I was in hopes that things might be beginning to go better in consequence of my interference. Mrs. Oke had scarcely once alluded to Lovelock in the last two or three days; and Oke had been much more cheerful and natural since our conversation. He no longer seemed so worried; and once or twice I had caught in him a look of great gentleness and loving-kindness, almost of pity, as towards some young and very frail thing, as he sat opposite his wife.

But the end had come. After that sitting Mrs. Oke had complained of fatigue and retired to her room, and Oke had driven off on some business to the nearest town. I felt all alone in the big house, and after having worked a little at a sketch I was making in the park, I amused myself rambling about the house.

It was a warm, enervating, autumn afternoon: the kind of weather that brings the perfume out of everything, the damp ground and fallen leaves, the flowers in the jars, the old woodwork and stuffs; that seems to bring on to the surface of one's consciousness all manner of vague recollections and expectations, a something half pleasurable, half painful, that makes it impossible to do or to think. I was the prey of this particular, not at all unpleasurable, restlessness. I wandered up and down the corridors, stopping to look at the pictures, which I knew already in every detail, to follow the pattern of the carvings and old stuffs, to stare at the autumn flowers, arranged in magnificent masses of colour in the big china bowls and jars. I took up one book after another and threw it aside; then I sat down to the piano and began to play irrelevant fragments. I felt quite alone, although I had heard the grind of the wheels on the gravel, which meant that my host had returned. I was lazily turning over a book of verses—I remember it perfectly well, it was Morris's "Love is Enough"—in a corner of the drawing-room, when the door suddenly opened and William Oke showed himself. He did not enter, but beckoned to me to come out to him. There was something in his face that made me start up and follow him at once. He was extremely quiet, even stiff, not a muscle of his face moving, but very pale.

"I have something to show you," he said, leading me through the vaulted hall, hung round with ancestral pictures, into the gravelled space that looked like a filled-up moat, where stood the big blasted oak, with its twisted, pointing branches. I followed him on to the lawn, or rather the piece of park-land that ran up to the house. We walked quickly, he in front, without exchanging a word. Suddenly he stopped, just where there jutted out the bow-window of the yellow drawing-room, and I felt Oke's hand tight upon my arm.

"I have brought you here to see something," he whispered hoarsely; and he led me to the window.

I looked in. The room, compared with the out door, was rather dark; but against the yellow wall I saw Mrs. Oke sitting alone on a couch in her white dress, her head slightly thrown back, a large red rose in her hand.

"Do you believe now?" whispered Oke's voice hot at my ear. "Do you believe now? Was it all my fancy? But I will have him this time. I have locked the door inside, and, by God! he shan't escape."

The words were not out of Oke's mouth. I felt myself struggling with him silently outside that window. But he broke loose, pulled open the window, and leapt into the room, and I after him. As I crossed the threshold, something flashed in my eyes; there was a loud report, a sharp cry, and the thud of a body on the ground.

Oke was standing in the middle of the room, with a faint smoke about him; and at his feet, sunk down from the sofa, with her blond head resting on its seat, lay Mrs. Oke, a pool of red forming in her white dress. Her mouth was convulsed, as if in that automatic shriek, but her wide-open white eyes seemed to smile vaguely and distantly.

I know nothing of time. It all seemed to be one second, but a second that lasted hours. Oke stared, then turned round and laughed.

"The damned rascal has given me the slip again!" he cried; and quickly unlocking the door, rushed out of the house with dreadful cries.

That is the end of the story. Oke tried to shoot himself that evening, but merely fractured his jaw, and died a few days later, raving. There were all sorts of legal inquiries, through which I went as through a dream; and whence it resulted that Mr. Oke had killed his wife in a fit of momentary madness. That was the end of Alice Oke. By the way, her maid brought me a locket which was found round her neck, all stained with blood. It contained some very dark auburn hair, not at all the colour of William Oke's. I am quite sure it was Lovelock's.

THE GHOST OF
GUIR HOUSE

CHARLES WILLING BEALE

Guir House

1

When Mr. Henley reached his dingy little house in Twentieth Street, a servant met him at the door with a letter, saying:

"The postman has just left it, sir, and hopes it is right, as it has given him a lot of trouble."

Mr. Henley examined the letter with curiosity. There were several erased addresses. The original was:

"*Mr. P. Henley, New York City.*"

Scarcely legible, in the lower left-hand corner, was:

"*Dead. Try Paul, No. —, W. 20th.*"

Being unfamiliar with the handwriting, Mr. Henley carried the letter to his room. It was nearly dark, and he lighted the gas, exchanged the coat he had been wearing for a gaudy smoking jacket, glancing momentarily at the mirror, at a young and gentlemanly face with good features; complexion rather florid; hair and moustache neither fair nor dark, with reddish lights.

Seating himself upon a table directly under the gas, he proceeded with the letter. Evidently the document was not intended for him, but it proved sufficiently interesting to hold his attention.

GUIR HOUSE, 16TH SEPT., 1893.

MY DEAR MR. HENLEY:

Although we have never met, I feel sure that you are the man for whom I am looking, which conclusion has been reached after carefully considering your letters. Why have I taken so long to decide? Perhaps I can answer that better when we meet. Do not forget that the name of our station is the same as that of the house—Guir. Take the evening train from New York, and you will be with us in old Virginia next day, not twenty-four hours. I shall meet you at the station, where I shall go every day for a month, or until you come. You will know me because—well, because I shall probably be the only girl there, and because I drive a piebald horse in a cart with red wheels—but how shall I know you? Suppose you carry a red handkerchief in your hand as you step upon the platform. Yes, that will do famously. I shall look for the red silk handkerchief, while you look for the cart with gory wheels and a calico horse. What a clever idea! But how absurd to take precautions in such a desolate country as this. I shall know you as the only man stopping at Guir's, and you will know me as the only woman in sight.

343

Of course you will be our guest until you have proved all things to your satisfaction, and don't forget that I shall be looking for you each day until I see you. Meanwhile believe me

Sincerely yours,
DOROTHY GUIR.

"Devilish strange letter!" said Henley, turning the sheet over in an effort to identify the writer. But it was useless. Dorothy Guir was as complete a myth as the individual for whom her letter was intended. Oddly enough, the man's last name, as well as the initial of his first, were the same as his own; but whether the P. stood for Peter, Paul, or Philip, Mr. Henley knew not, the only evident fact being that the letter was *not* intended for himself.

Reading the mysterious communication once more, the young man smiled. Who was Dorothy Guir? Of course she was Dorothy Guir, but what was she like? At one moment he pictured her as a charming girl, where curls, giggles, and blushes were strangely intermingled with moonlight walks, rope ladders, and elopements. At the next, as some monstrous female agitator; a leader of Anarchists and Nihilistic organizations, loaded with insurrectionary documents for the destruction of society. But the author was inclined to playfulness; incompatible with such a character. He preferred the former picture, and throwing back his head while watching the smoke from his cigarette curl upward toward the ceiling, Mr. Paul Henley suddenly became convulsed with laughter. He had conceived the idea of impersonating the original Henley, the man for whom the letter had been written. The more he considered the scheme, the more fascinating it became. The girl, if girl she were, confessed to never having met the man; she would therefore be the more easily deceived. But she was expecting him daily, and should not be disappointed. Love of adventure invested the project with an irresistible charm, and Mr. Henley determined to undertake the journey and play the part for all he was worth. It is true that visions of embarrassing complications occasionally presented themselves, but were dismissed as trifles unworthy of consideration.

It was still early in October, while Miss Guir's communication had been dated nearly three weeks before. Had she kept her word? Had she driven to the station every day during those weeks? Mr. Henley jumped down from the table, exclaiming:

"Yes, Miss Dorothy, I will be with you at once, or as soon as the southern express can carry me." A moment later he added: "But I shall glance out of the car window first, and if I don't like your looks, or if you are not on hand, why in that event I shall simply continue my journey.   See?"

But another question presented itself. Where was Guir Station? The lady had mentioned neither county nor county town, evidently taking it for granted that the right Henley knew all about it, which he doubtless did; but, since he was dead, it was awkward to consult him, especially about a matter which was manifestly a private affair of his own. But where was Guir? In all the vast State of Virginia, how was he to discover an insignificant station, doubtless unknown to New York ticket agents, and perhaps not even familiar to those living within twenty miles of it? Paul opened the atlas at the "Old Dominion," and threw it down again in disgust. "A map of the infernal regions would be as useful," he declared. However important Guir might be to the Guirs, it was clearly of no importance to the world. But the following day the Postal Guide revealed the secret, and the railway officials confirmed and located it. Guir was situated in a remote part of the State, upon an obscure road, far removed from any of the trunk lines. Mr. Henley purchased his ticket, resolved to take the first train for this *terra incognita* of Virginia.

The train drew up at the station. Yes, there was the piebald horse, and there was the cart with the gory wheels, and there—yes, certainly, there was Dorothy, a slender, nervous-looking girl of twenty, standing at the horse's head! Be she what she might, politically, socially, or morally, Mr. Henley decided at the first glance that she would do. With a flourish of his crimson handkerchief he stepped out upon the platform. "Rash man! You have put your foot in it," he soliloquized, "and you may never, *never* be able to take it out again." But he could as soon have passed the open doors of Paradise unheeded as Dorothy Guir at that moment.

"Mr. Henley! So glad!" said the girl in recognition of the young man's hesitating and somewhat prolonged bow. "He's a little afraid of the engine," she continued, alluding now to the horse, "so if you will jump in and take the reins while I hold his head—"

Paul tossed in his bag and satchels, and then jumping in himself gathered up the reins, while the girl stood at the animal's head.

Although Mr. Henley had hoped to find an attractive young woman awaiting him at the station, he was surprised to discover that his most sanguine expectations were exceeded. Here was no blue-stocking, or agitator, or superannuated spinster, but a graceful young woman, rather tall and slight, with blue eyes, set with dark lashes that intensified their color. Her complexion, although slightly freckled, charmed by its wholesomeness; and her hair, which shone both dark and red, according as the light fell upon it, seemed almost too heavy for the delicate head and neck that supported it. Although not strictly beautiful, she had one of those intelligent and responsive faces that are often more attractive than mere perfection of feature and form.

"It does seem funny that you are here at last!" she said, when seated beside him with the reins in her hand.

"It does indeed!" answered Paul, with a suspicion that he was a villain and ought to be kicked. For a moment he scowled and bit his mustache, hesitating whether to make a clean breast of the deception or continue in the role he had assumed. Alas, it was no longer of his choosing. He had commenced with a lie, which he now found it impossible to repudiate. No, he could not insult this girl by telling her the truth. That surely was out of the question.

Miss Guir touched the horse with the whip, and the station was soon out of sight. They ascended a long hill with gullies, bordered by worm fences and half-cultivated fields. Such improvements as there were appeared in a state of decay, and, so far as Henley could see, the country was uninhabited. Presently the road entered a wood and became carpeted with pine tags, over which they trotted noiselessly. Where were they going? Dorothy had not spoken since starting, and Paul was too much disconcerted to continue the conversation. He hoped she would speak first, and yet dreaded anything which it seemed at all probable she would say. The novelty was intense, but the agony was growing. At last, without looking at him, she said:

"You haven't told me why you never answered my last letter. You know we have been expecting you for ages."

Paul coughed, hesitated, and then resolved to tell a part of the truth, which is often more misleading than the blackest lie.

"I—I did not get it," he answered, "until a day or two ago."

Miss Dorothy looked surprised.

"Strange!" she said; "but, after all, I had my misgivings, for I never could believe that a letter like that would reach its destination. But you know you told me——"

"Yes, I know I did," interrupted Paul. "You were perfectly right. You see I got it at last, and 'all's well that ends well!'"

"Not necessarily; because if you are as careless about other matters as this, why—I may have—that is, *we* may have to part before really knowing each other, and do you know, *I* should be awfully sorry for that."

Although she laughed a quick, nervous laugh, the words were uttered as if really meant. Paul suffered, and tried to think of something non-committal—something which, while not exposing his ignorance of the real Henley's business, might induce the girl to explain the situation; but no leading question presented itself. He thought he could be happy if he could but divert the conversation from its present awkward drift.

There was a quaintness about the young lady's costume that reminded Henley of an old portrait. Evidently her attire had been modeled after that of some remote ancestor, but it was picturesque and singularly becoming, and Paul found it difficult to avoid staring in open admiration. Inwardly he concluded that she was a "stunner," but in no ordinary sense; and despite the novel and somewhat embarrassing situation, he was conscious of a fascination not clearly accounted for. Thoughts of the defunct Henley, with his store of inaccessible knowledge, were discouraging; but then the memory of the girl's smiles was reassuring; and, come what might, Paul determined to represent his namesake as creditably as possible.

The loneliness of the country road begot a spirit of confidence, so that Miss Guir soon appeared in the light of an old friend, to deceive whom was sacrilege. Mr. Henley realized the enormity of his conduct each time he glanced at her pretty face, but had not the courage to undeceive her. And why should he? Was not Dorothy happy? "Would it be right," he argued, "to upset the girl's tranquillity for a whim, for a scruple of his own, which had come too late, and which, for his as well as the girl's peace of mind, had better not have come at all? No, he would continue as he had begun. Doubtless he would be discovered ere long, but would not anticipate the event."

The forest was beginning to take on its autumnal tints, but Mr. Henley's conscience barred his thorough enjoyment of the scene. They followed the bank of a brook where wild ivy and rhododendrons clustered. They climbed steep places and descended others, and crossed a little river, where rocks and a rushing torrent made the ford seem dangerous. It was lonely, but exquisitely beautiful, and the mountain ridges closed about them on every hand.

The twilight was rapidly giving way to the soft illumination of a full moon; and it was not until Paul noticed this, that he began to ask himself, "Where are we going?" He could not put the question to the girl, and expose his ignorance of a matter which he might reasonably be supposed to know.

After a prolonged silence, Henley ventured to observe that he had never been in the State of Virginia before, hoping that the remark might lead to some information from his driver; but she only looked at him with a wondering expression, and after a minute, with eyebrows lifted, said:

"And I have never been out of it."

Paul would have liked to pursue the conversation, but did not know how to do it. So far from gaining any information, he felt that he was sinking deeper in the mire. "After all," he reflected, "there are worse things in life than being run away with by a pretty girl, even if one doesn't happen to know exactly where she is taking him, and even if she doesn't happen to know exactly whom she is taking." He stretched out his feet and leaned back, resigned to his fate.

Not a house had been passed in more than a mile. The road was deserted, and Paul's interest in future developments steadily growing.

Suddenly there was a terrible crash, and Mr. Henley's side of the cart collapsed. Dorothy drew up the horse and exclaimed:

"There! It is the spring. I was afraid it would break!"

"Too much weight on my side, Miss Guir," said Paul, jumping to the ground.

"It is not that; it was weak; and I should have remembered to place your luggage on my side. It is too unfortunate."

"What are we to do?" inquired Henley.

"It is difficult to say. We are miles from home, and the road is rough."

She was examining the broken spring by the uncertain light, and seemed perplexed.

"Can I not lead the horse while we walk?" suggested Paul.

"We could, but the break is too bad. I fear the body of the cart will fall from the axle. But stop; there is one thing I can do. There is a smith about half a mile from here, upon another road, which leaves this about a hundred yards ahead. I will drive on alone to the shop, and, although it is late, I feel sure the man will do the work for me. You, Mr. Henley, will wait here for the stage, which will be due directly. Tell the driver to put you off at the Guir Road, where you can wait until I come along to pick you up. The distance is not great, and I will follow as quickly as possible."

She was off before he had time to answer, leaving him standing by the roadside, waiting for the promised coach. It was not long before the rumbling of a heavy vehicle was heard, and but a few minutes more when an antiquated stage with four scrubby horses emerged from the shadow of a giant oak into the open moonlight, scarce fifty yards away. Mr. Henley hailed the driver, who stopped, and looked at him as if frightened. The man was a Negro, and, when convinced that it was nothing more terrible than a human being who had accosted him, smiled generously and invited him to a seat on the box.

"I 'lowed yer was a *hant*," observed the man, by way of opening the conversation, when Paul had handed up his bags and taken his place on top. Henley lighted a cigar, and the cumbersome old vehicle moved slowly forward.

Their way now lay through a beautiful valley, beside a picturesque stream, tunneling its course through wild ivy and magnificent banks of calmia, and under the wide spreading limbs of pines and hemlocks. The country appeared to be a wilderness, and Paul could not help feeling that the real world of flesh and ambition lay upon the other side of the ridge, now far behind. The night was superb, but the road rough, so that the horses seldom went out of a walk. Presently the driver drew up his animals for water, and Henley took the opportunity to question him.

"Do you know these Guirs where I am going?" he inquired.

The man paused in the act of dipping a pail of water, and seemed puzzled. Thinking he had not understood, Paul repeated the question, when the man dropped the bucket, and staring at him with a look of horror, said:

"Boss, is you uns in airnest?"

Henley laughed, and told him that he thought he was, adding that Miss Guir was a friend of his.

"Now I knows you uns is jokin', 'case dey ain't got no friends in dis 'ere country."

"But I am a stranger!" argued Paul.

"Well, sah, it ain't for de likes o' me to argify wid you uns, but ef you wants to know whar de house is, I kin show it to you; leastways I kin show you de road to git dar."

"That's it; but tell me, don't the people about here like the Guirs?"

"Boss, ef dey's frens o' yourn, I reckon you knows all about 'em; maybe more'n I kin tell you, and I reckon it's saiftest for me to keep my mouf shet tight!"

"Why so? Explain. Surely Miss Guir is a very charming young lady."

"I reckon she be, boss; dough for my part I ain't nebber seed her. Folks says as how it ain't good luck when she trabels on de road."

"What do you mean? Are any of her people accused of crime?"

"Not as ever I heerd on, sir."

"Then explain yourself. Speak!"

But not another word was to be gotten out of the man. He was like one grown suddenly dumb, save for the power of an occasional shout to his horses. A mile beyond this the driver drew up his team, and turning abruptly, said:

"You see dat paf?"

After peering doubtfully through the moonlight into the black shadows beyond, Paul thought he discerned the outline of a narrow wood road, and placing a tip in the man's hand, picked up his satchel and climbed down to the ground.

"Tank 'ee, sir, and de Lawd take keer o' you when you gets to de Guirs'," called the driver, as he cracked his whip and drove away, leaving Mr. Henley standing by the roadside listening to the retreating wheels of the coach. The forest was dense, and the moonlight, struggling through the tree-tops, fell upon the ground in patches, adding to the obscurity. Henley seated himself upon a fallen tree, to await the arrival of the cart. Although quite as courageous as the average of men, he could not help a slight feeling of apprehension concerning the outcome of his enterprise. Of course, he knew nothing about these people; but the girl was prepossessing and refined to an unusual degree. It seemed impossible that she could be acting as a decoy for unworthy ends. He laughed at the thought, and at the fun he would some day have in recounting his fears to her, and at her imaginary explanation of the driver's silly talk. At the same time he examined his revolver, which he kept well concealed, despite the law, in the depths of a convenient pocket.

When twenty minutes had passed, he began to grow impatient for the girl's arrival, and, when half an hour was up, started down the road to meet her. Scarcely had he done so when the sound of approaching wheels greeted his ears, and directly after Miss Guir was in full view.

"I hope you have been successful," Paul asked as she drew up beside him.

"Quite," answered the girl; "indeed, they put in a new spring for me; and we can now drive home without fear."

"Do you know, I have been half frightened," said Paul, climbing into the cart beside her.

"And about what, pray?"

"Absurd nonsense, of course; but the old man who drove the coach talked the most idiotic stuff when I asked him about your people. Indeed, from his manner, I believe he was afraid of you."

Miss Guir did not laugh, nor seem in the least surprised. She only drew a long breath and said:

"Very likely!"

"But why should he be?" persisted Henley.

"It does seem strange," said the girl, pathetically, "but many people are."

"I am sure I should never be afraid of you," added Paul, confidentially.

"I hope not; and am I anything like what you expected?" she asked with languid interest.

"Well, hardly—at least, you are better than I expected—I mean that you are better—looking, you know."

He laughed, but the girl was silent. There was nothing trivial in her manner, and she drove on for some minutes, devoting herself to the horse and a careful scrutiny of the road, whose shadows, ruts, and stones required constant attention. Presently, in an open space, bathed in a flood of moonlight, she turned toward him and said:

"I can not reciprocate, Mr. Henley, by saying that you are better than I expected, for I expected a great deal; I also expected to like you immensely."

"Which I hope you will promptly conclude to do," Paul added, with a twinkle in his eyes, which was lost on his companion, in her endeavor to urge the horse into a trot.

"No," she presently answered, "I can conclude nothing; for I like you already, and quite as well as I anticipated."

"I'm awfully glad," said Henley, awkwardly, "and hope I'll answer the purpose for which I was wanted."

"To be sure you will. Do you think that I should be bringing you back with me if I were not quite sure of it?"

He had hoped for a different answer—one which might throw some light upon the situation—but the girl was again quiet and introspective, without affording the slightest clew to her thoughts. How did it happen that he had proved so entirely satisfactory? Perhaps, then, after all, the original Henley was not so important a personage as he had imagined. But Paul scarcely hoped that his identity would remain undiscovered after arriving at the young lady's home; then, indeed, he might expect to be thrown upon his mettle to make things satisfactory to the Guirs.

They had been jogging along for half a mile, when, turning suddenly through an open gateway, they entered a private approach. Paul exclaimed in admiration, for the road was tunneled through such a dense growth of evergreens that the far-reaching limbs of the cedars and spruce pines brushed the cart as they passed.

"Romantic!" Henley exclaimed, standing up in the vehicle to hold a branch above the girl's head as she drove under it. The little horse tossed the limbs right and left as he burrowed his way amongst them.

"Wait until you know us better," said Dorothy, dodging a hemlock bough; "you might even come to think that several other improvements could be made beside the trimming out of this avenue; but Ah Ben would as soon cut off his head as disturb a single twig."

"Who?" inquired Paul.

"Ah Ben."

Mr. Henley concluded not to push his investigations any further for the present, taking refuge in the thought that all things come to him who waits. He had no doubt that Ah Ben would come along with the rest.

A sudden turn, and an old house stood before them. It was built of black stones, rough as when dug from the ground more than a century before. At the farther end was a tower with an open belfry, choked in a tangle of vines and bushes, within which the bell was dimly visible through a crust of spiders' webs and birds' nests. Patches of moss and vegetable mold relieved the blackness of the stones, and a venerable ivy plant clung like a rotten fish-net to the wall. It was a weird, yet fascinating picture; for the house, like a rocky cliff, looked as if it had grown where it stood. Parts of the building were crumbling, and decay had laid its hand more or less heavily upon the greater part of the structure. All this in the mellow light of the moon, and under the peculiar circumstances, made a scene which was deeply impressive.

"This is Guir House," said Dorothy, drawing up before the door. "Now don't tell me how you like it, because you don't know. You must wait until you have seen it by daylight."

She threw the reins to a stupid-looking servant, who took them as if not quite knowing why he did so. She then made a signal to him with her hands, and jumped lightly to the ground.

"Down, Beelzebub!" called Dorothy to a huge dog that had come out to meet them, while the next instant she was engaged in exchanging signals with the servant, who immediately led the horse away, followed by the dog.

"Why does the boy not speak?" inquired Paul, considerably puzzled by what he had seen.

"*Because he is dumb*," answered the girl, leading the way up to the door.

Paul carried his luggage into the porch where he saw that Dorothy's eyes were fixed upon him with that strange *quizzo-critical* gaze, with lids half closed and head tilted, which he had observed once before, and which he could not help thinking gave her a very aristocratic bearing.

"You should carry one of those long-handled lorgnettes," he suggested, "when you look that way."

"And why?" she asked quite innocently.

"To look at me with," answered Henley, hoping to induce a smile, or a more cheery tone amid a gloom which was growing oppressive. But Miss Guir simply led the way to the great hall door, which was built of heavy timber, and studded with nail-heads without. As the cumbersome old portal swung open, Paul could not help observing that it was at least two inches thick, braced diagonally, and that the locks and hinges were unusually crude and massive. He followed Miss Guir into the hall, with a slight foreboding of evil which the memory of the stage driver's remark did not help to dispel.

2

There are few men who would not have felt uncomfortable in the peculiar situation in which Mr. Henley now found himself, although, perhaps, he was as little affected as any one would have been under the circumstances. It was impossible now to retreat from the part assumed, and he resolved to carry it out to the best of his ability, never doubting for an instant that the deception would be discovered sooner or later.

Following Miss Guir across the threshold of her mysterious home, Henley entered a hall which was by far the most extraordinary he had ever beheld, and he paused for a moment to take in the scene. The room was nearly square, with a singular staircase ascending from the left. Upon the side opposite the door was a huge chimney, where a fire of logs was burning in an enormous rough stone fireplace, doubly cheering after their long drive through the cool October evening. A brass lamp of antique design, with perforated shade of the same material, was suspended from the ceiling, and helped illumine this strange apartment. From each end of the mantelpiece an immense high-backed sofa projected into the room, cushioned and padded, and looking as if built into its present position with the house. The walls were covered with odd portraits, whose frames were crumbling in decay, and the window curtains adorned with fairy scenes and mythological figures. The ceiling was crossed with heavy beams of oak, black with the smoke of a century; and the stairway upon the left was also black, but ornamented with a series of rough panels, upon each of which was painted a human face, giving it a somewhat fantastic appearance. Paul could not help glancing above, toward the mysterious regions with which this eccentric stairway communicated. An antique sofa, studded with brass nails, exhibited upon its towering back a picture of Tsong Kapa reclining under the tree of a thousand images at the Llamasary of Koomboom. There were scenes which were evidently intended to be historical, but there were others which were wild and inexplicable. The quaintness of the room was intensified by the flickering fire and the shafts of yellow light emitted through the perforations of the lamp.

A faint aromatic odor hung upon the air, possibly due to a pile of balsam logs in a corner near the chimney. Over all was the unmistakable evidence of age, and of a nature at once barbaric, eccentric, and artistic. Who had conceived and executed this extraordinary apartment? And what were the people like who called the place their home? Paul stood aghast and wondered as he inwardly propounded these questions.

The girl led the way to the fire, and, seating herself upon one of the sofas described, invited Paul to the opposite place. His bewilderment was intense, and with a lingering gaze at the oddities surrounding him, he accepted the invitation. Not another soul had been seen since he entered. Did the girl live alone? It seemed incredible; and yet where were her people?

Dorothy pulled off her gloves and warmed her fingers before the cheerful blaze, and then stood eying with evident satisfaction the costly gems with which they were loaded. The light seemed to shine directly through her delicate palms, and to fall upon her face and hair and quaint old-fashioned costume with singular effect. There was something so bizarre and yet so spirituelle in her appearance that Henley could not help observing in what perfect harmony she seemed with her environment. It was some minutes before either of them spoke—Paul loth to express his surprise for fear of betraying a lack of knowledge he might possibly be expected to possess, while Dorothy, in an apparent fit of abstraction, had evidently forgotten her guest and all else, save the cheerful fire before her. Presently she withdrew her eyes from their fixed stare at the flames, and, looking at Paul, said:

"You must be hungry."

There was something so incongruous with his surroundings and recent train of thought in the girl's sudden remark that Henley could not help laughing.

"One would scarcely expect to eat in such a remarkable home as yours, Miss Guir," he replied, looking into her earnest eyes, and wondering if she ordinarily dined alone.

"Nevertheless, we will in an hour," she answered, "and I shall expect you to have an excellent appetite after our long drive."

Paul wanted to ask about the members of her family, but thought it wisest to say nothing for the present. Surely they would appear in due season, for it was impossible the girl could live alone in so large a house, and without natural protection; and so he simply made a further allusion to the apparent age and great picturesqueness of the building.

"Yes," said Dorothy, again gazing into the fire, "it is old—considerably more than a hundred years. It was built in the Colonial days, when things were rougher and good work more difficult to obtain."

"But surely these portraits and historical scenes were the work of an artist," Henley ventured to observe, looking at a strange head of Medusa.

"Yes," she answered, "the one you are looking at was done by Ah Ben."

He had been led to believe that Ah Ben was a living member of the household, who would shortly appear, but this now seemed impossible, for these extraordinary pictures were as old as the house itself. What did the girl mean? Had this Ah Ben done them all? Should he ask her and expose his ignorance? Paul thought he would venture upon a compromise.

"And are these pictures as old as they appear?"

"Quite," answered the girl. "As you can see for yourself, the house and all that is in it date from quite a remote time, and many of the portraits were painted before the house was ever begun."

That seemed to settle the question. Ah Ben was evidently a deceased ancestor; possibly a friend of the family in the distant past, and Henley concluded that he had misunderstood the girl in her former allusion to the man.

Dorothy had not taken off her hat, nor did she seem to have the slightest intention of doing so; meanwhile Paul's appetite, which had been temporarily lulled by his novel surroundings, was beginning to assert itself, and as there was no prospect of an attendant to conduct him to his room, he was about to ask where he might find a bowl of water to relieve himself of some of the stains of travel. Before he had finished the sentence, however, his attention was arrested by the sound of a distant footstep. He listened; it came nearer, and in a minute was descending the black staircase in the corner. Paul watched, and saw the figure of an old man as it turned an angle in the stairs. Then it stopped, and coughed lightly as if to announce its approach.

"Come," cried Dorothy, "it's only Mr. Henley, and I'm sure he'll be glad to see you."

The figure advanced, and when it had descended far enough to be in range with the fire and lamplight, Paul saw a most extraordinary person. The man, although very old, was tall and dignified in appearance, with deep-set, mysterious eyes, and flowing white moustache and hair. The top of his head was lightly bound in a turban of some flimsy material, and a loose robe of crimson silk hung from his shoulders, gathered together with a cord about the waist. As he advanced Henley observed that the bones of his cheeks were high and prominent, and the eyes buried so deep beneath their projecting brows and skull, that he was at a loss to account for the strange sense of power which he felt to be lodged in so small a space.

"This is Ah Ben, Mr. Henley, of whom I have spoken," said Dorothy, rising.

The old man extended his hand and bowed most courteously. He hoped that they had had a pleasant drive from the station, and then took his seat beside the fire.

Paul was dumfounded. Probably he was expected to know all about the man, and he had only just decided that he had been dead for a century. How could he so have misinterpreted what he had heard?

Ah Ben stretched his long bony fingers to the fire, and observed that the nights were beginning to grow quite cold.

"Yes," said Henley, "I had hardly expected to find the season so far advanced in your Southern home."

"Our altitude more than amends for our latitude," answered the old man; and then, taking a pair of massive tongs from the corner of the mantel, he stirred the balsam logs into a fierce blaze, starting a myriad of sparks in their flight up the chimney. Dorothy was looking above, and Paul, following the direction of her eyes, observed a model of Father Time reclining upon a shelf near the ceiling. The figure's scythe was broken; his limbs were in shackles, and his body covered with chains. It was an original conception, and Henley could not help asking if Time had really been checked in his onward march at Guir House.

"Ah!" said Dorothy, "that is a symbol of a great truth; but I am not surprised at your asking"; then, turning to the old man, added: "Mr.

Henley has not yet been shown to his room, and I am sure he would like to see it. It is the west chamber."

"True," said Ah Ben, rising and taking a candle from the mantel, which he lighted with a firebrand; "if Mr. Henley will follow me, I shall take pleasure in pointing it out to him."

Paul followed the elder man up the black stairs, through devious passages, and past doors with pictured panels, until he began to wonder if he could ever find his way back again. At last they stopped before a rough door, hung with massive hinges stretching half way across it, discolored with rust, and looking as if they had not been moved in an age, and which creaked dismally as Ah Ben entered.

"This will be your room," he said, bowing courteously, and placing the candle upon the table near the chimney. He then reminded Henley that their evening meal would soon be ready. "If there is anything further which you will need, pray let me know," he added, and then retired.

"I should like my luggage," said Paul, having left it below, with the exception of a small satchel.

"It shall be sent to you at once," the old man answered, as he walked slowly away.

Left to himself, Henley looked around with curiosity. Every comfort had been provided, even to an arm-chair and writing-table by the fire; but the room, as well as its furnishing, was old and quaint, and rapidly going to decay. Everything he saw related to a past period of existence. The window was high, and deep set in the wall. There was a bench under it, upon which one was obliged to climb to obtain a view of the country, and Henley pulled himself up into the sill to look out.

The landscape presented an unbroken panorama of forest. No farming land was visible, and the distant mountains closed in the sky-line, and all bathed in the soft light of the moon, made a picture of extreme beauty and loneliness—a solid wilderness, shut in from the busy world without. There was a musty smell, as if the room had not been used in years, and he lifted the sash. The rich perfume of fir and balsam was wafted in, displacing the disagreeable odor.

The bed was a high four-poster, and there were steps for climbing into it. On examination, it was discovered to be built into the room with heavy timbers, and framed solidly with the house itself. A few faded rugs were scattered about the worm-eaten floor, and in every direction the wood-work was rough and unpainted, though massive enough for a fortress. Above the wash-stand was a strange picture, painted upon a fragment of coarse blanket, which had been stretched upon the wall. It depicted the setting sun, with red and gold rays, and a blue mountain in the distance. Around the entire scene, in a semicircle, was the word "Illusion," singularly wrought into the shafts of light, and undecipherable without the closest scrutiny. The figure of an old man in the fore-ground was contemplating the scene. It was a crude piece of work, but impressive. There was a large mahogany cabinet, mounted with brass; but its double doors were locked and its drawers immovable. Beside the bed was a worm-eaten door, and in idle curiosity Paul tried the handle. It opened easily, revealing a spacious closet, with hooks and shelves. Throwing the small satchel he had brought up with him upon the floor within, it struck something, but the closet was too dark for him to see what; so, taking the candle, he made an examination. In the farthest corner was a hand-rail, guarding a closed scuttle, in which was inserted a heavy iron ring. Henley took hold of the ring, and with some effort succeeded in opening the scuttle. Looking down, he found to his surprise that it communicated with a rough stairway leading below. He peered into the darkness, but could discern nothing save the steps, which seemed to go all the way to the cellar, and were just wide enough to admit of a human body. He then removed his belongings back into the room, shut down the scuttle, and closed the door. As there was no fastening, he wedged a chair between the knob and the floor, in such a manner that it could not be opened from within. He then threw himself upon the bed, wondering what would be the outcome of his unlawful enterprise, and while inhaling the tonic air of hill and forest, half wished he were well away from this uncanny house and its eccentric inmates. And yet, despite the mystery which enshrouded it, there was a charm, a fascina-tion, he could not deny. It was the dream-like unreality of his surround-ings—unreal, because different from all that he had ever known. Should he suddenly find himself a dozen miles removed, he felt certain that he would straightway return.

The musty smell had disappeared, and as the room was getting cold, Paul got up and closed the window. At the moment he had done so, there was a low knock at the door. He replied by a summons to enter, but there was no answer. The knock was repeated, and again Paul shouted, "Come in"; but, as before, there was no response. He now went to the door and opened it, and found a servant standing outside with his lug-gage.

"Why did you not come in?" Paul inquired.

But the man did not answer; he simply entered and placed the bags upon the floor. Henley now asked him another question, but the fellow did not even look at him, and left the room without saying a word. Suddenly Paul remembered that he had seen him before. It was the dumb man who had met them on their arrival. It was the only servant he had seen. Could it be possible that these people kept no other?

When Henley had completed his toilet, he blew out the candle and then groped his way down to the hall, where he found Miss Guir and Ah

Ben awaiting him. The girl came forward to greet her guest, and to reveal her presence, the fire having died away and the hanging lamp affording but a dull, copperish glow, barely sufficient to indicate the furniture and outlines of the room.

Dorothy was radiant, but peculiarly so. She was unlike the girls to whom he was accustomed in the city. Moreover, her manner was more quiet, more earnest and dignified than theirs. She looked more charming than ever in a white gown, while her burnished hair was held in place by a tall Spanish comb, and decorated with a flower. To be sure, the details of her costume were only suggested in the vague, uncertain light, but her pose and manner were unusually impressive.

"I hope you will not think that all Virginians are as inhospitable as we appear to be, Mr. Henley," she exclaimed, with a graciousness that was quite bewitching.

"I'm sure," said Henley, "that I have never been treated with greater consideration by any one; my room is simply perfect!"

"In its way, yes; but its way is that of a century past. But what I was referring to in the matter of special negligence was the time we have kept you from food."

"Do you know," Paul replied, "that I have been so absorbed with the many strange things I have seen since my arrival that I have scarcely had time to think of food?"

"But I told you that you would be expected to have a good appetite."

"And I have. In fact, when I think of it, I am ravenous," he answered.

"Then follow me," she said, leading the way toward a heavily-curtained door upon the right. They passed into a narrow passage, and then, turning to the left, entered a softly-lighted room. Paul was amazed at the sight that met his eyes. A round table, set for two, loaded with flowers, cut glass, and silver, and lighted with wax candles grouped under a large central shade of yellow silk, with a deep fringe of the same material. The distant parts of the room were in comparative shadow forming a proper setting for the soft candle-light in the center. Evidently no one else was expected, and Dorothy, taking her seat upon one side of the cloth, requested Paul to sit opposite.

"And will not Ah Ben be with us?" inquired Henley, glancing around to see if the old man were not coming.

"I'm afraid not," replied Dorothy; "he rarely dines at this hour."

If Mr. Henley had been told of the reception awaiting him at Guir House before leaving New York, he would doubtless have considered it a hoax. As it was, he was astounded. The odd character of the house and its inmates had already given him much ground for thought, even amazement; but to suddenly find himself face to face, *tête-à-tête* with a bewitching girl, at a gorgeous dinner table, laid for them only, was a condition of things calculated to turn any ordinary man's head. Never for an instant had the girl given the slightest intimation of why he, or rather the original Henley, had been wanted, and every effort to gain a clew of his business was thwarted—sometimes, it seemed, intentionally. The table was deftly waited upon by the same dumb man, who was a man-of-all-work and marvelous capacity, but his orders were invariably given by signals. Paul wondered if he were mistaken; could it be another servant with the same affliction? But that seemed incredible.

Miss Guir's eloquent face, her wonderful hair and eyes, doubtless interfered with Paul in the full enjoyment of his meal. In fact, he was bewildered—dazed. He could neither account for the situation or the growing beauty of the girl. Was it the candle-light that had proved so becoming? But there was another matter that disturbed him, perhaps, quite as much as this. It was the fact that Dorothy would not eat. Scarcely a mouthful of food passed her lips, although the dishes were of the daintiest, and she barely tasted many which she recommended heartily to him. Was she ill? or was it not the usual hour for her evening meal? Manlike, Henley was distressed for anything not endowed with a hearty appetite, and after the long cool drive he was sure she ought to be hungry. When he ventured to allude to the fact, and to remark that neither she nor Ah Ben ate like country people, the girl only smiled and declared that they both ate quite enough for their health, although she would never undertake to judge for others. With this he had to be satisfied.

From time to time Paul's eyes would wander around the table; and from its dainty dishes and exquisite flowers return to their true lodestone, his hostess. In fact, the girl possessed a mesmeric charm for him, which had grown with marvelous rapidity since his arrival.

"It is all wonderfully beautiful!" he said, looking straight into Dorothy's eyes.

"I'm so glad you like it," she answered smiling, "but you're not eating like a very hungry man."

She was helping his plate to a salad of cresses, to which she was adding an extra spoonful of dressing.

"I think you will find this quite the correct thing," she added, pushing the plate toward him.

"Everything is much more than perfect," answered Paul; "in fact, I am not accustomed——"

But he checked himself suddenly. How did he know what the real Henley was accustomed to? Possibly he was a millionaire, while he, Paul—was not.

Whate'er she was doing, in every pose, Miss Guir was a picture—a quaint, unusual picture, to be sure, but nevertheless a picture. In helping the fruit which was brought on after dinner, her white hands, ablaze with precious stones, shone to peculiar advantage.; and when she poured out the coffee that followed, Paul wished for his kodak, for he had seen nowhere, save in old-fashioned engravings, just such a picture as she made. But it became Miss Guir's turn to be critical.

"Do you know what I think?" she said, looking him full in the face, and without a suspicion of embarrassment.

"About what?"

She bent toward him with her elbows on the table, her chin resting upon her clasped hands.

"I think that if you had a flower in your buttonhole—you wouldn't mind it now, would you, if I were to give you one?"

And then without either smile or apology she took the chrysanthemum from her hair and tossed it over to Paul. There was something so odd, and yet so deeply earnest in the way the thing was done that Henley accepted the favor more as he might have accepted a command from royalty, than as a flirtatious banter from a girl. He placed the flower in his buttonhole without the faintest desire to respond with one of those frivolous speeches he would doubtless have used under most similar circumstances.

Before the meal was finished, Ah Ben entered the room, and poured himself a cup of coffee which he drank without sitting down. It was all that he took.

3

When Ah Ben had finished his coffee, the three retired to the great entrance hall, where the fire was burning brightly, and the hanging lamp lending its uncertain aid to the illumination of the curious old apartment. Ah Ben produced a couple of long-stemmed pipes, one of which he handed to Paul, with a great leather pouch of leaf tobacco which he showed his guest how to prepare for smoking. They seated themselves in the pew before the fire, Dorothy nearest the hearth, while Paul placed himself upon the lounge opposite.

A great stillness pervaded the house, and Mr. Henley could not help wondering again if there were not other members of the establishment. Dorothy was staring into the fire, her thoughts far away, while Ah Ben smoked his pipe in silence. "Perhaps they have theories about digestion," Paul reflected, while he pulled at his long Ti-ti stem, and watched the meditative couple before him. The firelight played upon Ah Ben's white moustache and swarthy features, and the colored handkerchief upon his head, and set the long thin fingers all of a tremble upon the pipe-stem, as if manipulating the stops of a flute. It danced over Dorothy's gown in a dazzling sheen of white, and flashed upon her jeweled hands in colored sparks of green and gold and purple and red, and lit up her face and hair with the soft warm tints of a Rubens. Such a picture did the twain combine to make; they looked indeed as if they might have stepped from the canvas of some old master and come for a brief season to taste the joys of flesh and blood and life.

The outer regions of the hall were in darkness, the ancient lamp barely revealing the oddities of brush, chisel, and structure, that combined to make the most remarkable living-room that Henley had ever seen. The decaying portraits, the singular carvings and peculiar furniture, now only revealed themselves by suggestion in the faint illumination of the lamp and uncertain flicker of the fire.

But what were these people, Dorothy and Ah Ben, to each other? It was out of the question that they could be husband and wife—it seemed equally so that they could be father and daughter. Paul searched the faces of each for traces of similiarity, but there were none. Their manner to each other, the girl's mode of addressing the man, all indicated the absence of kinship. Yes, Henley felt quite certain that Ah Ben and Dorothy Guir were neither related nor connected, and that they were never likely to become so.

From time to time the old man would arise to mend the fire, and a quiet conversation upon indifferent topics ensued, Dorothy uttering a few words occasionally, in a dreamy voice, with her head propped upon a cushion in the corner. At last she failed to answer when spoken to; evidently she had fallen asleep.

"My daughter, you need rest," said Ah Ben gently, and at the same moment a clock upon the stairs began striking eleven.

Dorothy opened her eyes and looked around.

"I must have fallen asleep!" she exclaimed quite naively.

She bade them each "Good night," and then started up the uncanny stairs. Near the top she paused in the darkness, and looking over the balustrade into the hall below, seemed to be waiting. Perhaps she was not so completely in the shadow as she imagined, and perhaps Paul did not see aright, but through the gloom he thought he caught the flash of a diamond as it moved toward her lips and away again. If tempted to return the salute, his better judgment prevailed, and while holding the stem of his pipe in his right hand, pressed the tobacco firmly into the bowl with his left. A troublesome thought presented itself. Could this girl have entered into any kind of entanglement with his namesake which would have demanded a tenderer attitude than he had assumed toward her? Had he neglected opportunities and failed to avail himself of privileges which he had unknowingly inherited? For an instant the thought disturbed Mr. Henley's equilibrium, but a moment's reflection convinced him that the idea was not worth considering. Whatever it was he had seen upon the stairs he knew was not intended for his eyes, even if it had been meant for himself.

"Shall we smoke another pipe?" said Ah Ben. "I'm something of an owl myself, and shall sit here for quite a while before retiring."

Paul was glad of the opportunity, and accepted with alacrity. He hoped in the quiet of a midnight conversation to discover something about this peculiar man and his home. Perhaps he should also learn something of the girl, her strange life, and the Guirs.

"We may not be so comfortable as we would be in our beds," continued the elder man, "but there is a certain comfort in discomfort which ought not to be undervalued. Sleep, to be enjoyed, should be discouraged rather than courted."

"Yes," answered Paul, "I believe Shakespeare has told us something about it in his famous soliloquy on that subject."

"True," replied Ah Ben, "and I suppose there is no one living who has not felt the delusion of comfort. Like many other material blessings, it is to be had only in pills."

Ah Ben had stretched his legs out toward the hearth, and while passing his hand across his withered cheek, had closed his eyes in reverie. The dim and uncertain shadows made the room seem like some vast cavern, whose walls were mythical and whose recesses unexplored. The lamp had expired to a single spark, and there was nothing to reveal their presence to each other except the red glow from the embers.

"No," said the man, continuing to speak with his eyes still closed, "luxury is not necessary to a man's happiness, although he has persuaded himself that it is so."

"Perhaps not," Paul admitted, "although I contend that a certain amount of comfort is."

"By no means. There was never a greater fallacy, although I am free to admit that under certain conditions it may conduce to that end. But tell me, have you never seen one happy amid the greatest physical privations?"

"Not absolutely."

"No, not absolutely; the absolute does not belong to the finite. I refer to what most men would consider happiness."

"Oh, if you're talking about saints, they're outside my experience."

A faint smile played over Ah Ben's face as he answered:

"Saints, my dear sir, are no more to me than to you. Have you ever seen a prize fight?"

"Oh, yes; several."

"Do you not believe that the winner of a prize fight, even when covered with bruises, and suffering in every bone of his body, is happier at the moment of victory than he was the previous morning while lying comfortably in his bed?"

"I dare say; but now you're speaking of——"

"Happiness," suggested Ah Ben; "and if you will pardon me for saying so—for possibly I may have thought more upon this subject than you have—I can tell you the one essential which lies at the root of all happiness, without which it can never be acquired, but with which it is certain to follow."

"And what is that?" inquired Paul, with interest.

"*Power*," said Ah Ben, with an assurance that left no doubt of the conviction of the speaker.

"I suppose that is a kind of stepping-stone to contentment," answered Paul, reflectively.

"Precisely; for no man who lacks the power to accomplish his desires can know contentment. But contentment is transitory, and rests upon power. Power alone is the cornerstone of happiness."

"Do you really believe that?" Paul inquired, half incredulously.

"I know it. With me it is not a matter of speculation; it is a matter of knowledge."

"Then let me ask you why it is that the greatest power in the world, which is undoubtedly money, so often fails of this end?"

Ah Ben was refilling his pipe. When he had finished, he raked a coal out of the fire with the bowl, pressed it firmly down upon the tobacco, and then said, reflectively:

"You are mistaken. Money does confer happiness to the full limit of its power, but this limit is quickly reached—first, because man's ambitions and desires grow faster than his wealth, or reach out into channels that wealth can never compass, or, and principally, because wealth is an impersonal power, and not a direct one. Give the earth to a single man, and it would never enable him to change his appearance or alter one of his mental characteristics, nor to do one single thing he could not have accomplished before—it giving him simply the power to make others do his will; and so long as his will is not beyond the power of others to do, he is to that extent happy. But to be really happy, a man must have *personal power*. Wealth is not power. Power is lodged in the individuality."

"I don't know whether I quite understand you," said Paul.

Ah Ben looked at him searchingly with his luminous, deep-set eyes.

"Can gold restore an idiot's mind," he inquired, "or a cripple the use of his limbs? Would a mountain of gold add one iota to the power of your soul? And yet it is gold that men have labored for since the earth was made. Could they once understand its real limitations, what a different planet we should have!"

"That is all very well," answered Henley; "but this personal power of which you speak is born in a man, and is not to be acquired by anything he can do; whereas, the battle for wealth can be fought in a field open to all."

"There again I must beg to differ from you," said Ah Ben. "There is a law for the acquirement of this soul-power which is as fixed and certain as the law of gravitation; and when a man has once gained it, he has no more use for worldly wealth than he has for the drainings of a sewer."

"Do you mean to say that by a course of life——"

"I do, and it is this: *Self-control is the law of psychic power*."

"Then, according to your theory, the better mastery a man has over himself, the more he can accomplish and the greater his happiness?"

"I go still further," the old man continued. "I claim that *self-control is the only source of happiness, and that he who can control his body—and by this I mean his eyes, his nerves, his tongue, his appetites and passions—can control other men; but he who is master of his mind, his thoughts, his desires, his emotions, has the world in a sling. Such a man is all powerful; there is nothing he can not accomplish; there is no force that can stand against him.*"

The fire had died out, save for a few glowing embers, but Ah Ben's singular face seemed to draw unto itself what light there was, and to hold Henley's eyes in a kind of mesmeric fascination. He had put off going to bed for the sole purpose of gaining some knowledge of the house and its inmates; and yet now, with apparently nothing to hinder his investigations, he felt an unaccountable diffidence about making the inquiries. An impression that the man was a mind-reader had doubtless increased this embarrassment, and yet he had had no evidence of this kind, nor anything to indicate such a fact beyond the keen, penetrating power of those marvelous eyes. Paul felt that there was a mental chasm, deep and wide and impassable, that yawned between him and the strange individual before him. Such stupendous power of will as lodged within that brain could sport with the forces of nature, suspend or reverse the action of law, disintegrate matter, or create it. At least such was the impression which Mr. Henley had received.

It was past midnight before a movement was made for bed, and when Ah Ben brought a lighted candle, inquiring if everything in the bed-chamber had been satisfactory, Paul was about to reply in the affirmative, when he suddenly remembered the staircase in the closet.

"I was about to forget," he said, "but would you mind explaining the object of a very peculiar staircase I discovered in the closet of my room?"

"This house is old," Ah Ben replied simply. "It was built when the State was a colony and full of Indians. The stairway communicating with the lower floor was doubtless intended as a means of escape. I had not thought of this annoying you, but can readily see how it might. You shall be removed to another room at once."

"*Removed?*" exclaimed Paul. "My dear sir, I had no intention of making such a suggestion. The most I thought of asking for was a bolt for the door, or scuttle; but since your explanation I do not wish either."

They bade each other good night, and Paul undertook to find his room alone, declining Ah Ben's offer to accompany him. But the house was full of strange passages and unexpected stairways, making the task more difficult than he had expected. After wandering about he found himself stopped by a dead wall, at least so it had looked, but suddenly directly before him stood Ah Ben.

"I thought you might need my assistance," he said quietly; and then without appearing to notice Henley's astonishment, led the way to his room.

When Paul found himself alone, he became conscious of a growing curiosity concerning the stairs in the closet. He opened the door and looked in, and then quietly lifted the scuttle by the ring. He peered down into the darkness, but, as the stairs were winding, could discern nothing for more than a half dozen steps below. He listened, but the house was perfectly quiet, Ah Ben's retreating footsteps having died upon the air. Somehow he half doubted the story which the old man had told him about the original intention of the stairway as a means of escape. It seemed improbable, and dated back to such a remote period that he could not help feeling distrustful. Candle in hand, he commenced to descend, looking carefully where he placed his feet. As everywhere else, the wood-work was worm-eaten, and the timbers set up a dismal creaking under the weight of his body, but he had undertaken to investigate the meaning of this architectural eccentricity, and would not now turn back. On he crept, noiselessly as possible, adown the twisting stairs, carefully looking ahead for pitfalls and unsuspected developments. Once he paused, thinking he heard the distant tread of a foot, but the sound died away, and he resumed his course. Some of the steps were so broken and rotten that extreme caution was necessary to avoid falling. At last he reached the ground, and found himself at the bottom of a square well, around the four walls of which the stairs had been built. He was facing a massive door, which occupied one of the sides of the well. Paul tried the lock, but it was so old and rust-eaten that it refused to move. There was no other outlet, and the place was narrow and damp. He looked wistfully at the solitary door, feeling a vague suspicion that it barred the entrance to a mystery, and resolved to return at some future time, when not so harassed with sleepiness and the fatigues of travel, and make another effort to open it. Paul looked above, and as he did so a gust of air swept down the narrow opening and blew out his light; at the same instant he heard the fall of the scuttle and realized that he was shut in.

"Trapped! and by my own cursed curiosity," he muttered, as he commenced groping his way up in the darkness. But it was not so easy as he had supposed. Twice he slipped his foot into a rotten hole, and once the stairs trembled so violently that he thought they were about to fall. Nevertheless he reached the top, as he realized when his head came in contact with the trap-door, upon the other side of which he pictured Ah Ben standing with an amused smile. Henley placed his shoulder against the door, and to his amazement found that it opened quite easily. He then procured a light, and having satisfied himself that there had never been the slightest intention to entrap him, the door having simply fallen, he went hurriedly to bed.

4

The breakfast room was a charming little corner reclaimed from a dingy cell, where in by-gone days guns and ammunition had been stored, but the peace-loving inhabitants of later times had rendered these no longer necessary. It was now the most modern room Paul had seen since his arrival at this great unconventional homestead, looking quite as if it had been tacked on by mistake to the dismal old mansion.

Upon entering, he found Miss Guir sitting alone at the table. She was attired in a charming costume, and looked as fresh as the flowers before her. She greeted him with a smile, and asked how he had slept.

"Perfectly!" he answered, seating himself by her side, where he looked out of a low French window opening upon a garden with boxwood borders and a few belated blossoms.

"But do you know," he continued, "the most extraordinary thing happened."

He went on to tell of his experience in the closet, thinking it best to take the *bull by the horns* and see if anything in Dorothy's expression would lead him to suspect foul play. She listened to his story with interest, and, as Paul thought, a slight display of anxiety, but nothing more. When he had finished, she simply advised him not to go down those stairs any more, as they were rotten and dangerous. This was all. Nevertheless Henley felt sure that the girl knew what lay upon the other side of the door at the bottom. They chatted along quite pleasantly, Paul endeavoring to lead the conversation into some instructive channel, but without success.

"I thought perhaps I should have met some of your people at breakfast," he said, while sipping his coffee.

Dorothy stopped with a piece of toast half way to her lips.

"*My people!*" she exclaimed.

"Yes," said Paul, unmindful of the impression he had made.

"Really, Mr. Henley, what are you talking about?"

"The Guirs!" said Paul, still unheedful.

Suddenly he looked up, and the expression on the girl's face startled him.

"Are you ill?" he cried. "Is there anything I can do for you?"

"No, no," she gasped. "It is nothing. I am nervous. I am always nervous in the morning, and you gave me quite a turn. There now, I shall feel better directly."

If Paul was astonished before, he was dumfounded now. He could not imagine how anything he had said could produce such an effect, but he watched the return of color to the girl's face with satisfaction. Presently she looked up at him with a smile and said:

"It is all right now, but you must excuse me for a minute. I shall be back immediately."

She got up and left the room, leaving Paul alone. His appetite had quite departed, so he turned his chair around and looked out of the window at the boxwood bushes and the trees beyond. Not a human figure was in sight, nor was there a sound to indicate that there were living creatures about the premises. Where was the family? Surely such a large house could not be occupied solely by the few individuals he had already met. If there were other members, where had they kept themselves? He would have given the world to have asked a few straightforward questions, but there seemed no opportunity to do so. Where was Ah Ben? Even he had not shown his face at the breakfast table. A painful sense of mystery was growing more oppressive each hour, which the bright morning sunlight had not dispelled, as he had hoped it would. If this feeling had confined itself to Ah Ben and the house, Paul thought he might have shaken off the gloom while in the company of the girl, but even she was subject to such extraordinary flights of eccentricity, such sudden fits of nervous depression, that he felt she was not surely to be depended on as a solace to his troubled soul. While he was meditating, the door opened, and Dorothy returned. She was full of smiles; and the color had come back to her cheeks.

"I can't imagine how I could have given you such a turn," said Paul apologetically, as he resumed his place at the table.

"It was altogether my fault," she answered. Then looking at him very earnestly, added:

"I hope, Mr. Henley, that you may never become an outcast, as I am. I hope *your people* will never disown you. But let us talk of something else."

As upon the previous evening, she was solicitous about his food, that it should be of the best, and that he should enjoy it, although apparently indifferent about her own.

"Of course, you will find us quite different from other people, Mr. Henley," she continued, sipping her coffee (she never seemed to drink or eat anything heartily); "our ideas and manner of living being quite at variance with theirs."

"Yes," Paul replied, as if he understood it perfectly. She was toying with her cup as though not knowing exactly how to continue. Presently she looked up at him appealingly, possessed of a sudden idea, and added:

"And what do you think about the brain?"

Paul was astonished at the irrelevancy of the question.

"I think it is in the head," he answered, smiling, in the hope of averting a difficulty. "That is, I think it ought to be there," he added in a minute, "although it is doubtless missing in some cases. Still, there can be but little dissent from the general opinion that the skull is the proper place for it."

She looked puzzled, and Paul began to wonder if he had offended her, but in another moment she relaxed into a smile.

"I'm sure you don't think anything of the kind," she answered, "for if you do, you're not up to date. The latest investigations have shown that brain matter is distributed throughout the body. No, I'm not joking. We all think more or less with our hands and feet."

"I've not the slightest doubt of it," Paul answered, applying himself to his food; "and even if I had," he continued, "I should never dispute anything you told me." And then, looking her full in the face, he added: "Do you know, Miss Guir, that you have exerted a most remarkable influence over me? It might not be polite to say that it is inexplicable; but when I recall the fact that no girl ever before, in so short a time—"

He paused for a word, but before he could discover one that was satisfactory, she said:

"Do you mean to say that you have formed a liking for me already?"

"It is hardly the word. I have been fascinated from the moment I first saw you."

"I'm so glad," she answered, without the slightest appearance of coquetry, and as simply and naturally as though she were talking about the weather. Paul was puzzled. He could not understand her, and not knowing how to proceed, an awkward silence followed. Presently she leaned her head upon her hand, her elbow resting on the table, and with a languid yet interested scrutiny of his face, said:

"You doubtless know the world, its people and ways, far better than I, and perhaps you wouldn't mind helping me with my book."

"Indeed! You are writing a book, then?"

"No, but I should like to do so."

"And may I ask what it is about?"

"It's about myself and Ah Ben, and the awful predicament into which we have fallen."

"I should like greatly to help you," said Paul, thinking the subject might lead to a clearer insight of the situation; "but even were I competent to do so, which I doubt, I can not see how any little worldly knowledge I might possess could possibly be of service in a description of your own life."

"It is only that I should like to present our story in attractive form—one which would be read by worldly people."

"A laudable ambition. But what is the predicament you speak of?"

"The predicament is more directly my own; the situation, Ah Ben's."

"Perhaps if you will explain them, I might aid you."

"You might indeed," she answered seriously, rising from the table; "but it would be premature. Let us go into the garden."

She led the way through the back of the house out into the old-fashioned yard, where boxwood bushes and chrysanthemums, together with other autumnal flowers, adorned the beds. They walked down a straight path and seated themselves upon a rustic bench in full view of the edifice. Paul lighted a cigarette and watched the strange old building before him, while Dorothy was content to sit and look at him, as though he were some new variety of man just landed from the planet Mars. Presently she arose and wandered down the path in search of a few choice blossoms, leaving Paul alone, who watched her until she disappeared among the shrubbery.

Sitting quietly smoking his cigarette, Mr. Henley became absorbed in a critical study of the quaint old pile which had so suddenly risen to abnormal interest in his eyes. A part of the structure was falling rapidly to decay, while other portions were so deeply embedded in ivy and other creeping things that it was impossible to discover their actual state of preservation. The windows were small and far apart, and Paul recognized his own by its bearing upon a certain tree which he had noticed while looking out upon the previous night. Following down the line of the wall, he was surprised to find a large space which was not pierced by either door or window, and naturally began to wonder what manner of apartment lay upon the opposite side, where neither light nor air were admitted. The wall, to be sure, was covered with Virginia creeper, which had made its way to the roof, but it was evident that it concealed no opening. Then his thoughts wandered back to the mysterious well, and he began to wonder if the closed door at the bottom connected with the unaccounted-for space behind this wall. His curiosity grew as he brooded upon this possibility—a possibility which he now conceded to be a certainty as he marked the configuration of the building. The blank wall was beneath his bed-room. The well descended directly into it, or upon one side of it, and communicated with it through the door mentioned. There was nothing to be learned by inquiry, and Henley determined to make another effort to force open the door. His resolution was not entirely the result of curiosity, for he had taken such a sudden and strong liking for the girl that he disliked the thought of leaving her; and yet the riddle of her environment was such that he conceived it to be no more than a proper regard for his own safety to take such a precaution while visiting her. Having reached this determination, he cast about for the means of executing it. He thought he should require a hammer and a cold chisel, but where such were to be found he could not conceive. Moreover, even were they in his possession, it was impossible to see exactly how he could make use of them without arousing the household. He thought of various devices, such as a muffled hammer, or a crowbar to wrench the door from its hinges, but these were discarded in turn as impracticable, from the fact that they were unobtainable. He looked about him among the shrubbery, but there was nothing to aid him; and, indeed, how could he expect to find tools where there were no servants to use them? He got up and walked down the path, absorbed in reverie, and although unable to devise any immediate plan to accomplish the task, his resolution became more fixed as he dwelt upon it. He would risk all things in opening that door, and was impatient for an opportunity to renew the effort. Then the girl's voice came floating through the air in a plaintive melody, and Henley was recalled to his surroundings. In another minute she had joined him.

"I was afraid you would be lonely without me," she said, "and so I returned as soon as I had carried the flowers to the house."

"I am so glad," he replied, with a look of unmistakable pleasure. "Do you know, this is the most romantic place I have ever seen in all my life, and you are certainly the most romantic girl."

"Am I?" she answered sadly, and without a glimmering suspicion of a smile.

They walked slowly down the path until reaching a decrepit old gate, where they stopped.

"This is the end of the garden," she said. "Shall we go into the woods for a walk?"

"Dorothy!" Paul began, "pardon me for calling you by your name, but do you know I feel as if any prefix in your case would be irritating, from the fact that you strike me as a girl who is utterly above and beyond such idle conventionalities. One would almost as soon think of saying Miss to a goddess."

"And may I call you Paul? You will not think me forward if I should do so?" she asked, looking up at him.

"I will think myself more honored than any poor language of mine could describe," he answered.

"You know I would not want to call you Paul," she added, "unless I believed in you—unless I thought you were true and honorable in all things."

Paul winced. Was he not deceiving the girl at that very minute? What could he say?

"Dorothy," he answered, after a moment's hesitation, "I am not true, nor honorable neither. Perhaps you had better not call me Paul. I do not deserve it."

She was looking him straight in the face, with her hand upon the gate. He felt the keen, searching quality of her eyes, but was able now to return the look.

"We sometimes judge ourselves harshly," she continued. "I have myself been often led by an idle temptation into what at first appeared but a trifling wrong, but which looked far more serious later. Had I acted with the greater knowledge, I had committed the greater fault."

What was she saying? Was she not describing his own position?

"Therefore, when I say Paul," she added, "I do it because I like you, and because I believe in you, and not because I think you perfect."

She lifted the rickety old gate with care, and he closed it after them; then they walked out over the dank leaves, through the brilliant coloring of the forest. The day was soft and tempting, while a mellow haze filled the air.

"I am going to show you the prettiest spot in all the world," said Dorothy, "a place where I often go and sit alone."

They walked side by side, there being no longer any path, or, if there had been one, it was now covered, and the sunlight, filtering through the tree-tops, fell in brilliant patches upon the gaudy carpet beneath their feet. They had walked a mile, when Paul heard the murmur of distant water, and saw that they were heading for a rocky gorge, through which a small stream forced its way in a jumble of tiny cataracts and pools. It was an ideal spot, shut in from all the world beyond. The restful air, barely stirring the tree-tops, and the water, as it went dripping from stone to stone, made just enough sound to intimate that the life principle of a drowsy world was existent. They seated themselves upon a rocky ledge, and Dorothy became absorbed in reverie; while Paul, from a slightly lower point, gazed up at the trees, the sky, and the girl, with mute infatuation.

"You lead such an ideal life here," he said, after some minutes of silence, "that I should imagine the outer world would seem harsh and cold by contrast."

"But I have never seen what you call the outer world," she answered, with a touch of melancholy in her voice.

"Do you mean to say that you have lived here always?"

"Yes, and always shall, unless some one helps me away."

"I don't think I quite understand," he replied, "who could help you away, if your own people would not. Pardon the allusion, but I do not grasp the situation."

"I could never go with any of the Guirs," she answered, with a shudder, "for I am quite as much afraid of them as they are of me."

Paul was again silent. He was meditating whether it were best to ask frankly what she meant, and risk the girl's displeasure, as well as his own identity, or to take another course. Presently he said:

"Dorothy, I would not pry into the secrets of your soul for the world, and am sure you will believe in my honesty in declaring that there is no one whom I would more gladly serve than yourself. I think you must know this."

An eager glance for a moment dispelled the melancholy of her face, and then the old look returned with added force, as she answered:

"Yes, Paul, I believe what you say, and admit that you, of all men, could be of service; and yet you have no conception of the sacrifice you would entail upon yourself by the service you would render. Could I profit myself at the cost of your eternal sorrow? You do not know, and alas! I cannot explain; but the boon of my liberty would, I fear, only be purchased at the price of yours. I had not thought I should be so perplexed!"

He had not found the slightest relief from the embarrassing ignorance that enshrouded him. The girl's utter lack of coquetry, and her depth of feeling, made his position even more complex than it might otherwise have been.

"As you must know, I am talking in the dark," he continued after a minute, "but this much I will venture to assert, that no act of mine could be a sacrifice which would put my life in closer touch with yours; for although it was only yesterday that we met for the first time, I love you; and I loved you, Dorothy, from the instant I first caught sight of you at the station. I do not pretend to explain this, but have felt an overpowering passion from that moment."

"And you will not think me unmaidenly, Paul, if I say the same to you?"

She made no effort to conceal her feelings, and they sat murmuring sweet things into each other's ears until a green bird came fluttering through the air, and lighting upon a bough just above their heads, screamed:

"Dorothy! Dorothy!"

It was a parrot, and there was something so uncanny in its sudden appearance that Paul started:

"He seems to be your chaperone!" he observed.

"He is my mascot!" cried Dorothy. "If it were not for his company, I fear I should go mad. I am so lonely, Paul, you can not understand it."

"Have you no neighbors?" he inquired.

"None within miles; and we live such a strange isolated life that people are afraid of us."

Paul thought of the stage driver, and his look of horror on hearing where he was going.

"I can't understand why people should be afraid of you simply because you live alone," he said. "For my part, I think your life here is most interesting. But you have not told me how I can help you."

"Nor can I yet," she answered. "There is a way, of course, but I can not consent to so great a sacrifice from you; at least, not at present."

"And would it compel me to leave you?"

"No; it would compel you to be with me always."

"And have you so little faith in me as to call that a sacrifice? I did flatter myself that you believed what I told you just now."

"But, Paul, you do not know me. Wait until you do. Then, perhaps, you will change your mind."

She spoke with emphasis and a strange depth of feeling, and he wondered what she meant.

"I could never change, Dorothy," he replied with fervor, "unless you wished it; but if you did, do you know I believe it would not be in your power to reverse the bewildering spell you have wrought, and make me hate you, for never before have I felt anything approaching this strange sudden infatuation. But do not keep me in suspense; tell me, I pray, what is this mystery in your life which you think would change my feelings toward you?"

"I belong nowhere. I have no friend in all the wide world," she answered bitterly.

"You have forgotten Ah Ben," suggested Paul. She did not answer, but continued stroking the parrot which had lighted upon her shoulder, demanding her caresses with numerous mutterings.

"Modesty prevents my reminding you of my humble aspirations to your friendship," added Paul, nestling closer to her side. Suddenly she looked up at him with an intense penetrating gaze, while she squeezed the parrot until it screamed.

"Do you think you could show your friendship and stick to me through a terrible ordeal?" she asked earnestly.

"I'm sure of it," he answered. "My love is not so thin-skinned as to shrink from any test. Only try me!"

"Then get me away from this place," she cried, "far, *far* away from it. But, mind, it will not be so easy as you think."

"Are you held against your will?" demanded Paul.

"No, *no!* You can not understand it. But I could not go alone. I will explain it to you some time, but not now. There is no hurry."

"Is Ah Ben anxious to keep you?" inquired Henley.

"On the contrary, he wishes me to go. You can not understand me, as I am quite different from other girls. Only take my word for what I tell you; and when the time comes, you will not desert me, will you?"

There was something wildly entreating in her manner and the tones of her voice, and a pathos which went to Henley's heart. What it all was about he could no more imagine than he could account for any of the mysteries at Guir House; but he was determined to stand by Dorothy, come what might.

Suddenly the girl had become quiet, rapt in some new thought. In another minute she placed her hand lightly upon Paul's shoulder, and said:

"Remember, you have promised!"

"I have promised," answered Paul. "Is there anything more?"

"Yes," said Dorothy.

She paused for a minute, as if what she were about to say was a great effort.

"Well," he continued, "after I have got you safely away—which, by the by, does not seem such a difficult task, as no one opposes your going —but, after we have escaped together, what further am I to do?"

"Naturally, I feel great delicacy in what I am about to say," said Dorothy; "but since you have told me that you love me, it does not seem so hard, although you do not know who or what I am—but, to be candid and frank with you, dear Paul, after you have gotten me away—why, you must marry me!"

Paul snatched her up in his arms.

"My darling!" he said, "you are making me the proudest man on earth!"

"Do not speak too soon," said Dorothy, releasing herself from his grasp. "Remember I have told you frankly that you do not know me. Perhaps I am driving a hard bargain with you!"

For a moment Paul became serious.

"Tell me, Dorothy," he asked, in an altered tone, "have you, or Ah Ben, or any member of your mysterious household or family, any crimes to answer for? Is there any good reason why I, as an honest man, should object to taking you for my wife?"

She turned scarlet as she answered:

"Never! There is no such reason. There is nothing dishonorable, I swear to you—nothing which could implicate you in any way with wrong-doing. No, Paul; my secret is different from that. You could never guess it, nor could I ever compromise you with crime."

Her manner was sincere, and carried conviction to the hearer of the truth of what she said.

"It is time we were going to the house," she added, rising, with the parrot still upon her shoulder; and side by side they retraced their steps along the woodland way homeward.

5

Although Mr. Henley had no doubt of the truth of Miss Guir's assertion, the mystery of her life was as real and deeply impressive as ever. Perhaps it was even more so, as seeming more subtle and far-reaching than crime itself, if such a thing were possible. Paul was determined to investigate the secret of the closet stairs; for while Ah Ben's explanation was plausible to a degree, the blank wall and heavy door at the bottom filled him with an uncanny fascination, which grew as he pondered upon them. Exactly what course to pursue he had not decided, but awaited an opportunity to continue his efforts in earnest. There were two serious difficulties to contend with; one was the want of tools, the other the necessity of prose-cuting his work in silence.

As upon the previous evening, Dorothy and Mr. Henley dined alone, although Ah Ben, appearing just before they had finished, partook of a little dry lettuce and a small cup of coffee. Dorothy, as usual, ate most sparingly, "scarcely enough," as Paul remarked, "to keep the parrot alive."

After dinner they went together into the great hall, where Ah Ben prepared a pipe apiece for himself and his guest.

The logs were piled high upon the hearth, and the cheery blaze lit up the old pictures with a shimmering lustre, reducing the lamp to a mere spectral ornament. It was the flickering firelight that made the men and women on the walls nod at each other, as perhaps they had done in life.

They seated themselves in the spacious old leather-covered pew; Ah Ben and Dorothy upon one side, while Paul sat opposite. The men were soon engaged with their pipes, while Miss Guir had settled herself upon a pile of cushions in the corner nearest the chimney.

"You have been absent from home to-day, I believe," said Henley to the old man, by way of opening the conversation, and with the hope of eliciting an answer which would throw some light upon his habits.

"Yes," Ah Ben replied, blowing a volume of smoke from under his long, white moustache; "I seldom pass the entire day in this house.

There are few things that give me more pleasure than roaming alone through the forest. One seems to come in closer touch with first principles. Nature, Mr. Henley, must be courted to be comprehended."

"I suppose so," answered Paul, not knowing what else to say, and wondering at the man's odd method of passing the time.

A long silence followed after this, only interrupted at intervals by guttural mutterings from the parrot, which seemed to be lodged somewhere in the upper regions of the obscure stairway. When the clock struck eleven, the bird shrieked out, as upon the previous night.

"Dorothy! Dorothy! it is bed time!"

Miss Guir arose, and saying "Good night," left Ah Ben and Mr. Henley to themselves.

"I am afraid I have been very stupid," said the old man, apologetically; "indeed, I must have fallen asleep, as it is my habit to take a nap in the early evening, after which I am more wide awake than at any other hour."

"Not at all," answered Paul, "I have been enjoying my pipe, and as Miss Guir seemed disposed to be quiet, think I must have been nodding myself."

"Do you feel disposed to join me in another pipe and a midnight talk," inquired the host, "or are you inclined for bed?"

Paul was not sleepy, and nothing could have suited him better than to sit over the fire, listening to this strange man, and so he again accepted eagerly. Ah Ben seemed pleased, declaring it was a great treat to have a friend who was as much of an owl as he himself was. And so he added fresh fuel to the dying embers, settled himself in his cosy corner by the fire, while Paul sat opposite.

"Every man must live his own life," resumed Ah Ben; "but with my temper, the better half would be blotted out, were I deprived of this quiet time for thought and reflection."

"I quite agree with you," replied Paul, "and yet the wisdom of the world is opposed to late hours."

"The wisdom of the world is based upon the experience of the *worldly prosperous;* and what is worldly prosperity but the accumulation of dollars? To be prosperous is one thing; to be happy, quite another."

"I see you are coming back to our old argument. I am sure I could never school myself to the cheerful disregard for money which you seem to have. For my part, I could not do without it, although, to be sure, I sometimes manage on very little."

"Again the wisdom of the world!" exclaimed Ah Ben, "and what has it done for us?"

"It has taught us to be very comfortable in this latter part of the nineteenth century," Paul replied.

"Has it?" cried the old man, his eyes fixed full upon Henley's face.

"I admit," he continued, "that it has taught us to rely upon luxuries that eat out the life while pampering the body. It has taught us to depend upon the poison that paralyzes the will, and that personal power we were speaking of. It has done much for man, I grant you, but its efforts have been mainly directed to his destruction."

"No man can be happy without health," answered Paul, "and surely you will admit that the discoveries of the last few decades have done much to improve his physical condition."

He was nestling back into the corner of his lounge, where the shadow of the mantelpiece screened his face, and enabled him to look directly into Ah Ben's eyes, now fixed upon him with strange intensity. There was a power behind those eyes that was wont to impress the beholder with a species of interest which he felt might be developed into awe; and yet they were neither large nor handsome, as eyes are generally counted. Deep set, mounted with withered lids and shaggy brows, their power was due to the manifestation of a spiritual force, a Titanic will, that made itself felt, independent of material envelopment. It was the soul looking through the narrow window of mortality.

"Health?" said Ah Ben, repeating Henley's last idea interrogatively, and yet scarcely above a whisper.

"Yes, health," answered Paul. "I maintain that the old maxim of 'early to bed' says something on that score, as well as on that of wealth."

"True, but you said that a man must needs be healthy to be happy."

"That's it, and I maintain that it's a pretty good assertion."

"There again we must differ. Happiness should be independent of bodily conditions, whether those conditions mean outward luxury or inward ease. I must again refer you to the prize-fighter. But if you will pardon me, I think you have put the cart before the horse; for once having granted that personal power, happiness must ensue, and your health as a necessity follow. First cultivate this occult force, and we need submit to no physical laws; for inasmuch as the higher controls the lower, we are masters of our own bodies."

"That is a pretty good prescription for those who are able to follow it, but for my humble attainments I'd rather depend on physic and a virtuous life."

"Quite so," answered Ah Ben, thoughtfully, "but, speaking frankly, this limitation of your powers to the chemical action of your body only shows the narrowness of your scientific training. Had men been taught the power of the will as the underlying principle of every effect, one drug would have proved quite as efficacious as another, and bread pills would have met the requirements of the world."

"But in the state of imbecility in which we happen to find ourselves," added Paul, "I should think that a judicious application of the world's wisdom would be better than trifling with theories one does not comprehend."

"As I said just now," observed Ah Ben, "I have no desire to force my private views upon another, but I must distinctly object to the word 'theory,' as associated with my positive knowledge on this subject. Every man must do as he thinks right, and as suits him best; but, for my part, I have disregarded all the physical laws of health during an unusually long life."

Paul straightened himself up, and looked at his host in the hope of a further explanation.

"I don't think I quite understand you!"

"Yes," said Ah Ben, repeating the sentence slowly and emphasizing the words, "*I disregard all laws usually considered essential to living at all!*"

Henley was silent for a minute in a vain effort to decide whether or not he were speaking seriously. He could not help remembering his abstinence from food, but at the time had not doubted the man had eaten between meals.

"Then you certainly ought to know all about it," he continued, relaxing into his former position, but quite unsettled as to Ah Ben's intention.

"You must admit that I have had sufficient time to be an authority unto myself, if not to others," added the old man. And then as he pressed the ashes down into the bowl of his pipe with his long emaciated fingers, and watched the little threads of smoke as they came curling out from under his thick moustache, Paul could only admit that the gravity of his bearing was inconsistent with a humorous interpretation of his words.

"You interest me greatly," resumed Henley, after scrutinizing the singular face before him for several minutes, in a kind of mesmeric fascination, "and I should like to ask what you mean by the cultivation of this occult power of which you spoke?"

"It is only to be acquired by the supremest quality of self-control, as I told you yesterday," answered Ah Ben; "but when once gained, no man would relinquish it for the gold of a thousand Solomons! You would have proof of what I tell you? Well, some day perhaps you will!"

Henley started. The man had read his thoughts. It was the very question upon his lips.

"You are a mind reader!" cried Paul. "How did you know I was going to ask you that?"

Ah Ben made no answer; he did not even smile, but continued to gaze into the fire and blow little puffs of smoke toward the chimney.

"You referred just now to the prize-fighter," Paul resumed after a few minutes, "but I am going to squelch that argument."

"Yes," Ah Ben replied, now with his eyes half closed, "you are going to tell me that, although the man may have been battered and bruised, he really feels no pain, because of the unnatural excitement of the moment; but there you only rivet the argument against yourself; for I maintain—and not from theory, but from knowledge—that that very excitement is an exaltation of the spirit, which may be cultivated and relied upon to conquer pain and the ills of the flesh forever!"

"It would go far indeed if it could do all that, although I believe there is something in what you say, for in a small way I have seen it myself."

"Yes, we have all seen it in a small way; and does it not seem strange that men have never thought of cultivating it in a larger way, through the exercise of their will in controlling their minds and bodies? This exaltation of spirit is only attained through effort, or some great physical shock. It is the secret of all power; it conquers all pain, and makes disease impossible."

"Makes disease impossible!" cried Paul in astonishment.

"Yes," answered the elder man quietly. "This soul power, of which I speak, is the hidden akasa in all men—it is the man himself—and when once recognized, the body is relegated to its proper sphere as the servant, and not the master; then it is that man realizes his own power and supremacy over all things."

"But," persisted Henley, "if you go so far as to say that this occult or soul power can conquer disease, you would have us all living forever!"

"We do live forever," answered Ah Ben.

"Yes, after death; but I mean here!"

"*There is no such thing as death!*" remarked Ah Ben quietly, as if he were merely giving expression to a well-established scientific fact.

"And yet we see it about us every day," Paul replied.

"There you are wrong, for no man has ever seen that which never occurs!"

"You are quibbling with words," suggested Henley.

"There is a change at a certain period in a man's life, which, from ignorance, people have agreed to call death. But it is a misnomer, for man never dies. He goes right on living; and it is generally a considerable time before he realizes the change that has taken place in him. He would laugh at the word death, as understood upon earth, as indeed he frequently does, for he is far more alive than ever before."

"You speak as if you knew all this," said Paul. "One might almost imagine that you had been in the other world yourself."

"*Had been!*" exclaimed the old man with emphasis. "*I am in it now, and so are you. But there is a difference between us; I know that I am in it, because I can see it, and touch it, and hear it; while you are in it without knowing it.*"

There was an air of authority that impressed the hearer with the conviction of the speaker. This was not theory; it was the result of experience. There was a difference as vast as the night from the day.

"I suppose, when I am dead, I shall know these things too," said Paul meditatively.

"No," answered Ah Ben, "not when you are dead, but when you have been born—when you have come into life."

"Pardon me," answered Paul, pondering on the man's strange assertion; "but this knowledge of yours is in demand more than all other knowledge. Positive information about the other world is what men have sought through all the ages; why do you not impart it to them?"

"Impart it!" exclaimed Ah Ben. "Can you explain to one who has been born blind what it is to see? Can you impart to such a man any true conception of the world in which he has always lived? But *couch* his eyes, remove the worthless film that has covered them, and for the first time he realizes the glorious world surrounding him. Likewise *couch* the body, remove the shell that covers the spirit, and it is born."

"I perceive, then, that it is only through death that most of us can hope to gain this knowledge."

"Death, if you prefer the word," said Ah Ben. "Yes, it is the death of the film over the eye that reveals the world to the blind; but I should hardly say that the man was dead because he had so entered into another existence."

"Would you mind telling me how it is that you have gained this knowledge in such obvious exception to the rule!"

"The power of the occult is dormant in all men," answered Ah Ben; "and as I have already said, may be developed slowly, through the exercise of the will, or suddenly, as in some great physical shock, and of a necessity comes to all in the event called death. Were I to tell you how *I* acquired this knowledge, Mr. Henley, it would startle you, far more than any exhibition of the power itself. No, I can not tell you; at least, not at present; perhaps some day you may be better prepared to hear it."

The spark in the hanging lamp had almost expired, and the fire was reduced to a mere handful of coals, casting an erubescent glow over the pew and its occupants. Ah Ben stretched his hand toward the chimney, and as he did so, a ball of misty light appeared against it, just below the mantel. It was ill defined and hazy, like the reflection a firefly will sometimes make against the ceiling of a darkened room; but it was fixed, and Paul was sure it had not been there a moment before.

"Do you see that?" asked the old man, breaking the silence.

"Yes," answered Paul; "and I was just wondering what it could be."

"Watch! and you will see."

They sat with their eyes fixed; but while Paul was staring into the mantel, Ah Ben was looking at him.

"Observe how it grows," and even as he spoke the strange illumination deepened, until it assumed the distinct and definite form of a lamp. Then the mantelpiece dissolved into nothingness, and Paul was staring through the chimney into a strange room, whose form and contents were dimly revealed by the curious lamp which occupied a table in the centre. Two persons sat at this table, the one a woman, the other a boy, and near at hand was an English army officer. The woman was small, with dark eyes and hair, and a skin the color of tan bark. Her head was bowed forward and rested upon her arms, which were crossed upon the table. The man was looking down at her with a troubled expression, and in a minute he stooped forward and kissed the top of her head; he then turned suddenly and left the room. The scene was distinct, although the outer part of the room was in shadow. Presently the woman threw herself to the floor with a heart-rending shriek, and Paul started up, exclaiming:

"What has happened? She will wake everybody in the house!"

He bounded to his feet; but as he did so, the lamp in the strange room went out, and the chimney closed over the scene, leaving him with his old surroundings. Looking up at Ah Ben, he said:

"I must have fallen asleep. I've been dreaming."

"Not at all," answered Ah Ben. "You've been quite as wide awake as I have, and we've been looking at the same thing."

Paul demanded the proof, which the old man gave by telling him what he had seen in every detail.

"Then it's magic!" said Henley, "for surely no room can be visible through that chimney."

"That," answered Ah Ben, "is mere assertion, which you can never prove."

"Do you mean to tell me that the thing was real? There is a secret about this house which I do not understand!"

His manner was excited. He felt that he had been the dupe of the man before him, the prey to some clever trick; the thing was too preposterous, too unreasonable.

"Be calm," said Ah Ben; "there is nothing in this that should disturb you. The room has disappeared from our sight, and will no more trouble us. Shall we have another pipe?"

The words had an instantaneous effect, so that Paul resumed his seat and pipe, as if nothing had happened. For several minutes he sat silently gazing at vacancy, and listening to the north wind as it moaned through the old pines. He was trying to account for what he had seen, but could not. The mystery was deepening into an overpowering gloom. The house, with its eccentric inmates; the girl Dorothy, with her freaks and manner of living; the odd circumstance of the stairway in his closet; these, and other things, flashed upon his memory in a confused jumble, and seemed as inexplicable as the vision just witnessed through the chimney.

Suddenly a thought struck him. Could this last have been hypnotism? He put the question straight to Ah Ben. The man passed his withered hand over his face thoughtfully as he answered:

"Hypnotism, Mr. Henley, is a name that is used in the West for a condition that has been known in the East for thousands of years as the underlying principle of *all phenomena*."

"And what is that condition?" Paul inquired.

"*Sympathetic vibration*," answered the elder man.

"Vibration of what?" asked Paul.

"Of the mind," said Ah Ben. "The condition of the universal mind vibrating in our material plane, or within the range of our physical senses, is represented in the trees and the rocks, in the earth and the stars. Our physical senses, being attuned to his form of vibration, are in sympathy with it, and apprehend all its phenomena. There is but one mind, of which man is a part. Thought is a product of mind. Thought is real, and, when sufficiently concentrated, becomes tangible and visible to those who can be brought into sympathy with its vibrations. There is but one primal substance, which is mind. Mind creates all things out of itself; therefore, to change the world we look at, it is only necessary to change our minds."

"Let me ask if what I saw was hypnotism?" repeated Henley. "I ask this, first, because I know it is impossible to see through a brick wall, even if there should be such a room in the house; and, secondly, because I can not believe that I was dreaming, consequently the thing could not have been real."

"Hypnotism is a good enough word," answered Ah Ben; "but that which men generally understand by the real, and that which they consider the unreal, are not so far apart as they suppose. You say the room was not real, and yet you saw it; had you wished, you might have touched it, which is certainly all the evidence you have of the existence of the room in which we are now sitting. Hypnotism is not a cause of hallucination, as is commonly supposed, but of fact. Its effects are not illusory, but real. Perhaps it would be more correct to say that they are *as real* as anything else, and that *all* the phenomena of nature are mere illusions of the senses, which they undoubtedly are. But whichever side we take, all appearances are the result of the same general cause—that of mental vibration. Matter has no real existence."

Paul was meditating on what he had seen and what he was now hearing. Ah Ben's words were endowed with an added force by the vision of the mysterious room.

"When you tell me that there is practically no difference between the real and the unreal, and that matter has no real existence, I must confess to some perplexity," observed Henley.

Ah Ben looked up and smoothed the furrows in his withered cheek thoughtfully for a minute before he answered:

"Unfortunately, Mr. Henley, language is not absolute or final in its power to convey thought, and the best we can do is to use it as carefully as possible to express ourselves, which we can only hope to do approximately. Therefore when I say that a thing is hot or cold, or hard or soft, I only mean that it is so by comparison with certain other things; and when I say that matter has no existence, I mean that it has no independent existence—no existence outside of the mind that brought it into being. I mean that it was formed by mind, formed out of mind, and that it continues to exist in mind as a part of mind. I mean that it is an appearance objective to our point of consciousness on the material plane; but inasmuch as it was formed by thought, it can be reformed by thought, which could never be if it existed independently of thought. It is real in the sense of apparent objectivity, and not real in the sense of independent objectivity, and yet it affects us in precisely the same manner as if it were independent of thought. What, then, is the difference between matter as viewed from the Idealist's or the Materialist's point of view? At first there is apparently none, but a deeper insight will show us that the difference is vast and radical, for in the one case the tree or the chair that I am looking at, owing its very existence to mind, is governed by mind, which could never be did they exist as separate and distinct entities. Therefore I say with perfect truth that matter does not exist in the one sense, and yet that it does exist in the other. I dream of a green field; a beautiful landscape, never before beheld; I awake and it is gone. Where was that enchanting scene? I can tell you: for it was in the mind, where everything else is. But upon waking I have changed my mind, and the scene has vanished. Thus it is with the Adept of the East, with the Yoghis, the Pundit, the Rishis, and the common Fakir; through the power of hypnotism they alter the condition of the subject's mind, and with it his world has likewise undergone a change. You say this is not real, that it is merely illusion; but in reply I would say that these illusions have been subjected to the severest tests; their reality has been certified to by every human sense, and when an illusion responds to the sense of both sight and touch, when the sense of sight is corroborated by that of touch, or by any other of the five senses, what *better* evidence have we of the existence of those things we are all agreed to call real? Yes, I know what you are about to say, you object upon the ground that only a small minority are witnesses of the marvels of Eastern magic; but you are wrong, for I have seen hundreds of men in a public square all eye-witnesses to precisely the same occult phenomena at once. Now if certain hundreds could be so impressed, why not other hundreds? And with a still more powerful hypnotizer, why could not a majority—nay, all of those in a certain district, a certain State, a certain country, *in the world*—be made to see and feel things which now, and to us, have no existence? In that case, Mr. Henley, would it be the majority or the minority who were deceived? *All is mind*, and the hypnotizer merely alters it."

"You said just now," answered Paul, "that matter, being mind, was governed by mind, and that the tree or chair before me, owing its existence to mind, is subject to that mind; do you mean by that to say that the existence of that sofa, as a sofa, may be transformed into something else by mental action alone?"

"I do," said Ah Ben, "under certain conditions; namely, the condition called hypnotism. On this material plane we are imprisoned; the will is not free to operate upon its environment, but in the spiritual state this dependence and slavery to the appearances we call realities is cast aside; the will becomes free and controls its own environment—in short, we are out of prison. But even here, Mr. Henley, by practicing the self-control we were speaking of, the will becomes so powerful that it can sometimes break through the bondage of matter, which, after all, is no more real than the stuff a dream is made of, and mold its prison walls into any form it chooses; in which case, of course, it is no longer a prison, and the other world is achieved without the change called death!"

"And why do you call it a prison, if no more real than a dream?"

"Have you ever had the nightmare? If so, you must know that your will was insufficient to free you from the horrid scene that had taken such forcible hold of you. Was the nightmare real or not?"

Paul was silent for several minutes. He could not deny the reality of the scene through the chimney, for it had the same forceful existence to him as anything in life. Ah Ben, seeing that he was still puzzling himself over the problem of mind and matter, the puzzle of life, the great sphinx riddle of the ages, said:

"Let me ask you a question, Mr. Henley—I might say several questions—which may possibly tend to throw a little light upon this subject, and perhaps convince you that matter is really mind."

"Ask as many as you like."

"Pantheism," continued Ah Ben, "is scoffed at by many people calling themselves Christians as being idolatrous, and yet to me it is the most ennobling of all creeds. Without knowing anything of your religious faith, I would first ask if you believe in God?"

Paul answered affirmatively.

"Do you look upon him as a personal Deity—I mean as an exaggerated man in size and power—or as a Spirit?"

"As a Spirit," Paul replied.

"Very well, then; do you believe that Spirit is infinite or finite?"

"Infinite."

"Then, if it is infinite, there can be no part of space in which it does not exist."

"That is my idea also."

"If, then, that Spirit exists everywhere, it must penetrate all matter; in fact, all matter must, in its very essence, be a part of it; it must be formed out of the very substance of this infinite Spirit or Mind. Hence all is mind!"

"That seems clear enough," said Paul; "in which case it seems to me that we are a part of God ourselves, and God being spirit, we must be spirits now."

"Of course we are," answered Ah Ben; "as I have already told you, we are in the spiritual world now, although much of it is screened from our view, because we are temporarily imprisoned in a lower vibratory plane, called matter."

Ah Ben arose, and procuring candles, which he lighted by the expiring fire, the men went to their beds.

6

It was past midnight, and the house quiet, when Paul determined to have another look at the mysterious door at the foot of his closet stairs. He had sat for more than an hour before his bedroom fire, after bidding Ah Ben good-night, to make sure that the inmates of Guir House had retired; and as not a sound had been heard since locking his door, he sincerely hoped they were asleep. Before descending into the noisome depths, however, he concluded to climb up into his window, and have another look at the beautiful panorama of mountain and woodland shimmering in the meagre light of a hazy sky and a moon past full. The uncertain outline of a distant horizon; the interminable stretch of forest, which bore away upon every hand; the rugged heights, now soft and colorless; the aromatic smell of pine and fir; the distant murmur of falling water; and the assonant whispering of wind in the tree tops, had all become strangely fascinating to him, more so than such things had ever been before. "Never was a house so situated, so lost to the world, so tightly held in the lap of unregenerate nature," thought Paul; "no laugh of child, no shout of man, no bark of dog, nor bellowing beast to break the stillness of the midnight air; an impenetrable, imperturbable, and silent wilderness shuts out the busy world, as we know it, forever and forever. It is a fitting place for such witchery as the old man seems master of, and I do not wonder that he has chosen it for his home; but the girl—the poor girl!—she must get away!" He closed the window, and prepared for his descent into the well.

Removing his shoes, he put on a pair of soft felt slippers, and then, with candle in his hand, a box of matches and a revolver in his pocket, entered the closet, and opened the scuttle in the floor. A mouldy smell rose upon the air, and Henley recoiled at the thought of what might be in waiting below. He had not the slightest idea of how he should open the door at the bottom, but would make a careful study of the situation, hoping that a solution of the difficulty would present itself. The steps creaked dismally as he placed his weight upon them, and it was necessary to use extreme caution to avoid breaking through the more rotten ones. He had not descended more than a dozen, when there was a terrible crash above his head, and he found himself in absolute darkness. The trap had fallen as upon the previous night, he having forgotten to fasten it back, and the wind had blown out his candle. Henley hastened back up the stairs, fearful lest the noise had waked some one in the house, and without relighting his candle threw himself upon the bed to await developments. After listening for some minutes, and hearing nothing, he became convinced that no one had been disturbed; and so, creeping out of bed, and lighting his candle by the dying embers in the fireplace, started in afresh. This time he was careful to fasten back the scuttle door, and in doing so discovered that one of the great iron hinges was loose. It was more than two feet long, and with very little difficulty he managed to wrench it off, thinking it might possibly be of service in forcing the door at the bottom. He was careful this time to let the scuttle down quietly after him, thinking it safer to do this than to prop it open.

The bottom was reached in safety after the usual doleful crunching and creaking of the timber, and Paul sat down on the bottom step, with his candle, to rest and quiet himself, before proceeding with his work upon the door. A dead stillness reigned all about him, broken only by the occasional resettling of the steps above his head, but which, to his excited brain, was like the report of a pistol; still even this ceased in a few minutes, and the silence was undisturbed. He now made a careful examination of the door. It was very heavy, and solid. Holding his candle close against the crack, he could see, to his surprise, that it was bolted upon the inside. Placing his ear close against the keyhole, he listened, but it was silent as a tomb within; and how the door became fastened upon the inside was inexplicable, unless indeed there was another outlet, which from his examination of the building had seemed improbable. Then, taking out his knife, he stuck it into the wood in various directions to ascertain the condition of its preservation. The door itself was in an excellent state; but in examining the lintel, the blade of his knife suddenly sank into the rotten wood up to the handle. Here, then, was the place to begin operations, and fortunately it was on the side from which the door opened. Henley had soon dug away a great segment of decayed wood, exposing the bolt clearly to view. Then taking the hinge which he had brought with him, and slipping the small end between the bolt and the frame of the door, he used it as a lever to pry against the bolt within. The iron was so old and rusty, and his purchase so poor, that he only succeeded in making a rasping sound where the two metals scraped against each other, and so stopped, discouraged. Presently he bethought him of his handkerchief, which he wrapped carefully around the end of the hinge, and thus not only gained a better purchase, increasing his leverage, but was able to operate without the slightest sound. It was a long time before the bolt moved, but to his intense gratification it did move at last, and Henley took a fresh grip upon his hinge. Backward and forward he worked his lever, and with each turn the old bolt slipped back a little. At last he could see the end of it, and then it was clear of the frame entirely. He had expected no difficulty in opening the door when the hinge was once slipped, but to his surprise it was still immovable. He pulled and tugged and pushed, but it would not budge; then suddenly, just as he was about to give up, it came tumbling down upon him, so that he was barely able to save it from falling against the stairs with a terrible crash, but fortunately caught it upon his shoulder, and lowered it to the floor without a sound. Imagine his surprise in going to what he now believed to be the open portal, to find that the doorway had been bricked up from within, and that the door itself had simply been the back of a solid wall. Naturally, he was disappointed at finding himself no nearer the inner chamber than before. A careful examination of the masonry showed that the work of bricking up the entrance had undoubtedly been done from the other side, and after the door had been closed and bolted. This was evidenced from the fact that there was no mortar next the door, against the smooth inner surface of which the bricks had been closely laid. Henley worked his hinge between some of the looser joints, and found, just as he expected, that the mortar had been laid from within. By degrees he managed to wedge one of the bricks out of its place, and then pulled it bodily from the wall. The inner surface was plastered over. He tried another, which he got out more easily, and it told the same tale. Then he went to work in earnest, and had soon dug a hole large enough to admit his body. Leaning over into the aperture, with his candle at arm's length, the place looked dark and empty, with faint masses of lighter shadow. Then, with a certain indescribable awe, Henley commenced crawling through the breach. Stepping upon an earthern floor, he found himself in a vault-like chamber—damp, mouldy, and foul of atmosphere. He glanced hurriedly about, and then turned to examine the wall through which he had come. Just as he had surmised, the bricks had been laid from the inner side, and plastered over within. The person who had done the work must have had some other means of escape. This set him to wondering where the other entrance could be, and to a careful search around the wall; but there was no door, no window, nor opening of any kind. How had the work been done? While he was wondering, he stumbled over something in the floor, and, recovering, threw back his head, holding his candle high above it. He was startled by the sight of what appeared to be four shadowy human faces, looking directly at him from above. Instinctively he sought his revolver, but before drawing it perceived that what he had taken for living people were simply four portraits, of the most remarkable character he had ever beheld. Paul stared in bewilderment at the sight before him. The pictures were so old, their canvases so rotten and mildewed and stained with the accumulated fungi of time and darkness that it was only by degrees that the intention of the artist became manifest. In the hall and other apartments of the old house, Henley thought he had seen the most original and inexplicable pictures ever painted; but here, buried forever from the sight of human eyes, were the most dreadful countenances ever transcribed from life or the imagination of man. Torture was clearly depicted upon each face; but not torture alone, for horror, fright, and mental agony were strangely blended in each. Not a face that looked down upon him from those antiquated frames but bore that agonized, heart-broken, terrified expression. Paul was paralyzed; a kind of mesmeric spell held him to the spot, so that he could not remove his eyes from the uncanny scene before him. Then a wild desire to be rid of the place forever seized him, and he stepped backward. At the same minute he observed for the first time what looked like some faded letters painted upon the wall directly beneath the four mysterious portraits. Examining these with his candle, he saw that they formed the words:

"The last of the Guirs."

"No wonder Dorothy said that she was afraid of them," Paul reflected; "their portraits alone would drive me mad." He took another long searching look; and as his eyes grew accustomed to the faded coloring, he observed how cleverly the work had been done. Evidently the pictures had been painted from life, though under what circumstances Henley could never imagine. The faces were all those of a feminine type; they were of young women, apparently but little more than girls, and each with this life-like, though dreadful expression. As Paul stood marveling and wondering, a new interest seized him. At first he could not quite understand what it was, but it became stronger and better defined, he knew, for he recognized one of the faces. Yes, there could be no mistake about it; the picture on the left was a *portrait of Dorothy herself.* Henley rubbed his eyes, and looked again and again; he could not believe their evidence, but they had not deceived him. He tried to make himself believe that it was the likeness of some ancestor, to whom she had a strange resemblance; but, despite the look of pain, it could be no other than Dorothy, and indeed this very expression helped to heighten the likeness, for had he not seen a similar expression at the breakfast table? The longer he gazed at it, the more convinced he became that this was a portrait of Miss Guir. At last, thoroughly mystified, he turned away, intending to leave this grewsome chamber of horrors forever; but now for the first time the heap of rubbish in the center of the floor engaged his attention. Taking his hinge, he stirred up the mass; some shreds of cloth, which fell to pieces on being touched, and beneath them some human bones. This was all, but it was enough; and overwhelmed with horror, Henley rushed out of the room, bounding through the aperture he had made in the wall, and up the rickety stairs into his own bed chamber. He carefully closed the scuttle, heaped some firewood upon it, shut the closet door and fastened it securely from without. He then built up a roaring fire, lit another candle, and sat meditating over what he had seen until the dawn of day. When the light of the sun came streaming into his room, he undressed and went to bed.

Whatever may have been Mr. Henley's suspicions concerning the implication of the Guirs with the crime which he could no longer doubt had been committed in their house, they were promptly dispelled, so far as the young lady was concerned, upon meeting Dorothy at the breakfast table. Her innocent though serious face was a direct rebuke to any distrust he might have entertained; and he even doubted if she had any knowledge of the state of things he had discovered in the vault. This, of course, only added to the mystery; nor was Mr. Henley's self-esteem fortified by the memory of how unscrupulously he had become the guest of these people, and of how equivocal had been his treatment of their hospitality. All this, however, related to the past, and, as he felt, could not be now undone. He must act to the best of his ability in the extraordinary position in which he found himself.

After breakfast they walked again into the garden, and while Paul smoked his cigarette, meditatively, Dorothy gathered flowers for the house. There was an earnestness in everything that she did, quite unusual in a girl of her age, and at times her manner was grave and sad, but strangely attractive, nevertheless. When she had completed her labors in the garden, she came and seated herself beside him.

"Some day, Paul, we'll have a cheerier home than this; won't we?" she said, looking wistfully up at the quaint old pile before them.

"I don't think we could have a more romantic one," he answered; and then, hoping to elicit an explanatory answer, added, "but why should Guir House not seem cheerful to you?"

"I don't know; it has always been gloomy; don't you think so?"

"Not having known it always, Dorothy, I am not in a position to judge; but it will always be the sweetest place on earth to me, because I met you here for the first time."

"Yes, I know; but you must not forget your promise."

She seemed nervous and anxious concerning his fulfillment of it.

"And do you suppose that I could ever forget anything you asked me? No, Dorothy, while you will it, I am your slave; but, as I told you before, you exert such a strange power over me that you could make me hate and fear you. I don't know why this should be so, but I feel it!"

"Hush!" she said, extending her outstretched hand toward his mouth; "do not talk in that way; you frighten me; for, O Paul! I was just beginning to hope that in you I had found a friend who would never shrink away from me. Do not tell me that you will ever become afraid of me like the others. I could not bear it."

"I shrink! God forbid," he answered, "but tell me why are other people afraid of you? You mystify me."

"Because I am different—so different from them!"

"I'm quite sure of that," he replied, "else I should never have come to love you within an hour of meeting you."

She did not smile; she did not even look up at him, but sat gazing at nothing, with countenance as solemn and imperturbable as that of a Sphinx.

"How am I ever to understand you, Dorothy, you seem such a riddle?" said Paul presently.

"You will never understand me," she answered with a sigh. "No one ever has understood me, and you will be just like the rest!"

"But you will never let me be afraid of you, like the others, will you?" he exclaimed half in earnest.

"I don't know; others are; why should not you be?"

She was still staring into vacancy, with her hands clasped, and Paul thought he detected a little, just a little, of the same expression he had seen in the portrait. He started, and Dorothy saw him.

"What is the matter?" she inquired, looking around at him for the first time.

"Nothing; only you looked so dreadfully in earnest, you startled me."

"But surely you would not be startled by so simple a thing as that!"

"Why not? I am only human," he answered.

"Yes, but I am sure there was something else. Now tell me, was there not?"

"Why, how strangely you talk!" he replied, searching her face for an explanation. "Of course there wasn't; why should there be?"

She leaned back, apparently still in doubt as to his assertion, while her countenance grew even more grave than before. Henley was puzzled, and while Dorothy had not ceased to charm him, he was conscious of a very slight uneasiness in her presence. This, however, wore off a little later when they went together for a stroll in the forest. The girl's extreme delicacy of appearance, her abstracted, melancholy manner, and sincerity of expression, both attracted and perplexed Paul, and kept him constantly at work endeavoring to solve her character and form some conception of the mystery of her life. He had not yet had even the courage to ask her if Ah Ben were her father, dreading to expose himself as an impostor and be ordered from the place, which, despite his discovery of the previous night, he could only regard as an unmitigated hardship in the present state of his feelings; and so he had let the hours slip by, constantly hoping that something would occur to explain the whole situation to him. And yet nothing had occurred, and now upon the third day he was as grossly ignorant of the causes which had produced his strange environment as at the moment of his arrival.

"One thing I do not understand," Paul observed, as they wandered over the vari-colored leaves, side by side; "it is why you should be so anxious to leave this ideal spot."

"Have I not told you that it is because I am out of my element; because I am avoided; because I have not a friend far nor near! Oh, Paul, you do not know what it is to be alone in the world!"

"And do you believe that a simple change of locality would alter all this?" he asked.

She paused for a moment before answering, and then, looking down upon the ground, said as if with some effort:

"No, not that alone."

"What then, Dorothy?" he asked with solicitude.

"I have already told you," she replied without looking up. "Oh, Paul, what a short memory you must have!"

"Of course I understand that we are to be married," he responded hastily, "but how can that alter the situation? Dorothy, if we have not found congenial friends in that position in life in which God or nature has placed us, how can we hope to make them in another? Do you not think there may be some deeper reason than simple locality and single blessedness? Would it not be natural to look for the cause in the individual?"

"Undoubtedly you are right," she answered, "but your premises do not apply to my case, for neither God nor nature ever intended that I should live this life. Oh, Paul, believe me when I tell you that I know whereof I speak. Do not judge me as you would another; some day you may know, but I can not tell you now."

She spoke pleadingly, as imploring to be released from some awful incubus which it was impossible to explain. Paul listened in deep perplexity, and swore that the powers of heaven and earth should never come between them. So different was she from any girl that he had ever seen, that her very eccentricity bound him to her with a magic spell. When he had again asked her if Ah Ben would oppose their marriage, or indeed if any one else would, she declared that no human being would raise a voice against it.

"Then what is to hinder us?" he asked; "I am poor, but I can support you; not perhaps in such luxury as you are accustomed to, but I can give you a home; and if you are so unhappy here, why submit to unnecessary delay?"

He had become impassioned and enthused by the girl's strange influence over him.

"True, Paul, there are none to hinder us," she replied seriously, "that is, no one but—but——"

She paused, not knowing how to proceed.

"Then there is some one," cried Paul earnestly. "I thought as much. Who might the gentleman be?"

"Yourself!" exclaimed Dorothy, her eyes still fixed upon the ground.

"Myself!" shouted he in amazement. "Do you mean to say that I should oppose my own marriage with the girl I love?"

"You might," she answered demurely, casting a side glance up at him, and allowing the very faintest, saddest kind of smile to rest for an instant upon her face.

"Well!" said Paul, "I do not suppose you will explain what you mean, but it would be only natural that I should like to know."

"I only mean," she replied, resuming her meditative attitude, "that you do not know me; that you neither know who nor what I am. If I did not love you, I might deceive and entrap you, but not under the circumstances."

Later they returned to the house.

7

It was not until Mr. Henley had made another and longer visit to the dark room that he became convinced beyond all doubt that the work of sealing up the place had been done from within, and that there was, and had been, no other outlet but that through which he had entered. To suppose that the main wall of the house had been closed in at a later period would be preposterous, and for manifest reasons. His examination of the room's interior had been most thorough and exhaustive. The place was smoothly plastered upon the inside, and even the mason's trowel had been found upon the floor within, so that it became at once evident that those who had done the work had been self-immured. Although the reason for such an act was utterly beyond his comprehension, Paul felt a certain satisfaction in having reached this conclusion, as it showed the impossibility of Dorothy's being in any way implicated in the affair. It seemed even possible that she was ignorant of it. But this discovery in no wise lessened the mystery; it rather increased it.

A few evenings after Paul's decision regarding the self-immurement of those discovered in the vault, he and Ah Ben were again enjoying their pipes by the great fireplace in the hall. The elder man was generally disposed to conversation at this hour; and after Dorothy had retired, Paul alluded to the strange scene he had witnessed through the chimney, and expressed a desire to learn something of occultism. Taking his long-stemmed pipe from his lips, the old man gazed earnestly into the fire. He seemed to be thinking of what to say, and to be drawing inspiration from the glowing embers and dancing flames before him. At last he spoke:

"Occultism, Mr. Henley, is difficult—nay, almost impossible—to explain to a layman; or if explained, remains incomprehensible; and yet a child may acquire its secrets by its individual efforts. Spiritual power comes to those who seek it in proper mood, but, injudiciously exercised, may cause insanity."

"Nevertheless," urged Paul, "if you won't consider me a trifler, I should like to see a further manifestation of the power."

Ah Ben looked at him compassionately.

"Pardon me, Mr. Henley," he said, "but it is not always well to gratify our curiosity upon such a subject; but if you seriously wish it, and can believe in me as an honest and honorable custodian of the power, and will prepare yourself for a serious mental shock, I will show you something."

"Before proceeding," said Paul, "I should like to ask you a question. Was the room I saw through the chimney a real room? I mean had it any material existence upon earth?"

"Most assuredly. It was a scene in my early childhood, and originated in the Valley of the Jhelum, in the Punjab. The officer and lady were my parents. It was the last time I ever saw them. I was the boy."

"May I ask how it is possible to reproduce a scene so long passed out of existence, and which took place so many thousand miles away?"

"Easily told, but not so easily understood by one whose mind has never been trained to think in these occult channels," answered the elder man; "for to understand the thing at all, you must first divest your mind of time and space as outside entities, for these are in reality but modes of thought, and have only such value as we give them. India, doubtless, seems very far to you, but to one whose powers of will have been sufficiently developed, it is no farther than the wall of this room. So it is with time. How can we see that which no longer exists? But a little reflection will show us that even on the physical plane we see that which does not exist every day of our lives. Look at the stars. The light by which some of them are recognized has been millions of years in transit, so that we do not behold them as they are to-night, but as they were at that remote period of time; meanwhile they may have been wrecked and scattered in meteoric dust."

"But that is hardly an explanation of the scene referred to," answered Paul. "Whenever I direct my eyes in the right quarter, the stars are visible; whether they be actually there or not, they are there to me; but not so with the vision of the room. In my normal condition there is no room there, while in my normal condition the stars are always there."

"True, and because your normal condition is sympathetically attuned to the vibrations of starlight. Your consciousness is located in your brain, and so long as those vibrations continue to strike with sufficient force upon the optic nerve, you will be conscious of the light. But suppose the machinery of your body were finer—suppose your senses were absolutely in accord with those vibratory movements, instead of only partially so— do you not know that the starlight would reveal far more than it now does? Then you would see not only the light, but the scenes that are carried in the light, but which by reason of their obtuseness can not penetrate your senses. Were this improvement in men really achieved, our conceptions of time and space would be modified, and the condition of other worlds as plainly seen as our own."

"Yes," said Paul, determined to follow up the original question, "but what of a scene that occurred in this world some years ago, and whose light vibrations would require but the fraction of a second to reach our point of consciousness—no matter where situated on earth—and which vibrations have long since passed beyond the reach of man, and been lost in infinite space?"

"Nothing is ever lost, and infinite space is but a phase of infinite mind. All that is necessary to review such a picture is to change our point of consciousness from the brain to a point in space or *mind*, where the vibratory movement is still in progress. In other words, to overtake the scene by transposing our consciousness. Granted these powers, which are born of the soul, and we may behold any event in history with the clearness of its original force. Man is mind, and mind is one; but all mind is not self-conscious. The consciousness of mind is in spots, as it were, and here its consciousness is fixed in a spot called brain, where with most men it remains until the will, or some abnormal condition or the event called death, liberates it from its prison. You believe that with your God, the scenes of yesterday, to-day, and forever are alike visible?"

"Even admitting all that you say," answered Paul, "I can not see how it was that I, who have no such power, could see clearly an event in your life."

"Again the power of sympathetic vibration. The scene was reflected from my mind to yours."

"But you just now said there was but one mind."

"Perhaps then it would be more correct to say, from my point of consciousness to yours; or, to be still more accurate, to say that the intensity of my thoughts struck a sympathetic chord in yours, and vibrated through you as one consciousness. Without undue familiarity, Mr. Henley, I have found in you a responsive temperament. There are few men I can not influence, and with some the effort is trifling."

Paul was interested, and sat quietly reflecting upon what he had heard. Naturally the ideas were not so clear as they would have been had he given more thought to the conditions of spirituality, which for so many years had been a part of Ah Ben's existence, and which state was as familiar to him as the body in which he appeared. Time and reflection alone, as this strange man had declared, could bring one to comprehend and realize a condition of existence so totally differing from that of our material plane. The inability of language to express that of which we have no parallel, and of which we can not conceive, is a grave obstacle to our understanding; but the man was ever ready to exert himself to make the matter clear when he found his listener interested.

"If I am not tiring you," continued Paul, "I should like to call your attention to another point. You said that nothing was absolute; that all was relative; and yet when it comes to fixed measures, I think you must admit that this is not so. For example, a mile is a mile, and a mile must always be a mile under every conceivable condition. Am I not right?"

"At first thought it would seem so," answered Ah Ben. "A mile certainly appears to be an absolute unchanging quantity of so many feet, which must always and under every circumstance affect us in the same way; and yet a little reflection will show that this can not be so, and that a mile, after all, is only fixed so long as our mind is fixed. In other words, it is a mental conception, and relative to other mental conceptions. Let us, for example, suppose that the world and all its contents, and, in fact, the entire universe, were exactly twice as large as it is, the mile would then be twice as long as it is now; and that which we *now* call a mile would only make the impression of half as much distance as it now does. And so with all material conditions; I say *material*, for in the spiritual life we see these things more truly as they are, and not as they appear. There is but one class of facts which is absolute. I speak of the emotions. These are the realities of life—the soul qualities. Could we measure *love*, *hate*, or *happiness*, the standard would be fixed."

"Do not forget your promise to show me something more of your power in the region of occultism," said Henley, "for I am greatly interested."

"I will keep my word, but I warn you to prepare for a shock!"

"I am ready, and should like nothing better than to witness an example of your greatest power!"

The old man looked solemn, and then slowly answered:

"You shall be gratified. It is now past midnight. Dorothy is asleep, and it is a fitting time. If you will follow me to my own room, I will show you a mystery."

For a moment Paul hesitated. The thought of following this strange man at such an hour into the realm of the unknown, to investigate the supernatural, was uncanny, and he half wished he had not made the request. He knew the man to be no trifler. That which he promised, he would surely perform. Then, procuring a candle, Ah Ben led the way.

They walked along the narrow passage at the rear, Ah Ben stopping to close the door quietly behind them. They then mounted a still narrower stairway at the back, Paul following closely. Presently they entered a passage which led in the opposite direction from Henley's bedchamber, and then, turning sharply to the right, found a narrow hallway which terminated in a door. Here the men stopped.

"I am going to take you into my sanctum, and you must not be surprised if you find things different from the ordinary. The circumstances of my life have set me apart from most men; and if my surroundings are at variance with theirs, you must set it down to these facts."

Here he opened the door.

The room was lighted with the same lamp that Paul had seen through the chimney. There were odd-looking things, such as a skeleton with artificial eyes; a glass manikin with a reddish fluid that meandered through his body in thread-like streams; a horoscope and a globe, suspended from the ceiling, with the signs of the Zodiac. Various old parchments, covered with quaint cabalistic figures, were tacked against the walls. In a cabinet, embellished with hieroglyphics, stood another human form, a mummy wonderfully preserved.

"Here we are alone," said Ah Ben; "it is the quietest hour of the night, and therefore we are least apt to be disturbed."

"And what do you propose?" asked Paul with a misgiving he was loth to admit.

"Whatever you may desire, Mr. Henley; for you must know that which is born of spirit is not subject to the restrictions of matter. But remember that all is natural; there is no supernatural, and therefore no cause for alarm."

Ah Ben led the way to the window, and having drawn aside the curtain, threw up the sash. To Henley's amazement they walked directly through the open casement and found themselves upon a broad stone terrace in the glaring light of day. Beneath them lay a city of marvelous beauty, whose streets were lined with palaces, surrounded by their own parks, and whose inhabitants were walking in and about the shaded thorough-fares, or resting in the public seats beside them. The change was so sudden, so bewildering, that Paul drew back, his hand pressed against his head; whereupon Ah Ben took him by the arm and said:

"There is nothing here to alarm you. Come, let us descend these steps, and walk through the town!"

The voice and touch of the man reassured him.

Walking down the broad stone steps, they found themselves in a noble avenue lined with trees and adorned with sparkling fountains. Everywhere the people looked happy. There was neither hurry nor effort, but the grandest monuments to human action were visible upon every hand. Such palaces of dazzling marble; such lace-like carvings in stone; such noble terraces and gardens; and open to all the world alike.

"See," said Ah Ben, "the people here are of one mind. There is no wrangling nor struggling for place. These palaces are the property of the public; and why should they not be, since man's unity is understood? Exclusiveness is the result of ignorance, but privacy and seclusion may even be better enjoyed in the conditions prevailing here than in our own state of existence, and because of the unlimited power and material to draw upon. No man can crowd another after he has come to realize that all is mind, and that mind is infinite."

"But where is Guir House, and the estate?" inquired Paul, feeling as if the whole thing were an incomprehensible illusion.

"They have not been disturbed," the old man answered. "They are where they always were, *in the minds of those who perceive them, and upon whose plane they exist.*"

"It is too utterly bewildering. These things appear as real as any I ever saw."

"Appear! They *are as real.* Let us go into one of these bazars, and see what the people are doing."

They turned through an open doorway resplendent with burnished metal and sculpture to where great corridors, halls, and galleries, stocked with properties and merchandise of every description, were crowded with people. No one was in attendance; and those who came and went, carried with them what they pleased. No money was passed, nor did compensation of any kind seem forthcoming.

"If anything strikes your fancy, take it," said Ah Ben. "All things here are free, and yet everything is paid for."

Paul asked for an explanation, which Ah Ben gave as follows:

"The city before you is located in the year 3,000, more than a thousand years in advance of our time. It is called *Levachan*, and will appear upon earth about 700 years hence; in about four hundred years from which time it will attain the size and splendor you now behold. We here see it in its spiritual state, which precedes and follows all material forms. It will begin its descent into matter, through the minds of physical man, about the time I have mentioned. It is merely a type of a class toward which we are tending, and I show it to you that you may see the vast strides we shall have made by that time. In the state of society in which we find ourselves, compensation is made by a system of absolute freedom in exchange. Here, if a man wants a coat, he takes it, and the owner reimburses himself from the great reservoir of the world's goods, which is open to all men as integral parts of a unit."

"What check have you upon the unreasoning rapacity of a thief, who will take ten times as much as he requires?"

"The system operates directly against the development of that trait. Here, men are only too anxious to have their goods admired and taken; for, being certain of their own maintenance, they feel a pride in contributing to that of others, and there is no temptation to take that which can not be kept, since his neighbor has equal right to take from him an idle surplus. Here the laws are the reverse of ours, for here a man is encouraged in the taking, but never in the holding. Wealth is measured by what a man disburses; hence all are anxious to part with their individual property for the advancement of the commonwealth, knowing that the *one* can only thrive when the many are prosperous."

They continued their walk amid the marvelous wealth that surrounded them. There were fabrics of untold value; jewels of indescribable splendor; men, women, and children with strangely eager faces. They seated themselves upon revolving chairs in the midst of a great space to watch the glittering show.

"But tell me what it all means," inquired Paul. "I feel as if it were a dream, and yet I am absolutely certain that it is not."

"You are right; it is not a dream. Levachan is as real as New York, Boston, or Chicago, although invisible to men of earth. Its inhabitants are as conscious of their existence as you and I are of ours. They are quite as alive to their history and probable destiny as any well educated citizen of America or Europe."

"But where is Guir House, and all it contained?" repeated Henley, unable to understand.

"Nothing has been changed by this any more than if you were in your bed dreaming it all. But to you it is incomprehensible, as I told you it would be, because your mind has never been trained to think in these realms."

"No," answered Paul, turning uneasily in his chair, dazed by the marvelous pageant that moved constantly about them. "No, I admit that it has not, and that the whole thing is utterly beyond me; and this, none the less, because I am aware that one of the fundamental facts of nature is that two things can not occupy the same space at the same time. My previous education, instead of helping me, makes the situation more difficult. The Guir estate and this city can not both be here at once; of that I am sure."

"That is a mere assumption on the part of materialists," answered Ah Ben. "Not only two things, but ten million things, can occupy the same space at the same time; for what is space, and what is time? They are mental conditions, as are all the phenomena of nature. Even your scientist will tell you that the infinite ether penetrates all substances, and that cast-steel or a diamond contains as much of this mysterious element as any other space of equal size. The varying vibrations of this ether, or universal akasa, make the world and all that is in it; and these vibrations are interpenetrable and non-obstructive. Even on the material plane we see how the vibrations of light and heat penetrate those of visible and tangible substance, and how, in your more recent discoveries, light rays penetrate solid metals formerly called opaque. When I say that these vibrations are interpenetrable and non-obstructive, the statement must be taken as approximating the truth, and not as a finality, independent of all conditions; for by the power of the will, or as a result of mental habit, a man may either exclude or admit to his consciousness the thought vibrations of others. But you may set it down as a fundamental fact that there is nothing or no condition of which the mind can conceive that may not become an objective reality, which is the creative faculty in all of us. This city is here to us just as really and actually as were the trees of Guir forest a short time ago. By opening our inward sight, and putting ourselves in accord with another vibratory plane of existence, we are in full *rapport* with a condition that makes no impression upon the members of the sleeping world not so impressed."

"But we left the house at midnight, and here we are in the broad light of day. Do you mean to tell me that the mind controls the sun itself? The thing is so astounding that I feel as if I were losing my reason."

"And did I not tell you that it was unwise to gratify curiosity in this realm when unprepared by a long course of training? But let me quote you a few words from one of our greatest philosophers"; and Ah Ben quoted the following from Franz Hartman's "Magic, White and Black":

"Visible man is not all there is of man, but is surrounded by an invisible mental atmosphere, comparable to the pulp surrounding the seed in a fruit; but this light, or atmosphere, or pulp, is the mind of man, an organized ocean of spiritual substance, wherein all things exist. If man were conscious of his own greatness, he would know that within himself exist the sun and the moon and the starry sky and every object in space, because his true self is God; and God is without limits."

"These thoughts are utterly beyond me," said Paul uneasily.

"As I told you they would be," replied Ah Ben, turning his chair and looking at his pupil with a kindly expression; and then, with his usual earnestness, he added: "But they will not be so always."

"And you tell me that these things are actually as real as the furniture in Guir House?" inquired Henley.

"Quite!" answered the guide. "Test them for yourself. Do you not see this magnificent dome above our heads, supported upon these wonderful pillars? Try them, touch them, strike them with your hand. Are they not solid? Apply every test in your power to their reality; they will not fail you in one—and, let me ask, what further evidence have you of the furniture of which you speak? Thought is real; and the man who can hold to his thought long enough endows it with objectivity."

"It is a mystery involving mysteries," sighed Paul; "and I could never even ask the questions that are crowding into my mind."

"So it is with all life," the old man replied thoughtfully, pressing his hand against his forehead as he gazed into the brilliant scene without seeming to look at anything especial; "and so it is with all life," he repeated in a minute; "it is a mystery involving mysteries! What are dreams? Give them a little more intensity, as in the case of the somnambule or clairvoyant, and they are real. The trouble is, Mr. Henley, that few of us ever come to realize that life itself is a dream; and when science recognizes that fact, many of the difficulties she now encounters will vanish. Let me repeat a few lines from the Song Celestial, or *Bhagavad Gita*.

"Never the spirit was born; the spirit shall cease to be never;
Never was time it was not; end and beginning are dreams,
Birthless and deathless and changeless remaineth the spirit forever;
Death has not touched it at all, dead though the house of it seems.

"These thoughts are better understood in the East," continued Ah Ben, "where the people give less time to *religion* and more to the *philosophy* of life. And what are dreams but a part of our inner existence? None the less mysterious because we are so familiar with them. There are numerous authenticated records of dreams that have carried a man through an apparently long life, but which have really occupied less than a second of time as counted with us; through all the minutiæ and details of youth, courtship, marriage, a military career, war with all its horrors, the details of the last battle where death was inevitable, and where the last shot was fired and heard that brought the great change—of *awakening*, and the sudden perception that the entire phantasmagoria had been caused by the slamming of the door, which the exhausted sleeper had only that second opened as he dropped into a chair beside it. The facts in this case are proven; no perceptible time having elapsed. Time—time is nothing. Time is only what we make it. An hour in a dungeon might be an eternity, while a million years in the Levachan of the Hindoo would seem but a summer's day."

8

Continuing their walk, they followed an avenue of dazzling beauty, which led to a green hill overlooking the town, upon which stood a temple of transcendent splendor. The sunlight flashed upon its marble walls and *chevaux de frise* of minarets. Paul was filled with amazement, and demanded an explanation.

"Let us climb the hill and see for ourselves," answered his guide, leading the way.

Crowds of people passed in and out through the open portals of the temple; and when sufficiently near, Paul read the inscription above the principal entrance:

"*In Commemoration of the Birth of Human Liberty.*"

"I am as puzzled as ever," he declared, with a look of resignation. "It is the most stupendous and remarkable edifice I ever beheld!"

They passed up by a marble terrace and entered the building through an archway so wide and lofty that it might have spanned many ordinary houses. Windows of jeweled glass scattered a thousand tints over walls and columns of barbaric splendor, where encrusted gems of every hue, scintillating with strange fires, were grouped in dazzling mosaics portraying historic scenes in endless pageant. It was a miracle of art and trembling iridescence. White pillars, set with jewels, rose and branched above their heads like the spreading boughs of gigantic trees. The throng of humanity surged hither and thither, and yet so vast was the nave of the temple that nowhere was it crowded. Paul clung closely to his comrade's arm, fearful lest his only friend in this strange world should be lost to him. On they walked; Ah Ben having an air of long familiarity with the scene, while Paul was dazed and bewildered. Occasionally they would stop to examine some object of special interest or to take in with comprehensive view the marvels surrounding them. But the temple was too grand, too glorious for a hasty appreciation of its wonders.

Entering an elevator, they ascended to the roof and stepped out upon a mosaic pavement of transparent tiles. Looking over the parapet, they beheld a country of vast extent, where field, forest, and watercourse combined in a landscape of rare beauty. Beneath lay the marble city with its palaces, parks, and fountains. In the distance were shadowy hills and gleaming lights; and above, a sky whose singular purity was reflected over all. The height was great, but the roof so extensive that it seemed more like some elevated plateau than a part of a building. A multitude of spires rose upon every side like inverted icicles, and Paul was amazed to discover an inscription at the base of each.

"I have a distinct impression of the meaning," he said, looking up at his guide; "but how, I can not tell."

"Yes," answered the old man solemnly, "you now perceive that this stupendous temple commemorates the birth of liberty, or the death of superstitions, and the consequent liberation of the human mind from the slavery of false belief. The temple itself is a monument to the whole, while each minaret commemorates the downfall of some scientific dogma, and the consequent release of the human mind from its thralldom. The limit of man's power over his environment has been extended again and again; and even in your day, Mr. Henley, you have witnessed such marvelous advances as have adduced the aphorism, that this is an age of miracles. We speak from one end of the continent to the other. We sit in New York and sign our name to a check in Chicago. We reproduce a horse race or any athletic sport just as it occurred with every movement to the slightest detail, so that all men can see it in any part of the world at any time quite as well as if present at the original performance. We photograph our thoughts and those of our friends. We reproduce the voices of the departed. We commune with each other without the intervention of wires. We have lately pictured the human soul in its various phases. We see plainly through iron plates many inches in thickness, and look directly into the human body. Our food and precious stones are made in the laboratory, and a syndicate of scientists has recently been formed for the transmutation of the baser metals into gold. When man can produce food, clothing, and all the precious metals at will; when he can see what is occurring at a distance without the necessity of lugging about a cumbersome piece of machinery like his body—when all these and many other discoveries have been brought to perfection, the farmer and manufacturer may cease their labors. The necessity for war will no longer exist, as the righting of wrongs, the acquisition of territory, and the payment of debt will not demand it. But all these things and many more, Mr. Henley, will be brought to perfection before the liberation of man shall have been effected, which will be when he comes to understand that, with proper training and the ultimate development of self-control, there is no limit to his power. As I have told you before, self-control is the secret of all power. The day is not distant when the dogmas of science will be set aside for the spirit of philosophic inquiry. Then men will no longer say that they have reached the goal of human capacity or that they can not usurp the prerogative of the gods, for it will be known that we are all gods!"

Later they descended to the ground and passed into the superb public gardens of the city. Seating themselves beside one of the numerous fountains sparkling with colored waters and perfumed with strange aquatic plants, they watched the brilliant scene that surrounded them. Aerial chariots flashed above, and men, women, and children moved through the air entirely regardless of the law of gravitation. Occasionally a passer-by would nod to Ah Ben, who returned the salute familiarly, as if in recognition of an old friend; but no one stopped to talk.

"And you know these people!" cried Paul in astonishment.

"Some of them." But a look of intense sadness had settled upon the old man's face, quite different from anything Henley had seen. For a moment neither spoke, and then Ah Ben, passing the back of his hand across his forehead, said: "Yes, Mr. Henley, I know them, but I am not of them; and as you see, they shun me."

"I can not understand why that should be," answered Paul, who was conscious of a growing attachment for his guide.

"I can not explain; but some day, perhaps, you may know. Let us continue our walk."

Looking up at the marvelous examples of architecture that surrounded them, Paul observed that many of the houses had no windows, and inquired the reason.

"Windows and doors are here only a matter of taste, and not of necessity," answered the elder man; "the denizens of Levachan enter their houses wherever they please without experiencing the slightest obstruction. Likewise light and air are not here confined to special material and apertures for their admission. We are only just beginning to discover some of the possibilities of matter upon our plane of existence. Here these things are understood; for matter and spirit are one, their apparent difference lying in us."

"Yes," said Paul, "and I perceive that the inhabitants move from place to place through the upper atmosphere in defiance of all law!"

"Law, Mr. Henley, is the operation of man's will. Where man through uncounted eons of time has believed himself the slave of matter, it becomes his master. I mean that the belief enslaves him, and not until he has worked his way out of the false belief, will he become free."

They continued their walk through gardens of bewitching beauty, and amid lights so far transcending any previous experience of Henley's

CHARLES WILLING BEALE

that he no longer even tried to comprehend Ah Ben's labored explanations. At last his guide, turning, abruptly said:

"Come, let us return; the time is growing short!"

"Time!" said Henley, with an amused expression. "I thought you told me that time was only a mental condition!"

"True, I did," said Ah Ben, with a return of the same inexpressibly sad look; "but did I tell you that it had ceased to belong to me?"

There was no intimation of reproof, no endeavor to evade the remark; but Paul could not but observe the change in the man's manner as they retraced their steps. Indeed, he was conscious of an overpowering sadness himself, as he turned his back upon the strange scene.

"Come!" said Ah Ben, with authority, leading the way.

They passed up the grand stairway to the terrace, entering the room at the same window by which they had left it, and Ah Ben closed the sash and drew the curtains behind them.

A moment later Paul went to the window and looked out. There was an old moon, and the forest beneath lay bathed in its mellow light. The sudden transition to his former state was no less astounding than the first.

"Which, think you, is the most real," asked the old man, "the scene before us now, or the one we have left behind?"

Paul could not answer. He was revolving in his mind the marvels he had just witnessed. He could not understand how hypnotism could have created such a world as he had just beheld. It was not a whit less tangible, visible, or audible than that in which he had always lived, and he could not help looking upon Ah Ben as a creature far removed from his own sphere of life. How had the man acquired such powers? These and other thoughts were rushing through his mind. Presently his host touched him lightly upon the shoulder, and said:

"Come, let us descend into the hall again, and finish our pipes."

And so they wandered back through the silent house to the old pew by the fire; and Ah Ben, stirring up the embers and adding fresh fuel, said:

"Although it is late, Mr. Henley, I do not feel inclined for bed; and if you are of the same mind, should be glad of your company."

Paul was glad of an excuse to sit up, and so settled himself upon the sofa, absorbed in meditation. The firelight flickered over their faces and the strange pictures on the wall, and the head of Tsong Kapa shone more plainly than ever before. The portraits on the stairs were as weird and incomprehensible as they had appeared on the first night of his arrival; and the old man and the girl, and their strange life, seemed even more deeply involved in mystery than they had upon that occasion. Paul was now beset with conflicting emotions. The gloom of the house was more oppressive than before; and were it not for his sudden and un-accountable affection for Dorothy, he might have left it at once, had it not again been for the vision of splendor and happiness just faded from his sight. He could not bear the thought of losing forever the sensation of life and power and ecstasy just beginning to dawn upon him, when so cruelly snatched away; and but for Ah Ben he knew he should hope in vain for its return. Naturally, his emotions were strong and tearing him in opposite directions. The old man perceiving the depression of spirits into which his guest had fallen, reminded him gently of his warning regarding the shock of occult manifestation to those who were unprepared.

"It is not that so much," answered Paul, "as the regret I feel at having left it all behind. When a man has only just begun to experience the sensation of life—*of real life*—to find himself suddenly plunged back into a dungeon with chains upon his shoulders, you must admit the shock is terrible."

"Do I not know it?" answered the old man feelingly. "The return is far more to be dreaded than the escape into that life which you were at first inclined to call unreal; and yet, Mr. Henley, you must admit that it is difficult to decide the question of reality between the two worlds."

"True," answered Paul; "and yet I know that what I have just seen can be nothing else than a hypnotic vision; it is impossible it should be otherwise, for it has gone—and beyond my power to recall. What amazes me to the point of stupefaction is the marvelous impression of truth with which hypnotism can fill one. I had always imagined the effect was more in the nature of a dream, but this was vivid, sharp, and perfect as the everyday life about me. I am more bewildered than I have words to express."

"And yet," answered Ah Ben, "you still insist that the things you saw were unreal, because, as you say, they were the result of hypnotism. It seems difficult to convince you of what I have already told you, that hypnotism is not a cause of hallucination, but of fact. You insist that because the minority of men only are subjected to hypnotic tests, the impressions produced must be false. You will not admit that a minority has any claim to a hearing, although their evidence is based upon precisely the same testimony as that of the majority—namely, the five senses. You have no better right to assume that your present surroundings are any more truthfully reported by your senses than those of your recent experience. You see, you hear and touch; did you not do the same in Levachan?"

"I did, indeed," answered Paul, "and with a clearness that makes it the more difficult to comprehend; still, of course, I know that the vision of Levachan was a deception, while this is real!"

"And because you are convinced that a majority of men would see this as you see it. What if it should be proved that you are wrong?"

"That would be impossible," answered Paul.

"You think so, indeed," answered the old man with a strange look in his eyes; "and yet, if you will look above you and about you, you will see for the first time the way in which this old house looks to the great majority of mankind—indeed, to such a vast majority, Mr. Henley—that your individual testimony to the contrary would be regarded as the ravings of a madman. Look!"

Paul lifted his eyes. The roof was gone, and the stars shone down upon him through the open space. About him were rough walls of crumbling stone, rapidly falling to decay; there were no pictures, there were no stairs with their uncanny portraits, there was no great open fire-place with the blazing logs, nor hanging lamp, nor cheery pew—all—all was gone—and nothing but ruin and decay remained, save some bunches of ivy which had climbed above the edge of the tottering wall, outlined dimly in the moonlight. The floor had rotted away, and dank grass and bushes and heaps of stone had filled its place. A pool of water in a distant corner reflected the sky and a star or two, and the dismal croaking of a frog was the only sound he heard. Through the open casements wild vines and stunted trees had thrust their boughs, and beyond were the pines and hemlocks. Paul stood erect, and stared around him in blank amazement. Where was Ah Ben? He too had departed with the rest. Dazed and wondering, Henley sauntered toward the door, or rather to where the door had once stood, now only an open portal of crumbling stone, from the crevices of which grew bushes and a tangled network of vines. Climbing down over a mass of fallen bricks, he wandered out into the grounds. The lawn was buried beneath a confused jumble of rubbish and weeds, and the forest encroached upon its rights. The graveled road was no longer visible, wild grass, moss, and piles of fallen stone having covered it far below. As he looked above, the moon shone through the casement of a ruined window, and an owl hooted dismally from the open belfry. The old house was a wreck, a tottering ruin, from whatever point he looked; and no room above or below seemed habitable. He walked around to see if the blank wall which guarded the secret chamber was still intact. Yes, there it was; it alone remained untouched by the ravages of time or war. The portraits and human remains were probably safe in their hiding place, and Paul shuddered at the thought. What hand had bound them up in that strange old corner to be hid forever from the eyes of men? He had heard no human word, nor was there apparently any shelter where man or woman could live. Presently amid the deep shadows of the forest something moved. It came nearer, and then from beneath the trees walked out into the moonlight. Paul started; but at the same moment a familiar voice spoke to him. It was Ah Ben's.

"Do not let what you see alarm you, Mr. Henley, for it is the first time in which you have perceived Guir House in what you would call its normal state. As you now behold it, the majority of men would see it."

"Then I have been duped ever since my arrival!" exclaimed Paul in a slightly irritated tone.

"Not at all," answered the elder man complacently. "I have simply presented the house to you as it stood a hundred years ago. The impression you have had of it is quite as truthful as the one now before you. Indeed, it is as truthful as the view you now have of yonder star," he pointed to a twinkling luminary in the north; "for time has put out its fires more than a thousand years ago, so that you now behold it as it then was, and not as it is to-night."

"This hypnotism of yours is quite undoing me," answered Paul, passing his hand across his eyes.

"And yet what you now behold is not hypnotism at all, but fact, as the world would call it. It is what the vast majority of all men would see if here to-night. But I perceive that it is troubling you. Let us return to our old place by the fire, and the house as it was a century ago. In that state of the past I think you will find more comfort than in the melancholy ruin before us."

They climbed back over the fallen piles of bricks, stone, and mortar; and then Ah Ben lifted his withered hand, and touching Henley lightly upon the forehead, said:

"And now we are back in our old seats, just as they used to be in the days of yore!"

Paul looked about him. The fire was burning brightly. The pictures had been restored to their places on the walls. The old lamp and the strangely decorated staircase were all restored, just as he had left them a few minutes before. He gazed long and earnestly at the scene around him, and then fixing his eyes upon Ah Ben, helplessly, said:

"If then I am to understand that this is no longer real, but that the old ruin just beheld is the existing fact, might I ask in what part of the wreck you and Miss Guir have been able to fix your abode, for I saw nothing but crumbling walls—a roofless ruin?"

"The question you ask involves a story, and if you care to listen I will tell it to you, although the hour is late and the night far gone."

"I should enjoy nothing more," said Paul.

And the men filled and lighted their pipes, and Henley listened while Ah Ben told him the following:

9

"In the early settlement of this State, an Englishman by the name of Guir pre-empted a large body of land, near the center of which he erected this house. Although his intention in coming from the old country was to make his permanent home in the colony, his reasons for doing so were quite different from those which usually induce immigration. Guir was an artist, and a man of some means; and his object in colonizing was not so much to cultivate the soil, or to trade with the Indians, or engage in any business enterprise, as to gratify a craving for nature and surround himself with such scenery as he loved to paint. It would be folly to pretend that Guir was a man of ordinary tastes and disposition; for had he been such, he would never have undertaken a journey, with a family of girls, into such a wilderness as Virginia was at that time. No; from the very circumstances of his birth and education, he was unfitted to live with his countrymen; hence his early adoption of the colony as a home for himself, wife, and daughters. This happened a hundred and fifty years ago."

"He was an ancestor of yours, I presume," said Paul, hoping to gain some clew to the man's identity.

"No," answered Ah Ben, "he was not."

"Pardon the interruption," added Paul, fearing he had annoyed the speaker.

"Naturally, in a country without roads, or even wagon trails," continued the old man, without noticing the apology, "it was years before a house of this size could be completed, as every brick and nearly every stick of timber was brought from England. These, of coure, were conveyed by water as far as the rivers permitted, the rest of the journey being performed upon sleds drawn by oxen. But it was Guir's hobby, and in the course of a dozen or fifteen years the job was completed, and the house stood as you see it now. Then the owner set himself to work with brush, canvas, and chisel to decorate his home, and make it, according to his ideas, as beautiful and suggestive of his early youth as imaginable. With his own hands, Mr. Henley, he painted most of these pictures, although his three daughters, inheriting his tastes, assisted him. And thus, as the years rolled by, Guir House became more and more a museum of artistic efforts, embracing many unusual subjects, and in every degree of perfection. The broad acres of the estate produced much that was necessary toward the maintenance of life, and what they lacked was supplied once a year from a distant settlement near the coast. As you can readily understand, there were no neighbors, and but occasional visits from the red man, who looked distrustfully upon the pale-face. This feeling became mutual, and trifling acts of hostility on the part of the natives grew both in frequency and magnitude. Depredations upon

Guir's fields and cattle were at first ignored, in the effort to maintain peace, but in time it became necessary to resist them. Upon one occasion, a raid upon a distant field was successfully repulsed, with the aid of his wife and three daughters, attired in men's clothing and mounted upon fast horses. The Indians were so completely surprised by the ruse, being apparently attacked by five men, where they had believed there was only one, that they fled, completely routed, nor did they return for several years. Meanwhile, fearing another and closer attack, Guir converted one of the lower rooms of his house into an impenetrable and unassailable place of refuge. The windows were walled up, to correspond with the stonework of the house, leaving no suspicion of there having been once an opening. Likewise the doors were treated, and then carefully plastered both within and without, with the exception of one, which he made anew, to communicate with a private stairway leading from one of the upper bedrooms. This was the only entrance to the dark retreat, and a heavy bolt was placed upon the inside, to be used by the family in case of attack. There was no reason to suppose that a marauding party would ever find the way to this secret chamber, as the entrance was carefully covered by a scuttle in the floor of a dark closet; and the place being thoroughly fire-proof, the family felt unusually secure in the possession of their new retreat."

"I think I have seen the stairway you speak of," said Paul.

"Yes," answered the old man, "it communicates with the closet of your room.

"One day Guir had left his home. He had ridden alone into the distant hills to dispute the range for some cattle with his natural enemy, the red man. The pow-wow had been long and trying, and it was only with the setting sun that he had come to a proper understanding, as he supposed, with the ugly chief who dominated the region about.

"It was midnight when he reached his home. He pounded sharply on the door; but his good wife, who never retired without him, failed to answer the summons. So, after repeated knocks, Guir forced the door and entered. All was dark. An unearthly stillness pervaded the air, and a horrid suspicion forced itself upon him while groping his way forward to secure a light. Finding the chimney, he raked together a few coals, which he blew into a flame, and then, with trembling hands, lighted the candle upon the shelf above. Looking about him, Guir's heart sank. His house had been wrecked. His pictures, the work of years, were scattered in fragments about the floor. The windows were smashed, and the hall starred with broken glass. Not an ornament, not a treasure remained intact. But this he knew was as nothing to the horrible sight which he expected momentarily to greet his eyes. He called aloud to each member of his family, in the failing hope that some one would answer; but no sound broke the awful stillness. Suddenly he bethought him of the secret chamber, and with a wild prayer that his loved ones had been able to reach it in safety, and were still in hiding there, he started down the narrow stairs in search. Reaching the bottom, he found that the door had been wrenched from its hinges and thrown to the ground; and then Guir's heart sank, never to rise again. Stepping across the threshold of the room, candle in hand, a vision of blood swam before his eyes, and the dimly-burning light revealed the horror-stricken faces of his murdered family. Not one was left to tell the tale, but the story pictured before him was unmistakable in every detail. The treacherous natives had first tortured and then butchered them. For a time he stood transfixed with horror, unable to remove his eyes from the awful scene, or his feet from the spot where he had first beheld it; then, with the cry of sudden madness, he threw himself beside the bleeding corpses and lost all consciousness. How long he remained there was problematical, but on awaking Guir was still in the dark, and where he had fallen. At that moment a strange and overpowering desire seized him. He must paint the portraits of his murdered family before it became too late. Had he been sane, such a ghastly thought would never have possessed him; but Guir was crazed, and for days and nights following he worked in that dismal vault, by the light of a smoking lamp, at the task he had set himself, his fired imagination even intensifying the horrors of the grewsome tableau.

"Upon each canvas he depicted the awful countenance which fact and fancy had imprinted upon his brain. Guir painted not only what he saw, but what he imagined he saw—dreadful faces, loaded with torture and despair. When completed, he hung them upon the walls of the room, and then with his own hands bricked up the entrance from within, having first carefully replaced and bolted the door. When Guir had thus entombed himself, he lay down again upon the floor, and then, still a madman, opened a vein in his wrist. The letting of blood may have sobered him or restored his mental equilibrium; for suddenly, with a wild change in his feelings, he bounded to his feet and repented. Again he was in darkness, and could not guess how much time had elapsed since his fatal act. Staggering to the closed doorway, he endeavored to tear away the bricks he had so recently placed there, but the mortar was hardening fast, and he was unable to find his trowel. Groping frantically along the floor, he searched in vain for some tool to open the vault in which he was buried, and then, with the anguish of despair, dropped again upon the ground to await his fate. Thus Guir died, in an agony of remorse, and with the intensest desire to live."

Ah Ben stopped suddenly, and fixed his eyes upon Henley, as if trying to read his thoughts.

"There is one thing in that story that strikes me as very peculiar," observed Paul, returning his host's look with interest.

"And what is that?" answered the old man, his eyes still fixed on Henley's face.

"The fact that you are able to repeat with such circumstantial detail the feelings and actions of a man who died under such peculiar conditions, and quite alone."

"It might indeed appear strange to you, Mr. Henley, but my familiarity with the case enables me to speak with knowledge and accuracy."

"And would you mind telling me how that is possible?" inquired Paul.

"*Because I am the man Guir himself; and I have lived on through such ages of agony that I have no longer the will or desire to appear other than as the ancient wreck before you.*"

Paul started.

"Do you mean to tell me then that I am talking to a ghost?" he cried in dismay.

"As you please, Mr. Henley; but ghosts are not so different from ordinary people—that is, when they have become materialized. I have just now shown you the real condition of this old house, or rather the way in which the majority of men see it. I do not hesitate, therefore, to show you the ghost that haunts it; nor do I object to explaining the dreadful cause of the haunting, or a little of the philosophy of hauntings in general."

Paul looked aghast. Easy enough was it now to comprehend how the man had talked so familiarly of death and the next life after having actually crossed the threshold and passed into the realm of experience. But there was something too real, too natural about this personality to accept the remark as literal. Familiarity with Ah Ben had shown him to be a man. Paul felt sure of it. And yet here were revealed mysteries never dreamed of; one of which was even now producing an occult spell. Henley drew a deep breath in agony of spirit.

After a moment's pause, the old man continued:

"Ghosts, Mr. Henley, are as real as you; and when a spirit returns to earth in visible form, it is the result of some disquieting influence immediately before the death of the body, or, as I might say, previous to the new life. At the hour of physical birth, such influences cause idiocy or such imperfection of the bodily functions that death ensues, and the spirit returns to seek another entrance into the world of matter. When a man dies dominated by some intense earthly desire, his mind is barred against the higher powers and greater possibilities of spirit; his whole nature is closed against their reception, so that he perceives and hopes for nothing save the continuance of that life which has so completely filled his nature. His old environment overpowers the new by the very force of his will; and if this continues, he becomes not only a haunting spirit, but a materialized one, visible to certain people under certain conditions, and compelled to live out his life amid the scenes which had so attracted him. This, Mr. Henley, has been my case. I shall live upon earth, and be visible to the spiritually susceptible, until the strong impression made at the hour of death shall have worn away."

"And the young lady, is she your daughter?" inquired Paul.

"She is my daughter," answered the old man solemnly.

"How comes it, then, that she addresses you by so singular a name?"

"It is the one she first learned to use in infancy. As I partially explained to you, my mother was a Hindoo, while my father was English. The name Ah Ben belongs to the maternal side of my family."

"Another question—more vital than any I have yet asked, because it concerns my own well-being and happiness," continued Paul; "how is it possible that Dorothy can live in a place like this with a being who is only semi-material?

"Because her nature is double, as is mine," answered the old man. "Dorothy, like her sisters and mother, passed out of this life more than a hundred and fifty years ago."

"And did the same causes operate to bring her back to earth?"

Ah Ben became more serious than ever as he answered:

"You have touched upon the sorest point of all, and one which requires further elucidation. Sudden and unnatural death has a retarding tendency upon the spirit's progress; but where one has caused his own destruction, the evil resulting is incalculable. I was a suicide; and ten thousand times over had I better have borne all the ills that earth could heap upon me, than have stooped to such folly. For in what has it resulted? A prolonged mental agony, such as you can never conceive; for I have no home in heaven nor earth, but am forced to wander amid the shadows of each world, unrecognized by those either above or below me. Here I am shunned upon every hand, and, as you saw for yourself, I was equally avoided in Levachan. But that is not all; in the ignorance and selfishness of my grief, I yearned for my lost ones with a solicitude, a consuming fierceness and power of will which insanity only can equal. By nature I was intense; and even had I not committed the fatal act, my vitality would have burned itself away with the awful concentration of feeling. But it must be remembered that I was not the only sufferer from this pitiful lack of self-control. The stronger desires and emotions of the living influence the dead—I use the words in their common acceptation for the sake of convenience—and here is where I caused such incalculable injury to my own child; for Dorothy, having entered the spirit world with inferior powers of resistance, fell under the spell I had wrought, and joined me in the haunting of this old house. Here, Mr. Henley, am I, a suicide, justly deserving the punishment I receive; but there is my child, as innocent as the air of heaven, forced to suffer with me, and it is no small part of my chastisement to realize this fact. People fly from us as they would from pestilence, both in this world and the other, although many of the dwellers in the higher state, from their greater knowledge and loftier development, simply avoid us. And we can not criticise their action in either world, for we are not adapted to either state. We are outcasts."

Ah Ben paused for a moment, and then became deeply impressive, as he added:

"Mr. Henley, let the experience of one who has suffered, and who will continue to suffer more than you can possibly understand—let his experience, I say, warn you against the unreasonable yearning for the return of those who have passed on to their spiritual state! Here our eyes are blinded to the blessedness to come, and it is well it is so; for, were it otherwise, the discipline of earth life would be lost, as too monstrous to be endured. No man could submit to the restraints of matter, with the power and freedom of spirit in sight. If once I could have realized the dreadful results entailed upon what I had lost, by my effort to recover it, I would have known that the blackest curse would have been trifling by contrast. Let the dead rest! and let one who knows persuade you that their entrance into spirit life is a time rather for rejoicing than regret!"

"And is Dorothy to suffer as you have suffered, for what was no fault of hers?" demanded Paul.

"Yes," said Ah Ben; "the law of Karma is the law of nature and the law of God; and while ordinarily she would have passed safely on in the possession of her new-born powers, the pitfall which I blindly laid beset her unwary feet, and she fell. There is but one course open; but one way in which Dorothy can reach either heaven or earth, by a shorter road than that which I am compelled to travel. It is simple, and yet one which, under the circumstances, is almost impossible to achieve; and this from the fact that it requires the coöperation of a human being."

"I should imagine that any one with the ordinary feelings of humanity would gladly do what he could to assist such an unhappy fellow-creature!" exclaimed Paul.

"But she is not a fellow-creature," urged the old man.

"True, but I understood you to say that she might become one with the coöperation of a human being."

"I did," Ah Ben replied; "but where is that to be found?"

"Not knowing the nature of the task, it would be difficult to say," answered Paul, "but I will adhere to my first proposition, that one with the ordinary feelings of humanity would gladly do what he could."

"Mr. Henley, have you the ordinary feelings of humanity?"

"I hope so," answered Paul.

"Would you be willing to marry a ghost, and be haunted for the rest of your life; for the ghost would be sure to outlive you?"

Paul started.

"I have put the case too strongly," continued Ah Ben; "Dorothy is not a ghost in the ordinary sense. She is a materialized spirit, and that, my dear friend, is exactly what you are, with this difference: you have practically no control over your body; while she, having returned from the summer land abnormally, can, like myself, become invisible at will; but, upon the other hand, she is not always visible, even to those whom she would like to have see her. In short, as I have told you before, we belong to neither one world nor the other. But through union with a human creature, Dorothy can once more assume the functions of mortality, and after another period of earth life, become fitted again for the land of spirits."

"I understand you entirely," answered Paul, "and can say, without hesitation or reservation, that I love your daughter, and, be she whom or what she may, will gladly marry her, if she can say as much for me."

"I thought I could not be mistaken in my man," answered Ah Ben. "I have believed in your frankness, honor, and courage from the beginning; and although you came to this house with the intention of deceit, I feel sure that in the more serious situations of life you are to be relied upon. You have spoken to Dorothy, Mr. Henley, and I am confident she shares my trust in you."

"I hope so," answered Paul.

"I know it," the old man replied; "and let me tell you further that this match is not one subservient to the ends of utility or profit; for, were such the motive, the very end would be defeated. Dorothy must love the man she marries, with all her heart and soul; and you can readily understand, ostracized as we are, how difficult it has been to find such a one. For more than a century we have sought in vain, and I have pressed every opportunity and strained every power to bring about such a meeting and such a result as I trust will shortly follow; but the world has given us no chance, and those few who have been able to see us have only fled in terror!"

"Am I at liberty, then, to prove my devotion to your daughter by asking her to marry me?"

"You have already done so," replied Ah Ben, "and I have already given my consent; but I warn you, Mr. Henley, that in your intercourse with my daughter you should remember that you are dealing with a nature far more intense, and with far greater capacity to love, than any you have ever known. While the most fervid desire of Dorothy's life has doubtless been to meet some creature with whom she might affiliate,

I believe she would forego even that happiness if convinced that it would prove disastrous to the object of her affection."

Paul extended his hands to Ah Ben, who took them with fervor.

"Dear old man!" he said, "although I am speaking to a ghost, I am not afraid of you; and knowing how much you have suffered, it shall be my aim to help and comfort you; for have you not shown me how close is the other world, and so in a measure removed the dread of death? How truly do I feel that those who have left us may be close around us, although we can not see them."

And then, with a new light on all that surrounded him, Paul bade Ah Ben good-night, and went to his room.

10

The following morning, Mr. Henley was puzzled, in thinking over the conversation of the previous night, to remember that he had not been alarmed at the revelations which Ah Ben had made. The things he had seen and the words he had heard were amazing, but they had not terrified him; and when he recalled the easy and natural manner in which he had talked, he attributed the fact to the same mental change whereby he had perceived the visions.

The breakfast room was deserted, neither Dorothy nor Ah Ben being present; and so Paul partook of the meal alone, which he found prepared as usual. He lingered over his second cup of tea in the hope that the young lady would join him; but after loitering quite beyond the usual hour, he sauntered out into the garden, trusting to find her there. But Dorothy was nowhere to be seen, and Henley sank dejectedly into the old rustic bench to await her coming.

An hour passed, but no token of a human being was in evidence; not even the voice nor the footstep of a servant had been heard, and Paul sat consuming cigarettes at a rate that showed clearly his impatience. At last he returned to the house, and going to his room took pen and paper and wrote, in a large hand:

> Will Miss Guir kindly let me know at what hour I may see her? I shall await her answer in the garden. PAUL HENLEY.

Not being able to find a servant, he took this downstairs and suspended it from the hanging lamp by a thread, and then returned to the garden to tramp up and down the neglected paths, between the boxwood bushes, and to burn more cigarettes. He had not the slightest hope of finding Ah Ben, as that individual never put in an appearance until the day was far spent—in fact, not generally until after the shadows of evening were well advanced; and the only servant he had seen was the dumb boy alluded to, and even he had only appeared occasionally. Clearly there was nothing to do but wait. But waiting brought neither Dorothy nor Ah Ben, and Paul began to wonder seriously where his hosts could have taken themselves. The time wore on, and the shadow of a tall fir showed that the hour of noon had passed. Had he been left in sole possession of this old mansion, whose history was so amazing, and yet whose very existence appeared mythical? He wandered back into the house, and passing through the hall, stopped suddenly. His note was gone. Surely it had been taken, for it could not have fallen. Examining the lamp, Henley saw that a short end of the thread was hanging, indicating that it had been broken and the note carried away. Some one had passed through the building since he had left it. Could it have been the girl? and if so, why had she avoided him? One thing appeared certain; she would know where to expect his letters, and he would now write another. In twenty minutes he had prepared the following, which, having sealed, he again suspended from the lamp in the hall:

> DEAREST GIRL—I have waited all the morning to see you, and am growing fearfully impatient. Is it business or pleasure that keeps you away? Why not tell me frankly just what it is, as I can not bear to think that I am avoided from indifference, or because you are getting tired of me. Have I outstayed my welcome at Guir House? I entreat you to give me an answer and an interview, as I am so lonely without you; just how lonely I will tell you when we meet.   PAUL.

Having left this dangling from the same thread, he went out for a walk; and thinking it possible that he might meet Ah Ben in the forest, went in that direction.

The leaves were now falling rapidly, and the clear sky was visible through the bare limbs above; and the open spaces were beginning to give the woods quite a wintry aspect. Guir House was visible from a greater distance than he had ever seen it, and Paul sat down upon a fallen log to take in the picture of the quaint old mansion, buried in the depths of a trackless, almost impenetrable forest. He sang a verse of a familiar song in a loud voice, with the hope of attracting attention, but the distant echo of the last words was the only response that he got. Then he threw himself upon the ground and whistled and smoked alternately, his anxiety constantly growing; but the gentle sighing of the wind in the tree tops, and the uncertain rustling of the leaves, were but poor comfort. Was this to be the end of his strange visit? Was he to start back upon his homeward journey without an opportunity to bid his phenomenal hosts good-bye? He could not bear the thought. Dorothy at all events must be found. He would search the grounds and ransack the house. Surely she must be somewhere within reach of his voice. But then she was so strange, so different from any woman he had ever known. How could he tell, perhaps she had left the old place forever! Henley had not realized until now what a deep and overpowering dependence had suddenly developed in him toward these people. They seemed to hold the key to another world in a more practical and tangible way than he had ever deemed it possible for any mortal-appearing man to do. Even to be shut out from the wonderful city of Levachan would be an overwhelming loss, and how could he ever hope to see it again without their aid? To be deprived forever of the spiritual influence of these eccentric, half-earthly acquaintances was a thought he could not tolerate. Even the horrors through which they had passed appeared trivial as compared with the glimpses they had afforded him of happiness. But to see these things—to feel the mystery of their power and beauty just beginning to descend and take possession of him—and then to be snatched back to earth, with the inability to return, was too horrible, and like the ecstatic visions of a drowning man cut short by rescue. While he had Ah Ben and Dorothy within his reach, he felt the possibility of return; but suddenly they had gone, and for the first time he realized what they had been to him. Then it began to dawn upon him what these people must have suffered in a century and a half, and what they must continue to endure for untold time to come, in their inability to return in full to that world they had left, or even to take part in the affairs of this. Surely their case was far worse than his, for after a few years he would be freed from the bondage of matter, and would grapple with the mysteries which had become so fascinating; but with them it was different. Unfitted for either world, without a friend and alone, they must drag out their weary existence until the law of Karma was satisfied. But he would not give them up; he could not; for were they not the new life, the new atmosphere, the very essence of his newly discovered self? He had felt, and seen, how possible it was for a man to tread on air—to walk the upper regions of the sky, and he could never again be contented to crawl upon the surface of the ground like a worm. But without Ah Ben he must crawl. With him, Paul felt that all things were possible, which powers he felt that Dorothy also possessed; though, alas, through the crime, and earth-bound cravings of his host, these powers had been sadly curtailed.

Nerveless and dispirited he returned to the garden gate. Some one had been there since he had passed, for there were fresh foot-prints along the walk, of a small, feminine type, and directed toward the forest. The steps had passed outward, and their track was lost in the leaves beyond. Surely Dorothy had left the house and gone for a ramble in the woods without having seen him. How could he have missed her, and could it have been intentional, were thoughts which came unpleasantly to Paul at that moment. He stood gazing long and earnestly in the direction taken by the departing footsteps, and doing so, his attention was attracted by the flight of a bird which came swooping towards him from the depths of the woodland glade. Nearer and nearer it came, uttering a strange, shrill cry, as if to attract his attention; and then, after circling in the air above his head, came fluttering down, and lighted upon the gate-post at his elbow. It was Dorothy's parrot. But what did it mean by this unusual freak of familiarity? Paul spoke to the bird, which pleased it; and when he put out his hand to smooth its feathers, the parrot lifted its wings, and with a loud cackle exhibited a note which had been carefully tied beneath one of them. Henley relieved the animal of its burden, and discovered that the note was addressed to himself. When he looked around again, the parrot had flown away. This is what the note contained:

GUIR HOUSE.

My Own Dear Comrade—I call you my own because you are all that I ever had, but even now the memory of our few brief interviews is all that is left to me, for I must go without you. So happy was I when we first met, that I don't mind telling you, since we shall not meet again, how, in anticipation, I rested in your dear arms and felt your loving caresses; for you were all the world to me then—the only world I had ever known —and the break of day seemed close at hand. But soon the thought of drawing you down into that awful abyss 'twixt heaven and earth, which has whirled its black shadows about me for more than a century, seized me, and I could not willingly make a thrall of the one I loved; and so I leave you to those for whom you are fitted, while I shall continue my solitary life as before. You say that you are lonely without me! But what is your loneliness to mine? I, who never had a comrade; who never felt the joy of friendship; and who was dazed with the sudden flush of love, of hunger satisfied, of companionship! Have you ever felt the want of these, dear Paul? Have you ever known what it is to be alone—to live in an empty world—and that, not for a time, but for ages? Yes, you will say, you under-stand it, and that you pity me, and yet you do not know its meaning; for you at least can live out the life for which God and nature have fitted you, while I am fit for nothing. You know not what it is to be shunned; to be avoided; to be feared! You go your way, and smile and nod to those you meet, and they are pleased to see you. You are welcome among your friends, as they to you. Live on in that precious state, and feel blessed and happy, for there are worse conditions, although you know it not.

And now I am going to tell you a strange thing. It is this: I have shadowed your life from the hour of your birth. I have watched your career, and where able have guided and helped you, knowing that you were one whom I could love. I have helped to make you what you are, and therefore my right of possession is doubly founded, even though my love be too great to lead you astray. Gradually I led you up to the hour when all was ripe, and then mentally impressed you with the letter which you thought you received, and which I knew would affect you through your strongest characteristics—love of adventure, and—curiosity—as well as from the fact that you were susceptible to mental influence. You came, and I was happy—more happy than you will ever know—until my unsated Karma thwarted my plan, and showed that while seeking my own peace, I might possibly endanger yours. That ended all. I could go no further. But even now, as before, I shall come to you in spirit, during the still hours of night; for my love is more intense and strangely different from that which waking men are wont to feel. It is that which sometimes comes in dreams. Do you not know what I mean?

You will feel bewildered on reading this, and at a loss to understand many things, but remember that your inward or spiritual sight has been opened through the power of hypnotism, and you must not judge things as in your normal state.

When you reached our little station of Guir, you were expecting to find me there, and expectation is the proper frame of mind in which to produce a strong impression; and therefore, although you did not know what I was like, Ah Ben and I together easily made you see me as I was, together with the cart and horse; and although you actually got into the stage which was waiting, you thought you were in the cart with me. The incident of the broken spring was merely suggested as a fitting means to bring you back physically from the coach to the cart, where for the first time, in the moonlight, you saw me in semi-material form, visible as a shadow to some men, but wholly so to you. Had I appeared thus at the station, I should have alarmed all who saw me, and so I came to you only. The two worlds are so closely intermingled that men often live in one while their bodies are in another, and to those who are susceptible, the immaterial can be made more real than the other. I know these things, because, while at home in neither, I have been in both.

And now, dear comrade, think sometimes of her who loves you, and to whom you have been the only joy; and she will be with you always, although you may not know it, except in your dreams.

One more word. Think happily of the dead, for they are happy, and in a way you can not understand. If you love them truly, rejoice that they have gone, for what you call their death is but their birth, with powers transcending those of their former state, as light transcends the darkness. Disturb them not with idle yearnings, lest your thought unsettle the serenity of their lives. Let the ignorance which has ruined me be a warning. Some day I shall complete my term of loneliness, and begin life anew. We will know each other then, dear Paul, as here. Remember, I shall always be your spirit guide.   DOROTHY.

Henley folded the letter and looked about him in bewilderment, and with a sense of loneliness he had never known before. He thought he could realize the emptiness of life, the dissociation with all things, of which Dorothy had spoken. He was adrift, without anchor in either world. Heart-broken and crushed, he determined to find the girl at all hazards, and bounded down the garden path in search of Ah Ben, who alone could help him. At the last of the boxwood trees he stopped, and then, *in an agony of horror, beheld the roofless ruin of the old house as Ah Ben had shown it to him.* The crumbling walls and broken belfry, half hidden amid the encroaching trees, were all that was left of Guir House and its spacious grounds. Heaps of stone and piles of rubbish beset his path, and the open portals, choked with wild grass and bushes, showed glimpses of the sky beyond. In a panic of terror lest his reason had gone, Paul flew madly on in the direction from which Dorothy had first brought him. But not an indication of what once were ornamental grounds remained. Beyond, an unbroken forest was upon every side, and the growth was wild and dense. On he rushed, with both hands pressed tightly against his head, neither knowing nor caring whither he went. But at last two shadowy forms emerged from a dense thicket of calmia upon his left, and Paul felt that their influence was kindly, and that they had come to guide him back into the world he had left behind.

Sources and Acknowledgments

The texts in the present volume are reprinted from the following editions:

"The Uninhabited House" by Mrs. J. H. Riddell. From *Routledge's Christmas Annual* for 1875. Routledge, London, 1875.
The Amber Witch by Wilhelm Meinhold. David Nutt, London, 1895.
"Monsieur Maurice" by Amelia B. Edwards. From *Monsieur Maurice, A New Novelette*. Bernhard Tauchnitz, Leipzig, 1873.
A Phantom Lover by Vernon Lee. From *Hauntings, Fantastic Stories*. Frank F. Lovell, New York, 1890 (the title there is "Oke of Okehurst").
The Ghost of Guir House by Charles Willing Beale. Editor Publishing Co., Cincinnati, 1901; second edition, copyright 1897.

Thanks and acknowledgments are due to Dr. Frederick B. Shroyer of Los Angeles State College; Miss Maria B. Fletcher of Fletcher, North Carolina; Beale Fletcher of Asheville, North Carolina; and Mrs. Margaret Beale Umsted of Jamestown, Rhode Island.

A CATALOGUE OF SELECTED DOVER BOOKS
IN ALL FIELDS OF INTEREST

A CATALOGUE OF SELECTED DOVER BOOKS
IN ALL FIELDS OF INTEREST

AMERICA'S OLD MASTERS, James T. Flexner. Four men emerged unexpectedly from provincial 18th century America to leadership in European art: Benjamin West, J. S. Copley, C. R. Peale, Gilbert Stuart. Brilliant coverage of lives and contributions. Revised, 1967 edition. 69 plates. 365pp. of text.
21806-6 Paperbound $3.00

FIRST FLOWERS OF OUR WILDERNESS: AMERICAN PAINTING, THE COLONIAL PERIOD, James T. Flexner. Painters, and regional painting traditions from earliest Colonial times up to the emergence of Copley, West and Peale Sr., Foster, Gustavus Hesselius, Feke, John Smibert and many anonymous painters in the primitive manner. Engaging presentation, with 162 illustrations. xxii + 368pp.
22180-6 Paperbound $3.50

THE LIGHT OF DISTANT SKIES: AMERICAN PAINTING, 1760-1835, James T. Flexner. The great generation of early American painters goes to Europe to learn and to teach: West, Copley, Gilbert Stuart and others. Allston, Trumbull, Morse; also contemporary American painters—primitives, derivatives, academics—who remained in America. 102 illustrations. xiii + 306pp.
22179-2 Paperbound $3.50

A HISTORY OF THE RISE AND PROGRESS OF THE ARTS OF DESIGN IN THE UNITED STATES, William Dunlap. Much the richest mine of information on early American painters, sculptors, architects, engravers, miniaturists, etc. The only source of information for scores of artists, the major primary source for many others. Unabridged reprint of rare original 1834 edition, with new introduction by James T. Flexner, and 394 new illustrations. Edited by Rita Weiss. 6⅝ x 9⅝.
21695-0, 21696-9, 21697-7 Three volumes, Paperbound $15.00

EPOCHS OF CHINESE AND JAPANESE ART, Ernest F. Fenollosa. From primitive Chinese art to the 20th century, thorough history, explanation of every important art period and form, including Japanese woodcuts; main stress on China and Japan, but Tibet, Korea also included. Still unexcelled for its detailed, rich coverage of cultural background, aesthetic elements, diffusion studies, particularly of the historical period. 2nd, 1913 edition. 242 illustrations. lii + 439pp. of text.
20364-6, 20365-4 Two volumes, Paperbound $6.00

THE GENTLE ART OF MAKING ENEMIES, James A. M. Whistler. Greatest wit of his day deflates Oscar Wilde, Ruskin, Swinburne; strikes back at inane critics, exhibitions, art journalism; aesthetics of impressionist revolution in most striking form. Highly readable classic by great painter. Reproduction of edition designed by Whistler. Introduction by Alfred Werner. xxxvi + 334pp.
21875-9 Paperbound $3.00

CATALOGUE OF DOVER BOOKS

VISUAL ILLUSIONS: THEIR CAUSES, CHARACTERISTICS, AND APPLICATIONS, Matthew Luckiesh. Thorough description and discussion of optical illusion, geometric and perspective, particularly; size and shape distortions, illusions of color, of motion; natural illusions; use of illusion in art and magic, industry, etc. Most useful today with op art, also for classical art. Scores of effects illustrated. Introduction by William H. Ittleson. 100 illustrations. xxi + 252pp.
21530-X Paperbound $2.00

A HANDBOOK OF ANATOMY FOR ART STUDENTS, Arthur Thomson. Thorough, virtually exhaustive coverage of skeletal structure, musculature, etc. Full text, supplemented by anatomical diagrams and drawings and by photographs of undraped figures. Unique in its comparison of male and female forms, pointing out differences of contour, texture, form. 211 figures, 40 drawings, 86 photographs. xx + 459pp. 5⅜ x 8⅜.
21163-0 Paperbound $3.50

150 MASTERPIECES OF DRAWING, Selected by Anthony Toney. Full page reproductions of drawings from the early 16th to the end of the 18th century, all beautifully reproduced: Rembrandt, Michelangelo, Dürer, Fragonard, Urs, Graf, Wouwerman, many others. First-rate browsing book, model book for artists. xviii + 150pp. 8⅜ x 11¼.
21032-4 Paperbound $3.50

THE LATER WORK OF AUBREY BEARDSLEY, Aubrey Beardsley. Exotic, erotic, ironic masterpieces in full maturity: Comedy Ballet, Venus and Tannhauser, Pierrot, Lysistrata, Rape of the Lock, Savoy material, Ali Baba, Volpone, etc. This material revolutionized the art world, and is still powerful, fresh, brilliant. With *The Early Work*, all Beardsley's finest work. 174 plates, 2 in color. xiv + 176pp. 8⅛ x 11.
21817-1 Paperbound $3.75

DRAWINGS OF REMBRANDT, Rembrandt van Rijn. Complete reproduction of fabulously rare edition by Lippmann and Hofstede de Groot, completely reedited, updated, improved by Prof. Seymour Slive, Fogg Museum. Portraits, Biblical sketches, landscapes, Oriental types, nudes, episodes from classical mythology—All Rembrandt's fertile genius. Also selection of drawings by his pupils and followers. "Stunning volumes," *Saturday Review*. 550 illustrations. lxxviii + 552pp. 9⅛ x 12¼.
21485-0, 21486-9 Two volumes, Paperbound $10.00

THE DISASTERS OF WAR, Francisco Goya. One of the masterpieces of Western civilization—83 etchings that record Goya's shattering, bitter reaction to the Napoleonic war that swept through Spain after the insurrection of 1808 and to war in general. Reprint of the first edition, with three additional plates from Boston's Museum of Fine Arts. All plates facsimile size. Introduction by Philip Hofer, Fogg Museum. v + 97pp. 9⅜ x 8¼.
21872-4 Paperbound $2.50

GRAPHIC WORKS OF ODILON REDON. Largest collection of Redon's graphic works ever assembled: 172 lithographs, 28 etchings and engravings, 9 drawings. These include some of his most famous works. All the plates from *Odilon Redon: oeuvre graphique complet,* plus additional plates. New introduction and caption translations by Alfred Werner. 209 illustrations. xxvii + 209pp. 9⅛ x 12¼.
21966-8 Paperbound $5.00

DESIGN BY ACCIDENT; A BOOK OF "ACCIDENTAL EFFECTS" FOR ARTISTS AND DESIGNERS, James F. O'Brien. Create your own unique, striking, imaginative effects by "controlled accident" interaction of materials: paints and lacquers, oil and water based paints, splatter, crackling materials, shatter, similar items. Everything you do will be different; first book on this limitless art, so useful to both fine artist and commercial artist. Full instructions. 192 plates showing "accidents," 8 in color. viii + 215pp. 8⅜ x 11¼.   21942-9 Paperbound $3.75

THE BOOK OF SIGNS, Rudolf Koch. Famed German type designer draws 493 beautiful symbols: religious, mystical, alchemical, imperial, property marks, runes, etc. Remarkable fusion of traditional and modern. Good for suggestions of timelessness, smartness, modernity. Text. vi + 104pp. 6⅛ x 9¼.
                                                   20162-7 Paperbound $1.25

HISTORY OF INDIAN AND INDONESIAN ART, Ananda K. Coomaraswamy. An unabridged republication of one of the finest books by a great scholar in Eastern art. Rich in descriptive material, history, social backgrounds; Sunga reliefs, Rajput paintings, Gupta temples, Burmese frescoes, textiles, jewelry, sculpture, etc. 400 photos. viii + 423pp. 6⅜ x 9¾.   21436-2 Paperbound $5.00

PRIMITIVE ART, Franz Boas. America's foremost anthropologist surveys textiles, ceramics, woodcarving, basketry, metalwork, etc.; patterns, technology, creation of symbols, style origins. All areas of world, but very full on Northwest Coast Indians. More than 350 illustrations of baskets, boxes, totem poles, weapons, etc. 378 pp.
                                                   20025-6 Paperbound $3.00

THE GENTLEMAN AND CABINET MAKER'S DIRECTOR, Thomas Chippendale. Full reprint (third edition, 1762) of most influential furniture book of all time, by master cabinetmaker. 200 plates, illustrating chairs, sofas, mirrors, tables, cabinets, plus 24 photographs of surviving pieces. Biographical introduction by N. Bienenstock. vi + 249pp. 9⅞ x 12¾.   21601-2 Paperbound $4.00

AMERICAN ANTIQUE FURNITURE, Edgar G. Miller, Jr. The basic coverage of all American furniture before 1840. Individual chapters cover type of furniture—clocks, tables, sideboards, etc.—chronologically, with inexhaustible wealth of data. More than 2100 photographs, all identified, commented on. Essential to all early American collectors. Introduction by H. E. Keyes. vi + 1106pp. 7⅞ x 10¾.
                          21599-7, 21600-4 Two volumes, Paperbound $11.00

PENNSYLVANIA DUTCH AMERICAN FOLK ART, Henry J. Kauffman. 279 photos, 28 drawings of tulipware, Fraktur script, painted tinware, toys, flowered furniture, quilts, samplers, hex signs, house interiors, etc. Full descriptive text. Excellent for tourist, rewarding for designer, collector. Map. 146pp. 7⅞ x 10¾.
                                                   21205-X Paperbound $2.50

EARLY NEW ENGLAND GRAVESTONE RUBBINGS, Edmund V. Gillon, Jr. 43 photographs, 226 carefully reproduced rubbings show heavily symbolic, sometimes macabre early gravestones, up to early 19th century. Remarkable early American primitive art, occasionally strikingly beautiful; always powerful. Text. xxvi + 207pp. 8⅜ x 11¼.   21380-3 Paperbound $3.50

ALPHABETS AND ORNAMENTS, Ernst Lehner. Well-known pictorial source for decorative alphabets, script examples, cartouches, frames, decorative title pages, calligraphic initials, borders, similar material. 14th to 19th century, mostly European. Useful in almost any graphic arts designing, varied styles. 750 illustrations. 256pp. 7 x 10. 21905-4 Paperbound $4.00

PAINTING: A CREATIVE APPROACH, Norman Colquhoun. For the beginner simple guide provides an instructive approach to painting: major stumbling blocks for beginner; overcoming them, technical points; paints and pigments; oil painting; watercolor and other media and color. New section on "plastic" paints. Glossary. Formerly *Paint Your Own Pictures.* 221pp. 22000-1 Paperbound $1.75

THE ENJOYMENT AND USE OF COLOR, Walter Sargent. Explanation of the relations between colors themselves and between colors in nature and art, including hundreds of little-known facts about color values, intensities, effects of high and low illumination, complementary colors. Many practical hints for painters, references to great masters. 7 color plates, 29 illustrations. x + 274pp.
20944-X Paperbound $2.75

THE NOTEBOOKS OF LEONARDO DA VINCI, compiled and edited by Jean Paul Richter. 1566 extracts from original manuscripts reveal the full range of Leonardo's versatile genius: all his writings on painting, sculpture, architecture, anatomy, astronomy, geography, topography, physiology, mining, music, etc., in both Italian and English, with 186 plates of manuscript pages and more than 500 additional drawings. Includes studies for the Last Supper, the lost Sforza monument, and other works. Total of xlvii + 866pp. 7⅞ x 10¾.
22572-0, 22573-9 Two volumes, Paperbound $11.00

MONTGOMERY WARD CATALOGUE OF 1895. Tea gowns, yards of flannel and pillow-case lace, stereoscopes, books of gospel hymns, the New Improved Singer Sewing Machine, side saddles, milk skimmers, straight-edged razors, high-button shoes, spittoons, and on and on . . . listing some 25,000 items, practically all illustrated. Essential to the shoppers of the 1890's, it is our truest record of the spirit of the period. Unaltered reprint of Issue No. 57, Spring and Summer 1895. Introduction by Boris Emmet. Innumerable illustrations. xiii + 624pp. 8½ x 11⅝.
22377-9 Paperbound $6.95

THE CRYSTAL PALACE EXHIBITION ILLUSTRATED CATALOGUE (LONDON, 1851). One of the wonders of the modern world—the Crystal Palace Exhibition in which all the nations of the civilized world exhibited their achievements in the arts and sciences—presented in an equally important illustrated catalogue. More than 1700 items pictured with accompanying text—ceramics, textiles, cast-iron work, carpets, pianos, sleds, razors, wall-papers, billiard tables, beehives, silverware and hundreds of other artifacts—represent the focal point of Victorian culture in the Western World. Probably the largest collection of Victorian decorative art ever assembled—indispensable for antiquarians and designers. Unabridged republication of the Art-Journal Catalogue of the Great Exhibition of 1851, with all terminal essays. New introduction by John Gloag, F.S.A. xxxiv + 426pp. 9 x 12.
22503-8 Paperbound $5.00

CATALOGUE OF DOVER BOOKS

A HISTORY OF COSTUME, Carl Köhler. Definitive history, based on surviving pieces of clothing primarily, and paintings, statues, etc. secondarily. Highly readable text, supplemented by 594 illustrations of costumes of the ancient Mediterranean peoples, Greece and Rome, the Teutonic prehistoric period; costumes of the Middle Ages, Renaissance, Baroque, 18th and 19th centuries. Clear, measured patterns are provided for many clothing articles. Approach is practical throughout. Enlarged by Emma von Sichart. 464pp. 21030-8 Paperbound $3.50.

ORIENTAL RUGS, ANTIQUE AND MODERN, Walter A. Hawley. A complete and authoritative treatise on the Oriental rug—where they are made, by whom and how, designs and symbols, characteristics in detail of the six major groups, how to distinguish them and how to buy them. Detailed technical data is provided on periods, weaves, warps, wefts, textures, sides, ends and knots, although no technical background is required for an understanding. 11 color plates, 80 halftones, 4 maps. vi + 320pp. 6⅛ x 9⅛. 22366-3 Paperbound $5.00

TEN BOOKS ON ARCHITECTURE, Vitruvius. By any standards the most important book on architecture ever written. Early Roman discussion of aesthetics of building, construction methods, orders, sites, and every other aspect of architecture has inspired, instructed architecture for about 2,000 years. Stands behind Palladio, Michelangelo, Bramante, Wren, countless others. Definitive Morris H. Morgan translation. 68 illustrations. xii + 331pp. 20645-9 Paperbound $3.00

THE FOUR BOOKS OF ARCHITECTURE, Andrea Palladio. Translated into every major Western European language in the two centuries following its publication in 1570, this has been one of the most influential books in the history of architecture. Complete reprint of the 1738 Isaac Ware edition. New introduction by Adolf Placzek, Columbia Univ. 216 plates. xxii + 110pp. of text. 9½ x 12¾. 21308-0 Clothbound $12.50

STICKS AND STONES: A STUDY OF AMERICAN ARCHITECTURE AND CIVILIZATION, Lewis Mumford.One of the great classics of American cultural history. American architecture from the medieval-inspired earliest forms to the early 20th century; evolution of structure and style, and reciprocal influences on environment. 21 photographic illustrations. 238pp. 20202-X Paperbound $2.00

THE AMERICAN BUILDER'S COMPANION, Asher Benjamin. The most widely used early 19th century architectural style and source book, for colonial up into Greek Revival periods. Extensive development of geometry of carpentering, construction of sashes, frames, doors, stairs; plans and elevations of domestic and other buildings. Hundreds of thousands of houses were built according to this book, now invaluable to historians, architects, restorers, etc. 1827 edition. 59 plates. 114pp. 7⅞ x 10¾. 22236-5 Paperbound $3.50

DUTCH HOUSES IN THE HUDSON VALLEY BEFORE 1776, Helen Wilkinson Reynolds. The standard survey of the Dutch colonial house and outbuildings, with constructional features, decoration, and local history associated with individual homesteads. Introduction by Franklin D. Roosevelt. Map. 150 illustrations. 469pp. 6⅝ x 9¼. 21469-9 Paperbound $5.00

CATALOGUE OF DOVER BOOKS

THE ARCHITECTURE OF COUNTRY HOUSES, Andrew J. Downing. Together with Vaux's *Villas and Cottages* this is the basic book for Hudson River Gothic architecture of the middle Victorian period. Full, sound discussions of general aspects of housing, architecture, style, decoration, furnishing, together with scores of detailed house plans, illustrations of specific buildings, accompanied by full text. Perhaps the most influential single American architectural book. 1850 edition. Introduction by J. Stewart Johnson. 321 figures, 34 architectural designs. xvi + 560pp.
22003-6 Paperbound $4.00

LOST EXAMPLES OF COLONIAL ARCHITECTURE, John Mead Howells. Full-page photographs of buildings that have disappeared or been so altered as to be denatured, including many designed by major early American architects. 245 plates. xvii + 248pp. 7⅞ x 10¾. 21143-6 Paperbound $3.50

DOMESTIC ARCHITECTURE OF THE AMERICAN COLONIES AND OF THE EARLY REPUBLIC, Fiske Kimball. Foremost architect and restorer of Williamsburg and Monticello covers nearly 200 homes between 1620-1825. Architectural details, construction, style features, special fixtures, floor plans, etc. Generally considered finest work in its area. 219 illustrations of houses, doorways, windows, capital mantels. xx + 314pp. 7⅞ x 10¾. 21743-4 Paperbound $4.00

EARLY AMERICAN ROOMS: 1650-1858, edited by Russell Hawes Kettell. Tour of 12 rooms, each representative of a different era in American history and each furnished, decorated, designed and occupied in the style of the era. 72 plans and elevations, 8-page color section, etc., show fabrics, wall papers, arrangements, etc. Full descriptive text. xvii + 200pp. of text. 8⅜ x 11¼. 21633-0 Paperbound $5.00

THE FITZWILLIAM VIRGINAL BOOK, edited by J. Fuller Maitland and W. B. Squire. Full modern printing of famous early 17th-century ms. volume of 300 works by Morley, Byrd, Bull, Gibbons, etc. For piano or other modern keyboard instrument; easy to read format. xxxvi + 938pp. 8⅜ x 11. 21068-5, 21069-3 Two volumes, Paperbound $10.00

KEYBOARD MUSIC, Johann Sebastian Bach. Bach Gesellschaft edition. A rich selection of Bach's masterpieces for the harpsichord: the six English Suites, six French Suites, the six Partitas (Clavierübung part I), the Goldberg Variations (Clavierübung part IV), the fifteen Two-Part Inventions and the fifteen Three-Part Sinfonias. Clearly reproduced on large sheets with ample margins; eminently playable. vi + 312pp. 8⅛ x 11. 22360-4 Paperbound $5.00

THE MUSIC OF BACH: AN INTRODUCTION, Charles Sanford Terry. A fine, nontechnical introduction to Bach's music, both instrumental and vocal. Covers organ music, chamber music, passion music, other types. Analyzes themes, developments, innovations. x + 114pp. 21075-8 Paperbound $1.50

BEETHOVEN AND HIS NINE SYMPHONIES, Sir George Grove. Noted British musicologist provides best history, analysis, commentary on symphonies. Very thorough, rigorously accurate; necessary to both advanced student and amateur music lover. 436 musical passages. vii + 407 pp. 20334-4 Paperbound $2.75

JOHANN SEBASTIAN BACH, Philipp Spitta. One of the great classics of musicology, this definitive analysis of Bach's music (and life) has never been surpassed. Lucid, nontechnical analyses of hundreds of pieces (30 pages devoted to St. Matthew Passion, 26 to B Minor Mass). Also includes major analysis of 18th-century music. 450 musical examples. 40-page musical supplement. Total of xx + 1799pp.
(EUK) 22278-0, 22279-9 Two volumes, Clothbound $17.50

MOZART AND HIS PIANO CONCERTOS, Cuthbert Girdlestone. The only full-length study of an important area of Mozart's creativity. Provides detailed analyses of all 23 concertos, traces inspirational sources. 417 musical examples. Second edition. 509pp.   21271-8 Paperbound $3.50

THE PERFECT WAGNERITE: A COMMENTARY ON THE NIBLUNG'S RING, George Bernard Shaw. Brilliant and still relevant criticism in remarkable essays on Wagner's Ring cycle, Shaw's ideas on political and social ideology behind the plots, role of Leitmotifs, vocal requisites, etc. Prefaces. xxi + 136pp.
(USO) 21707-8 Paperbound $1.75

DON GIOVANNI, W. A. Mozart. Complete libretto, modern English translation; biographies of composer and librettist; accounts of early performances and critical reaction. Lavishly illustrated. All the material you need to understand and appreciate this great work. Dover Opera Guide and Libretto Series; translated and introduced by Ellen Bleiler. 92 illustrations. 209pp.
21134-7 Paperbound $2.00

BASIC ELECTRICITY, U. S. Bureau of Naval Personel. Originally a training course, best non-technical coverage of basic theory of electricity and its applications. Fundamental concepts, batteries, circuits, conductors and wiring techniques, AC and DC, inductance and capacitance, generators, motors, transformers, magnetic amplifiers, synchros, servomechanisms, etc. Also covers blue-prints, electrical diagrams, etc. Many questions, with answers. 349 illustrations. x + 448pp. 6½ x 9¼.
20973-3 Paperbound $3.50

REPRODUCTION OF SOUND, Edgar Villchur. Thorough coverage for laymen of high fidelity systems, reproducing systems in general, needles, amplifiers, preamps, loudspeakers, feedback, explaining physical background. "A rare talent for making technicalities vividly comprehensible," R. Darrell, *High Fidelity*. 69 figures. iv + 92pp.   21515-6 Paperbound $1.35

HEAR ME TALKIN' TO YA: THE STORY OF JAZZ AS TOLD BY THE MEN WHO MADE IT, Nat Shapiro and Nat Hentoff. Louis Armstrong, Fats Waller, Jo Jones, Clarence Williams, Billy Holiday, Duke Ellington, Jelly Roll Morton and dozens of other jazz greats tell how it was in Chicago's South Side, New Orleans, depression Harlem and the modern West Coast as jazz was born and grew. xvi + 429pp.
21726-4 Paperbound $3.00

FABLES OF AESOP, translated by Sir Roger L'Estrange. A reproduction of the very rare 1931 Paris edition; a selection of the most interesting fables, together with 50 imaginative drawings by Alexander Calder. v + 128pp. 6½x9¼.
21780-9 Paperbound $1.50

AGAINST THE GRAIN (A REBOURS), Joris K. Huysmans. Filled with weird images, evidences of a bizarre imagination, exotic experiments with hallucinatory drugs, rich tastes and smells and the diversions of its sybarite hero Duc Jean des Esseintes, this classic novel pushed 19th-century literary decadence to its limits. Full unabridged edition. Do not confuse this with abridged editions generally sold. Introduction by Havelock Ellis. xlix + 206pp. 22190-3 Paperbound $2.50

VARIORUM SHAKESPEARE: HAMLET. Edited by Horace H. Furness; a landmark of American scholarship. Exhaustive footnotes and appendices treat all doubtful words and phrases, as well as suggested critical emendations throughout the play's history. First volume contains editor's own text, collated with all Quartos and Folios. Second volume contains full first Quarto, translations of Shakespeare's sources (Belleforest, and Saxo Grammaticus), Der Bestrafte Brudermord, and many essays on critical and historical points of interest by major authorities of past and present. Includes details of staging and costuming over the years. By far the best edition available for serious students of Shakespeare. Total of xx + 905pp. 21004-9, 21005-7, 2 volumes, Paperbound $7.00

A LIFE OF WILLIAM SHAKESPEARE, Sir Sidney Lee. This is the standard life of Shakespeare, summarizing everything known about Shakespeare and his plays. Incredibly rich in material, broad in coverage, clear and judicious, it has served thousands as the best introduction to Shakespeare. 1931 edition. 9 plates. xxix + 792pp. 21967-4 Paperbound $4.50

MASTERS OF THE DRAMA, John Gassner. Most comprehensive history of the drama in print, covering every tradition from Greeks to modern Europe and America, including India, Far East, etc. Covers more than 800 dramatists, 2000 plays, with biographical material, plot summaries, theatre history, criticism, etc. "Best of its kind in English," New Republic. 77 illustrations. xxii + 890pp. 20100-7 Clothbound $10.00

THE EVOLUTION OF THE ENGLISH LANGUAGE, George McKnight. The growth of English, from the 14th century to the present. Unusual, non-technical account presents basic information in very interesting form: sound shifts, change in grammar and syntax, vocabulary growth, similar topics. Abundantly illustrated with quotations. Formerly Modern English in the Making. xii + 590pp. 21932-1 Paperbound $4.00

AN ETYMOLOGICAL DICTIONARY OF MODERN ENGLISH, Ernest Weekley. Fullest, richest work of its sort, by foremost British lexicographer. Detailed word histories, including many colloquial and archaic words; extensive quotations. Do not confuse this with the Concise Etymological Dictionary, which is much abridged. Total of xxvii + 830pp. 6½ x 9¼. 21873-2, 21874-0 Two volumes, Paperbound $7.90

FLATLAND: A ROMANCE OF MANY DIMENSIONS, E. A. Abbott. Classic of science-fiction explores ramifications of life in a two-dimensional world, and what happens when a three-dimensional being intrudes. Amusing reading, but also useful as introduction to thought about hyperspace. Introduction by Banesh Hoffmann. 16 illustrations. xx + 103pp. 20001-9 Paperbound $1.25

POEMS OF ANNE BRADSTREET, edited with an introduction by Robert Hutchinson. A new selection of poems by America's first poet and perhaps the first significant woman poet in the English language. 48 poems display her development in works of considerable variety—love poems, domestic poems, religious meditations, formal elegies, "quaternions," etc. Notes, bibliography. viii + 222pp.

22160-1 Paperbound $2.50

THREE GOTHIC NOVELS: THE CASTLE OF OTRANTO BY HORACE WALPOLE; VATHEK BY WILLIAM BECKFORD; THE VAMPYRE BY JOHN POLIDORI, WITH FRAGMENT OF A NOVEL BY LORD BYRON, edited by E. F. Bleiler. The first Gothic novel, by Walpole; the finest Oriental tale in English, by Beckford; powerful Romantic supernatural story in versions by Polidori and Byron. All extremely important in history of literature; all still exciting, packed with supernatural thrills, ghosts, haunted castles, magic, etc. xl + 291pp.

21232-7 Paperbound $2.50

THE BEST TALES OF HOFFMANN, E. T. A. Hoffmann. 10 of Hoffmann's most important stories, in modern re-editings of standard translations: Nutcracker and the King of Mice, Signor Formica, Automata, The Sandman, Rath Krespel, The Golden Flowerpot, Master Martin the Cooper, The Mines of Falun, The King's Betrothed, A New Year's Eve Adventure. 7 illustrations by Hoffmann. Edited by E. F. Bleiler. xxxix + 419pp.

21793-0 Paperbound $3.00

GHOST AND HORROR STORIES OF AMBROSE BIERCE, Ambrose Bierce. 23 strikingly modern stories of the horrors latent in the human mind: The Eyes of the Panther, The Damned Thing, An Occurrence at Owl Creek Bridge, An Inhabitant of Carcosa, etc., plus the dream-essay, Visions of the Night. Edited by E. F. Bleiler. xxii + 199pp.

20767-6 Paperbound $1.50

BEST GHOST STORIES OF J. S. LEFANU, J. Sheridan LeFanu. Finest stories by Victorian master often considered greatest supernatural writer of all. Carmilla, Green Tea, The Haunted Baronet, The Familiar, and 12 others. Most never before available in the U. S. A. Edited by E. F. Bleiler. 8 illustrations from Victorian publications. xvii + 467pp.

20415-4 Paperbound $3.00

MATHEMATICAL FOUNDATIONS OF INFORMATION THEORY, A. I. Khinchin. Comprehensive introduction to work of Shannon, McMillan, Feinstein and Khinchin, placing these investigations on a rigorous mathematical basis. Covers entropy concept in probability theory, uniqueness theorem, Shannon's inequality, ergodic sources, the E property, martingale concept, noise, Feinstein's fundamental lemma, Shanon's first and second theorems. Translated by R. A. Silverman and M. D. Friedman. iii + 120pp.

60434-9 Paperbound $2.00

SEVEN SCIENCE FICTION NOVELS, H. G. Wells. The standard collection of the great novels. Complete, unabridged. *First Men in the Moon, Island of Dr. Moreau, War of the Worlds, Food of the Gods, Invisible Man, Time Machine, In the Days of the Comet.* Not only science fiction fans, but every educated person owes it to himself to read these novels. 1015pp. (USO) 20264-X Clothbound $6.00

LAST AND FIRST MEN AND STAR MAKER, TWO SCIENCE FICTION NOVELS, Olaf Stapledon. Greatest future histories in science fiction. In the first, human intelligence is the "hero," through strange paths of evolution, interplanetary invasions, incredible technologies, near extinctions and reemergences. Star Maker describes the quest of a band of star rovers for intelligence itself, through time and space: weird inhuman civilizations, crustacean minds, symbiotic worlds, etc. Complete, unabridged. v + 438pp.   (USO) 21962-3 Paperbound $2.50

THREE PROPHETIC NOVELS, H. G. WELLS. Stages of a consistently planned future for mankind. *When the Sleeper Wakes,* and *A Story of the Days to Come,* anticipate *Brave New World* and *1984,* in the 21st Century; *The Time Machine,* only complete version in print, shows farther future and the end of mankind. All show Wells's greatest gifts as storyteller and novelist. Edited by E. F. Bleiler. x + 335pp.   (USO) 20605-X Paperbound $2.50

THE DEVIL'S DICTIONARY, Ambrose Bierce. America's own Oscar Wilde—Ambrose Bierce—offers his barbed iconoclastic wisdom in over 1,000 definitions hailed by H. L. Mencken as "some of the most gorgeous witticisms in the English language." 145pp.   20487-1 Paperbound $1.25

MAX AND MORITZ, Wilhelm Busch. Great children's classic, father of comic strip, of two bad boys, Max and Moritz. Also Ker and Plunk (Plisch und Plumm), Cat and Mouse, Deceitful Henry, Ice-Peter, The Boy and the Pipe, and five other pieces. Original German, with English translation. Edited by H. Arthur Klein; translations by various hands and H. Arthur Klein. vi + 216pp.
20181-3 Paperbound $2.00

PIGS IS PIGS AND OTHER FAVORITES, Ellis Parker Butler. The title story is one of the best humor short stories, as Mike Flannery obfuscates biology and English. Also included, That Pup of Murchison's, The Great American Pie Company, and Perkins of Portland. 14 illustrations. v + 109pp.   21532-6 Paperbound $1.25

THE PETERKIN PAPERS, Lucretia P. Hale. It takes genius to be as stupidly mad as the Peterkins, as they decide to become wise, celebrate the "Fourth," keep a cow, and otherwise strain the resources of the Lady from Philadelphia. Basic book of American humor. 153 illustrations. 219pp.   20794-3 Paperbound $2.00

PERRAULT'S FAIRY TALES, translated by A. E. Johnson and S. R. Littlewood, with 34 full-page illustrations by Gustave Doré. All the original Perrault stories—Cinderella, Sleeping Beauty, Bluebeard, Little Red Riding Hood, Puss in Boots, Tom Thumb, etc.—with their witty verse morals and the magnificent illustrations of Doré. One of the five or six great books of European fairy tales. viii + 117pp. 8⅛ x 11.   22311-6 Paperbound $2.00

OLD HUNGARIAN FAIRY TALES, Baroness Orczy. Favorites translated and adapted by author of the *Scarlet Pimpernel.* Eight fairy tales include "The Suitors of Princess Fire-Fly," "The Twin Hunchbacks," "Mr. Cuttlefish's Love Story," and "The Enchanted Cat." This little volume of magic and adventure will captivate children as it has for generations. 90 drawings by Montagu Barstow. 96pp.
(USO) 22293-4 Paperbound $1.95

THE RED FAIRY BOOK, Andrew Lang. Lang's color fairy books have long been children's favorites. This volume includes Rapunzel, Jack and the Bean-stalk and 35 other stories, familiar and unfamiliar. 4 plates, 93 illustrations x + 367pp.
21673-X Paperbound $2.50

THE BLUE FAIRY BOOK, Andrew Lang. Lang's tales come from all countries and all times. Here are 37 tales from Grimm, the Arabian Nights, Greek Mythology, and other fascinating sources. 8 plates, 130 illustrations. xi + 390pp.
21437-0 Paperbound $2.75

HOUSEHOLD STORIES BY THE BROTHERS GRIMM. Classic English-language edition of the well-known tales — Rumpelstiltskin, Snow White, Hansel and Gretel, The Twelve Brothers, Faithful John, Rapunzel, Tom Thumb (52 stories in all). Translated into simple, straightforward English by Lucy Crane. Ornamented with headpieces, vignettes, elaborate decorative initials and a dozen full-page illustrations by Walter Crane. x + 269pp.
21080-4 Paperbound **$2.00**

THE MERRY ADVENTURES OF ROBIN HOOD, Howard Pyle. The finest modern versions of the traditional ballads and tales about the great English outlaw. Howard Pyle's complete prose version, with every word, every illustration of the first edition. Do not confuse this facsimile of the original (1883) with modern editions that change text or illustrations. 23 plates plus many page decorations. xxii + 296pp.
22043-5 Paperbound $2.75

THE STORY OF KING ARTHUR AND HIS KNIGHTS, Howard Pyle. The finest children's version of the life of King Arthur; brilliantly retold by Pyle, with 48 of his most imaginative illustrations. xviii + 313pp. 6⅛ x 9¼.
21445-1 Paperbound $2.50

THE WONDERFUL WIZARD OF OZ, L. Frank Baum. America's finest children's book in facsimile of first edition with all Denslow illustrations in full color. The edition a child should have. Introduction by Martin Gardner. 23 color plates, scores of drawings. iv + 267pp.
20691-2 Paperbound $2.50

THE MARVELOUS LAND OF OZ, L. Frank Baum. The second Oz book, every bit as imaginative as the Wizard. The hero is a boy named Tip, but the Scarecrow and the Tin Woodman are back, as is the Oz magic. 16 color plates, 120 drawings by John R. Neill. 287pp.
20692-0 Paperbound $2.50

THE MAGICAL MONARCH OF MO, L. Frank Baum. Remarkable adventures in a land even stranger than Oz. The best of Baum's books not in the Oz series. 15 color plates and dozens of drawings by Frank Verbeck. xviii + 237pp.
21892-9 Paperbound $2.25

THE BAD CHILD'S BOOK OF BEASTS, MORE BEASTS FOR WORSE CHILDREN, A MORAL ALPHABET, Hilaire Belloc. Three complete humor classics in one volume. Be kind to the frog, and do not call him names . . . and 28 other whimsical animals. Familiar favorites and some not so well known. Illustrated by Basil Blackwell. 156pp.
(USO) 20749-8 Paperbound $1.50

EAST O' THE SUN AND WEST O' THE MOON, George W. Dasent. Considered the best of all translations of these Norwegian folk tales, this collection has been enjoyed by generations of children (and folklorists too). Includes True and Untrue, Why the Sea is Salt, East O' the Sun and West O' the Moon, Why the Bear is Stumpy-Tailed, Boots and the Troll, The Cock and the Hen, Rich Peter the Pedlar, and 52 more. The only edition with all 59 tales. 77 illustrations by Erik Werenskiold and Theodor Kittelsen. xv + 418pp. 22521-6 Paperbound $3.50

GOOPS AND HOW TO BE THEM, Gelett Burgess. Classic of tongue-in-cheek humor, masquerading as etiquette book. 87 verses, twice as many cartoons, show mischievous Goops as they demonstrate to children virtues of table manners, neatness, courtesy, etc. Favorite for generations. viii + 88pp. 6½ x 9¼.
22233-0 Paperbound $1.50

ALICE'S ADVENTURES UNDER GROUND, Lewis Carroll. The first version, quite different from the final Alice in Wonderland, printed out by Carroll himself with his own illustrations. Complete facsimile of the "million dollar" manuscript Carroll gave to Alice Liddell in 1864. Introduction by Martin Gardner. viii + 96pp. Title and dedication pages in color. 21482-6 Paperbound $1.25

THE BROWNIES, THEIR BOOK, Palmer Cox. Small as mice, cunning as foxes, exuberant and full of mischief, the Brownies go to the zoo, toy shop, seashore, circus, etc., in 24 verse adventures and 266 illustrations. Long a favorite, since their first appearance in St. Nicholas Magazine. xi + 144pp. 6⅝ x 9¼.
21265-3 Paperbound $1.75

SONGS OF CHILDHOOD, Walter De La Mare. Published (under the pseudonym Walter Ramal) when De La Mare was only 29, this charming collection has long been a favorite children's book. A facsimile of the first edition in paper, the 47 poems capture the simplicity of the nursery rhyme and the ballad, including such lyrics as I Met Eve, Tartary, The Silver Penny. vii + 106pp. (USO) 21972-0 Paperbound $2.00

THE COMPLETE NONSENSE OF EDWARD LEAR, Edward Lear. The finest 19th-century humorist-cartoonist in full: all nonsense limericks, zany alphabets, Owl and Pussycat, songs, nonsense botany, and more than 500 illustrations by Lear himself. Edited by Holbrook Jackson. xxix + 287pp. (USO) 20167-8 Paperbound $2.00

BILLY WHISKERS: THE AUTOBIOGRAPHY OF A GOAT, Frances Trego Montgomery. A favorite of children since the early 20th century, here are the escapades of that rambunctious, irresistible and mischievous goat—Billy Whiskers. Much in the spirit of Peck's Bad Boy, this is a book that children never tire of reading or hearing. All the original familiar illustrations by W. H. Fry are included: 6 color plates, 18 black and white drawings. 159pp. 22345-0 Paperbound $2.00

MOTHER GOOSE MELODIES. Faithful republication of the fabulously rare Munroe and Francis "copyright 1833" Boston edition—the most important Mother Goose collection, usually referred to as the "original." Familiar rhymes plus many rare ones, with wonderful old woodcut illustrations. Edited by E. F. Bleiler. 128pp. 4½ x 6⅜. 22577-1 Paperbound $1.00

TWO LITTLE SAVAGES; BEING THE ADVENTURES OF TWO BOYS WHO LIVED AS INDIANS AND WHAT THEY LEARNED, Ernest Thompson Seton. Great classic of nature and boyhood provides a vast range of woodlore in most palatable form, a genuinely entertaining story. Two farm boys build a teepee in woods and live in it for a month, working out Indian solutions to living problems, star lore, birds and animals, plants, etc. 293 illustrations. vii + 286pp.

20985-7 Paperbound $2.50

PETER PIPER'S PRACTICAL PRINCIPLES OF PLAIN & PERFECT PRONUNCIATION. Alliterative jingles and tongue-twisters of surprising charm, that made their first appearance in America about 1830. Republished in full with the spirited woodcut illustrations from this earliest American edition. 32pp. 4½ x 6⅜.

22560-7 Paperbound $1.00

SCIENCE EXPERIMENTS AND AMUSEMENTS FOR CHILDREN, Charles Vivian. 73 easy experiments, requiring only materials found at home or easily available, such as candles, coins, steel wool, etc.; illustrate basic phenomena like vacuum, simple chemical reaction, etc. All safe. Modern, well-planned. Formerly *Science Games for Children*. 102 photos, numerous drawings. 96pp. 6⅛ x 9¼.

21856-2 Paperbound $1.25

AN INTRODUCTION TO CHESS MOVES AND TACTICS SIMPLY EXPLAINED, Leonard Barden. Informal intermediate introduction, quite strong in explaining reasons for moves. Covers basic material, tactics, important openings, traps, positional play in middle game, end game. Attempts to isolate patterns and recurrent configurations. Formerly *Chess*. 58 figures. 102pp. (USO) 21210-6 Paperbound $1.25

LASKER'S MANUAL OF CHESS, Dr. Emanuel Lasker. Lasker was not only one of the five great World Champions, he was also one of the ablest expositors, theorists, and analysts. In many ways, his Manual, permeated with his philosophy of battle, filled with keen insights, is one of the greatest works ever written on chess. Filled with analyzed games by the great players. A single-volume library that will profit almost any chess player, beginner or master. 308 diagrams. xli x 349pp.

20640-8 Paperbound $2.75

THE MASTER BOOK OF MATHEMATICAL RECREATIONS, Fred Schuh. In opinion of many the finest work ever prepared on mathematical puzzles, stunts, recreations; exhaustively thorough explanations of mathematics involved, analysis of effects, citation of puzzles and games. Mathematics involved is elementary. Translated by F. Göbel. 194 figures. xxiv + 430pp.

22134-2 Paperbound $3.50

MATHEMATICS, MAGIC AND MYSTERY, Martin Gardner. Puzzle editor for Scientific American explains mathematics behind various mystifying tricks: card tricks, stage "mind reading," coin and match tricks, counting out games, geometric dissections, etc. Probability sets, theory of numbers clearly explained. Also provides more than 400 tricks, guaranteed to work, that you can do. 135 illustrations. xii + 176pp.

20335-2 Paperbound $1.75

MATHEMATICAL PUZZLES FOR BEGINNERS AND ENTHUSIASTS, Geoffrey Mott-Smith. 189 puzzles from easy to difficult—involving arithmetic, logic, algebra, properties of digits, probability, etc.—for enjoyment and mental stimulus. Explanation of mathematical principles behind the puzzles. 135 illustrations. viii + 248pp.
20198-8 Paperbound $1.75

PAPER FOLDING FOR BEGINNERS, William D. Murray and Francis J. Rigney. Easiest book on the market, clearest instructions on making interesting, beautiful origami. Sail boats, cups, roosters, frogs that move legs, bonbon boxes, standing birds, etc. 40 projects; more than 275 diagrams and photographs. 94pp.
20713-7 Paperbound $1.00

TRICKS AND GAMES ON THE POOL TABLE, Fred Herrmann. 79 tricks and games— some solitaires, some for two or more players, some competitive games—to entertain you between formal games. Mystifying shots and throws, unusual caroms, tricks involving such props as cork, coins, a hat, etc. Formerly *Fun on the Pool Table*. 77 figures. 95pp.
21814-7 Paperbound $1.25

HAND SHADOWS TO BE THROWN UPON THE WALL: A SERIES OF NOVEL AND AMUSING FIGURES FORMED BY THE HAND, Henry Bursill. Delightful picturebook from great-grandfather's day shows how to make 18 different hand shadows: a bird that flies, duck that quacks, dog that wags his tail, camel, goose, deer, boy, turtle, etc. Only book of its sort. vi + 33pp. 6½ x 9¼.
21779-5 Paperbound $1.00

WHITTLING AND WOODCARVING, E. J. Tangerman. 18th printing of best book on market. "If you can cut a potato you can carve" toys and puzzles, chains, chessmen, caricatures, masks, frames, woodcut blocks, surface patterns, much more. Information on tools, woods, techniques. Also goes into serious wood sculpture from Middle Ages to present, East and West. 464 photos, figures. x + 293pp.
20965-2 Paperbound $2.00

HISTORY OF PHILOSOPHY, Julián Marias. Possibly the clearest, most easily followed, best planned, most useful one-volume history of philosophy on the market; neither skimpy nor overfull. Full details on system of every major philosopher and dozens of less important thinkers from pre-Socratics up to Existentialism and later. Strong on many European figures usually omitted. Has gone through dozens of editions in Europe. 1966 edition, translated by Stanley Appelbaum and Clarence Strowbridge. xviii + 505pp.
21739-6 Paperbound $3.50

YOGA: A SCIENTIFIC EVALUATION, Kovoor T. Behanan. Scientific but non-technical study of physiological results of yoga exercises; done under auspices of Yale U. Relations to Indian thought, to psychoanalysis, etc. 16 photos. xxiii + 270pp.
20505-3 Paperbound $2.50

Prices subject to change without notice.
Available at your book dealer or write for free catalogue to Dept. GI, Dover Publications, Inc., 180 Varick St., N. Y., N. Y. 10014. Dover publishes more than 150 books each year on science, elementary and advanced mathematics, biology, music, art, literary history, social sciences and other areas.